GODS AND GENERALS

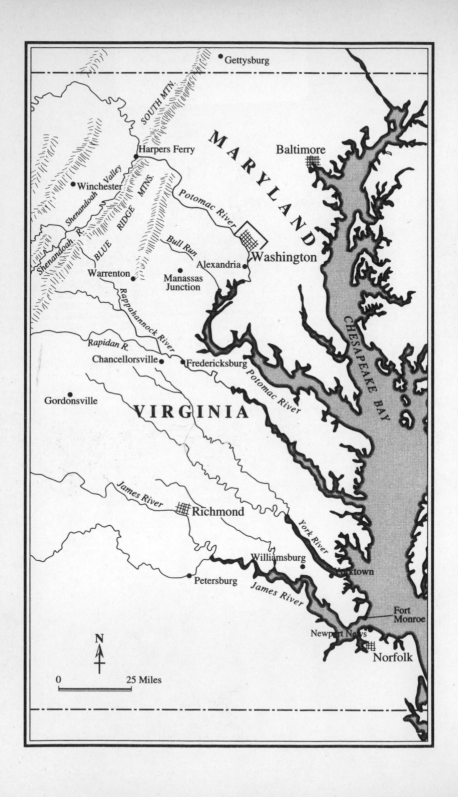

Gettysburg

MARYLAND

SOUTH MTN.

Harpers Ferry

Baltimore

Winchester

Shenandoah Valley

Shenandoah R.

BLUE RIDGE MTNS.

Potomac River

Bull Run

Washington

Alexandria

Warrenton

Manassas
Junction

Rappahannock River

Rapidan R.

Chancellorsville

Fredericksburg

Potomac River

CHESAPEAKE BAY

Gordonsville

VIRGINIA

James River

Richmond

Williamsburg

Petersburg

James River

York River

Yorktown

Fort
Monroe

Newport News

Norfolk

N

0   25 Miles

GODS
and
GENERALS

JEFF SHAARA

Birlinn

This edition published in the UK in 2000 by
Birlinn Limited
8 Canongate Venture
5 New Street
Edinburgh
EH8 8BH

First published in July 1996 by
Ballantine Books, New York

ISBN 1 84158 065 1

British Library Cataloguing-in-Publication Data
A catalogue record for this book is available
from the British Library

Printed and bound by
Creative Print and Design, Ebbw Vale

To Lynne

TO THE READER

IN 1974, MICHAEL SHAARA PUBLISHED *THE KILLER ANGELS*, A
novel about the men who led the fight at the Battle of Gettysburg.
It was not an attempt to document the history of the event, nor
was it a biography of the characters who fought there. Both have been
done, many times, before. What Michael Shaara did was to tell the
story of the battle by telling the story of the men, from their points of
view, their thoughts, their feelings. It was a very different approach,
and it was possibly the first novel of its kind. It also won the Pulitzer
Prize. Michael Shaara died in 1988. He was my father.

The impact of his approach, the feeling that the reader truly
knows these characters, has drawn an emotional response from a great
many people. Over the years, many have expressed their appreciation
for my father's work, whether in letters or in person. They continue to
do so. Some have ancestors who shared the battlefields with Lee or
Chamberlain, some are people who have simply come to know these
characters well, to understand the impact that these men had on
the history of this country and on our lives today. And there have
been others who have said "I never liked history, but I loved these
characters." It is to all these people, but especially those who learned
their American history in often impersonal textbooks, that this story is
written.

This is primarily the story of four men: Robert E. Lee, Thomas
Jonathan "Stonewall" Jackson, Winfield Scott Hancock, and Joshua
Lawrence Chamberlain. Woven throughout the story of these men are
the stories of many others, their wives and families, the men who served
with them on the field, names many of us know well: James Longstreet,
Winfield Scott, "Jeb" Stuart, George McClellan, and characters important

not just to the telling of this story, but to history as well: Jefferson Davis, Sam Houston. As *The Killer Angels* gave readers a connection to the characters *at* Gettysburg, this story takes them further back, to the first rumblings of the Civil War, the tragedies and successes of their personal lives, and their experiences as soldiers, to paint a picture of each character as he might have understood his own world. In 1861 every American was faced with the horror of watching their young nation divide, and every soldier—and a great number of civilians—had to make an extraordinary decision, a question of loyalty, of principles, of duty. Those individual decisions in many ways changed our history as a nation. Each character in this book is faced with the same choice, and each makes his decision for different reasons.

This story begins in late 1858 and concludes in June 1863, just prior to the Battle of Gettysburg. I have tried to follow a time line that accurately describes the history as it follows each character. That history and the events that propel this story are true. Most of the dialogue, the thoughts, the characterizations of the men and women, are my offering, my gift to the memory of these extraordinary individuals.

JEFF SHAARA

ACKNOWLEDGMENTS

INSPIRATION FOR A WORK SUCH AS THIS IS A DEEPLY INDIVIDUAL EXperience, yet my own adventure in bringing this story from some unknown and unexplainable place to the printed page suggests that there is much more to be said.

I am deeply indebted to Ronald Maxwell, who was the first to suggest that I could, and should, continue the story that my father began. Ron held the torch high for *The Killer Angels* for fifteen years, until his own dream of bringing that story to film was realized. His screenplay and his directing talents gave the world the film *Gettysburg*, and so he too is continuing my father's legacy.

For assistance with the considerable research for this project, I must thank the following:

Patrick Falci, of the Civil War Round Table of New York, who is a tireless source of information and materials, and whose willingness to open doors for this project is most appreciated.

Lieutenant Colonel Keith Gibson, of the Virginia Military Institute, and his wife, Pat Gibson, who opened up their home and allowed me to explore their considerable insight into these characters.

Ms. Michael Anne Lynn, of the Stonewall Jackson House, in Lexington, Virginia, for her gracious hospitality, and her willingness to impart her own suggestions for research materials.

Dr. Jeffrey Pasley, Department of History, Florida State University, for his enthusiastic assistance in providing valued sources of reference.

Ms. Clare Ferraro, publisher, Ballantine Books, for her extraordinary support, and her belief that this book could stand beside *The Killer Angels*.

Mr. Doug Grad, editor, Ballantine Books, who has listened with much patience and has lent a skilled hand to guiding a first-time author through this process.

I give most special thanks to my wife, Lynne, who proofread my hasty typing, and always, *always* gave me unqualified support throughout this often unnerving process.

Finally, there can be no greater acknowledgment than to my father, Michael Shaara. His long career as an accomplished writer, the highs and lows, are strong memories from my earliest years. Ultimately, his greatest achievement, *The Killer Angels*, opened an enormous door for me, allowed my apprehensions to be set aside, and brought forth the first words of this book. His greatest wish, what drove him through a difficult career all his life, was the desire to leave something behind, a legacy to be remembered. Dad, you succeeded.

GODS AND
GENERALS

INTRODUCTION

TWO EXTRAORDINARY EVENTS OCCUR IN THE MID-1840S. FIRST, the United States Military Academy, at West Point, in a stroke of marvelous coincidence, graduates several classes of outstanding cadets, a group of young men who at the time are clearly superior to many of the classes that have preceded them. The second event is the Mexican War, the first time the armed forces of the United States takes a fight outside its own boundaries. The two events are connected, and thus, together, they are more significant than if they had occurred separately, because the events in Mexico served almost immediately as a brutal training ground for these cadets, who are now young officers.

They are a new breed of fighting man, the college-educated professional soldier, and the Mexican War is the first war to which West Point has given commanders. It is not a popular war, is seen by many opponents as nothing more than a land grab, the opportunity for the United States government to flex its muscles over a weaker enemy, and thus gain the spoils: South Texas, New Mexico, Arizona, California. What no one can know at the time is that the experience these young soldiers receive will have a profound effect on the battlefields of their own country in 1861. Not only do these men bring home the terrible visions of death and destruction, the experience that wars are not in fact great and glorious exhibitions, but they bring home something more—the discovery that the old way of fighting a war, the Napoleonic School, is becoming dangerously outdated.

The discovery comes from the use of the latest improvements in technology, for the rifleman and the cannoneer, for the observer and the bridge builder. Mexico is very much a testing ground for the new killing machines: greater range, accuracy, and firepower. And so, these young officers are schooled not only in the skills of traditional command and tactics, but in the vastly improving knowledge of the art itself, of engineering and mathematics.

The effect that all of this will have thirteen years later, on the battlefields of our own country, cannot be underestimated. One of the many great tragedies of the Civil War is that it is a bridge through time. The old clumsy ways of fighting, nearly unchanged for centuries, marching troops in long straight lines, advancing slowly into the massed fire of the enemy, will now collide with the new efficient ways of killing, better rifles, much better cannon; and so never before—and in American history, never since—does a war produce so much horrifying destruction.

But this is not a story about the army, or about war, but about four men. Three of them serve their country in Mexico, two of them spend the decade of the 1850s in a peacetime army with very little constructive work to do. They are not friends, they do not share the same backgrounds. But their stories tell the stories of many others, weaving together to shape the most tragic event in our nation's history, and so their story is our story.

ROBERT EDWARD LEE

Born 1807, Lee graduates from West Point in 1829, second in his class, with the unequaled record of never having received a single demerit for conduct in his four years as a cadet. He returns home to Virginia to a dying mother and a scandal-laden family, and so resolves that his life shall bring atonement. Lee possesses an unwavering sense of dignity, and is thus often considered aloof, but his dedication to duty and his care for those around him reveal him to be a man of extraordinary compassion and conscience. His faith is unquestioning, and he believes that all of his accomplishments, all events around him, are the result of God's will.

Lee marries Mary Anne Randolph Custis and has seven children, but he is rarely home—the sacrifice of being a career soldier. He distinguishes himself as a Captain of Engineers, goes to Mexico, and his reputation lands him on the staff of General in Chief Winfield Scott, the grand old man of the army. Lee performs with a dedication and a skill that makes heroes, and Scott promotes him twice, to Lieutenant Colonel. After the war he is named Commandant of West Point, finds it stifling, finds himself growing older with little prospect of advancement beyond his present rank, and he is not a man who will pull strings, or play politics for favors.

In 1855 the army forms the Second Regiment of Cavalry in Texas, and Lee astounds friends and family by volunteering for command. He sees this as his last opportunity to command real troops in the "real" army, and thus spends five years in the cavalry, which ultimately becomes another thankless and unsatisfying job. Serving under the harsh and disagreeable thumb of General David Twiggs, Lee asks for and is granted leave, after receiving word that his father-in-law, George Washington Parke Custis, the grandson of Martha Washington and the patriarch of his family's home, has suddenly died.

WINFIELD SCOTT HANCOCK

Born 1824 in Pennsylvania, one of twin boys, he graduates West Point in 1844. Hancock serves in Mexico with the Sixth Infantry, but only after waging war with his commanders to let him fight. He leads troops with some gallantry, but misses the army's great final victory at Chapultepec because he has the flu. He watches from a rooftop while his friends and fellow soldiers, Lewis Armistead, George Pickett, James Longstreet, and Ulysses "Sam" Grant, storm the walls of the old fort.

After the war, Hancock marries Almira Russell of St. Louis, considered in social circles, and by most bachelors there, to be the finest catch in St. Louis. She is beautiful and brilliant, and accepts her role as the wife of an army officer always with good grace and a superb ability to charm all who know her. They have two children, a son and a daughter.

Hancock, a large, handsome man, has the unfortunate talent of making himself indispensable in any assignment he is given, possessing an amazing talent for the drudgery of army rules and paperwork. This launches him into a dead-end career as a quartermaster, first in Kansas, then in Fort Myers, Florida, where the Everglades assaults the soldiers there with crushing heat and disease, snakes and insects, and the constant threat of attack from the Seminole Indians. He soon is transferred back to "Bloody Kansas," as the army tries to maintain control of rioting civilians confronting each other over the issue of slavery. Moving farther west with the army, he is named Quartermaster for Southern California and assumes a one-man post in the small but growing town of Los Angeles. But Hancock is never content to be a quartermaster, cannot forget his days in Mexico leading infantry, and aches for duty as a real soldier.

THOMAS JONATHAN JACKSON

Born 1824, Jackson arrives at West Point as a country bumpkin with homespun clothes and no prep school training, unlike the brilliant George McClellan or the aristocratic Ambrose Powell Hill, and has great difficulty at the Point. Jackson struggles with the studies, but has no vices, and so spends his time improving, and acquires a reputation as rigid and disciplined, and graduates in 1846 in the upper third of his class. All who know him there are certain that if the courses had gone a fifth year, Jackson would have reached the top.

In Mexico, as an artillery officer, he quickly shows his commanders he is not only suited for the heat of battle, but thrives on it. Jackson leads his two small guns into the fight with an intensity that puts fear into the enemy, and into many who serve with him. He is promoted three times, more than anyone in the army, and returns home a major.

After the war, Jackson grows weary of peacetime army life and applies for a position as an instructor at the Virginia Military Institute, in Lexington, Virginia. He is far from the most qualified candidate, but his war record and the fact that he is a native of western Virginia, and might assist in drawing recruits from that area, gain him the job. Thus he resigns from the army in 1851; he becomes a major in the Virginia Militia and embarks on a career in academics, for which, justifiably, he will never receive praise.

Jackson becomes a Presbyterian, and earns a reputation in local circles as a man of fiery religious conviction, if not a bit odd in his personal habits. He is seen walking through town with one hand held high in the air, thought by many to be constantly in prayer, and he is often sucking on lemons. He violates the law by establishing a Sunday school for slave children in Lexington, and justifies it by claiming it is the right of all of God's creatures to hear the Word.

In 1854 Jackson marries Eleanor Junkin, daughter of the president of Washington University, but a year later she dies in childbirth, as does the baby. Jackson's grief overwhelms him. He takes a long tour of Europe to recover emotionally, but his physical health, and his eyesight, give him constant trouble.

In 1857 he marries again, this time to Mary Anna Morrison, the daughter of a minister who is the founder of Davidson College in North Carolina. Their first child survives only a month. The tragedies of this time in his life place him more firmly than ever into the hands of his God, and he sees every aspect of his life, every act, as only a part of his duty to please God.

JOSHUA LAWRENCE CHAMBERLAIN

Born in 1828, Chamberlain graduates from Bowdoin College, Brunswick, Maine, in 1852. He is considered brilliant, with an amazing talent for mastering any subject. He enrolls in the Bangor Theological Seminary, considers the ministry as a career, but cannot make the final commitment, for though he often preaches Sunday services, he does not hear the calling. Chamberlain returns to Bowdoin as a teacher and is named to the prestigious Chair formerly held by Dr. Calvin Stowe. Chamberlain is now Professor of Natural and Revealed Religion, and speaks seven languages.

While part of Stowe's circle, Chamberlain becomes well acquainted with Stowe's wife, Harriet Beecher Stowe, who at that time is working on *Uncle Tom's Cabin*. The book has considerable influence on Chamberlain and causes him to see far beyond the borders of Maine, to the difficult social problems beginning to affect the country.

He falls desperately in love, and marries Frances "Fannie" Adams, daughter of a strict and inflexible minister. Fannie is a complex and difficult woman, burdened by her own family's awkward collapse—her father marries a woman barely older than she is. Fannie is moody and seemingly hard to please, but Chamberlain loves her blindly. While his distinguished position and title satisfy her, he begins to slide into a long period of discontentment and to focus more on the gathering tide of conflict, the loud and bloody threats to his country.

PART
ONE

1. LEE

THE COACH ROLLED THROUGH THE SMALL IRON GATES, UP THE slight rise, toward massive white columns. Lee had not seen Arlington for nearly three years, saw again the pure size, the exaggerated grandeur. It was the home of George Washington Parke Custis, the grandson of Martha Washington and Lee's father-in-law, and the old man had built the mansion more as a showplace for the artifacts of President Washington than as a home for a living family. The design was cold, impractical, but to Custis, the impression was the important thing, the shrine to his revered ancestors. But now Custis was dead.

Lee had received the wire from his wife, the first news from her in many weeks. They had written often, always, and he sent letters to all of them; not just Mary, but his children as well. He had missed a father's great joy of watching his children grow and learn, and so all he could do was offer the steady stream of advice and counsel, and try not to miss them too much, try not to think about what his career had done to his family. For several weeks the letters had been few from Mary, which was unlike her, but Lee had not thought much on it. He focused instead on his work, the absurd job of the cavalry, chasing Comanches over the vast Texas wilderness, *their* wilderness.

But there had finally come a letter, a wire, special courier, unusual, and the shock of the news hit him hard—that Mary now had no one, could not possibly manage the old estate—and so the army had granted him emergency leave, and he was returning home to Virginia.

He rode closer to the grand house, felt a chill, realized how much the house looked like a tomb, pulled his coat tighter around him. He was not yet accustomed to being away from the Texas heat, and November had settled in around Arlington like a gray shroud. As he climbed the slight rise, he could see out over the lands and untended fields. There had been little planting that year, and ragged brown grass filled the fields in matted lumps. Lee tried to think back, to recall the beauty, but he could not recall the lush green, the neat rows of corn, knew it had never really been like that; the old man had never been much of a farmer.

He wheeled the coach now to the short steps, reined up the horse, and stepped down onto dirty white brick. He looked, all directions, saw no one, thought, Very strange, there was always some activity, even the field hands, Custis's slaves, and though they did not spend much time in the fields, they could usually be seen out and around. He walked up the short steps, stood between the absurdly huge columns. The porch was empty, no chairs, and none of the white clay pots had been planted. There was no sign of any life anywhere. Lee began to feel the coldness; not the Virginia weather, but more, deeper.

He went to the doors, tried to see first through the small glass panes, could not—curtains lined the inside, and so he thought of knocking, felt a hesitation, then felt foolish. This was his home too, and he turned the large brass knob and walked into the house.

He slowly closed the door behind him, the silence broken by the sharp squeaking of the hinges, the sound startling him. He moved farther into the vast hall, looked toward both side rooms for anyone, then finally heard a voice, a girl. Lee turned, saw a whirl of black lace, and down the wide round stairway came his daughter Agnes.

She stopped, stood for a brief second with mouth open, a look of shock, said only, "Oh!"

Then she ran down, bounded past the last few steps and threw herself hard against her father's chest. Lee wrapped her in his arms, held her, felt her crying, her soft sobs buried into his coat, and he rocked her slightly, was suddenly uncomfortable, had not expected this. He lifted her away, put his hand out and touched her soft hair.

Agnes said, "Oh, Papa, Papa," and he felt her let go. She pressed to him again, pouring the pain out against him.

"It's all right, child, I am home now," he said. "Home." She began to loosen her hold, lifted her head and looked at him through swollen red eyes. She laughed then, a short sweet sound, and he put his hand on her cheek, realized now how much she had grown, thought, She is sixteen, and soon she too will leave and be gone.

"Papa, it was so . . . sudden. Why did God take him? He is buried next to Grandma. You must see the grave. Oh, Papa, it makes me so sad to go there." Her words began to pour out in quick bursts, overwhelming him.

He held her by the shoulders, said, "Wait, slow, slow, my child. We will talk . . . we have time to talk now. But where is your mother? I have not seen her."

Agnes felt words boiling inside of her, wanted to tell him so much, but saw his face, the lines, the gray hair, began to see him as older, different.

"She is upstairs. In her room. Your room. Oh, Papa, I am so glad you are home."

She hugged him again, and he turned, did not want her to start crying again. Moving toward the stairs, he looked up, expected to see Mary at the top, tall thin Mary, smiling and scolding him. She must have heard Agnes crying, he thought, and felt a chill—it was odd she hadn't come to greet him.

He climbed in quick steps, stared up toward the railing that led away from the top of the stairs, expecting still to see her. He reached the broad, open hallway, moved quickly to their room, saw a closed door and knocked, a gentle tap. She must be asleep, he thought, and pushed the door open, another squeaking hinge, and frowned because he did not want to wake her.

"Robert. Is that you?"

He stepped in, looked at the bed, thick and white, but she wasn't there. Then he saw her, sitting by the window, and he made a sound, a small gasp. He couldn't help himself, felt his knees give way, then stiffened, gained control, said, "Mary . . . are you not well?"

"No, Robert, I am not well."

She sat in a small leather chair, leaned slightly to one side, and Lee saw her right arm, hanging down, the hand twisted in a grotesque curl.

"I am sorry I did not greet you at the door. I saw you ride up. It is difficult for me to walk."

Lee stared at her, did not understand, did not know what to say.

"Please don't look at me like that."

"I'm sorry, but what is wrong? Are you getting better?"

"I have arthritis. The doctor says I will likely get worse. It's been a year or so. I could not tell you. I am ashamed that you should see me like this."

"No, no, it's all right. I am home now, I will take care of you."

"For how long?" Lee felt the edge in her voice, had heard it before, the bitterness she tried to hide, that the letters *did* hide. But now it could not be concealed, and he felt a sudden wave of guilt, as though if he'd been here, she would not be this way, it would all be different.

"I am . . . I have a two-month leave. General Twiggs . . . the army was very understanding."

"Understanding? I doubt the army has ever understood what it is like around this house."

Lee turned away from the argument, felt only the need to help, to mend the wounds.

"I was shocked at the news. I did not realize your father was ill."

"He wasn't. It was pneumonia. He had only a few days. We were with him . . . the girls were with him when he died."

She tried to stand, raised herself up with her left arm, pushing against the chair. He rushed forward, held her, lifted her under the arms, pulled her against him and felt the frail stillness, the dead right arm. She groaned suddenly, pulled back.

"I'm sorry. It hurts. It . . . always hurts. I just wanted to see outside."

Gently, he reached for her again, could feel her bones, had a sudden fear he might break her, and she turned, left his hands and faced the window.

"Would you please ask Agnes to bring me some tea?"

He backed away, still held his arms out toward her, and she moved closer to the window, a slow painful step, placed her left hand on the sill and looked out toward the gray sky. He watched her, felt sick inside, shut out. Behind him, in the hallway, he heard soft steps. He turned, said, "Agnes? Are you there?"

There was a silence, and then the girl answered, "Yes, Papa." Lee opened the door, stepped into the hallway and, in one motion, went to his daughter and held her, felt her strength and gave her back some of her tears.

HE SAT AT THE OLD MAN'S DESK, SURROUNDED BY HIGH WALLS and thick oak shelves. The dark office was suffocating, every space occupied by some memento, some piece of history, and Lee had begun to feel it all as a great weight.

He read through a stack of papers, the massive confusion of the old man's will. Custis had drawn it up himself, had felt no need for lawyers, and now Lee agonized at the contradictions, the grand pronouncements and the wholly impractical way Custis had divided his holdings. But it was the first page, the first paragraph that had given Lee the greatest dread, because the old man had named Lieutenant Colonel Robert Edward Lee as the principal executor of the estate.

There was land, thousands of acres on three plantations, and Lee's sons, Custis, Rooney, and Robert, Jr., inherited that. Then there was cash to be paid to the girls, but there was no cash in the estate: the money was to come from the farming operations of the lands. So, if the older sons were to come home and give up their careers to manage the farms, they would do so only to raise funds to give to their sisters. And, as Lee continued to plow his way through the documents, he noticed that Custis had not made any mention of existing debts, of which there were plenty. Thus, funds first had to be raised to settle those, or the Virginia courts would not approve the final settlement of the estate.

All of this was challenging, but Lee had the experience to handle it—he'd managed complicated budgets and administered financial dealings both in the Corps of Engineers and at West Point. The only thing he needed was time.

He studied the mound of papers for most of the afternoon. His eyes and his concentration began to wander, and so he left the study, walked through the large house, became acquainted again with the odd design, the vast clutter of artifacts. He stopped at the main parlor, admired the portraits, Custis and his wife. The old man was fiercely proud of his legacy, considered the home to be of great value to his country, a place where the name of George Washington would forever be preserved in the souvenirs of the first presidency. Lee began to see the artifacts differently now, the pieces of silver, large porcelain plates and tall vases, the small and large portraits cluttering the walls. He turned slowly, looked in detail around the room, the fireplace mantel, the shelves and glass cabinets. How strange to live in a museum, he thought. It took something away, some part of home. He hadn't noticed that before, and so had never missed it. He looked at the portraits again, saw a smaller painting and looked closer at the small gold frame. It was Mary as a girl, probably done when she was Agnes's age.

He knew she was never beautiful, not by the standards of the other boys. But he'd loved those things that were there, clearly, in the portrait: the frailty, a girl who needed caring for—*his* care.

Her father had not been happy with this young Lieutenant Lee, had thought his daughter fit for a husband of considerably higher breeding. Lee's own father, the great hero of the Revolution, Light-Horse Harry Lee, had died in shame and exile, with huge debts and failed dreams, a great soldier with no talent for business, and it was a disgrace and a reputation that haunted the young soldier. His mother had suffered as well, and when Lee graduated from West Point, he returned home to a dying woman, a woman worn away by the scandals, who had only one pride now, the success of her son. She died soon after, in his arms, and left him with soft words and the deep hurt of a mother's love, and he had told her, the last words she would hear, that he would make her proud.

Lee had pursued the young Mary despite the old man's hostility, and it was finally Mary's mother who had intervened, knew her daughter would do well to be cared for by this serious and soft-spoken young gentleman, and so finally they were allowed to be married.

He smiled at the memories: Mary the spoiled girl, his own easy patience, her mother scolding her for her carelessness, her inability to do anything for herself, and years later, her daughters scolding her again for the same reason. Lee remembered waiting, late for church, and she was never ready, would not come, had more "fixing" to do. So he and the children would go off anyway, and Mary would finally arrive in a flutter of mismatched colors, and the girls would ask her what it was she had "fixed."

He left the portrait, walked into the huge front hall, the cavernous entranceway that added no comfort to the house. He turned toward the back, went past small sitting rooms, a hallway, and then outside, where he stood on the small rear porch and looked out over the fields. It would be spring soon, the planting season, and there was no one here to handle it. He thought of the will, the debts, the old man's generous gifts to his grandchildren, gifts that would never be given, unless someone took charge. Lee stepped down to the brown grass, the thick patches of old, dirty snow melting now. He thought of the army. He would have to request further time, an extension of the leave, and realized that he had friends in Washington. That came from years of being the good soldier, never asking for the favors others sought with regularity. Walking out through the yard, toward a small stone wall, he thought of names, men he had known well, served well in Mexico. He did not have the political stomach for reminding his superiors what he had done, had done for *them*, and so he was a lieutenant colonel still, and probably would be for the rest of his career.

Sitting on the rough stone, Lee looked away, down a long clear hill to a row of far trees and beyond, to the wide river, the Potomac, and the buildings of Washington. He thought of General Scott, so much like his own father had once been. Scott was the finest soldier of his day, a man you could trust absolutely, who would fight for his cause and his men, and a man who had little use for the double-talk of politics. But in the peacetime army there was no other place for Scott

to be than across the wide river, in those white buildings, surrounded
by men who saw him as an outdated annoyance. He was still in command of the army, however, and Lee knew Scott was his friend. And
he would only need a few months. . . .

He looked again, closer, at the near fields, and thought, What
would it be like to be a farmer?

2. JACKSON

MAJOR JACKSON STOOD WITH A SOLEMN STIFFNESS, FACING THE seated rows of cadets. The classroom was small, with white walls, a solid oak floor, and one tall window, toward which the cadets would occasionally gaze, though not for long. He had completed today's lesson, a thorough explanation of the practical applications of geometry on the trajectory of artillery. He had recited the lesson exactly as he'd memorized it the night before.

"So, gentlemen, you will see that with a proper grasp of the principles I have laid before you today, you may eventually apply these principles with great effectiveness in your own field experiences, and indeed, these principles may be applied to a great many other practices as well."

Eyes were fixed on him in a daze, and there was no sound. The room was a small tomb, and he led the class with a somber intensity that invited no comment from his students.

"Sir?" A hesitating voice rose from one side of the room, from the sharp glare of the window.

Jackson stopped, tried to see the boy's face, obstructed by the sunlight. "Did someone speak?"

"Yes, sir. I am a bit confused, sir, about your principle of application. Do you mean that we may apply mathematical principles to the pursuit of, say, romance, sir? Or perhaps the appreciation of a beautiful girl can be explained by one of these formulas, sir?"

Jackson stared in the direction of the question. There were a few stifled giggles, and Jackson knew this boy, knew the reputation as a clown, and had no use for it.

"Cadet, have you found yourself in a position to pursue romance?"

There was more stifled laughter, all heads turned toward the boy. Jackson could see him now, his eyes had pierced the glare. The young man looked at his professor with a slight sneer, the cockiness of the aristocrat.

"Well, sir, of course, some of us are fortunate in the pursuit of the fairer sex." He smiled, glanced around at his audience.

Jackson stared at the boy, felt his neck turn red, looked back toward the class. Faces turned back to him, and he said, "Gentlemen, if you are going to succeed at this institution, you have one common goal—to learn your lessons. If you are placing your energies elsewhere, you will not succeed, either with me or with your careers as military officers."

The laughter had stopped, the joke was over, and the young cadet by the window made a low comment, which Jackson could not clearly hear.

"Does Mr. Walker have another valuable thought to share with us today about the usefulness of the principles of geometry?" The question held no sarcasm. Jackson did not play the game, had only one purpose in this room, to impart the lesson.

"No sir, I have nothing further. Um, except, sir, I am confused about the principles regarding the application of triangulation in the placing of the observation sights for artillery." It was a serious question. Jackson knew that this cadet, for all his bluster and arrogance, was not doing well in his lessons. He sagged, thought, This is inexcusable, a clear lack of effort from the boy. He knew others in the class were having some difficulty as well, and he often received questions that had the unnerving effect of disrupting his presentation.

"Mr. Walker, I am forced to conclude that I must repeat this lesson tomorrow, word for word, and if you, if all of you, will pay a bit closer attention, perhaps it will be understood. We are out of time today."

There was a low groan, and the cadets understood that Jackson was serious, that tomorrow's lesson would be the same as today, *exactly* the same, and they would absorb the words again, or try to, and there would be little room for questions.

He turned, reached toward the small desk behind him, picked up his copy of the large gray textbook which all the cadets carried. They rose, a great collective sigh, and filed from the room.

Jackson was annoyed. He had spent the greater part of the previous evening memorizing today's lesson, had spoken it aloud to himself in the dim lamplight of his room. It was perfectly clear to him, and he had recited it with the same clarity today. He turned back, watched the cadets, frowned. Many of these young men would not survive the academic load at VMI. He saw the fault lying with the outside influences, recalled West Point, the local taverns that had attracted so many of his classmates. Lexington, Virginia, was not as sophisticated, there was not a bustling social scene, and so it mystified him why these young men were so distracted, why they could not seem to grasp the lessons that were so clear to him.

He held the heavy book under one arm, waited for the last cadet to exit, then walked out into the hallway. He saw many faces watching him, heard some laughter, comments, the brashness of boys who are briefly anonymous, out from your control. He did not look at them, had heard it before, walked past the building's wide oak doorway and to the cool air outside. He stopped, took a deep breath, then another, tried to rid himself of the stale air of the classroom. It has been going fairly well, he thought, most of them do want to learn. He could not understand the others, could not understand why they made the effort to be here if they had no sense of duty.

Major Jackson walked again, with long loping strides, kept the book tightly under his arm, allowed the other arm to swing freely. Conversations stopped when he passed, cadets pointing, more comments. He didn't see them, kept his eyes straight ahead in an intent stare—he had an appointment to keep.

Moving out across the wide parade ground, he glanced once toward the row of brass cannon, *his* cannon, which he used to teach the skills of artillery. It was the one part of their lessons the cadets enjoyed. Jackson's reputation in the classroom was clear and appalling. He was nicknamed "Tom Fool," a teacher with no talent for teaching, whose daily routine tortured his cadets, but out here, with the guns, there was something else, something the cadets could feel. The professor was, after all, a soldier, and with his beloved guns his lessons became animated, energetic. Though he forced them through the torture of the classroom, they knew that out here, in the open air, Jackson and his guns would show them a small glimpse of the *fire*. Out here they did not ridicule him, and though many of these young men would never become soldiers, they would know at least what a soldier *was*.

He moved beyond the gates now, passed through the campus of Washington University, which spread out alongside VMI. The atmosphere here was very different. There was laughter, young people moving in pairs under great sweeping trees. He did not look at them, stared straight ahead, moved in long strides toward a distant church steeple.

He was uncomfortable now, would not look around, would avoid the modest brick home that sat in the center of the campus, the home of Dr. Junkin, the university president. Jackson had lived in that home, had married Junkin's daughter, Ellie, and it was a part of his life that he put aside, kept far away. Ellie had died in childbirth, and the pain of that moment filled him when he was weak, when he could not wall it away. The Junkins were still his family, but he had married again, to Anna Morrison, the daughter of a minister, and his life had begun again. But he was not safe from the unspeakable, from the sad face of God, and he stared hard ahead, but knew the house was there, *right* there, and he tried, braced hard against the pain, pushed it away into some untouchable place.

He glanced up, saw the sharp point, the small cross at the top of the distant steeple, lowered his eyes again. Looking down the dirt street, he moved quickly now, with purpose, thinking, I will not be late.

The little girl had been only a month old, a small piece of pure light, and Jackson had thought, This is our reward, God is pleased and has allowed us to feel this joy. But this baby too did not live, was suddenly gone, and he felt the loss as if a piece of him had been torn away. Blessedly, Anna had survived, and no, there would be no pain, God had shown him something important, a lesson he must not forget. And so, while Anna had grieved, and her health had suffered, Jackson had gone back to his classroom.

He had often struggled with the notion of God, was not raised with any strict adherence to one church, but the gradual ending of the war in Mexico had taken something from him. When the duty that had driven him with such pure energy was drifting away, his real search began. He even considered becoming a Catholic then, defying the prejudice that many of the soldiers held. He learned Spanish and spoke often with local priests. But there was something about the papacy he found uncomfortable. He had difficulty accepting that authority, preferring to pursue instead a more personal service to God. In the peacetime army his duty was stripped down to mundane and pointless tasks, and so his religion had given him a new purpose, another place where his duty was clear. If he could not serve the army, he would serve God, and his enemies would be any temptations, any distractions, from that course.

He was in the street now, away from the campus. Cresting a short hill, he glanced at the high steeple. He felt excited, thinking of Dr. William White, the Presbyterian minister who had given him a comfortable home for his young religion, a man who did not insert himself into Jackson's worship, who understood that God was to be found well beyond the walls of White's own church.

Jackson did not look at the people along the street, did not feel the eyes watching him, staring at the sharp uniform, the crisp white pants, the blue jacket, brass buttons tight to the neck. He did not feel them staring as he reached into his pocket, felt for the hard round ball, pulled it free and shifted the book to his other arm. He reached into another pocket for a small knife, and then, with a quick slice, cut the ball in half and abruptly stuffed one piece, dripping and sticky, into his mouth. It was a lemon.

It was another experience from Mexico—the variety of strange and exotic foods. He had discovered lemons, tasted the sour tartness with the enthusiasm of a child, allowed himself one small piece of pleasure. He felt some guilt even for that, but knew, unlike many of the others, he had kept his path straight, that God had perhaps given him this small gift, this one small treat. Now, as the sharp ribbon of juice filled him, he thought of the baby. The pain tore through him, and he stopped, closed his eyes, said quietly, "No . . ."

Now he saw the people, their eyes, and he nodded, touched the brim of his cap, and continued his walk toward the church.

H E STARED DOWN, BETWEEN HIS KNEES, THOUGHT OF WORDS, how to begin. Dr. White sat behind the old desk, a thin man, slightly bent, waiting, patient.

"I am in something of a turmoil, Doctor. I was hoping I could have a few moments of your time to dig through it, or, perhaps, help me understand what is happening."

White sat silently, waited for Jackson to continue. The silence lasted over a minute, and White finally said, "Major Jackson, I have always considered you not only a guiding force in this church, but I have also considered you my friend. There are few in this congregation who share my devotion to doing God's good work as much as you. Please do not hesitate to freely discuss with me anything, anything at all. I had hoped you would visit me sooner. You have suffered a loss that no one can realize unless they have lived through it."

Jackson sat without moving, stared at White's desk, then looked up, into his eyes. "I have heard . . . that God punishes us for loving each other too much. There are those . . . who have come to visit . . . friends . . . I suppose. They offer kind words, advice. I have been told . . ." He stopped, tried again to form the words.

"I have been told that if we do not suppress our love for human things, and give more to God, He . . . makes us pay with great pain. I . . . am not sure I believe that. And yet . . . I am finding it harder to keep the pain away."

"It's an interesting doctrine, but I must say, not a very comforting one. Do you feel you and Anna have been punished?"

Jackson thought, glanced at the ceiling, then around the room.

"I . . . well, no. God has His reasons . . . Anna has suffered a great deal. I have told her we must try harder to please Him, that He has given us a lesson. It does not seem to help her. The path I chose, marrying Anna, was the correct one. I truly believe that. But I may love her too much. Is it possible . . . God has given us . . . a warning?"

White put his hands together, under his chin, and looked down.

Jackson continued. "If it is wrong for me to love anyone but God . . . if I have to, I can do that."

White looked up, said, "You have made a giant leap of interpretation there, I must say. You are accepting what has happened in your life as a direct result of an act of God. Step away, Major, back away from your own pain, and look around you. Your loss is not yours alone. What of your family? What of the people in your life, who share the pain of your loss? And, excuse me, Major, but what of the baby?"

"The baby?" Jackson stiffened, did not want to think about the baby.

"Was the baby punished because you gave it love? Major, I do not know why God does the things He does, but I believe you have the same duty to God as you have always had: to follow the right path, to live your life with a clear conscience. If God decides to inform you why He is doing whatever it is He chooses to do, then please come and tell me. But I suspect, Major, that you may only learn the Great Answers when He calls you away from this life."

Jackson pondered again, absorbed the words, began to feel a release, a load removed. He had assumed an awful guilt for the baby's death, had assumed it was his fault. He sat silently, scolded himself for his ego, his presumptions.

After a long, quiet pause, White said, "Major, do you miss your mother?"

The question caught Jackson by surprise. He looked at White, puzzled, thought about his mother. "I suppose . . . well, I try not to. It serves no purpose. She died when I was very young. God would not want me to dwell on that . . . the pain."

"Well, maybe. But do you miss her? Do you ever talk to her, pray to her? If we believe that all our departed loved ones sit with God, then maybe it is *she* who watches over you, who might provide you some guidance."

Jackson stared at White, fought, pushed away the image of his mother. "I . . . don't think I can do that. It seems odd to pray . . . not to God."

"Don't look for answers, Major, look for guidance, for comfort. And do not fear love. I believe that God would be happy if you sought out the guiding hand of someone who loves you as much as your mother loves you."

Jackson thought again, did not like thinking of her. When she entered his mind, the brief glimpses, the memories, always brought pain, so he did not pursue it. But if it would please God . . .

"Doctor, thank you." Jackson stood abruptly, and White leaned back in his chair, saw the look he had come to know as Jackson's own, the face that says, It is time to move on, to take the next step.

S HE STOOD HIGH ON THE SMALL PORCH, ABOVE THE HARD DIRT street, watched him slap at the horse. The carriage lurched, then began to roll slowly away.

He saw the look, the dull pain, and tried to make her smile, waved foolishly, exaggeratedly, then stood up precariously. Now she laughed, softly, and shook her head. He sat back down on the small wooden seat, pulled at the horse, and the carriage stopped.

"It will be soon. Really."

She nodded. "I know, Thomas. It is a good thing. . . ."

"You can come along . . . still. . . ."

"No. This is for you. I will be fine. The garden needs tending."

He turned to the horse, nodded quietly, thought, Yes, the garden . . . that will also please God. He looked at Anna again, thought, There will be comfort for you as well. She waved now, the smile faded, and she began to back away, into the house, and he knew it was time to go.

He drove the horse with a long whip, bounced along, holding straps of worn soft leather in his hand. There were high hills and thick woods, then a farmhouse, orchards, vast fields of ripening corn. He rode down the Shenandoah Valley, northward, through the most beautiful land he had ever seen, the treasured land of home. He would gaze, marveling at a farmer's good work, the neat rows that covered the countryside, and then in the distance the high mountains, the Blue

Ridge, the Alleghenies. He rode with purpose, the passion of the good mission. He did not feel the painful bouncing, did not fight the dust. It was bright, and warm, and perfect, and he stopped only to rest the horse. After many hours and many miles, he reined up, saw a small wooden sign with crude letters, HAWK'S NEST.

He stepped down from the carriage, looked for . . . something, not sure what. He saw no people, a few small wooden buildings, one of old brick, a general store, a broken sign hanging loosely over the door. He walked stiffly over, working the kinks out of his legs, patting his chest and pants, freeing the dust.

The store was dark, with one small, dirty window. It did not appear to be open for business, but behind a dust-covered counter sat an old man, deep wrinkles in dark, weathered skin. He slept on the floor, propped up against a sack of flour. Jackson leaned over the counter, studied the strange old face, the etchings of long hard experience. The old man let out a muffled noise, a small snore, twitched a wiry shoulder, and Jackson thought, Let him be, and began to turn away. But the weight of his boots sent a loud squeak from the worn wooden planks of the floor, and the old man suddenly woke, snapped to, looked at Jackson with the fear of a wounded animal.

"Who are you . . . what . . . ohhh." The old man grabbed his head, looked away in obvious pain, then back at Jackson, the fear now annoyance.

"What can I do for you, there, stranger? Pardon me for not getting up . . . bad leg. Bad most everything else too. Damned apple cider . . . A word to you, friend. Don't mix good corn whiskey with bad apple cider."

He closed his eyes, groaned again, one hand on top of his head, holding it in place. Jackson stood quietly, wanted to leave, but this was the only person he had seen.

"Pardon my interruption, sir. I am Major Thomas Jackson, of Lexington. My mother is buried here, around this place. I am trying to find her grave."

"Your mother?" The old man squinted up at Jackson's face, tried to recognize him, didn't. "What's her name? When was the funeral? Indians get her?"

Jackson thought, Indians?

"Her name was Julia Neale Jackson Woodson. She died in 1831."

"Twenty . . . uh . . . twenty . . . some-odd years ago?" The old man laughed, wiped his nose. "You just now find out about it?"

Jackson did not smile, did not want to explain, had not expected difficulty finding the gravesite.

"Is there a cemetery here, a churchyard?"

"I don't reckon there is, son, um . . . Major, you say? Woodson? You in the army? Indian fighter?"

"It's Jackson, my mother married again just before she died. I'm Virginia Militia. I'm a professor at VMI."

"VMI—what's that? A professor?" The old man was obviously disappointed. "I'm an old Indian fighter myself, Texas, the cavalry. Back then, well, we had it really rough, not like these boys today. You see them fancy repeating revolvers? Well, Major . . . Jackson, I don't know no one with any of them names around here. Check with the lieutenant outside, we have our troops stationed here, all good men, good Indian fighters. Just come back from Texas, you know, cavalry. Watch that cornfield over there, they sneak up every now and again. Arrow flew in here just . . . well, there, over there. Dang near got me too. Stay down here, the floor, safe." The old man made a cracked wheeze, coughed.

Jackson followed the man's gesture, saw no arrow, began to understand.

"Thank you, sir. The . . . the lieutenant seems to be off duty. Can you tell me where I might find someone who can tell me more?"

"Yep, check with old McLean . . . yep, McLean, he's around the town most of the time. Old guy, older than me even, hee. Gray head. Jake it is, Jacob McLean."

The old man coughed again, kept talking. "You bring a regiment with you? I heard drums last night, they're planning something, I tell you that. I stay here, on the floor."

Jackson nodded, turned, and stepped gratefully back into the sunlight. Across the road, away from the few buildings, was a huge cornfield, stretching to the hills beyond. He walked to the edge of the field, thought, Maybe a farmhouse, saw no one, and a voice behind him said, "You, hey, you there! You aim to steal some corn?"

Jackson turned, saw an old man, bent, gray, with a crooked cane. The man was well dressed, dark wool suit, looked out of place.

"Sir, I'm trying to find some information . . . a man named McLean. I'm looking for—"

"Well, you found him, son. I seen you come outta the store, there. You been talking to Jasper?"

"I didn't get his name," Jackson said. "He told me to watch for Indians."

The old man laughed, shook his head. "Yep, old Jasper brought all those Indians home with him from Texas. Brought a good love of the strong spirits too. There's a lot of that around here. If these people ain't shootin' at their neighbors, they're drinking themselves crazy. We had to take his gun away, his old musket. He was prone to takin' a potshot over that countertop every now and again. Doubt he'd ever hit anything, but it weren't good for the mood of the town."

The man began to laugh, stopped, eyed Jackson again. "We don't see many newcomers around here. Not a place many people happen on . . . visitors usually stay to the east of here, on the big road."

Jackson began to feel the frustration, wondered if everyone here did nothing but talk, felt a warmth creeping up the back of his neck.

"Sir, if you please, I am looking for the grave of my mother. Julia Neale Jackson Woodson, died near here many years ago."

The smile slowly left the old face, and Jackson saw clear eyes looking him over, studying him.

"Julia was your mother?"

"Yes, sir. My name—"

"You're Tom. Her youngest boy. I remember you, see it in your eyes."

Jackson felt a rush of relief. "Yes, yes, did you know her? Do you know where she is buried? I'm here to see her . . . to see her grave. I haven't been back here since . . . since then."

"I reckon I oughta know. I helped dig the grave." The old man turned, pointed his cane down a rough trail. "Down this way, a mile or so, by the river."

"The river?" Jackson didn't recall water.

The old man turned, looked at him. "I reckon it has been a while since you been here, eh, son? The New River, at the end of this road here. Not much of a river actually. Dries up now and again. But a nice spot for a grave. As I recall, she picked it out herself."

Jackson looked down the dim road, branches hung low across, barely room for a carriage to pass.

"Would you mind showing me . . . taking me there?"

"Well, no, I wouldn't mind. Wouldn't mind a'tall."

Jackson led him toward the carriage, and the old man walked around to the far side, warily eyed the climb up.

Jackson mounted, reached out a hand to the old man, who struggled, grunted, then, with Jackson's help, reached the seat. He looked at Jackson and studied him, but Jackson was looking toward the small road, the high grass. He slapped the horse with the leather straps.

The old man steadied himself against Jackson's arm as the carriage rolled onto the old road, then said, "You don't live around here . . . I'd know it. What you doing here, son? Why you come back here after so long? This is not a place people just happen by."

Jackson drove the carriage, didn't speak. They bumped along past thick clumps of bushes and tall trees, and Jackson felt the delicious coolness of the thick woods, realized he was sweating, anxious. He felt the old man's hand, holding on to his arm, could not think of the right thing to say, the answer to the old man's question.

"I came back here to see her. I miss her."

The old man nodded, said, "I reckon we all miss somebody."

The road became muddy, and Jackson knew the river was close. The old man put up a hand. Jackson stopped the horse.

"I believe . . . wait, no . . . there, over this way." The old man pointed the way, and Jackson steered the carriage through the woods.

The carriage splashed through a thick muddy bog, the horse kicking black mud in the air, and then the road appeared again, a slight rise. They entered a clearing and Jackson could see flat ground, the edge of a small river, a small meadow of green grass, a huge oak tree, and across the meadow, on the far side, before the old man could point to it, the depression in the earth, the unmarked resting place of his mother.

Jackson reined the horse and stepped off the carriage, jumping down onto soft ground. His hands were sweating and he felt his heart pound.

The old man said, "If you don't mind, I'll just sit here. I 'spect you want to be alone anyhow."

Jackson didn't answer, walked softly, silently, toward the sunken grave. At the lower end, away from the river, he stopped, knelt, reached out a hand and touched the grassy ground. He ran his hand along the edge of the depression, felt the lush grass between his fingers, the cool moisture wetting his hands, and put a hand to his face, touched the wetness to his cheek. He sat now, closed his eyes. He thought of Dr. White, tried to pray, not to God, to her, but it would not come, he could not talk to her. He sat quietly, thought back, stared at the small sounds of flowing water, began to remember her, the strong arms, the soft voice.

His mind began to carry him, drifting through the sweet smells of her kitchen, the clear summer days and the snows of the winter. He could see his sister, just a baby, and began to feel what it was like, being the great protector of her tender helplessness. He saw the small bedroom, saw himself, just a young boy, seven, and his sister, older now, holding on to him, reaching up to grip his hand, and they were very quiet, staring at her in the bed . . . *and now he was there, and it was real,*

and he saw the pain, the awful hurt in his mother's dying face, and he leaned over, touched her face, held her now, felt her breath fading away, and she reached for him, wrapped him in her arms, and spoke, soft words, but he could not hear and he tried to answer, and she spoke again, the words coming in clear, quiet sounds, and now he heard, understood, he felt her warmth, her love, and he knew that God was there, and it was all right. . . .
He began to pull away, remembered it all now, gently closed the dark and silent place, felt the dampness of the grass again, knew now that she sat with God and loved her children still.

3. CHAMBERLAIN

NOVEMBER 1859

IT WAS COLD, VERY COLD, AND HE FELT THE STING IN HIS CHEEKS, A slight burning pain in the edges of his ears, the delicious feeling of being totally alive, every nerve, every part of you totally awake, every breath of the cold air filling you with the sharp and wonderful bite of the Maine winter. In front of him the hillside stretched far below, spread out in a deep white carpet broken by clusters of dark green, the tall fir and spruce trees, branches holding on to clumps of snow. He looked farther out, over to the next hill, saw more trees, a solid, thick mass, the snow hidden underneath.

He had climbed the wide hill, moved slowly across the crest, resting between slow, deliberate steps, sinking into the deep powdery snow. He began to move downhill now, and stopped, stared at the tall ridges in the distance. How high are we, how far up? he wondered. He took a long, cold breath, thought, Easier going down, and . . . I am tired—Tom is so much younger.

Chamberlain turned, looked sideways across the wide slope for the figure of his brother, knew the boy would be moving through the smaller trees to the left, the short, thick ones where a man could hide his movements, sneak through, then suddenly glimpse the far side without detection. He waited, heard nothing, and realized, Yes, you can hear *nothing*. He listened hard, focused on any sounds, and there were none, no birds, no breeze. Remarkable, he thought. How many places can you go where you hear nothing?

He kept watching the cluster of small trees, suddenly saw movement, the trees first, a small shower of loose snow from the low branches, and then a quick brown flash, and a deer burst out, ran along the hillside toward him. He did not move, and the deer stopped, looked back to the trees, then raised its long, thick, white tail and began to make long prancing strides right toward him, still not seeing him. Chamberlain stood completely still, and the deer stopped again, now saw him, stared at him from a few yards away, and Chamberlain stared back, looked into the large round eyes, saw, not panic, but intense curiosity. They stood motionless for several seconds, and the deer suddenly raised its tail again, the thick flag, had seen enough of this unknown thing, and jumped quickly into motion, ran off, down the hill, away from him, and then darted below through the larger trees.

He watched the animal, could still glimpse the high bounding tail, thought, How odd, they hide so well, masters of camouflage, and then display their tail so everything in the woods can see them.

"Lawrence . . . did you see him?"

The boy emerged from the small trees, running now, fought his way through the deep snow, and he looked down, saw the tracks of the deer, then looked at Chamberlain, called out, "Lawrence, he ran right by you. Did you see him?"

He watched the boy, plowing his way closer, and Tom looked again at the tracks punched through the snow, a solid line leading away down the hill.

"Yes, Tom, I saw him. He went off, down there." He pointed a gloved hand down the hill.

"Well, yes, Lawrence, I can see where he went. Did you get a shot? I didn't hear you shoot."

Chamberlain looked down at the musket, the long barrel of the old flintlock, had not even thought of using it. "No, I didn't get a shot."

"Lawrence! You let him go. God in heaven, you did it again! I been trailing that fellow from clear across that last valley, and he flushed out right by you . . . and you let him go. I swear, Lawrence, you do cause me some aggravation."

The boy was out of breath, and Chamberlain swung the gun up, laid it backward on his shoulder, said, "We best be getting back. Over there, some clouds moving up. Could be more snow."

The boy looked toward the thickening sky, then stared back at Chamberlain, and suddenly kicked at the soft snow.

"Phooo! I am never going hunting with you! Not ever again! If you wasn't going to shoot the deer, why'd you come along anyway?"

Chamberlain turned, began to walk, stepping slowly through the snow, up the broad hill. He looked back, saw his brother following, holding his musket firmly in both hands, ready, always ready. Chamberlain stopped, smiled at the boy, who puffed up the hill and moved up beside him, short bursts of steam from tired breathing.

"Why do you come out here if you don't want to shoot anything?"

Chamberlain raised his free hand, waved it about, a grand sweeping turn, said, "I love it. I love hunting. The woods, all of this. I don't need to shoot, it's more than that . . . it's just being here."

The boy let his gun drop into one hand, rested the butt in the snow. "I reckon I understand that, Lawrence. There's something out here, something in these hills that makes everything else seem . . . all right, somehow."

Chamberlain looked at the boy, surprised. "It's good you see that. You may need this someday. You may need to get away from . . . something. I hope you always have . . . all of this."

"Get away? What you getting away from, Lawrence? My God, you've got everything a man could want. You're a teacher, a big-time college professor. You make good money, I bet. You got a wife . . . a real beauty too, and that baby, Lawrence, I swear . . . I only hope I can have what you have."

Chamberlain looked at the boy, saw red cheeks and wide eyes, saw a young piece of himself. "You're only eighteen," he said. "You've got plenty of time to make your own life. Just don't forget about this place. No matter where you end up, and you may move very far away someday . . . come back here when you can. Climb up here, and listen to the silence."

Tom frowned, did not understand, saw something, a dark mood in his older brother he had not often seen. "Lawrence, you telling me you're unhappy? I can't hardly believe that."

"No, no, certainly not. Let's go, those clouds are getting a bit darker."

They walked together, did not speak, followed their own tracks back through the soft snow, over the crest, began to move down, into the chilling shade of the taller trees, and Chamberlain suddenly felt a brief flash of depression—he was going back down, back to the real world.

He knew that Tom was right, that there was much to be thankful for. He had been named to the prestigious Chair, vacated by the famous Calvin Stowe, with the title of Professor of Rhetoric and Oratory. It was a stunning accomplishment for a man in his mid-twenties, and the prestige focused even more attention on this brilliant young man with the certain future. He thought, Yes, I have so much . . . Fannie is so happy. And he thought of the baby, the precious little girl, and the tiny face gave way to images of classrooms and the pages of black writing, the lectures he had already prepared for next week.

He kicked his boots through the snow and saw the dark hallways of Bowdoin, endless tunnels in gray buildings, and he felt something, a small twist in his stomach, and he did not understand: What is wrong with me?

As he moved down the long hill, the trees became thicker, darker, and the walking was easier, the snow harder and thinner under the great pines. His brother moved ahead of him, darting between the trees along the familiar trail. Chamberlain watched him slide over the small slick patches, the glazed areas of ice, hardened by many footsteps. He began to pay more attention to his own feet, the treacherous footing, and he marveled at his brother's recklessness, slipping, nearly falling, then upright again. Chamberlain moved carefully, feeling his way over the glassy ground, and soon Tom was gone, farther down the hill, and Chamberlain could hear him, faint whoops as he ran and slid, closer to the house of their parents. He'll make it without a bruise, Chamberlain thought, and I'll move slow and easy, and break my leg.

He leaned against a thick fir tree, held on to low, stiff branches, steadied himself, listened, knew Tom was at the house by now, and he caught a faint smell, smoke, from the chimney. He looked back up the hill, through the dark trees, saw heavy clouds, there *would* be snow tonight, and he released the branches, slid a few inches, took a step down, tested the firmness, then thought, No, I'm not ready to leave, not yet. He turned, looked out through the trees, carefully took a long step up, out of the trail, climbed up to softer snow, began to move away from the trail, from tree to tree, felt better footing now, the snow not hardened by the constant travel.

He walked along the dark slope, felt his way over fallen branches, old stumps. The weight of the gun was tiring him, and he thought of laying it down, leaning it against a tree. But no, not a good idea, he might not find it until spring, and his father would go through the roof, so he raised it up, rested it on his shoulder, and moved farther along, into the trees. He came to an old flat stump, capped with thick snow that he pushed away with a sweep of his arm, and sat down.

He knew the house was just below, maybe a hundred yards, and he could see them, could imagine the scene: Fannie was there, with the baby, and his other brothers, Hod and John. His mother would be in sublime control, preparing the great dinner, and Fannie would offer to help, a polite and insincere gesture, and his mother would say, "No, it's all done," and the young men would sit impatiently in front of the fire, waiting for the feast, and make conversation about very little, and yet the whole house would be filled with a common feeling, a sense that they were all loved, all of them, by each other, and as one family. And by now Tom was there, shaking snow from his boots and excitedly telling them all about the deer and his older brother, the hunter who would not shoot, and Chamberlain knew that his father would say nothing, make some small gesture of unspoken hopelessness, another disappointment.

He should have gone to West Point. That was the first disappointment. He had heard that now for years, especially after his graduation from Bowdoin, when he enrolled instead at the Theological Seminary. It had been the happiest day of his mother's life, her dream that her oldest son would become a man of God, and his father had just turned away, did not share his wife's closeness with the Almighty. But Chamberlain did not find the great spark, the powerful commitment to his faith, and so after his courses at the seminary, he had gone back to Bowdoin, and not to West Point, to teach the subjects he had so mastered; and so, to his father, there was another disappointment.

He was named Lawrence Joshua Chamberlain, but had switched the two, thinking "Joshua Lawrence" had a more formal sound, a better rhythm, and yet in a stroke of illogic preferred to be called Lawrence. His father preferred it as well—he had named him to honor the famous military hero of 1812, Commodore Lawrence, the man forever known for the quote, "Don't give up the ship." His mother would not relent, preferred the more biblical Joshua, and though both his father and grandfather had been named Joshua, his father had settled on calling him Lawrence, and Chamberlain had always wondered if it was because his mother did not.

He stared down the hill, closed his eyes, felt a great weight of gloom.

By now they would begin to wonder. Fannie would say something, ask Tom to go out and see what was keeping him, and he felt guilty, did not want them to worry, but knew they had no idea, could not understand why he sat alone on a cold stump in the thick, darkening woods.

Everyone, he thought . . . all of them, even my father, they're all happy for me, they see me now as a success. But he did not feel like a success. This should be the happiest time of my life, he thought, and he searched for it, tried to feel the self-satisfaction, the sense of standing at the entrance to a long and prestigious career, a doorway to great academic achievement, and he felt nothing, no sense of thrill, no anticipation. He thought of Tom's comment, back on the hill, "You make good money," and he smiled. Any salary would seem like good money to someone who had never had a job. But Chamberlain was not pleased with the meager living he was offered for his teaching, had even added to his own workload, was now teaching languages as well, anything he could do to supplement his income. He scolded himself: There is something foolish about all this, I am, after all, in the very position I had sought. This was what he was meant to do, clearly. He was a natural scholar, could master any discipline put before him, but when he thought of that, he felt it again, the twist in his stomach.

I need to come up here more often, he thought, the hills, the great wide silence. Give it time.

Fannie had been reluctant to marry him, had worried about his career, their ability to raise a family. But Fannie was already happier, and there would be more children. He smiled at that, thought, A son, I would truly love to have a son, to bring him up here, show him this world, maybe even teach him to hunt, if he wants to. He might be better at it than I am.

He felt a cold wetness coming up through his pants, the melting dampness from the icy stump, but he did not move, sat still for a while longer, felt a great weariness, the need to go back. He looked down at the musket, cradled in his arms, looked along the dull metal of the barrel, saw rust spots, small brown circles, thought, Better work on that, I will certainly get the blame. He straightened his back, began to reach his arms up, a long stretch, and in the thick silence he heard a noise, a slight crunch of snow. He turned quietly, saw movement a few yards away, behind a tree, and then a deer emerged, a few short steps, and was clear of the tree.

Its head was down, searching along the ground, prodding small openings in the snow, for some small piece of brown grass, and Chamberlain saw he was huge, antlers wide and tall and heavy, and a thick neck, a chest like a brown barrel, larger than any deer he had ever seen, and the deer eased along, did not yet see him, and he brought the gun slowly up to his shoulder, pulled the hammer back with his thumb, slowly, slowly, and the hammer clicked lightly into position. The deer raised its head, froze, looking at him, and he sighted down the barrel, placed the small metal bead on the animal's shoulder and pulled the trigger. There was a loud snap, and the gun did not fire. Chamberlain had leaned forward, anticipating the heavy recoil from the old gun, nearly fell off the stump, and there was a quick flash of the white tail and the deer was instantly gone.

He stood up, his heart pounding heavily, thought of running after the deer, another chance, but knew it was pointless. He looked at the gun, said aloud, "Well, I'll be damned," and he started walking, began to move back through the woods, toward the trail.

They will never believe me, he thought, and laughed nervously, stopped, felt his hands shaking. An icy chill ran down his legs, and he knew it wasn't just the cold; he had never felt like this before. He had never enjoyed shooting anything, but this had been pure instinct, without thought—he had never wanted to kill something so badly in his life, and now it shook him, frightened him. He started walking again, quickly followed his own tracks back toward the trail, smelled the smoke again. He reached the trail, began a quick stumbling descent to the house. Far above, drifting down through the tops of the tall trees, it began to snow.

4. LEE

November 1859

A T LAST THE HOUSE WAS QUIET. HE HAD TRIED TO DO SOME work, sat at the desk in the old man's study, but the girls seemed especially playful that morning. Young Robert, Jr. had been their victim, and the joyous cries had echoed through the vast rooms like the sound of bells. Lee hadn't stopped them, would not interfere, had just sat back in the old chair and listened with a quiet smile. It was Monday morning, and the schools were calling, and Lee wondered if the chance of getting out, of spending time away from the grim house was having an effect.

Mary was still upstairs, and Lee knew she was still in bed. The nights were difficult, the pains kept her awake for long hours, and Lee could do nothing to soothe her, to stop the pain.

Now the children and the happy sounds were gone, outside and away, and once again the house was still. Lee picked up a sheet of paper, ran his finger down a long list of materials, the lumber and hardware still needed for repairing the house.

Of all the tasks he was facing, the repairs came slowest. The fall harvest was completed, and there was more time, and so he looked to the house, the work that had been put aside for the more important job of getting the farm into production.

He rechecked the list of lumber, refigured the roofing for the outbuildings, and heard a carriage, the sound of a horse on the bricks of the front entranceway. He stood, put on the dark gray coat that hung across a chair and went out into the barnlike foyer. He could see a figure through the glass, a soldier. The man did not ring the brass bell, had seen Lee coming, waited.

"Yes, what is it?" Lee pulled the door open, then straightened in surprise. "Well, my word. Mr. Stuart, Lieutenant Stuart! Quite a surprise!"

"Sir! I am honored to see you again, Colonel."

Lee opened the door wide, stepped back and motioned the young soldier into the house.

"Lieutenant, I regret to say you have just missed the girls. They have grown up . . . and I'm sorry, my wife . . ."

"Yes, Colonel, I heard about Mrs. Lee. I am dreadfully sorry for her condition. Please pay my respects, sir, when you are able."

Lee led the young cavalryman into the study, felt a flood of energy, had not seen him since he graduated from the Point. It was no secret that J.E.B. Stuart had been Lee's favorite cadet.

"I heard you had been assigned out West, but after I went to Texas, I didn't hear much more. My word, it is good to see you!"

Stuart was embarrassed, was not used to a show of emotion from Lee. He held a plumed hat firmly at his waist and clutched the brim with both hands.

"Yes, sir, I was in Kansas. Sent to fight Indians, spent more time chasing the guerrillas, the insurrectionists. Quite a mess out there, sir. The army seems caught in the middle . . . seems like no way to make people get along. Sad, bloody place. But, sir, I have news!"

Lee smiled. Stuart always had a way of turning the conversation, any topic, back to himself.

"Sir, I am married! And, a child! Perhaps you know Colonel Cooke, Philip St. George Cooke, a Virginian, of course. I married his little girl! And, well, we have come back here . . . a visit . . . the colonel was helpful in arranging a leave for me so that he could see his new grandbaby."

"Well, Lieutenant, it seems you have been busy. I never doubted that . . . not for a moment. I am honored you found the time to call on me."

Stuart suddenly brought a hand up to his mouth. "Oh, sir . . . no . . . thank you, but I am here officially, from the War Department, actually. I was there this morning, hoping to arrange a meeting with the Secretary. I have this invention, you see, a means of attaching the sword—"

Lee knew he would have to steer the young man back to the main subject, gently interrupted, "Lieutenant, the War Department? You have a message for me?"

"Oh . . . yes, sir. I was sitting in the clerk's office, waiting for the chance to see the Secretary, when Colonel Drinkard suddenly appeared, handed me this." He reached into his coat pocket and brought out a small envelope. "He asked me if I knew the way to Arlington. I have been instructed to give this to you."

Stuart looked at the note, studied it for a brief moment, then suddenly remembered his duty, came to noisy attention, and handed it with a snap of his arm to Lee.

Lee could not help a smile. "Thank you, Lieutenant, you may stand at ease."

Stuart complied, then leaned slightly forward, looked at the envelope, waited impatiently for Lee to open it.

Lee unfolded a small piece of linen stationery, read aloud, for Stuart's benefit. " 'From the chief clerk, Colonel Drinkard, at the request of the Secretary of War, Mr. Floyd, Colonel Lee will report to the Secretary's office with all haste.' "

Lee looked at Stuart, and Stuart said, "That's it? Just . . . report?"

"Appears so. Well, Lieutenant, would you be obliged to give me a ride over the bridge? We can leave . . . right now, actually."

"But your uniform, sir. You are not dressed."

Lee looked at his civilian clothes, the dark wool suit. "Nothing in the note about a uniform, Lieutenant. They seem to prefer haste to dress. I suspect the Secretary will forgive the oversight."

Lee pointed the way, and Stuart went quickly to the front door and held it stiffly open. Lee stopped and looked up, glanced at the top of the vast stairway, knew Mary was sleeping, would stay in bed all day. A note, he thought. I should let her know.

He moved back into the office, pulled out a sheet of clean paper, wrote a few words, paused. Stuart had moved to the office doorway, watching him, and Lee looked at the bright young face, eager, full of life, then finished the note: "I might be gone awhile." He wondered how she would react to that. He was always to be gone for just a while. Without speaking, he folded the note, passed Stuart and moved quickly up the stairs toward the silence.

THEY CLIMBED THE CLEAN WHITE STEPS THAT LED TO THE OFfices of the Secretary of War, and above them, from the wide doorway, came Secretary Floyd himself, leading a cluster of young clerks.

"Ah, Colonel Lee, greetings, yes, left a message upstairs for you. We are off to the White House, please accompany us."

Lee said, "Certainly, at your service, sir," thought of asking more, knew it would wait for now. Behind him, he heard Stuart, a rough whisper, and Lee understood, asked Floyd, "Do you mind if we are accompanied by Lieutenant Stuart? He is serving as my . . . aide."

Floyd nodded, did not look at Stuart. "Fine, fine, let's move a bit, shall we?"

The crowded carriage rolled quickly to the President's home, and the group of men walked swiftly into the building, Stuart jumping in front to open doors.

Lee had met President Buchanan at social functions, really did not know much about him, about the man. But he realized that all this commotion was serious; there was none of the social banter of politicians.

Lee and Floyd were escorted past guards into the President's office. Stuart, knowing he had to remain outside, sat deeply into a thick chair, pouting silently.

Lee followed Floyd into a wide office, sunlight pouring through great windows. Aides were moving away, and Lee could see Buchanan sitting across a vast desk.

The President said, "Colonel Lee, welcome. Allow me to dispense with pleasantries, if you will. Colonel, we have what seems to be an emergency, a situation. We need you to command a military force, to lead troops against . . . well, we don't know what. A revolution, an insurrection, call it what you will."

Lee's eyes widened. He had heard nothing of any trouble.

Buchanan continued, "Harper's Ferry . . . from what we have heard, the Government Arsenal has been captured, trains have stopped running. We've heard as many as five hundred, maybe more, a slave uprising."

Floyd nodded vigorously. "Five hundred at least, slaves rising up, yes, a great deal of bloodshed."

Buchanan glanced at Floyd, impatient, went on. "Colonel, you are to take command of a company of marines that is currently en route, and three companies of infantry from Fort Monroe that are preparing to move. The militia has been called out as well, mostly Maryland men, I believe, some Virginians."

Floyd nodded sharply. "Yes, Maryland and Virginia."

Lee sat quietly, absorbed, waited for more.

"Is there a problem, Colonel?"

"No, not at all, Mr. President, I am honored to be your choice . . . but I am confused why—"

"Because you are *here*, Colonel. Washington is full of ranking officers who haven't led troops in decades. There's no time to bring in anybody from the field. According to General Scott, you're the best man we've got, under the circumstances. There should be no further need for explanation, Colonel."

"No, sir, certainly not. I will leave immediately for Harper's Ferry. Do we know anything about . . . any idea who or what this is about, who we are dealing with?"

Floyd spoke up: "Kansas ruffians, insurrectionists, slaves. That's all we know. It's chaos, Colonel."

Lee thought, There are few slaves at Harper's Ferry. But . . . the Arsenal—if there was an uprising, it was a prime target, a huge store of guns that could supply a massive revolution. But something nagged at Lee, some feeling that he had heard this before: the rumors that flew through Texas, huge hordes of Indians terrorizing the plains, frightened civilians, the constant alert for a crisis that was never there. Still, there was the Arsenal.

"Good luck, Colonel. Keep the Secretary posted on events, if you don't mind. It seems that real information is in short supply."

"Yes, Mr. President, I will do my best."

The meeting was over, and as the men left the President's office, passing through the heavy oak door, Stuart jumped to his feet, his eyes imploring Lee for details, and Floyd stopped, turned to Lee and said, "I don't have to tell you what this means, Colonel. This could look very bad for us here, very bad for . . . the President. The public is very nervous. All this talk of slave revolts, and now . . . my God." His voice quieted and he leaned closer to Lee. "You must protect us!"

Lee slid away from Floyd, said, "Will the Secretary provide us a ride to the train station? We will secure a car immediately. And perhaps a courier. I should . . . could you please send word to my family."

Floyd nodded, excited. "Certainly, Colonel. Right away."

Lee turned away, moved past the huddle of clerks, past grand portraits on stark white walls, down the wide steps to the lush green lawn, Stuart following close behind. He heard Stuart comment, a low curse, something about politicians. Lee did not answer, let it go by, thought now of Mary, tried to see the soft face, but the image would not come, and so he began to think of his new command.

T HE MARINES WERE UP AHEAD, WAITING FOR THEIR NEW COM-mander. Lee had wired to the station in Baltimore, told them he was close behind, instructed them to stop at Sandy Hook, just outside Harper's Ferry. It was long past dark when Lee and Stuart caught up, and as the two men stepped from the train car, a young officer approached, saw only Stuart's cavalry uniform, saluted him with a puzzled look.

"Sir, are you. . . ? I was told to expect a Colonel Lee."

"I am Colonel Lee, this is Lieutenant Stuart, my aide. Forgive my appearance, Lieutenant, there was not time for proper dress."

"Yes, sir. I understand, sir. Lieutenant Green at your service. I am to turn command of the marines over to you."

"Very well, Lieutenant, I assume command." Lee looked past the young man, saw neat rows of crisp blue, men waiting for orders. "Lieutenant, is there anything you can tell us?"

"Well, yes, sir. The bridge over to Harper's Ferry is wide open, no resistance that we can see. We've heard a few shots, but nothing major."

Lee was not surprised. A more accurate picture was beginning to form in his mind.

"And over there, Colonel, state militia has been arriving since we've been here, several companies. I don't know who is in command there, sir."

Out beyond the station platform Lee saw troops gathering in the darkness, a ragged formation of volunteers, numbers swelling by the minute, and he had an uneasy feeling, did not look forward to commanding men who were not used to command. He stepped down off the platform, walked out toward the uneven groups of men, saw someone who appeared to be in charge.

"Excuse me, sir, are you in command of these men?"

The man turned, gave a quick glance to the older man in the dark suit, sniffed with the air of a man of importance.

"Pardon me, sir, but I have no time for interviews. I must organize these men here—"

"That's good to hear, sir. I am Lieutenant Colonel Robert E. Lee, and by order of the President I am assuming command of your militia."

The man turned again, looked Lee over doubtfully, said, "I do not know you . . . Colonel. Forgive me if I'm somewhat cautious. We don't know who the enemy is here. Have you some orders, some documentation?"

From the platform behind him, Lee heard the voice of Stuart, calling out, "Colonel, a wire for you. The infantry is in Baltimore, awaiting your orders. And the marines are ready to move out on your command, sir."

The militia commander began to respond, puzzled, then realized Stuart had been talking to Lee.

"Well, forgive my suspicions, Colonel. I am Colonel Shriver of the Maryland militia. I suppose . . . my men are at your disposal."

"Thank you, Colonel. Perhaps you can tell me exactly what we are confronting here."

"From what we have learned from the townspeople, sir, there is a group of men barricaded in the Arsenal, with some hostages, local citizens."

"How many, Colonel? How many men, how many hostages?"

"Perhaps twenty, or more."

"Hostages?"

"Oh, no, sir, the insurrectionists, the rioters. There may be ten or twelve hostages. The insurrectionists fought with some local militia for most of the day, and then holed up in the engine house, inside the Arsenal."

"Any notion who is in charge?"

"I have heard, a man named Smith . . . something like that."

"Very well, Colonel. Have your men fall into line behind the marines. Keep them together, good order. Let's move out."

Stuart had walked down toward the road, the wide bridge over the Potomac. He turned, ran back up the short hill, met Lee at the platform, motioned to the bridge.

"There are people, Colonel, wagons, moving across the bridge, both ways. Looks awfully . . . normal."

"I know, Lieutenant. I believe this situation will soon be under control. Would you please go to the telegraph window and wire the Baltimore station my orders to return the infantry to Fort Monroe. I don't believe we will be needing an army here."

"Yes, sir, right away."

"And, Lieutenant, send a wire to Secretary Floyd. Tell him his revolution has an army of twenty men."

"Sir?"

"No, you had better just tell him the situation is in hand and not as serious as rumor would suggest."

"Yes, sir, I understand."

Lee walked over to the lines of marines, saw curious faces watching him, said, "I am Lieutenant Colonel Lee, Second Regiment of Cavalry. Forgive my lack of uniform. I don't know what you have heard about what is happening over that bridge, but I assure you, it will not be as bad as you've been told. Now, gentlemen, if you will move out behind me, we may proceed."

Lee glanced at Lieutenant Green, who saluted, and put the men into motion, then Lee walked down and away from the platform, toward the dim lamplights of the bridge.

THERE WERE SEVERAL DOZEN CITIZENS ARMED WITH OLD MUS-kets, some with pickaxes and shovels. As Lee approached, the crowds moved aside, cheering the troops. They had made a makeshift barricade around the engine house, overturned wagons and broken barrels. He saw a man point a rifle, fire blindly into the dark, then an answering shot came from the engine house, and the civilians ducked behind their crude wall.

Lee halted the men behind the barricade, and Green and Stuart began to move the people back. There were shouts, mostly toward the engine house—curses, taunts of what they were going to get now.

Colonel Shriver walked up beside Lee, said, "It's been like this all day, Colonel. Potshots back and forth. There was a good scrap earlier, before they holed up. A couple of their men didn't make it inside, killed by civilians. The hostages are mostly workers, Arsenal workers who walked right into the fight."

A woman suddenly appeared out of the dark, older, bent, head wrapped in an old scarf. She looked at Lee, then Shriver.

"Who's in charge, one of you?"

"I am Lieutenant Colonel Lee, madam, in command."

"Well, *Lieutenant Colonel* Lee, one of the men inside that building is my good friend, and a distinguished gentleman. He tried to stop this, wanted to talk to them, and they kept him! Took him prisoner! He's kin to President Washington, he is. Lewis Washington. You take care with him in there, Lieutenant Colonel Lee."

Lee knew Lewis Washington well, his wife's cousin, the President's grandnephew. He sagged, looked at the engine house. Putting a familiar face on the hostages should not have made a difference, but he could not help it. His first plan had been to storm the building immediately, but in the dark and in the confusion it was likely that there would be more blood than necessary. He turned to the young marine.

"Lieutenant Green, have your men take up position here, spread behind these barricades. Colonel Shriver, would you please deploy your men in a wide circle around the building. I want it perfectly clear to these people they are surrounded. Make some noise, be obvious about it, but keep your heads down. And Colonel Shriver, before you go—we will be moving in at daylight. Would your men like the honor of capturing these troublemakers?"

"Thank you for the offer. I am honored, sir. But, well, these men are volunteers, they have wives . . . families. Your soldiers here . . . the marines . . . are paid for this sort of thing, are they not?"

Lee looked at the fat face, lit by dim firelight. "Of course, Colonel. The marines will handle this."

Lee saw Green placing his men, waited until he had completed the job, then motioned to Stuart to join him with the young marine.

"Lieutenant Green, I want you to pick out a dozen men, good men. They will be the assault team. Lieutenant Stuart, I will prepare a message to the insurrectionists, which you will deliver. It will say that they are surrounded, and I will guarantee their safety, and so forth. When they accept the terms, the marines will move in quickly and subdue the men, removing their weapons. Once they understand the hopelessness of their situation, this should end quickly. Now, post guards, Mr. Green. Let the others get some sleep. We will talk again at daylight."

There was a commotion down the line, a marine guard held a man roughly by the arm, brought him toward the officers.

"Excuse me, Colonel, Lieutenant. This man claims to have information."

Green excused his man, and Lee watched the civilian in lamplight, adjusting himself from the gruff treatment by the marine.

"Colonel, my name is Fulton, I'm a newspaperman, from Philadelphia. I know who your man is, there." He pointed toward the engine house.

"How do you know, Mr. Fulton?" Lee asked. He looked the man over, saw a good suit, dark gray wool, like his own.

"I've been in Kansas, covering the trouble there. I have interviewed many of the insurrectionists, Colonel, they seem to favor reporters. I suppose we provide them a soapbox, if you will. Colonel, I have no doubt that the man you are facing is Mr. John Brown."

It was a name faintly familiar to Lee, did not carry great weight. But Stuart said, "John Brown? Here?"

Lee looked at Stuart, heard the pitch in his voice. "What do you know of the man, Lieutenant?"

"He is trouble, Colonel. He led some of the radical antislavery people out West. Slipped through our fingers more than once."

Fulton said, "He is a violent man, Colonel, a man who will not hesitate to kill himself and everyone around him for his cause."

"He's right, Colonel. Brown is . . . well, I think he's crazy. Wants the slaves to rise up, thinks he can start a revolution. I saw a paper, something he spread all over Kansas, telling the white people, his *own* people . . . they were all going to die."

Lee stared at Stuart, let it sink in. "Mr. Fulton," he said, "how can you be so certain?"

"Colonel, I've been following Brown for some time, written a few stories about him. He didn't seem to mind me snooping around. I knew he was headed this way, might try for the Arsenal."

Stuart's voice rose. "You knew he was coming here, and you didn't warn anybody?"

Lee put a hand on Stuart's arm, said, "We're here now, gentlemen, let's work on solving our situation here. Mr. Fulton, thank you, you are excused."

"Thank you, Colonel. Best of luck." Then the man slid away, was gone in the dark.

Lee thought of the hostages. His mind began to work, he absorbed the new information, the uncertainty of a man like Brown. His simple plan might result in a bloodbath. He felt his stomach tighten, a chill in the cool night.

"Gentlemen, this is a new situation. Our priority is the safety of the hostages. Lieutenant Stuart, if Mr. Brown rejects the terms, and I suspect he will, you are not to negotiate. The marines must storm the entrance immediately."

Both men nodded approval, and Green said, "Sir. Begging your pardon, sir, but we need a signal, something to tell us when to move."

Lee looked at Stuart, who touched his hat.

"If they . . . if Brown rejects the surrender," Stuart said, "I will remove my hat, drop it downward. That will be the signal to move in."

"Very well," Lee said. "Mr. Stuart, I will have the message ready for you shortly. Mr. Green, we must use the bayonet. We do not know the situation in there—we cannot have your men firing at will."

"I understand, sir. It will be bayonets. I will have the men prepare a battering ram. We will make good work of it, sir."

"Very well. Get some rest, Lieutenant, I will speak with you at dawn."

"Sir!"

Lee found a wooden box, sat down. Stuart grabbed a lantern, a careless target left sitting on top of the barricade. He brought it closer, out of sight of the engine house, and Lee pulled a pen from his pocket, the same pen he had used that morning to figure his list of lumber, and wrote out the terms of surrender.

I T WAS JUST DAYLIGHT, A COLD, THICK MORNING, FOG ROLLING OFF the river into the small town. Lee climbed up a small hill, a short distance behind the barricade, to find a clear view, and was suddenly aware that the hills around him were covered with people. In the night, the town had poured from its homes, and now everyone, Lee guessed a thousand, maybe more, was watching the proceedings. He looked back to the engine house, saw the militia stirring, forming into line all around, a toothless presence that might at least intimidate Brown into surrender. Through the mist he saw the blue form of Lieutenant Green, moving up the hill toward him.

"Colonel. Good morning. We are ready when you are, sir. We await the order."

Below, Stuart was tying a white handkerchief to a short pole with quick, nervous motions, and then he turned, saw Lee and ran up the hill. "All set, Colonel!" Stuart was breathless, shivering.

Lee looked at Green, gave him a nod, and the young marine went toward a small group of men, his handpicked troops. Lee waited for him to leave, out of earshot. Then he put a hand on Stuart's arm, a brief clench from his cold fingers. "Lieutenant," he said, "it would please me if you would use some caution this morning. We have no way of knowing how this man Brown will respond."

"Colonel . . ." But there were no words, both men knew it was just duty. "I await your order, sir. Let's take these people out."

Lee nodded. "You may proceed, Lieutenant."

Stuart ran back down, picked up his flag of truce, pulled Lee's message from his pocket, and, with a glance toward the waiting marines, walked past the barricade, across the open ground, to the engine house door.

Lee heard Stuart's voice, firm and unshaking, and he held his breath, said to God, *Please, let there be reason, protect him from harm.* Suddenly, the door opened, a slight movement, and Lee could only see a dark, faceless crack.

Stuart looked into the slight gap, saw a short barrel of a rusty carbine pushing out through the opening, pointing at his head. He focused on the small black hole, the end of the barrel, stood without motion, said quietly, "I have a message . . . a request from Colonel Robert E. Lee. Please allow me to read it."

There was noise from inside, hushed sounds. Stuart could hear people moving, and from behind the rifle came a face, smeared black dirt in a wild mass of tangled beard, and Stuart recognized the glare of the deep black eyes, the face of John Brown.

Stuart showed the paper, held it up, could not look away from the eyes, and Brown said with a quick burst, "Read it!"

Stuart began, emphasized the part about their safe passage, the impossible nature of their position. Lee's words were brief, to the point, and as Stuart read, he glanced at Brown, at the small black hole pointing at his head, wished the message had been shorter.

Brown began to make a sound, a hissing grunt. The barrel of the rifle stuck farther out, closer to Stuart's face, and Brown began to speak, a quick stream of words, his own terms, his version of the day's fighting, a flurry of talking that Stuart tried to follow. Behind Brown there were other voices, joining in, and Stuart knew the situation was falling apart, felt the tightening in his body like a coiled spring, and said, "Colonel Lee will hear no discussion. . . ." and Brown began again, made demands for safe conduct, mentioned the hostages. The voices became louder behind Brown, hostages were calling out, pleading for help, the voices blending together in a dull roar, and Stuart began to feel overwhelmed, stared into the barrel of the rifle. Then one voice, clearer, older, yelled out, and even Lee heard the words, the voice of Lewis Washington.

"Never mind us, fire!"

Stuart backed away one step from the rifle, said, "Colonel Lee will not discuss your demands," and suddenly the rifle was gone, back into the dark, and the door closed with a loud thump. Stuart stared at the door, then turned, looked at the marines, took a deep breath, reached his hand up, a slight quiver, and removed his hat.

From the barricade the marines rushed forward, and men in sharp blue uniforms began to pound on the thick wooden door. After several heavy blows the door splintered and a hole was punched through. Green threw himself into the hole. Behind him, his men lined up, pushing their way in one at a time.

Lee saw the marines disappear inside, a painfully slow assault. Then there were shots, and Lee knew it would not be the marines.

Inside, Green was frantic, he had only a sword, and he saw the face of the man who had spoken to Stuart, focused on him, saw the rifle, and hurled himself in a screaming rush. He brought the sword down and knocked the rifle away. Brown lunged at the young man, tried to grab him around the neck, and Green raised the sword again, brought it down heavily on Brown's head. The sword hit sideways, the blade bent at a useless angle, and Brown tried again, grabbed for Green's neck, but the young man turned the sword, swung the heavy handle against Brown's head, and with a cry of pain Brown went down.

Behind their lieutenant the marines made use of their bayonets. The shooting stopped and men lay wounded all around the inside of the building. Green turned, saw the hostages huddled in a group against one wall, then looked back to the door, daylight through the ragged opening, and he saw blue coats, two of his men on the ground. They had just made it through, were shot down just inside the door, and Green went to the men, saw the blood and yelled out. They were dragged aside, the door was pulled open, and the rising sun flooded the dark space. It was over.

B ROWN WAS HELD IN A SECURE ROOM IN THE ARSENAL, AND NOW the politicians came, to see for themselves how the great rebellion had been crushed. Lee stood aside, performed his official duties, while Brown was questioned by anyone who had the influence to see him.

Lee and Stuart went about the business of identifying Brown's cohorts, dead and alive, captured a small store of arms Brown had accumulated, but to Lee, his work was done. He notified Secretary Floyd that the matter was concluded, that in his opinion there was little for Washington to be concerned about.

The marines and Lieutenant Green remained in Harper's Ferry as security, and served as escort when Brown was moved to Charlestown for trial. Despite wild rumors of new riots elsewhere and threats of attempts to free him, Brown was tried and convicted without incident, and was sentenced to be hanged.

5. JACKSON

NOVEMBER 1859

THE DIRT SIFTED THROUGH HIS FINGERS LIKE FINE BROWN SUGAR. Jackson sat, dug his hands into the soft soil again, held it up, watched it pour down. It was his, his dirt, his land. From where he sat, he could look across the twenty-acre patch, down the long straight rows, the newly planted winter crops. The green sprouts of the collards and turnips had broken the soil a few weeks before, and now the new life in the garden was stronger, ready for the coming cold. He slid along on the seat of his pants, between the thickening green lines, plucked out the intruders, the errant weeds. Winter was sliding across the mountains, and he looked up, toward the west, saw the cold gray line of thick clouds. There will be snow tonight, he thought, and frowned, looked out over the patch, concerned.

He stood up, stretched, raised both arms above his head, reached upward, felt the pressure in his back, scolded himself for sitting so long on the cold ground.

"Not healthy, not at all," he said aloud.

These days his health seemed to come and go, the pains in his side, his poor vision. He had taken trips to the hot springs and water spas over the summer, but it was Anna who worried him. She had still not recovered from the baby's death, and he missed her quick energy, her playfulness. She had taken the water treatments with him, had seen the same doctors, but seemed to be no better.

He stood stiffly, put his hands on his hips, made dirty handprints on his cotton trousers, looked out over the garden. Surely, this will please God, he thought, an offering, the labor of new life. He bent down, rubbed his fingers along a short green stem, prickly and rough. These are Your children too, he thought.

Townspeople had passed by throughout the day, small carriages and lone riders, and at midday he had seen the stage to Staunton. There were friendly greetings, and he had acknowledged them, returned waves. There was space behind his home, a fine spot for a small garden, but it was not enough, and so he had bought this piece of plain land, barely outside the expanding boundary of the town, a flat field hugged by the rolling hills, and people would stop just to admire, to point and wave at the major, this odd professor who so thoroughly groomed his small farm.

He looked again at the clouds, the dark movement, thought of home, the good smells of supper, wiped his hands on an old rag and began to step past the neat rows, toward the main road, when he heard a shout.

"Major! Major Jackson!"

It was a cadet. Jackson could see the uniform bouncing on the back of a horse, riding wildly toward him from the town. The boy was waving one arm, then had to use it to steady himself, then waved again. Jackson thought, Not a very good rider, something we should work on . . .

"Major Jackson, sir!" The boy reined up, jumped from the saddle, stumbled sideways and landed in a heap of gray and white. The horse did not stop, ran on a short way, contemptuous.

The boy gathered himself, grimaced, felt a knee, then stood at attention and saluted. Jackson returned it, though, as the boy quickly noted, his ragged farming clothes did not present him as any kind of officer.

Jackson waited for the boy to catch his breath, then said, "You all right, cadet? Nasty fall."

"Yes, sir. Not my horse, sir, had to grab the closest one, and well . . . Sir, I have been instructed by the commandant, by Colonel Smith himself, sir, to request in the strongest terms that you report to the colonel as soon as is possible, sir."

Jackson straightened, wiped his hands again. "Now? Is there some problem?"

"Sir, I have only heard reports that we have been called to duty, sir. By the governor."

"The governor? Well, all right, then. You return to Colonel Smith, report that I am right behind you. You are dismissed."

"Yes, sir. Thank you, sir."

The boy walked gingerly toward the horse and took the reins. The horse allowed him to mount, and with a quick yelp from the boy, it turned and carried its rider toward the town.

Jackson started down the road at a quick pace. His house was on the way to the institute, and it would not take him long to dress. Behind him, in the west, the thick clouds rolled forward, the unstoppable flow of the coming storm.

I T WAS DARK WHEN JACKSON ARRIVED AT THE COMMANDANT'S OF-fice. There were other officers there, small quiet talk, anxious whispers. Jackson closed the heavy door behind him, stood in the entranceway, nodded to the others, saw both dress and casual uniforms, a hasty assembly.

From down the hallway there was a voice. Cadets moved quickly by, saluting the officers. Jackson watched the young faces, tried to recall the names, as Colonel Smith stepped noisily into the room.

"Gentlemen, as you were. Sorry to call you out like this, evening meal and all, I know . . . but we have received some orders, a rather important assignment. Allow me to read it."

He reached into his vest pocket, drew out a folded paper, opened it, and Jackson could see a ribbon, the seal of some importance.

"From: The Honorable Henry A. Wise, Governor, the Commonwealth of Virginia.

To: Colonel Francis H. Smith, Commandant, Virginia Military Institute.

By Special Order, the Officers and Corps of Cadets, Virginia Military Institute, shall report to Charlestown, Virginia, on the twenty-eighth day of November, 1859, for the purpose of maintaining the general security, for the protection of the town and its inhabitants, and for the prevention of any violent uprising from interfering with the execution by hanging of Mr. John Brown."

Jackson felt a sudden lump in his stomach. The insurrection that John Brown had attempted was a hot topic, and reckless rumors had flooded over the countryside after his capture. But he had believed the Federal Army would handle the matter. Someone spoke, Jackson turned and saw Major Gilham.

"Colonel, are we to be the only security?"

"Let's just say, Major, we're the only *organized* security. The governor has already issued a call for militia, and units from all over the state have been assembled, but I would not place much stock in their ability to do anything more than cause trouble. Oh, and there's one more thing." Smith looked back to the paper, found his place, stopped.

"Well, no need to read it all, point is, not only are we to provide security, but it appears the good governor has decided that I am to be the executioner in charge. I don't have to tell you that, in fact, our Corps of Cadets, with you gentlemen in command, may find itself up against . . . well, God knows what."

Jackson felt a low fire deep in his gut, thought of his guns, the artillery crews. They were very young, and some of them were not very good, but he began to run the faces through his mind, assess the skills.

"Gentlemen," Smith continued, "your commands will cover your areas of expertise, of course. In the morning, we will issue the order to the corps to move out. Major Jackson . . ."

Jackson's thoughts scrambled, he snapped to attention and stared straight, past the colonel.

"Major, you will bring a two-piece battery of your cannon. Pick some good boys, Major. This could be a difficult assignment."

"Yes, sir. Already working on it, sir."

Smith spoke to the other officers individually, and Jackson did not hear, had his orders. Then they were dismissed, and he moved back outside, felt the cold chill of the night, looked across the parade grounds, the wide space guarded by his guns. He looked at them, each one, and nodded, a brief greeting to the heavy brass, then he graded, appraised, silently chose the two he would take, and smiled, a quick, cold clench of his mouth. Then he turned and marched home through a starless night.

ON THEIR FIFTH DAY CAMPED AROUND CHARLESTOWN, THE cadets woke to an early breakfast and new orders. Then there were drums, a slow cadence, giving a rhythm to the troops, who marched in line, filed into a large field, and formed their units. The artillery were first, had set up on the high ground, and Jackson stood by one of his cannon and faced the tall wooden scaffold, looking across to his other gun, pointing out, away from the forming troops. The units of cadet infantry filed in behind the scaffold, a vast rolling field, neat blocks of bright red, new field uniforms the cadets were wearing for the first time. Jackson's handpicked gun crew stood at rigid attention, and there was no talking, no looking about. From the vantage point of the rise, Jackson could see all the others, the ragged formation of volunteer troops, and beyond, the buildings of the town. A

crowd of people filled the road with the temper and bluster of a careless mob, following a wagon, and Jackson knew the cadets could not
control a riot, that they had to depend on these people to control
themselves.

The wagon climbed the rise, rolled closer. Jackson could see a soldier on horseback leading the way, and then the wagon itself, carrying
several officials and the local sheriff. High up above the rest, the figure
of John Brown sat on the head of his coal-black coffin.

The wagon rolled on slowly, approaching the scaffold, and Jackson watched with a tense gripping in his gut. The first chilling days of
December had arrived without incident, but to the experienced officers, the wild rumors had become troublesome; the cadets could be
easily spooked. There was talk of a vast number of Negroes, arming,
heading in a crazed mass toward the town to free their leader. It was
said that the Federal Army had abandoned the area, had assumed the
worst and fled, leaving these boys to fight off a revolution.

Jackson knew of rumors, had heard a continuous stream of them
in Mexico, knew they followed an army like flies. He did not believe
there was a revolution, that there would be a fight here. But if there
was . . . he glanced at the polished brass of his big gun. The townspeople spread out, people scrambling for the good view. Then they
began to quiet, a great weight pressing down upon them all, any sense
of celebration pushed away by the presence of the troops, these quiet
boys with guns.

The wagon passed close to Jackson, turned, and stopped at the
scaffold. He tried to see Brown's face, to get a close look at the eyes.
How different this was from war, he thought, to wait for death slowly,
to know with total certainty it was coming, would not catch you in the
heat of action, snatching you suddenly from your duty, but was there
in front of you, and you approached it with slow, steady steps. He felt
an odd respect for that, watched Brown move deliberately from the
wagon up the wooden stairs. As he reached the platform, Brown
smiled, made a comment to the sheriff, and said something to Colonel
Smith, who stood somberly to one side. Jackson looked up at the few
men now on the platform, saw no minister, no man of God, and he
was surprised, could not understand that, the rejection of God. Jackson
thought, He seems . . . cheerful, does not show any sign of fear, is not
appealing for mercy. . . .

Now Colonel Smith gave a quiet order to the sheriff, who said
something to Brown, then placed a white cap over Brown's head, covering the smiling face. The crowd now began to move, the slow pulse

of expectation, and Jackson heard the anxious muffled voices. It would be very soon.

Colonel Smith then read from a document, and Jackson could not hear the words, knew it was the death warrant, the governor's order. Then Smith motioned to the sheriff, a brief nod, and the sheriff leaned toward the colonel, made certain, and Jackson saw the sheriff's hand, the simple instrument of death, saw the blade flash, cutting the rope. The trapdoor, the floor beneath Brown's feet, opened with a clatter that startled the crowd, made them all jump in one sharp beat. Brown's body dropped down quickly, then caught, and Jackson heard the small sound, the rope tightening, and Brown's arms jerked up, bending at the elbows, small twitches in the stillness, and then down again, and then no motion. The body hung with a stillness that froze all who saw it. There was a light breeze, and the body began slowly to turn, to spin, and Jackson looked down and said a prayer. *Dear God, let this man pass over and be with You, even if he did not ask . . . did not understand . . . he is Your own.*

Then he heard a voice, a mad scream from the crowd, "Burn in Hell!" and others followed, hard shouts and small cries for damnation.

He looked back to Brown's lifeless body, thought, Perhaps it is meant for him to pass below, into the fires of Hell. Jackson clenched his fists. He could not bear that, could not believe that men could be judged to be so wicked, and that others would be so eager to condemn their brothers to a flaming eternal death.

6. HANCOCK

THEY RODE IN SINGLE FILE, TWELVE OF THEM, DRESSED IN THE bright colors of the Spanish army, or what they knew of that army, so far away. Wide red sashes were wrapped around their waists, and their hats sprouted long thick plumes, plucked long ago from birds no one here had ever seen. They rode slowly, deliberately, on horses that had been decorated with as much care as their riders. As the men passed the front of Hancock's house, they turned their heads, faced the house, a fixed stare, fierce and defiant.

"This is very odd."

Hancock reached out an arm, and Mira moved closer. He pulled her to him, wrapped his arm around her shoulders. They watched from inside, through the wide front window of the house, as the procession moved past. Hancock watched each man carefully, looked for weapons, any sign the display would turn into something else, something more aggressive.

"I've been expecting this, actually. General Banning told me about this—this custom."

"What does it mean? Is it a threat?" She turned, looked instinctively toward the small cradle where the baby lay sleeping.

"Probably not, but it could be the first step. They're showing their displeasure against the authority of the government, and ... I guess that's me."

He had been here only a few months, ordered to the new post from up north, Benicia, near San Francisco, the headquarters of the California command. It was a promotion, if not in rank, at least some prestige, a reward to a man who had demonstrated great skill in managing property, a flair for the paperwork of equipping an army.

They had come to California nearly by accident. The Sixth Infantry had moved west from Fort Leavenworth, Kansas, a long march to the Utah Territory, to confront the rebellious Mormons, who were threatening to reject the authority of the federally appointed governor. But with the show of force closing in, the Mormons had avoided the fight, had finally agreed to accept the government's authority, and so the Sixth Infantry, under the new command of General Albert Sidney Johnston, had been ordered to keep going, farther west, and provide manpower for the new Department of California.

The march had taken many months, and in all had covered over two thousand miles, the longest overland march by infantry in military history, and it was the job of this young quartermaster, Captain Winfield Scott Hancock, to supply the troops. And, as he had done from his first days of service, he had exceeded the army's expectations, had arrived at Benicia better equipped than when they left Kansas. It was an extraordinary accomplishment, and so Hancock had been appointed to command the new Department of Southern California, which consisted of . . . him.

His first concern had been the Indians, the Mojaves, but there had been no trouble, and Hancock had even become acquainted with some of the tribal chieftains. But the Spanish residents had deep loyalties to the old territorial government, a government that had been forced to surrender control to these new Americans, one great price for the defeat of Santa Anna in Mexico, and it was a control that most in Southern California never recognized, because little around them had changed.

The protesters had completed their ride past his house, sped up their horses and disappeared down the street, toward the older buildings of Los Angeles. Hancock turned from the window, went into his small office, opened a desk drawer and pulled out a small pistol.

Mira came in behind him, saw the dull metal of the old gun. "Win, are we in danger?"

He didn't answer, was thinking about the warehouse, the piles of government stores, weapons and powder, as well as the various hardware, tents, and blankets. He always thought it foolish of the army to store these supplies in Los Angeles, with only one man, one quartermaster, as the military presence in the area. The Quartermaster's Depot was a simple storage building, a barnlike warehouse with a wide door, secured by crude strap hinges and one old lock, and the nearest military unit was over a hundred miles away, the cavalry detachment at Fort Tejon.

He held the pistol, felt the solid power, ran his fingers over the oily surface, then turned and handed it to Mira.

"How long has it been since you fired this?"

She pointed it down to the floor, turned her hand sideways, then back.

"Kansas. Mr. Benden took me out to the cornfields, set up a box. He was concerned that with you gone I might need it."

He watched her handle the gun, thought of the huge Irishman, the man he had hired to look after her. Kansas was a dangerous place, had become a war zone, the issue of slavery for the new state a source of growing conflict. Hot-tempered radicals on both sides of the issue were crowding in, hoping to vote the issue their way, whether the state would be free or slave. The conflicts had become vicious and bloody, and the army had been squarely in the middle. Hancock knew that an officer's wife could be a vulnerable target, and he had hired Benden, a fierce giant whose fists had long ago earned him a reputation as a man you did not confront. Benden had taught Mira how to shoot, and she had a knack for it, a steadiness, could outshoot many of the officers. But she did not enjoy guns, saw them as the tools of the soldiers, did not understand the compliments the men gave her.

"Maybe we can go out, the big field down the road, set up a target."

She looked at him. "You didn't answer my question. Are we in danger?"

"I'm not sure. We are certainly vulnerable. I need to learn more about these Spaniards, this . . . protest. In the meantime, it can't hurt to be prepared." He reached for his coat.

"Where are you going?"

"To see Banning. He deals with these people, maybe he's heard something."

She put the gun down on his desk, reached up, and he caught her hands, pulled them into his chest, held them.

"If there is any trouble, it will certainly be at the warehouse, not here. I won't be long . . . don't worry."

He lifted her hands up, kissed them, and then turned and went out through the front door. She followed him, leaned against the open doorway, watched him cross the hard dirt street, then closed and locked the door.

General Phineas Banning was not a general at all, had not been a military man, but had come to Los Angeles some years earlier, recognized the great potential for shipping and commerce, and organized the first modern port facilities. His command of engineering projects, his natural ability to organize the local workers, had given him the military nickname. Banning had a strong appreciation for the army's usefulness, as did most of the Americans in the area, and so the Hancocks had been warmly received. Hancock knew Banning better than most in the area, knew that his close involvement with the larger community, the Spanish-speaking community, could provide him with a clearer picture of what was going on with the protests.

Hancock was well known now in the town, the only blue uniform that anyone saw walking the street. People smiled, polite, as he passed, though most did not speak English and there were few words of greeting. Banning's office was a large adobe house, had been converted from an old Spanish villa, and sat on the main road that led out to the coast. He reached the open yard, saw several young men sitting on the steps. Hancock guessed them to be laborers, men waiting for their foreman, for instruction. They were short and brown, tough, hard-looking men, heavy arms and broad chests, and they watched Hancock with quiet black eyes. He climbed the stone stairway to the veranda, reached the door and turned to see a dark face watching him closely; there was no politeness, no smile.

Inside, he heard voices, the first words of English since he had left his house. He called out, "Hello? Mr. Banning?"

From a dark hallway he heard a sound, then a door opened and light filled the long space. He saw two men walking toward him, carrying papers, rolled-up drawings. One of them was Banning.

"Well, Captain Hancock, a surprise! Come on back, please." Banning waved the other man away, said something briefly in Spanish, and the man was out the door. Hancock heard commotion outside, the stirring of the men.

"Forgive my visit, I'm sorry if I have interrupted your work. I do need to talk to you."

"Nonsense, always time for a few words."

Hancock followed Banning down the hall, turned into a large office containing a huge, heavy desk and windows filled with pots of flowering plants. Banning went around the desk, sat in a heavy leather chair, wheeled it closer, folded his hands in front of him in a gesture of attention.

"Now, Captain, what's on your mind?"

Hancock sat in a wooden chair, saw reflected sunlight in a rich mahogany glare, did not put his hands on the desk.

"We had a demonstration today, in front of my home. It was as you had described: men dressed as Spanish soldiers, formal uniforms, riding by and staring."

"Hmmm, so. It's been coming. A lot of talk. Anything happen, any problem?"

"No, they didn't approach the house, just rode by, then took off."

"That's the way it works. The key is, what happens next."

"That's what I was hoping you could tell me."

"Captain, have you seen Hamilton's newspaper this week? The *Star*?"

"No, missed it."

"That damned idiot. He's filling his paper with all kinds of stories about what's happening back East, the election and all. I know him, he thinks he's fair, I suppose. But he's the only news these people have about Washington. I get letters, some correspondence from Delaware, friends in New York, a great deal of commotion about the election, none of it too positive, but then I read about the same events in Hamilton's 'news' and I see his slant, his opinions coming through. And that, Captain, is where your trouble might come from."

"About the election? What kind of trouble?"

"This fellow Lincoln, this Republican ... he's got a strong following in the North. Too strong, probably. The Democrats are splitting up, fighting it out with each other. From what I can gather, the Southern cause is hurting itself. But when you read Hamilton, you see Lincoln as the devil himself, and the election as a vote to preserve the American way of life. That kind of rhetoric talks to people's passions, not their good sense. You a Democrat, Captain?"

"Yes, I suppose I am. My father had pretty strong views on politics, can't say I ever disagreed with him much, but most soldiers I know are Democrats. What is so dangerous? It's just an election."

"There's more and more talk that if Lincoln wins, the country could divide up, fall apart altogether. The slavery business, the government sticking itself into the affairs of the states, there's a good many people who see Lincoln as the man who will destroy the country. And you've got loose cannons like Hamilton throwing this stuff out at people like it's the word of God. Around here we're pretty far removed from what the government says, Captain. Things like 'law' and 'Union' don't mean much to people who don't even speak your language. Sounds pretty scary to me, Captain."

"And, the Spanish . . ." Hancock paused, began to understand.

"The Spanish, the Mexicans, are sitting back, taking it all in. I tell you, Captain, if the country splits apart, there's talk, right outside this

damned window, these boys don't think I know what they're saying. . . .
They're waiting for the day, because the bet is they can walk right in and
grab California away from the army. Hell, they already know there's
American soldiers who are talking about quitting, going home to their
states. You scared yet, Captain?"

He looked past Banning, out the wide window. He had heard
some talk, most of it coming from San Francisco, from Benicia, the angry talk of politics. He had never been too political, had supported the
Democrats because it was what his father had done. He felt there was
some logic in their issues, the right of the states to determine their own
course. But . . . the collapse of the Union? It seemed too far beyond
reason, too irrational to be taken seriously.

"You expecting any help here, Captain, any troops?"

"I haven't asked for any. There has never been any trouble." He
realized now he sounded naive, that the demonstration in front of his
house could be far more serious than he wanted to admit.

"The local boys might need some discouraging, Captain, so keep
the lid on. If they start feeling their strength, thinking they can push the
army a little harder, they will."

Hancock began to think, his mind seemed to come awake, clear.
The warehouse . . . the property of the army . . . the munitions . . .
could not fall into the hands of anyone.

"Phineas, you could do your country, and me, a great service."

Banning smiled, nodded. "At your service, Captain."

"Spread the word. There's cavalry coming, several squadrons, no, a
regiment. Captain Hancock is . . . outraged . . . that local citizens would
defy the military authority, by the . . . the . . . disgraceful lack of respect
paid to me and my wife, the threats against my home. How's that?"

Banning laughed. "I must say, Captain, I have never seen such
fury from a military man. It could be . . . my God, the army could be
coming here to . . . oh, my Lord, it could be a massacre!"

Hancock felt the rush of energy, but did not laugh with Banning.
It had to work, a show of bravado, throw uncertainty into a growing
mob. It would slow them down, at least until he could send to Tejon
for real troops to back up his rumors.

Hancock stood, made a slight bow. "You are a friend, Mr. Banning. Thank you for your time."

Banning sat back in his chair, and Hancock saw he was already
planning how he could spread the word. He said quietly, "Hamilton,"
and Hancock knew, of course, the newspaperman would jump on this
story, a military invasion, full-scale occupation, martial law . . .

Hancock left Banning's office, walked out into hot sunlight, thought, Go to the warehouse, just to be sure. He turned a corner, passed several new shops, with Spanish and English signs, then made his way out beyond the street where his house sat, where Mira waited for him. He reached the long wooden building surrounded by a short picket fence with flaking white paint, saw the sign over the wide doors, U.S. ARMY SUPPLY DEPOT. He suddenly felt naked, very weak, unarmed. He pulled keys from his coat pocket, found the one for the old brass lock, swung open the thin wooden door. Inside were stacks of goods, high piles in neat rows, cloth and canvas. This is insane, he thought. All this, enough to equip, what? A small army? At least, to supply a good-sized bit of trouble. In a far corner he saw a wooden box, large and square, and he leaned over, pulled at the wood planking. It came loose, and he put his hand inside, felt through thick straw, worked his fingers in until his hand touched hard steel. He pulled the large pistol out through the top of the box, held it up toward the open door of the warehouse, aimed at nothing, then tucked it in his belt. He reached back into the box, pulled out another, then paused, thought, Maybe one more.

The wide flat door began to move, pushed by an afternoon breeze, and he jerked to attention, startled, and grabbed at a pistol. He laughed at himself, felt his heart beating with icy quickness, and thought of Banning. Are you scared yet, Captain?

T HE SPANISH "SOLDIERS" HAD COME AGAIN, MORE OF THEM THIS time, another absurd parade, and there had been others with them, people on foot, following along, yelling at the house, at *him* as he watched from the window. He could still see the faces, the infection spreading in the crowd.

They sat together in the fading light. Mira had brought him supper, and he was finishing the last piece of bread, drinking a cup of coffee. Outside the cavernous warehouse the last bit of orange glow was fading on the flat western horizon.

"You had better leave soon. It's already dark."

She took the plate from his hand, set it on the ground, slid closer and leaned against him. They sat on the wooden box that held the pistols, and he wrapped his arms around her, leaned back against the side of the building.

"In a moment, there's no hurry. Consuela stayed late today, probably has the children in bed by now. She's been a godsend, really."

Hancock thought of the sweet old woman Mira had found to help with the house. She knew almost no English, but he could see in her hands, her touch, an understanding. She seemed to know just how to deal with the children, what they needed. Hancock had never actually spoken with her. She would not look at him, always looked at the floor when he was there. Very strange, he thought, and he wondered if it was fear, respect, or just old Spanish custom. She had been in Los Angeles since she was a child, and Hancock guessed she was maybe sixty-five, seventy years old. He began to think out loud.

"I wonder what these people think of us."

Mira stared ahead, still pressed against him. "What people, you mean the Spanish, the Mexicans?"

"Yes. We won the war, took over their government here, and they just go on like they always did. Maybe they never considered themselves Mexicans, any more than they consider themselves Americans."

"It's the Church. They worship at the same place they have since they were children, the same priests. I don't think Consuela even understands what the government is. She talks about the priests as the authority."

"She told you this?"

"In not so many words. The priests always were in control here, even before the war. If the people have problems, that's who they see."

"And now the Americans are having problems, and the priests see an opportunity to regain control."

She sat up, turned, tried to see his face in the darkness.

"Do you really think it's the Church?"

"I don't know. Someone is organizing this resistance, the protests. Those people today, the protesters, they have leaders, behind the scenes. They're smart enough not to show us who they are. All it takes is one, one man who knows how to use words, charismatic, who commands their respect, a man like Santa Anna."

"Surely not the Church . . ."

"I don't know. We may never know."

She stood, stretched her arms upright, and he could barely see her. We should have a lantern, he thought, but no, if they come, they must not know I am in here. It's the only advantage I have.

The word was out, Banning had seen to it, and the Spanish citizens were buzzing, hostile and afraid, and Hancock knew it had been a risk, but no one had come near the warehouse, not yet. But now the rumors came back at him. At a meeting, even a rally, tonight, the militant leaders of the Spanish community were going to take their own actions. Many of the locals had been speaking out, calling for a rebellion, taking back control from the Americans.

And though his rumors had seemed to work, and slowed down the hot talk, there were still no American soldiers, they had not come, no great military presence to keep down the talk of rebellion. He had sent a message to Tejon and a civilian courier to Benicia, but it was slow, no telegraph, no railroad. There had been a squad of infantry passing through, going to Arizona. They stopped briefly for provisions, the normal function of the Quartermaster's Depot, but they had not stayed, could not. Their captain had orders, an Indian raid near Yuma, did not see Hancock's problems as a priority, and so they loaded a few wagons with supplies from the warehouse and were gone.

"This is all because of the election."

She bent down beside him, put a hand on his, and she knew he wanted to talk, did not want her to leave, not yet. "What do you mean?"

"This trouble—it's all because of the election, all the talk in the paper, Hamilton's damned newspaper, his great oratory about the collapse of the country if Lincoln is elected. It's madness, pure idiocy."

She sat quietly beside him. "It's his right, he can print anything he wants," she said. "I don't think people pay much attention to that kind of talk."

"But they do. They are—it's not just Hamilton, it's the South . . . the states. The infantry unit that just came through, their captain told me that soldiers at Benicia are talking about going home, quitting the army if Lincoln wins the election. The newspapers come from back East and fights break out over pieces of news. They are talking about the slave states pulling out of the Union, making a new country . . ." He paused, lifted his hat from his head, ran his hand through thick hair, and she sat closer again, next to him, felt his tension.

He took a deep breath, said, "We have a system, a democratic system, and if one man is elected, it's because the people choose him. But not this time. This time if the wrong man wins, the system gets torn down. And not just back East, but right here. Most of the local Americans are Southern sympathizers. Hamilton speaks to them, they listen. Banning . . . at least Banning is reasonable, some of the others I guess, too. But if the Union collapses, what will these men do? We are so isolated, so far from the Federal government. It's not just the Spanish who want California to be independent, it's men like Hamilton. How easy it is to be so reckless, to make grand pronouncements about rebellion and independence, when the authority, the system, the responsibility is so far away." He paused, held her gently away from him, stood up and began to pace, feeling the nervous energy.

"I wear the uniform of that authority, I'm the only piece of the government here, and this post is *my* responsibility. No one will start any rebellion with *these* guns."

She watched in the dark, felt his movement, and then he stopped, leaned down and took her hand, helped her stand.

"You had better leave, go on home, before it gets much later."

"Please, Win, please, be careful. These are just ... *things*. The army can replace them."

He hugged her, held her hard against him. "It's all right. Besides, it's only rumors. You know what rumors are like. Help should be here soon anyway. It's probably just for tonight."

He didn't sound convincing, knew it, didn't believe it himself. He was glad she could not see his face; he could never lie to her.

"All right, my dear husband. I'll be back in the morning, I'll make a big breakfast for you."

"Wait, do you have—"

"Yes, Captain, I have the pistol right here. I will be fine."

He walked her over to the doors, pushed them open slowly, quietly. The moon was coming up over the far trees, and he was relieved to see the street was not as dark as the inside of the warehouse and it would be a short walk to their house. She kissed him, quickly, did not want to draw it out, make it worse than it was, and then she moved away. He followed her with his eyes until she was gone in the dark.

He went back inside, pulled the doors together, could see the moonlight coming in between them, through an opening a half-inch wide. He felt his belt, the pistols, felt a little foolish, thought, You must look like some kind of buccaneer. He sat down on the box, adjusting the pistols, a one-man army. He leaned back against the hard wall, maybe would try a nap, but he was wide-awake, began to listen to the silence. He looked away from the doors, from the small sliver of moonlight, tried to see in the dark, the high stacks of supplies, up to the tall ceiling. He thought of wild animals, the night creatures. What was so different about their eyes? Damned dangerous beasts if they could see in this.

He did not know how much time had passed, could not see his watch. It was late, near midnight, certainly. He stood up slowly, flexed stiff knees, walked toward the crack of the doors. He peered out, saw nothing, no movement, and felt relief, confident Mira had made it home all right. He thought of the children, told himself, purposefully, they would be fine, there would be no danger to them, it was the supplies they would want, the munitions. He went back again to his corner, to the open box of pistols, sat and leaned against the wall, listening to the quiet night.

His hand rested on something, a tin cup, his coffee. He brought it up, smelled it, took a small sip of cold mud, made a face Mira would have scolded him for, set the cup back down on the hard ground beside the box. He heard a horse whinny in the far distance, and a dog barking. He froze, listened hard, heard nothing else, leaned his head back now, his hat a thin pillow against the wood siding.

He heard a horse again, closer this time, and he sat up, felt a burst of cold in his stomach, and quickly he was standing. He moved over against the far wall, listening, and now there were more. He heard the dull rhythm of slow hoofbeats. The cold spread through his body, his heart pounding his brain into a clear alertness. He pulled a loaded pistol from his belt, touched the cartridge box in his coat pocket, moved in a silent glide to the doors, peeked out and waited.

The horses came closer, outside the picket fence, and he saw them now, saw the riders, could not tell much, just gray shadows, no voices. He watched the men dismount, tried to count ... five, six. One man walked to the gate, pushed it open, and they began to move toward the building, to the wide doors, quiet slow steps, and Hancock stood straight, took one step back from the crack, raised the pistol, could see one man's form moving up closer, blocking out the moonlight, and he held the pistol with both hands, felt a rising heat, his heart sending a roar of sound through his head.

He set the barrel of the pistol in the crack of the door, aimed at the man's chest, and the man stopped and said in a loud whisper, "Captain Hancock? Captain, you in there?"

It was Phineas Banning.

Hancock pulled the pistol back, stood for a moment in the dark, fought the urge to laugh, then slid a steel bar through heavy metal rings on the door and pushed it open.

"Captain? We heard you were in here. I called on your house earlier, saw your wife. She damn near shot me. Guess it was late ... sorry ... but she said you were here, standing guard."

"What are you doing here? Who is with you?"

Hancock tried to see faces, now others began to speak, familiar voices, men he knew well from the town. Banning quieted them, said, "Captain, we have been hearing things, talk of trouble, and we're here to help."

Another man spoke, Joseph Brent, a lawyer, a man who dealt with the Spanish people.

"Captain, you are in some danger here. There is organizing going on, men gathering west of town, talking about a raid on this warehouse. We got together to see what we can do to help."

"Gentlemen, this is dangerous business. I can't ... I'm not authorized to issue guns to civilians. This is the army's problem, I can't ask you—"

"Captain, we can't have the army treated like this. It's bad for business." Banning laughed and pulled back his coat. Hancock could see the reflection from a pistol in his belt. Now he saw other guns, men held up rifles, old muskets.

Another man spoke, Ben Wilson, a rancher. "Captain, we are your friends. Just tell us what to do. We're here to help."

Hancock looked at the faces, tried to see them in the dark, began to feel a sense of confidence, of strength. He pointed to the fence, said with a quiet firmness, "There, one of you in each of the four corners of the fence. One at the gate, one with me, here, by the doors. Use your ears, you'll hear them before you see them. Don't hesitate. If you hear anything, call out, be loud. Let them know we're here. And, gentlemen, don't shoot at anything without my order. No innocent casualties. Are we clear?"

There were short murmurs, nods, and the men began to spread out. Banning moved up and stood beside him.

Hancock said, "Phineas, thank you. I am fortunate to have such friends."

Banning put a hand on his shoulder. "So are we, Captain, so are we."

T HE RAID DID NOT COME. HANCOCK SAT QUIETLY, A FEW FEET from Banning, leaned against the wooden doors of the warehouse, began to see the bright glow in the east, heard the men begin to stir, standing, stretching, and now it was light enough to see faces clearly. He called them together, watched as the small army assembled. He wanted to say something, something more than a thank-you, but from down the road, away from town, there were hoofbeats, many horses, and a cloud of rising dust. His men turned, started to move, and Hancock listened, felt a rising alarm at the growing sound of many horses; too many. Then he saw them—a small flag, dull blue coats in the dim morning light: it was the cavalry.

The front of the column stopped at the picket fence, the line stretching down the road and around a curve, a full squadron, maybe a hundred men. Hancock's civilian army came back together, stood in their own kind of formation, and he felt their pride, his friends standing at attention—they were being relieved.

An officer dismounted, came through the gate and saluted Hancock, a gesture of greeting, not rank.

"Captain William Lorman, at your service, sir. Second squadron of cavalry, Fort Tejon. Understand you have a bit of a problem here, Captain?" Lorman glanced at the civilians, saw the weapons, and looked back at Hancock, puzzled.

"Captain Lorman, these men are good citizens of Los Angeles, and have provided volunteer service to their country in time of crisis. They are to be commended."

Lorman looked over the men again, shrugged. "Whatever you say, Captain. They may be excused now. We have been ordered to encamp here, to act as security for your command until the infantry arrives." He looked again at the line of men, saw the ancient Tennessee rifle held by the rancher, Ben Wilson, said to Hancock in a low voice, "They didn't have to shoot anybody, did they?"

"No, Captain, all is peaceful here for now. Their presence was a deterrent, I am certain of that. Please have your men set up their camp around the depot, as you see fit. Did you say *infantry?*"

"Yes, Captain, I am to tell you that a regiment of infantry under the command of a Major Armistead is being sent down from San Francisco."

"*Major* Armistead?"

"That's the message I was given. You know him?"

"I know him as *Captain* Armistead." Hancock smiled, shook his head. Chasing bandits around Benicia must have its rewards, he thought. He turned back to his friends, who had eased their stance, were watching the horse soldiers dismount.

"Well, Captain," Banning said. "Looks like you don't require our services anymore. My word, it is a good feeling, isn't it?"

"What's that?"

"The army . . . the troops. Calms things down a bit, I'd say. Gives me a bit of credibility too. Now, our friend Hamilton will really pay attention when I bring him some news. Could be very useful indeed." Banning laughed, gave Hancock a crude salute, and the others, smiling now, yawns and more stretches, began to move away in a weary stagger back to their homes.

He watched them leave, then turned to find Lorman again, to offer assistance, when he heard her voice, then saw a bright wave. Mira came to the gate, the soldiers parting with an admiring stare, letting her pass. She didn't rush to him, knew about decorum, the dignity of officers. Hancock glanced at Lorman, who had moved up to ask for something, and Lorman caught the look and backed discreetly away, then barked something to his men Hancock did not hear. Mira held out her arm, which Hancock hooked into his, and she led him out, through the gate, back toward their home and their waking children.

7. LEE

SEPTEMBER 1860

HIS OLDEST SON, CUSTIS, HAD ARRIVED HOME THE NIGHT BEfore. Lee had secured a post for the young man in Washington so he could live at Arlington, and continue the good work Lee had started managing his grandfather's estate.

Lee sat at the breakfast table, a hand on his round stomach, groaned, thought, I should not have eaten that last biscuit. Custis sat at the other end of the table, still eating, reached again toward the plate of biscuits.

Lee looked at the young man, tried to see his own face, but saw so much of Mary. Mary sat at the table as well; the arrival of her son had been an effective tonic, and she had come to breakfast for the first time in weeks.

Custis finally sat back, stretched. "Oh my, how I've missed Aunt Becky's biscuits!"

Rebecca was the old black servant and cook who had been at Arlington since Mary had been a child. Now frail and half blind, she was devoted to Mary, a valuable help to her, as much as Mary would allow.

Custis yawned, stood, raised long arms over his tall frame. "So, Father, when do you report to Texas?"

"I will leave this week, probably on Friday. They want me there as soon as possible, though I can't . . . well, they need a commander, somebody to fill the office. General Twiggs will be back down there before much longer. The command is his and he won't stay around Washington for long. I will make the best of it, temporary as it may be."

Custis smiled. "Well, you have no worries here. Your reinforcements have arrived."

Lee rose from the table, made way for Rebecca as she cleared the table. He went to Mary's chair, but Custis intervened.

"Excuse me, Father, but Mother and I have made plans for this morning."

The young man slid Mary's chair back, and he helped her stand. Lee saw a faint smile cross her worn face. "Yes, my son and I are going for a ride."

Lee thought it was not a good idea, she was so frail, but he saw his son's firm grip, the two of them standing close, and he felt Mary's enthusiasm, so rare now.

"Well, you be careful. Custis, you drive—"

"Robert, enough!" Mary said. "I have managed around here without your help for too long. I believe I can take care of myself, and my son too!"

She was teasing him, but the words stung. Lee nodded, backed away, and walked down a wide hallway to the study. He stood at the large desk and looked at the ledgers and the paperwork. He thought, I will sit with Custis later, go over the records. He sat down heavily in the soft leather chair, rocked back, felt great relief that his son was home, then thought again of his post, of San Antonio and Fort Mason.

He knew it would be more of the same, uneventful and frustrating, and his career still had little chance of advancement. While in Washington, he had learned that more than twenty colonels were ahead of him in seniority, and the news struck him like a hammer, made him think of retirement. But he could not sit still at Arlington and grow corn. And so, his long leave was finally expiring, and he was assigned to fill the temporary vacancy left by General Twiggs's prolonged visit to the capital, appointed mainly because he was the only colonel currently assigned to a post in Texas.

He had gone there for one reason, volunteered for the cavalry because it was the only chance he might ever have to be a soldier again; the satisfaction that came from the praise, the respect from General Scott, the good work in Mexico. He had spent three years as Commandant of West Point, appointed over many others, a job politicked for by men who sought the prestige, the opportunity to grow old in the quiet surroundings of their own authority, absolute control over a corps of cadets. But Lee had tired quickly of the mundane responsibilities, the annoying administrative duties, conflicts over ridiculous infractions of outdated rules. It had been no better than his long career as an engineer, and to the surprise of all who knew him, he jumped at the opportunity to command the newly formed Second Regiment of Cavalry, an honest command of real troops, and so he'd gone to Texas.

But Texas was not like Mexico, and he was under the authority of General David Twiggs, a thoroughly disagreeable and bitter old man, who had a complete dislike for Winfield Scott. The Department of Texas was Twiggs's private domain, and Lee learned quickly that Twiggs had little regard for his abilities and a great suspicion of his warm relationship with General Scott.

The Second Regiment was stationed far from the comforts of San Antonio, far into the miserable heat and incredible hostility of the wilderness. And if Lee was to receive no support from Twiggs, he would receive less help from the elusive Comanches he was sent to control. But contemplating the coming winter, the changing seasons, the fresh chill of the Virginia winter, he thought, I do miss Texas . . . and I am not a farmer.

"Colonel Lee?"

It was Rebecca.

"Yes, what is it?" It came out gruffly, and he was instantly sorry. "Is there something I can do for you, Rebecca?"

The old woman padded slowly into the study, pointed out toward the front door. "Colonel, there's a visitor, sir. It's Nate, ol' Nate."

Lee did not know who she meant. He stood and walked past her and to the front door, opened it and faced a huge black man, with broad shoulders and thick neck, one of Custis's former slaves. As Lee looked up at the massive frame, the name came back to him.

"Nate! Yes, yes, Nate, why, come in. It's been a while since you left."

The man leaned slightly, stepped through the front door, seemed shy, hesitant, and Lee realized he had probably never come through the front door before.

"Thank you, Colonel. I comes to ask you somethin' if you have the time." He spoke slowly, with a deep cavernous voice, did not look Lee in the face. Lee motioned for him to follow, went into the study, saw Rebecca looking at the familiar black face, squinting, trying to see him clearly. Nate leaned over, gave the old woman a gentle hug, said only, "You ol' woman."

Lee could see that Rebecca was moved, teary-eyed, and she quickly turned away, moved down the hall, scolded, "Now you don' take up the colonel's time, you heah?" and she was gone, back toward the kitchen.

Lee had often wondered how old the woman was. She didn't know herself. He turned to the big man, said, "It appears she misses you."

"Sweet ol' woman, that she is, Colonel. Hope she lives forever. Reckon she will as long as she has Miss Mary to tend to."

"You may be right. What can I do for you . . . Nate?" Lee realized that was the only name he could recall, did not know his last name, felt foolish.

"Colonel, you did me a great thing, sir, when you gives me my papers. I wanted you to know, I done real good. The man you sent me to, Mr. Van Dyke, they is good Pennsylvania folk, they right happy to have ol' Nate on their farm. I been blacksmithin'."

It all came back to Lee now. He had heard there were opportunities in the Pennsylvania Dutch country for freedmen to find work, vast new farms in a rugged land, and he had inquired, learned of several farmers who would hire good help. Nate had been one of the first, one of the most able men the old man had, and Lee had watched him leave with mixed feelings. But Arlington could not afford to hire the freedmen.

"Colonel, the reason I come back here . . . I raised some money. They payin' me good. Never been . . . not good at spendin' much money . . . it just gatherin' up. So's I come back here to ask you about my brother, Bo. I wonder, sir, if you would allow me to buy him."

Lee had been listening to the man's deep voice, and noticing his clothes, a nice homespun suit, well made. Now, he looked up at the dark, rugged face, let the words sink in, began to feel awkward.

"You want to . . . buy your brother?"

"Yes, sir, he's not fit for much. He been crippled up most of his life, not much good to you here."

Lee realized now who Bo was, the man with a missing foot, bad farm accident long ago. He hobbled about with a cane, did odd work for the other field hands, work that didn't require much mobility.

"Nate, the people who are still here are not for sale. I am pleased, greatly pleased, to allow any of them to leave, who want to. The problem has always been that most of them have nowhere to go. It was . . . easier finding work for you, you are . . . well, quite fit. Men like Bo, and the women like Rebecca, they don't have much hope of finding any work."

"But sir, Bo don' have to work. I can take care of him now. I done talked it over with Mr. Van Dyke, he say it all right."

Lee sat down at the desk, reached for a blank piece of paper, pulled out his pen and began to write, then stopped, stared down for a moment, said, "Nate, forgive me. I don't recall your last name."

The man smiled, a wide toothy grin. "They give me a name. Mr. Van Dyke says when he first seen me, he thought I was black as coal, so they calls me Nate Cole. I even hear some people call me *Mistuh* Cole."

"Well, Mr. Cole, I suppose your brother should have the same last name, so . . . here." Lee wrote out the document, signed it with a broad stroke. "Here are his papers. He's a freedman."

Nate kept smiling, shook his head, wanted to say something, still felt reserved in front of Lee, took the paper and held it up to his face.

"I reckon I cain't read this, Colonel, but I knows your name, your signin'. I looked at the papers you give me . . . still looks at 'em, carries 'em here." He tapped at his wide pants pocket. He folded the new paper carefully, the tender freedom of his brother, put it into the same pocket, started to go, then stopped. "Colonel, how many you gots left here?"

"You mean, how many still work the land? How many . . . hands?" Lee felt a sudden cold shock. He could not say the word slave to this man, had almost never used the word at all. "Thirty . . . or so, I believe."

"When they gonna be freed, if you don' mind me askin', Colonel?"

The question sank deep into Lee. It was the same question he had asked himself when he first read the old man's will. The will called for release of all Custis's slaves within five years of his death, and Lee had seen the mandate as a relief, the added incentive to take care of an unpleasant burden. But there had always been a problem. Many of the slaves simply did not want to leave, had no thoughts of any other home, but once freed, they would have to be kept on as paid labor, and Arlington had enough financial struggles as it was.

"I'm working . . . hard at it, Nate. You know those people. Most of them have no idea what lies beyond these hills. I cannot just . . . send them away. Where would they go?"

"I didn' know about much of nothin' either, Colonel. Now I'm doin' good. I knows some of 'em . . . they been hearin' about Africa . . . this Liberia. I knows some of 'em wants to go there."

"I'm happy to hear that—Liberia is a good solution. But it's expensive. I cannot . . . Mr. Custis's estate does not have the money to pay for that. Not now."

Nate looked down, rubbed his chin with a hard hand. "Colonel, you think there ever come a time when everybody . . . do like you?"

"You mean, give all the . . . slaves their papers?"

"Yes, sir. Everywhere."

Lee thought, ran a hand through his hair, said, "I believe . . . the Negroes are where God wants them to be, and when God wants the Negroes to be free, then He will free them. God has set you free, through my hand. He has set your brother free through your hand. There will come a time—"

"Colonel, you is a good man, a decent man, and I thanks you for what you done for me, and for Bo. But forgive me, Colonel, not meanin' no disrespec', this here is *your* name on this paper, not God's. If'n we waits for God to set all of us free, we be waitin' for a long time."

Lee stared now into the man's eyes, the deep lines in the black face. "You may be right about that. It may be a long time. But I must do what I believe God wants me to do. I can't do anything else."

"It ain't you, Colonel, that I'm talkin' about. You done good, you *is* doin' good." Lee began to see a small light, a flash of anger in the dark eyes. "But they is plenty of white folks who don't depend on God for much of nothin'. They ain't about to change the way things is."

"Nate, all I can say . . . well, I promise you that God will decide one day it is time, and it will happen."

Nate nodded, but Lee saw he did not agree, did not have the faith that Lee so cherished.

"Colonel, I be goin' now. I gots to find my brother, then I be on my way. Thank you, Colonel, I hope God blesses you."

The man turned and was quickly gone, soft respectful steps. He went out the front door, closed it quietly behind him.

Lee sat back against the soft leather, stared toward the hallway, felt something strange, a new sensation. He had never had such a conversation with one of . . . them. He thought, God has had a hand here, in this. He thought of John Brown, the reckless calls for abolition made by people who did not live with slaves, who took no responsibility for what happened to them. But the speeches went on, and there was great anger in the South, especially down in the cotton states, where there were many more slaves than here, around Arlington. Nate is right, he thought. These people are not letting God decide. There had been blood in Kansas, blood at Harper's Ferry.

Lee stood, walked toward the small window that looked toward Washington. *God, please let them see reason. . . .*

S AN ANTONIO HAD NOT CHANGED, AND LEE SPENT HIS BRIEF TIME
of command once again swallowed up by the same monotony
and aggravations that he had left. As he'd expected, Twiggs came
quickly back from Washington and assumed command of the Department of Texas once more, his ego too tender to spend much time that
close to his commanders in Washington. So Lee found himself back in
command of the Second Regiment, and Twiggs had sent him north, to
Fort Mason, back to the routine Lee thought he'd missed.

As Lee's coach rolled into the dusty walls of Fort Mason, he did
not wait for the escort to open the door or even the coach to stop
before he was out, moving across the hard dirt of the compound.
He needed no greetings, no introductions. It was all too familiar. He
reached the door to the headquarters offices, paused, looked around.
He was surprised there were not more troops around. Only a few
groups of men were scattered about, and no formations of drilling
squadrons. The fort was a good deal quieter than he had left it more
than a year ago.

He pushed open the door and walked into a thick cloud of cigar
smoke. Behind the small desk sat a corporal reading a newspaper, feet
up on the desk. The man had a huge cigar stuffed in one side of his
mouth, did not look at Lee.

Lee waited, felt an unusual lack of patience, drained away by the
heat and dust of his trip.

"On your feet, soldier."

"What . . . ?" The man looked up, annoyed at the interruption,
did not recognize Lee's face, finally absorbed his rank, and placed the
paper gently across the desk. He stood noisily then, pushing back the
chair.

Lee stared at the cigar, still poking through the man's mouth, and
the man caught Lee's look, removed the cigar, raised his hand in a
sloppy salute, and dropped it down prematurely, not waiting for Lee's
response.

"Excuse me, Colonel. We don't get many visitors around here."

Lee felt a hot rush, a sudden impatient anger, wanted to tell the
man who he was, how long he had served this army, all the good things
he had done, only to be treated with such lazy lack of respect. Seconds
passed, and the man looked down at the cigar, then reached for it, and
Lee suddenly felt great despair. He continued to watch as the man grew
impatient, painfully wanting to return to the chair and his newspaper.

Looking around, Lee felt embarrassed now at his anger, saw the door to the smaller office open, *his* office, asked, "Is Major Thomas here?"

"No sir, he's out right now. But if you would like to leave your name, I'll see he gets your message. You do have a message for him, sir?"

"Yes, Corporal, you may tell Major Thomas that Colonel Lee has returned. And if you don't mind, Corporal, you may retrieve my bags from the coach outside, put them in my quarters, and then—"

"Right . . . Colonel . . . Lee . . ." The man was writing on a corner of the newspaper; Lee's name meant nothing to him.

Lee wanted to say more, to put this arrogant little man in his place, remind him he was in the army, but he sensed the futility, felt swallowed up in the heat, abruptly had no energy.

"Uh, Colonel, you want me to get those bags now?"

"Now would be helpful, Corporal. If you don't mind telling me, just when may we expect Major Thomas to return?"

"Any time now. He's gone over to find a bite to eat, at the mess. Do you know where the mess is, Colonel?"

"Yes, I do, Corporal. Thank you for your help."

Lee turned and walked back into the sun. He saw a few men moving about now, followed a young lieutenant into a low white building. The man did not see him until they were inside, then said, "Oh, sir," and saluted.

Lee saw recognition, a familiar face, tried to think of the man's name.

"Welcome back to Fort Mason, Colonel. Please, would you join . . ." The man looked around, tried to find reinforcements, saw one table in the rear with a group of officers and motioned nervously for Lee to follow. "This way, sir. Please, join us."

Around the table were four men, faces Lee did not know, except for his old friend and second in command, George Thomas. They were quietly arguing, had not noticed him.

The lieutenant spoke up. "Gentlemen, please. It's Colonel Lee."

Thomas turned around, surprised, rose suddenly, knocking his chair back, a noisy clatter. "Colonel, forgive me. I didn't know you had arrived. Good to see you again, sir."

"Thank you, Major. Please, sit down. I just came in to let you know I was here."

"Have a bite to eat, Colonel. Some bread left, not too hard."

He seemed rattled to Lee, but still, it was a friendly face, and Lee suddenly was very glad to see him. "Well, I'm sorry to interrupt your conversation, but a bit of bread might do, yes."

The men spread their chairs, made room for Lee and the young lieutenant, and Thomas made introductions, names Lee did not recall. The men greeted him with formal respect and few smiles.

Lee said to Thomas, "I was wondering, it seems there are not many troops here. Are they out on patrol, something up?"

Thomas glanced at the others, looked down at the table. "Colonel, there aren't many troops here at all. The men have been assigned, scattered out all over Texas, spread pretty thin. Begging your pardon, sir, but since you've been gone, the situation here, all over, has gotten a good deal worse."

"Worse than before?"

Thomas nodded. "The army won't send any more men, they say it's money, but I'm guessing they just don't see we're doing much good out here. We've got new outposts clear up . . . well, just about everywhere there's Indians. We're spread out so much, even the forts themselves aren't safe anymore. We lose horses and mules every day. Forgive me, Colonel, but, well, I'm glad to have you back in command, but I'm not sure just what your command is."

Across the table a man with a dark, full-bearded face and deep-set, angry eyes, introduced to Lee as Captain Barlow, said, "The reason is pretty clear, Colonel. What George isn't saying is that Washington has bigger problems than a bunch of wild Indians. We all know what you did to John Brown. What George doesn't seem to understand, Colonel, is a lot of us folks from up North see that Brown fella as a symbol of what's wrong, what's got to change in the South. If it comes down to it, a lot of us . . . the army is willing to do what it takes to straighten things out."

Lee was shocked, had no idea anyone outside of Washington knew anything about the Brown raid. He looked at Barlow, saw anger, saw the deep feeling directed at *him*.

"Captain, John Brown was just . . . it was a group of rioters. There was no uprising, no slaves."

"Colonel, John Brown was hanged because he tried to educate the slaves, tried to unite them in a cause of justice. Read the papers! I'm from New Jersey. I get the Trenton papers every week, and there's a lot of people, Colonel, who want the South to own up to its responsibilities."

Lee felt shaken. Surely, he thought, this man does not speak for many. He looked at the big man, tried to sort through the hostility.

"The South? You are referring to the slave states as one . . . community? Captain, I am from Virginia, as is Major Thomas. I do not consider Virginia . . . to be united in some way with any other states, whether Alabama or New Jersey, except by the Constitution."

Thomas saw the look on Lee's face, knew Lee did not understand the man's anger. "Colonel, have you not heard the news, about the elections?"

Lee realized he hadn't been reading much. He had received some Virginia papers from his son, but could not recall any mention of John Brown.

"I'm sorry, I have not paid much attention. I have been rather . . . my duties in San Antonio kept me rather involved . . . the Mexicans, mainly, the bandits. I have spent a great deal of time in the field."

Another man spoke, older, gray-haired, a lieutenant, and Lee heard the distinct drawl of the southern accent. "Colonel, the Republicans are going with Abraham Lincoln as their candidate. Many in the South see Lincoln as nothing short of a threat to this nation."

Lee said, "I have always assumed Mr. Breckenridge . . . I always felt he was the popular choice and would be elected without . . . controversy."

"Controversy?" Barlow laughed. "Colonel, since Harper's Ferry there is nothing but controversy. The abolitionists and the moderates have united, the way is clear. Mr. Lincoln will be elected, and the talk of secession will grow."

Lee had heard the word before, secession.

"I am not very political, Captain. God would not allow . . . I always had the faith that this country would elect those who knew best, who could follow the best course through any situation. I certainly never thought what happened at Harper's Ferry would be seen as such a political—"

Thomas interrupted, "The problem, Colonel, is that the army is becoming divided as well. What Mr. Barlow is saying is that we may be asked to take action where we may find it difficult. I have talked to men from South Carolina. . . . There is much talk that if the Republicans are elected, South Carolina will withdraw from the Union, will secede. If that happens, what would you expect the officers from South Carolina to do? What would we do if it were Virginia?"

Lee was becoming overwhelmed. "Surely you gentlemen are overstating the situation. I cannot believe that one state would withdraw from the Union just because a Republican is elected President. And, Virginia . . . Gentlemen, I have heard nothing of this kind of talk. Virginia is certainly not a part of this destructive talk, talk that does nothing but stir emotions. No, gentlemen, I believe you are wrong, I believe reasonable men will find a reasonable path and that all this talk of secession is just talk. What of Texas, what of right here?"

The older man spoke again, in a quiet tone. "Colonel, there is no support for Mr. Lincoln in Texas. We consider him to be quite the enemy. And that, sir, is the point."

"The President of the United States is your commander, Lieutenant!" Barlow had stood, and his voice boomed.

Lee looked at the man, then rose, moved his chair away from the table, said, "Gentlemen, please. I am a soldier in the United States Army, as are all of you. I cannot believe that any of us will be called on to fire upon any state. I would never allow myself to bring violence upon my home of Virginia, and I believe there are enough men of reason in this country who feel the same way."

Barlow glared at Lee and leaned forward, his palms down on the table. "With all due respect, Colonel, I am not sure I understand your blind loyalty to your home, but my home is the United States of America, and I believe that what is going on in the South is a threat to our country, and I will do everything I can to preserve the integrity of the Union. If there is a rebellion against a legally elected President, whether he be Lincoln or Breckenridge or my aunt Mary, then I will serve my country by putting down that rebellion!"

Now the gray-haired lieutenant stood, said to Barlow, "Captain, there *will* be a rebellion against a government that illegally inserts itself into the private, constitutionally protected affairs of the states. . . . The Federal government has *no* right—"

The two men faced each other, and Lee raised his hand, looked into Barlow's black eyes, felt helpless, saw a deep chasm between him and these men who carried such passion. "Gentlemen, we are all officers here."

They looked at him, stared, waited. He wanted to say more, to end this, but there was nothing else he could say. He had calmed them, however, their tempers softened. As he turned and moved toward the door, the men sat down again, watched him leave, then resumed their discussion.

O N NOVEMBER 6, 1860, ABRAHAM LINCOLN WAS ELECTED President. Within a few weeks the state of South Carolina had called a convention, to vote on withdrawing from the Union.

The governor of Texas, Sam Houston, was in San Antonio to

confer with the army. Lee had been summoned to the meeting, and made the dusty trip back from Fort Mason once more.

General Twiggs sat behind his huge desk, reached out and with a flourish of motion straightened an imposing stack of official papers. When Houston wired him of the need for a meeting, Twiggs insisted it be here, in his office. So, the three men sat, with Twiggs clearly in control.

Lee had great admiration for Houston, the great hero of Texas's fight for independence from Mexico, and the *first* to defeat Santa Anna's army, ten years before Scott. In person, Lee could see that Houston fit all the legends, all the great tales. He was a large, handsome man whose presence dominated a room. Of course, Twiggs would not allow himself to be dominated.

"Colonel Lee," Houston said. "I'm glad you could be here. I have wanted to meet you for some time."

"Thank you, Governor."

Twiggs sniffed, brought the meeting back to the subject at hand. "Governor, the army has learned that it is likely the state of Texas will secede very soon. This office is concerned that the transition proceed smoothly and that violence is minimized. I would like to hear your thoughts on how this might best be accomplished."

Houston shifted in his chair, glanced at Lee and said, "General, there will be a vote on this issue within a few days, and I am reasonably certain that despite my strong desire for Texas to remain a part of the Union, there is a great deal of strength on the part of those who would pull us apart."

It was a politician's words, Lee thought, but he also saw a painful look on Houston's rugged face.

Twiggs said, "Well then, let's make this a simple matter. The army is prepared to vacate the forts and turn over all equipment at your request."

Lee was stunned. Twiggs was offering the surrender of the army's property and territory, when secession had not even been called to a vote. He felt words boiling up, could not stay quiet.

"General, forgive me, sir, but has General Scott approved this transfer?"

Twiggs glared at him. "Colonel Lee, General Scott is busy in Washington sitting on the right hand of God. He does not know the situation here, he is not in a position to make the best decisions."

"General, have you notified anyone in Washington of your offer to the governor?"

Twiggs stood and leaned out over his desk, toward Lee. "Colonel, I do not need any instructions from you on how to perform my duties. You are in attendance here today because you command a regiment that will be involved in the transfer. There is nothing else for you to say."

Lee clearly remembered Mexico. There was always the deep rift between Scott and Twiggs, the jealousy that Twiggs had for command, for the popularity of the troops. Twiggs was making a last grand show now, Lee thought, displaying an independence in his command that would never be tolerated in Washington. He was an old man, had voiced his opinions for weeks that the Union would be dissolved, and Lee realized that if the pressure came down on him, he would simply leave, retire, and return to his home state of Georgia. By complying peacefully with the Texas secessionists, he would be able to return to Georgia in a positive light, a friend of the South. It was all very neat, very convenient, and Lee felt a fire crawl up the back of his neck. He gripped the arms of his chair. Twiggs was right, there was nothing else he could say.

Houston sat without speaking, watched Lee. He was a good soldier as well as a politician, and he also understood what Twiggs was doing.

"General," he said, "I believe we should meet again, once the convention vote is taken. It is perhaps premature to plan any specifics."

Houston rose, made a slight bow to Twiggs, then turned to Lee, who caught a glance, a meaning in the look. Houston walked to the heavy oak door, paused, turned back to Lee and said, "Colonel, please, if the general will permit, will you accompany me?"

Twiggs had not expected the meeting to be this brief, had not finished basking in his own importance, and he tried to speak, to rescue the situation. "Governor, we have much to . . . there are many details—"

"Yes, General, I will call on you when the matter is more clear. Thank you for meeting with me. Do you mind if Colonel Lee is excused?"

Twiggs glanced at Lee, then looked back at Houston, said nothing, but nodded dumbly. Lee stood then, and in an awkward moment saluted Twiggs before moving toward the door.

In the outer office, he waited for Houston, curious. Twiggs's aides stood as Houston came out, and the two men walked through the outer door, where Houston's aides were waiting, three men in identical gray suits. They rose in unison from their chairs.

"Gentlemen, please remain here for a few moments," Houston said. "I would like to speak to Colonel Lee."

The men sat back down, expressionless, and Houston led the way outside, down the stone steps, into the cool December air.

From a distance, Lee saw people stop, staring. There were waves and greetings. Houston was the most beloved Texan of his day, and Lee could see it in the faces.

"We may draw a crowd, Governor."

"They'll keep their distance, they usually do. I never get tired of hearing the calls, though, the warmth. I just wish these people would understand . . . they are on a reckless course."

Lee did not speak, knew there was a reason for this, felt very comfortable speaking with the big man.

"I take it you and General Twiggs do not often confide."

Lee nodded. "No, I believe he sees me as General Scott's spy."

"Are you?"

Lee smiled. "Certainly not. I rarely see the commanding general these days. General Scott is a good man, Governor. It is a shame to see him grow old."

"We are all growing old, Colonel. The important thing is to grow old doing the right thing. Forgive me for saying so, Colonel, but I do not believe your commander here is doing the right thing."

"General Twiggs? I do not pass judgment on my superiors, Governor."

Houston laughed. "Well put, Mr. Lee."

They walked around a corner, and Lee glanced up, knew Twiggs's office window was just above them.

"Tell me, Colonel. As a Virginian, are you sympathetic to the Southern cause?"

"Governor, forgive me, but I have learned that with events, emotions, as they are now, it is best for a military commander to keep his opinions to himself. It seems there is a lot of hostility in the air. An army that is swayed by politics and rumors stops being much of an army."

"Colonel, I regret to say that these days we are all swayed by politics, whether we choose to be or not. And it is not a rumor . . . your army is falling apart around you. Your commander is about to jump ship and throw his command to the wolves. And I believe the new President is about to send troops to stop a rebellion . . . maybe right here."

Lee stopped walking and said, "Do you really see that . . . do you think this lack of reason will prevail?"

"Colonel, you heard what I said up there. The state of Texas is about to vote to withdraw from the Union. I have spoken with the governors of four other states, all of whom support secession, and all of whom expect their states to follow South Carolina."

This was all new to Lee. He suddenly felt very small. "Governor, will God allow this to happen?" Lee knew it was a question Houston could not answer.

"Colonel, I know of your duty in Mexico, your duty here. I know you to be a good soldier, and I believe you are a decent man. I must admit to feeling a good bit isolated these days. I am wondering if I am the only one around here who believes that there is a bountiful surplus of stupidity in all this."

Lee glanced up, toward Twiggs's office, thought of the harsh talk from his officers, the rising anger, the feeling that the world was falling out of control.

"Governor, allow me to say you have a gift for words."

8. HANCOCK

DECEMBER 1860

" COME IN, CAPTAIN, THANK YOU FOR COMING. PLEASURE TO
finally meet you."
Hancock felt wary, moved into the small office slowly,
and the man said again, pleasantly, with a warmth Hancock did not expect and did not trust, "Come in, please."

"I received your invitation, Mr. Hamilton. The note said you had
a message for me."

"Yes, yes, we'll get to that in a moment. Please, sit down. We
have some coffee, if you would like. Cigar?"

"No, that's all right, thank you."

Hancock looked around the newspaperman's cluttered office, saw
clippings tacked to the wall, some framed, some loose, large headlines,
small columns. There were pages from cities back East, from papers
Hancock had read in St. Louis and Philadelphia.

"Surprised we haven't actually met before now."

Hancock looked at the man, saw a small bald head on a short
round body, and he studied the face, looked for something, some sign.
Hamilton was not what he had expected.

"Fine uniform you have there, Captain. I've heard you've been a
captain for quite a while. Any chance of a promotion soon? Certainly
you deserve one. You're in charge of a wide area, a good deal of responsibility, and a good reputation too. A man who knows his duty."

"Staff officers aren't promoted as quickly as the line, the men in
the field. If there's a vacancy above me, there's always a chance I will be
considered."

A brief look on Hamilton's face betrayed him, and Hancock now
saw he wanted more, wanted him to say something about the army,

make some complaint. He stiffened in his chair, felt foolish for having given the man even a small piece of information. He was cautious now, felt that behind the charm, the polite banter, this man could not be trusted.

"Well, Captain, I hope your fortunes change. That is, in fact, why I asked you to stop by. Have you heard the news from back East? The election?"

Hancock said nothing, knew the word would be received soon, it had only been three weeks.

"No? I thought not. I seem to get the news before most here. My job, you know. A newspaperman learns to talk to a great many people, make a great many friends, people who love to pass along information. Fact is, Captain, there's a steamer anchored this morning on the coast, just arrived from the Isthmus. The captain brings me the newspapers, and in return he goes home with a little gold. A fine arrangement, works with most of those fellows, certainly works for me. Let's see. . . ." Hamilton bent down, reached under his desk, lifted up a newspaper and pretended to read. Hancock knew there was some game being played, some little piece of strategy that Hamilton was enjoying.

"Mr. Hamilton, I should return to my post. You said you had a message for me?"

"Oh, certainly, Captain, forgive me. It's just, well, when events happen around us that are certain to change our lives, well, it's momentous. Today is such a day!"

"How? What has happened?" Hancock began to lose patience, leaned forward with his hands on the desk. Hamilton did not flinch, and Hancock thought to himself, Careful, this man does not intimidate, too much arrogance. Find out what he knows.

"Captain, the election, as you know, was held just a few weeks ago. What we greatly feared has happened. All of us who value the sanctity of our freedoms, those of us who treasure the sacred right of the American people to determine our own futures, are sickened, sir, mortified at the outcome. Mr. Abraham Lincoln has been elected President of the United States. The Democrats beat themselves, split their vote between Breckenridge and Bell, a foolish, fatal mistake."

Hancock absorbed the news, had not believed it would happen, had thought Breckenridge would carry the vote.

"I take it by your silence, Captain, you do not approve of Mr. Lincoln?"

Hancock stood up. "Is there anything else, Mr. Hamilton? I really must be leaving."

"Please, Captain, a moment more. Please, sit."

"If you have a point, sir, please make it."

"Really, Captain, there is no need for that tone. I have no ill feeling toward the army, and certainly not toward you. I have an instinct for these things, Captain. I sense you have your own strong feelings about Mr. Lincoln, and I know that you are in fact a Democrat."

Hancock felt a curiosity, wanted to leave, but more, wanted to know what Hamilton was up to. "Go on."

"Captain, I'm sure you have heard, from your own sources, that the army is going to face a severe crisis because of this election. I know that in San Francisco this news is going to be received, *is* being received, with a great deal of anger, and I also know that many good men, officers of high rank, will resign from the army and return to their homes in the southern states. Many men, men you know well, I'm sure, anticipate hostilities to break out. Mr. Lincoln is a misguided fool, a puppet for the radical elements in the North who want nothing less than total domination and control over the South." Hancock said nothing.

"Forgive me, Captain. I didn't mean . . . I didn't ask you here to preach to you. The point is, where do you stand, Captain?"

"I'm an officer in the United States Army. I took an oath to defend my country—"

"Please, Captain, set aside the standard doctrine for a moment. We are a long way from West Point. Your army is about to dissolve, fall to pieces. The commanders, generals, colonels, men to whom you place your admirable loyalty, are about to resign. The reality is that the southern states will secede, forming their own independent nation. What do you think will happen to California, Captain? Let me tell you. The good people of California have no more loyalty to Mr. Lincoln's government than do the people of South Carolina, or Alabama, or Texas. California will become an independent nation, Captain. A rich nation, welcoming all those who recognize the great bounty we have here. A man like yourself, a man of strength, duty, a man who understands order . . . we will need order, Captain. There is a place for you here, a command, a position of great prestige. California will need her own good soldiers."

"Mr. Hamilton, California is governed by the laws of the United States government, as are you, sir. If I believed you had the authority to offer me any such position, I would arrest you for treason."

"Captain Hancock, when you leave here, look around you. Count the flags you see, the illegal flags of the Bear Republic. The only

American flag you will see is on your own building, and when the army leaves, that flag will come down. That is the reality, Captain."

"Please excuse me, Mr. Hamilton. I have duties to attend to." He began to back away, reached behind him for the door, still watched the round little man.

"The offer stands, Captain. Don't place your loyalties foolishly. You have a family to think of—their future . . . their safety. . . ."

Hancock felt something break inside him, lunged forward, put one knee up on the desk, reached across and grabbed Hamilton's shirt, pulled him forward heavily onto his desk. He stared a long second into the man's eyes, expected fear but did not see it.

"If you . . . if anyone comes near my children . . . my family, I will kill them. I will shoot them dead, Mr. Hamilton. Do you understand?"

He released the man's shirt, and Hamilton slid back down into his chair, smiled slightly.

"No one is threatening your family, Captain. I'm just a news-paperman. This was a friendly conversation, that's all. I thought a man in your position should hear the latest news, the election. I'm always here, Captain, my door is always open."

Hancock backed away, stared at the man's face, the cold smile, the maddening smugness, and he wanted to grab him again, suddenly felt very weak, powerless, and left the office. He rushed outside through a narrow doorway, felt the coolness, the December breeze, and a motion caught his eye. He looked up, across the street, saw up on a building the short pole and, snapping crisply in the wind, the flag of the Bear Republic.

CAPTAIN LORMAN'S CAVALRY HAD BEEN CAMPED AROUND THE supply depot now for several weeks, longer than expected. Hancock knew that the longer the infantry was delayed, the greater chance the cavalry would be needed somewhere else and called away. He had sent inquiries to Benicia, asking when the infantry would arrive. Messages were moving back and forth to Fort Tejon, and from there communications were being received from Benicia. It was the only communication line the army had, but there was no definite word about the infantry. It was a five-hundred-mile march down a coastline used by many bandit groups, and no one expected the army to pass through without some problems. All Hancock knew was that they were on the march.

It had been only three days since his meeting with Hamilton, but

by now everyone knew of Lincoln's election, and the men had begun
to react here, just as everywhere else.

Hancock knelt on the hard dirt floor, his head close to the ground,
reading faded labels on wooden boxes, making notes on a thick
inventory pad.

"Captain? Oh, there . . . do we have the tents?" Lorman stepped
up beside him, leaned over.

"No problem, Captain," Hancock replied. "Some of them are
here, underneath. It would be helpful if your men could lend a hand,
moving this stack, maybe . . . over there, that empty corner."

"Sure thing, Captain." Lorman turned, moved back outside,
called to his men, and instantly soldiers were around Hancock, waiting for instructions. He stood up, pointed to the tents, and the men
began to work, lifting boxes, shifting piles. He could feel the energy, a
new eagerness. The men knew they would not be here much longer,
had begun to itch for a change, the return home to Tejon, or a new
assignment.

Hancock watched the labor, saw it was handled, began to leaf
through the inventory sheets, and Lorman said, "Captain, a minute, if
you don't mind?"

"Certainly." They walked outside, Hancock following Lorman's
lead. Lorman was a younger man, clean-shaven, smaller than Hancock,
with a sturdy build and the compact stance of a good horseman. They
walked out to the picket fence, and Hancock saw the men moving
about, tending their horses, cleaning rifles, the daily chores of camp.

"We received new orders, Captain," Lorman said. "This morning.
Colonel Blakely is sending us to the coast, south of here a ways. The
navy has been losing some property to bandits around the San Diego
Mission. They don't have the manpower, or the inclination, to chase
them around the countryside. The colonel has told me specifically to
defer to your judgment. If you feel it is too dangerous for us to leave
just yet, we can delay a few days."

"That's very good of the colonel. But . . . it seems a little unusual
to send your men out without returning to Tejon first. Other units
could—"

"Captain," Lorman said, "I don't question the colonel's orders."

"No, certainly, I didn't mean that. I just—" He stopped, could see
the look on Lorman's face, knew there was more, something the
young man was not saying. Hancock glanced around the depot,
waited.

Lorman said, quietly, barely above a whisper, "Captain, we don't need to go back to Tejon, not now. The colonel feels we need to keep the men moving, keep them out in the field. Until . . . the tempers calm down."

"Do you think they will calm down?"

"As long as my men stay busy, they don't talk. As long as they have a mission, they all point in the same direction."

Hancock listened to the man's words, tried to hear an accent. "If you don't mind, Mr. Lorman, where are you from?"

"Illinois. My family's up near Lake Michigan."

"Pennsylvania, myself. Please, forgive my personal question. I was just . . . well . . ."

"You were wondering if I was one of the Southerners. It's all right, Captain. We're all asking the same questions. I have men I've served with for five years, men I thought I could always depend on, who were always where you put them, doing their job. I have a lieutenant, there, that tall fellow with the red beard, Calloway, been with me from the beginning. He says he's going home, quitting, says he has to defend Alabama. I ask him, defend them from what? He says, Lincoln. Do you understand this, Captain? What are they defending?"

Hancock looked at the ground, thought of Hamilton, the fierce oratory, pulling people along by their fears.

Lorman put a hand out, rested it on the fence rail. "You know, I thought it would be best if I supported Mr. Lincoln, nice to see someone from Illinois that made good like that. I never gave much thought to being a Republican or a Democrat or anything else, I figured it was the right thing to do, and now I hear men talking like he's the devil. I don't see what it is he's done that people hate him so."

Hancock saw the innocence, saw himself, a soldier who learns late the dangerous power of politics, said, "There's been too much talk, I think. Too many loud voices. If someone disagrees with you, you shout back a little louder, and so he does the same. The words get nastier, the threats grow . . . and that's how wars start."

Lorman looked at him, and Hancock said the word again, to himself: *war.*

"But . . . we're all on the same side," Lorman said. "One country—"

"Mr. Lorman, you and I are from one country. Maybe your lieutenant from Alabama doesn't see it that way. These people here, these Californians, don't seem to see it that way. I don't know how you change that."

Lorman turned, and Hancock saw a man running over, calling out. "Captain, a rider . . . a courier."

They turned toward the sound of hoofbeats, saw a blue uniform riding up, but from a different direction, not the road to Tejon.

The two officers moved toward the gate, and Lorman said, "He's not cavalry—the uniform, infantry."

The man dismounted, looked around, saw the officers approaching, saluted and said, "Lieutenant Phillips, sirs, Sixth Regiment of Infantry. Begging your pardon, I have a message for Captain Hancock."

Lorman gestured in Hancock's direction. "Right here, Lieutenant."

"Sir, Major Armistead sends his compliments, wishes me to inform you that units of the Sixth Regiment will be camping just north of town this evening. He also requests . . ." The man felt in his pocket, pulled out a rumpled piece of yellow paper. "Major Armistead respectfully requests an invitation to dinner with the captain and his commanding officer, Mrs. Hancock."

Hancock laughed, startling the dusty lieutenant, who said, "Excuse me, sir, but may I assume that the captain understands the major's message?"

"Quite well, Lieutenant. Please pay my respects to your major. Tell him . . . the commander will expect his presence at seven o'clock. It's all right, I'm authorized to speak for my . . . commanding officer."

The man saluted, climbed back on his horse, and with a quick graceful spin, a self-conscious move in the face of a crowd of cavalrymen, spurred the horse down the road, into a dusty cloud.

Lorman waved his hat at the dust. "I assume, Captain, we may begin to break camp. Sounds like you are in capable hands. And, forgive the personal observation," he said, smiling, "it sounds like this Major Armistead is a good friend of yours."

Hancock watched the dust rising on the road, turned, looked at the young man from Illinois.

"That he is, Captain."

9. LEE

FEBRUARY 1861

A T FORT MASON THE OFFICERS HAD GIVEN UP ON MAINTAINING good order and discipline in the troops. The tensions were high, fights were common, and it seemed that no one gave much thought to Indians, or any other aspect of their duty.

Lee sat alone in the commander's office. He still allowed Major Thomas to share the small space, felt it relieved the boredom by having a companion, especially someone from Virginia. But Thomas was away now, and Lee passed the days in painful ignorance. Occasional newspapers would make it to the fort, passed through San Antonio, and always now the news was bad.

He turned his chair toward the small window, looked out beyond the wall and saw the Lone Star, the flag of an independent Texas flying from a high pole, placed purposely, defiantly, where the soldiers would see it.

What will happen? he wondered. Will we become prisoners, or will they simply tell us to leave? He reached out, ran his finger along the windowsill, pushed up a small line of gray dirt, the dust of the frontier. He felt a part of some great disaster, some great piece of history, and yet, he was not part of it, was not connected. He turned back to his desk, wiped his hand on his pants, said aloud, "I have always been too far away."

He suddenly felt very lonely, thought of Mary, his family, wondered what they knew, what news they heard, what wild rumors were cascading through Virginia. Of course, there would be rumors. There were always rumors. But no rumor could be any worse than what already *was*, nothing could make less sense. The country was falling apart, and he was helpless, could do nothing, was stuck in Indian country.

"Sir?"

It was the voice of Sergeant Morgan, a small, cheerful man who did not seem affected by all this, which Lee found curious and a bit entertaining. He simply loved being a soldier.

"Yes, Sergeant, come in." Lee leaned back in the chair, stretched, did not feel like a commander.

"Forgive the interruption, sir, but a message has come for you."

"Read it to me, Sergeant, if you don't mind."

"It's sealed, sir. From General Twiggs's office, sir."

"Read it, Sergeant. Not much in the way of military secrets passing through there these days."

Morgan broke the seal with a flourish, sent a piece of wax flying past Lee, hitting the window.

"Oh, sorry, sir. I'm not used to opening these things."

Lee tried to smile, felt very tired, didn't have it in him. "Go on, read it, Sergeant."

"Yes, sir, 'To Lieutenant Colonel Robert E. Lee, dated February fourth, 1861, by direct order of the War Department, you are hereby relieved of duty with the Second Regiment of Cavalry and are hereby ordered to report in person to General in Chief Winfield Scott in Washington, prior to April first.' Good God."

Abruptly, Lee was awake. He reached out, and Morgan stared at the order, reluctantly handed it to him.

"I assume, Sergeant, that last comment is from you, not from the War Department?"

"Oh my God! Oh . . . yes, sir. Sorry, sir. I never read one of these before. You have been . . . relieved of command, sir? I'm terribly sorry. What did you do?"

"Sergeant, I have no idea. But it appears my services here are . . . concluded."

He looked at the order, and saw there were no added remarks from Twiggs, he had simply passed it along, and Lee thought, probably with pleasure. He stood, pulled his blue coat from a hook on the wall, put it on.

"Sergeant, thank you. That will be all."

Morgan saluted, said, "Colonel, I'm . . . I have enjoyed serving in your command. You will be missed, sir."

"Thank you, Sergeant. You are dismissed."

The man left the office, closed the door gently behind him. Lee smiled, thought, I should have told him to keep this quiet.

He went to the window, bent over, put his hands on the dirty sill, looked out, saw nothing moving, no troops. He straightened, pulled down on his coat.

"I don't suppose it makes much difference anymore."

As HIS COACH ENTERED SAN ANTONIO, LEE KNEW IMMEDIATELY there were changes. The streets were filled, people carrying all manner of weapons, a ragged army caught up in the passions he had feared.

The coach approached the hotel, his stopover for the night. He planned to leave the city the next day, making the roundabout trip back home, to Washington, and to Arlington. There was a late winter chill, a cold wind that washed down the streets, and as Lee stepped from the carriage, he drew attention. Several armed men approached, and Lee saw they were all wearing red armbands.

"Whoa, there, we got an officer here!" Lee looked at the man, saw a rough face, ragged clothes, and a rusty rifle. The man stepped closer, looked Lee over, did not point the rifle, but held it high, ready.

Lee saw others, more rough faces, and he thought, Get inside the hotel, now. Then another man moved up and onto the steps, blocking his way, and Lee turned to the first man, said, "Who is in charge here? Do you have a . . . commander?"

"Yep, reckon we do. Ben McCulloch. Now, soldier, if I was you, I'd be a-moving on out of here real soon."

Lee knew the name. McCulloch was commander of the Texas Rangers, a man who certainly would side with his home state.

"Gentlemen, I have no intention of staying here any longer than it may take me to arrange transportation."

He looked across the wide street, toward the buildings that belonged to the army and the one building that had briefly been his office. On top he saw a new flag, moving slowly in the cold breeze, the Lone Star.

Up on the wagon his driver, a corporal, waited for his instructions, and Lee saw the young man's growing fear, knew that could be bad. He nodded silently to him in an attempt to reassure, then turned back to the man closest to him.

"Excuse me, gentlemen," he said, polite, respectful. "May my aide and I be allowed into the hotel?"

The man moved closer. His face hardened as he stared at Lee. He took another step closer, put his hands on his hips and leaned forward, his face close to Lee's. It was a taunt, bait for a hotheaded soldier, a clear clean shot at the man's chin.

Lee knew the man wanted him to swing, to take a shot, and he stood still, said quietly, "Sir, may we pass?"

The man straightened up, looked at Lee with disappointment, then backed away. The others stood aside, and Lee sensed the mood clearly, the itch for a confrontation, and knew he must not give them one. The young corporal jumped down from the wagon, did not bring his rifle, and Lee nodded again to him, thinking, Good, good, leave it there, let them have it, the spoils of the fight. The corporal picked up his bags, and they moved with deliberate steps up into the hotel.

LEE WALKED BACK DOWN INTO THE BUSY STREET. HE HAD CHANGED, now wore civilian clothes. He moved quickly across, did not look into faces. He climbed the steps into his old headquarters, saw three men, civilians with red armbands, and no other men, no blue uniforms anywhere.

"Well, howdy, here's another dandy! Something we can do for you, mister?"

"I was wondering if you men could tell me where I might find General Twiggs?"

The men laughed, short and without humor, and Lee suddenly felt very alone.

"Twiggs is gone, friend. He packed up and flew out of here this morning, he and his flock of blue birds." The man made a raw laugh, and the others, enjoying the moment, joined in, one man slapping the other's shoulder.

Lee had to know more, to find out, but knew these men would not show much patience.

"Is the army . . . gone? I have been away, just come from Fort Mason. May I be told what is happening?"

From behind, Lee saw another man, coming out of the office in the back, Twiggs's old office. The man walked up beside the others, looked Lee over carefully, and Lee saw familiarity, recognition.

"You are Colonel Lee, are you not?"

Lee was relieved. The man seemed reasonable, he sensed some authority. "Yes, I am Lieutenant Colonel Robert E. Lee, formerly commanding the Second Regiment of Cavalry, Fort Mason. I would like to speak to General Twiggs, if that—"

"Colonel Lee, I am pleased to tell you that your kind General Twiggs has surrendered to the authority of the state of Texas. The state

of Texas now controls all property formerly held by the United States
Army. Including, I might add . . . you."

So it was done. Lee felt a rising anger, felt his hands shake, and he
clenched his fists. "Sir, I am not a participant in this . . . madness. The
War Department has ordered me back . . . to leave here, to leave Texas.
With your . . . permission, I will arrange for transport and be on my
way. I am trusting in your good judgment, and your courtesy, not to
prevent my leaving."

"Colonel, the services of the United States Army are no longer required in Texas. You *will* leave immediately. However, your equipment, your weapons, your possessions, will remain the property of the
state of Texas."

Lee's fists clenched harder, his nails dug into his palms. He spoke
in a slow hiss, fought the urge to explode at this man. "I have no equipment. I have only my personal belongings, my clothes, books. *Surely*,
you will—"

"Colonel, I have made myself clear. You will leave Texas immediately. You may keep the clothes you are wearing. There is nothing else
to discuss."

Lee looked at the others, who stood leaning against the desk,
watching his moves. He thought, I have been given a chance to leave,
to get out. They are in control, can do anything they want. Thank God
for this one reasonable man.

He looked back to the man in charge, nodded, and backed slowly
toward the door. As he turned toward the street, he felt the tightness
in his fists and slowly spread them, loosening the clench. It was beyond his control, beyond sanity. There was nothing he could do but
go home.

MARCH 1861

H
E STOPPED BRIEFLY IN THE HALLWAY, WAITED, TOOK A
breath, then opened the heavy door and stepped into the dark
outer office, meeting the gaze of Colonel Keyes.

"Well, Colonel Lee, we have been expecting you. Tell me, how
was your experience in Texas? I understand you and General Twiggs
performed an admirable job, a flawless surrender."

Lee took another breath, did not speak, looked at the sharp eyes
of Keyes, a man named to a position Lee had turned down years ago,
secretary to Commanding General Scott.

Lee understood, he was back in Washington. All the reasons he had for not settling into a position here were more plain than ever. Opinions rattled through these offices like dried bones, and facts were often disregarded if they caused a conflict with rumor.

"I have an appointment with the commanding general. Will you kindly inform him I am here?"

Keyes stood, could not hide a sneer, retreated behind a door and then returned, saying, "Colonel, the general has decided to see you now."

Lee did not answer, walked past Keyes's desk and into the bright, sunlit office of General Winfield Scott.

Scott sat in a huge leather chair, watched Lee with a slight tilt of his head, then stood with a painful effort. Lee saw the stiff movement, the slow struggle. Scott held out a huge, worn hand, smiled with a warmth Lee remembered well, and the two men sat, facing each other across the shiny plane of Scott's oak desk.

"I see that look, Colonel. It's the same look I get from the President. I'm what is referred to around Washington as an old soldier. There is no kindness in the description. Most of these fools have no idea what old means to a real soldier. They assume it means it's time to retire. I rather take it as an accomplishment, a mark of survival. There are a *lot* of *young* soldiers."

Lee studied the old red face, the deep lines, the gray hair now thinner, and realized that he had never seen Scott so fragile . . . so unkempt.

"Sir, it is good to see you again. I must say, things are . . . difficult . . . in the field. I hope the general is maintaining his command—"

"Enough, Colonel. I'd prefer it if you didn't speak to me like you're speaking to Davy Twiggs. Yes, we have some problems. Big problems. But we have good men in this army, men who are used to *solving* big problems. Men like you, Mr. Lee. That's why you're here."

Until this moment, Lee did not know why he had been recalled from Texas, had considered many alternatives: his own weak performance, Twiggs's dislike of him, the shifting politics in Washington. It had not occurred to him that Scott had called him there for a specific duty.

"General, I am happy to be at your service."

"Well, maybe so, maybe not. Tell me, Colonel, what are your feelings about this rebellion? Your home is in the South. How do you feel about what is going on?"

"Sir, forgive me, but I am curious why so many people assume that because Virginia sits below the Potomac, we are in a tight alliance with the cotton states. I do not see Virginians making speeches such as anything prevailing in South Carolina or Mississippi, or Texas. Since my return, I am relieved to see that Virginia does not have the secessionist passion that has infected the deep South."

"There is slavery in Virginia, Colonel. How do you feel about that?"

"I believe in emancipation, but I believe it is ultimately in God's hands. I do not agree with the radicals of the deep South. And, I must say, General, I also do not agree with the talk in the North, the calls for radical abolition, made by people who have no involvement with the situation, who propose no solution to the problem."

"Colonel, how did you feel about General Twiggs giving in so easily to the rebellion in Texas?"

Lee looked down at his hands, turned his palms up, then over, said in a low voice, "I was outraged, sir."

"I'm glad to hear that, Colonel. You might be interested to know that General Twiggs has been relieved. Damned fool."

"I had not heard that, sir."

"Colonel, if you had been in command there, in Texas, what would you have done? Would you have held out, possibly confronted by an armed force? Would you have fired on civilians?"

Lee absorbed the question. He had hoped he would never make that decision, had considered the utter lunacy of being placed in that position, had tried to maintain his faith that it would never happen.

"I take it, Colonel, that by your hesitation in answering, it would have been a difficult decision."

"Yes, sir. Most difficult, sir."

"It should be. Damned difficult. These people are American citizens. Imagine, Colonel, what kind of courage it takes to make that decision. I happen to believe that you have that courage."

"Thank you, sir. But I have never—"

"Colonel, they don't believe I can run this department anymore, that my days are numbered. But—they don't know how to run it either."

"They . . . ?"

"The President. The new administration. Let me tell you, Colonel, they have their hands full of troubles. Full. This man Lincoln . . . good man, I think. If he gets the chance to . . . well, if the radicals don't drown him out . . . There's quite a few people around here that think old Davy Twiggs is a traitor, would have him shot.

Would probably have had *all* of them shot. Probably wouldn't have hesitated, like you just did."

"But . . . why?"

"Who knows, Colonel—moral outrage, the love of country, the damned flag? People like to be inflamed, get their dander up, and the problem is, it's too easy. It's too easy to make a speech up in New York and scream about killing the rebels when you don't have to look 'em in the eye. Hell, Colonel, you've seen men die. It's not something you get all fired up to enjoy."

"No, sir. But I believe there is some of that same . . . passion in the South. I saw it in Texas, men who just want to fight, to strike out at something, you can see it in the eyes."

"That's what I like about Lincoln. He's done his damnedest to keep all sides of this apart, find a solution, make everybody happy. Hell, he's a politician, that's what they're supposed to do. The problem is, Colonel, it isn't working. Not this time. And that too is why you're here."

Lee sat up, straightened his back, looked at the hard old face.

"I need some help, Colonel. I need a second in command. The President hasn't told me directly, but he will. He will come to me and with that politician's smoothness, that comforting look, he will say that I am too damned old to run this army, that things are likely to get out of hand faster than a feeble old soldier can handle. And, Colonel, he may be right."

"Sir, I know of no one in this army more qualified—"

"Colonel, I'm seventy-five years old. I wake up each day with new pains, new weaknesses. I've got this great big office, with these damned great big windows, and you know what happens when the sun shines in here in the afternoons? I take a damned nap. Fall asleep, right here in this chair. Can't help it. You should see your friend Keyes out there when somebody important calls. He peeks in first to make sure I'm awake."

Lee could feel Scott's mind moving away, drifting from the subject, and he saw the anger, Scott's disgust for politics, for Washington. He remembered President Polk, the long arm of the administration reaching down to Mexico, trying to control Scott, to fight a politician's war. It was no way to handle a good soldier, not then . . . not now.

"General, you are offering me . . . a position as your second in command?"

"What? Oh, yes, Colonel. There's going to be a great deal more trouble with this rebellion before much longer. A great deal. You familiar with Fort Sumter? Charleston?"

"Yes, sir. I spent some time in that area, before Mexico."

"Well, Mr. Lee, the President is going to use Fort Sumter as the justification, the spark that lights the powder."

"I'm not sure I understand, sir."

"The army still controls the fort—Major Anderson there hasn't been as gracious to the rebels as your General Twiggs. So far, it's been a standoff. But they're running out of supplies. I have advised the President to withdraw the men, pull out of the fort. It's a regrettable move, another surrender, if you will, but for the time being it will preserve the peace. But the President is going to send down a ship, into the harbor, not to evacuate, but to resupply the troops. I can't argue with the fact that it is Federal property, but, Colonel, there are a number of rebels in Charleston sitting on some very big guns who aren't going to let that ship in, who aren't going to allow the fort to be supplied. And there, Colonel, is your spark."

"The President knows this?"

"Of course. This is his game: politics. The army can't fire the first shot, and so far, nothing violent has happened."

"But General, if the fort is fired on, the army will respond. They will have to."

"You have the picture, Colonel. Now, think back to all that moral outrage that's spreading like a plague in the North, and . . ." Scott raised his hands, a slow, rising motion, then spread them apart. "Boom."

"A war."

"Yes, Colonel, a war. But at least the President can say it's a *good* war, a war for what is right. And so . . . we will need commanders who will accept that as the truth, commanders who will understand their duty, their loyalties, who will not hesitate if ordered to fire on American citizens. What do you say, Mr. Lee?"

"A war . . . will involve everyone. There will be no neutral ground. If Virginia sides with the southern states . . . General, I cannot fire upon my home."

Lee stood, walked to the window and looked out, across the Potomac.

"General, my home is right there. My family is spread all over this part of Virginia." He turned back, felt a shock, the clear vision. "If you . . . invade the South, this is where it will happen. Your enemy territory will be there . . . right across that river, and so, that is where it will begin. I would not . . . I could not accept that assignment, General."

"Colonel, you said yourself there is no great cry for secession in Virginia. I do not believe it is a foregone conclusion that Virginia, or Tennessee, or Arkansas, or Kentucky will join in the rebellion."

"I hope you're right, General. I pray you are right. But if there is fighting, many things could change. I must request time to consider your offer. Please, allow me some time."

"All right, Colonel. Think about it. You know where to find me."

Lee sensed an abruptness, knew it was time to leave. He moved toward the door, then stopped. "General, please understand, I am honored you would consider me—"

"Colonel Lee, there is a great deal more at stake here than honor."

APRIL 1861

ON APRIL 12, P.G.T. BEAUREGARD, A MAN WHO HAD SERVED with Lee as a fellow engineer in Mexico, commanded the Confederate troops who opened fire on Fort Sumter.

Major Robert Anderson had held solidly to the fort for two days, with no loss of life, but ultimately had to concede to the hopelessness of his position.

In Richmond, the state convention to debate the calls for secession met secretly. Lee heard that the voices of reason dominated the sessions, and he was confident Virginia would remain neutral. On April 17 he received an urgent request to come to the house of Francis P. Blair, father of an old friend from Lee's days as an engineer in St. Louis, before the Mexican War. He was also a close acquaintance of President Lincoln.

Early the next day, Lee rode his small carriage over the bridge into Washington. The river flowed peacefully beneath him, and along the banks, rows of young trees were speckled with the fresh buds of a new spring. He could see couples, lovers walking along the water, wrapped with the sublime peace of romance. For a moment he felt lost, away from all the turmoil. He left the bridge and rode through the wide streets, feeling as good as he had in weeks. It must be the air, he thought, and had a sense that everything would be all right, the troubles would pass.

Then he reached the Blair house, climbed out of the carriage, and saw an old man standing on the porch. The look on the man's face, a stony, sobering stare, brought Lee back down, back to the place and the time. It was Francis Blair.

As Lee reached the porch, Blair turned, without speaking, walked into the house and held the door open for Lee, who followed. Lee was ready with a warm greeting, inquiries about Blair's son, still in Missouri, but the old man did not speak. He led Lee into a study, a large and impressive room with shelves filled with hundreds of books.

Lee looked around the room admiringly, and finally Blair said, "Colonel, have a seat. Welcome to my home. I thank you for your promptness."

"Thank you, Mr. Blair. I am happy to see you. I would like to hear about your son—"

"Colonel, allow me to get to the point. I have been authorized by President Lincoln himself, with the full blessings of the War Department, to offer you the position of Major General, in command of an army, an army that is being formed to put down the rebellion and preserve the Union."

Lee had not expected anything of the sort, did not know Blair was that close to the President. His mind danced, jumped in all directions, and he sat for a long moment before replying. "I am . . . grateful, but an army? Where . . . when is this army being formed . . . ?"

"The President is issuing a call for volunteers, from every state. *Every* state. The President expects to build an army of seventy-five thousand men, maybe more. You are the choice, his choice, for commander of that army."

"But, General Scott . . . ? Has he . . . ?"

"The general still retains the title of Commanding General, but it is only a title. The President will not remove the general from his post. He feels that General Scott is entitled to leave his command in his own fashion. The general is also strongly in favor of your appointment to this post.

"If you don't mind, Colonel, the President is in somewhat of a difficult position. This army must be raised, equipped, and organized as quickly as possible. I'm sure you are familiar with the difficulties of that. We require your acceptance of this position . . . well, immediately."

Lee stared at the old man, tried to think, to clear his mind. "I am assuming, Mr. Blair, that this army is to be used to . . . invade those areas . . . to eliminate the rebellion by force."

"Of course, Colonel. The Federal government has been violently attacked by elements of an unlawful band of criminals, who have been most effective in turning the sentiments of several state legislatures against their central government, against the Constitution. The President has no choice. The situation is quite clear."

Lee stared at the wall beyond Blair's desk, the rows of books, then looked down, looked at his own hands, realized he was shaking. He said a small prayer. *God, how can You have let this happen?* But it *was* happening, and he was being asked to sit in the center of it all. He thought of the long, dull years spent wondering if there would ever be the satisfaction, the reward for a good career, the advancement he so wanted but could not politic for. And now it was there, from the President himself, and with it came the horror of what he would have to do. He prayed again, silently asked God, *Why must there be such irony?*

He looked at Blair, saw patience. The question had been asked. Lee broke the silence with a small cough. "Sir, would you please convey my deepest sense of honor and gratitude to the President, but I must decline your offer. Please understand, I am sorely opposed to secession, as I am opposed to the violent path that the southern states seem bent on following. I decided months ago that my greatest loyalty is to Virginia, to my home. I would rather resign from the army and return to my fields at Arlington than to lead an invasion such as this. I hope, with all prayers to God, that Virginia stays within the Union, but I fear that with this call for an army, this building of an invasion force . . . I fear that the President will now unite his enemies. And that may include Virginia. Please tell him, please be clear, I have never taken my duties lightly, not to my country nor to my home. But I have no greater duty than to my home, to Virginia."

Blair did not speak, sat with his head down, rubbed an old hand on the back of his neck, then looked up and nodded. "Well, Colonel, we have your answer. I hope . . . in the end . . . your home is a safe place."

HE RAN UP THE STEPS TO GENERAL SCOTT'S OFFICE, DID NOT stop outside the door, pushed through and halted at Keyes's desk.

Keyes jumped, startled. "Oh! Colonel . . . I am not aware you have an appointment—"

"Please, Colonel, may I see the general? It is very important."

Keyes knew instinctively that Lee was serious, would not be there to waste anyone's time. He opened Scott's office door, said something Lee could not hear, then opened the door farther and stood aside.

"Thank you, Colonel Keyes. I am grateful."

Scott sat back in his chair, watched Lee pull the door shut, and Lee saw there was no humor in the man's face.

"General, forgive the intrusion. I have just spoken with Francis Blair. Permit me to be blunt, General, but I must assume you knew of this meeting."

"Yes, Colonel, I knew. I also had a fairly clear notion of how you would respond."

"Sir, I did not accept the offer. I could not . . . take up arms. . . ."

"An explanation is not necessary, Mr. Lee. I know your position. You are aware how much I admire you as a soldier. I believe the country has lost an opportunity here, the best use of perhaps its best commander."

He stopped, and Lee saw his face grow darker, a sadness he had not seen before. Scott looked at him through red, tired eyes, the eyes of a man whose time is past.

"I also believe, Mr. Lee . . . Robert, if I may . . . that you have made the greatest mistake of your life, but I feared . . . it would be so."

Lee sat down, did not want this, did not want the old man feeling this. "I regret if I have disappointed you. I understand that my duty . . ." He paused, carefully picked the words. "I understand that by stating my reasons for turning down this post, I have compromised my effectiveness as a commander. I have expressed my conclusion that I will not raise my sword against my own people. If I remain in the army, I may be asked, again, to do just that. It would force me to resign under orders."

"Yes, Colonel, it would, and your career would conclude with disgrace. The army does not have room for those men who cannot answer the call. You have stated your position. Now you have only one course. I have always known you to be a man who would do what is right."

Lee knew the next step, what he must do. He thought of his career, the years, the slow advances and thankless jobs. And Scott could not understand, could not see a soldier's loyalty replaced by a different loyalty, to his home, his family. Lee thought, I have not been there, for Mary, for the children, but I must be there now.

"Sir, I will prepare a letter, which I will forward to you as quickly as possible."

Lee did not want to look at the old man's face. The bond that had always been between them would now be gone. He stood, stared down at the desk, bowed slightly, and Scott did not move, stayed back, sunk deeply in the big chair. There were no words, nothing was said, and Lee looked up, saw the old face once more, turned, softly wiped his eyes and went to the door.

O N APRIL 20, THE SAME DAY LEE SENT HIS LETTER OF RESIGNA- tion to General Scott, the Virginia convention, in response to the President's call for troops, voted overwhelmingly to se- cede from the Union.

10. JACKSON

April 1861

THEY WERE STUDENTS, A HUNDRED OR MORE, BUT JACKSON knew it was more like a mob. The flagpole of Washington University now carried the new flag of the rebellion, the Confederate flag, and the students cheered wildly as it waved with a sharp snap in the brisk spring breeze.

Jackson kept his distance from the crowd, moved past unnoticed, heard young speakers, voices of careless protest, the bravery of the untested, and he continued on, toward the home of the university president, Dr. Junkin.

There were a few students gathered outside the Junkin home, some calling out rude, hostile remarks. Jackson pushed his way through. They saw his uniform and there were a few cheers. The door was locked, but it immediately opened partway, and he was invited in with a brief greeting. It was Julia, Junkin's youngest daughter, and Jackson saw the dark eyes, the fear. She took his hand, a brief squeeze.

"Major, thank you, thank you for coming. Father is—"

And from behind her, an unsteady voice, the bitterness of a man who has seen too much.

"Major, glad you could make it. A wonderful day, truly. The enlightened students, the leaders of our intellectual future, are screaming for the destruction of our nation."

Jackson watched the old man turn away, walk into the parlor. He noticed a slight bend in his back, a weakness in the bones. The old man had lost three of his children, and Jackson still shared the horror that was in this house, of the terrible black night when his own dear Ellie had died giving birth. He tried to push it away again, but here, inside the house, the memories were everywhere. He watched the old man, thought, You are with this every day . . . *always.* He shook, a brief, cold jolt. God must be of comfort, he thought. Junkin was a deeply devout man, and they had spent great, long hours discussing their faith. The old man had always been there with the right words, and now, Jackson thought, it is *my* turn to provide the comfort, the words.

"Come in here, Major, if you please. Take a seat."

Jackson followed, and Julia went away, toward the rear of the house. Jackson wanted to say something to her, something consoling, but she was gone. He moved into the parlor, sat across from the old man, could still hear the calls, the loud voices from outside.

"Sir, are you all right? Have you been assaulted?"

"Oh yes, Major, very much so. My university, my students, have assaulted me in ways they don't even understand. Those children out there," he waved a thin arm to the front of the house, "they think they know what is best for this country. They read about some fancy politician in South Carolina making some flaming ridiculous speech about revolution, and off they go. They have no sense of what . . . no sense of the reality . . . My God, what is happening to us, Major?" He stopped, put his head down, rested his face in soft, open hands.

Jackson thought of words, but nothing came. There were not many in Lexington who were still holding on, who had heard of the secession votes and were still fighting it, who did not share the loyalty to the new cause, the defense of Virginia.

"Sir, President Lincoln is raising troops, says there will be a war, there will be an army sent here, we are to be attacked. . . ."

The old man raised his head, looked at Jackson with red eyes. "You miss the point, Major. All of that is . . . out *there,* somewhere. What is right here is our lives, our homes. *My* home. Right now the students of this school are openly preaching the overthrow of our country. The townspeople here are gathering themselves into militia units. People are talking about Virginia as though she is some sort of Holy Land!"

"But the President . . . Lincoln is—"

"What Lincoln is doing is responding. There are vast numbers of . . . idiots—yes, that's the word—in these state governments, who believe that they can make a good speech, rouse the people into a rebellion and defy . . . defy the word of God!"

Jackson sat still, absorbed the old man's words, felt confused. "The word of God?"

"Major, this country was founded by good Christian men, on the principles of equality, justice, and all of it *under God.* That has never been done before, *never*, in the history of the world! This country is God's model, God's message to the rest of the world. '*Look here!* We are God's chosen land, this is how God intends man to be governed.' "

The old man's voice cracked, he was losing control, trembling. Jackson waited, leaned forward, caring.

"Point is, Major—the *real* point, that is—the reason I wanted to see you: I'm leaving."

"Leaving . . . the university?"

"Leaving Virginia, Major. Going up to Pennsylvania. I have already resigned my position. These young fools outside don't even know it yet. I cannot live in a place that does not want me. Any control I have in this university is gone. It has been made quite clear to me by a good number of the local citizens that my views are *treasonous.*"

"Doctor, you cannot . . . just *leave.* This is your home, your family. . . ."

"My family is in shambles, Major. My children . . . those that are . . . not gone . . . my sons are scattered . . . my wife sits now with God . . . and you may be assured, Major, be assured, *they* understand why I am leaving." He stopped, wiped at his nose, and Jackson saw the old man was crying.

From the hallway, Julia quietly walked in, sat softly by her father, looked at Jackson. "Major, my father has been through . . . well, you know. It is not right for him to spend the rest of his life fighting a war. He has given all he should have to give, all God ever expected him to give."

Jackson nodded, did not see things the way the old man did, did not see the blessings of God on Mr. Lincoln's war, but he was not prepared to argue with the old man. If he could not be of comfort, could not say the right words, he would have to just say nothing and let them go.

"When will you be leaving?"

Julia looked at her father, and the old man took her hand, smiled weakly at her, turned to Jackson.

"She's going with me, you know. So much like her mother . . . I suppose this old man needs to be looked after."

Julia said, "We'll be leaving this week, Major. We have some family waiting for us. The sooner, the better, wouldn't you agree?"

Jackson heard more voices outside, louder now, saw Julia look toward the front windows, saw the fear, and he stood.

"Doctor, we all must do what we believe God wants us to do. I have prayed for this country, I have prayed that God would stop this, would end all this talk of war, of this rebellion. . . ."

He paused, suddenly realized this would be the last time, that the old man would never come back. But he could not let it go, could not let the old man leave without understanding why he himself would stay. He knelt down on one knee, close to the old man.

"I have spoken to the church, to Dr. White. Many others . . . We have tried, we have prayed and asked all good Christians to pray, that this might not go any further. How can a nation founded on the principles of the Almighty allow this . . . destruction? I have no answer to that . . . except that we do not make the war. The God-loving people of this country are not making this war. The people up there . . . Mr. Lincoln . . . this is their . . . they are . . ."

He stopped. The old man's eyes were not looking at him, he did not hear him, and Julia looked at him pleading no, not this, not now, and Jackson understood, he could not make this fight with the old man. He stood up, held out a hand to Julia, and she rose.

The old man said, "What, you leaving, Major? Well, my my . . . there it is, I suppose. . . ." He tried to stand, struggled, and Jackson leaned to help him, lifted him under the arm.

The old man straightened himself, looked at Jackson, stared straight into his eyes and spoke very slowly, deliberately, "Major, I will only say . . . you are wrong. God will damn all those who fight to destroy this country."

"Father, please!" Julia said, and looked at Jackson. "He doesn't mean that . . . really, Major. You must understand. They have taken his school from him. It's all he has left. You must understand."

Jackson nodded, put out a hand, let it hang in the air toward the old man, a last gesture. The old man looked at the hand, then looked at Jackson's face, a part of his family still, and he took the hand, gave it a weak shake, let go, turned and walked slowly out of the room.

Jackson watched him go, did not speak, and gave a short prayer: *God please watch over him, he has always been Your good servant.* Then he turned to Julia, who was crying silent tears. He wanted to say the right thing, to heal the hurt, but it was not there, there were no more words, and so he turned away and went to the front door.

The students began to cheer him when he stepped out, and a young voice called out, "Did you straighten him out, Major?" and others joined in.

Jackson stopped at the edge of the porch, looked at a small sea of youth, said, "There is nothing for you to do here. Go back, join your friends at your celebration."

He stepped down through the small crowd, and they followed

him. He made his way toward the open green, where the larger crowd still cheered the new flag, and now more people noticed him, the uniform, began to call out to him. He looked up at the flag, and they cheered again, assumed he was with them, and he felt sick, a twisting in his gut. He stepped up on a marble platform, the base of the flagpole, thought for a moment, looked over the crowd, was surprised to see some uniforms, cadets, but then he saw the faces, the fire, the pure untarnished lust for the glorious fight.

"You are all quite eager for a war," he said, and there were whoops, a jumble of hot words and the loud cries for blood. He waited, wanting to tell them, to give them some of the wisdom that had been taught to him only where the blood flows and men scream, the horrible sounds of raw death.

"In Mexico . . . I have seen a war. You do not know what . . ."

But they had stopped listening, heard only each other, the growing pulse, the throbbing rhythm of passion, the voices now together in one long, high, frightening sound. Jackson stepped down, moved through outstretched hands, the deafening cries of a world gone mad, and walked away, left the noise, a swelling horror, behind him. He walked toward the town, felt his mind drift off, floating away, out past the hills, thought of his path, his duty to God. He weighed again, as he had so many times, why he would fight, why it was the right thing to do, but all the politics and causes ran together, scrambled his mind into a mass of confusion, and the one clarity was that God was here, was with him, had shown him the Path, and the reasons men gave no longer mattered.

ANNA ROSE EARLIER THAN USUAL, THE SUN JUST OVER THE TREES on the eastern rim of the mountains. Jackson was already gone, out for his morning walk, and she dressed quietly, with special care, with respect for the Sabbath. She thought, The services will be good today, a break from the turmoil of the past week.

Jackson had been occupied with preparations for the deployment of the cadet corps, the readiness required to send these boys off to train an army, a new army. The week had ended with nothing definite, though constant rumors had kept the entire town on edge.

Anna walked down the stairs that wound through the center of their home. She stopped midway, stood on the small landing, paused to listen, could hear her husband's footsteps, the unmistakable rhythm. She listened, waited for him to climb the back stairs, and heard his every motion, could see him in her mind, removing his boots, the long, high stretch, organizing his body, seeking out the pains and probing them. Then he quietly opened the back door and padded inside.

He came into the hallway, tiptoeing, would not wake his little *esposita*, rounded the base of the stairs. Anna stood above, looked down on his tall frame, and he saw her suddenly, smiled up at her. She did not smile in response, did not share his good mood.

"My darling, you startle me. Did I wake you? I'm sorry."

"No, Thomas, I . . . just fell awake, had to be up. This is a special Sunday."

"Why? Oh, forgive me, I know it is special. I have missed the good prayer sessions, the good company. . . ."

"No, Thomas, this is special because you will be leaving soon. We both know that. All the prayers, all our hopes, have not been answered. There will be a war."

He was surprised at her gloom, tried to put it aside. "There is no war yet. I am still here, with you. There is still hope. The Almighty may yet make them see, may turn us away from this course. It can still happen."

"No, Thomas, it will not happen. God does not change our course, that is for us to do. All we have done is plan one course, and only one course, and there is only one end."

He was stunned, had not heard her speak this way before. He realized he had been so busy this week, had spent so much time at the institute, he had not been with her, had not been of much comfort. She heard the rumors, all the buzz in the town, and he understood how rumors affected people.

"We are preparing, we must be ready. But that is not for today. This is the Lord's day, and we shall spend it with Him, you and I together."

He started up the stairs, to be close to her, but she passed by him, to the bottom of the stairs, said, "I expect we should start with breakfast," and she disappeared around the corner. He watched her, wanted to tell her . . . something, make her understand that his duty was his greatest responsibility to God, that God would protect them as long as he did his duty. He felt a pain in his side, reached up high with his left arm and stretched. The pain lessened, but did not go away. He began to climb up to the bedroom, to change his clothes and make ready for the Sunday services, at least there would be that, the comfort of church, and he thought of Dr. White. Maybe Dr. White could talk to Anna, help her understand. But we will have this day, at least, he told himself, this blessed day.

They both heard the sharp noise from the small brass bell at the front door. Anna stood in the kitchen, heard the bell ring again, heard the urgency, the strain on the thin metal. She could not go, could not answer the door. There could be nothing good about a caller this early on Sunday morning.

Jackson hurried down the stairs, opened the door and saw: a cadet.

The boy snapped to attention, said with crispness, unsmiling, "Good morning, Major. This just arrived for you."

Jackson took the envelope, saw the wax seal, thought he should wait and send the boy away, but he could not stop himself from opening it. He felt his hands shake, looked up at the boy, embarrassed, but the cadet was staring straight ahead, was not seeing, the good discipline of the soldier.

The paper slid out into Jackson's hands, clean and white, and there were only a few lines, the beauty of the skilled pen. Jackson read the message silently, looked back behind him, looked for Anna, and she was not there, had not come out, and he knew she had expected this, had seen it coming sooner than he had, already knew what it said.

Jackson turned back to the boy, said, "Cadet, return to the institute. Give Colonel Smith my compliments, and inform him that I will be at his office within the half hour."

The boy saluted, said simply, "Sir," and in one quick motion was down the steps and gone.

Jackson looked again at the message, the neatly scribed words:

> You are ordered to report immediately with the Corps of Cadets to Camp Instruction, Richmond, to begin the formal training and organization of the Provisional Army, for the defense of the Commonwealth of Virginia.

He turned, did not look for Anna, ran up the stairs to find his uniform.

Anna stayed in the back of the house, the kitchen, prepared a small meal for herself, knew he would not eat now. Then she heard him, the heavy boots on the old stairs. He called out, said something, she couldn't hear it all, and then he was gone.

She walked out to the back, down the porch steps, looked across the yard, the new furrows in the clean brown soil, the bed of the new spring garden, waiting for the seeding, the new crop, and she knew he would not be planting it, that he would not be working his beloved field outside of town. She looked up to the porch, saw the cloth bags, the seeds. She had just bought them this week, had hoped to sit with him, to poke small fingers into waiting dirt, the beginnings of the new life, and she thought of him, the look of pure joy, sitting in the dirt, part of it, brown smudges all over his clothes and face; thick, caked dirt on his hands. He loved it, would ask her to sit with him, share the feeling, the good work with God's earth.

She stood in the yard for a long while, lost track of time. She could hear noises drifting over the town from the big hill to the north, where the cadets were preparing. She could hear drumming, the hollow sounds echoing through the streets, and the townspeople, excited voices. She went back to the porch, sat on the steps. Looking up, she saw the spring birds flying past, circling, landing on the freshly turned soil, then away in a flutter, spooked by the noises from the street, and then she heard him, calling out in his playful Spanish from the front of the house, and she stood, hurried up the steps and inside.

"My *esposita*, I have only a few minutes. I must get back . . . we have a church service. . . . Dr. White is going to lead . . . then we are moving out, to Richmond." He was out of breath, and she knew he had run all the way from the institute.

"Come, before I leave, we must sit, read together. There is a verse . . ." and he led her into his study, found his Bible, hurriedly thumbed through. "Yes, yes, here. Corinthians, Second Corinthians, chapter five, please, sit by me. I have been thinking about this verse."

Anna sat, put her hand on his, and they read it together.

"For we know that if our earthly house of this tabernacle were dissolved, we have a building of God, a house not made with hands, eternal in the heavens . . ."

When they had finished, he turned, knelt before her, looked at her with a softness she had never seen, then closed his eyes and said, "I pray, O Almighty God, I pray that You feel our love, You feel that we do only what You ask, that our path is the right one, and that we may sit by Your side . . ." He went on, a long and earnest plea, and Anna pulled her mind away, watched him, saw the passion, the determination to do *right*, and she lay a hand gently on the side of his face, waited.

He finished, the final Amen, then she pulled him closer, and he opened his eyes, and she knew it was to be, his way was clear. They rose, stood with hands together, and she smiled. He saw the first smile from her today, and suddenly he hugged her, clamped his arms around her, pulled her into him and held her . . . and then it was done.

She stood at the open door, watched him move in a quick motion down the steps, watched the long strides marching up the street, away. He turned, one more wave, and she tried, could not raise her hand, watched him crest the hill and drop out of sight. She looked up then, tilted her head toward a bright sky, the sharp unblemished blue, and asked aloud, "How could You make this day so beautiful?"

11. LEE

April 1861

H E STARED OUT THE WINDOW OF THE MOVING TRAIN, SAW THE buildings of Richmond grow in size and number. He had not been through this part of Virginia in years, and he marveled at the changes, the vast number of new houses, the sleepy farmlands absorbed by a spreading city.

Barely two days after his resignation, Lee had received a messenger from Governor Letcher, a request that he accept the command of the Provisional Army, the defense forces for the state of Virginia.

The train ride was his own idea. He did not receive an invitation to meet personally with the governor, but assumed it would be best if he was closer to the rush of events that would certainly follow the secession vote.

As the train began to slow, Lee continued to gaze intently at the buildings, stately homes of red and white brick with tall, peaked roofs. They reached the station, and the train lurched to a stop. He climbed down onto the platform into a fever of activity, the hot energy of people moving with a purpose. Through the moving crowd he spotted a line of horse-drawn taxis, carried his one leather bag and climbed aboard, alone and unrecognized. The taxi began the climb up the streets of the city in turmoil, toward his temporary home, the Spottswood Hotel.

The Spottswood was a grand place, and as such, the focal point for important meetings and gatherings. Lee walked slowly through the hurried clatter of the lobby, saw groups of men, some huddled in intense conversation, others waving big cigars, broad-chested men with loud voices, proclaiming their opinions with the mindless flourish of those who share no responsibility for the consequences of their grand ideas. Lee stopped briefly, listened to one such speech, felt uncomfortable and began to wonder what reckless policies and self-indulgent planning was going on elsewhere.

His room was large, with white walls and dark oak furniture. He placed his bag on the bed, deciding to unpack later, for he wanted to waste no time before seeing the governor. From the large window he gazed down at the streets, saw tightly packed carriages, men on horseback, noticed that everyone was hurrying, the wagons and carts bouncing about on the rough cobblestones. He began to feel anxious, excited, could not help but be caught up in this, whatever it was.

There was a mirror hanging on the wall across from the window, and Lee checked his appearance, the fine dark suit, looked down at the fresh polish on his black leather shoes, and with quick, precise steps, went out to meet the governor.

The walk to the capitol was longer than he had anticipated. He climbed hills and walked down streets that intrigued him. There was much of his own history here, and he felt a strong sense of kinship, the revolutionary spirit that had filled this place nearly a century before. He kept a brisk pace, felt the cool spring air, and up ahead could see a statue, a man on a horse, standing high in the middle of a circle, a wide plaza. He approached with curiosity, then saw: George Washington.

He stopped. People were walking past, few looking at the tall figure, the sharp bronze features. Lee felt himself breathing heavily, the exhilaration of the walk, and he looked into the face of Washington, thought, We too are in the midst of a revolution. He wondered what Washington would do in his situation, and felt, of course, he *had* been in this same situation, accepting the cost of fighting for independence.

Lee spoke, in a low voice unheard by people dashing past. "What has changed? Why has it not worked?" He began to think of history, the great men: Madison, Franklin, Adams. They did not design a government to control the people.

He shook his head, looked around at the crowded street. He watched a family, a young mother pulling along two reluctant children, then saw more children, a small park across the plaza, parents sitting on benches while children crawled about in thick green grass.

I have so missed that . . . all of that, he thought. But I did that myself . . . the army, my whole life.

Now he thought of Mary, watching him write his letter to Scott, giving up his career. He'd cried, put his head down on his arm there at the big desk and wept, and she was there, put a frail hand on his shoulder, tried to help, and he realized for the first time what she had given up. She had married a young soldier, had shared the life that his career demanded. She was confined to a wheelchair now, could barely walk at all, and now he was gone again, leaving behind advice, as he always had, to move the family, take the girls and leave Arlington. He knew, as she could not comprehend, what a war would do to his home.

And so, Lee knew he would accept this command, would defend his home, because in the end he had nothing else, he had given up all of it.

He looked back up at the face of Washington. We are all revolutionaries, he thought. If we understand that, we will have great strength, we will defend our homes, we *will* prevail.

He turned, began to move through the crowds, toward the capitol.

L EE WAS SURPRISED HOW QUICKLY HE WAS ESCORTED INTO Governor Letcher's office.

"Colonel Lee, a surprise, to be sure. Good of you to come, however. Please, please, be seated. Cigar?"

"No, thank you, Governor. I received your gracious request, and thought it best that I come here. . . ."

"Excellent, yes, Colonel. Oh . . . excuse me, I don't believe I should refer to you . . . excuse me, *Mister* Lee."

"It's quite all right, Governor. I still refer to myself as Colonel."

"Well, Mr. Lee, I would prefer to call you Major General Lee. Are you, um, pleased with that title?"

Lee began to feel swallowed by the energy, the enthusiasm, of this man who, he suddenly thought, did not look much like a governor. He thought of the imposing figure of Sam Houston, the image pressed into his brain, a contrast to the bald man with the puffy red face who sat across the wide desk. Around the wide office sat several others whom Lee did not recognize, men in dark suits. There was a sense of celebration, and Lee wondered, Has something else happened, what have I missed?

"Sir, I am honored that you would offer me the position."

"Well, you come highly recommended, most highly. This won't be official of course, there's the convention . . . the formalities. Your name must be brought before the body, then voted. Well, it's all very ceremonial."

"Whatever is required, sir."

"Good, good. This is a ghastly business, Mr. Lee. We did everything,

everything to convince the convention to stay neutral, but as I'm sure you were made aware, when Mr. Lincoln called on us, on *Virginians*, to supply troops to *his* army, well, sir, the response was . . . well, I must say, even I began to feel the call to secede, to defend against this kind of tyranny. Well, I seem to be making a speech."

There was laughter from around the office, good-natured jabs at Letcher's political side. Lee tried to relax, to flow into the good feelings, but could not, felt himself pull together, deflecting their good humor.

"Sir, may I inquire as to my first duties? Do you . . . is there a plan, a strategy? Pardon my directness, sir, but I need to be informed on just what is happening."

"Yes, certainly you do, Mr. Lee. The government of the new confederation of southern states is currently quartered in Montgomery, and is seeking to reach an agreement with Virginia to relocate here, in Richmond. They are also requesting that the Provisional Army forces, which you will command, be incorporated into a central army, a joining of all the state forces. This matter is still under some discussion."

Lee heard murmurs from around the room, sensed this was a difficult topic.

"I believe you are well acquainted with the President of the Confederated States, Mr. Davis, Jefferson Davis?"

"Yes, sir, we attended West Point together. I haven't been in touch with him in a number of years."

"No matter. He has great respect for you, Mr. Lee, and I expect you will be working closely with him and his people on establishing our defense. It is likely, Mr. Lee, as you may already know, that with Virginia's siding with the Southern cause, we are clearly the front door to any invasion force. Your first duties will be quite explicit. Form a line of defense."

There were some nods of approval, and one man, a large, round man with a deep raspy voice, said, "Hit them. Hit them hard."

Another round man, shorter, with a higher-pitched voice, said, "Yes, we must attack them, quickly. Show them they can't push us!"

Lee listened, respectfully, said nothing. Of course, it would be popular to go on the offensive, the people would cheer the marching troops, the call to battle.

Letcher cut off the discussion, saying, "Good, good, well, Mr. Lee will begin his duties as quickly as we can formalize the post. If there is nothing else, Mr. Lee?"

"Gentlemen, I look forward to serving the Commonwealth of Virginia, and I will defend her from harm as best I can."

There were more murmurs, approving, confident. He stood, ready to leave, waited for others to rise. As he reached the wide door, the big man placed a heavy arm on his shoulders and breathed a thick voice into his ear.

"Remember, hit them hard!"

12. HANCOCK

MAY 1861

THE ROUTE STARTED WEST IN KANSAS, FORT LEAVENWORTH, where the last of the telegraph wires stopped. The man rode hard and fast and as long as the horse would carry him, then, trading one horse for another, climbed toward the great mountains, following the trails through the high passes. The horse carried him quickly over the shrinking ice fields, slippery patches of melting snow that were just now warming under the springtime sun. There were stations along the way with fresh horses, small and crude outposts, and the man would hand over his heavy cloth sacks, the precious mail, newspapers, to a new man, who would take a fresh horse farther, higher, then down through the hard red rocks of the western flatlands, across the plains of Utah and Nevada, along the edges of small rivers that cut through the dry sands. He would climb again, into California, the breathtaking views across the Sierras, more snow now, and the horse slowed, could not move as quickly as the rider pushed him. Often it did not survive, brought the rider to the next station, only to collapse, dead from brutal exhaustion. Once across the mountains, the ride became easier, the green hills and valleys of northern California, a blessed relief to the man who had begun the trip hundreds of miles back, had survived the dangers of the mountains.

At last, there was the Sacramento River, the wide, calm waters that fed San Francisco Bay. Here, the rider knew, there would be time to rest, to play a bit, the wild and restless city, where the prospectors drank beside the rough men of the sea. But there was no play until the sacks were delivered, and the rider pushed his horse just a little harder as the town of Benicia, the walls of the old fort, appeared over the low hills. He dropped the sacks into the hands of a waiting officer, and both men saw relief in the eyes of the other, the rider because his duties were over, and the officer because they had some news.

Now, letters and papers went south, to Los Angeles, held by the leather pouches of the army, carried by soldiers this time, not the free and rugged civilians who brought the news across the great expanse of prairie and mountain and desert. Now they rode in numbers, protection from bandits who did not know what the pouches carried but knew there could be value, there could always be value. The soldiers were well armed, rode only during the day, and arrived at Los Angeles more rested, with horses that could take them back home.

Lewis Armistead saw them first, a cloud in the distance rising above the narrow road from the north. He was on his horse, had just left the Hancock home, stuffed with a truly marvelous dinner, and was now riding back toward the depot, the camp of his men.

The soldiers rode up fast, saw his uniform and slowed. He saw the faces, men who had ridden all day, hard dust on their burnt faces, the horses sagging, soaked in the lather of the hard ride.

The soldiers pulled up beside him, saluted, and he saw one officer, a captain, an unusually high rank for this duty.

"Major . . . Captain Billings, sir. Company D, Sixth Infantry. Oh . . . Major Armistead, sir."

"That's right, Captain. You're a long way from home."

"Major, these are handpicked men, a security detail. My orders came from General Johnston himself. We are to deliver these pouches to Captain Hancock, and in your presence, sir, if that is possible. The general was quite insistent in his instructions, sir."

Armistead felt a twinge, deep in his gut, a small icy hole. "Gentlemen, I have just come . . . well, follow me. Captain Hancock's house is just . . . there, up this road."

He led the men up the narrow strip of hard dirt, halted his horse in front of the small house with stucco walls and low, flat windows. The men dismounted together, stood ready, looking out in all directions, away from the house, standing guard. Against what? Armistead wondered.

He led the captain to Hancock's door, pulled back a rickety screen and knocked.

It was Mira who greeted them, smiled at Armistead and started to say something funny, a joke, to tease him about his appetite. Then she saw the captain, the brown leather bags, saw past them to the horses, soldiers with guns, and stepped back, pulling the door open wide. She nodded for the two officers to enter, then went to find her husband.

Armistead led the captain inside and waited with him. From the rear of the house, the room where his children had been put in bed, Hancock came out in civilian clothes, smiling at the words of his son. Armistead looked at his friend, but did not smile, said, "Captain, this man has ridden from up north, has some information."

"Captain Billings, sir. Company D, Sixth Infantry. I have orders from General Johnston to give this to you personally, and in the presence of Major Armistead."

Hancock took the bags, looked at Armistead, the smile gone. "Thank you, Captain. Is this . . . all?"

"Yes, sir. This concludes my mission. If you will excuse me, I will escort my men to a convenient campsite, and we will return to Benicia in the morning."

"Captain," Armistead said, "two companies of the Sixth Regiment are camped about a quarter mile from here, at the supply depot, just down the main road you were on. Please take your men there, they can have a decent meal and a tent. See Lieutenant Moore, tall, thin fellow, tell them I said to fix you up."

Billings saluted, nodded. "That is most kind, Major. Thank you." He backed toward the door, took a last glance at the bags hanging over Hancock's arm, and left.

Hancock felt the weight of the bags, smelled the old leather, the gray dust rubbing off on the sleeve of his white shirt. "Well, Lewis, shall we have a look?"

Armistead had often come to dinner, had made it a habit years before, in Fort Myers, Florida, on the edge of the Everglades, when the Sixth Infantry had been sent to the worst place any of them had ever seen—suffocating heat, bugs and snakes, quiet diseases—to pursue and contain the Seminoles. Mira had been the only woman on the post, and the officers took turns for the wonderful opportunity to share the Hancocks' dining table, but it was Armistead who always seemed to have his place set, and the friendship between the two men was understood. They had served together even before Florida, in Mexico, and Hancock had known Lewis Armistead as the jokester, the Virginia gentleman who could feign the embarrassed look of the proper aristocrat and then, with a sly grin, embarrass the unsuspecting victim with his own crude wit.

Armistead was older, had carried with him the shameful reputation of having been booted out of West Point, the jokes then having done more harm. The shame did not come from him, however, but from the others, the gentlemen. Those like Hancock, who knew him well, knew that West Point had wasted its heavy-handed discipline on a fine soldier.

After Mexico, the post around Leavenworth had been a happy time for all of them, but that was before the conflicts over slavery, and before the *influenza*. It was a word most of them had never heard, and it took away the joy, and many of the laughing faces, and one of them was Armistead's wife. Hancock and his own family had been spared, and the bond between them had grown solid then, strengthened by the terrible loss of one and the knowledge that it could have been any of them.

Mira stood quietly behind Hancock as he opened one of the bags and pulled out a heavy brown envelope stuffed with papers, letters, the usual contents of the mail run. He set the contents down on a chair, opened the second bag, and saw a round bundle, newspapers wrapped with string and enclosed by a letter, with the seal of General Albert Sidney Johnston.

"What's this?" he said, sliding the string off. A newspaper slipped out and fell on the floor, the front page with a headline bigger than any he had ever seen, one word, wide letters of black ink: **WAR!**

They stared at the paper, then Armistead bent down, picked it up and read.

"Oh, dear God . . . dear God . . ."

Mira came forward, put her hands around Hancock's arm, and he unrolled the other paper, held the official letter aside, and saw another headline, not as large. FORT SUMTER FIRED UPON!

Mira said, "Fort Sumter?"

"South Carolina . . . Charleston harbor." Hancock read further, scanning the words. The room began to fill with a thick silence, and after a long minute he put the paper down and said to Mira, "They've done it. The southern states have started a war. Major Anderson . . . held his ground, wouldn't surrender the fort . . . so they shelled it."

Armistead stopped reading. "It says no one was killed, no casualties."

"Does it matter?"

"It might. There could still be a way to settle it—much harder once there is blood."

Hancock looked now at the official letter, straightened it out, read it aloud.

"To, Captain Winfield S. Hancock, Chief Quartermaster, District of Southern California. From, General Albert S. Johnston, Commanding, Department of California.

You are hereby advised that a condition of war now exists between the United States of America and a confederation of states that have elected to withdraw their allegiance to that union. Those states are: South Carolina, Georgia, Texas, Alabama, Florida, Mississippi, and Louisiana. There is great sentiment in this army for men to adhere first to the loyalty they feel is appropriate to their homelands, as taking a greater priority, and being a greater cause than their oaths taken in service to this army. This office shares those sentiments, and I have advised the War Department of my resignation, to be effective only when the department may appoint a replacement for this office, and only when such a replacement is able to take official command of this office. By my example, I hope to inspire the officers and men under my command to delay hasty action, perform your duties as good soldiers, and pursue with care and dignity whatever action is dearest to your conscience. May God have mercy on us all."

Hancock put the letter down, and Armistead said, "He's resigned. Dear God. But, of course, he's a Texan. But . . . he's the commanding general."

Mira picked up a newspaper, said, "It could be all over by now. This paper is dated April fifteenth, that's over two weeks ago."

"Damn the mails . . . damn the distance." Hancock tossed Johnston's letter into a chair and angrily began to pace, taking long steps in the small room. Mira backed away, gave him room.

Armistead read the paper again, said, "It doesn't say anything about Virginia."

Hancock stopped, looked at Armistead with a fierce glare. "Is that important? If Virginia was on that list, would you quit too?"

Armistead felt Hancock's anger, moved away to an empty chair, sat. "I would have to, Win. I could not go to war against my home. How can anyone do that?"

"Your home? Your home is the United States of America! You took an oath to defend her from her enemies."

"Virginia is not anyone's enemy."

"No, not yet. But Mira's right. Two weeks . . . a lot can happen in two weeks. Seven states! Now what happens? Read the letter: 'A condition of war' exists. This is not an argument, this is not a matter of disagreement between points of view. They fired cannon at a government installation. All right, no one was killed, but this is just the begin-ning. Have you ever seen a war where no one is killed? There will be a response, there has to be: Lincoln . . . General Scott . . . they won't just turn away and say, fine, you shot first, so you win this little war. Now go and form your own country. Damn the distance! We are so far away!"

Armistead leaned forward, rested his arms on his knees, stared down at the newspaper still in his hands. "I don't think . . . I can't be-lieve Virginia would side with the rebels. No one wants this. The last letter I received, my friend Hastings, in Richmond? He said the legisla-ture is solidly pro-Union. No one wants a war."

Hancock began to move again, pacing back and forth like an an-gry cat.

"No one wants a war? I'm sorry, my friend, but you're wrong. There's two sides to this, two sides that have been pushing us toward a war for months. One side says, 'It's Lincoln! He's the cause!' And the other side says, 'It's slavery! That's the cause!' And the people out here want me to believe it's simply a need for independence, keep the gov-ernment from telling us what to do. And so, pointing fingers become pointing guns, because nobody listens to fingers."

He looked at Mira, staring down at the other paper, and moved closer to her. "We can't stay here," he said. "Our country is falling apart, and I'm the custodian of a pile of blankets. I have to know . . . we are too damned far away!"

She looked up from the paper, and he saw tears. She nodded, but did not say anything. He looked at Armistead, who put down his pa-per, stood, slowly moved to the window and looked out to growing darkness.

"General Johnston is right," Armistead said. "May God have mercy on us all."

WITHIN A WEEK ANOTHER GROUP OF RIDERS CAME DOWN with more official letters, and with them the news that Armistead had not wanted to hear. Virginia, along with Arkansas, Tennessee, and North Carolina, had joined the confedera-tion of rebellious states. There was other news as well, Lincoln's call for troops, the organization of a Confederate Army, and the inaugura-tion of Jefferson Davis.

The rumors of threats to American control of California came more frequently now, and so the infantry stayed at Los Angeles, at

Hancock's discretion. Other supply posts in far-reaching districts, not easily protected, were dismantled, brought to Los Angeles, and added to Hancock's command.

Armistead was with his men, slept in his tent, when he heard the commotion, the sounds of another fight.

"Yaah . . . that's it! Get him! Yeeahhh!"

He rolled off his cot, grabbed his jacket, heard more yelling now, men gathering. Poking his head outside, he saw the crowd, men in uniform and out, surrounding a dusty struggle. He pulled on his pants, grabbed his pistol, and moved unsteadily into the early morning sunlight.

There were other officers approaching, from other directions, and they pulled the spectators back, away from the fight, tried to get closer to the action. Armistead could see the men now, rolling on the ground, torn clothes, one very bloody face, and he pushed past more men, raised his pistol and fired.

The onlookers backed away, and Armistead stood alone over the combatants, kicked lightly at one, rolled him over, looked at the faces. He didn't know them, thought one face familiar, and then other officers were there, lifting the men up. They looked at Armistead through beaten eyes, swollen red faces, one man bleeding furiously from his nose.

"Good morning, gentlemen. Do we have a problem here?"

One of the men, wiping at a cut on his lip, replied, "Major, sir. We was . . . having a disagreement, sir."

The other man, smaller, felt the blood on his face, held his sleeve up against his nose, then said, "He called me a shit-kicker. Said my whole family was shit-kickers. Ain't gonna take that from any man. Sir."

Armistead heard the man's distinctive accent, the deep drawl. "Where you from, soldier?"

"Miss'ippi, sir."

"And you, soldier, you consider that a good reason to insult the man's family?"

"Sir, begging your pardon, but we all knows what's happening. The Southerners are deserting the army, quitting. Heard talk that even you, Major . . ."

Armistead looked at the man's face, saw the cold anger, looked back at the man from Mississippi, who said, "Major . . . I ain't decided if I'm going back home or not. We got a farm . . . my folks . . . my wife is raisin' the kids, the livestock. I don't want to fight nobody. But the army's breakin' up. That's all we been hearin'. I hear tell you headed back to Virginia too, Major."

The other man grunted, and Armistead could tell he had the better of the fight. He was a bigger man, older, with heavy, broad shoulders.

"He's just like the others," the bigger man said, "begging the major's pardon. This here unit's going to pieces because of this war. I been in this outfit since Mexico, sir. I seen you join this outfit, seen you move up from a wet-eared cadet to command of the regiment—"

A lieutenant, holding the man, snapped him up under the arms, said "Watch your mouth, soldier."

Armistead raised a hand. "No, Lieutenant, let him talk. Talking is one thing maybe we all need to do. You may speak freely, soldier. What's your name?"

"Corporal Garrett, sir. Thank you, Major. I just want to say . . . it makes me sick, sir, to see what's happenin' to this army. These farm boys got no understanding, no respect, it seems mighty easy for some to up and quit. I never been much in the South. I ain't never spent no time around the darkies, I got no call to tell nobody what they oughta do. But this here's the army. We got a duty . . . we all got the same duty, all of us, Major."

Armistead looked up, spoke louder, to the broad circle of men. "I know many of you have been with this regiment for a long time . . . some of you, like Mr. Garrett, from the beginning. You are known in this army, you have a reputation, you have always conducted yourselves with honor. To those of you who do not understand why some are leaving, I can only say, it is honor as well. Since both of these men seem to have heard about my decision, I will tell you all. No more rumors. Yes, I have resigned my commission. I will be returning to Virginia as soon as my duties here can be concluded. You men may also be aware that General Johnston has also resigned, as have many of the officers of the Sixth Infantry. I will not defend this decision. It is a personal one, and is the most difficult decision I have made in my life. If you have served under my command as long as Mr. Garrett, then you will know this to be true."

"You plannin' to fight against this army, Major?"

"Mr. Garrett, I plan to go home, to Virginia, and if necessary, I will defend Virginia. Some of you might be going home looking for a fight. The point is, we must all do what we believe is right."

"That ain't a good answer, Major. No disrespect, sir, but it just ain't. This here farm boy I had a go with, he's just a dumb soldier like me. But you're an officer. This army follows you, does what you tell it to do. No sir, I can't accept your answer, Major. You can put me in the stockade, but I reckon I can't salute you no more."

Armistead saw pain in the man's eyes, a deep hurt, and he realized that he had taken something away from the man, from all of them. He had not felt before how much they had respected him, he just took it for granted they followed him because of the uniform he wore, the rank he carried. Now he saw it was much more, and he had pulled it away. He could not look at the man's face anymore, said slowly, in a quiet voice, "Lieutenant, release Mr. Garrett. There will be no punishment for these men. Clean them up, let's get the day started, shall we?"

He turned, looked toward his tent, and the men parted, let him pass. He heard small comments, did not listen, knew what they were feeling now. Reaching the front of his tent, he lifted a flap, and heard a rider, men calling out, and saw a man dismount and men pointing toward him, directing the man his way. The soldier moved with the official step of a staff officer, clean uniform, and Armistead saw a young face covered in freckles.

The man said, "Major Armistead, sir, you are requested to report to the home of Captain Hancock. General Johnston has arrived."

HANCOCK STOOD AT HIS FRONT WINDOW, LOOKED OUT AT THE wagon in his yard, the covered carriage that had brought Johnston and his staff to Los Angeles. He turned to a room full of blue coats, Johnston's staff, who milled around, not used to having nothing to do.

"Captain, your hospitality is most gracious, indeed. My compliments to Mrs. Hancock as well."

"Thank you, General. I would have made better preparations. We were not informed you were coming."

"Please, Captain. We will not intrude on your privacy for very long. I have instructed the men to begin the search for a house."

"A house, you mean, a residence? Are you moving here, General?"

"Gentlemen, please sit down! Good Lord, you're like a hive of bees!" Johnston's voice boomed through the small house, and from the back he heard Mira, trying to quiet the baby's cries. The aides sat around the room, some in chairs, some on the floor. For a brief moment the room was completely quiet, and Hancock heard a horse, looked out and saw Armistead, who rode up beside the carriage, peeked curiously inside, then came to the front door and made a formal knock.

Hancock said, "That would be Major Armistead, sir. Excuse me." He went to the door, pulled it open and saw a look on Armistead's face, a question: Why? Hancock gave a slight shrug, knew only that Johnston had simply arrived.

"Ah, Major, good to see you again!" Johnston stood, held out a hand, and Armistead took it, smiled weakly, looked around the room at the assembled staff.

"General. Welcome."

Johnston went back to his chair, sat heavily on the creaking frame, said, "I was just telling Mr. Hancock about my search for a house. I am moving here. Heard a great many things about the area, better climate than the bay, warmer."

Hancock moved back to his window, stepped over the legs of the seated men.

"Excuse me, General, but are you moving your headquarters . . . down here?"

Johnston stood up again, tried to move around the room, stepped on a young lieutenant's foot, stumbled, said angrily, "All right, enough. Out of here, all of you! Outside! This is the man's home, not a damned staff room."

The officers jumped up, filed quickly out the front door, and Hancock smiled. He looked at Armistead, who watched Johnston, followed him with his eyes back to the chair.

Armistead said, "You have been replaced."

Johnston looked up, did not acknowledge Armistead's words. "They're like damned children," he said. "No, not true. Children will go off and do what they damned well please. They're more like pets. Won't move a bit until you tell 'em to."

There was a quiet pause. Johnston leaned back, rested his hands on his thighs, looked at the floor.

"They're good men. A good staff. Finest in the army. Wish I knew what to do with 'em. They're too damned loyal. Gave up their careers to stay with me. Not very smart, but to a man, not one of them would listen. They all resigned."

Armistead sat in one of the vacant chairs, said again, "You've been replaced."

"Yes, Major, I have been replaced. No, no, make that I have been *removed*. A quick, clean operation. They were afraid, I guess." He stared down again, sagged into the chair, and Hancock saw now a growing sadness.

"Excuse me, General, but they were afraid of . . . what?"

"Captain, let's get one thing straight right here and now. I am no longer 'General.' I am *Mister* Albert Sidney Johnston, private citizen. Your new commander is old Bull Sumner himself. They sent that old man out here to boot me out of my office. No formal notice, no notice at all, he just . . . arrives. Comes busting into my office . . ."

Hancock said nothing, thought, Of course, they were thinking of Twiggs, the surrender of Texas, and had to act quickly so that Johnston would not do the same. But Johnston was not Davy Twiggs.

"Damn them. Damn them all. I kept my honor, gentlemen. I did my duty, just like I said I would. I had no mind to leave until I was replaced, even offered to stay around awhile, help the new people get settled in. They snuck up on me. I thought . . . hell, I thought for a while they were going to arrest me! Hell of a way to end a career."

They sat without speaking, a long pause until Armistead said, "You're going to stay here? What about Texas . . . your home?"

"My home is gone, Major. Burnt down. Got a letter from my cousin. Local militia most likely, thought I was staying loyal to the army. Might go back there yet, but thought this might work out, might be a nice place to live."

"What about the rebel . . . the Confederate Army? I saw a newspaper, your name on a list, possible commanders."

Johnston looked at Hancock, and Hancock suddenly realized this conversation could be dangerous, that Johnston's plans could be information he might have to report. And Johnston knew it.

"Tell me, Captain, are you planning on joining Mr. Lincoln's war?"

"If you mean, am I planning to leave California? I hope so. I have requested a new assignment. Forgive me, General, but I sent the request directly to the War Department, and to General Scott. I thought there might be a greater delay if I sent it through your office."

"Don't explain, Mr. Hancock. We're all looking out for our own best interests these days. And what about you, Major? I *did* receive *your* resignation."

Armistead shifted in his chair, and Hancock knew he felt uncomfortable. It had been unspoken, until now. Hancock knew the papers had gone north, but they had not discussed it, would not argue.

"I will be leaving in two weeks. There's a ship stopping here, on the way to the Isthmus." He looked at Hancock. "I'm sorry, Win. I just learned of the ship yesterday. It seems like the best opportunity."

Hancock stared at him, had known Armistead's decision was made the instant the news of Virginia reached them, had gone through all the feelings, the anger, the sadness, the gut-wrenching frustration that this was all complete and utter madness.

Armistead looked at him, then away. "What else am I to do? Tell me, Win."

Hancock glanced out the window, to the cluster of blue coats sitting around Johnston's wagon, the show of perfect loyalty to their commander. He looked back, across the small room, saw both men looking at him, felt the weight of the gaze, as though it was *him*, he was the one not doing the right thing.

"Gentlemen, I offer you no advice. I will fight for my country, my whole country. I do not believe we are a collection of independent states, but one nation, and my duty is to preserve that nation. I do not sympathize with your pain, or the torment of your decision. Your conscience must guide you, and in the end only you will know if your decision was the right one."

Johnston stood, went slowly to the door, pulled it open, turned to Hancock and said, "Captain, we are all men of honor. Remember that. God will judge our choices."

Hancock moved to an empty chair and stood behind it, resting a hand on the back. He rubbed the smooth dark wood, looked up and into the face of his former commander. "Sir," he said, "it is not God who will assemble us on the battlefield, nor position our troops, nor place the cannon, and it is not God who will aim the musket."

13. LEE

MAY 1861

IN THE DAYS THAT FOLLOWED LEE'S OFFICIAL APPOINTMENT, HE presided over an extraordinary effort at organizing a defensive line across northern Virginia. Governor Letcher had provided him with a long list of volunteer officers, with many names from the old army. He began the delicate balancing act of placing good men in key positions, while tolerating the political appointments given to "distinguished citizens," whose grasp of military service was usually limited to their ability to look good on a horse, wearing a dashing new uniform.

He was alone in his new office, across the street from the governor's offices, pondering the most recent list, the names from which he would organize an army. His finger slid down the pages, stopping at names he recognized, and he thought, Good, good, yes, this is very good indeed.

It was not surprising to Lee that most of the Virginians who had served in the old army would rally to their state's defense, and his confidence began to build as he saw the names, the experienced officers: A. P. Hill, Dick Ewell, George Pickett; men who had been in Mexico. He searched for some names in particular, and was surprised at their absence—his friend George Thomas from Fort Mason—and Lee thought, Well, there is still time.

The offices around Lee's were buzzing with a mild chaos, and Lee knew his next priority would be the formation of some sort of staff. The paperwork on his desk began to pile ominously, the requests for appointments, local dignitaries from smaller towns, who had organized their own units with themselves at the top, letters of recommendation for friends and relatives from those with political pull. The experienced officers did not make the requests—they would wait for their assignments.

Lee made notes on a separate page, checked a map that hung on the wall to his side, and saw a man standing in his doorway, stiff, silent. The face was familiar. Lee said, "Yes, hello, may I be of assistance?"

The man stepped into the office. He was tall, lean, and sturdy, wearing a dark blue coat, knee-high cavalry boots, and a small billed cap, which Lee could now see carried the insignia of the Virginia Military Institute.

"I believe I know you. . . ." Then Lee remembered Scott's grand review in Mexico City, the great victory celebration in the center of the capital.

Scott had wanted them all together, would shake the hands of the officers, and so the army had lined up in formation, the troops spread out down the streets to the square, and this one man, this young artillery officer, had stopped the procession, had received a loud and personal congratulations from Scott. It was recognition of more than just duty, but of an officer who had taken his small guns up close, to the face of the enemy, had led his men out in front of the slow advance of the infantry and moved the enemy back on his own, pushed away the Mexican guns that stood in their way. Lee remembered clearly now, had sat on the podium behind Scott, watching the embarrassed face of this rigid soldier. The young man had been promoted three times, began as a second lieutenant fresh from the Point, and left Mexico as a major.

Lee smiled at the sharp face, the deep blue eyes watching him carefully, and he nodded quietly at the face of a hero. "Yes, you are Thomas Jackson."

"Sir." Jackson gave a crisp salute, which Lee returned, and Lee pointed to a chair, heaped in papers. "Major, please, sit down. Excuse the mess. Things are a bit hectic."

Jackson went to the chair, set the papers on the floor, sat down, straight, did not touch the back of the chair.

"General, I am reporting with the Corps of Cadets from VMI. The young men are prepared to assist in the training of the new volunteers, sir. I, however . . . I have received orders of a different nature. Please allow me, General . . ."

Lee saw a look on Jackson's face, discomfort, urgency.

"What is it, Major? Is there a problem?"

"General, the concerns of one officer do not have priority where duty is concerned, however, I feel I may have been . . . I seem to have been made a Major of Engineers. General, I am not an engineer."

"Who made you an engineer?" Lee was puzzled.

"The Executive War Council, sir. However, I have received a letter from Governor Letcher." He reached into his pocket, drew out an envelope, handed it to Lee.

Lee felt a small anger at these people who were throwing commissions around the state like prizes at a county fair, with little understanding of the value of experience. He read the letter. ". . . recommend that General Lee appeal the appointment, and place Major Jackson in field command, at the rank of colonel . . ." At the bottom, he saw the now-familiar signature of John Letcher, Governor.

"This should not be a problem, Major. The council has been somewhat hasty with many of their appointments. In fact . . ." Lee turned and looked at the map on the wall, lines of red X's marking those places requiring the most troop concentration. "You are familiar with the area around Harper's Ferry, Major?"

"Yes, sir, quite familiar. My home . . . my family is from the valley area."

Lee thought, Of course, this is ideal. "Major, you will soon be commissioned colonel in the Virginia Provisional Army, and as such I am placing you here." He reached out to the map, placed a finger on Harper's Ferry.

"You will assume command of the volunteer units forming there. Organize them into brigade strength and defend the Arsenal there, until we can remove the equipment to a safer location."

Jackson stood, went closer to the map, squinted. "Sir, I am honored. I will hold the position as long as necessary."

"Major, I don't believe you should concern yourself with digging in there. The area is not defensible. The town sits in a low bowl, if you will, surrounded by high hills. But we need the machinery in the Arsenal. If we can maintain some strength there, just long enough to keep the Federal forces hesitating, we will have accomplished a great deal."

"I understand, General. I will leave immediately." Jackson turned, took long noisy steps toward the door, then stopped abruptly, made a neat turn back toward Lee and said, "Excuse me, General. A very good friend of mine, he's my brother-in-law, actually . . . no, he's my wife's brother-in-law. . . ." Jackson stared at the ceiling, spoke to himself, "No . . . well, yes, he's married to Anna's sister, so . . ."

Lee winced, No, not this one too, a good soldier who should know better.

"He is nearly my brother-in-law. He is a mathematics professor at the University of North Carolina . . . a very intelligent man, not lacking in a sense of duty. I believe if he were to be asked, he would return to the army."

"Return . . . ?"

"Yes, sir. He was in Mexico, left the army as a major."

Lee let out a light breath. At least this brother-in-law had some experience. "What is his name, Major?"

"Daniel Harvey Hill, sir."

Lee nodded, the name was familiar to him. He looked down the list on his desk, turned a page, then another. Jackson stood stiffly, watched, curious about what Lee was doing.

"Ah, yes, right here. Major, this army thanks you for your efforts on Mr. Hill's behalf, but it is not necessary. He has already volunteered."

Jackson nodded, said quietly, "Good . . . he knows his duty," then he turned again.

Lee said, "Major, wait."

Jackson froze, realized suddenly he had not saluted, spun around with his hand to the bill of his cap.

"No, Major, I mean . . . I just wanted to say, the state of Virginia is pleased to have your services. You are a valuable asset to her defense."

"General, duty has called me, and I can think of nothing that will please the Almighty more than my performing my duty. I will do whatever I must do to defeat my enemies."

Lee watched the serious face, saw something new, a grimness he had not seen before, had not seen in the others.

"Major, the men you will command are signing up for one-year terms. Most here say that is far too long, that this will be a brief affair, that we may be done with this business after one good scrap. It is the consensus among the political leaders here that the Federal forces will not fight, that with our first good show of strength, they will turn and run. I do not share their view, I would not count on that, Major. Nothing would please me more, but I fear this fight will not be brief."

"General, I will do everything in my power to make it as brief as possible. If they do not run, then they will die."

Lee saw the stern face, staring beyond him, looking at the wall above his head. "Very well, Major. May God be with you."

Jackson turned once more, marched from the office, and Lee heard him speaking, heard soft words hidden by the sharp sound of his boots on the oak floor, and Lee could tell only that it was a prayer.

THE NEW CONFEDERATE ADMINISTRATION UNDERSTOOD THE strategic need to defend Virginia. Lee's decision to occupy the key geographic points, from the western mountains to the vulnerable coastline and river systems, was supported by Davis's government. Lee had quickly established strong posts at Harper's Ferry and at the naval yards at Norfolk. The Federal Army had abandoned both positions, had attempted to burn what equipment was left behind, but alert militia units had rescued the materials, which were vital to Lee's plans for equipping his troops.

It was only logical that since Virginia was of such general importance to the defense of the rest of the Confederacy, their relationship should be formalized. Lee and Letcher had been able to convince President Davis that Virginia would bear the brunt of the Federal Army's moves, and thus they had few objections when, after Lee had established effective lines of defense, the rapidly organizing army of the Confederacy began to assume control.

As this balance shifted, Virginians whom Lee had appointed, men who filled necessary commands in the Virginia forces, began to make the transfer, accepting equivalent rank and positions in the Confederate Army. While politically minded men jockeyed for positions of command, Lee spent his days with the vast mundane details of building an army, and while the growing corps of officers began to make grandiose plans for the quick defeat of their enemy, Lee was struggling with finding enough flour, blankets, and cartridges for the men.

By early May, Lee had reached a point of near exhaustion and a sense of growing frustration with his own duties. There was simply too much to do.

On the floor beside his desk was an old brown cardboard box, and Lee tossed another pile of letters down, watched them bounce and flood over the sides. He thought, I will need another box. He began to sort another stack, separating the official messages from the governor and President Davis from troops reports and other military matters. Into the box had gone the private letters, the flowery recommendations, the long insistent lessons on warfare from people who had read about Napoleon, or who had their own theories for whipping these soft soldiers to the north. Occasionally there was the simple prayer, the sincere hope for peace, for a bloodless struggle, but those were rare. Across the office, Lee saw another bag on the one chair, a pile of mail he had not yet sorted, but all addressed to him.

He stood, stretched, loosened stiff bones, said aloud, "Enough."

He went to the door, pulled his coat from a hook, and walked out through the hallway, past offices of noisy officers. He avoided the faces, thought, Please, allow me to get away, just for a while. And then he was safe, outside, walking down the hill away from the building, from the government. He took deep breaths, walked under the full green canopies of the trees, opened up the dark creases of his mind to the warming spring breeze.

He walked to the Spottswood, still his home, thought of something cool to drink, just for a moment, a guilty pleasure. He reached the grand dining room and was relieved to find it nearly empty. He saw the perfect spot, a delightful corner table, and hurried, as though racing against unseen competitors vying for the same chair, then sat down, the victor. A waiter approached; no, not a waiter, a soldier, a tall, thin boy in an officer's uniform, the uniform of Virginia.

"Sir . . . you are General Lee, are you not, sir?"

Lee knew the escape was over, felt his duty creep back out, pushing away the sunlight. "Yes, Lieutenant, I am."

"Oh, sir, it is a great pleasure to meet you, sir. I am at your service."

"Service?" Lee thought of the waiter again, looked past the boy, trying to find someone to bring him . . . something.

"Yes, sir. Lieutenant Walter Taylor, sir. I have been assigned to your staff. My orders, sir."

Taylor pulled an envelope from his pocket, held it out, and Lee saw the governor's seal, looked at the boy's face, handsome, the eagerness of the young.

"My . . . staff. Yes, it appears the governor is providing for my assistance . . . hmmm." Lee finished reading the orders, returned them to the waiting hand.

"Tell me, Lieutenant Taylor, do you know how to write?"

"Write? You mean, can I read? Well, yes sir, certainly, sir."

"No, I mean, write letters. Capture a good phrase, the gracious message."

Taylor was puzzled, thought, then said, "Well, yes sir, I believe I can. I write home . . . as often as I can."

"Good. Then by all means let's get started." Lee stood, put aside the thoughts of a cool drink, and Taylor backed up a step, not sure what was happening. Lee put a hand on the boy's shoulder, turned him around gently, said, "Follow me."

Taylor glanced over to his own table, his food untouched on a plate, just delivered the moment he saw the general enter the room. He made a quick sidestep, grabbed a piece of bread, stuffed it into his pocket, then galloped after his new commander, who was already outside, returning to his work.

B Y JUNE, LEE HAD ASSISTED IN THE TRANSFER OF ALL THE VIR-ginia forces into the Confederate Army. While he assumed there would be a place for him in that army, once again he did not have the political outspokenness to grab a choice position for himself. As he entered the new offices of the Confederate government for a meeting with President Davis, Lee knew he was now in command of a nonexistent army.

He passed through large double doors, and there was no one in the outer office, no voices, none of the manic activity that seemed to fill his own building. He slowed, eased toward Davis's office, then knocked. There was a muffled sound from inside, a voice, and Lee turned the old brass handle, opened the door.

"Yes? What is it? Oh, General, do come in."

"Thank you, Mr. President. I didn't see . . . there's no one out here."

"Yes, I know. Sent them home."

Davis was a tall, angular man. His face carried a fierce expression that rarely softened. He sat behind an enormous desk, signing documents in steady succession.

"Sir, do you have a moment? If this is not a good time—"

"No, do come in, General. Just finishing up some orders here, you know how it is. There, that will hold those people for a while. Damned nuisance, these supply people."

"Sir, if I can assist—"

"This is the Confederate Army supply, General. I would imagine your hands are full worrying about your own state."

"Well, sir, that is precisely why I came to see you. It seems that my duties in command of Virginia's army are coming to a close. The army has been incorporated into the Confederate Army, and the strategic positions along the northern border have been secured by your generals. It has not been entirely smooth, but the job—"

"The job has been handled, General, handled most efficiently. I thank you. So, you have a run-in with Joe Johnston, eh? I heard he took over your men in Harper's Ferry, bit of a problem. He is not . . . well, he has his own way. Good man, though, good man."

Joseph Johnston had been the only high-ranking Virginia officer in the old army to sign up immediately with the new Confederate Army without first joining the Virginia forces. Lee knew Johnston always had a keen eye for politics, and so had secured himself a senior position immediately. Now, he commanded the newly promoted General Jackson and the other forces around Harper's Ferry, and did not recognize Lee's authority, would not even correspond with him.

"Sir, permit me to . . . be direct." Lee was growing more uncomfortable. There should not be this formality, he thought. We have a long history . . . I knew this man when we were at the Point. We were . . . well, not close, but . . . there should not be this wall, this political boundary. This was all too familiar to Lee, the coldness of politics, the lack of recognition, being ignored in favor of the men with louder voices. He felt very alone, very unsure. But as the responsibilities had gradually passed to the other commanders, he had stiffened, vowed to himself he would not allow this to simply slide by.

Davis looked up at Lee, looked into his eyes for the first time. Davis had assumed the role of commander in chief with a fanatical attention to detail. He tried, often at great expense of energy, to control all aspects of his government, and often had no trust for subordinates, and so his aides were usually left with nothing to do, while Davis assumed command of even minute details. It was Lee who seemed to win his confidence, because Lee was the only commander who did not challenge Davis's authority, who did not confront Davis with a great ego.

"General, you have performed an admirable . . . well, you have proven to me anyway that you were just the man we needed."

"Thank you, sir." Patience, Lee thought, be careful.

Davis continued, "Yes, of course. We're old soldiers, you and me. I understand what you've done, what steps had to be taken. There has been some talk, talk that you have been too gentle on our enemy, talk that we should have launched a full-scale attack into Washington, stopped this thing in its tracks. There has been some criticism of your defensive strategy."

"Sir, do you believe we should have attacked?"

"No, no, of course not. That's the point. You can't attack an enemy until you can take the fight to him. We weren't ready for that, didn't have the means. Now, however, I believe we do. That's why I'm glad to have men like Joe Johnston and Beauregard up on those lines. They may not be exactly . . . thinkers. But they will fight."

"Sir, I do not have a position in the Confederate Army."

"What? Of course you do, here, wait." Davis slid papers around

on his desk, lifted one tall stack, shoved it aside, sent pieces fluttering
away to the floor.

"Yes, right here. Mr. Lee, you have been named one of five
brigadier generals commanding Confederate forces. Your Governor
Letcher was most insistent, helped me convince the convention. There,
that what you wanted?"

Lee thought, No one told me . . . I should feel honored. But he
felt hollow, an emptiness.

"Thank you, sir. May I ask, what are my orders? What troops do
I command—where do I go?" He scolded himself for being too anxious.

Davis looked through papers again, began to read, absently, and
Lee saw distraction.

"Sir, do you have duty for me?"

"What? Duty? Of course, General, right here, with me."

"Here . . . ?"

"You're too valuable to the operation of this army—the supplies,
the detailed work. Can't have you up there, in the middle of the fighting."

Lee sank into his chair, felt a great weight press him down.

Davis shoved papers aside again, looked at Lee. "Invaluable, General. You are what we need here. Behind the scenes, running the show.
No one better at it, no one at all."

Lee stood, pulled himself slowly from the chair. "Thank you for
your confidence, Mr. President. I have to get back to my office . . . a
great deal to do."

"Yes, I'm sure, General. Busy times, busy indeed. Keep me
informed."

Davis turned back to his work, and Lee moved slowly out
through the quiet offices, back to his own vast piles of paper.

14. HANCOCK

JUNE 1861

"NOTHING. NOT A WORD, NOT A DAMNED WORD!" HE SAT on the floor, shuffled again through the mail pouch, scattered the letters around him.

Mira stood over him, put a hand on his shoulder. "It takes time. They haven't forgotten you."

"Are you sure? We're a long way from Washington, a long way from the war. I'm just another officer who happens to be far enough away that he can be overlooked. What do I have to offer? Right now they're looking for fighters, company commanders, brigade commanders. I'm a supply officer. They've probably got men lined up in the street for the field positions. Damn!"

He gathered the mail, straightened the bundles, put them back into the pouch, and she knelt down, picked up a handful of letters, mail for the soldiers of the Sixth, Armistead's men, helped him put them in order.

"Is there anyone else you can contact?"

"I've written General Scott, the War Department, the Quartermaster General's Office. I suppose I could try Governor Curtin. He knows my father well, might be able to find me something in the Pennsylvania volunteers."

"When will the next mail run be?"

"Hard to say. They're a bit quicker now, maybe three, four days. All we can do is wait."

He got up off the floor, lifted the pouch over his shoulder, reached for his hat.

"I'll be back soon. Once I deliver this, I'll come help you get the house ready. Anything you need?"

"No, I have it all. It should be a nice dinner, we'll try to make it a fun evening. The piano should be here soon; the church is sending it over in a wagon."

"The piano?"

"I thought it might be nice, some music . . . this doesn't have to be a sad evening."

"But it will be. This whole thing is sad. But yes, music will be nice. You've been practicing?"

"Win, if you came to church more regularly, you would hear quite an improvement in my playing. If I know soldiers, and my playing is not satisfactory, there will be at least one of you who will show me how it's done."

He laughed, pulled open the door. "Soon."

She pushed the door closed behind him and locked it, her habit now. Her mind began to work, to plan. She mentally counted heads, went back to the kitchen, the pantry, lifted a small sack of flour, put it down heavily on the thick wood table. She reached up to a high shelf, brought down a large clay bowl, set it by the flour, then paused and thought of Armistead, waiting with a bright smile, the eagerness of a child, as she kept him waiting, waiting for the cookies to cool. He would eat an entire sheet full if she let him, and so she would make him wait, torture him playfully with the smell, until he begged, please. Then finally she would produce the flat pan, and he would gobble the first one in one bite, then savor the rest, slowly. Win would have to wait until Lewis picked out the ones he wanted, the big ones, before he could get to them. She smiled, thought, yes, I'll make those too. It would be good to see him smile again.

THEY BEGAN TO ARRIVE ABOUT SIX. HANCOCK ANSWERED THE door, opened to see officers in civilian clothes.

"Mr. Garnett, Mr. Wiggins, welcome, come in."

"Thank you, Captain. Mighty fine of you to do this. Most kind." The men entered the house.

Hancock pointed to a small table, bottles and glasses, said, "Wine, gentlemen? Help yourself. Mrs. Hancock will be bringing out some trays of food . . . ahh, here."

Mira entered from the kitchen, brought a large platter of bread and cheese, set it down on another table, and the men bowed to her, a short, formal greeting, and then reached for the wine.

Hancock heard a carriage, looked out through the screen, saw

Johnston climbing down with a large bundle of flowers wrapped in brightly colored paper. Hancock did not see the staff officers, and felt relief, for there would be plenty of food now, the house would not be so crowded. With generals, you never knew what they assumed. Johnston came to the door, Hancock stood back, and Johnston held out a large hand. Hancock took it, and both men knew they were not yet enemies.

"Please, allow me to present these to our hostess."

"Certainly. She is back in the kitchen . . . come. . . ."

"No, I'll wait here. Don't want to interfere."

Mira appeared again, brought another bottle of wine, and Johnston made a great show, a low sweeping bow. "On behalf of all the new civilians who have gathered here this evening, we offer you this gift, our warmest thanks for your fine hospitality."

"Well, goodness, Mr. Johnston, thank you, these are quite impressive."

She took the flowers, saw the variety, knew this had taken some time, and carried them back into the kitchen to find a vase.

"Tell me, Captain, in all honesty. This party was her idea, was it not?"

Hancock was still by the door, looking outside for one more guest.

"Well, now that you mention it, yes, I must confess. I'm not a big party man myself."

"Quite all right, Mr. Hancock. I don't believe any of us have felt much like celebrating, certainly not now. I appreciate your wife's sense of sentiment. It's important we don't forget . . . that we can do this . . . that we are all still friends."

Outside, horses rode up, two more officers in civilian clothes. Hancock tried to recall the names, men from Benicia. Johnston moved up closer, followed Hancock's gaze, said, "Ah . . . Captain Douglas . . . that is, Mr. Douglas. Mr. Harrison. Good, good. Hope you don't mind, Captain. They came down this morning, on the steamer. I asked them to join me here."

"Not at all, *General.*" Hancock laughed, and Johnston got the joke, nodded.

"Yes, well, we do cut a wide swath, Captain."

Hancock welcomed the men, and after greetings were exchanged all around, Hancock said to Johnston, "Will there be more, *sir?*"

"No, not tonight. There's a few more arriving tomorrow, another boat." Johnston seemed more serious now.

Hancock said, "So, when do you leave?"

Johnston looked at him, and the sound of voices behind him grew, the talk of soldiers, glasses of wine moving about. He said quietly, "How did you know I was leaving?"

"I have many good friends here, Mr. Johnston."

"It's not what I had hoped for. This place doesn't offer what I had . . . well . . . it's not important."

He turned, left Hancock at the door, went to the table where the half-empty wine bottle waited. He poured a glass, the others gathered around him, and Johnston joined the party. Hancock turned, looked outside again, the sun was on the far trees, and the light was slipping away.

Mira appeared again, brought out more wine, to the great happiness of the men, and Hancock watched them toast her, a rowdy salute. She glanced at him, knew he did not share the mood, and he turned again and looked out, waiting.

The horse came at a slow trot, and Hancock did not recognize him at first, had not seen him in civilian clothes for a long time. He pulled the horse into Hancock's yard, dismounted by the others, unhooked a hanger, a thin bag, from the side of the saddle, carried it carefully above the ground, then saw Hancock standing, waiting at the door.

"Good evening, Captain. Sorry to be late. I had to stand over my aide to get him to clean this just right. Couldn't give it to you dirty."

Armistead passed through the door, did not look at Hancock's face, and Hancock closed the door, followed him into the party.

The men gathered around the new arrival. A glass was presented, and Mira came out of the back, the men parting. She hugged him, and the others began to make the sound, the rowdy hoots, then saw that she was crying and quickly stopped. The room was silent for a long pause.

Mira stood back, smiled through red eyes, said, "Gentlemen, we have a great deal more wine."

The men began to loosen again, and Armistead raised his free hand, said, "No, wait. I have a special presentation to make." The men quieted again, and Armistead turned to Hancock and held out the hanger. Hancock took the cloth bag, slid it from around the contents, saw: Armistead's uniform.

"Captain Hancock, it is the sincerest wish and boldest prediction of those present that you will not remain a captain forever. In anticipation of the army's wisdom, and in the interest of eliminating the normal administrative delays, I present you with the uniform of a major. Congratulations in advance."

There was applause, and Hancock ran his hand over the blue cloth, saw the gold oak leaf on the shoulder, looked at Armistead, who held up a glass of wine and nodded slightly. Hancock smiled and looked at Mira, who applauded as well, and he moved forward, closer to the men, and joined the party.

I T WAS CLOSE TO MIDNIGHT.
"Gentlemen, another toast, to our hostess."
"Yes! Hear! Hear!"

Mira had finished her work, had let the empty platters and used glasses gather in the kitchen. Her only distraction now was the children, and she slipped away, back to their room, checking, astonished at the soundness of their sleep, what with the noise from the front of the house. She watched the angelic faces, thought, We will pay for this in the morning, probably very early in the morning.

She went back to the front room, saw the door opened, men saluting with a drunken stagger, laughing and good humor, and the party grew smaller, then smaller again.

There had been piano playing earlier, lively songs and bad singing, and Mira had been right, the men had taken over, some reminiscing about old drinking halls and indiscreet women, brought to life again with poor examples of musical skill.

There were only a few remaining. Johnston sat in the corner, propped up by a firm grip on an empty wineglass, nodding peacefully to the conversation of the others, betrayed only when he could not rise to salute departing guests.

Hancock was closing the door, moved toward the wine bottle, and now Mira saw Armistead across the room, watching him. They had not spoken, had not been together all night, and she knew it would come, that it was too close, too deep to share with the others. Then she remembered, turned quickly and went back to the kitchen. She reached behind the cloth curtain of a high cupboard, brought out a straw basket, white linen, a soft cradle for the batch of cookies. She carried them gently, moved back toward the party, and Armistead was waiting for her.

"I wondered how long it would take."
"You knew I made these?"
"I smelled them the minute I entered the house. You live around

soldiers as long as I have, the smell of anything else is a piece of heaven." She pulled back the flap of linen, and he reached in, grabbed one, stuffed it in his mouth, then grabbed a handful, counted the remainder.

"Hmm, there's . . . six more. Two for Win, two for you . . ." He glanced over his shoulder, saw no one else worthy. "I guess the last two are for me." He reached for a cloth napkin, wrapped his treasure gently, pulled a small parcel from his coat pocket, making room for the feast. He held the parcel up, stared at it, said slowly, serious now, "My dear Mrs. Hancock, I have something for you. I would be honored if you would be the caretaker of this. . . ." He handed her the parcel, wrapped in layers of white tissue, tied with a small string. "There are some things I wish you to keep. Please . . . would you see to it that this be given to my family . . . in the event I do not survive this war?"

"Certainly, Lewis." She took the parcel, looked at him, thought, He is not drunk. She had watched him sip from a single glass of wine for over an hour.

"Lewis . . . when are you two going to talk?"

"My dear Mrs. Hancock, would you do us the honor of playing some more? This party seems to have dwindled a tad." He exaggerated the soft drawl, and she nodded, knew not to push. She looked across the room at her husband, who stood over Johnston, a meaningless conversation so that he did not have to face Armistead.

She moved to the piano, gathered in her dress, sat on the small bench and looked up at Armistead. "What would you like to hear?"

"Something quiet . . ." He looked over at Hancock. "Something . . . appropriate."

She thought, flipped through the music books that had come with the piano, came to one book, thin and coverless, and the book fell open at her touch. She saw the title, "Kathleen Malvourneen," and softly touched the keys, began to sing quietly. She did not want to interrupt the others, the conversations. Suddenly, the room was quiet, her voice calling them together:

"Kathleen Malvourneen, the gray dawn is breaking,
The horn of the hunter is heard on the hill,
The lark from her light wing the bright dew is shaking,
Kathleen Malvourneen, what? Slumb'ring still?
Kathleen Malvourneen, what? Slumb'ring still.
Oh, hast thou forgotten how soon we must sever?
Oh, hast thou forgotten this day we must part?

It may be for years, and it may be forever;
Then why art thou silent, thou voice of my heart?
It may be for years and it may be forever;
Then why art thou silent, Kathleen Malvourneen. . . ."

Hancock moved close to her, stood by her side, and he looked at Armistead, the tanned, rugged face, and saw that Armistead was crying, staring down at the piano, at Mira's soft hands on the keys. Hancock moved around behind her, put a hand on Armistead's shoulder, and Armistead looked up. Hancock saw the pain, saw him shake slightly. Armistead fell forward, put his head on Hancock's chest, and Hancock wrapped his arms around his friend, felt his own tears, could not ignore it any longer, knew this would be the last time.

Mira played the song again, did not sing, felt them standing behind her, heard the soft sounds, and after a minute Armistead took a deep breath, composed himself and stood back, keeping his hand on Hancock's shoulder.

"I must do what I am meant to do. I hope you will never know . . . you will never feel what this has cost me. If I ever . . . raise my hand . . . against you . . . may God strike me dead." He looked down, saw Mira's upturned face, the soft eyes, said again, *"May God strike me dead."*

H E RODE HARD, SPURRED THE BLACK MULE DEEP IN ITS haunches, leaned forward as the animal strained its way up the steep hills, the rocky ground. Behind him was the town, the tile roofs of Los Angeles, smaller now and far below. He rode up higher, along any trail that led up, any trail the mule could climb. He reached a long crest, could see the other side now, to the east, the wide, flat desert, and he stopped, felt the mule breathing under him, gasping for thin air.

He climbed down from the tired animal, felt better now, relaxed, his anger drained by the long climb. He looked around, was not sure exactly where he was, looked back to the west, over the town, could see the coastline, the distant islands off the coast, and he thought, My God, this is a beautiful spot.

He climbed a big rock, pulled himself up with his hands, found a flat place on top and sat down. It was cooler now, he was far above the choking heat of the summer sun. He looked at the mule, grateful, and the mule seemed refreshed as well, began to poke its nose around the rocks, looking for anything green.

He turned back to the east again, to the dull flatness, thought of the Indians, the only people out there, wondered how far you would have to go to see a white man. But you would not go, because before the Indians would bother you, the desert itself would take you, bake you in suffocating heat. He turned slightly, could see more to the south, long rows of mountains fading, smooth and round, not like the stark roughness he had seen in Wyoming, in Utah. He gazed over the smaller peaks, toward the far trails that had carried some of them back East, the long routes through Arizona and Texas where the new soldiers of the South would be welcomed to the new war.

He reached into his coat, pulled the envelope from his pocket, opened it again, held the letter up to the sunlight behind him, read it again, calmer this time, no surprises.

Captain Winfield S. Hancock, Chief Quartermaster, Department of Southern California.

You are hereby ordered to report to the Quartermaster General, Washington, pursuant to your assignment as Supply Officer, the Department of Kentucky, General Robert Anderson, Commanding.

He read it again, stared at the words "Supply Officer." He looked up, stared out at the wide, clear space, said aloud, *"Damn!"*

He folded the letter, put it in his pocket, thought of Mira. She had always been right, always said, "You are too good at your job." He wondered how many old soldiers, former soldiers, friends of politicians—anyone looking for a place in the new pages of glory—how many had volunteered to be *supply officers*? And worse, Hancock knew that without good supply officers, the army would not function, and so, of course, that was where they would send him. But it was not where he wanted to go.

He thought of Mexico, of his long fight to be sent there. He had been assigned as a recruitment officer, to sign up new volunteers for the war, and he was too good at that as well, made himself indispensable. Finally, after long months of tormenting his superiors, he had been assigned to the Sixth, and had accompanied some of his recruits south to join Scott's army. He'd been in the good fight too, the key battles around Mexico City, had led infantry into stupid assaults, ordered by bad generals who did not understand that you did not push your outnumbered troops straight into fortified positions, and so many had died. Hancock had brought that home with him, would always know what it was like, *out there*, in front of the lines. And so it was difficult to live with the peace, more difficult than he could ever admit to Mira. He tried not to see Armistead's face—he was gone, probably in Virginia by now—but Hancock knew: Armistead would *fight*, it was all he was, and unless Washington noticed him in the great crowd of the growing army, Hancock would have to settle for being a supply officer.

He stood up, high on the perch, felt a sudden breeze, balanced himself, could see down, through a small canyon, sharp, steep rocks. Steady, he thought. No need to end up down *there*. He eased himself down from the big rock. The mule was ignoring him, had found a small patch of coarse grass, tugged at it noisily, and Hancock put his hand on the animal's back, looked back to the town, thought, I suppose we will miss it here, the weather, good friends. But I have never been in one place for long, that's just not the way the army works.

He climbed up on the mule, which raised its head and turned to look at him. Hancock saw something that looked like annoyance, and he laughed, patted the animal's neck, said aloud, "Yes, my friend, you have your duty as well. Now, I would appreciate it if you would re- move us from this big damned hill without any major injury. Then you may carry me home. I have to tell my wife we're leaving."

15. LEE

LIEUTENANT TAYLOR MOVED WITH NOISY HASTE, BOUNDED UP the stairs to the old office building, his boots echoing in heavy steps down the wide hallway to Lee's office. Lee heard him coming, looked up from his writing to see the young man stumble around the corner, supporting himself against the doorway, gasping for breath.

"Lieutenant, are you all right?"

"Sir . . . the War Department . . . it's an attack . . ."

"Slowly, Lieutenant. There's been an attack on the War Department?"

"No, sir . . ." Taylor panted, then adjusted himself, took a long, deep breath. "Sir, I was just at the War Department, delivering the dispatches as you requested. There is a great deal of . . . activity there. I stayed as close as I could, and heard the staff relaying messages from General Beauregard. It seems, sir, that he is being attacked. I heard them talking about General McDowell moving against our forces at Manassas Gap, sir. Beauregard . . . that is, General Beauregard, is calling urgently for reinforcements from General Johnston."

Lee stared at the young man, who was still trying to catch his breath.

Lee knew the attack made sense, the Manassas Gap Railroad was a key strategic position below the Potomac. McDowell's Federal forces had stayed to the north far longer than Lee had expected, and he assumed that the same political pressure that the Confederate Army had endured, the wild calls for mindless attack, had been just as loud in Washington, and so McDowell's forces finally were moving southward.

Joe Johnston had withdrawn out of Harper's Ferry, south to Winchester, protecting the Shenandoah Valley, but now it was apparent that McDowell had focused closer to Richmond, on Manassas, and so Johnston would be called to move in next to Beauregard.

Lee thought it through, glanced up at the map on his wall, the markings of troop placements. If McDowell's troops pushed through the Confederate line, there would be little to stop the Federals from marching straight into Richmond. Lee stood, closer to the map, went over the defensive lines again, thought, We are in place, we have the ground. Now we will find out if we have an army.

Taylor watched Lee, knew when to be quiet. Finally, Lee turned to him, said, "I suggest we make our way over to the President's office."

"Yes, sir, right behind you, sir."

Lee led the young man through the hall, down the steps, and immediately there was a sense of action. The street was alive, everyone was in a hurry. He moved quickly, felt the energy, began to run now, a bouncing step up into the administration building. Taylor stayed close behind, marveled at Lee's enthusiasm, smiled a wide grin, felt, finally, this was what it was about, the real duty of a soldier.

Lee approached the wide doors of Davis's office, saw couriers, a steady flow of men moving from the office, new orders and fresh legs, and finally made his way through the noise and activity. Davis was standing tall above the others, and Lee waited, thought, Wait for the right moment.

Then Davis saw him, his eyes fierce, flashing, and he shouted above the others, "General Lee, we are in a fight!" Lee moved closer, and the office began to clear out, quieter, and Davis said, "I'm heading up to the front, to Manassas. I can't just . . . sit here. I have a train leaving immediately."

Lee waited, felt the intensity, knew Davis shared his anxieties, which most of the others did not feel—that they were an unorganized, untested force, and that one great battle could decide the issue; the entire rebellion could end here.

Lee felt a strange urge, suddenly held out his hand, a warm gesture, affection for a man who did not show affection. Davis took the hand, political reflex, did not look at Lee, passed by him, hurried out. Lee turned to Taylor, saw a puzzled look, and then they both knew what was happening, that Davis was gone.

Lee moved out, past Taylor, into the outer office, and saw the last of Davis's staff close the broad door.

"Sir, we must . . . we can't stay here."

"Lieutenant, it is clear that this is our post. Our duty is in Richmond."

"But, sir, there is an attack. . . ."

"We have good men in command, Lieutenant. It is their battle now."

Lee felt the energy drain from his body, the familiar hollowness. Do not focus on this, he thought. This was, after all, not the issue. He walked outside, saw wagons and horses moving, streams of people, all moving toward the trains, all rushing to the great battle.

"Sir, with your permission."

Lee turned to Taylor, saw the youth, the wounded look, knew he had to go, to be a part. He nodded. "Yes, Lieutenant, you are authorized to join in the fight. Find an infantry unit, give the commander my compliments. They will find a place for you."

"Sir!" Taylor saluted, made a high yelp, turned and ran toward the depot. Lee watched him, all long legs and wild leaps, and he turned toward his office and walked across the wide street, against the flow of people rushing out from his building.

THERE WAS A DEATHLY SILENCE. LEE STOOD AT HIS WINDOW, above the empty street, felt amazingly alone. The city seemed abandoned. He had spent the day in feeble attempts at work, could not sit, went to the window every few minutes, and when there was nothing to see, would return to his desk and try again to attack the papers.

He stood back from the window, went, again, to the map, considered the lines, *his* lines, the defensive design he had put into place, now being commanded by others, others who would receive the credit if the positions were good, if he had chosen the right ground. No, he would not think of that. It does not matter who does the duty, he thought, if the duty is done. I am here because God wants me here, I will serve in other ways. He repeated that, had repeated it all day, trying to ease his feelings, the sense that he was out of place.

The long day began to dim, and he watched the sunset all the way to the darkness, and still there had been no news. He realized for the first time that there were people still, downstairs, in some of the other offices, but no one brought him any information. They probably did not know he was there. Hungry, he decided to go back to the

Spottswood, pondered the long walk, heard a long low whistle, and from the north saw a distant flicker of light. The train moved closer, into the station beyond the buildings. Lee stared, listened, heard more whistles now, and then he saw a rider in a furious gallop. The man rode up close to Lee's building, dismounted and yelled something Lee could not understand, then was gone, into the offices below. Lee started for his door, waited, heard more noise, another rider, several horses now. People began to come out, to fill the street. He went back to the window, was surprised to see so many, had assumed most of them were gone. There were cheers, wild cries, and he could not stand it anymore, left his office and went down to the dark, lamplit street.

Spotting a uniform, a young bearded man covered in dirt, he asked, "Soldier, do you bring news of the battle?"

The man looked exhausted, regarded Lee with wild joy. "We whipped 'em, we whipped 'em good. They's a-runnin' back to Washington, hee hee."

Lee put his hands on the man's shoulders. "Please, can you be more detailed?"

Lee felt the man squirm, itching to get away, to join the growing celebration in the street around them, but he stilled under Lee's grasp.

"Yes, sir. It was General Jackson. Saved the day, he did. Drove them bluebellies all the way back to Washington! They's sayin' he stood his men up like a stone wall!" The man slipped away, a quick turn and Lee could not hold him. He let the man go, but he could not celebrate, had to know more than rumors.

He left the street, went back up to his office. Through the window he could see wagons now, crowds of people returning from the battle. He heard another train whistle, knew this would go on all night, and he would have to wait till tomorrow to find out the details. He sat back in his chair, stared at a dark ceiling, thought of the lone soldier, his only piece of news, and kept hearing the words: General Jackson saved the day.

THE FEDERAL FORCES HAD FLED FROM THE FIRST MAJOR BATTLE of the war in a complete panic. The troops under Beauregard and Johnston did not pursue, ordered into inactivity by generals who did not understand how completely they had won the day. The lack of action now spread over the armies like a thick blanket. Thousands of spectators had lined the edges of the battle-field at Manassas, only to view incredible horrors that none had anticipated. After the battle both sides seemed infected with a gloom, a sense that this was now very real, the abstract political rhetoric replaced with the clear, sickening knowledge that many men were going to die.

16. HANCOCK

SEPTEMBER 1861

THE CARRIAGE BROUGHT THEM TO THE FRONT STEPS OF THE Willard Hotel, a white brick building that stood over a wide square. Mira was helped from the carriage by the firm hand and pleasant smile of the doorman, a tall black man in a foolish top hat, who bowed deeply as he released her. Hancock climbed out the other side, watched as the man picked their bags from the rear of the carriage, thought of offering to help, but the man was gone, up the short stairs, into the hotel.

"Well, my husband, this is not at all what you expected, is it?"

He looked around, saw people in all forms of dress, some hurrying, some in a leisurely stroll through the square, down the broad streets of Washington.

"No. This is . . . strange."

From the moment of their arrival in New York, and all during the train trip to the capital, they had heard the rumors: a city under siege, the savage rebel army on the outskirts, a general panic. Hancock knew not to trust rumors, but in some ways they made sense. He had read of the early skirmishes, unprepared armies colliding in sloppy battles like two small children in a fistfight, swinging wildly, arms flapping in a flurry of misdirected motion. But then there were the reports from Manassas, what the northern papers called Bull Run, where there were too many troops and too many bad generals, and one general in particular, Irvin McDowell, who believed the cocky assurances from the men in expensive suits, the congressmen and dignitaries who happily followed the army in grand carriages, who brought along their women, sitting under brightly colored parasols, watching the splendid event from a hillside; an eager audience, picnicking and partying as

155

their gallant heroes under fluttering flags would crush the dirty riffraff of the rebellion.

It was McDowell who learned that the dirty little rebel army had come to fight, would not run from the loud brass bands or the neat lines of blue troops, and were not there to perform for his audience. The bloody rout sent the Union troops back through their admirers in a panic, and the stunned audience was swarmed by the real sounds of war, loud piercing screams, the cries of wounded and terrified men. They saw blood, great bursts of red covering the troops and the ground, and the men in the fancy suits did not cheer, but pulled their women back, moving with the great flow of panic back into the city, pursued by the brutal honesty of death.

And so, the rumors had flown. This army of savages was on the brink, ready to overwhelm the decent people of Washington. But the attack hadn't come, and while Hancock had not expected the rumors to be accurate, he was amazed at the calmness, the jovial mood of the people, still so close to the bloody fields.

"Very strange." He moved around the carriage. Mira took his arm and they went up into the hotel.

The man behind the desk glanced at his uniform, noticed it was not new, seemed surprised, and Hancock now saw that the lobby was filled with officers, men with loud voices, crisp blue coats, the men of the new army. No one noticed him, and he did not think of saluting anyone, though he passed by men of high rank, men who were strutting about like swollen birds.

"Excuse me, we have sent word . . . we have a room, I believe?"

The clerk looked at him again, then saw Mira. His eyes brightened and he nodded in her direction. "Name?"

"Captain Winfield Hancock. And Mrs. Hancock."

"Hmmm, let's see . . . oh, here. Yes, you have Room 6D."

The man motioned to a waiting bellman, another black man in a formal gray suit and red hat, who had been waiting for the cue. The man picked up their bags and led them to the stairway. Hancock paused, glanced out through the noisy throng of uniforms, thought there might be someone he knew, some familiar face. But he recognized no one, saw officers speaking to civilians, men with pads of paper, reporters, of course. He turned back to Mira, who was waiting for him, smiling.

"Let's go up to the room, please. I'm covered with dust."

He felt her arm in his again, and she pulled him along, following the bellman. The man led them up to their room, pushed open the heavy oak door and led them inside. Mira directed the placement of the bags, and Hancock went to the window, looked out to the street, the rooftops, saw the larger buildings, the grand spectacle of the Capitol building, the great white monuments to the government he served. He began to feel a hopelessness, a dark futility, surrounded not by the symbols of his country, the great cause of the Union, but by men sealed away in their offices, men who made decisions based on the preservation of their jobs, men who would distrust Albert Sidney Johnston and could never understand the passion of Lewis Armistead, and so they did not understand that they were in great danger, that this army was in for a real fight and could not be run by puppets and peacocks.

He did not notice the bellman leave, suddenly felt her hand, sliding up his back to his shoulder. He wrapped an arm around her waist, pulled her in tightly, and she said, "It seems so quiet . . . like there is no war at all."

"I know. A few weeks ago, the bloodiest battle ever fought on this land took place a few miles from here, and they have already forgotten."

"Maybe it's better forgotten."

"No, it is better remembered. Because if they don't, it will happen again, and keep on happening until they realize . . . this is a war. The Southerners are not an unruly mob that comes at us with sticks and torches. They have leaders, men who know how to take men into combat. Those men downstairs . . . in the lobby . . . those men have never led anything . . . and they will learn what that can cost."

She looked up at him, saw his hard stare, and she felt him tighten, his jaw clench. She said, "You won't be content to be a supply officer. . . ."

There was a long pause, and he took a deep breath. "I have never been content to be a supply officer."

"Then *tell* them. Volunteer for something else."

He dropped his arm, turned away from her, from the window. "I'm not a politician. I don't have the friends, the pull, that those people . . . downstairs have. I have been given a job, and ultimately it comes down to that, to do what the army orders me to do."

She moved toward him, and the sun came in behind her, silhouetting her. He reached out, touched her face with gentle hands, and there was a knock at the door.

He stared at her a moment longer, then turned, pulled open the heavy door, and was surprised to see an older man, an officer.

"Forgive me . . . are you Captain Hancock?"

"Yes, please come in."

The man moved quickly, then saw Mira and looked uncomfortable. "Forgive the intrusion, Captain, they told me downstairs you just arrived. We've been waiting for you."

"We, being . . . ?"

"I am Colonel Randolph Marcy, General McClellan's chief of staff."

"General McClellan?"

"Yes, Captain. The general has sent me to request that you not report anywhere until the general can see you."

"Forgive me, Colonel Marcy, but I am not familiar with a *General* McClellan. I knew of a McClellan in Mexico, knew him at the Point. . . ."

"You have had a long journey, Captain. General George McClellan has been appointed Commander of the Army, to assume those duties General Scott is . . . no longer . . ." He paused, did not want to say the words. "You *are* familiar with General Scott?"

Hancock nodded. "Of course, sir. Forgive me. I have been out of touch."

"Quite all right, Captain. Events occur at a rapid pace these days. The President feels that General McClellan is more suited to the operation of an effective fighting force than is General Scott. General Scott is . . . beyond his time, wouldn't you agree?"

"If that is the President's judgment."

"General McClellan will send word to you here. Again, forgive the intrusion." He turned to Mira, bowed, said a curt "Madam," and backed out the door.

Hancock went back to the window, began to feel hot, blood rising in the back of his neck. "So, we have a real war, and they shove aside the only real warrior we have."

"What do you suppose General McClellan wants with you, dear? He said they were waiting for you. It sounds terribly important."

"McClellan. I remember him now, feisty little fellow, a couple years behind me. Brilliant . . . graduated at the top of his class, should have stayed in the army. I think he went up north somewhere, ran a railroad or something. Now he's the commanding general?"

"And he wants to see *you*."

THERE WAS CONSTANT MOTION, MEN MOVING IN ALL DIRECtions, office doors opening and closing in a jerky rhythm, the manic activity of headquarters. Hancock felt suddenly embarrassed, saw the clean blue coats, the sharp gold braids, knew his uniform was a bit ragged. There had not been time to have it cleaned, the call from McClellan coming the morning after Marcy's visit. The best he could do was a clean white shirt, and he saw they all had clean white shirts.

"This way, Captain. The general can see you now."

He was led by a young major, another new uniform, past aides and piles of paperwork, desks covered with lists and figures, paperwork he knew well.

McClellan sat behind a massive desk, shiny mahogany trimmed with gold-painted strips of wood shaped like the braids of a rope. The office was full of men, and McClellan was signing orders and requisitions, handed to him by each man in succession. Hancock was instantly impressed, knew the efficiency of motion, felt he was indeed in the presence of a commander.

"General, sir, this is Captain Hancock."

McClellan looked up, did not rise, pointed to a chair without speaking, and the major followed the instructions, pulled the chair out, motioned for Hancock to sit.

McClellan did not stop working, did not send the men away, and Hancock knew that whatever the reason for this visit, it would not be private.

"Captain, we are building an army here. A good army. A goddamned big army. You understand that?"

Hancock cleared his throat, tried to make himself heard above the noise of the staff.

"Yes, sir. I can see that, sir."

"Do you know what goes into this, Mr. Hancock? Well, of course you do, you're a damned quartermaster. Best in the army, I've heard."

Hancock did not feel complimented, instead felt a small, cold hole in his stomach. He thought, He wants me to be a quartermaster general. A tremendous need, and you can do it, you're the right man for it, for quite possibly the worst job in the army. He waited for more, saw the papers flow across McClellan's desk in a smooth stream, stopping only for a brief glance, a short explanation, and a quick stroke of black ink.

"They don't understand, you know. They have no idea."

Hancock looked at the face, the eyes that were not looking at him but darted at the papers, piercing and aware. Hancock said only, "Sir?"

"The politicians. The President. They have no idea what this army needs. *None.* No idea what this war is about . . . what we are up against. You cannot command from an office, from a comfortable backside, Mr. Hancock. I believe you know that."

"Yes, sir. I suppose I do."

"The President has called for seventy-five thousand troops. We need three times that, and more. The rebel army that sits right out there, right across that river, numbers over two hundred thousand, gets stronger every day. If we don't move on them, and move with a well-trained, well-equipped, and well-commanded force, we will be massacred. You hear about Bull Run?"

"Yes, sir. I read the reports on the trip east."

"Bloody disaster. Could have been worse . . . they could have marched right into Washington. Hell, they could have marched all the way to New York! Point is, we weren't ready, and they were. No more of that. This is my command now."

Hancock was beginning to relax, began to feel part of the office, the flow of activity, knew McClellan understood. "How may I help, sir?"

McClellan looked at him, shifted his attention away from the papers for the first time. "You know why I called you here?"

"No, sir. I assume, sir, because you want me to assist the quartermaster—"

"Quartermaster? That's for clerks. I have plenty of clerks, Mr. Hancock. I need soldiers. I need men who fought in Mexico, who know what gunfire sounds like, men who don't run when the enemy shoots at them. So far, this army hasn't shown much stomach for a real fight. This whole damned city is filling up with officers, men who can't wait to be heroes, who have no idea *how.* We need leaders, Mr. Hancock. I believe that includes you."

Hancock sat up straighter, felt a new stirring in his gut, said, "I have received orders . . . to report to General Anderson . . . as his supply officer. Does the general have a new assignment for me?"

"Anderson? Good man. Held on at Fort Sumter without losing a man. So, now the War Department sticks him out there in Kentucky, when we need him right here. Mr. Hancock, do you know General 'Baldy' Smith . . . William Smith?"

"Not well. He was at the Point, a year behind me. I can't say I've heard anything about his career in the army."

"Of course not. He barely has one. But he has friends in important places, and so the War Department has given him a division. Never mind that he's barely led anybody anywhere. The department specializes in rewarding politicians. Point is, Smith needs some brigade commanders, men who *do* know how to lead, men who can keep him out of trouble. That's you, Mr. Hancock. I am recommending to the President that you be promoted to Brigadier General and assigned to General Smith's division."

"Brigadier General? Sir, I'm only a captain."

"There is a war, Mr. Hancock. Look around you. You can't fire a cannon down any street in Washington without hitting a newly appointed general. Your promotion will have no difficulty. You are, after all, one of the few around here who is a real soldier. I am grateful for your service, Mr. Hancock."

McClellan turned back to his papers. Impatient aides moved closer to the desk, and the procession began again. Hancock felt overwhelmed, wanted to say something appropriate, saw that the moment was passing, the army was moving on in front of him.

"Sir . . . General, I am honored."

"It is we who are honored. We have a difficult job to do, Mr. Hancock. We have enemies in front of us and behind us. It is the army, alone, that must win this war. Are you with me, Mr. Hancock?"

Hancock did not understand McClellan's concerns, but let the words go, understood that he had been given an extraordinary opportunity, the chance, again, to be a soldier. He stood, saluted, said, "Certainly, sir. I am with you."

McClellan glanced up, returned the salute, then the young major was by his side. He placed a hand on Hancock's arm, a subtle pull, and Hancock knew it was time to leave. He turned, nodded to the young man's expressionless face, then made his way through the blue coats, passed through the maze of offices, past a line of well-dressed civilians, waiting to see Someone Important. He found the crowded stairway which led him back outside, into the clear September morning.

Hancock moved with long strides, passing statues and small patches of green grass, crossing the wide streets, dodging horses and wagons carrying soldiers. He knew Mira would be waiting for him, anxious, staring out the window of their room, looking at the soldiers, trying to spot him in the crowds below. He hurried now, hopped up the curb, glanced up at the windows of the hotel, could not see her, too much glare. He pushed into the lobby, saw more blue coats, women in bright dresses gathered around the men who posed and preened, and he made his way toward the stairs, rounded a corner and bumped into a man, a uniform.

The man turned, saw Hancock's insignia, sniffed, said, "Watch where you're going, there, *Captain*. I'm the new *colonel* of the Forty-ninth Ohio Volunteers. I suggest that if you are going to survive in this army, you learn to respect your superiors."

Hancock stepped back. "Sorry," he said, then looked at the soft, pale dough of the man's face, the short round body, recalled McClellan's words, thought, Which way will *you* run when the cannons fire?

As THE MONTHS PASSED, THE CONFEDERATE ARMY ALLOWED ITS first great advantage, the hot surge of momentum, to slip away, and Lee had been right after all, the war would last well beyond the twelve-month terms of the volunteers.

As Lee had experienced in the new Confederate Army, the clash of egos, the struggle of ambitious men with private agendas, had rendered quick actions and smooth organization impossible. It was no different in the North. General McClellan had finally been persuaded to make another major move, a new offensive strategy designed to capture Richmond. Moving his entire army by boat to the Virginia peninsula, he would invade from the east coast, up the rivers, driving the small Confederate forces inland. It was a long winter of inactivity, while both sides waited for McClellan to finally do something with his huge army.

17. LEE

APRIL 1862

THROUGHOUT THE WINTER MONTHS, LITTLE HAD CHANGED FOR
Lee. He had officially been named Davis's military adviser,
which still meant that he continued to perform those duties
that Davis didn't want.

Joe Johnston was named commander of all forces in the northern
Virginia area, and Beauregard, whose ego would predictably clash with
Johnston's, was transferred to command of the army of northern Mississippi. With the new movement by McClellan, the threat to Richmond had changed directions. There was a growing lack of confidence
that McClellan's huge Federal force could be stopped.

Lee was the last to enter Davis's office, saw the men seated in a
half-circle. He had grown accustomed to meetings such as this being affairs that were anything but friendly and sociable. Davis sat behind the
big desk, rested his lean face sideways against one hand, appearing tired
to Lee, and impatient. As Lee reached his own chair, he nodded to Joe
Johnston, who sat upright, combative, glancing at Lee but not smiling.
To Lee's right sat Secretary of War Randolph, a man Lee respected for
his reasonableness and his seeming lack of political ambitions. Lee felt
he could freely discuss his problems and strategies with Randolph,
who, like him, could not escape the stranglehold that Davis maintained
on military decision-making.

There were two other men, seated behind Johnston, and both of
them stood when Lee entered. Lee knew one to be General Gustavus
Smith. The other was introduced by Davis.

"General Lee, General Johnston has been accompanied by two of
his ranking commanders. I believe you are acquainted with General
Smith."

163

Lee nodded, Smith sat down, and Lee regarded the other man, much larger, a grim serious man who had been close to the fight.

"This is General James Longstreet."

Longstreet made a brief nod, Lee returned it pleasantly. Longstreet seemed surprised, curious at Lee's cordial greeting.

Both men sat, and Davis said, "Gentlemen, General Johnston has brought to Richmond grave concerns. He does not feel . . . well, General, I will not speak for you. Please inform us as to your need for this meeting." There was nothing pleasant in Davis's voice.

Johnston, who had small features and a short, pointed beard, stood and turned slightly, facing Lee and Randolph. Lee noticed the slight to Davis, saw Davis quietly move his chair to see Johnston's face.

"We are in the midst of the greatest crisis of our rebellion, the greatest crisis of my command. General McClellan is massing his entire army on the peninsula and will very soon be able to make a broad sweep, brushing our meager forces out of the way, until he sits gloating in this very office!"

There was no reply; Lee knew Johnston would have more.

"Our army is scattered so far and wide that we cannot possibly concentrate enough manpower to stop this assault. As we speak, the forces of General McDowell are moving toward Richmond from the northwest, clearly aiming to join flanks with McClellan's. When this happens, Richmond will be surrounded, cut off. It is clear to this command that we have but one alternative, and that is to pull forces from the southern coasts, from the Shenandoah Valley, the Carolinas, Tennessee . . . from any areas where troop positions are strong, and concentrate them for a great defense, the defense of Richmond!"

Lee looked at Davis, who did not speak. It was Secretary Randolph who broke the silence.

"General, do you propose to abandon Yorktown and Norfolk?"

"Of course. We cannot possibly hope to hold back McClellan's forces along the coast. His superior artillery will destroy our defenses there in short order."

Randolph spoke again. "Sir, I must disagree with your plan. If you pull out of Norfolk, we will lose the naval yard, the ships that are currently under construction. We will concede the absolute domination of the seas to the Federal navy. Their gunboats would then move up the James River unimpeded and be in position to shell the city."

"General Lee?" Davis said. "Do you have an opinion regarding General Johnston's plan?"

Lee knew that Johnston was too stubborn to hear alternatives, could not be persuaded away from his own plans. The friction between him and Davis was largely a result of Davis's insistence on keeping a hand in Johnston's operations. Johnston, rather than argue, would simply cut off communications, leaving Davis and Lee totally ignorant of planning and troop movements.

"Mr. President, I do not believe it is a wise course to remove our forces from the Southern coastline. We would be offering the Federal Army uncontested control of Savannah and Charleston. We are in a serious situation in Tennessee and Mississippi, and troops cannot be spared."

Davis nodded, said nothing. Johnston still stood, glared at Lee, said, "We have no choice but to concentrate our forces here, to defend Richmond, and if possible to strike out at the Federal Army from a strong position."

Lee glanced at Longstreet, knew of his good work at Manassas. He looked back to Davis, waited for some sign, some hint that Davis was going to take a stand. But the president sat still, leaned his head against his hand and stared straight ahead. Now, Lee realized that Davis would act when Johnston was not there. He had been pressed into silence by Johnston's grand pronouncement, would not enter into simple squabbles, on which Johnston seemed to thrive. Lee realized that this was Davis's way of maintaining control. The orders would be issued after the meeting was over, and Davis would not have to explain, could be direct, authoritative on paper, and not be challenged.

Lee felt a growing frustration, a sense that no one here was really in charge, that Johnston would go back to his troops and do precisely what he wanted, and if Davis pushed him, he would simply ignore it. Finally he spoke, carefully picking his words.

"General Johnston, it is my feeling that if we begin mass withdrawals, we will announce to the enemy our plans to settle into a defensive posture around Richmond. We will open up all avenues for him to move his troops, concentrating at his own pace and with his own methods. Is it not possible that, since we have already seen that General McClellan is prone to great caution, we might delay him even further by vigorously defending the peninsula? Is it not possible that we could then find opportunities to attack him, far from Richmond?"

Johnston smiled slightly, said, "Well, General Lee, I suppose from your vantage point here, that may seem like a workable strategy, but you can be sure that for us in the field, who confront the guns of the enemy, these decisions must take into account the overwhelming forces that face us. . . ."

Lee clenched his teeth, did not look at Johnston, heard the words flow out with oily smoothness, the patronizing tone that Johnston would use to disarm any disagreement to his plans. The men had been friends for thirty-five years, had gone through the Point together, through Mexico, and now Lee knew it would never be again. Johnston was alone, had cut off everyone, had placed himself in an isolated position from which he could not be moved.

Randolph spoke again, repeated his position, and General Smith made a comment, lamenting the thinness of his lines. Lee withdrew further, began to see the others from a long distance, the voices hollow and droning. Davis still would not speak, and Lee again watched Longstreet, who focused on each speaker with a determined stare.

The meeting lasted all afternoon, and finally Davis suggested a break for the evening meal. The men rose, limbered stiff legs, and began to file from the President's office.

As Johnston reached the door, Davis said, "General, Yorktown must not be abandoned."

Johnston spun around, faced Davis and said, "If I fight there, I will be pushed back, and then they will have Yorktown anyway." Davis did not speak, and Johnston turned and left the office.

Lee sensed Davis's anger, knew the two men would expend great energy on their differences, that Johnston had made it clear he would have his way, something Davis would not swallow. Lee suddenly realized that there might be an opportunity, and his mind began to move, the wheels of the engineer, as he formulated his own plan.

L EE AGREED WITH JOHNSTON THAT MCDOWELL'S FORCES WOULD try to link up with McClellan, that McClellan had shown he would not move forward until he had every piece of strength available. There was an opportunity to delay McClellan from moving by keeping McDowell away. The man in a position to do this was General Jackson.

McDowell's army was spread over an area that began in front of Jackson, in the Shenandoah Valley, and arched eastward, up toward Washington, then down near Fredericksburg, where they were a short march down the Rappahannock River from McClellan's right flank.

Lee was not in a position to give direct orders to Jackson, could not assume that authority without stepping on the toes of both Johnston and Davis. But he had seen Jackson's reports, his urgent requests to be allowed to attack the Federal forces in front of him. While Johnston

FEDERAL POSITION—
McCLELLAN'S INVASION OF
THE VIRGINIA PENINSULA

SOUTH MTN.

Harpers Ferry

MARYLAND

Baltimore

Winchester

Shenandoah Valley

BLUE RIDGE MTNS.

McDOWELL

Washington

Manassas
Junction

CHESAPEAKE BAY

Fredericksburg

Potomac River

Gordonsville

VIRGINIA

Rappahannock River

James River

Richmond

York River

McCLELLAN

Williamsburg

Petersburg

Yorktown

James River

Fort
Monroe

N

Newport News

Norfolk

0   25 Miles

maintained actual command over Jackson, and over General Ewell's division, which was positioned across the Blue Ridge near Jackson, Lee assumed that Johnston would be completely absorbed in his plans on the peninsula.

Because of his distance from Johnston, Jackson had been operating more or less as an independent force, and Johnston's lack of concern for correspondence included Jackson and Ewell. Thus, for long stretches the two commanders had no direct orders from Johnston. Lee saw the opportunity to fill that void.

Lincoln, and his Secretary of War, Stanton, had made it clear that the protection of Washington was a top priority. This was frequently discussed in Northern newspapers, which Lee occasionally saw. He began to reason that if Lincoln felt Washington was threatened, McDowell's troops would be withdrawn from Virginia and brought back closer to the capital. The best way Lee saw to convince Washington there was a threat was to allow Jackson to move aggressively north, attacking McDowell's forces at the mouth of the Shenandoah Valley.

Jackson had sent his own letters to Johnston, which had passed through Lee's offices, in which he stated his desire to attack the forces to his front. His reasons were clear: to stall any movement by McClellan. It was not difficult for Lee to "suggest" to Jackson what his course of action should be.

Jackson's small force had been used primarily to observe the movements of Federal troops in that area, but by adding Ewell's division, he would have nearly sixteen thousand troops, a sizable force when commanded by a man like Jackson, whose single-minded sense of aggression Lee was coming to appreciate.

The greatest threat to Lee's quiet plan was a sudden southward move by McDowell into the center of Virginia, down through Fredericksburg, which would cut off Jackson from Richmond and effectively cut Virginia in half. This was a risk Lee accepted, confident that the Federal commanders would remain as sluggish as they had always been.

JACKSON ACCEPTED LEE'S SUGGESTIONS AS THE AUTHORITY HE needed, and began a campaign that resulted in the defeat of four Federal armies, including Generals Milroy and Fremont, who threatened the valley to the west, plus the complete destruction of the forces under Generals Banks and Shields. With his force of sixteen thousand men, Jackson defeated and drove from the valley Federal forces numbering nearly seventy thousand. The defeat of Banks was so complete, and the retreating troops so panicked, that Banks's force was pushed all the way back across the Potomac. The response from Washington was as Lee had predicted. McDowell's movements were reversed and his forces were recalled to the defense of what Lincoln believed was Jackson's imminent assault on Washington. McClellan did not get his reinforcements, and so, true to form, McClellan did not attack.

In the newspapers and among the troops, both North and South, the name of Thomas "Stonewall" Jackson was becoming legendary.

LEE STOOD AS SECRETARY RANDOLPH ENTERED, THEN THE TWO men sat across the vast desk from President Davis.

Both men had been given a frantic summons, and Lee could see that Davis was not well. His thin face appeared hollow, his eyes dark and heavy. Davis sat with his hands under his chin, supporting his head only a few inches above the desk.

Randolph had just returned from Norfolk, to see for himself what dangers were threatening the naval yard, and his report to Davis had only added to the President's anxieties. While at Norfolk, Randolph received a courier from Johnston, ordering the troops there to withdraw from Norfolk. The message contained no other information, did not even advise where they should go. It was plain to Randolph that there was no Federal force threatening the city and there was no need to abandon the equipment at the yard. Randolph furiously issued an order countermanding Johnston's, so the valuable machinery could be moved before the city was evacuated.

Davis lifted his head, spoke slowly. "Gentlemen, my authority . . . is it plain to the two of you that I am the commander in chief?"

Lee glanced at Randolph, who nodded, said, "Yes, sir, of course."

"General Lee? Is it plain to you as well?"

"Certainly, Mr. President."

"Then can either of you explain to me why I am unable to persuade our General Johnston, our commanding general in the field, to inform us what he is doing? Have either of you been able to communicate with the general?"

Randolph said, "No, sir. It is most . . . difficult, sir. We have sent wires, couriers to his headquarters requesting his position . . . his intentions. He does not respond."

"Gentlemen, as you may know, we have received word that

Yorktown has been abandoned. General Lee, do you have some idea where our army might be headed?"

Lee had received only one communication from Johnston, a suggestion for a full-scale invasion of the North by an assembly of all the troops in the East, with a similar invasion of Ohio by the troops of the West. The suggestion had been so irrational, and without serious regard for the actual problems of moving troops, that Lee had not shown the letter to Davis. Lee now saw that regardless of the kind of collapse that was affecting Johnston, Davis was falling apart as well.

"Mr. President, I have not been informed of General Johnston's plans. We have . . . My staff has spoken with soldiers . . . men who have come from the front. . . . We have tried to put together some information from these stragglers—"

"Stragglers?" Davis's voice rose, cracked. He looked away, past the two men, spoke to no one. "We rely on the word of stragglers."

"Sir . . ." Randolph spoke with a gentle tone. "Sir, we must consider that if the general is in a full-scale retreat, the Federal Army could appear at the outskirts of Richmond at any time. This might well throw the city into a panic. It may be prudent for us to consider evacuating the city."

Lee stiffened. Randolph continued, "The general abandoned Yorktown because he had great fear of the Federal artillery, the guns from their ships. Those same guns will most certainly follow him up the James River. We cannot hope to defend Richmond against that kind of assault. The city could be destroyed."

Davis stared ahead, then turned to Lee. "General Lee, is it time for us to . . . evacuate?"

"I don't believe it is necessary quite yet, Mr. President. I agree that we must not make Richmond a battlefield, and it may be that General Johnston feels he is retreating from indefensible positions, but I do not share that view. If he has withdrawn completely from Yorktown, he may have established a defensive line at Williamsburg, using the fortifications constructed by General Magruder. If so, that should slow McClellan's advance even further. If he withdraws from Williamsburg, there are a number of other strong positions, still far enough from here to keep the city safe. Frankly, sir, I am pleased to see McClellan sitting where he is. His forces are spread across a part of Virginia that is very difficult for the movement of troops. The swamps, the wide creeks . . . he is vulnerable. If we can persuade General Johnston to stand his ground, McClellan will never get as far as Richmond."

Randolph looked at Lee, said, "We don't know where our troops are. How can you be sure we are capable of making a stand?"

"There are lines of defense ... every river, every stream—not only can we make a stand in that country, Mr. Secretary, but I believe that General McClellan can be pushed back, driven off the peninsula altogether. We have some good commanders leading good troops. We must persuade General Johnston of that fact."

Randolph turned back to Davis, shook his head. "I don't see how we can persuade General Johnston to do much of anything. We can't even get him to respond to our inquiries."

Lee looked at the faces of the two men, saw Davis staring blankly away. A sense of defeat hung in the air like a dark mist, and Lee could not sit still.

"If you will permit, sirs, I must return to my office."

Davis did not speak, continued his stare, and Randolph raised one hand slightly, a weak gesture, said only, "Good, General."

Lee walked across a darkening street, knew this day was over, nothing more would happen. He climbed up to his office and saw that his staff had already gone. He went to his window and looked out, past the government buildings. In the street below came a small group of soldiers, men who carried the dirt of the Virginia swamps, men who had left their army but had not walked far.

18. HANCOCK

APRIL 1862

H E SAT ON HIS NEW HORSE, A GROUCHY MARE HE CALLED
Annie. His men filed from the steamer, marched gladly down
the long ramp, happy to leave the cramped ship. They formed
in companies on the wharf, in front of the walls of Fort Monroe. They
had come down the Potomac, had reached the mouth of the James, and
now the pieces of McClellan's army would wait for the rest, until it
was all assembled and the commander would begin his invasion up the
peninsula.

Hancock watched them, the tight formation, the smooth movements. He had spent the long Washington winter training these men,
and he knew that regardless of McClellan's fear of the enemy's superior
preparations, his brigade was ready to fight.

Gradually, all four of his regiments were formed and began to
march away from the wharf, creating space for more troops. He pulled
his horse toward the colors of the Fifth Wisconsin, the first regiment to
move out, rode up beside Colonel Amasa Cobb, a distinguished political leader before the war who had learned the art of drill only under
Hancock's direction.

"Colonel, it's a fine morning, is it not?"

"General Hancock, sir, this unit is prepared. You shall be proud
of us, sir."

Hancock looked back over the neat lines, the steady marching, officers on horseback riding beside the lines of fresh troops, men who
now felt like soldiers. He pulled his horse out of the line, sat alongside
the moving men, thought, Let them see me, let them feel the pride. He
sat tall in his saddle, gave them each a look, and the men responded
with waves and some cheering. The company commanders, young

captains and smooth-faced lieutenants, saluted him crisply as they rode by, made a show of tightening the lines of their small commands. Hancock thought, These men will not run. It's in their eyes, their step. General "Baldy" Smith had come through the camps throughout the winter, had given the customary speech, the rousing call to the flag, the great honor in duty, and the men were always enthusiastic, always responded. Smith, and the others, men who tried to inject some great spark of patriotism into the troops, would ride away satisfied that they had done their bit to train the men, to prepare them for the bloody war. Hancock stood at the front, always listened with respect, and watched his men, knew that this was not what made them soldiers, that if the fight were not in them already, no great speech about loving the flag would change that. He did not understand why the generals did not see, would not accept, that those other fellows, those boys in the ragged uniforms who wanted to burn your lovely flag, had already shown they could hurt you, would stand up to your patriotism and put the bayonet through your beloved uniform. But still the words came, and Hancock began to understand. It was all they knew how to do: make speeches. Very few of them had ever led troops under fire, had ever led troops at all. And when the time came, many of them would fail, and many men would die because they did not have leaders.

His head began to feel heavy—he'd had little sleep since they boarded the steamer—and he slumped in the saddle, looked down at the ground, the short grass his horse was now exploring . . . *the ground a smooth, shining carpet of red, soaked in the blood of the army, a man was screaming, then more, many more, thick gray smoke and burning powder, and the sounds of artillery shells exploding and the stench of death—*

Hancock jerked awake, sat up straight, felt his heart pounding. He looked around, saw his troops in line, forming again in a wide field, and felt foolish for the small, terrifying daydream. Then he thought, No, it is foolish if you lead these men into the face of the enemy and are not prepared for them to die.

Across the field he saw Cobb again, directing his men, and the order was given to make camp. The men began to spread out, unloading the wagons. Hancock saw a flag moving quickly up the road that came from the walls of the fort, saw General Smith and a group of aides, and they spotted him and rode in his direction. Hancock met the general with a salute.

Smith said, "General Hancock, greetings to you, sir. Your men are positioned well, yes. This field will be filling up over the next few days, we hope to have the entire corps here by Wednesday."

"Corps, sir?"

"Yes, Mr. Hancock, have you not heard? We have been placed under the command of General Sumner. General McClellan has organized the army into corps. Better use of the chain of command and all that. I suppose I should have told you."

Hancock thought, Yes, that's your job: chain of command. He thought of Sumner. Edwin "Bull" Sumner, the man who had gone to California to remove Albert Sidney Johnston—interesting coincidence.

"Sir, my men are ready for orders, at your discretion."

"Very good, General. Our next move is up to General McClellan. Once the army is all here, I expect we will begin some real action, probably sweep on into Richmond."

Hancock wondered if they all believed that, that the rebel army would simply be brushed aside like so many bugs. He nodded, polite, said only, "We're ready for a fight, General."

"Good, good. Well, I'll keep you informed. Got to check on my other commanders, General. Good day to you."

Smith rode away, the aides trailing behind, and Hancock prodded the horse, which protested mildly, then moved toward the spreading troops and the fresh campfires. The afternoon was wearing on, and he looked out to the west, beyond the field, to great thickets of trees, miles of nothing, except . . . out there, somewhere, men waited with bayonets.

HANCOCK'S BRIGADE WAS ENCAMPED IN THE WIDE FIELD FOR nearly a month. McClellan made it plain, both to his commanders and to Washington, that he believed his army to be greatly outnumbered, and that a rapid, forceful move up the peninsula would result in certain disaster. As the army formed in front of Yorktown, McClellan's force of over ninety thousand men faced the Confederate general Magruder's command of fifteen thousand. Rather than assault this force, McClellan decided to lay siege to the city, and sent a continuous stream of requests to Washington for more men and more guns. When on May 4 he finally reported to the President that Yorktown was in his possession, he did not mention that it was a Confederate withdrawal that had handed it to him.

The army was finally put into motion, moving several miles inland, through the abandoned positions of Joe Johnston's retreating army. As they advanced to Williamsburg, they met the troops of the

Confederate rear guard, a strong solid line that had been placed before them by General Longstreet.

Hancock's men were well back in line, and he knew little of what was in front of him, except for the scattered sounds of skirmishes. He rode beside the lines of his men, spoke with each commander as they passed, answering the same questions with a simple, "I have not been informed."

The roads were sandy and soft, and he watched a small squad of men helping push a wagon through a bog. He looked at the sky, thought, No rain today, thank God. They had sat in the mush of a campground, softened by days of rain, a hard, soaking spring storm that had drowned the fires and dampened the enthusiasm of the whole army.

Up the line in front of him, his men were stalled again by some obstruction he could not see, and he spurred the horse, rode forward feeling a boiling wrath. He moved the horse along the edge of the road. The men moved aside, the waves and shouts muted now; the men had an instinct for the mood of their commander. Along with Hancock, they all were wondering if this army had any idea where it was going.

He heard a shout behind him, turned the horse and saw a courier, a man covered in mud. The troops watched the man pass, began to laugh, called out, mocking the man's obvious distress.

"General Hancock, sir. I have a message, from General Smith." The man paused, took some air, and Hancock saw a stream of brown water flowing from the man's boots, the blue pants smeared with shiny brown sludge, saw eyes looking at him through a wet paste of brown goo. He began to smile, felt himself let go, a tightness in his chest loosen, and now he laughed, and around him his men took the cue, laughed as well.

The courier glanced at the men, then back at Hancock, who saw the man's embarrassment growing and said, "Are you all right, Captain?"

"Sir, I had an accident. My horse doesn't seem to care for this sand, and he threw me. Forgive my appearance, sir."

"At least wipe off your face," Hancock said, laughing.

The man felt his face with his hand, saw the mud on his fingers, said, "Oh," and pulled a handkerchief from his pocket, wiped painfully at the drying crust.

"Sir, if I may . . . General Smith is at the rear of this column, and he requests your presence as soon as possible. He has orders deploying your men, sir."

Hancock stopped laughing, turned away from the stalled troops, who were continuing to gather, and motioned to the man to follow. They rode off the road, through a small gap in the brush, and Hancock turned back, spotted a lieutenant leaning back in his saddle, allowing the men to break their lines. He shouted at the man, "You there! Lieutenant! Get these men back into line. Prepare to move them forward. We are on the march, not in camp."

The man jumped up straight in his saddle, began to shout at the men, who were already moving back in place, straightening their lines on the road.

Hancock looked at the courier, could now see his face, said, "Captain, in the future you will impart your messages to me out of earshot of the troops, do you understand?"

"Sir? Yes, sir. I didn't see any need—"

"Captain, we are in the enemy's country. Have you ever heard of spies?"

The man stiffened, glanced around, said in a whisper, "Spies? Do you really think there are spies?"

Hancock stared at the man, felt the rage beginning to build again. "Captain, we are at war...." Then he thought, No, let it go. He took a long breath. The man leaned closer to him, whispered again, "Sorry, sir. I will pay more attention next time. General Smith requests your presence. He is in the rear of this column, with General Sumner, sir."

Hancock turned his horse, climbed back to the road, began to move toward the rear. He did not see where the courier went, and did not care. He thought, Maybe, *finally*, something will happen.

MAY 4, 1862

H E HAD MET GENERAL SUMNER SEVERAL TIMES, HAD SERVED under him briefly in St. Louis, had even seen him in California, but he did not expect the man to have aged so badly.

"General Hancock, do come in, thank you." Sumner was an old man, and Hancock saw now that he might be too old. His headquarters was a large tent, and he sat alone at a small table. Behind him was a map, hung between two thin sticks, small trees that had been cut and pushed into the soft ground. General Smith stood beside Hancock, nervous, clasping and unclasping his hands. He greeted Hancock only with a small nod.

Sumner turned in his chair, motioned to an aide, who handed him a pointer, and he held it up to the map, waved it unsteadily.

"Gentlemen, this map is all wrong. It's the only map we have, but it's all wrong. Turns out, the roads we've been using don't go where they're supposed to go. Damned nuisance." He stopped, coughed, turned back to the men in front of him.

"We've got the enemy in front of us, dug in, ready for a fight. General McClellan is not here. He is ... God knows ... back there, somewhere, trading complaints with Washington. So, I am in command of the field. This is not my choice, but it is the circumstance. General Smith?"

"Yes, sir."

"General, you must deploy your division across the roads in front of you. Then push out through the woods to the right. General Hancock, I would like that to be your job. Take five regiments, yours and some from ... from whoever General Smith designates. Move north, out on our right flank. There's supposed to be some fortifications out there, part of what they call Fort Magruder. You know John Magruder? Artillery man, hell of a fighter. Did some fine work in Mexico."

Hancock nodded, said, "Yes, sir. I am familiar with him."

"Well, that place could be a threat to our position. The enemy is dug in heavily around their so-called fort. General Hooker is in contact with the direct center of the fortifications. He probably has his hands full. General Hancock, I want you to take this man here."

He raised a thin arm, and Hancock looked toward a cavalry officer, standing to one side, who stepped forward.

"I'd like him to go with you, be my observer. He has scouted the woods already, may be of some help."

Hancock looked at the young man, saw blond hair falling in loose curls, a red scarf tied loosely around the man's neck, a long feather sprouting from the band in the man's hat. The man saluted, said, "It will be an honor to serve with you, General."

Sumner coughed again, and Hancock stared at the strange cavalry officer a moment longer. Then Sumner said, "General Smith, are you yet engaged?"

"Sir, we have forces in our front, and ... well, yes, we have been moving against them. Not fully, though. Shall I give the order to advance, sir?"

Sumner stared up at Smith, leaned back in his small chair, paused for a long moment and said, "General, have you heard fighting on your left?"

"Yes, sir. About an hour ago. Seems to be somewhat heavy."

"Well, General, that fighting involves two divisions, Hooker and Couch. I imagine they are expecting you to move up in support. Does that seem like a reasonable plan to you?"

Smith felt the sarcasm, glanced at Hancock self-consciously, said, "Yes, sir. Right away. If you will excuse me, sir. I will move my units up in support and engage the enemy."

Smith hurried out of the tent, and Hancock saluted Sumner, followed Smith outside. Smith climbed up on his horse, turned around unsteadily, said, "General . . . best of luck. This day may make heroes of us all."

Hancock wondered if he was serious, said nothing. He looked over to the young cavalryman, who pulled his horse up beside Hancock's. "Do you have a name, soldier?" he asked.

"Lieutenant George Armstrong Custer, at your service, sir."

"Well, Lieutenant Custer, shall we get started?"

FOR OVER A MILE THEY SLID BETWEEN HUGE LIVE OAKS, PUSHED through the thickets of scrub pine. Behind them, off to their left, they could hear the sounds of a growing battle, the deep rumble of artillery and the high chatter of musket fire.

Hancock stayed on foot, led the column through the woods, Custer his guide. The battle sounds were solid now, no wavering, no gaps. If it goes badly, Hancock thought, if they push the rest of Smith's division back, if Hooker doesn't hold his ground, we are out here by ourselves, cut off.

The woods began to thin, and he saw an opening, the trees spreading far apart now. The woods ended suddenly, giving way to a wide-open plain more than a mile long. He put his glasses to his eyes, heard Custer say, "There it is," then saw their objective across the long, undulating field: the small dam. Behind him the regimental commanders had been assembled, and Hancock turned, saw the troops stretched out in ragged lines, disappearing back through the thick trees.

"Gentlemen, we have to cross this field and reach that dam. I don't see any sign of the enemy, but the field has some elevation, some depressions, they could be waiting for us anywhere. Once we reach the dam, it's a tight line over the top, only a few feet wide, and from what Lieutenant Custer tells me, the enemy's entrenchments are on the other side. We will form battle lines here at the edge of the woods, then move across the field as quickly as we can. Keep the noise to a minimum, and no firing."

He scanned the faces, saw an aide, Hughes, with small round glasses on a long point of a nose. "Lieutenant, send word to Colonel Wheeler: I want his batteries brought forward to the edge of these trees, focused on that dam. If we can't get across it, we'll blow it to hell, maybe drive 'em out with a flood of water. Any questions?"

There were no questions. He looked at the faces, the commanders he had trained, knew they were ready. He focused the field glasses out across the open field, and the men went back to their units, began moving them up.

Custer stepped out of the trees, walked out into the open, then turned and said, "Give me a squad, General, a picket line maybe. Let me ease across and draw their fire. I can't see anybody, but those far trees could be full of artillery."

Hancock thought, Yes, good, it could work. Tempt some nervous gunner, a sweating hand holding a tight lanyard, and they could start a reckless fire that would reveal the entire position of the enemy. He nodded, waved back to another aide, said "Give Lieutenant Custer fifty men, tell them to keep low, move fast, cross that field."

The man ran back, and men quickly came forward, men who had not yet seen the enemy, who would be the first.

They moved out into the open. Custer spread them into a thin line, spaced a few feet apart. Then, with a quiet wave of his arm, they were moving away through the field. Behind them the regiments poured neatly out of the trees, began to form in lines three deep, then moved forward, made room for the units behind. Hancock climbed on his horse, rode out to Custer, watching, looking ahead for the small puff of smoke coming well before the sound, the first telltale sign of an impatient gunner, the high screech of the shell that would rip the air as it tumbled toward them. But there was nothing.

"Proceed, Lieutenant. With speed."

Custer saluted, waved to the line of men, and they began to move in a quicker step, jogging through the thick green grass, moving up a slight incline. Hancock braced, waited for the volley, but it did not come. The men were now out of sight and he was watching an empty field, then they came up again on a far rise, still in line, still with the quick step. Now the regiments began to move, the slow, steady march, and Hancock rode along the front, watched the officers spread the

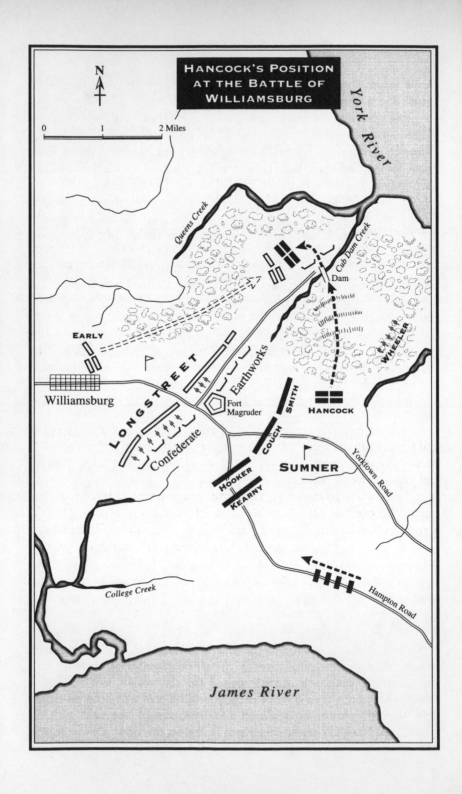

HANCOCK'S POSITION
AT THE BATTLE OF
WILLIAMSBURG

N

0   1   2 Miles

York River

Queens Creek

Cub Dam Creek

Dam

EARLY

WHEELER

LONGSTREET

Earthworks

Williamsburg

Fort
Magruder

SMITH

COUCH

HANCOCK

Confederate

SUMNER

HOOKER

KEARNY

Yorktown Road

College Creek

Hampton Road

James River

formations. He prodded the horse, moved quickly down the lines, and the men waved hats. There were some careless cheers, quickly silenced by the officers.

He rode out now to the top of the first rise, could not see Custer's men, and so rode farther, dropped down, then climbed the gentle slope to the next rise, and then they were there, very close to the dam now, a small dirt ridge blocking an unseen creek. He looked behind him, saw the troops coming up over the first rise, then studied Custer through the glasses again, saw them reach the dam. He held his breath, felt the pounding in his chest, careful, careful, but there was still no sound, and now he saw Custer, saw the ridiculous hat held high in the air, waving, and now the small line of men were on the dam and moving across.

He rode forward again, down the slight hill to the long flat plain, could see the dam plainly now, and behind him the men were up the second rise, spread out in a beautiful wave of blue. He saw movement on the dam, held up his glasses and saw Custer standing in the middle of the dam, waving crazily, both arms, and he understood, knew what they had done.

The fighting behind them continued to be steady, and he listened carefully, could not detect any movement, any change in the flow. Good, he thought, hold your ground. He rode now to the dam.

The troops were coming up behind him, across the flat ground, and Custer ran toward him, waving the men forward. "Sir! It's empty!" he said, excited, panting. "There's no one there! We can cross the dam and occupy the fortifications!"

Hancock dismounted, handed the reins to an aide and walked quickly across the soft dirt of the dam. He saw his men, the first ones across, in line behind a great round wall, a wide trench. Then he saw more trenches, spreading out in several directions, and he climbed up on a high mound of brown dirt. The men waved, threw hats quietly in the air, and he thought, This is incredible, we have flanked the enemy and no one knows we're here.

Beyond the earthworks there was shooting, distant musket fire, and the men began to move in that direction. Rifles came up on the far side of the works, pointing out at the scattered shots. Hancock walked along the top of the earthworks, and now other officers were eyeing their front, toward the shooting, and he saw an officer motion to him, a quiet, urgent wave. He jumped down into the trench, moved to the man's position and followed the man's point with his glasses.

Across the wet grassland, dotted with small marshy ponds, he saw lines of brown, Confederate troops in line, moving to the left, toward the battle they had been hearing. Beyond those troops were more earthworks, larger, heavier, the walls they called Fort Magruder. Light musket fire was increasing in their direction, and Hancock lowered his glasses, saw, closer, another fortification, trenches and earthworks, smaller, like this one. He saw a rebel officer, a man in a tall black hat, pointing the rifles of the troops in a new direction, *their* direction, aware now of this new threat.

Hancock called for a courier, and a red-faced lieutenant scurried over the dirt embankments and saluted clumsily. Hancock said, "Go, now, to General Smith. Tell him we have flanked the enemy. We are only lightly opposed, but that will change. If he can shift his units in this direction, we can assist both him and General Hooker. We might be able to push the enemy out of the fortifications to Hooker's front. Stress the point: we are on the enemy's flank. Move *fast*, Lieutenant."

His troops were nearly all across the dam, and the trenches were filled, became lines of solid blue. Hancock spied the closer troops again, saw thin lines, maybe one regiment, and he shouted at the other officers, "Up . . . over the wall, advance on those troops! Tell your men to hold their fire until you order it. Move out!"

The officers shouted the orders, and men began to climb the earthen walls. They slid down into the tall grass, lines formed, and they moved forward. There was more noise now, shots coming in quicker succession, the balls whizzing by, some high over his head. He sat on the wall, heard the balls thumping the sides of the thick dirt. His men continued to move out, a spreading swarm of blue down through the grass, and within minutes they had reached the lines of the enemy. Suddenly, they stopped, poured a volley of thick fire into the rebel troops, and instantly he could not see, the lines hidden by a thick white cloud. He slid down, jumped into the thick grass, pulled his pistol and began to move forward with his men.

He stumbled, followed the shouts of the men in front of him, was not sure of distance, how far he had come. Then the smoke gave way, the shooting slowed, then stopped, and he was climbing another wall, a low, thick hill of dirt. In front of him his men were pushing on, through the new fortifications, and now he saw the first bodies, men in gray and brown uniforms, those who did not escape the assault. He did not wait, ran over the tops of the earthworks, reached the far side, saw his men ready to climb out, to press on, and he waved them back, no, not yet.

He saw the rebels moving away, no more than a hundred men, and he realized they had pushed back only a small outpost, an isolated unit. He looked toward Fort Magruder again and the heavy sounds of battle, and saw nothing to their front, nothing to stop them from pushing on, into the side of the Confederate position.

He turned, looked back toward the distant dam, said out loud, to the reinforcements that were not yet there, "Come on, dammit!"

Then he saw a horseman, a man riding on the dam, a tricky move, and the man came forward, a different face, not his courier, and he began to walk back through his gathered troops.

The courier saw him, dismounted, and climbed the wide dirt wall. "General, sir. General Sumner orders you to withdraw from your position. You are in a tenuous spot, General. You are ordered to withdraw back to General Smith's lines . . . back there. You are too far in advance, sir."

Hancock stared at the man, disbelieving. He saw the snotty confidence of the untested staff officer, the smug arrogance of a man with a big message and no responsibility for it, and he moved closer to the man, leaned hard into the man's face.

"Listen, son. You go back and you tell General Sumner . . ." He paused, felt the anger screaming in his ears, and the man's face changed, the arrogance turned to fear. Hancock was surprised, and a voice in his head said, No, careful, be careful. He turned away, looked for another courier, saw his aides now, gathering around, and no one was talking, they were all watching him. He pointed at one, the young Lieutenant Crane, motioned him closer.

Crane moved up, saluted, and Hancock took a slow, deep breath, loosened the tightness in his jaw, said, "Lieutenant, you will take a message to General Sumner. You will inform the general that we are on the open flank of the enemy, and that reinforcements have already been requested from General Smith. You tell General Sumner that I do not understand his . . . order for withdrawing these troops. I would like it made clear. Do you understand, Lieutenant?"

"Yes, sir. Perfectly," and the man was off, ran to a waiting horse and rode quickly away.

Sumner's man watched Hancock warily, like a trainer watching an angry lion, and Hancock ignored him, moved forward, toward the eyes of his men, stepped through the earthworks and climbed up, studied the heavy Confederate lines, still in place, through his glasses. The battle had begun to slow, the volleys were irregular, but the sounds still came from in front of the fort, no big push either way: it had been a stalemate. He thought, It won't be a stalemate if we hit them from here. But he knew Longstreet would react, his presence was known by now. He looked at his watch, nearly three o'clock. Plenty of time . . . if Smith would just come.

"Sir, a rider!"

He looked around, saw a horseman coming through the thick swampy grass, a different man, not one of his, and the man dismounted, ran in a crouch over the earthworks, hearing a battle that wasn't there.

"General Hancock, sir, General Smith regrets to inform you that he has been ordered by General Sumner not to send any troops to your position. General Smith understands that you have been ordered to withdraw. General Smith is of the opinion . . . sir . . . that you may withdraw at your convenience, sir. At a time you see as best, within the limits of General Sumner's order." The man paused, and Hancock saw his discomfort.

"Sir, the general is not in agreement with General Sumner's order, and wishes you to know that. But General Sumner is in command of the field."

Hancock nodded, knew Smith was playing it as carefully as a good politician can.

"Please return to General Smith and thank him for his intentions. You may tell the general that I will remain here until such time as General Sumner's orders are clarified. I did not completely understand them the first time. His courier was . . . vague."

"Yes, sir. Thank you, sir." The man ducked low again, moved back across the earthworks.

Sumner's man stood with Hancock's remaining aides, and stepped forward, prepared with a mild protest.

"Sir, General Sumner's orders—"

"You may return to General Sumner. Relay to the general that our position here continues to be strong. We are in a position to carry the field. Request General Sumner to repeat his order. You were *vague*."

The man swallowed his protest, mounted his horse and was quickly gone.

Hancock went back to the front wall, continued to glass the far positions. The shooting began again, a fresh volley, then slowed, and now there was silence. From behind him, he heard another horse, turned and saw Crane. The look on the young man's face told him what he did not want to hear.

"Sir, General Sumner has ordered you again to withdraw from your position. He is insistent, sir."

Hancock turned away from the man, felt a heavy fist inside his chest, pressing down hard on his own disgust, forcing it down deep inside him. You do not criticize generals, you obey them, he thought. But this is pure stupidity. We are losing our opportunity. A glorious piece of good luck has been erased by the hesitation of a cautious old man.

He looked at his watch, five o'clock. Now there was not much time, and it was clear that no more troops were coming from General Smith.

Men began to call out, pointing, and Custer suddenly appeared, climbing over the far end of the earthworks, plucking at briars on his hat.

"I hope you, for one, have enjoyed this day, Lieutenant. Gone for a walk in the woods?"

"General, sir, I have been doing a bit of reconnaissance. The enemy is beginning to move this way. At least two regiments, maybe more, are forming behind those woods to the right. They appear to be units of Early's brigade, sir."

Hancock thought, We can hold out here for a while, but this fortification is too small, we are too tightly bunched. If they should bring up artillery . . .

"Good work, Lieutenant." He motioned to Crane, sent him to the commanders, gave the word to begin pulling back, out of the fortifications, back toward the dam.

The orders were called out, and men began to climb out, going back the way they had come, and he saw the looks, the disappointment. They didn't understand either, he thought. Even the troops knew they should have kept going.

He followed the last of the companies through the winding trench works, then climbed up and over the dirt embankment, and now the earthworks were empty, except for the neat row of Confederate dead, which his men had arranged respectfully. They moved quickly back through the thick grass, reached the first fortification, filled it, and Hancock climbed up on the wall, watching his men. He looked out past the works, back across the dam to the great open field, the plain of green grass that they had first crossed, saw a rider suddenly appear on one of the low crests that ran across the field. It was Smith's man again, and he knew there would be nothing he wanted to hear. But he watched the man disappear again, between the crests, completely out of sight. Then the man topped the second crest, came down across the flat plain toward the dam.

Hancock turned, suddenly, shouted, "Regimental commanders . . . I need the commanders here . . . *now!*"

The word went out, and through the trenches below him he saw the officers approach, snaking their way through the troops. Behind him Custer was glassing the fortification they had abandoned.

"General, the rebels have returned."

Hancock turned, put his glasses on the flags that were moving into the works, saw three, four, then men on horses, more troops, and now shots began, from out of the woods, closer to them, from the right, where Custer had seen the units forming.

He turned, saw the faces of his colonels, said, "Gentlemen, we have been ordered to withdraw. So, we will withdraw. Right now, lose no time, move across the dam as quickly as you can. Lots of noise, let them know we are leaving. We are running away, their numbers are overwhelming us." He laughed, and the officers did not understand, looked at each other, and Custer stood up beside him, followed his gaze out to the wide-open field.

Hancock said to his commanders, "Gentlemen, when you top that first rise, form your men into battle line . . . facing *this* way. Then you will wait for my orders."

The officers spread out through the troops, and the column formed quickly, began to cross the dam.

Hancock saw Lieutenant Hughes, called him over and said, "Lieutenant, are Wheeler's batteries where I wanted them, in those far trees there?"

"Yes, sir. Colonel Wheeler understood your orders plainly, sir."

Good, he thought. Very damned good. Wheeler would not move his guns without word from him first, no matter who sent the order.

"Lieutenant, I want you to ride like hell across that field, find Colonel Wheeler and tell him to prepare for an assault. Tell him we are withdrawing across his line of fire, and to keep a sharp watch on our movements. I will give him a signal. I will wave my sword in the air—tell him, once we pass across his line of fire to keep watching me. He will know what to do."

"Yes, sir." Crane moved toward the dam, pushing through the line of men, and Hancock watched him ride out across the open grass.

Behind him rebel troops, Early's troops, were cutting their way through the dense woods, and now the pickets had made it through, began to fire at the blue coats filing out of the works. Hancock pointed Custer in their direction, and the young lieutenant ran toward the sound of the muskets, collecting men, placing them on the dirt wall, and quickly they fired a volley, then another, and the annoying fire was slowed, the pickets driven back into the cover of the dark woods.

Hancock pointed the glasses back toward the other earthworks, saw lines of men moving out, toward him, blending into the tall swamp grass. The rebels were now in pursuit of his retreating troops.

Custer ran toward him, and Hancock saw they were nearly alone in the earthworks. The last men were crossing the dam, and his troops were marching in ragged formation across the field, beginning the slight climb up toward the first crest.

"Excuse me, General, but there are rebel troops on two sides of us, advancing rapidly. I suggest, sir, it is time to leave."

Hancock hopped up on the wall that faced the woods, saw lines of men pouring out through the trees, easy musket range away, and he jumped down, said, "Yes, Lieutenant, we must join the retreat. Try to look as panicked as you can."

"Sir?"

"Let's *move*, Lieutenant."

Hancock ran across the dam, Custer close behind. The balls began to fly by now, poorly aimed at a rare target. They reached the horses and received the reins from a very nervous aide, who quickly ran toward the withdrawing lines of his own unit. Hancock spurred his horse, thought, This is not the time to be stubborn, old girl, and the mare moved in a quick jump, began to glide up the long incline, past the swiftly marching troops.

He stopped at the crest of the hill, could see it all now. The Confederate troops had swarmed over the works, were crossing the dam, hard in pursuit. He saw the whole picture now in his head, the plan came to him like a clear blue light, like a window opening in his brain, a sudden flow of clean, cool air, and he smiled. Yes, *yes*. He turned, looked back to the line of trees that had brought them there, felt the presence of the big guns, Wheeler's guns, and he knew Wheeler was watching him, somewhere, up in a tree. Keep watching, my good man, you are about to see it unfold.

His troops reached the crest of the hill, began the descent into the trough between the two crests, and quickly the officers directed them into line. Hancock watched as they filled the depression, a solid blue wall growing stronger as each man came over the hill.

He glassed back down toward the dam, saw cannon being rolled up on the other side, then scanned down to the lines of gray troops coming up the hill. Their cannon will not fire, he thought, it is too close to their own men, right over their heads, and now they can't see

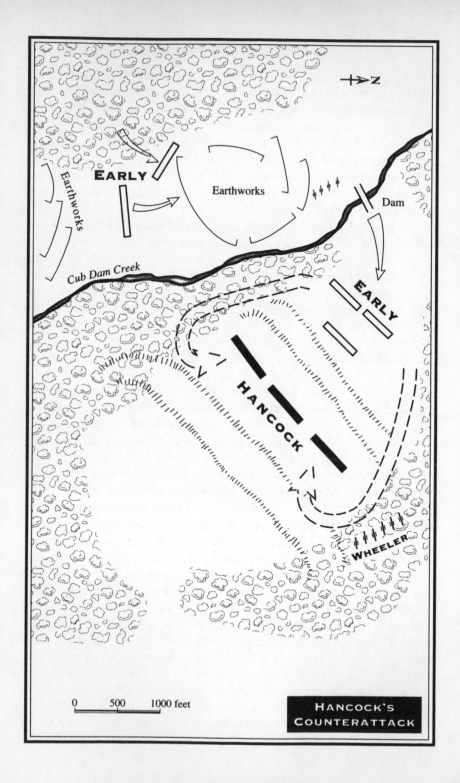

Earthworks

EARLY

Earthworks

Dam

Cub Dam Creek

EARLY

HANCOCK

WHEELER

0   500   1000 feet

HANCOCK'S
COUNTERATTACK

us at all. He looked back to the trees, saw motion through the low branches, and took one last glance at the lines of men chasing him. Then he grabbed at his belt, felt the solid brass handle, pulled his sword from the scabbard and waved it in a wide circle over his head.

In an instant puffs of smoke blew out from the line of trees, and shells began to scream across, in front of the crest, and into the lines of rebel troops. He sat high on his horse, just enough to peer over the top of the hill, saw the cannon far below turning, taking aim on his guns, of course, they would try to duel the artillery. They could not shell the troops. He waited until the rebel guns began firing, smoke grew in a thick cloud over the dam, shells began to burst back in the trees to his right.

The lines of rebel troops were moving faster now, began a wild yell, feeling the full effect of the cannon fire. Wheeler's shells continued to burst among the rebels, flashes of fire and smoke began to blur the lines, and now the first gray troops made it to the top of the hill and faced the solid blue line. The first volley went out, a thousand muskets opened together, a long, thin line of white smoke pouring their shot into the first lines of gray troops. The rebels stopped cold, only a few yards from the lines of blue, began to turn back into themselves, and more men reached the top, saw what lay on the other side, and another volley was fired, and the rebel lines fell to pieces. Hancock watched the collapse of the attack, saw the rebels backing down, off the crest, and he turned, yelled to Custer, gave the order, yelled for him to carry the order through the lines, then yelled to Colonel Gray and Colonel Cobb, whose men waited in line close beside him, *"Charge!"*

His men moved up the gentle slope in one motion and met the jumbled and broken lines of gray troops at the crest of the hill. The strong advance by his deep rows of men, visible now across the open field as one long blue wave, sent the rebel lines back down the slope in complete confusion. Hancock's men crossed over the rise, began to pursue the rebels back toward the dam. He rode to the top of the crest, could see nothing for the thick smoke, gradually pushed his horse forward, rode slowly for several minutes down the gradual slope, over the bodies of the Confederate troops, a bloody carpet across the entire ridge. The sounds of the battle faded. The only musket fire came from far away now, across the dam, and now his men began to come back up the hill. The chase was over, the rebel soldiers were pushed back to their defenses.

The smoke began to clear, and he noticed for the first time that it was nearly dark. A light breeze blew toward the trees where Wheeler had his guns, and now the field showed the signs of battle, a stark change to the way he had first seen it, the smooth green grass pockmarked by the craters of exploded shells, the heaped dead and crawling wounded, nearly all from the Confederate side. He saw an officer running toward him, holding a flag, saw: Custer. The young lieutenant came up the hill, had lost his hat, and his hair flew about in a great blond tangle.

"General, sir, I have captured this here flag. Took it right out of the man's hand. He just . . . gave it to me. I reckon we won this one, General. That was some fine work, if I am allowed to say, sir."

"Thank you, Lieutenant. We have a fine brigade here. They should be proud. But I may have some explaining to do at headquarters."

A s HANCOCK'S MEN PULLED BACK FROM THEIR FIELD OF BATTLE, they sent nearly six hundred Confederate prisoners to the rear, with a total loss to their own forces of barely thirty men. McClellan arrived at Sumner's headquarters in time to learn of Hancock's battle, and rode immediately to the scene. His first order was to General Smith, to reinforce Hancock's position. McClellan understood what Hancock had tried to do, and planned an assault to complete the job. But Longstreet understood as well, as did Joe Johnston, and the following morning, when the Union lines moved forward, they found Fort Magruder abandoned and the Confederates again in retreat.

19. LEE

JUNE 1862

HE ENTERED HIS OFFICE, SAW TAYLOR BEHIND HIS DESK, THUMB-ing through a stack of letters. The new title that had been given to Lee, Military Adviser to the President, a title with nothing of significance attached, no real duty other than remaining near Davis, also provided for promotions for his staff. Taylor had received a commission of Major.

Lee paused, watched the young man, smiled at the quick movements, the efficiency. He is just a boy, Lee thought, and he's a major. It took me nearly twenty years. . . .

"Oh, good morning, sir. You're early, I didn't expect you this soon."

"Good morning, Major. Any news? Anything from General Johnston's headquarters?"

"Sorry, sir, nothing. I spoke this morning with some men from General Hood's brigade . . . Texans."

Lee smiled, could not hide the reaction to the name, saw the huge man, John Bell Hood, the bright blond hair and beard, the only man Lee knew from his days in the cavalry who actually *liked* it there, chasing impossibly elusive Indians through the suffocating dust.

"You certain it was General Hood's men?"

"Yes, sir. They came from Seven Pines, sir."

"Seven Pines? So, our army is closer still."

"Yes, sir. They told of being whipped at Williamsburg, said General McClellan had pushed them out of the trenches at Fort Magruder."

"They said that? We have abandoned Williamsburg?"

"Yes, sir. They didn't know much else, so I talked to some others, and they said pretty much the same thing. McClellan is apparently hot on their heels."

Lee turned, went to his window, expected to hear something, cannon, some sign. There was no sound. He thought, This is madness. McClellan has never been hot on anybody's heels. And did Davis know this, know of losing Williamsburg?

"Major, I am going to take a ride. It is not necessary to inform anyone in what direction I am riding."

Taylor was puzzled. "Direction . . . ?"

"Major, I can no longer stay here and endure General Johnston's silence."

Lee heard the heavy sound of boots in the hall, then a young man, Major Marshall, another boy with the new responsibility of a senior officer, entered. Marshall stopped, startled to see Lee, and saluted, jarring his wire-rimmed glasses to one side.

"General, sir. Please forgive me for being late, sir."

He glanced at Taylor, asked quickly under his breath, "*Am I late?*"

Lee's mind was moving ahead, beyond the office, and he stepped toward the door, put a hand on Marshall's shoulder. "Let's go, Major, we're taking a ride."

Marshall trailed after Lee, then turned back to Taylor, still confused. Taylor laughed, seeing the young man's awkward expression, waved him away with a loud whisper, "Good luck on your mission, Major!"

T HEY WERE NOT FAR FROM THE CITY WHEN THEY CAME UPON the first troops, men of Gustavus Smith's brigades. The men were down, lying about in large clusters, trying to avoid the vast patches of thick mud from the hard rains that had soaked these swamps the last few days.

Lee and Marshall rode on, passed more resting troops, then reached an intersection where a large building was identified with a makeshift sign, THE OLD TAVERN. Across from the tavern was a farmhouse, and Lee stopped, saw horses, officers moving in and out. To the east, in the distance, he heard the sound, the soft rumble of artillery, then a steady rattle, a flow of musket fire.

"This way, Major."

Lee dismounted by the horses, and the men coming from the house stopped and gave a surprised salute. Lee led the young man in, looked through a doorway into one of the rooms and saw staff officers, Johnston's men. He motioned to Marshall to wait there, and the young man went in. Lee moved away from the pleasantries shared by officers who did not dirty their uniforms. He went toward the other doorway, peered in, and saw Joe Johnston.

Johnston looked up, did not stand, and Lee felt the tension, the dense air of trouble. He saw Gustavus Smith, nodded, and Smith made a quick unsmiling acknowledgment. There was a third man, General Whiting, another Johnston favorite, another quick nod. There had been no talking, and Lee sensed he had not caused an interruption. The men sat apart, did not face each other.

Lee broke the silence. "General, have you heard the firing?"

Johnston looked up, and Lee saw nothing in the eyes, a cold stillness. He made a quick wave with his hand. "Some artillery. Nothing to be concerned about."

Surely he has heard the muskets, Lee thought. He saw an empty chair, sat down, and still no one spoke, no attempt at conversation. Lee waited, had not expected this kind of reception. He studied Johnston, who did not look at him, did not look at anything, sat staring at the floor.

From outside there was the sound of a horse, a shout, and through the house came a burst of noise, a courier, who stopped in the doorway and began a frantic recital of his message: "General, sir, General Longstreet offers his compliments and wishes to report that he is engaged with the enemy and is moving them back. He requests with some urgency that the general provide support on his left flank."

Johnston rose, passed quickly by Lee and was gone, then the others were up, and Lee heard Johnston call to his staff. There was a flurry of activity, men running for horses, and in a few seconds Lee was alone. He still had no idea what was going on.

He walked outside, found Marshall watching the men leave, and then from up the road, from the west, the road to Richmond, he saw a group of men and a familiar rider. It was President Davis, who rode closer, spotted Lee and smiled; in a good mood, Lee saw, which was strange.

"Well, General, I see you have also decided to use the direct approach with Joe Johnston. Have you learned what is happening? I hear musket fire."

Lee could still see Johnston in the distance, and Johnston looked back, then spurred his horse and rounded a bend, out of sight.

"Mr. President, it appears that General Johnston has a full schedule today. He did not take the time to reveal his plans."

"Yes, well, I know he saw me, I watched him leave. I suppose we have no choice but to follow along. Would you please accompany me, General?"

The men rode down a muddy road through thick woods. Troops were moving up on all sides, and Lee saw the flags, the units from Hood's brigade. He looked about, hoped to see their commander, but the woods were too thick, and Lee knew it would not be a good time for conversation. From straight down the road came a sudden burst of musket fire, and in the distance smoke began to rise.

Davis pointed, said, "That's Fair Oaks."

Now cannon fire began to slice the air, heavy thunder poured toward them, and Lee knew the sound: Federal guns.

They rode forward, staying on the road, then came to a wide-open field filled with lines of moving men. To their front the woods turned thick again, and they watched the lines move forward, disappearing into the thick mass. Smoke began to fill the open spaces, and Lee heard units coming together, men screaming in confusion, officers trying to direct the lines, and he knew this was not good, there was no order.

After a few minutes men began to pile out of the woods, filling the road. Lee saw a flag: Texas, more of Hood's men. The firing had moved away now, farther down the road. Lee saw an officer, a colonel, and yelled to him, "What are your orders?"

The man rode closer, saw Davis, saluted and shouted back, "We cannot locate General Longstreet's flank, it is too thick. I'm trying . . . the men cannot fight through these woods!" The man saluted again, rode quickly away, tried to push his horse back into the trees.

The cannon fire continued in uneven bursts, and the daylight began to fade until the trees became a solid gray wall. Lee knew it would not go on much longer. Davis was speaking to the troops, a crowd had begun to gather around them, and then the wounded began to appear, carried out of the woods, and the sounds of battle were replaced with the cries of the men.

There was nothing left for them to do. Soon they would see the commanders and there would be answers to the confusion. Through the soldiers that crowded the road came a horseman, yelling, waving his hat, an officer Lee had just seen, one of Johnston's men. The foot soldiers cleared a path, and he rode closer.

"Sirs, General Johnston is wounded," he shouted. "They are bringing him . . . there." The man pointed across the open field, where the smoke was beginning to clear.

Johnston was carried by two of his staff, who laid him down under a tree as Davis and Lee rode up. Davis jumped down, kneeled, put his hands on Johnston's shoulders, and Lee stayed back, watched from behind. There were shells still falling, mostly in the distance, and Lee could not hear the men speaking, but he saw Johnston's face, saw he was awake.

Davis turned and glanced at Lee, said something to Johnston, then mounted his horse. "We must find General Smith. He is in command now."

They began to move back toward the farmhouse, would wait for the officers to come together, out of the dark.

Gustavus Smith was already at the house when they arrived and went inside. Smith was pacing, a manic display. "There was no . . . communication. I had no idea what we were . . . Longstreet was not on the road. . . ."

Davis did not speak, and Lee stepped forward, said to Smith, "What was General Johnston's plan?"

Smith stopped moving, looked at Lee, glanced past to Davis, said, "General, I don't know. He didn't tell me."

Smith began to pace again, looked at Davis, then Lee. "Where are my men? What do we do now?" He turned to Lee, and Lee saw a wildness in his eyes, a man not in control. "What do we do now? The men are all over. The Federals are right . . . out there!"

Lee backed away and followed Davis outside. Davis mounted his horse, motioned to him.

"General, would you please ride with me?"

"Of course, Mr. President."

They rode slowly through the dark. The sounds of the wounded filled the woods, and small flickers of light were moving about. Lee could smell the mud, the rain, knew the weather was again turning wet. Good, he thought. It would slow down the troops, swell the rivers. There would be time to regroup, to make new plans.

They moved farther from the troops, toward the west, closer now to the city, and the signs of battle were gone. The only sounds were those of horses stepping through the thick mud.

Davis had his head down. Lee thought he was sleeping. Abruptly, Davis sat up straight, leaned toward Lee and said, "General Johnston is not mortally wounded. He will survive."

"I'm relieved to hear that, sir. He is a valuable man."

"Maybe. He is a good soldier. I am not sure he is a good commander."

Lee didn't answer. They rode in silence again, and Lee began to think back, to drift away, Johnston in Mexico, at West Point, the fiery temper, which would give way to a quick joke, a big laugh.

"General, I am placing you in command of the army."

Lee was jolted from his thoughts. "Sir?"

"This army needs the right man to lead it. These men . . . they want to fight. I have no doubt you are the man to give the commands . . . make the decisions."

Lee felt his heart pound, looked at Davis through the dark, tried to see, to be sure. Davis said nothing else, and Lee took a long, deep breath, said, "Sir, I will do my best."

They rode on, toward the dark shapes of Richmond, the horses moving in a slow rhythm. Lee stared at the flickering lights, distant lamps and streetlights. His mind was turning, moving beyond the night to the days ahead. It began to rain then, a steady, cool mist, but he did not notice, was deep into thought, and feeling very, very good.

PART TWO

20. LEE

I T HAD BEEN JUST SEVEN DAYS, THE LAST OF JUNE AND THE FIRST few days of July. Each day had brought a new fight, at places they would remember as Frayser's Farm and Gaines Mill, Mechanicsville and Malvern Hill. The armies fought and struggled and moved about and made blind and stupid mistakes and brilliant and heroic attacks, and for both sides the losses had been staggering. But now McClellan had pulled his army back down the peninsula, away from Richmond, and in Washington his political enemies had their day. He had not taken Richmond, despite fighting battle after battle, though he had not once been truly defeated or even driven from the field. McClellan had pulled away by his own choice, backing toward the safety of the big gunboats, escaping from demons that Lee did not command.

Lee knew he had missed an opportunity, that McClellan in his retreat had repeatedly left himself open to assaults at a variety of places, but Lee had discovered his own army's weakness, his reliance on his commanders, and those commanders had not always been up to the task. Troop movement was inconsistent, communications were poor, attacks had been uncoordinated. The great weakness of choosing generals through politics had shown itself, and now, with McClellan tightly bound away from Richmond, Lee finally had both the authority and the breathing space to reorganize the army.

His headquarters was at the home of an old woman, the widow Dabbs, whose large house sat in the midst of an old, underused farm. His office was one of the smaller rooms, at the back of the house, and he had his own entrance so he could go outside when he chose, to slip away when he needed the rest or to just take a short walk.

The room reminded him of his office at Fort Mason, small and plain, the low ceiling and close walls, with one small window, but outside, he faced a stand of thick trees, saw the rolling green hills he loved. Beyond, the narrow, soft roads led out toward the bloody fields.

It had been a long day, couriers moving rapidly in and out, officers moving through the little office in a steady stream. Major Taylor had learned, had grown into the job, and Lee was grateful for the endless flood of minute details Taylor handled, diverting them from his attention.

For the first time, the army began to acquire an identity. Johnston had commanded units that he felt were his alone. Other generals not directly associated with Johnston's command, such as Magruder, incorporated their own aura of political importance to the running of their commands. Thus, the army had been a group of smaller armies, where coordination and communication was a matter of both ego and convenience. Lee understood the necessity of eliminating the independence of division commanders, and thus formed a system over which he had more control, and more confidence. Longstreet had been the backbone of the Seven Days' battles, had shown an ability to both move his troops and carry the fight, and Lee felt an instinctive trust for his abilities. Jackson had not performed as well during the series of fights, but Lee knew him well enough to know that given a specific task, there was no one who would move forward with more energy or ruthlessness. These qualities persuaded him to place Longstreet and Jackson in command of two large wings, bringing the various division and brigade commanders closer together and under his central authority. Others, men who simply had no place leading large numbers of troops, were removed, delegated to commands in distant fronts, out of harm's way.

The most immediate difference between Lee and Johnston, however, came in Lee's communications with Davis. Lee sent a continuing stream of messages to the President, kept him informed all through the Seven Days, and now passed along messages of all kinds, from important command decisions to the more mundane. Lee knew this would put Davis in a better frame of mind, and though Davis insisted on providing him with constant advice, Lee knew that simply by the existence of the open lines, Davis would convince himself he was still in tight control, while Lee did his job in his own way.

In Washington, the administration had heard enough of McClellan's strange logic, and the general's paranoia about those who conspired against him became reality. He was relieved of command, and the Army of the Potomac was given to General John Pope.

21. CHAMBERLAIN

July 1862

THE UNIFORMS WERE FRESH AND BLUE AND SHARPLY CREASED, and most seemed to fit their wearers well, but occasionally the taller boys or the shorter would self-consciously glance at their too-short pants legs or the sleeves that rode down over their hands. They marched down the main street, and people came out from the shops to watch and admire. There had been no great patriotic fever in Brunswick, no loud breathers of fire, abolitionist orators, radical Unionists screaming out from soapboxes, but these boys, this new company of clean-faced boys, the sons of the shopkeepers and bankers and longshoremen, the boys who had responded to the calls for volunteers, stirred something in them, brought them together in a new way, and so they watched quietly as the slightly uneven lines paraded by.

Chamberlain had come into town to see the tailor. He now carried his package, a bundle of new shirts, all crisp and white and neatly folded, encased in a tight wrapping of brown paper. He tossed the parcel up onto the seat of the small carriage, began to pull himself up, and heard a drumbeat, a rhythmic pounding that surprised him. Then he saw the line of blue rounding the corner a block away. There was a flag, held up high by a boy in front of the line, and beside him was the drummer, who bounced the drum awkwardly in front of him, suspended by a thin strap around his neck, somehow maintaining the steady beat. Chamberlain climbed up into the carriage, sat sideways on the small seat and waited, saw the townspeople now, the small crowd gathering along the edge of the street. Then he saw the flag, a bright red A on a blank field of blue. They marched four abreast, and the line stretched back, still emerging from around the corner. He began to count, and made a quick guess, maybe two hundred. They reached him and passed at a deliberate march, the drummer setting the pace. He saw the faces, felt a cold thump in his chest; they were the faces of children.

Chamberlain had built a reputation at Bowdoin for respecting his students as much as they respected him. He advocated less strict discipline, and more equal exchange of ideas, and this put him in conflict with the old professors, the men who treated the students with a mindless rigidity, an inflexible doctrine of study and examination. The attitude appalled him, and he did much to show the students that they not only had the right to question their instructors, but were obligated to do so. He taught them to accept the responsibility for their own education, because, sadly, many of the professors would not. Now he saw the same faces, the young men he had taught, several marching in line alongside the local boys, the farmers' sons who did not go to school, who had been taught only that they would do as their fathers had done. But now there was a war.

As the troops marched by him, some of the students saw him, turning discreetly, nodded in his direction. And he saw the looks, the pride, and he thought, No, they are too young. They are not old enough to become an army. But the uniforms were new, shining buttons and black leather belts, and he turned away, felt a sudden sickness, knew the image would be with him for a long time, boys and their uniforms, marching happily to war. He waited for the last of the troops to pass, slapped the horse with the leather straps, turned the carriage toward his home.

THERE WERE EMPTY CHAIRS, GAPS AMONG THE CROWD OF SEATED students. He walked to the front of the classroom, placed his notes down slowly, on the podium, and looked out at the young faces. They watched him as they always did, the talking stopped, and there was a moment when there was no noise at all.

"Some of you are missing. I did not realize, until today, why attendance was falling off. Forgive me, I feel somewhat foolish."

There were a few giggles. He saw heads turning to look at empty chairs, and he lowered his eyes, stared down at the podium.

"Some of you have decided to fight in this war. Some of your friends are on their way to join the army, have already joined. President Lincoln's call for volunteers is being answered. To many of us, this is a surprise. Not because we did not believe people would join the fight, but because so many of them—so many of *you*—would do so with such . . . enthusiasm.

"I am embarrassed to tell you that I am among those who never believed this country would fall into this situation. I always have felt that we are a nation that is very different . . . unique, perhaps. We were founded by thinking men, brilliant men, men who designed a system where conflicts were resolved in debate, where the decision of the majority would prevail. These men had confidence in that majority, they had faith that the design of the system would, by definition, ensure that reasonable men would reach reasonable conclusions, and so we would govern ourselves, all of us, by this new type of system, a system where our conflicts and differences would be resolved by civilized means. There is no other system like this, anywhere. And if this war is lost . . . if the rebellion is successful, it is possible there may never be another."

He paused, cleared his throat.

"Forgive me, I did not intend to talk about this . . . I do have a lesson prepared here. But . . . and you may know of this, the new regiments are being formed, and they are marching off to war, and of course . . . I knew that, I have been reading the papers, just like you. But I watched them today. They marched right by me, and I saw . . . *you*. And I felt a sense of history, of familiarity . . . as though I have seen this before, great columns of troops, men with strong, proud hearts and polished weapons, marching . . . just the same as they have done for centuries, since the dawn of man. Some of us have been naive enough to believe it would not happen again, that we have gone beyond that. We were wrong.

"I don't mean to sound . . . political. I've never been one who gives much weight to the opinions of politicians, but we are living in a time when those opinions threaten the existence of this nation. That's . . . extraordinary, but it is true. Those who lead the rebellion are trying to prove a point . . . a point that we are not one nation, that we are a group of separate countries, we are Maine, and Vermont, and Virginia and Georgia and Texas and New York . . . and that if any one of us disagrees with the policies of the Federal government, we have the right to erase whatever binds us together, disregard the existence— or the importance—of the Union. They have simply said, 'We quit— and if you don't approve of our right to quit, then you will have to send a great army down here and point your bayonets at us and maybe shoot us, and you may expect that we will do the same thing to you.' If that seems a bit simplistic, forgive me. I know some of you are students of Dr. Coleman, who is imminently better qualified to explain political science."

There were giggles, a few heads were shaking no, and he paused, scanned their faces, wondered why he was doing this, but they still watched him, waited silently.

He moved away from the podium, walked toward the tall window, looked out across the grounds of the college.

"We are so far removed, and yet, it is right here, right out there. We are all a part of it."

He turned back to the faces. "Does this mean we are simply patriots? If we say you cannot destroy the Union, you cannot simply cut the ties that hold us together, is that a reason to pick up a rifle? Do any of you believe that President Lincoln has the right to ask you to . . . kill someone? I believe Dr. Coleman would agree that this nation was founded on the notion of self-determination, that we are all individuals with the right to choose, and so, how much responsibility do we have to politicians? But . . . look around you. It is more than that . . . more than politics, more than Mr. Lincoln, more than some vague principle that you might be required to recite for Dr. Coleman. A great army has come together, has *volunteered* to fight for this union. I have heard numbers . . . hundreds of thousands of men. It's astonishing. And so, if you live up here in Maine, and you never go outside New England, and you have never seen a slave, or even read the Constitution . . . you must take notice. When you see the faces of these soldiers, in their new uniforms and their shining bayonets, try to understand why this is important. If you don't feel it here, in your heart, then feel it here." He tapped the side of his head with a finger.

"If you believe something is truly important, you have an obligation to fight for it. How many times have we heard words like that, especially from great figures of authority, like . . . our parents?"

There were nods, laughter.

"And how many times have the words really meant anything? Well, my young friends, if it has never mattered before, it matters now. And if I did not believe that I would ever see young men—the men from the empty seats in this room—if I did not believe I would ever see any of you put on a uniform and pick up a musket, well, I saw it today. And . . . if there are more of you who plan on doing the same . . . God bless you."

H E STOPPED IN THE DOORWAY OF THE SMALL OFFICE, SAW AN older woman, a tight bun of silver hair, thick glasses, sitting behind a small desk. "Excuse me," he said. "Is the meeting . . . in here?"

"What? The meeting? Yes, there, in Dr. Woods's office. Are you a member of the faculty?"

"Yes, madam, I am Professor Chamberlain. I am the—"

"Can't say I'm familiar with you, young man. No matter, I forget faces all the time. If you say so . . . go on in."

He moved warily through the small room, approached the old dark door to the president's office, stood for a moment, reached slowly for the knob, turned it quietly, and behind him the woman startled him.

"Go on in, son. They won't bite you."

He had rarely been in the president's office, had never had reason to call on Dr. Woods personally. There was a distance between them, mainly in age, but Chamberlain had respect for Woods, knew the president was at odds with most of the older faculty, men who rejected the modern notions of education. Woods had been gradually pushing through a policy of enlightenment with respect to the students' off hours, their free time. Many had felt their behavior should be regulated around the clock, that students should be monitored closely, lest they succumb to the horrors of unspeakable temptations, most of which were not identified.

"Ah, Mr. Chamberlain. Good, you made it."

Woods stood behind his desk, and there were a half-dozen men in the large office, men whom Chamberlain knew, some by reputation, others socially. There were always faculty meetings, mostly informal affairs, and Chamberlain had learned early on that attendance was rarely an issue, but this time there had been a memo directed to him, by name, a specific invitation.

He saw the always grouchy Dr. Caldwell, who nodded without smiling, and Grodin, the philosophy professor, a tiny man with a high, nervous voice, a man not much older than himself. Grodin came forward, held out a small friendly hand, which Chamberlain shook.

"I think we should begin," the president said. "Gentlemen, if you can find a chair." Woods sat down in his tall, cushioned chair, pulled himself forward, closer to the desk, leaned out toward the others, waiting for them to find seats. Chamberlain slid a straight-backed wooden chair out from the corner of the room, sat to the side of Woods's desk.

"Good, now gentlemen, let us begin." He turned and looked at Chamberlain, and Chamberlain felt the sudden stares of the others, wilted slightly.

"Professor Chamberlain, we have received some . . . somewhat disturbing reports. Please understand, this administration is not attempting to guide you in any direction. In fact, it is widely known here that your teaching is top of the line . . . first-rate. You are highly thought of . . . most highly."

Chamberlain waited, began to get impatient. "Sir, if you don't mind, can you tell me the nature of these complaints?"

Woods looked uncomfortable, glanced over to Caldwell, who said, "Professor Chamberlain, I have the highest regard for your abilities. But several of the faculty members have been hearing reports of some unusual discussions . . . unorthodox goings-on in your classroom. It is said that your views on this war—"

"Your views on this war are causing some disruption in this school." Chamberlain looked for the voice, saw a man lean forward from the far corner, Dr. Givins, the old mathematics professor, thin wisps of white hair scattered over a pale spotted scalp.

"Professor Chamberlain?" Woods saw the need to speak up, and took charge. "Have you been advising your students to volunteer for the army?"

Chamberlain looked around the room, saw the stern old faces, and the small smiling face of Grodin. He looked at Woods, saw the weary expression of a man who has better things to do.

"President Woods, I have expressed to my students that there is a significance to the events down South . . . that it is quite likely our nation is in jeopardy. I have not had to recommend to anyone on what course they should follow, they are quite capable of deciding for themselves."

"Ridiculous!" It was Givens, and he stood up, a bent old man, pointed at Chamberlain and said, "Wars are not fought by children! Young man, if you care about the well-being of this institution, then your time could be better spent teaching these students to consider the greater good!"

Chamberlain stared at the man, tried to understand what he was talking about. "The greater good?"

"This college! The enrollment. What is going to happen to this fine institution if the students rush off and join the army? It's madness! What of their futures? You're teaching them foolishness!"

Woods raised his hands, leaned toward Givens, said, "Please, Doctor, we are all gentlemen here. Your point is understood—"

"No, Dr. Woods, I'm afraid his point is not understood at all." Chamberlain stood up, could see Givens now, small in his distant chair.

"Wars are indeed fought by children, by young people who have little say in where they are sent to die. The greater good? These students may not have a greater good if this nation is dissolved. If this war goes on, we will all feel the consequences, whether we understand them or not. It is our job, our responsibility, to prepare these young people for life out there ... outside these buildings. And right now that life is very uncertain. I'm sorry if you feel your responsibility ends in your classroom."

Caldwell stood, did not look at Chamberlain, spoke to Woods. "I'm sure that Professor Chamberlain will concede that there is not much that any of us can do that will affect the outcome of this war. The government's problems go well beyond the needs and influences of one small college. Dr. Woods, we have made a great deal of progress in building the reputation of Bowdoin as a place where students may come to receive a modern and practical education. Professor Chamberlain has contributed greatly to that reputation, and will continue to do so. Certainly he can understand the benefits of not allowing himself to be sidetracked by issues that are so far removed from that goal."

"With all respect to you, Dr. Caldwell ..." Chamberlain paused, spoke slowly. "If we attempt to teach these students that the most important lessons they will learn are the lessons to be found within these buildings, then we have done them a most serious injustice. And they will discover that quickly, once they leave here. You ... some of you may be satisfied with the job you do, you may pat yourselves on the back after your daily lectures and sit back in your offices, confident that you have done some great service for our young people, but I am having an increasing difficulty with that. Right now ... there are professors, men just like us, just as educated, and just as experienced, who are facing their students at the University of Georgia, or the University of Virginia, and telling them that the course their rebellious states are following is the right one, and that they are growing up into a world where the concepts of the United States and a Federal government, and the Constitution, and ... even the concept of individual freedom for all men, will have no meaning, are obsolete. They will study the history of the United States of America just as we now study the history of England. I'm sorry, gentlemen, I cannot stay focused on my lectures on oratory, or my lessons in German semantics, and pretend that the outcome of this war has no significance."

Woods stood, said, "Gentlemen, let us adjourn. Mr. Chamberlain has made some valid points, and I believe little else can be served by debating these issues here. I, for one, do not believe that anything of Mr. Chamberlain's ideas hold any threat to either this college or his students, and that accordingly, the matter is settled. This meeting is adjourned."

The others sat for a moment, surprised by the quick end to the meeting. Chamberlain continued to stand, thoughts pouring through his mind, a great tide of energy, and he felt he could have gone on, had a great deal more to say, and then realized Woods knew that as well. Gradually, the men rose, went to the door, and there were glances, small voices, and Givens moved by him with fragile old steps, did not look at him, and then Grodin, who held out the hand again, smiling again, and Chamberlain could not tell if he had even heard anything he'd said, wondered if any of them had.

"Mr. Chamberlain, would you remain? If it is not inconvenient . . ." Woods was motioning to the chair, and Chamberlain looked at him, saw kindness in the old face, something fatherly, and he sat down, waited. The last of the others filed out, and the door was closed behind them. Woods put his hands on his head, rubbed his temples, as though wiping away a headache.

"They probably haven't been lectured to in a long time, Mr. Chamberlain. They're not used to it."

"I'm sorry, I didn't realize I was lecturing."

"No matter. They'll recover. No doubt I'll hear from one or two of them privately, the friendly advice of my colleagues, that maybe I should talk to you myself, set you straight." He laughed, prodded the headache again.

Chamberlain watched him, pulled his chair over toward the front of the desk, felt himself heating up again, said, "So, is that what this is? Are you going to tell me that I should watch what I say, that I should pay no attention to my instincts, my fears about the war? I should not disrupt the blind serenity of Bowdoin College?"

"Certainly not. Mr. Chamberlain, I share many of your concerns. Unlike many of those distinguished men, I have traveled somewhat throughout the South, and I know that what you are saying is probably true. But I also know that these men are right, that there is very little that any of us can do to affect these matters, and that if we open up our worst fears, if we convince these students that our nation is in a deep crisis, it is possible, don't you see . . . they may take that seriously. They may stop applying themselves, what's the use, and so forth. Some of them will go off and be soldiers—young people are good at that sort of nonsense—but it's the rest that concern me, the ones who stay, who look to us for a foundation, something they can build on. It is possible, Mr. Chamberlain, that what you are telling them is taking that foundation away."

Chamberlain felt suddenly betrayed.

"But you said you agreed—"

"Yes, Mr. Chamberlain, I do agree. I understand, and I share your concerns. That much is true. But I question the wisdom of sharing those concerns with young minds."

"There is no one else better suited to solve these problems. Certainly, you don't believe this office full of gray-haired academicians is going to solve anything." He looked at Woods's gray hair. "My apologies, sir."

"No, you are quite right. But my concern is you. I believe you need something . . . to take you away from these distractions. This war is not likely to last very long, you know. And when it is over, we will need to get back to the job at hand, which is teaching these young people. Right now, you are distracted. I would like to propose a possible solution."

Chamberlain waited, watching the kind old face, then realized he was about to be fired, felt a sudden lump in his stomach.

"Mr. Chamberlain, I would like you to consider a leave of absence. Have you ever been to Europe?"

"Europe? No, sir, I haven't."

"Well, this might be the perfect time. Take a leave of absence. We'll grant you two years. Travel, study, visit the great universities, the museums, the cathedrals, immerse yourself in the culture. You have a great talent for languages, so use it. It should be easy for you . . . and your family. It will be the opportunity of a lifetime for them. When it's over, come back here, to your Chair, and I am confident your attitude will have tempered. The war will certainly be over, and all this . . . disruption will be gone."

"Two years?"

"That should be plenty of time. It's an opportunity, Mr. Chamberlain. A rare opportunity."

"I would like to think about it, if you don't mind, discuss it with my wife."

"Of course, I'm not looking for an answer right now."

"Thank you, sir." He stood, felt a fog in his brain, a sudden numbness, his mind flooded with the idea of leaving, and . . . Europe . . . and he nodded, went slowly to the door.

Woods said to him, "It's the opportunity of a lifetime!"

HE HAD GIVEN HER AN ABSURD EXCUSE, FELT GUILTY IMMEDI-ately, but she would not understand, and there would be time for explanations later.

Augusta was a short coach ride from Brunswick, and he had wired a request, had received a positive response, and so today he would see the governor.

The coach reached the city, and he saw immediately the government buildings, the state capitol. There was little about the town to impress, but he felt impressed anyway, had never dealt with a seat of power, did not consider that these were just politicians, but the men who were close to it all, who had the facts, had up-to-date knowledge of the war and made their decisions accordingly. He felt childlike, excited.

He had excused himself from his classes for a couple of days, and Woods, and the rest, did not know where he was. It was assumed he had taken some time to be with his family, to weigh the great decision of accepting the leave. He told Fannie that he had to attend a meeting in Augusta, but did not mention the governor, said something that he could not even remember, some fictitious name of an academic conference. It had been a lie, and he knew it, and she had said nothing. He thought, She knows. But then, No, she knows you the same way they all know you, you're the bright young scholar, the man with the future firmly planted in academics, and they have no idea what it is doing to you.

The coach hit a pothole, lurched through the rough stone streets of the capital. He watched the unfamiliar scenes roll past, shops and bakeries and offices. She would never understand this, he thought, and none of them will listen, they will tell me I'm a fool, a college professor who knows nothing of life beyond academics, who has no business anywhere close to the war.

The coach slowed, pulled into the depot, and he stepped down, could still see the top of the capitol building, high above the rows of shops and houses, and he moved quickly in that direction. He looked at his watch: one-thirty. He was early, had time, but did not slow down, would sit and wait for hours if he had to. He paid little attention to the people, the storefronts, kept his eyes on the capitol, then finally he turned a corner and saw the entire building, perched in the center of a square, waiting for him to arrive.

"SIR, GOVERNOR WASHBURN CAN SEE YOU NOW."
He was startled, had let his head fall, sleepily, and he snapped awake, stood, saw the young man holding the door for him, and he tried to say something, his mouth dry and

thick. "Thnn uuu," he said, and cleared his throat, stepped through the door.

Washburn sat behind his fat desk, framed by heavy flags, the state of Maine and the Stars and Stripes. It was a picture that Chamberlain had expected, what a governor's office should look like. Washburn was a man of medium height, showed signs of a prosperous life; a large roundness pushed his coat forward. He wore glasses, peered over them at the young professor, then glanced over to another man, a thin, older man in a blue uniform, who sat beside the great desk, examining Chamberlain carefully.

"Professor Chamberlain. We received your request.... A bit unusual, but these are unusual times. I understand that you wish to volunteer for service. Exactly what did you have in mind?"

Chamberlain stood stiffly, said, "Governor, I would like to volunteer for military service in whatever capacity you consider appropriate. I am an educated man, I have considerable experience instructing young people, and I am willing to serve where the army considers me the most useful. Sir."

"Professor, that's a fine offer. Are you familiar with General Hodsdon, our adjutant general for the state of Maine?"

Chamberlain looked at the man in the uniform, who nodded pleasantly, and Chamberlain stiffened again, said, "No, sir."

"Well, Professor, General Hodsdon has the unenviable responsibility of organizing and equipping our volunteer regiments, and seeing that they are staffed with commanders who may lead them out safely beyond the border of our state, so they may lend a hand to President Lincoln's army. General, would you like to ask the professor here some questions?"

"Certainly, Governor. Professor, I took the liberty of wiring your President Woods, asking about you. Nothing too personal, of course, but we do need to know what we are dealing with here."

Chamberlain looked at Hodsdon, felt a lump forming in his stomach.

"Professor, in all honesty, I was surprised to find that President Woods did not seem to be aware that you were making this visit."

"No, sir, I did not inform him."

"May I ask why?"

"Because, sir . . ." He paused, sorted the words. "I am considered to be a good teacher. I have a prestigious position at Bowdoin. It is unlikely that Dr. Woods would appreciate my desire . . . to leave."

"You're quite right about that, he did not seem to appreciate it at all. However, he did respond to my inquiry with some highly positive comments. I don't mean to embarrass you, Professor, but he considers you a brilliant man. He made mention of your value to the college, and he considers you to be the . . . how did he put it . . . the 'new light of the future' or something like that."

"Dr. Woods is very kind. I do not consider myself destined, however, to remain behind the walls of a university. I have a strong belief in the need, our need, to win this war."

"That's good, Professor. Tell me, do you have any military experience?"

He paused again, thought of just saying no, but considered that anything might help. "Sir, when I was younger, I attended Major Whiting's Military Academy." He felt instantly foolish. He had been barely a teenager.

"Yes, I'm familiar with Major Whiting. Is there anything else?"

"No, sir. But before you pass judgment, please allow me to express that . . . I will accept the challenge of studying military tactics, and I will apply myself to training as I have applied myself to . . . many things."

Chamberlain stared straight ahead, looking past Washburn's head, heard a slight chuckle.

Hodsdon said to Washburn, "Governor, President Woods gave me a lengthy description of this young professor. He speaks seven languages, teaches four different disciplines, and Woods says he will likely master any subject that is placed before him."

"It's no wonder President Woods is unhappy with your running off to join the army." Both men laughed now, and Chamberlain nodded slightly, felt himself relaxing.

Washburn waved his hand, said, "Professor, it is not necessary for you to stand at attention. You're making me nervous. Sit down, please, over there."

Chamberlain turned, saw a wide dark chair, sat slowly down, thought, At least, keep your back straight.

Washburn moved some papers on his desk, studied one, said, "Professor, I have an order here from President Lincoln, requesting five new regiments of infantry. *Five.* We're talking about five thousand men. General Hodsdon has already sent them fifteen regiments, but it's not enough."

Hodsdon said, "Professor, what do you know of the war?"

Chamberlain considered the question, said, "I know that we are fighting against a rebellion that . . . if we are not successful—"

"No, Professor, the *war*. The fighting."

"I have seen newspapers, some reports."

"Professor, what the newspapers will not tell you is that the Federal Army has shown that when it confronts the forces of the rebels, when we bring superior numbers and superior armament against an enemy that is poorly equipped, underfed, and outnumbered, *we lose*. The war could well have been over last July, after that mess at Bull Run, had the rebels marched on into Washington. They sent our troops scurrying back across the Potomac like a bunch of schoolchildren. We are in sad shape, Professor. I for one am pleased to accept your offer. We are in desperate need of good officers."

Washburn said, "General, how about this? I see here . . . we have no one yet in command of the Twentieth Regiment. Professor, how would you like to be commissioned the rank of colonel and placed in command of the Twentieth Regiment? How does that sound?"

Chamberlain stood again, looked over at Hodsdon. "Well . . . Governor . . . thank you, but . . . commander? I must admit, I would have no idea how to begin. I had thought, maybe a lower position . . ."

Hodsdon leaned across the desk, pointed at something in Washburn's papers that Chamberlain could not see, then said, "Governor, I believe the professor is correct, perhaps immediate command of a regiment may be a bit premature. As you can see, here, we have Colonel Ames arriving back here next month. I had expected to appoint him to command that regiment."

"Hmmm, all right, yes I see." Washburn nodded, then looked up over his glasses at Chamberlain. "Well, then, Professor. How about Lieutenant Colonel? You would serve as second in command, the Twentieth Maine Regiment, under the command of Colonel Adelbert Ames."

Chamberlain absorbed the words "Lieutenant Colonel," felt a bursting need to yell at the top of his lungs, run around the wide office, and he pulled himself together, knew he was smiling, could not help it.

"I am honored to serve, sir. May I ask . . . when would I—"

Hodsdon said, "You will receive orders within a few weeks. Most likely, you will report to the adjutant's office in Portland, it's the closest to you. This should give you enough time to arrange your personal affairs."

Washburn stood, held out a thick hand. "Good luck, Professor. Oh . . . one piece of advice."

"Yes, sir, please."

"When you take command of your troops, it might be better for discipline if you're not smiling like that."

THE COACH RIDE FROM THE CAPITAL SEEMED TO TAKE FOREVER. Now he walked, and sometimes ran, from the depot, and reached his house in a panting, sweating excitement.

He stopped outside the front door, said to himself, Slow, calm down, and let his body breathe heavily. He waited a moment and then opened the front door. Inside he heard the cries of his small son, Wyllys, now barely three, and he stopped, was struck by a wave of guilt, felt that he had somehow betrayed his family. He listened to the boy, the sound echoing through the house, and then heard Fannie, saying something, trying to calm him. Chamberlain walked slowly through the house, went down the hallway, toward the sounds, reached the doorway into the children's room and paused.

Fannie sat on the floor beside the boy, holding something, a toy, waving it toward him in a playful tease, and the boy quieted. Up on the small bed, Daisy, who was now five, watched them both, began to laugh as the crisis passed. They did not see him, and he stayed quiet, framing the scene before him like a treasured picture, one he knew he would carry with him.

Fannie had given birth to four children, and two had not survived. There had been doubts about Wyllys's health as well, and his first year had been difficult. Chamberlain had grown weary of doctors, of somber pronouncements and vague predictions, and through it all he had feared more for Fannie. Their home had become the warm nest she needed, and the deaths of the children had shaken her, but Chamberlain was amazed that she had come back, had learned to smile and laugh and play again. Even after the second death, it was as though she had expected it, a price for the happiness, and so it too had passed, and now the boy was growing, the problems were behind them, and the family was complete.

"Daddy!" Daisy saw him now, jumped off the bed, ran to him and clutched his leg.

Fannie turned around and smiled, saw his expression, and the smile faded. She turned back to the boy, made sure he was all right, then stood up and said, "You're back so soon. I wasn't sure . . . you said it might be a couple of days."

"Yes, it did not take long. The ride is fairly short. Come, we need to talk."

"Let me get them ready for bed. It's been a rather long day. They seem to have some new energy these days, or maybe . . . I have less." She forced a small laugh, and he knew she was preparing herself for something, some news, his face had betrayed him. He went outside, to the small front porch, sat in a rickety chair, saw lights now, the day was done. He pushed back carefully, felt the chair twisting, groaning, and he looked up, saw the first stars, looked back on his day, his meeting, what he had done, and realized now that he actually felt alive, and happy, and it shook him, he had not felt this way in years. Now he would have to explain that to her.

It was not long, a few minutes, and she came out, had wrapped a sweater around her shoulders, moved in front of him, to the other chair. He could barely see her now, her silhouette in the dim lamplights of the town.

"I don't think I could have gotten them to bed if you had not come home. That's all I heard this afternoon, 'Where's Daddy?' "

They sat quietly, and Chamberlain felt himself tensing up, felt his heart beating. His hands began to sweat, and he took a deep breath, then another. Fannie heard him, knew he was finding the words, waited a few minutes, then said, "Are we moving?"

"What? Moving?"

"I thought . . . maybe you have been offered a new position."

"Well, no, but . . . ." He stopped, could put it off no longer. "I saw the governor today, Governor Washburn."

"The governor? Really?" She laughed, "My father calls him Old Breadball."

Chamberlain smiled, knew many reasons why he did not discuss politics with Reverend Adams.

"The governor has offered me . . . a commission. He has offered me a command position, a lieutenant colonel's rank . . . in the Maine volunteers."

She sat up straight, and he felt her eyes. "Why would he do that?"

"Because I requested it. I volunteered for service."

She stared at him in the dark, and he leaned forward, brought the chair slowly back down onto four legs.

"You volunteered . . . to join the army? Why on earth . . . you mean, you want to leave here? Leave us?"

"No, I didn't do it for that. Please. I love you, I love you all. But . . . this has been coming for a long time . . . maybe since the war started."

"You can't mean this, Lawrence. You're not a soldier."

He heard the edge in her voice, knew she was not going to take this well. He turned in the chair, faced her.

"The closer I came to doing this, the more I thought about it, the more I knew it was something I had to do . . . I wanted to do. I cannot let this war happen without doing something. If I don't do . . . something . . . I will regret it for the rest of my life."

Her voice was quiet, softer. "But what about your career? You can't just . . . quit. Have you told them?"

"No. I will do that tomorrow. They already know, probably. Woods knows. I'm sure I will hear a lot of . . . criticism. Those old men, they have no idea what this is about. I doubt I could ever convince them, so I won't try. They can't stop it. They've granted me the leave already."

"I thought we were going to Europe, I thought that was the news. You haven't told me if you were accepting the leave or not. It's been weeks, and I thought, finally, you had made up your mind. I did not expect you to join the army. How could you do this . . . without discussing this with me first? Do I not have any say in this?" She was angry now, and he looked away from her, out into the dark, did not have an answer for her, had never been able to tell her that he was simply . . . unhappy.

"I'm sorry. Please try to understand. . . ."

"I thought we were finally . . . doing so well. I thought you enjoyed . . . doing what you did. You never gave me any notion that you would ever do anything like this."

He looked at her again, tried to see her face in the dark, said, "I had come to believe that I would grow old standing in front of students, reciting my lessons, and that it didn't matter if I was happy or not. If this is where I am supposed to be, then I would accept that. But . . . something changed. I look into their faces, and they expect answers, and I began to realize that the answers they want are the same ones *I* want. My colleagues . . . they stopped asking about anything a long time ago . . . they know all they need to know, and their lives are as complete as they will ever be, and that works for them. I am not ready to grow old, to accept that what I am today is what I will always be."

She stood, moved away, to the edge of the porch, leaned against the thin railing, stared out to the night sky. "So, that's it."

He stood, moved toward her. She lowered her head, said slowly, her voice calmer now, "So . . . when do you leave? How long will you be gone? What will you be doing?"

"I'm not sure . . . of any of that. They'll send me orders . . . soon
. . . a few weeks. It's a new regiment, the Twentieth. I'll be serving
under a fellow named Ames, Colonel Ames. I expect we have a good
deal of training to go through. I have a lot to learn."

"You'll learn it. If you want to do this, you will learn it."

He smiled, thought of Woods, Hodsdon. "They seem to believe
that too."

He moved close behind her, wrapped his arms around hers, held
her against him. They stood quietly together for a long moment, then
she said, "What of us, the children? Are we to stay here?"

"Well, yes . . . I suppose so. I will be able to send money home,
my salary. We'll have to see . . . it's up to you, really."

"Up to me?" He heard the anger again, her voice cutting through
him. "How much of anything is up to me? You have made a decision
that will change all our lives. A soldier . . . my God, you may be injured . . . you . . . might never . . ." And now she began to cry, shook
against him softly. He reached into his pocket, pulled out his handkerchief, held it out to her, and she wiped her eyes.

"No, no . . . don't think on that. I will probably be sent to some
office somewhere, writing speeches for some general."

He tried to sound convincing, but she turned in his arms, faced
him now, said, "No, Lawrence, that is not what you will do. That is
not why you volunteered." She had stopped crying, stared at him hard
in the dark. "Go, do this thing . . . but be honest about it. Do not tell
yourself that everyone here is happy for you, that you are doing something wonderful for us all. I will not spend my nights happily thinking
about what could be happening to you. I will not send you away from
here with a lie. If you are not happy, then change that, but remember
that what you are doing may have a price for the rest of us . . . for
me. . . ." She began to cry again, sobbed hard against him.

He held her, put his head down gently against hers and said, "I
will try to be careful . . . I *will* be careful. I *will* come home to you.
I will miss you . . . I will miss the children."

She grew quiet, still leaned tightly to him, then he felt her stiffen,
pull away slightly, and she said calmly, "I know you will. And I know
you will write us, and I know we will be all right. There is my father,
and your family too." She moved away from his arms, along the porch,
turned back and said, "Lawrence, when you come home, you will be a
different person. I am afraid for . . . what that will be like. I don't want
you to change. But if you must do this, then go do it, and we will pray
for you, and when it is over, your family will be here."

He nodded quietly, knew it was all she could give him, that he had done something for himself, and that not all of them could understand, not even her.

To the east, out toward the vast open water, the moon began to climb above the treetops and the peaks of the houses, and he could see her face reflected in the faint light, said in a whisper, "I *will* come home . . . and I *will* make you proud."

He went to her then, pulled her up to him, and she softened against him, and he kissed her, a soft and long caress. Far off, beyond the town, the hollow wail of a great long train cut through the night, the cars heavy with men in rich blue uniforms, sharp creases and polished buttons, rocking in a steady rhythm down the southbound tracks.

22. LEE

August 1862

"SIR, IT APPEARS THAT THINGS ARE A BIT MORE QUIET. DO YOU have any orders?"

Taylor stood in the small doorway, and Lee turned away from the window, studied the young man for a moment, said, "No, Major . . . actually, I don't. We seem to have . . . a pause. It's been a long time. I'm waiting to hear more of Pope. Have we heard from General Stuart today?"

"No, sir. I will inform you when he arrives. Sir . . . might I suggest . . . begging your pardon, sir."

Lee waited, knew Taylor was still slow to speak frankly, often treated him as he would an overly stern father who would lash out angrily if the words did not come out just right. Lee did not understand that, had never been angry or harsh with him.

"Please, Major, you have something to say?"

"Sir, we feel it might be a good opportunity for you . . . to visit your wife, sir. It's a short ride . . . and you could be back by dark. We can handle anything that comes up today. You said yourself . . . it's pretty quiet, sir."

Lee looked at him, saw a slight smile, knew the young man was trying to be helpful, and he thought of Mary, living now at the Spottswood. Taylor was right, it was a short ride into Richmond.

"Thank you for your suggestion, Major. However, we are in the midst of organizing a new army . . . new commanders, a new way of doing things. It is not appropriate for me to suddenly leave . . . make a journey to Richmond for my personal benefit."

"Sir, only for the day—"

"Major, thank you for your concern. You are dismissed."

Taylor looked hurt, like a scolded pet, and Lee watched him turn, disappear from the doorway. He does not understand, Lee thought.

Mary had come to Richmond, carried through Union lines by the generosity of McClellan. The plantations were under Federal control now, and months before, Arlington had been ransacked and vandalized, despite assurances from General McDowell that the historic home would be protected. Though McClellan had guaranteed she would be safe at her son's home, it was risky, and McClellan was receiving criticism for providing a guard for the wife of the enemy commander. So, she had been granted safe passage. More fragile and crippled than ever, she made the journey to Richmond without incident. Lee met her there, saw her for the first time in months, and her condition was worse. The visit had not gone well, and seeing her had depressed him. His appearance had changed as well—he now was fully gray, and had grown a full, short beard. The change made him seem older, and she absorbed that reality poorly. Now, he was deep into his command, had buried himself totally in the running of this army, and could not bear to think of her . . . could not face what they had become, the permanent distance between them.

Lee turned back to the window, stared out at the trees, watched the heavy branches sway slightly, the leaves flickering in a summer breeze. He thought of going out, walking down to the small grove of apple trees that stood at the end of a far field, a field that had once grown corn and wheat, but now, after the marching feet of his troops, was only patches of thick short grass, dotted with bare spots of dried mud. He tried to stand, felt suddenly weak, saw her face again, the younger face, the way it had been before. But it was not a clear memory, and the early years, when the children were small, the brief times together, did not seem real, did not even seem to be his. The only life that was real to him was this one, the army.

He heard horses, several, riding hard up to the house, and he knew from the sound it was too fast and too much show: *Stuart*. He smiled, heard loud voices and took a last look out the window. How strange, he thought, I feel more like a father here than anywhere else. They are all my children: Taylor, Stuart, sometimes . . . even Jackson. Maybe this whole army . . .

Is that not what a commander must do, earn respect, give them discipline and . . . love them? The thought jarred him. He felt suddenly guilty, thought, No, it's all right, I do not love my own family any less. But I have not been a good father . . . and now God has placed me here, to redeem myself. And if my own children don't know . . . then these men will. He turned back toward the doorway, waited for the inevitable burst of Stuart.

But it was Taylor first. "Sir, General Stuart has returned, and has asked to see you."

Lee was still smiling, tried to hide it, said, "Of course, Major, send him in."

Stuart was instantly through the door, and Taylor backed out. Stuart had kept his hat on, rich gray felt and a long black plume, waited for the right moment, removed it with a flourish and made a deep bow to his commander. Lee let him go through the routine, could not hide the smile. Abruptly, Stuart came to attention, slapped his heels together sharply.

"Sir, with your permission, may I present the latest newspapers from the North." He reached into his coat, withdrew a handful of clippings, laid them carefully on Lee's desk. Lee leaned forward, picked through them, all items about McClellan and Pope and the recent battles.

"Good, General, thank you. I see there's quite a bit about their new commander."

Stuart made a sound, a grunt, and Lee looked at him, questioning. "With the general's permission," Stuart said, "I have heard of General Pope's dispatches, sir. He has ordered his men to pursue a policy of barbarism, sir, pure barbarism. His army has been instructed to take whatever they can from our farms, from our stores. He has ordered anyone conversing with any of our people to be arrested as a spy." Stuart began to move, pacing in the small space, obviously angry. Lee sat back in his chair, watching, surprised. "General Lee, this man is no gentleman. McClellan . . . at least you could depend on him to conduct himself like a civilized man . . . but this fellow Pope is . . . a barbarian!"

Lee picked up one of the clippings, read briefly, *My headquarters shall be in my saddle.* Lee paused, knew there would be jokes about that. He read on, a message Pope had given to his troops, trumpeting his victories in the West, which Lee stopped to consider, some minor battles that had little influence on the war. He read on, *I come from where . . . we have always seen our enemies from the rear . . . let us not talk of taking strong positions and holding them, lines of retreat, bases of supplies.* The story quoted him further, bombastic statements about crushing the enemy with quick and direct blows, and Lee looked up at Stuart, who was still moving about.

"Well, it seems we have a new problem."

"Sir, I have learned that General Pope has taken command of the forces under Banks and Fremont, and has at his command, sir, something over fifty-five thousand men. General McClellan has not yet left his base on the James River, but according to . . . those reports, there, sir, in the Washington paper . . . the wounded from his forces have already been seen coming up the Potomac. If General Pope is planning a large-scale operation, he will need General McClellan's forces. It's only logical, sir. . . ."

"Yes, General, I see that." He pushed through more of the clippings. "It seems that McClellan is no longer a priority with Mr. Lincoln. Certainly, his troops will begin to move, to unite with Pope's."

"Sir, they cannot be allowed to treat our civilians with such lack of respect."

"There's more to it than that, General." Lee felt something, an uneasiness in his stomach, thought, Pope is a dangerous man, a man who will say anything to create a name for himself, who will say and do anything to rally support from Washington.

"General Stuart, please excuse me . . . you are dismissed."

"But sir, I have . . . I have other details . . . troop positions—"

"It's all right, General, we will talk in a little while. I just need a few moments."

Stuart snapped to attention again, saluted, and left the room. Lee turned back to the window, thoughts rolling through his mind in waves. He took a deep breath, began to sort out a plan, thought, This is a great opportunity. We can use Pope's own ego to trap him.

He pondered, watched the slow motion of the big trees, then turned, said in a loud voice, "Major Taylor," and instantly Taylor was in the doorway. Lee looked at the bright face, said, "Major, send for General Jackson."

B Y LATE AUGUST, POPE'S ARMY WAS CENTERED IN THE AREA BE-tween the Rappahannock and Rapidan Rivers, north of Fredericksburg. Lee ordered Jackson's troops north, to move between Pope and Washington, which would have the easily predictable effect on Lincoln, who would see Jackson's move as a direct threat to the capital. Pope would certainly be called upon to move back to the northeast, removing his pressure on central Virginia. Lee also suspected that Pope would convince himself he had been given a glorious opportunity, that Jackson's army by itself was no match for his superior numbers. By assuming correctly that Pope would focus completely on Jackson, Lee knew he could maneuver the rest of his army, under Longstreet, and bring the attack to Pope while he was exposed.

The move by Jackson's troops also achieved a direct benefit for his own forces. Their sudden advance put them quickly at the Manassas Gap railroad junction, where Pope's supplies were stored. The small number of troops guarding the depot were easily routed by Jackson's surprise arrival, and so they not only disrupted the flow of material to Pope's army, but found themselves awash in vast stores of food and equipment. Pope reacted as Lee had predicted, and began to move back up to crush the greatly outnumbered Jackson, with little regard for the rest of Lee's army, which, unknown to Pope, had moved by a slightly different route, to unite with Jackson's forces.

McClellan's troops were indeed being withdrawn from the Virginia peninsula, and were moving up the Potomac to join with Pope. Thus, Lee knew his opportunity for meeting Pope on more even terms was a brief one. But Pope was in a hurry as well, would not sit and wait for the rest of his army to arrive while the ripe target of Jackson sat alone.

LEE AND LONGSTREET RODE TOGETHER, IN FRONT OF THE LONG columns, quietly, feeling the August heat. Out in front, nervous skirmishers, a handpicked squad of Texas sharpshooters, cleared the way of any Federal snipers and scouted the advance of the army for detachments of Federal troops who might have been sent to scout the Confederate positions. They were the only advance guard the two men had. Behind them, Hood's division led the long column.

Lee rested his head, his hat pulled low, and appeared to be sleeping, but he was very awake, his mind focused on what might be ahead of them and where Jackson might be. They had received no word since last night, knew only that Pope's army was scattered, the result of a hasty march, and that somewhere, up ahead, Jackson was preparing for the assault.

They had climbed a long hill, had crested the top, surrounded by the familiar signs of a bloody fight. It was Thoroughfare Gap, where General John Buford's Federal cavalry had slowed the march, holding the pass against a brigade of Georgians, commanded by George Anderson. Buford's cavalry had been stubborn, had held up the march for nearly half a day, but finally General Hood had been sent over the mountain through another route, a nearby pass, and the flanking movement had worked. Buford's men and a small detachment of supporting infantry finally gave way.

Now, the Federal troops were gone, pulling back, to unite with Pope's larger army, and so Longstreet's men kept moving forward, up and over the mountain, toward their rendezvous with Jackson.

They rode slowly, a steady rhythm, and behind them the officers were shouting now, for the hills were steep and the heat was draining the men. Lee could hear the commands, "Keep up," "Stay together," and he sat up straighter, crested the hill, saw shattered trees and broken wagons, noticed the fresh smell of yesterday's fight. Along the wide ridge, in the rocks and beyond, the bodies of men still lay, exposed. Lee saw the uniforms, both sides, a vicious fight in a tight area, and the army was now pushing through, quickly, too soon for even the burial parties. They had marched nearly thirty miles in thirty hours, and so it was not just the heat that deadened their steps.

Lee saw the Texans moving below, keeping a tight line, spread far to each side, and he smiled, thankful. Behind him, he heard voices, then one voice, the deep, booming sound of John Bell Hood.

"Well, dammit, move them along! It's just a hill!"

Lee turned, saw Hood approach, a small staff following.

"General Lee, forgive me, I had meant to ride with you earlier. We're having a bit of trouble getting these men up this damned hill . . . begging your pardon, sir."

Lee nodded, and Longstreet turned in his saddle. Hood abruptly saluted, and it was an awkward moment. Longstreet was Hood's commander, and Hood knew he should have spoken to Longstreet first. It was a small error, one of those annoying pieces of military etiquette that Hood had not yet mastered.

"General Longstreet, I have ordered the company commanders to push the men hard, get them up this hill with all speed."

"That's good, General." Longstreet spoke from under a wide-brimmed hat, pulled low so his face was half hidden. Hood looked at Lee, and Lee saw the eyes, the wide, excited face, the thick blond beard, and he thought of Texas, knew Hood had not changed. He had performed brilliantly as a commander, had led his Texans with a fire that infected them all, and Lee knew that if it was critical, if one man could be sent into the furnace, could face the deadly hell and turn the tide, it would be Hood.

Hood said, "I'd best get back down the line . . . see how we're doing." He saluted, Longstreet returned it, and Hood glanced at Lee with sharp, smiling eyes. Lee nodded, knew that Hood remembered Texas too, the shared experiences, unspoken feelings men have when they both know they are good soldiers.

Lee turned to Longstreet, who was staring ahead, peeking out under the brim of his hat.

"We shall need him, I believe, before this is through. Make good use of him, General."

Longstreet did not turn, kept staring to the front, said, "I've seen him work, General. He will have his chance again."

Lee followed Longstreet's stare, tried to see what held his attention. He had seen the look before, as though Longstreet were seeing something far away, well beyond the horizon.

Longstreet was partially deaf, and others who did not know him well often mistook it for aloofness or simple rudeness. He was not a man for fluent conversation, did not join in around the campfire, the jovial, drunken revelry that too often surrounded the headquarters. Lee had learned to respect him as a commander, knew Joe Johnston had relied on him often. He had not known Longstreet long, had not known him at all before the war.

Longstreet came home from Mexico with a wound that hadn't healed for a long time. He settled into a career as a paymaster in the old army, had spent most of the peacetime years out West, in El Paso and Albuquerque, and never had shown the ambition to press further. At the start of the war he was a major, and had come back to the South expecting nothing more, volunteering for a job as paymaster again. But President Davis knew him from Mexico, knew that Longstreet had led infantry, the great assault on the big fortress of Chapultepec, knew of his training at West Point and his abilities to command, and so Longstreet was surprised to be commissioned a brigadier general. Only a few weeks after his arrival in Virginia, he was leading troops at Manassas.

But Lee knew something had changed, there was a new darkness in Longstreet's eyes, in his moods, and Lee tried to understand it. The cause seemed obvious at first. During the previous winter, while his family was staying in Richmond, all four of Longstreet's children had contracted a fever. Within a few days three of them died. All of Richmond was shaken by this news, and no one expected that he would return to duty so quickly, resume command of that part of the army that would play such a large part in turning McClellan away.

Lee had heard the earlier stories, the poker playing, the long nights of drinking and bawdy storytelling, and he could not believe any of that, did not see those things in this big, dark man. There was a hollowness, a deep opening in the man's soul, and Lee had wanted to talk about that, to be of some ... comfort. He didn't know if

Longstreet was particularly devout, had never heard him mention God, thought, If he knew that God is with him, that all of this . . . his tragedies, are part of a Plan . . . But there was never the right moment; the two men did not share that kind of close conversation. To Lee, that sort of closeness had never been easy, but he'd grown very fond of Longstreet, was not even sure why, and so wanted to do . . . something. They often were together now. Longstreet seemed to gravitate toward Lee's headquarters, but the conversations were brief and military, strategy and planning, and Lee sensed an edge, as though Longstreet held himself in some tightly bound, angry place. Longstreet seemed to know it himself, and Lee began to hear more caution in his planning, more need to avoid the big risks.

Jackson was very different. Lee had come to understand that if left alone, Jackson held nothing back, would operate with a fury and an anger that was simple and straightforward. He was given credit for military genius. The newspapers referred to him as the greatest general in either army, though Jackson never seemed to pay attention to that kind of praise. Around Lee he was like a young child, eyes wide, eager to please the fatherly Lee, and so Lee had learned to treat him that way. But he did not see just a child. He saw a very strong and dangerous animal that would do whatever you asked him to do, with complete dedication and frightening efficiency.

Lee did not know how Longstreet and Jackson felt about each other. There had never been a dispute, or any other reason to examine their relationship. Longstreet clearly considered himself the ranking officer, which technically was true: his commission had come first. Jackson had often deferred to that seniority when the two were together, but Longstreet understood Jackson's value, and if he thought Jackson reckless and headstrong, he did not express it to Lee.

The strength of the forces under the two generals was now nearly equal, due mainly to the transfer of Ambrose Powell Hill's division from Longstreet's command to Jackson's. A. P. Hill was a difficult, moody, and egotistical man, and a dispute had arisen between him and Longstreet after the Seven Days' battles. A correspondent for the Richmond *Examiner* had written glowing and exaggerated accounts of Hill's role in the army's confrontations against McClellan, indicating that Hill's division was responsible for most, if not all, of their successes. Longstreet responded angrily by authorizing his chief of staff, Major Moxley Sorrel, to write a letter to a rival newspaper, the *Whig*, setting the record straight. After heated and nasty correspondence between Hill and his commander, Longstreet finally had Hill arrested, which so inflamed Hill that he challenged Longstreet to a duel. By this time Lee had no choice but to intervene. The solution was simple, and served a useful purpose. Hill's division was moved, increasing Jackson's strength, and Longstreet was relieved of a headache.

The columns were closing up behind them, and still Longstreet stared ahead, not moving. He spurred his horse then and moved slowly forward, starting down through the gap. Lee followed, and Longstreet stopped again, and now Lee heard it. There was a rumble, straight ahead, the rolling thunder of cannon, and Lee knew it was Jackson.

They began to move again, and behind them the column of soldiers reacted to the distant sounds, the men quickening their steps with a new flow of energy. Lee strained toward the horizon, looked for smoke, and then from below he saw riders, the gray hat and the tall plume: *Stuart*.

The horses reined up, and a cloud of hot dust followed, enveloping the group of men. Lee closed his eyes, waited, and Stuart said, "General Lee, General Jackson is engaged, in a line facing to the southeast. He is deployed along an unfinished railroad cut and is in a position of some strength. I suggest, sir, that you direct this column to his right flank. There is a small town, Gainesville, where you may turn to the left, taking the Warrenton Turnpike toward Groveton. You will find General Jackson's right flank anchored there."

Stuart was breathing heavily, and Lee waited for the flood of words to pass, then said, "General Stuart, my compliments. We will proceed as you have suggested. Can you advise us as to the concentration of General Pope's army?"

"Sir, General Jackson is facing a heavy concentration of troops. We have located three corps, with at least three more corps approaching the field."

Longstreet rubbed his nose, said quietly, "That's near seventy thousand men. Jackson has twenty-two thousand. I hope that railroad cut is a deep one."

Lee turned to Longstreet, said, "General, I have confidence that General Jackson will not engage the enemy unless he is confident of holding his lines. It is up to us now. We still have an opportunity. Let us move forward."

Longstreet saluted, turned his horse around, saw the approach of Hood, who was hurrying toward the group of commanders.

Longstreet said, "General Hood, your men will lead the column, and speed is a priority. We will proceed to Gainesville, turning left and filing out in a line away from General Jackson's right flank."

Instantly Hood was away, riding back to his officers with the instructions, and now Lee said to Stuart, "General, take your men out to the right, to the northeast, see if you can determine if more troops are close to joining Pope's forces. McClellan's army is out there somewhere, and if they are moving this way, we need to know. Be mindful that your position will also serve to protect General Longstreet's right flank."

Stuart smiled, nodded. "Sir, I have a squadron out that way now."

"Good, General. You will keep me informed?"

Stuart removed the hat, made a sweeping motion. "I serve only you, *mon Général*."

Salutes were exchanged and Stuart rode back down, away from the column. Lee turned, saw the men pressing forward, motioned to his staff, the waiting couriers. He could feel the movement from behind, the pressure of the column, unstoppable, and he spurred his horse, leading them forward. Down the hill he saw the lines of sharpshooters, watching, waiting for him to begin moving again, and now they continued forward, down through the thinning trees.

Longstreet rode alongside, still stared out ahead, toward the low sound of the guns, which was now constant. He pointed, but Lee had already seen a flat cloud of smoke beginning to rise over far trees.

Lee said, "General Stuart has proven himself valuable again."

Longstreet said nothing, and Lee knew he did not approve of Stuart's style, the flair for the dramatic.

Lee waited, then said, "He is of great value to us, General."

Longstreet nodded, said, "I do wish . . . begging your pardon, General, but he needs to be kept on a shorter leash. He has a great love of headlines. It may cause some problems."

"General Stuart has his ways . . . certainly different from our ways, you and me. But he is young, and he inspires the men. And if the newspapers love him, then he can inspire the people as well. There is no harm in that."

Longstreet said nothing, and Lee focused again to the front, could see small buildings now, a few houses, and he motioned behind him. A staff officer rode up, the young Major Marshall, and Lee said, "Major, ride forward into that town, make certain there is an intersection, and determine that a left turn will lead us toward that fighting."

"Sir!" and Marshall was quickly gone.

Longstreet looked over at Lee, smiled slightly. Lee stared straight ahead, said, "I have great confidence in General Stuart. But, General, there is no harm in being certain."

As LONGSTREET'S MEN REACHED THE FIELD, JACKSON ABSORBED a daylong pounding from Pope's forces. Waves of Federal troops poured against Jackson's lines, were beaten back, and then replaced by fresh troops. As Jackson held to his precarious position, Longstreet's troops spread out to the right, at a slight angle forward, so that by the next morning, Lee's army lay in the shape of a V, with Jackson on the left and Longstreet on the right. The bulk of Pope's army lay just outside the mouth of the V.

That night, Lee called the commanders together. He had set his headquarters up just behind the junction of the V, and his staff had secured an old cabin for him to sleep in. Jackson, Longstreet, and Stuart all arrived at eight o'clock, as requested. Lee rarely issued orders for his meetings, made the more cordial suggestion of when they should attend, but there was no confusion in the minds of his generals. Now, they had all gathered, their staffs at a respectful distance, and Lee emerged from the cabin, paused, stared up into the dark sky. It was a warm and humid night, and he welcomed the relative cool of the old log house. Stuart was the last to arrive, had just dismounted, and Jackson and Longstreet had made themselves crude seats from a pile of cut firewood.

Lee stood at the door of the cabin, adjusted his uniform, saw the three men outside watching him, lit by the bright glow from the nearby fire. Taylor stood to the side, waiting. Lee asked, "Coffee, gentlemen?"

Stuart said, "Thank you, yes, if it's all right, sir." Taylor moved quickly away. Lee looked at the other two.

Longstreet shook his head silently, and Jackson rose, said, "Thank you, General, I do not partake."

"Of course, General, no matter, please, be seated." He walked out among them, found his own seat, a thick-cut log propped upright on the bare ground. Taylor appeared, handed Stuart a tin cup and then moved back, behind Lee, and sat on the ground, his back against the side of the cabin.

Lee spoke first, always spoke first. "General Jackson, your troops performed an admirable service today. How are they faring?"

Jackson rose, stood stiffly, said, "General, I have pulled most of the units back, into the cover of the thick trees. They are somewhat battered, but they will hold their lines."

"Back . . . into the trees? You pulled them away from the railroad cut?"

Jackson glanced at the others, then looked back at Lee. "Yes, sir. It should be better for their . . . relief. They will be ready tomorrow."

"General, what do you suppose will happen if General Pope discovers the railroad cut has been abandoned?"

"I did consider that, sir. It can only be to our advantage. My troops can move out of the trees quickly if he attempts an advance."

"Yes, I know. This is not a criticism, General. It might be a good plan. Our best advantage lies in the ground we now hold. It is up to General Pope to advance against that ground."

Jackson sat, and Longstreet stared down, scratched at the ground with a stick, said slowly, "General Lee, I do not believe General Pope knows our disposition. Our deployment on the right was barely contested. He does not seem to have made any serious move to confront our lines."

Lee stared at him, could not see his face for the wide floppy hat. All that afternoon, Longstreet had been in position to advance into the battle, could have possibly relieved the great mass of pressure on Jackson, but had not done so, had told Lee that it was not a good time, that there were too many uncertainties about the ground, about the location of Pope's other units, those not pressing Jackson. Lee had been frustrated by the lack of action, but now it was done, and he could do nothing but look ahead. Lee knew, if Longstreet was right, if Pope did not realize the strength that lay behind the trees to his left, he might be inclined to make a very serious mistake.

"General Longstreet, are you prepared to advance your troops in the morning?"

Longstreet knew there was something implied in the words, let it go. He did not share Jackson's raw lust for plunging ahead, had not been comfortable in an area where rolling hills and thick lines of trees made visibility difficult.

"General, we are prepared to meet the assault."

"General Stuart, have you observed any additional forces coming our way?"

Stuart stood stiffly, held the big hat in his hands, had quickly tossed the cup aside. The presence of Jackson and Longstreet had a subduing effect on him; the brutal seriousness was intimidating. He began slowly. "General, yes, we did observe a column of troops moving down from the northeast . . . at least a corps. By dark, they were still several miles away."

"Good. I do not expect that General Pope will receive much more assistance on this field, not by tomorrow. These are, after all, General

McClellan's troops marching toward him. They are likely to be somewhat . . . slow to advance."

Longstreet looked up, and Lee saw his face in the firelight. Longstreet said, "General Pope is not a well-liked man. Even at the Point he had a way of talking too much, saying the wrong thing. If he has even met with his own commanders, it is likely he has very little . . . coordination."

Lee stared at him. "What do you mean, General?"

Longstreet tossed the stick aside, stood up, stretching his back. "I mean, General, that even if General Pope is seeking the advice of his commanders, he is not likely to listen to it. He does not have confidence in anyone's ability to lead his forces . . . but his own."

"If you are correct, General, then he may yet pursue General Jackson's 'retreat.' That will be our opportunity."

Jackson stood again, following Longstreet's lead, said, "General Lee, I did observe on my way here . . . there are a large number of

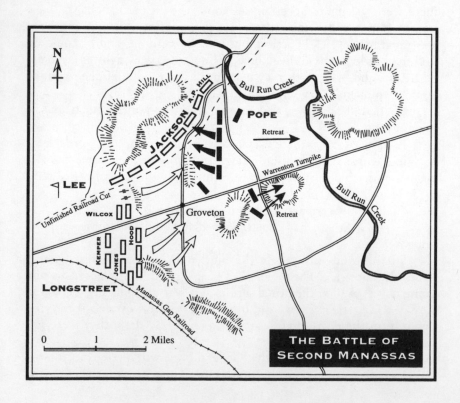

THE BATTLE OF
SECOND MANASSAS

General Longstreet's batteries digging in on my right flank. These could be very useful if I am attacked."

Lee smiled. "Yes, General, General Longstreet and I have placed a heavy concentration of guns at the junction of your two lines. There is a slight rise at that point. They may have a clear view of the field, and so far it appears that General Pope is not aware they are there."

"Then, General Lee, let us hope he provides them with a fine target."

AUGUST 30, 1862

POPE HAD INDEED CONVINCED HIMSELF THAT JACKSON WAS IN RE-treat, and despite the observations from Generals Porter and Reynolds, who cautioned against Longstreet's position, Pope believed that the bulk of Longstreet's strength had moved back behind Jackson, not alongside him. The next morning, after long hours of conflicting advice and his growing impatience at what he believed was Jackson's potential escape, he ordered his men forward.

Lee sat on a flat stump, still behind the center of the V. He had simply waited, nervous, praying, hoping that Pope would bring the attack forward. It was now past noon, and he stood, began to pace again, as he had done all morning. He knew his location was important, he should stay between the commands, but he could not see anything. In front of him the batteries were spread along a wide ridge, hidden by a thick line of trees, but it was these trees that kept him blind to the field. Suddenly, he heard a loud and distant noise. He had expected guns, an artillery barrage first, but this was not cannon, it was . . . men. Out to the left, in front of Jackson's waiting troops, heavy lines of Federal infantry had emerged from the far woods, over distant ridges, and were in pursuit of what they believed to be Jackson's withdrawal.

Lee started forward, began to run up into the trees. Behind him, his staff was moving quickly, grabbing horses, following him. He reached the tree line, and the men on the guns turned, cheered him as he moved past. He did not look at them, focused in front, trying to see. Finally, he stood at the edge of the trees, the ground dropping away in front of him, a long, shallow bowl, and he saw three lines of blue, moving from right to left, toward the railroad cut. Then he heard another sound, one he'd heard before, the sound of Jackson's men, a high, steady, terrifying chorus. Farther to the left, behind the cut, the gray lines flooded forward, out of the trees. The field filled quickly with smoke, the sound of voices replaced by that of muskets.

"Sir!" Lee turned, saw Taylor and other staff officers. He looked back at the guns, saw the men moving, ready, and he motioned to his staff, started back to the rear. The orders came, and the guns began their deafening fire. Flashes of light and thick smoke filled the tree line. Lee watched from behind, could no longer see the great lines of troops, but knew what was now happening to them.

The Federal forces pushed hard against Jackson's left, the troops of A. P. Hill. Once the shock of Jackson's surprise advance had worn off, the reality was that Hill's forces were outnumbered, and the Federals kept pushing, kept coming. Pope sent more strength into the assault, and Jackson knew that Hill was in trouble, was beginning to waver.

Lee sat again on his stump, waited anxiously. There had been little word from the fighting, and he thought, Jackson must not hesitate, he *must* ask for help. This time we have the troops. Behind him, Taylor stood, holding two horses, his and Lee's, the beloved gray the general called Traveller. Lee thought, I should ride up, try to see something, and he turned, motioned to Taylor. Down to the left he saw a rider, coming hard. It was Henry Kyd Douglas, of Jackson's staff.

Douglas dismounted, saluted hastily, said, "General Lee, General Jackson sends his compliments, and requests reinforcements, sir. He requests at least a division on his left flank, to support General Hill, sir!"

Lee looked at Taylor, said, "Major, tell General Longstreet to move. . . ."

He paused, saw another rider to his right, one of Longstreet's staff. The man pulled up but did not dismount. "General Lee, General Longstreet is advising that he believes the time has come to advance his army into the attack, sir. He believes that the Federal Army is exposed to a counterattack from his position."

Lee felt his heart thump, the cold chill of the moment. "Yes, tell General Longstreet to advance with all speed. Major Douglas, return to General Jackson, tell him General Longstreet is advancing in force on his right."

Both staff officers were quickly gone, and Lee looked at Taylor, saw the young man moving around with jumpy, nervous energy, and Lee said, "Major, this could be a glorious day!"

T HE EFFECT OF LONGSTREET'S SUDDEN PUSH INTO POPE'S FLANK caused an immediate collapse of the Federal lines. While small pockets of blue troops fought stubbornly, the tide of the battle had turned for good, and now Jackson's weakened lines pushed forward as well. Within a couple of hours Pope's army was in a panicked retreat toward the Potomac.

Lee rode Traveller out through the line of trees, followed close behind Longstreet's advancing infantry. Smoke filled the air, and he could not see the Federal troops, only the backs of his own lines. They continued the rapid advance, and the solid roar of musketry deafened him. Behind him, Taylor raced to keep up, yelling out, trying to convince Lee this was not the place to be.

He climbed up a long ridge, reached the top, and his men were moving ahead down the other side, pursuing the Federals down a long hill. Now he could see across to another ridge. A steady stream of blue flowed over the hill, men in a dead run, moving away without firing. He stopped, sat high on Traveller and watched the scene. The sunlight was starting to fade, heavy clouds darkening the fields. His mind was racing, filled with thoughts and pictures.

He thought of Pope, where he might be. Was he watching this as well, or was he caught in the flow, pulled away by the tide of a beaten army? He thought of Longstreet, who had delayed yesterday, would not attack until the time was right, and now it did not matter because the time was right today. He knew Jackson would be out with his troops, pushing them forward. He turned back, looked to the row of trees where the artillery was, saw the gunners standing along the ridge, waving, cheering, and then he thought of the lone soldier, the man who had come back into Richmond after the first battle, the man he had tried to talk to, who spoke only of Jackson's great success, and he wondered if he was here, today, a year later, and had seen it all again.

Taylor was beside him now, and Lee looked at the young man, said, "Remember this, Major. There are not too many days like this . . . when you have swept your enemy from the field and you can watch him run. You don't need official reports or newspapers or the gossip of stragglers . . . you don't need anyone to tell you what has happened."

Taylor nodded, staring wide-eyed at the frantic withdrawal of Pope's army.

Lee pulled on the reins, turned the horse around, said, "We had best get back . . . they will be looking for us." Then he paused, looked out one last time, saw his own troops now, moving over the far ridge, still in pursuit, a deadly chase that would last until it was too dark to see.

I T RAINED ALL NIGHT AND ALL THE NEXT DAY. LONGSTREET'S fresher troops were assigned the dismal task of burying the dead, and the men dug their way through the soft ground of the farmlands, now turned to vast seas of thick mud. The pursuit of Pope's army had been bogged down by the rain and by the arrival of more of McClellan's troops, which Pope now used as a rear guard as he limped his way slowly back toward Washington.

Lee's staff gathered at the edge of a stand of trees. They had just come across Bull Run Creek, following the slow advance of the army, pressing closer to the Federal troops. Out in front, the advance lines had confronted the Federal skirmishers, who did not run, and so both armies moved sluggishly in the rain, staring at each other like two tired animals, one slowly backing away.

Lee stood beside Traveller, holding the reins, and around him the rest of his staff waited for further news of Pope's movement. Taylor stood near Lee; the others mostly sat on their horses. There was no dry place, and the thick black rubber of their raincoats wrapped each man like a glistening shroud. Lee focused, tried to hear, caught the occasional dull pop of musket fire from the distant skirmish lines, but it was infrequent and had no meaning. There will be no fight today, he thought, and even with McClellan's reinforcements, Pope would not make a stand. He would go back to Washington and tell of a great battle where he was lucky to rescue his troops, could only back away because his troops were sadly underprepared or overmatched, and he would inflate the enemy's strength and claim he fought the good fight against tall odds, because that was the kind of man he was. He will not tell his President that he stumbled blindly into a disaster, Lee thought. That observation would be made by others.

Lee put his hand on Traveller's neck, felt his uniform pull at him, soaked by the wetness, the hot and stifling humidity, held hard against him by the dripping raincoat. He patted the horse's thick, wet hair, and the horse turned slightly, cocked his head. From behind, a man came through the trees, said in a quick yell, "Yankees!" and a shot rang out, the ball whistling over Lee's head.

Traveller jumped, lunged forward, and Lee's hands were still holding the reins, were tangled in the tight leather straps. He was suddenly pulled, snatched ahead by the motion of the horse. His knees dragged the ground, and he tried to release the reins but could not, and then quickly the horse was stopped, grabbed by Taylor.

"There, boy, whoa . . . calm down." And now Taylor looked toward the soldier, saw others moving up with him, muskets raised, yelled out in an angry burst, "You damned fool, this is General Lee!"

The men put their guns down, saw now that the horsemen in the black raincoats were not Yankees. A sergeant emerged from the men, came closer, saw Lee and said, "Oh, my God . . . oh, my God."

They helped the general up, and he found his feet, his hands loosening from the straps. The officers were quickly around him and he was held under the arms, carried to the trunk of a fallen tree, sat down on soggy wood. Now he looked at his hands, felt the pain twisting through his hands and arms like fire. He heard someone call out, and from the woods men began to gather. He heard someone yell for a surgeon, and he stared at his hands, thought, this is bad . . . and it is very very painful.

A man was pushed through the crowd of soldiers, and Taylor brought the man forward, said, "General, this is a doctor."

Lee looked at the man, saw an older face, gray beard, felt some comfort in that, and the man said, "Dear me, General, what have you done to yourself?"

Lee rested his elbows on his legs, and the doctor put his hand under the elbow, lifted it gently.

"You have a broken bone in your hand, General," the doctor said. "I can set that . . . and the other one. . . ." He lifted the other arm, bent down, looking it over. "Nothing broken, it seems, but quite a sprain." He looked at Lee's face, and Lee was staring down, was trying not to look at his hands. The doctor said, "General, you are in a great deal of pain. Let me get you something—"

"No," Lee said, shaking his head. "You cannot drug me, Doctor. Not now. I will be all right."

"Whatever you say, General. But I do have to set that bone. You will feel better if you at least drink something. I have some whiskey, here, always carry it. Just a small swig—"

"Thank you, Doctor, no. Just do what you can."

The doctor handled the arms carefully, and Lee stared ahead, past the men, who were now being scattered, sent away by his staff. The pain in the right hand, the hand with the broken bone, was not nearly as bad as the other, and he wondered at that: bending is worse than breaking, he mused, I would not have thought that . . . but . . . either way . . .

He tried to focus on other things, Pope, the battle, but the pain was enormous, and he felt as if the one arm was on fire. Now there were bandages and splints, the doctor working quickly. Taylor stood behind, looking over the doctor's shoulder, and said, "It's all right . . . it's all right," and Lee knew Taylor was convincing himself.

He turned, tried to see the young face, said, "Yes, Major, I will be fine." But his voice shook, betraying the effect of the pain, and he thought, Of course, this is punishment . . . God's way of saying every victory has a price. Yesterday was . . . too easy. It must never be too easy.

The doctor finished his work, and the staff lifted him up, helped him to a wagon, an ambulance that had been brought up. He was helped aboard, sat on a thin mattress, and the driver saw his face, recognized him, snatched his hat from his head and held it against his chest as he began to cry, "Oh Lord, what has happened to General Lee?"

There was an embarrassed pause, and Lee looked at the man, surprised at the outburst. "Soldier," he said calmly, "I have been inconvenienced, that's all. It is a small price for the inconvenience we have given General Pope."

POPE CONTINUED TO PULL BACK, AND HIS TROOPS FILED NOW into the massive fortifications near Washington. Lee did not pursue, there was too much strength. McClellan's army was united with Pope's, and for now they were safe. Lee knew there would be no fighting for a while, that it would take a fresh start of some kind, a new Federal commander, new bluster and new pressure from Lincoln. For now, he began to look toward his own troops and the serious problems confronting his own army. A majority of the men had no shoes at all, or wore pieces of cloth wrapped around their feet. Clothing was becoming an embarrassment—many of the men were covered only partially by rags that were barely strung together. The only uniforms visible were on the officers, and those had become so worn that most showed rips at the knee and frayed cuffs and sleeves. But it was not their clothing that affected the men's ability to fight—it was food. The farms of Virginia had been assaulted not only by the needs of the army, but by the pillaging of Pope's army as well, and what crops and livestock were available were barely able to support the needs of the civilians.

Lee rode everywhere now in the ambulance. He could do nothing with his bound hands without great pain, and so relied completely on his staff. Taylor became ferocious at protecting him from unnecessary visitors. They tried to make him comfortable, made the ambulance a rolling office, and he was thankful there was a lull in the fighting—he knew that if things were hot, he would have to turn the command over to someone else, probably Longstreet.

The ambulance hit a deep pothole, bouncing him high off the fat cushion that served as his seat. The driver stopped, peered back through the flaps, worried, said, "Begging your pardon, sir. It's a bit rough since the rain."

Lee nodded, said nothing. It had been several days, and the discomfort did not bother him anymore. His hands had stopped hurting with every movement, every small gesture, and now it was just the wait, the healing, and the frustration of not having the freedom to move, to take Traveller out through the tall trees, to ride with dignity among the men. He loved that the men were inspired, cheered when he rode past, and he saw it as a blessing, the good fortune of high morale in these men who knew the joy of victory. Now, they watched him go by with a painful silence, an occasional yell of condolence, good luck. He understood the importance of that intangible spirit the commander carries with him, riding with his staff and the flags, the response that comes from the hearts of men who have no shoes and little to eat. And if there was to be no enemy in front of them, there must be something else, to make the best use of the opportunity. They could not sit on this same trampled ground and wait for another big fight.

Jackson arrived first, rode up on his little sorrel carrying the dust of many days. Lee watched him from the back of the wagon, his legs dangling. Jackson rode alone, upright in the saddle, stiff, never seemed comfortable on his horse. He still wore the old small-billed cap from VMI, which now sat flat on his head like a crushed tin can. The bill was pulled forward, came down barely over his eyes, and as he rode he cocked his head slightly back, in order to see. Lee smiled, thought, He could ride right past Federal sentries, and they would never know who he was.

Jackson dismounted, and an orderly took the reins. The general tossed something aside, and Lee smiled, saw it was a lemon, spent, crushed into a flat mass. Jackson walked quickly with long strides, and now Lee saw something in the sharp face, a painful sadness. Jackson reached out a hand, then froze, awkward, wanted to touch Lee's bandaged hands, could not.

"General Lee, I pray you are not in pain."

"Thank you, General, it is better now. I must keep them wrapped for a while, though. We heal slower with age, an unfortunate fact."

There was a voice behind the wagon: Major Walker. "Sir, General Longstreet is arriving."

The horses thundered closer, Longstreet and his staff. Jackson backed away from Lee, saluted toward the sound, and Lee waited, could not see where Longstreet was, then heard the heavy steps, the slow, deep voice.

"Afternoon, General Jackson." Then Longstreet was around the back of the wagon, saw Lee. "Well, my word . . . you look a fright, General, begging your pardon. I heard you went at Pope's rear guard with both fists." He laughed, a quiet chuckle, and Lee smiled, was surprised, had not seen Longstreet in such a jovial mood for a long time.

"I will leave the hand-to-hand to the men from now on, General. It is not a pleasant thing for an old man."

They both were smiling, and Jackson stood stiffly, puzzled, did not share the joke.

"Come, gentlemen, if I may be assisted . . ." Walker was there quickly, lifted Lee off the wagon, and he settled on the ground, arched his back, stretched slightly. "This wagon is not for comfort. Let us walk, gentlemen."

The three men moved away from the horses and the staffs, walked out into a field, stubs of cornstalks, now pressed into drying mud. It was hot again, and they moved away from the shade trees.

Longstreet said, "The weather should break soon, cool things off."

Lee adjusted his hat, turned now to face away from the sun. "General, do you believe General Pope will attempt another advance before spring?"

Longstreet kicked at a spot of hard ground, knocked thick mud off his boots. "General, I don't believe we will see General Pope again, not in the spring, or ever."

"You may be correct, General, but his army is still there, and now they are safe and so they will refit and resupply, and Mr. Lincoln will send them out again. The question is not so much who will lead them, but when they will come, and where."

Jackson said, "We should have pressed them back to Washington. They were running. God sent the rain, to slow us. He wishes us to fight again, in a better place."

"I don't know if there is a much better place than this one," Longstreet said. "That army left this field as quickly and as completely as any army ever has."

Jackson tilted his head back slightly, looking at Longstreet. "But we did not destroy him. We must still destroy him."

Lee nodded, looked at both men. "General Jackson, as much attention as I would like to devote to the Federal Army, we have a closer problem at hand, the condition of *this* army. I have been thinking . . . it's about all I have been able to do. Our greatest need is to feed this army, and we can do that in either of two ways. We can withdraw, to the Shenandoah Valley, where the crops are still in good supply. That would expose this part of Virginia to occupation by the Federal Army yet again. While this army could restore its health in friendly country, the damage to the morale of the people could be great. It is also likely that President Davis would not approve of that move."

Jackson shifted his feet. "Nor would I, sir. We would lose what we have gained by chasing the Federals back into Washington. You have a second plan, sir?"

"Yes, General. I propose we advance our army north, into Maryland. The farms there are plentiful and nearly untouched. With the fall harvest, we can feed our troops well. And there is one other consideration. The people of Maryland have expressed neutrality. It is my belief that the constant use of their land by Federal troops is felt as a hostile occupation. It is quite possible that our intervention there will be viewed as a liberation. We might receive a great deal of hospitality, and we might even receive a number of volunteers for service in the army."

"General, if they have proclaimed neutrality," Longstreet said, and paused, "would we not be seen as an army of occupation as well?"

"I don't believe so, General. The invasion of Virginia, of the entire Confederacy, by Federal forces, made clear to any neutral party that the Confederacy is not the aggressor here. We did not bring this war, and we fight now only to free the South of Federal occupation. If Washington will end their side of the fighting, and recall their armies . . . General, this war will be over. And, gentlemen, that is another reason why I believe this plan can succeed. By moving into Maryland and strengthening our forces, we will then be in a position to push into Pennsylvania. If Mr. Lincoln sees that we are threatening to cause destruction against the Northern cities, Philadelphia, even New York, there will be a great outcry in the North to stop this. So far, gentlemen, the bloody fields are Southern fields. If we threaten to bring that blood into the North, there will be great pressure on Mr. Lincoln to end this war. We might not even have to fight, just our presence, just the threat, could be sufficient."

Longstreet stared down, spoke from under the brim of his hat. "General, we would be cutting ourselves off from our base of supply, from communications. We would be vulnerable from the rear."

"General Longstreet, you did march with General Scott, into Mexico, did you not?"

"Yes, sir."

"And did not General Scott cut himself off from his supplies, from all communication, and by doing so, did he not bring a rapid end to that war? And did he not accomplish all of that in a foreign land? Well, this is not a foreign land, and the citizens will see that we do not come to terrorize, as did General Pope. We come to end the war, quickly and without any need to conquer or subdue anyone. We have proven our superiority on the battlefield. The threat of that superiority may be all we need."

Jackson began to fidget, rocked back and forth on stiff legs. "My men are ready to move on your command, General."

"General Jackson," Lee said, "we do have one problem, which I will need you to address."

Longstreet said, "Harper's Ferry."

"Yes, General, you are correct. There are nearly twelve thousand Federal troops quartered there, and they could add to those numbers easily by moving men up the river. That would be the danger to our rear. Harper's Ferry must be secured. General Jackson, I want you to move your forces down that way, surround the town from the heights and secure it by any method that will ensure success. I will accompany General Longstreet's forces across the Potomac, masking our movements behind the mountains. We should be well into Maryland before anyone in Washington can do anything to impede us."

Longstreet said, "General, we are already greatly outnumbered, and by dividing the army . . . there is considerable risk, sir."

"This plan could end the war, General. Is that not worth risk?"

. Jackson looked at Longstreet, said, "General, my troops will move on Harper's Ferry and reunite with your army in short order."

Longstreet kicked at the dirt, said, "We need cavalry in the mountain passes, masking our movement, and in our rear, to keep anyone from following us."

"General Stuart will be so ordered. I will inform President Davis of this plan, and provide both of you with detailed written orders by tonight. It is a slow process. . . ." He held up his hands. "I must dictate everything to my staff."

Lee turned, began to walk back toward the wagons, and the

others followed close behind. They reached the edge of the shade, felt the cooler air, and Lee paused, said, "Gentlemen, you were both on this field a year ago. We won a great victory then, quite possibly could have ended this war, and we did nothing, we did not follow it up. That is why we had to fight here again, on this same ground. It is a lesson learned, gentlemen. It is time to take this war out of Virginia."

23. CHAMBERLAIN

AUGUST 1862

THEY STOOD IN GROUPS, SAT IN SMALL CIRCLES. SOME WERE LY-ing on the ground, some slept. He had walked from the train station, through the streets of Portland, had seen other men moving in the same direction. No one noticed him as he made his way into Camp Mason, the first assembly point for the volunteers of the Twentieth Maine.

He saw the faces of the young, the same kind of faces he had seen in the streets of Brunswick, but there were others too, older men, men with rugged, worn faces, big men, log cutters, farmers, and he was surprised, but it made him feel better. This was not, after all, an army of boys.

There were tents lined up in neat rows at the far end of the grounds, and he began to move that way, lugging a heavy cloth bag over his shoulder. He had thought of bringing his usual small trunk, then decided it would be too conspicuous. He did not want to appear to be too green. At least make a good first impression, he thought. He walked past the groups of men, heard conversations, most about where they had just come from, what was left behind, a few comments about the war, where they might go next. He heard a few accents, Irish, Scottish, but clearly, they were all Maine men, and they did not yet know that he would lead them.

He reached the tents, saw a man, an officer, the only uniform he had seen so far, sitting at a small table. The man was writing on a long sheet of paper, and Chamberlain said, "Excuse me, I'm looking for my tent. I'm Lieutenant Colonel Chamberlain."

The man looked up, glanced him up and down quickly, then stood, saluted.

"Sir, I am Major Gilmore, formerly of the Seventh Maine. I have been sent here to assist you . . . and . . . this regiment."

"Fine, Major, it's a pleasure to meet you. You are a veteran, then?"

"Yes, sir. Fought in General Hancock's brigade, on the peninsula, General Smith's division."

"We can use some experience here, Major, myself included. Are you the only officer here?"

"There are others, sir, the company commanders, but the uniforms have not yet arrived."

"And Colonel Ames?"

"The colonel is expected at any time. I have taken the liberty, sir, of preparing a schedule . . . a routine for the drills. I had thought Colonel Ames would want to begin as soon as possible. They're a pretty rough bunch, sir. If you'd like, we can begin right away, get a bit of a jump on it before the colonel arrives."

Gilmore handed him the paper. Chamberlain saw a list of march steps, formations, and column movements, and he examined the list with an attempt at a critical eye, hoped Gilmore did not realize that he would have no idea how to begin drills.

"Yes . . . well done, Major . . . but, this is Colonel Ames's command. I think we should let him decide the training schedule."

"Whatever you say, sir."

Chamberlain began to look around, studying the faces, the clothes, the mix of city and country, then turned toward the tents, said, "Major, can you point me—"

"Begging your pardon, sir, yes, you are over there . . . that large one, with the open flaps."

"Thank you, Major." He began to move that way, felt a childlike excitement, his own tent, sleeping right out here, on the ground, then he felt silly, forced himself not to smile. He leaned over, into the empty tent, saw only one small cot. He threw his bag toward the back, then gazed at the camp again, thought, Maybe I should walk among the men, introduce myself, get to know them. Then he thought, Well, no, maybe a commander shouldn't do that. But the officers . . . I should find the officers. . . .

"Beggin' yer pardon, sir, but I heared you was a perfessor?"

It was a comical voice, with a crude, exaggerated accent. Chamberlain turned, saw a man coming from between the tents, a small, thin man in baggy clothes. The man had spoken out from under a wide, floppy farmer's hat, then the hat lifted and he saw: Tom!

"What . . . you come to see me off? What are you doing here?"

"Lawrence, I joined up. I'm in this regiment. I'm going with you." Then he snapped to attention, threw up a crooked salute, said, "Colonel, sir!"

"How did . . . did Father approve this? How will he run the farm?"

"Lawrence, once he heard you was gonna be a colonel, he couldn't say no. You know him, he'll be all right, they both will. I just gave him one less thing to cuss at. And Mama said so many prayers for both of us . . . we got nothin' to worry about."

"Well . . ." He looked at the clean smile of the boy, felt the pride, then a hard tug in his gut. His brother, his little brother, was a soldier. "Well, I guess I have one more responsibility—I have to look after you."

"Me? Lawrence, Mama told me to look after *you*."

Chamberlain smiled, could picture that scene, his mother wrapping the tight arms around her youngest son, the last gift of pious advice, and his father standing to one side, grim and silent, maybe one nod, one grudging show of affection.

"This is really something, eh, Lawrence? Look at all these men. And you're gonna tell 'em all what to do. Think they'll listen to you? You're just a professor."

Chamberlain felt a sting, said, "They'll do what they have to do . . . it will take some time. But one thing has to change right away."

"What's that, Lawrence?"

"Stop calling me Lawrence."

H E LAY ALONE AND QUIET, HEARD NOTHING, THE CAMP DARK and silent. He thought, I had better sleep . . . I have to be sharp tomorrow. But there was no sleep, and he tried to move, lay on his side, hoping it would be more comfortable. But the stiff cot would not give in, and he rolled onto his back again, staring at white canvas. He sat up, stuck his head out through the flaps, saw the stars, a clear, lovely night, and stepped outside, stretched, looked out over the sea of tents. Nearly a thousand men, he thought, waiting for someone to tell them what to do. Waiting for *me*. No wonder you can't sleep. He looked farther out, saw a lone figure moving, walking, then toward the other side, another one: sentries. Major Gilmore had posted guards, something Chamberlain would not have thought of. Guarding against what? We're still in Maine. But, of course, the guards were there to keep these men *here*.

He thought of taking a walk, strolling through the cool air, but no, it would be a bad example. Try to get some sleep, Colonel, he told himself, and he moved back into the tent, sat on the cot. His brother was there. He had not counted on that. It shouldn't change things, he thought, but it does.

Stretching out on the cot, he stared up again, at the blank canvas. He tried to relax his mind, heard himself breathing, and then saw Fannie—God, I miss her already. He thought of the many nights he would reach over to her, run his hand gently over her arm, touch her hair. . . .

It was a terrible screeching, a dying animal, some horrible demon tearing through his brain, a hellish whine in his ears. It was dawn . . . and it was a bugle.

Chamberlain turned over, tried to find the floor, rolled off the edge of the cot and hit the hard ground with his whole body. Then he pulled himself up, tried to stand, and his head bumped the canvas above him. He tried to see, stumbled toward the opening in the tent, saw it was still dark, a faint white glare beyond the far trees. The bugle continued to blow, a broken and tuneless flow of sounds, and men were moving now. He heard voices and curses, and he backed into the tent, looked through the darkness for his clothes, realized he was already dressed, had never taken them off. He turned again, fought his way out through the tent, stood outside in the chilly morning and saw a man on a horse, a sharp silhouette in the faint light. It was Gilmore, and beside him, standing, was the man blowing the bugle. Chamberlain began to move that way, thought, I really do need a uniform, and as he approached, Gilmore saw him and saluted stiffly. Behind him, Chamberlain saw a horseman sitting stiffly, a smaller man in a wide-brimmed hat. The man moved his horse up beside Gilmore, the major said something, and, blessedly, the bugle stopped.

Then Gilmore said, "Colonel Ames, I am pleased to present Lieutenant Colonel Chamberlain."

He felt confused, then realized it was him, and he saluted in the man's direction. He could not see the face, but he heard, "Colonel Chamberlain, please accompany me to breakfast."

Food? he thought. "Yes, sir. When, sir?"

Ames stared down at him, said nothing, and now the men were gathering in numbers, most of them up and out of the tents.

Gilmore shouted, "Line up . . . here, across here."

The men began to fall in, and Chamberlain heard the voices, "Where's the coffee?" "Kill that bugler," and he thought, Yes, a brave man carries the bugle.

Gradually the men came together, a sea of bodies in the faint light, and Gilmore shouted, "Quiet! Men of the Twentieth Maine Regiment of Volunteers, this is your commanding officer, Colonel Adelbert Ames."

There were some cheers, applause, and Gilmore waved his arms frantically. "Quiet! You do not applaud your commander. You will learn to salute him. Now, here . . . this is Lieutenant Colonel Chamberlain, your second in command."

There were more cheers, and Chamberlain bowed, then heard Gilmore again. "Quiet!"

The noise lessened, and the men began to mumble, talking among themselves, waking up in a rising steady hum, and Gilmore yelled again, "Quiet!" and it had only minor effect.

Ames said, "Major, it's their first official morning. We'll give them a bit of slack today. You won't have much of a voice left if we don't. Let them eat . . . then we begin the drills. Colonel Chamberlain, come along, if you please."

Ames moved his horse away, and Chamberlain walked behind, was not sure where they were going, remembered breakfast, and thought, I really do need a horse.

"COLONEL, YOU WILL SHARE MY TENT."

"Sir?"

"It will work out better. We can spend our time more efficiently, teaching you the fundamentals."

"Certainly, sir."

They sat at a small table, under a flat open tent, and Chamberlain was holding his first cup of army coffee, was attacking it bravely, determined. It was his greatest challenge so far. The tent began to fill with other men, the officers of the regiment, who had learned that the officers ate separately from the men. They came slowly up, with some shyness, approached the mess table where assorted piles and pots of food were waiting. Chamberlain watched them come, stuffed a hard biscuit into his mouth, knew immediately it was a mistake, too large and too dry, but could not remove it. He saw Ames watching him, and so took a hard gulp from the coffee cup, washed it down.

Ames smiled. "Welcome to the army, Colonel."

Ames was a small, thin man. He had a wide, round face with a thick mustache, and Chamberlain was surprised to see he was young, much younger than him. He had graduated from West Point only a year before, and had seen action immediately at the first big fight, Bull Run. His assignment to command this new regiment was a questionable reward, but he was an ambitious man, and took his own advancement as seriously as he took his need for discipline.

"I've been told quite a bit about you, Colonel. General Hodsdon has a great deal of faith in your abilities. It's my job to teach you how to be a commander."

"Thank you, sir. I will do whatever it takes."

"We'll start immediately. This regiment is about as raw as any I have seen. That will not last, Colonel. They will learn how to be good disciplined soldiers, or they will be slaughtered."

Abruptly, he stood, said loudly to the other men under the tent, "Gentlemen, in fifteen minutes I want the regiment formed in lines of four, company A on the left, and so on down the line. We cannot waste time getting these men in shape."

Chamberlain looked at the other officers, saw nods, uncertain faces, and there was a noise off in the distance, the shouts of men, a line of wagons. A man ran to the tent, saw Ames's blue coat, said, "Sir, the uniforms are here!"

The officers rose from their breakfasts and the tent emptied as they moved quickly toward the small line of wagons. Men had crowded around, there were happy shouts, and now the officers took control, began to yell instructions, herding the men into formation.

Chamberlain stayed with Ames, following his lead, and Ames climbed on his horse, moved the animal slowly toward the forming men. Chamberlain walked behind, watched the officers waving and pointing, with minimal success. Men still gathered at the wagons, and suddenly Ames rode forward, pushing his horse through the men. Reaching the first wagon, he pulled his sword and yelled something Chamberlain couldn't hear. The men scattered, moved toward the familiar, less-threatening faces of their company commanders. Now the columns began to show some shape, rough formations, and Ames turned the horse around, rode to the front.

Gilmore rode up, began speaking, then Ames followed, giving instructions of what was expected of them, how the training would go. The company commanders were instructed to appoint a quartermaster officer, who would issue the uniforms. Chamberlain listened to the words, the commands, watched the strange mix of men standing before him, some looking up at Ames, some at him, some staring away into some distant place, and he began to get a feeling of dread, a feeling that this wasn't going to work. These men were not an army. Surely it was different in other units, men with a sense of order, an inherent knowledge of how to do all this. These were Maine men, a different breed, men used to a hard, tough life, a life as individuals, men who never had to listen to anybody tell them anything, and so many of them were not listening now.

He tried to spot Tom, looked for the floppy hat, did not even know what company he was in, and his eyes ran up and down the rows, past all variety of dress and stance and expression. Are they better than us? He thought of General Hodsdon's words, and he wondered if the rebel army was so much better, what it was that won battles. He still felt the dread, a sense of doom, and then he saw Tom, the bright face. He was not wearing the ridiculous hat, was smiling at him, directly at him, and Chamberlain could not stare back at him, because he would begin to smile as well. But he felt the look, the energy of youth, the enthusiasm, and now he began to see others, the faces that were staring to the front, listening to Ames's words, absorbing them, and he saw there were a lot of them, men who did not yet know how, but would learn, men who understood after all, what this meant, what they had to do.

He began to feel better, the dread slipping away, and imagined himself wearing the uniform, the deep blue, seated high on a horse, before neat rows of men with their own uniforms, straight lines of rifles, shining bayonets. He glanced up at Ames, heard the voice of the commander, and thought, No, they are not better than us, and we *will* have our chance.

SEPTEMBER 1862

THEY WERE AT CAMP MASON LESS THAN A MONTH WHEN ORDERS arrived to board the trains, trains that would pass through other towns and other states, adding carloads of men and equipment, bringing them all out of the cool hills of New England, toward the flat, hot plains around Washington.

Chamberlain had his horse finally, a gift from the town of Brunswick, a wonderful surprise. It was light gray, dappled with white spots, and he rode slowly, grandly, through the formations, watching the men of the regiment turning themselves into soldiers. And they had watched him as well, as he was taught and drilled night after night by Ames. Now, as they rode the long rails south, there was a feeling, shared by all of them, that they were ready for the only real test. Ames still pushed them, rode them hard, drilled them so often that they began to curse him, hate him, but they continued to learn, and if Ames was despised, they also knew he was a good soldier.

In Washington they continued to drill, lines and formations, columns of march and lines of battle, the bugle commands and the hand signals of the officers. Then they were issued muskets and ammunition, backpacks and blankets and canteens. Around them, in camps spread throughout the city and well beyond, great fields of blue troops and white tents, horses and wagons, began to move together, toward and across the river, lining up and flowing out along the narrow, hard roads. The men knew it was their turn, fresh troops for a battered army, and they began the march, not to the south, as they had thought, but northwest, toward a far corner of Maryland.

CHAMBERLAIN HEARD THE REPORTS, THE RUMORS AND GOSSIP, and sorted through it all, began to feel an instinct for what was accurate and what was absurd. Then there was the official announcement, passed along formally to each regiment: General Pope was gone, relieved. The reckless and pompous fool had been replaced, after he had led his army to a bloody disaster, another costly and painful embarrassment on the same ground that they knew as Bull Run, and it was the beloved McClellan who was getting his second chance.

What his troops, and General Lee, did not know was that an extraordinary piece of good fortune had fallen upon McClellan. Lee's Special Order 191, which detailed to his generals their movements and objectives, had been issued to all his commanders, and when they began to move away, units of the Federal Army had felt their way cautiously out, moving slowly over the ground the Confederates had left. It was here that a pair of soldiers, walking the abandoned camps, found a prize, three precious cigars, rolled up inside a piece of paper. They may have considered the cigars more valuable than the paper, but had the good sense to turn it over to an officer, who quickly took it to McClellan's headquarters. It was a copy of Special Order 191. So now there were no more ghosts, no great, unseen obstacles to McClellan's mission. He knew Lee's plan, his troop strengths, and their positions: that his army had been divided, Jackson to Harper's Ferry, and Longstreet moving north into Maryland.

Now they were marching in a great blue line, and Chamberlain rode the grand horse, crested the small rolling mounds, could see the vast army in a long curving line in front of him, the dark blue snake spotted by patches of white and brown, clusters of wagons and cannon. Behind him he saw more, much more of the same, his own troops, and behind them, a long cloud of thick dust, the rest of the great army.

They marched through farmlands, fields of corn, some just picked. The farmers, anticipating the destruction from a hundred thousand marching troops, had made a frantic effort to save what they could, because they did not believe the army's assurances.

Maryland was a neutral state, and though most were against the cause of the rebels, they did not welcome the blue-coated troops as their own. They did not want this war fought on their lands. But if they protested and anguished over the presence of the great blue masses, they regarded the move northward by Lee's rebel army as even worse, a hostile invasion, a violation. The warm welcome from the liberated people of the state that Lee had so expected was nowhere in evidence. And so both armies were now on neutral ground.

McClellan was moving with unusual speed, to avoid panic in the North, a speed that Lee did not anticipate, and when the armies began to find each other, Lee spread his greatly outnumbered troops along a small tributary of the Potomac, Antietam Creek, and waited for the assault McClellan was pushing toward him.

In Maryland, September is still summer, and there had been no break from the heat. Chamberlain rode in a thick daze, his body moving with a slow rhythm with the steps of his horse. There was no breeze, and he felt as if there was no air at all, just a thin mist of dry dust. He could see down to the surface of the road, saw the moving feet of the men in front of him, saw little puffs kick up from each foot, the tiny clouds rising slowly, coming together into one continuous line of hot, dry, choking dirt. Most of the cloud did not quite reach him, as it did the men on the ground, he was just high enough to escape most of it, but he knew the men behind him were breathing nothing but, and he felt guilty, avoided looking down at the hoofprints of his own horse, knew he was helping to choke his own men.

He looked out across a cornfield, wondered, Why don't we just . . . move over there, no dust? But he knew there was a reason, some reason, and thought, Of course, fences, and ditches, and we do not march for the convenience of the men.

Ames rode beside him, had said nothing for a long hour or more. Chamberlain wanted to look at him, wondered if Ames was sweating as much as he was, but thought, No, keep it to the front. So he drifted off again, now began to think of Maine, knew it was a bad idea, could not help it. September . . . the cool streams, the cool shade, his mother's cool apple cider . . . He sat up straight. Stop that!

Behind him the heat was pressing his men down hard, and men were falling out on the side of the road, lagging behind. This was their first real march, and if they were sturdy and fit and strong, they were not ready for this heat. The officers behind had tried to keep them in line, and there were shouts and cursing, but it had stopped now. The veterans knew this was the way it went, and tonight most would catch up and find their camps. By tomorrow they would begin it all again. They would be lighter as well—all day Chamberlain had stared at a continuous stream of discarded equipment lining the edge of the road, backpacks and blankets, small cloth sacks, boxes and pouches. Some of it was personal, the treasured memories of home, but most was army issue. New soldiers did not yet understand . . . they would issue you as much as you could carry, and the more you marched, the less you would carry, for even the precious gifts and memories lost meaning in the heat.

Chamberlain could see wider, fatter hills now, deep green mounds, and they began to climb, a slight incline. Down the road, coming toward him, was a line of men, walking slowly, with heads down, kicking through the dust, and he saw: prisoners.

The men were mostly barefoot, torn and ragged clothes hung loosely from thin bodies. There were pieces of an identifiable uniform. He saw one man who seemed to be an officer, and the man looked up at him as they passed by, glanced at the fine fat horse, and Chamberlain wanted to stop, talk to the man, but they were gone. Then there were more, thirty, forty, and they did not look up, moved steadily, their guards walking alongside with long bayonets they did not need. Chamberlain wondered, Are they still at war? Am I the enemy, even now? Their war is over . . . maybe. Or maybe it will never be over.

In front of him the line of troops began to climb the larger hill. He could see the blue moving up, toward a small pass, a slight break between two taller mounds. Please, he thought, let us reach those hills, let us stop up there, it would be cooler, it has to be. The sun hung just above a long line of low mountains that stretched far away, to the left. His mind drifted again. He began to focus on the sun now, talking to it: go on, move . . . down . . . He closed his eyes, willing it lower.

The climb became steeper. He had to lean forward now, and Ames suddenly pointed, stuck an arm out in front of him. Chamberlain focused, saw a tree split and shredded into a great pile of white splinters, and now there were more, and the smell of fresh earth, scattered sprays of dirt, small holes, then larger ones, and now beside the road there were broken and crushed wagons, pushed aside by the lead troops, pieces of lumber and metal, and some twisted forms that Chamberlain eyed with fascination.

Ames said, "A good fight here yesterday . . . Turner's Gap, they held us up for a while. Gibbon's 'Black Hats' pushed them back."

Chamberlain saw more evidence of the fight now, a small farm, the house burned, a thin line of black smoke still rising, drifting away finally, high above. Beyond, there was a shattered barn, torn into pieces, great rips in the thin walls. He saw men out in a field, working . . . a burial detail, a long line of fresh, open dirt, and he looked for the bodies, the dead, saw some blue and white and brown . . . things—they were too far away to see clearly. Now they were inside the gap, cresting the wide mountain, high hills rising on both sides of them.

He had seen a tornado once, just for a few brief moments, a hard storm of wind and rain, and a thick black funnel dropping down like some great evil claw. It had touched down only for a minute, had torn through the fields near his family's farm. He had stayed out in the fields, watched it through stinging bites of cold rain, until it lifted again, pulled back up into the blackness. He never forgot that, had followed with pure amazement the clean path it had cut, the total destruction weaving through the fields and woods and then suddenly stopping. Now, here, he saw it again, the total obliteration of trees and bushes and wagons and cannon, torn and ragged pieces of raw death alongside the untouched, the perfect.

It was cooler now. The sun had dropped behind the big hill, and he turned around in the saddle, looked back down the line of men, saw fewer than he had expected. The line seemed stretched out, pulled from the rear, and the faces of the men were down, the steps heavy and automatic. Soon, he thought, just a bit more.

They were moving downhill now, and he saw the sun again, the last piece of orange over far hills, and then there was a bugle, from far up ahead, and the lines in front of him began to slow. He pulled his horse up, saw a flood of blue spreading in both directions away from the road, filling small open spaces under great wide trees. The bugles became louder now, came down the line, closer, and the sound filled him with a vast joy, soothing notes. His own men had stopped, began to bunch up again. Ames said something to the color bearers, and a bugle rose up, blew loud and clear, the call to fall out, stack arms. They were done for the day.

SEPTEMBER 17, 1862

T HE BUGLES BEGAN EARLY, BEFORE DAWN. HE ROLLED OFF THE cot, stared ahead into black nothing, tried to focus his brain. Ames was already gone, up before the bugle, and Chamberlain could make out the empty cot, thought, Is that what it takes to be a commander? He reached for his uniform, laid carefully at the end of his own cot, struggled with the brass buttons, his clumsy fingers not yet awake. He tried to stretch, reached his arms out wide, could not raise them up, so he moved out of the tent, and heard the sounds of men moving, the slow hum of the army coming alive.

"A good mornin' to ye, Colonel."

"Huh?" He tried to see the face, a short man, thick, built like a bull, and the man held out a tin cup, steaming hot.

"Colonel Ames sent me to get you, Colonel. Says you might be needin' a touch of the elixir."

Chamberlain stared at the man, heard the accent, the hint of the Irish.

"Thank you . . . uh . . ."

"Kilrain, sir. Sergeant Kilrain. Glad to be of service, sir. The boys—we been a-watchin' you with some interest, that we have. You come a long way. Becomin' a pleasure to serve under you."

Chamberlain took the hot cup, drank a painful gulp, could see the face now, faintly in the first light, broad, round, familiar, maybe. There were so many.

"Thank you, Sergeant. Do I know you? You say you've been watching me?"

"Aye, Colonel. We ain't properly met, but bein' you're the second in command and all, and not long of this army, we have been takin' an interest, don't you see? Fact is, Colonel, when we go into line against those rebels up there, we need to know who's up front. We was a bit leery of you, some of us older gents. I been tellin' em you'll be turnin' out all right."

"You a veteran, Sergeant?" He realized from the gravelly voice, the heavy face, Kilrain was older, maybe near the limit, forty-five.

"Aye, Colonel, I suppose you could say that. Did me duty in the regular army for a while—made the great long walk with General Scott, down South. Not very many of us back then, and we did a mighty fine job, if I do say. A great many more of us now, and we're not doin' such good work."

Chamberlain could see now, across the sea of tents and men and wagons, and he felt clearer, not sure if it was the dawn or the coffee. He wanted to ask this sturdy little man some questions, felt something . . . some curiosity, as though this man had something he could use, some knowledge.

"It's a pleasure to meet you, Sergeant. Perhaps we can talk later." Chamberlain held out a hand, an old instinct.

Kilrain saluted, said, "Best be gettin' back, Colonel. We be movin' shortly. There's a mess of rebs up there, just a ways. Enjoy your coffee, Colonel."

Chamberlain watched him leave, then turned and began to look for Ames, thought, Maybe I should tell him what Kilrain said, about the rebs . . . the Confederate Army. But Ames would know, of course, and Chamberlain was still feeling slightly left out of things, too high above the flow of rumors and gossip of the men, too far below the official reports. But if Kilrain were right . . . it could be their first fight.

He tossed the last bit of coffee out of the cup, began to walk. Off to the west, down the hard, dry road they would march again, came a rumble, a brief burst of distant thunder, and he thought of rain, an early morning storm, but the men around him stopped moving and the faces turned, and he knew that it was not thunder, it was guns, the big long-range cannon. The sounds came again, more this time, some closer, the answering rounds, and the men began to move again, quicker now. He saw Ames talking to the company commanders, and he cursed quietly, trotted over, embarrassed for not being there sooner.

". . . and we will remain near this road . . . staying in reserve of the rest of the corps until needed. Tell your men . . . be ready, stay in formation." Ames turned, saw Chamberlain, said, "Good morning, Colonel."

"Sir, I'm sorry, I woke with the bugle—"

"If I had needed you, Colonel, I would have awakened you. I have just informed the officers that we have been instructed to remain in place, in our position in line of march. The army is spreading out in front of us, a couple miles up. The enemy is dug in behind a small creek, Antietam Creek, just this side of Sharpsburg. We may be put into the attack at any time. For now, get the men to step it up, finish their breakfasts, then wait for the orders to move. Got that?"

"Certainly, Colonel." He paused, listened again. The rumbling had stopped. "Colonel, whose guns are those? Is the attack begun?"

"Likely it's the first feeling out, probing, testing the strength. It's like a game to the artillery boys, letting you know they can hit you when the time comes. Let's grab some breakfast, Colonel."

Ames moved away, and Chamberlain followed, toward the wagons and the plates of food. The fare was much simpler now, hardtack, the thin bread with the consistency and flavor of old bricks, and bacon, nearly raw. He caught the smell: a steaming pot of thick coffee. He felt his stomach turn slightly, did not feel hungry, but he saw Ames putting hardtack in his pocket, thought, If today is the day . . . there might not be a mess wagon later. He grabbed a handful of thick, greasy bacon, stuffed it in his mouth, then the hardtack, and he followed Ames's lead, put a few pieces in his pocket, kept one out to eat now. He held out the tin cup Kilrain had given him, the mess orderly filled it, and suddenly there was a bugle, their own, and the men began to flow away from the tents and the wagons, and his stomach turned again. He looked at the coffee, tossed it out, and ran toward the front of the gathering troops.

T HEY REACHED A SMALL VILLAGE, PORTERSTOWN, AND MARCHED through wide streets, the townspeople standing in doorways, leaning out windows, some waving, others just staring. Farther ahead, on the creek itself, was the Middle Bridge, held by the Confederate division of Daniel Harvey Hill. The rebel forces were dug in, back, away from the creek, and to their front the Federal Army was spreading out, into lines of attack, were crossing the creek and preparing for the assault. The battle had begun on the far right, just after dawn, and now, as the sun began to rise up behind them, Chamberlain could hear the steady rumble, and as they moved closer, the sharp sounds of single cannon. He sat high on his horse, moving along with the same slow rhythm of the march, but now the men did not fall out, did not feel the weight of the hot September morning, but stared to the front, marching steadily, closer to the sound of the guns.

He heard the steady clatter of muskets now, still off to the right of the road, to the northwest. The battle is not in front of us, he thought. Strange that we should move this way . . . not up there.

In front of them Chamberlain saw a rise, a long, wide hill, and as they began to move up, he saw guns, rows of black cannon set into shallow, round depressions before the crest of the hill. Just then they began to fire, quick bursts of gray smoke, and a sudden shocking boom that startled him and his horse. He bounced around on the road, had to grab the horse hard to calm him. From over the hill he saw Ames, riding hard, past lines of troops that were moving away now, to the right, toward the sounds of the battle.

Ames reined up his horse, and Chamberlain saw he was sweating. "Colonel, we're here, right here. Keep the men in column lines. Let's move them out into this field. Wait for further orders. We are part of the reserve."

Chamberlain turned, and Ames rode past him, into the columns of men, and gave the command to the bugler. With the signal, the men moved quickly off the road. Then Ames rode up again, toward the front of the column, slowed his horse as he reached Chamberlain, said, "Colonel, keep them tight, keep them ready. I am to survey the field to our front."

Chamberlain watched him ride away, up the long hill, turning his horse to the side behind the rows of black cannon. The guns began to fire again, a loud and thunderous volley, and the hill became a great, thick fog bank.

He stayed on his horse, saw now across the road, on the left, vast numbers of troops, lines disappearing into a distant grove of trees, and the men not moving, keeping their formations. He rode out the other way, to the right, into the grass, saw more troops farther out that way, a great field of blue, waiting. He looked to his own men, saw the companies staying in their formations, coming off the road, and he rode up to the head of one column, saw Captain Spears of Company G, a small, sharp man who had also been a teacher. He had a narrow, thick beard, sat on a horse, watched Chamberlain approach, puffed on a large round pipe.

"Well, Colonel, do you think we will get our chance?"

Chamberlain looked back to the crest of the hill, could still not see through the smoke, and another volley thundered out, shaking the ground, startling his horse again.

"Whoa, easy . . . We'll see, Captain. Right now we must be ready . . . be ready to move forward on command!" He felt a little foolish, a vague order, felt again as if he were left out, didn't know what was happening. The battle sounds had continued to the northwest, and he wondered, Are they moving away, around us? He glanced at Spears, said, "I'll be right back . . . just going up the crest a ways, take a look maybe."

"We're right here, Colonel."

He turned the horse, then decided to dismount instead. This wasn't a parade. He jumped down, felt his belt, his pistol, began to walk toward the thick cloud of smoke.

The guns continued to fire, every minute or so, and he wondered, How far away is the enemy? There had been no explosions, no incoming shells, none of the sounds he'd been told about, coached about, by Ames, just the deadening thunder of their own big guns.

The smoke began to envelop him, and he kept moving. Suddenly he could not breathe, felt suffocated by the thick smell of burnt powder. He stopped, coughing hard, tried to see, caught a glimpse of one gun, saw men moving around it like ghosts, and then, abruptly, they all moved away and the gun fired, jerking backward with the recoil. He felt his ears deaden, shattered by the sound of the blast. He went farther, was moving up between the guns now, and suddenly the smoke cleared in front of him, a light breeze sweeping up the far side of the rise, blowing the smoke away to the rear. Down below he saw the wide, flat plain, farms and roads and trees, cornfields and small distant buildings. And to the right, far across the curving lines of the creek, there was more smoke, great, flat clouds of white and gray. The sounds of the battle were steady and loud now, and on either side of him the big guns boomed again, the shock knocking him off his feet.

He lay on soft grass, thought, I'm hit ... then, No, but I'm damned near deaf. He raised his head, could still see down, the fields and woods. Now, from the sounds of the battle, he saw his first troops, thick lines of blue, uneven and ragged formations, moving toward a cornfield, and then smoke, solid lines of gray, and in a few seconds the sound reached him, the chattering musket fire, and the blue lines were in pieces, men moving back, some still advancing, some not moving at all. He saw more lines now, solid blocks of blue spreading wide, advancing, and more smoke, and more sounds, and then, farther away, a glimpse through the smoke, other lines of men, some moving, some firing, quick flashes of white and yellow, and the big guns beside him firing again.

He saw down to the left the arch of a stone bridge, crossing the creek to the south. Down in front of him, where the creek swung closer to the base of the hill, he could see the Middle Bridge, saw troops moving across, a steady advance, and then he saw the rebels on the far side, moving into position, and he understood: the attack is moving, shifting this way, we will begin now, *here*. He turned to watch the men working the cannon, and was startled to see more men, his men, watching the battle, lying on the ground, creating a neat blue patch on the hill. He had not thought anyone else would be up here, should not have been up here; *he* should not be up here, but he knew they could not just wait, could not sit behind some big hill and hear it all and not see.

Chamberlain stood up, began to wave his arms, fast and high, motioning to the men, and another blast came from the guns. He braced himself, did not fall, kept waving, back, move back, wondered if they saw him or were ignoring him. He moved along the hillside, tried to yell, but the sound of the guns took his voice away, and suddenly he heard a high, distant scream, louder now, whistling toward him, dropping down on him from behind. He turned, saw nothing, but the sound pierced his ears, and the ground suddenly flew high around him, dirt spraying him, knocking him down, and he lay still, shook his head ... checked, all right, but ... a bad day for the ears. Then another scream, overhead, and behind the hill, down where the rest of his men sat waiting, there was another explosion, and he tried to see, but it was beyond the crest.

Suddenly, someone had him under the arms, lifting him, and he said, "No, I'm all right," and he saw the face of an officer, a man with black crust under his eyes, around his mouth and nose, glaring at him with eyes of cold steel.

"You are bloody well not all right, you damned fool! Get these men back off this hill. You're drawing fire to my guns!"

Chamberlain saw the uniform, a captain, realized suddenly he had done a supremely stupid thing, and the man turned away, was gone through a new cloud of smoke.

Chamberlain crouched down, ran along the hill, yelling at the men, "*Back, get back*, we're giving the enemy a target!"

They were watching him, understood, and moved fast and low, back over the hill and away from the guns.

He slowed as he came down out of the smoke, saw his men moving back in their lines, where most of the others, the ones who did not have to see, were down on the ground, resting. He saw the still smoking earth, the round fresh hole from the enemy shell, and he thanked God it had not gone farther, had not gone into the rows of men.

Captain Spear was standing, talking to another officer, and they looked at him, questioned silently, saw the dirt, the black grime that covered him, and he said, "The battle may be moving our way. Keep them ready!"

They nodded, looked at him without expression, and he wondered if they knew what he had done, that he had stood up high on a hill, out in front of his own carefully placed cannon, and waved his arms like some idiotic fire-breathing evangelist.

He moved away, felt thirsty, looked for his horse, his canteen, and saw a sergeant, the short and sturdy Irishman, Kilrain, standing, leaning on the barrel of his musket.

"Well, now, Colonel, did you get a fine look at what we're facin'?"

Chamberlain wiped at the dirt on his face, said, "Quite a sight . . . right over that hill, it's a few hundred yards, all of it."

"Impressive, ain't it, Colonel? Watchin' them line up and walk right into the fire."

"Yes . . . impressive." He stared back up the hill, the big guns quiet now, the smoke clearing, and he could see them again, lining the crest of the hill. The cannon are hidden, of course, he realized, hard to get the range on them that way. I will damned well remember *that*.

"The word is, Colonel . . ." Kilrain said, and Chamberlain turned, looked into the heavy face. "The word is, we'll be sittin' here all day. The boys reckon we been left behind. I been tellin' em, don't be in such a damned hurry . . . the time will come."

"I'm not sure. It looks like the battle might swing back this way. We had better be ready." He had said it again, felt foolish again. Telling them to be ready won't make them ready.

Kilrain looked up toward the hill, said, "It's already in front of us, Colonel, there."

Chamberlain listened, realized the noises to the right had faded, replaced now by a wave of new sounds, over the hill and out in front of where he had been. And now the cannon fired again and did not pause, and the smoke began to flow down the hill toward them and above them, darkening the sky. He heard the scream again, the whine of the incoming shell, and up on the hill the shell burst, a new thunder, and he felt the ground shake under his feet. More shells came high overhead, and behind him the men began to move nervously, some standing, some crouching, and the officers were shouting, keeping them in line—there was no other place to go.

The sounds were much closer now. He stared at the hill, wondered if this would be the place, if suddenly the rebels would pour over the hill, rush past the cannon and down. Easy, he thought . . . there's a whole army out there . . . we're in back, behind them all.

The cannon kept up the waves of firing, and the enemy's shells continued falling around them, but only a few, and not aimed at them . . . just chance . . . the shells that were missing their targets. He sat down now, and the men who had stood, expecting . . . something, sat as well, and there was nothing to do but wait.

It was now past noon, and out on the road men and wagons were moving back, away from the fight. The troops stared at the long procession, the solid line of wounded, heard the sounds, the wails and screams, and some would not look, turned their faces away, and others stared hard. Chamberlain had stood at first, a show of respect, but this too was not a parade, and he sat again and listened to the battle work its way along the creek far out in front of them. Now there was fire down to the left, toward the stone bridge, and it seemed to grow more quiet in front of him, and he had the strange feeling that the battle had been like some great, horrible wheel, rolling slowly from right to left, right in front of them, right past them.

It is not coming after all, he thought. This is what the reserves do, they sit back behind it all and hear the sounds, and wait for an attack that does not come. He realized then that he felt disappointment. He looked down along the lines, saw the faces that had been watching the hill, that like him had been expecting something and who now began to look elsewhere. There were a few fires, coffee being made, more laughing.

Well, then, it must be going well, he thought. They don't need us. He began to move toward the new smells, was suddenly very hungry. He brushed dirt from his pants, stepped around a small crater, then another. The men were letting go now, the tension releasing, and there was more laughter, a big sergeant teasing a small man with glasses.

Chamberlain did not feel like laughing, felt something dead, hollow in his gut. The hunger had become something else, more painful now. He stopped at a fence post, cupped his hand over the top, suddenly pulled hard on the post, pulled it down, the base uprooting from the soft dirt. He stood back, looked around, felt embarrassed, but more, he felt angry, denied. He turned toward the hill, looked up to the guns, silent now, the fight drifting, too far away.

24. HANCOCK

THE BATTLE HAD MOVED AWAY, OFF TO THE LEFT. HE HAD BEEN up front, in the center of the entire Federal line, for only an hour or so, and he expected a fight, a good fight. He could still see the gray lines spread out on the far side of the field, but they did not come.

He did not know Israel Richardson, knew only that the man was down, presumed dead by now, a terrible wound. It had happened just after noon, when the fighting was heaviest in front of where Hancock now stood. Richardson was the commander of the First Division, Second Corps, and McClellan had come immediately to Hancock, had brought the promotion as if asking a question, in that respectful way he spoke to those whom he trusted. Hancock had accepted with a thin veil over his eagerness. He did not forget that the position was vacant because a man had just been killed. His own brigade had not been engaged, had been placed by Baldy Smith around the division's batteries, who had tried to lend support to the first attack on the far right. Hancock had time for brief good-byes, had taken his staff with him, and now was in command of his own division, right in the middle of it all.

He had ridden his horse quickly to the front lines, had met the brigadiers in a hasty greeting, had passed along a message from McClellan, an embarrassing note that Hancock read flatly and without comment: "We will push them into the river, before the sun sets." But in front of him, across the narrow field, no one was running, and he had already sent a courier back, asking for instructions, had expected the word to come down the line, push ahead, advance. The Confederate lines were badly bruised, had withstood an assault by overwhelming numbers all morning, but the attacks were never coordinated, were fought piecemeal, and it was clear that Lee had been able to shuffle his units back and forth, meeting the greatest point of attack.

Now, the only serious fight was down to the left. He looked that way, heard big guns and muskets, thought, It has to be Burnside, trying to cross that damned bridge. He could not see it from where he stood, but he knew the location, knew Burnside's orders, and could only listen as one more small piece of McClellan's massive army was sent against Lee's thin lines.

He climbed back up on his horse, could see more clearly the lines across from him, and a musket ball whizzed by, above his head, then another, and he thought, Best not sit in one spot. Spurring the horse, he rode back over a small rise and dropped out of sight of the Confederate lines.

He dismounted, his small staff following him, and saw an officer, trailing aides, one holding aloft a bright green brigade flag. It was General Meagher, Thomas Meagher, of the Irish Brigade.

"General Hancock, sir, are we to be movin' forward now? The men . . . they're waitin for a fight."

Hancock stared behind, back toward headquarters, saw no one coming, no courier. "General Meagher, I have no orders to advance. The last word I received from General McClellan himself was that we were to hold this position against an assault by the enemy. General, have you seen any signs that the enemy is preparing to assault?"

"Not hardly, General. There's a pretty thin line out there in front of my men. Unless Bobby Lee's got a herd of ghosts backin' them up . . . I believe we have a good chance of bustin' right through."

Hancock looked again at the empty ground behind him, removed his hat, rubbed a hand across his head, felt a throb, the birth of a headache, the back of his neck tightening, squeezing up and over the top of his skull. He said aloud toward the empty field, "Dammit!"

Meagher watched him, understood, said, "General, I'll be gettin' back to my men. I will wait for word, General. We'll be sittin' tight."

Meagher spurred his horse and rode off, leading his aides, and Hancock watched him leave, saw the green flag in a quick flutter as it dropped away over the rise. He began to feel truly angry, once more the frustration of the commander who has the men, the strong position, and must wait while someone else sits in a fog. He turned, looked at the faces of his staff, saw Lieutenant Hughes, knew he was the best horseman, would move quickly.

"Lieutenant, go to General Sumner's headquarters. Maybe they decided to attack and forgot to tell us."

Hughes moved his horse closer. "Sir, might I word that differently? General Sumner is—"

"Lieutenant, please pay our *respects* to General Sumner, or General McClellan, or whoever else might be in charge of this damned army, and request some instructions. Tell them that we can hear General Burnside's activity on our left and are wondering if we should go to his aid. Please inform them that the lines in front of us can be pressed without much difficulty, if we are so ordered. You more comfortable with that, Lieutenant?"

"Yes, sir." Hughes jerked the horse, moved away over the open field, and Hancock pulled his horse the other way, eased up the rise until he could see the Confederate lines again. There was no movement.

M CCLELLAN'S ORDERS WERE REPEATED: "HOLD POSITION, AND prepare to receive an assault." Burnside's forces finally broke through and crossed Antietam Creek late in the afternoon, only to have their strong advance routed by the sudden arrival of the troops of A. P. Hill, the last of Jackson's forces to rejoin the army after the capture of Harper's Ferry.

Sumner, who commanded the Second Corps, had seen his divisions punished at the center of the Confederate position, at a place known as the Bloody Lane, but he had managed to push through, until Lee's more mobile units strengthened the position. Now, neither side had moved the other from the field, and the aging commander convinced himself that this amounted to a success. McClellan seemed to accept that logic, absorbed it himself, and so once Burnside was halted and the daylight began to fade, McClellan's preference was to wait and see if perhaps Lee would give them a better opportunity tomorrow.

25. CHAMBERLAIN

THE SUN WAS DROPPING TOWARD THE CREST OF THE HILL WHEN Ames rode up and dismounted.

Chamberlain stood, and Ames said, "We won't be needed today, Colonel."

Chamberlain looked at him, waited for more, and Ames turned, stared up the hill to the guns. Other officers began to gather, and Ames turned back to them, said, "The Fifth Corps was not needed today, gentlemen, not in the judgment of the commanding general. The battle has been extremely costly. The enemy has been pushed back, at great loss to both sides, and from what we can observe so far, we have gained little. It is possible that tomorrow the fight will resume." Ames stopped, looked slowly at the officers.

"I have been ordered to announce to you that the commanding general feels that this battle has been a great victory. Certainly I would not presume to dispute or contradict the words of General McClellan. I would only caution you to prepare your men for tomorrow, for what may yet follow." He moved away, began to walk out into the field, looking over the sight.

The company commanders spread out to their men, and the order was given to stack arms and make camp. Chamberlain watched the men unload the wagons, watched the camp form, the tents and new fires. Beyond the hill there were still faint sounds of the battle, scattered firing, and he had to see, to walk back up. He stepped through the thick grass, up toward the positions of the guns, and saw now they were being moved, their crews hitching them to the caissons and the horses pulling them away from their shallow pits. He looked for the captain, the man who had ordered him off the hill, to apologize, to tell him it was his mistake, but he could not see the faces. The teams were beginning to move away, toward the road and down closer to the battle.

Chamberlain reached the top of the hill, looked down again across the quiet fields and saw great masses of men, long battle lines, and small groups in formation, appearing just as they had that morning. Now the light was fading, and he watched, waiting for something to happen, expecting movement, some noise. The men did not move, however, and he felt a sudden wave of horror, realizing he was looking at long lines and vast fields of dead soldiers, the unspeakable conclusion, the bloody aftermath. He forced himself to look, felt a hot sickness rising in his gut, scanned the wide fields from the far right, where the sounds had first come, down toward the stone bridge, where it had ended. Every field, every open space, was dotted with clusters of the dead, every fence draped with dark shapes, every road a solid black line. He saw the cornfields, flattened and spotted with the dark shapes, and then he saw movement, the few men who wandered among them, and he felt sick again, thankful he was not down there, one of them. He wondered what they were doing, what they were thinking, what they were looking for. He stood for a long while, felt the breeze against his face, could still smell the smoke and powder, but not the dead. Not yet, he thought. The sun had dropped below the horizon, a distant line of trees, far behind the army in ragged gray uniforms that was still out there, was still facing them. Now the fields began to darken, the ghastly sight began to fade from his view, and he thought, They did not need us today . . . but the enemy is still out there, and there is still a war. . . . Could we not have helped?

THE FOLLOWING DAY THE TWO ARMIES FACED EACH OTHER without moving, like two fighters who have beaten each other senseless and don't know what else to do. McClellan outnumbered Lee's forces by better than two to one, had been given the best opportunity he would have to end the war, but he waited, again pleading with Washington for more reinforcements.

Lee realized his invasion to the north was no longer feasible, that even though his army had fought to a bloody draw, his smaller forces could not win that kind of war. And so, after bracing for a new attack from McClellan's army, an attack that never came, he waited until dark, and during the night of September 18 withdrew his badly bruised army back across the Potomac, into Virginia.

26. HANCOCK

"SIR, THEY'RE GONE."
It was just light enough to see, a cool morning. Hancock had reached the front lines, had ridden through a fine foggy mist until he saw the green flag.

"They're gone, General," Meagher said again. "The lines are empty."

Hancock did not stop, rode his horse past the shallow trenches, up over the low mound of earth that had protected his men, rode into the open field between the lines. Meagher rode out with him, and they guided their horses carefully, avoiding the scattered black masses, the bodies of the dead. Behind them the officers began to shout and men climbed up from the trenches, began to move out with the commanders, some running farther, to the advance, screening the generals. But there was nothing to screen against. They reached the Confederate lines, saw down long rows of shallow ditches, saw bodies piled out in front of and behind the lines; and in the trenches themselves, broken muskets, pieces of clothing and equipment, and nothing else.

Hancock stared at the empty ground, said aloud, "We let them get away."

"Aye, General, that we did."

Meagher moved his horse closer, and the two men sat quietly for a long minute. Finally, Meagher said, "We lost many a good man. Did ya know General Richardson, sir?"

"No, I'm sorry, I didn't. I heard he was a fine commander."

"Maybe . . . A general that gets himself killed isn't much good to anybody. We had a good fight of it, though, maybe better than some, maybe worse. I will say, beggin' your pardon, General, we was all pleased when we heard you was takin' over."

Hancock nodded, said nothing. He knew the reputation of the Irishmen, knew they had indeed given the good fight. And they will again, he thought, if someone will give them the chance.

Meagher looked at Hancock for a long moment, said, "You know General McClellan, do ya, sir?"

"Yes, I know him. He's a good friend, opened a mighty big door for me. More than once."

"Aye. Do ya think we can win this war, General?"

Hancock looked at the heavy, round face and the sharp, honest eyes that hid nothing. "You mean, do I think General McClellan can win this war?"

"Is it not the same question, General? This army wants Mac to lead it, they've shown that. And who else can we follow?"

Hancock looked away, did not want to think about it, had felt this way before, the sense that no one was really in command.

"Forgive me for speakin' freely, General. If you'd rather I'd button it—"

"No, General Meagher, your concerns ... are good ones. We have all been taught how to follow orders. I just wish someone was back there who understood *opportunity*. I have been in this position before, General. I watch this army fight and maneuver itself into great advantage, and then we just stop, as though someone, somewhere, does not truly believe we can finish this. I am loyal to General McClellan because he is our commander. I have always believed he knows what is best for this army, what is best for his troops. That's why the men love him ... he is *their* general. And that may be his problem. He may love them too much."

"I don't know about much of what goes on back there, sir, under those big tents. But my men, General, these tough old micks ... they been watchin' each other get shot up for over a year now, and it seems that nothin' ever comes from it. General, forgive me for sayin' it, but these soldiers ... they would have won this war by now if it weren't for the generals, maybe me included."

Hancock laughed quietly, but the humor passed quickly. "I expect Mr. Lincoln might agree with you."

LEE RETURNED TO CENTRAL VIRGINIA, MOVED HIS FORCES INTO the fertile comfort of the Shenandoah Valley. McClellan remained around Sharpsburg and Antietam Creek for over a month before the prodding from Washington had an effect. Lincoln himself had come to McClellan's camp, pushing him to make some pursuit of Lee's bloodied army, and so by the end of October, McClellan finally started the chase. While Lee's escaping army had crossed the Potomac in one night, McClellan took eight days. And now, while he marched slowly and carefully down the Blue Ridge, Lee had time to move east, placing Longstreet between the Federal Army and Richmond, so that McClellan would again stall, and begin the persistent calls to Washington for more troops.

NOVEMBER 1862

"WELL, GENTLEMEN, I FEEL WE HAVE LITTLE TO FEAR OF old Robert Lee now! Look, outside!"

Hancock turned, with the others, saw what McClellan was pointing to: snow. It had turned colder all day, and the army camp had begun the first preparations for winter quarters. The troops had started digging the small square pits over which they would build whatever form of shelter they could find. There were mixed feelings about the winter break. Some of the men welcomed the rest, the opportunity to write letters, play cards, nurse sore feet or small wounds. Others despised the waiting, the weeks of inactivity, and, if the weather was bad, the necessity of staying cramped together inside these small, makeshift shelters.

Hancock watched the new snow, thought, We have waited for over a month, and now here is the first honest excuse. Behind him the large, single room was glowing from the warmth of a large fire. One end of the simple house was a huge stone hearth, framing an enormous firebox. As the fire grew, the men had begun moving away, toward the other end of the long room. They were all familiar to Hancock, mostly generals, brigade and division commanders of the Second Corps, who were camped near McClellan's headquarters. Most had come through the recent campaigns weighed down with a sense of self-defeat, and privately, each man believed he had done the best that could be done, as though it was no one's fault. Excuses filled every conversation: the weather, the ground, the government, some mysterious power that seemed to be with Lee. No one talked now of the end of the war, there were no longer any grand predictions, no more fat boasting to the newspaper reporters. The sense of gloom was affecting the troops as well, spreading out through the entire army. But tonight, here, the mood was oddly buoyant. Men were laughing and talking, and McClellan himself sat on an old wooden chair, behind a crude table, smoking a cigar, the center of attention. A bottle of brandy had made its way around the room, was emptied, and another had appeared, began the same route.

Hancock knew the faces, men mostly around his age, many with long careers, and now some tough experience, and he did not feel attached, did not share the pleasant air of camaraderie, still stared out the window watching fat snowflakes and wondered, Why are they laughing?

He looked back into the room, through a haze of cigar smoke and blue coats, saw one man watching him. General Couch had been placed in command of the Second Corps after the apparent failure of Bull Sumner to again appreciate the value of initiative. While everyone bore some share of the failures at Antietam, Sumner had controlled the entire center of the line, and by keeping up the pressure, could have split Lee's army in half. When the time had come, he simply quit, and the talk began quietly that he had run out of nerve. Even McClellan had understood that Sumner had only one advantage that gave him seniority in the army, and that was his age. He was simply the good old soldier, the career man who had spent his long life rising gradually through the ranks. At the start of the war neither Winfield Scott nor the War Department had any reason to assume that Sumner was not qualified to lead large numbers of troops into battle. It finally fell on McClellan to pull him off the line.

Darius Couch was slightly younger than Hancock, a small man of light build. He had come out of West Point in 1846 with the same class that produced McClellan and Jackson. He left the army after Mexico, but returned to serve with his friend McClellan, and had shown a fiery competence for leading troops.

Hancock returned his look, saw Couch glance toward the door, a silent signal, and Hancock moved that way, followed Couch outside into the blowing snow. They walked out a way from the house, toward the camps of the troops, and Couch stopped, reached a hand out, his palm catching the snow.

"Winter."

Hancock nodded in the dark.

Couch said, "Nothing will happen now. We have wasted the last good month of the year. Have you spent much time in Virginia, General?"

Hancock looked out through the snow, toward a large field, a wide sea of small fires and huddled men.

"No, sir."

"A miserable place to move an army. The roads . . . after a snow like this, it will probably warm up, melt it all, and the roads will turn to deep mud. Doesn't get cold enough to freeze solid, so the cycle repeats. We'll probably sit right here for months, until someone persuades our commanding general to get started again . . . if he is still our commanding general."

"Yes, sir." Hancock held himself back, did not know Couch well, but there was something in the man, something quiet and dark and dangerous, something he had begun to see in a few of the others, had seen it now in himself, that nameless *thing*: Men who advanced with their troops and did not hear the muskets and stepped over their dead without looking down. He also sensed that Couch did not fit into that great warm celebration behind them, powerful men who drank too much brandy and toasted each other's empty successes. Couch pulled at his coat, wrapped his arms around his thin frame.

"I know how much Mac appreciates your work, General. I know he appreciates mine. He's a good friend, and once he's in your corner, he'll go all the way to Hell to back you up. There're a lot of people in this army who have never even met him, and they feel the same way, that he's their friend too." He paused. "I wish he was a better fighter."

Hancock could not see his face, knew the words were difficult, that since their days at the Point, Couch and McClellan had always been close.

Hancock felt the cold now as well. Snow was blowing into his collar. He said, "Well, excuse me, General, I believe I'll head back to my quarters."

Couch turned, held out a hand, said, "Good night, General," and Hancock took the hand, then started away.

There was a sound of horses on the road, between the house and the vast field, and Hancock saw four men. They rode up along the rail fence, reached the gate, where a guard halted them, then from a small shelter more guards appeared, and one horseman said, "Special courier, I have a message for General McClellan."

The guards gathered closer. One man lit a match, tried to see the man's papers, and Couch walked over, said, "Excuse me, gentlemen, I am General Couch, Second Corps commander, and this is General Hancock. You may give the message to us, we will take it to General McClellan."

The man who had spoken said, "Begging your pardon, General. I am General Buckingham, from Secretary Stanton's office. These men are my escort. I am to deliver this personally to the commanding general. If you will examine the seal . . ."

Couch stepped forward, took the papers, saw the heavy wax seal of the War Department, said, "General, please follow me. General McClellan is there, inside the house."

The men dismounted, and Buckingham stepped up beside Couch and waited.

Couch looked at Hancock, said, "Well, General, still off to bed?"

"No, I suppose not. Maybe one more look at the fire . . ."

The three men walked toward the cabin, and Hancock held open the door, moved into the big room behind the other two. The noise did not stop, no one paid attention. Couch and Hancock waited by the door, and Buckingham made his way to McClellan and announced himself quietly. McClellan looked up at the man, nodded without smiling, and Hancock saw Buckingham hand him the paper. McClellan pushed his thumb through the wax, unfolded the letter, read for a few seconds, then stood up.

"Gentlemen . . . please. May I have your attention? Quiet, please."

The talking wound down, faces turned, and McClellan said, "Is there any brandy left? This man is from the War Department. He has ridden hard through this weather and appears to need a drink."

A bottle moved from the far side of the room, was placed on the table in front of McClellan. He poured the last of the contents into his glass, handed it to Buckingham, and Hancock saw that the man's hands were shaking. He raised the glass slowly, said, "Thank you, General."

"Gentlemen, this man has braved this miserable night at the request of the Secretary of War. I could read the letter out loud, but it is simpler to just say that I have been relieved of command. Effective immediately, this army is under the command of . . ." He paused, and Hancock sensed it was dramatics, McClellan making the best of his last moment in the spotlight. ". . . Major General Ambrose Burnside."

There was a moment of stunned silence. The men began to look at each other, and Hancock dropped his head, stared at the floor, felt briefly sick, took a deep breath. Couch's hand was on his shoulders and he said, "We can only do our jobs, General."

TO THE TROOPS, BURNSIDE'S APPOINTMENT WAS NOT AS IMPORtant as McClellan's dismissal. Rumors began to fly immediately, angry men making big talk. The most radical story was that McClellan was to lead an armed force into Washington, unseating Lincoln. There was more widespread talk of a milder protest, men refusing to serve, resigning. The officers were more discreet. Most understood that angry talk was dangerous talk, and if rumors led to action, the effectiveness of the army could dissolve.

Hancock felt McClellan's dismissal as a blow, but understood that the affection he held for the commander did not mean that McClellan was the best man to lead the army, and so when the angry talk reached him, he was quick to put it down. He was, after all, a career soldier, and he had no doubts that his loyalty lay to the nation, not to any one man.

The troops considered Burnside just another in a line, a man who held a title, who inspired nothing else. To the commanders, Burnside's appointment was a serious mistake. Even Burnside himself had doubts, had been as surprised as the rest that his name had come down from Washington. He was thought of in the high ranks as a reasonably capable commander, a friendly, generous man with no particular talents. He had been as culpable as anyone else for the failures at Antietam.

Burnside immediately made two decisive moves. He reorganized the army, creating three large "Grand Divisions," putting them under the commands of the ambitious and temperamental Joe Hooker; William Franklin, Hancock's original commander from the Sixth Corps; and, surprisingly, Bull Sumner. Burnside did not explain his logic, and Hancock assumed that by creating a buffer of experience between him and the corps commanders, Burnside would be able to shield himself from direct criticism, and perhaps direct blame. Hancock's division, under Couch's Second Corps, was placed in Sumner's Grand Division.

Burnside's second decision was to abandon the pursuit of Lee's army through central Virginia, and instead make a sudden surprise move to the left, to the southeast, along the Rappahannock River, crossing below Lee's army, placing the Federal Army between Lee and Richmond. Burnside assured the President that this would bring a speedy end to the war, as Richmond would fall before Lee could react. The place he chose to make the crossing was the town of Fredericksburg.

THEY HAD MARCHED FOR TWO DAYS, WOUND THEIR WAY ALONG the high banks of the Rappahannock River. Hancock rode at the head of his division, and today Couch rode with him. They were in the lead, and would reach their destination before dark, the town of Falmouth, across the river from Fredericksburg.

The weather had warmed slightly, and Hancock rode without his heavy coat. The men moved at a good pace, knew the march was a short one, stepped through a layer of mud on the road that gradually deepened as more of the army passed. Couch had said little, stared away, toward the other side of the river.

"There's a few more."

Hancock looked across, saw gray-clad troops at what had been a bridge crossing, burned timbers now poking at angles out of the water. There was a shot, then two more, and Hancock turned around and watched the column. The men did not break ranks, kept up the smooth march, and now a small squad of skirmishers formed along the bank, fired back across at the rebel troops, and they quickly vanished.

"I wonder if Lee knows by now."

Hancock looked at Couch, said, "I expect he does. I heard earlier, a report of some cavalry watching us. Probably Stuart's men. They're keeping an eye on us."

"I have to admit," Couch said, "I think this might work. If we can get across the river quickly, move down toward Richmond . . . Lee will have a problem."

Hancock thought of Lee, tried to form a picture, had only seen him once since Mexico, at a party in Washington. He was a quiet Southern gentleman, graceful and proper, and he had given Mira some advice, had told her to go with her husband to California, to keep the family together. It was a brief conversation, but there was a quiet sincerity to the man that had caught Hancock's attention, and the advice had an impact on Mira as well. She had not told him of her doubts about going to California, but revealed something in conversation to Lee, and Lee's words carried a sadness, an awareness of what his own career as a soldier had cost him. Now, Hancock tried to see the face, wondered how Lee might have changed, what it was that made him such a good leader. So much has happened, he thought, we never could have known it would become this bloody insanity.

He thought of Albert Sidney Johnston and their last night, the party at his home. Johnston had already pulled away before he left California, his loyalties had already made him cautious. He was the first to understand that he was to be the enemy, and now Johnston was dead. Mira had written him, relaying the story from the papers, a battle at a place called Shiloh. There will be more, he thought, more familiar names, and he tried to stop it, said to himself, Do not do this. But he could not avoid it, saw now the rugged face of Lew Armistead. He'd heard little about him, knew he had been with Longstreet in the Seven Days' battles, but there was no real news. And he thought of Couch's words: "We all have our jobs to do. And our job now is to move this big damned army as fast as we can, and outsmart Robert E. Lee."

From down the road a rider came up, saw the colors behind them, pulled his horse alongside and saluted. "General Couch, sir. I am Major Spaulding, of the Engineering Corps. I am to guide your column into position for the crossing."

Couch nodded, said, "Very good, Major. You anticipate any problems?"

"Not at all, sir. The river is calm, and there appears to be little if any opposition on the other side. All we need are your pontoons, sir."

Couch looked at Hancock, puzzled, and said, "What pontoons, Major?"

Spaulding laughed, tried to be part of the joke, said, "Why, General, we can't send this army across the river without your pontoons."

Couch did not laugh, and Hancock saw the face of the engineer slowly change, the smile fading. "General, we have been waiting . . . we have orders from General Burnside to lay the pontoon bridges as soon as your corps arrives. I assumed, sir . . . you have them."

"Major, you had better look elsewhere. There are no pontoons with this column."

Spaulding's red face, bitten by the cold air of the fast ride, now drained of color. "General, we have already checked. . . . General Burnside requested the pontoons be delivered over from Harper's Ferry. The request went straight to Washington, to General Halleck. I heard him discussing it myself, sir. The pontoons were to be . . . were to arrive at the same time as your column. General Burnside was very plain on this, sir. I have my orders. I have to build a bridge."

Couch looked at Hancock, said, "General, you see any pontoons? Anybody in your division hiding any pontoons?" His voice began to rise, angry and without humor, and Hancock now understood. They would sit still again, the great power of this army would be held up one more time because something went wrong.

Spaulding abruptly saluted, said, "General, if you please, I have to return to Falmouth."

"Of course, Major, go about your business. We will arrive shortly."

The man turned, sent mud spraying over them as his horse kicked away, and Hancock said, "So, we have no way to cross the river."

"No, General, of course not. The plan was a good one too."

"They may find them yet, sir. Hard to lose something as big as a pontoon train."

"Oh, we'll find them, General. They'll make their way to Falmouth eventually. They might even get us across the river in time to do some good. But I have a feeling, General . . . surely, you share it. You've been with this army long enough." Couch stared ahead with dark eyes, and Hancock said nothing, now could see the small town, buildings, a church steeple, small neat houses, and to the right, down a long, steep embankment, the wide river, and across it, Fredericksburg.

I T SNOWED THROUGHOUT THE NIGHT, SLOW AND STEADY, AND early in the morning when he left his tent, the ground was covered with a thin white blanket. He walked through the camp, felt the cold, knew winter had yet to really show itself, that this army was preparing to move in what might be the worst conditions imaginable.

It had been two weeks, and the pontoons had still not come. The word came from Burnside to just sit and wait. Couch had gone to headquarters every day, meetings and informal gatherings of the higher ranks, but Burnside was adamant: They would cross the river at this place. The missing pontoons were simply an inconvenience.

Hancock walked downhill now, toward the river. He saw a thin glaze on the water, the first signs of ice, thought, If we wait long enough, we can walk across. He felt the ground soften, slippery mud under the thin layer of snow, and he backed away, thinking, Don't fall into that mess *this* morning. Mighty damned uncomfortable. He eased along the bank, looked across to the larger town of Fredericksburg, saw a long hill behind, stretching down to the left. The hill had the same layer of snow, and he stopped, admired it as he would a painting, a beautiful scene. Church spires rose sharply above the town, and the riverfront buildings were packed together in a neat row. He guessed at the distance, three hundred yards, maybe less.

Above him, upriver, there was some rough water, a few rocks breaking the smooth flow. He stopped, saw something moving among the rocks, waited, and now he could see. It was a cow.

Several more cows moved into the water on the far side, breaking through the thin ice as they moved out into the middle of the river. The first one had reached the near bank, climbed up through the black mud, disappeared into thick grass and short trees. He watched the others, watched the depth of the water, saw they did not go down more than three feet, and he turned, ran back up through the snow, toward the headquarters of General Couch.

Couch was eating breakfast, a pile of steaming hotcakes, and Hancock caught the smell, the butter, felt a hungry turn in his stomach. Couch watched him approach, saw the look, said, "Ah, General, news travels fast I see. A gift, from a local farmer . . . white flour and butter, and even a few eggs. No need to hurry, there's plenty. Join me, please."

Hancock stopped at the table, was out of breath, said, "No, oh no, sir . . . that's not why . . . sir, we can cross the river. Upstream, a quarter mile. It's shallow enough to ford."

Couch stuffed a forkful of hotcakes into his mouth, syrup dripping down his chin. He stared at Hancock, swallowed hard, said, "Ford the river? It's a long way across, General, and it's damned cold. You sure it's shallow?"

"Sir, I just watched a herd of cattle cross the entire way, no more than three feet deep. We can have the whole corps across by tonight."

Couch stood, glanced down at the hotcakes, looked over to a waiting aide and said, "Enjoy these, Captain," and the man leapt forward, picked up the fork and attacked the plate without sitting down.

Hancock followed Couch away from the table and the smells, and they walked quickly toward the grand house, the stately home overlooking the river that had once belonged to the family of George Washington. It was Sumner's headquarters.

Guards saluted as they passed, and Hancock glanced around the yard, saw vast gardens, vine-covered walkways, brown stems peeking out through the snow. They entered the house, and Hancock caught the strong smell of cigar smoke. Standing in the middle of the main living room, among a cluster of clean blue coats, was General Burnside.

Burnside was the only one wearing a hat, tall black felt with a wide brim, and from underneath, his thick whiskers washed down the sides of his round face. He turned toward the opening door, smiling, and Couch said, "Excuse us, General, we did not know you were here. We came to see General Sumner. General Hancock has some information you may find useful."

Burnside looked at Hancock, held out his hand, said, "Yes, General Hancock, a pleasure. Please, gentlemen, let's go this way. . . . I just left General Sumner in his office."

They moved away from the larger crowd, and Hancock saw civilians now, men with pads of paper: reporters. They passed into a smaller sitting room, were alone now, and Burnside peered around the corner of what had been a bedroom, said, "General Sumner? We have visitors."

Sumner stood, seemed annoyed at the interruption, and they crowded into the small room. It was dark, because Sumner had closed the curtains, and there was only one other chair, which Burnside offered to Couch.

"No, General, please, you are in command here."

Burnside nodded, smiling, said, "Quite right, quite right," and sat in the chair.

Sumner looked up at the other two, said, "What is it, Couch?"

"Sir, General Hancock reports that it is possible to ford the river, upstream a short distance. The crossing appears to be a fairly simple one. With your permission, we could begin moving the men right away."

Sumner stared at Couch with no expression, and Burnside chuckled quietly, said, "General Hancock, I certainly appreciate your efforts at reconnaissance, but that possibility has been considered and rejected. The pontoons will be here at any time, and then we will be able to not only send the men across, but the wagons and supplies as well. It would be foolhardy to send the men without the wagons."

There was a silent pause, and Hancock said, "Excuse me, General, but am I correct in my observation that there is little force opposing us across the river?"

"Yes, General, you are correct. As I have planned, we have caught old Bobby Lee by surprise."

"Well, then, sir, if I may suggest . . . it is possible that General Lee is moving this way. Certainly he is aware of our intentions. If we were able to occupy the town, it would make our job much easier when the bridges do arrive, sir."

Sumner grunted, and Hancock looked at the old face, and there was still no expression. Burnside said, "General, that's a bit risky, I'm afraid. Those men could be cut off. This weather . . . the river is already rising a bit. It will be best, I assure you, if we wait until the entire army can proceed across. I am not worried about General Lee. He will not move against such a large and formidable force as we have here." He paused, laughed, pleased with himself. "I do not share General McClellan's tendency to inflate the enemy's strengths. We have General Lee just where we want him."

Hancock said nothing, looked again at Sumner, who was staring at Burnside with a look that said they had already had this conversation. Beside him, Couch began to shuffle, and Hancock heard a deep breath come from the small man.

Couch said, "General Burnside, if we cannot cross the river very soon, I am confident that General Lee will make every effort to impede our movement to do so. I feel fairly certain that he will also make great efforts to prevent us from moving toward Richmond. We do not know the disposition of General Jackson's forces, and we could find them on our flanks if we move on toward Richmond prematurely. It is important, sir, that we make some attempt to gain even a small advantage by occupying the town, and possibly the heights beyond. Allow me, sir, to send at least General Hancock's division across the river. Surely, they can carry enough supplies with them, and the artillery from this side can protect them from any aggression by Lee—"

Burnside raised his hand, cutting him off, still smiled. "Gentlemen, please, we have beaten this to death. We will cross the river when the bridges arrive, and not before. You must understand, I do not have the luxury of deviating from the larger plan. The President has approved my strategy, and I will stick to it. Once this army is across the river, I assure you, General Lee will have little chance to do any more than nip at our heels as we move down to Richmond. Now, if you please, gentlemen, my presence is required outside."

Burnside stood, did not wait for salutes, was quickly gone. Sumner leaned back in his chair, rubbed at tired eyes, said, "Someone should tell him he can deviate from any plan he chooses. I've already done all the talking I can. This is his operation, and he means to make it work."

Couch pulled at Hancock's arm, moved toward the door, said, "Let's hope, General, that we get those bridges soon."

Outside, the growing bite of the November wind rolled down the long valley of the river. Behind the hills around the headquarters, great fields of troops built fires from whatever wood they could find, passed the time huddled together in tents, and most now expected they would sit here through the winter, that another opportunity had been missed, and so the work began again on the construction of winter quarters. Far upstream, long miles away, teams of horses pulled lines of heavy wagons, bringing the pontoons down the soft roads toward the army.

The two men walked out from the grand old mansion, down the short steps, and Hancock stopped, stared out across the river, to the hills that lay beyond the peaceful town, the pleasant scene he had admired that morning. We should be over there, on those hills, he thought. Couch was watching him, turned to see where Hancock was focused, and started to say something but let it go and left Hancock alone. Turning away, he moved back to his headquarters.

To the west, far behind the hills, the clouds began to grow darker. Another winter storm was moving toward them, more snow, and Hancock pulled at his coat, saw Couch moving away, down the slope. He thought again of the hotcakes, and began the walk back to his camp.

NOW, BEHIND THOSE HILLS, BEHIND THE PEACEFUL TOWN, OUT of sight of the men in blue, there was movement, a steady stream of men in ragged clothes and worn coats, horses and wagons and flags, moving up the sides of the hills, spreading along the ridges covered by the clean snow. They began to dig, long trenches and shallow artillery pits, and now one man rode to the top of the hill, sitting on a tall gray horse, and looked out across the river, toward the high bank, to the place where the generals had just met, the grand old house that had belonged to George Washington, and so had belonged to the family of his wife. Lee had arrived.

PART
THREE

27. LEE

NOVEMBER 1862

HE STRAIGHTENED HIS STIFF LEGS, STOOD HIGH IN THE STIRRUPS, the big gray horse not moving under him. The hill around him was mostly bare. A few trees broke the clean snow, and in front of him the slope was steep, dropping away toward the town. He could see clearly, see it all, the wide gap of open land the attackers would have to cross, broken only by a few fences, and one deep canal, which would disrupt any quick advance of troops. Fredericksburg itself was spread out against the edge of the river, and he knew he would not hold it, it had no value to the army, but even if he had wanted to, the Federal cannon were massed across the river, on top of the long rise known as Stafford Heights, perched high above the river, and so would control any movement in the town and make any defense there impossible. No, it was back here, these hills. He looked around, saw the troops working, dirt and snow flying, a few trees felled and moved into place. The cannon had arrived now, and the shallow pits prepared, and his own guns were moving into position. They too would control the ground, the open fields the Federal troops would have to cross to reach them. He looked back to that ground, the flat grassy plain, saw a few small houses, knew they would offer little protection.

Across the Rappahannock, on the far hills, he saw the camps, the masses of blue, and could see some movement, though not much detail. The heights were nearly a mile away, and the only really clear image was the house, the mansion, the ancestral home of George Washington. He glanced that way, did not want to look at it, avoided it, knew that again this war had taken something from him. He looked down, patted Traveller's neck, said a small prayer: *Please, don't destroy this one too.* He knew it was not just the war, that Mary's health was failing for reasons beyond what he was doing now, but he could not help the feeling that if this were over . . . if they were at home and he could be with her, she would be better. He realized he did not even know where she was these days, somewhere in Richmond, safe, for now. But across the river from him sat another piece of her, another symbol of loss, and he could not look at it, knew that there were other matters at hand.

He focused again, looked back to the open ground at the base of his hill, saw straight down to a deep road bed, a long stone wall that ran along the base of the hill. Surely, he thought, they will not do it here, not *here*. He looked to his right, to the south, along the ridge of the hills, saw his men working far into the distance, digging in. This is too . . . perfect. He felt a nagging sense of alarm: No, it will not happen here. Burnside is not a fool. But . . . there they sit, across the river, a great assembled force, and they are not moving.

The Federal Army had marched with uncharacteristic speed, had surprised him, slipping down the river this far. He hadn't expected the fight to be here, had waited for them to come at him from farther upriver, crossing at the shallow fords to the north. But Stuart followed their movement, the advance down to Falmouth, watched them all along the way, and they continued to move south, reaching the hills across from Fredericksburg a full day before Lee could move any troops in their direction. Lee then quickly brought Longstreet's army to these hills, and now Jackson had been recalled from Winchester, from the valley, and was on the march. Everything pointed to one conclusion: Burnside's plan was to cross here, he would fight here. And we have the good ground, Lee thought. Longstreet's army had grown to nearly forty thousand men, its greatest strength of the war. But Burnside had nearly three times that, and Lee knew that if they moved quickly, came across the river soon, even the good ground would not be enough. Jackson was on his way, with another thirty-five thousand, and if he arrived in time, it would be the largest force Lee had yet commanded, but Jackson had been nearly 150 miles away.

He turned Traveller around, began to ease him along the top of the ridge, moving slowly down to the south. The hills fell away slightly, down into thick trees, and he could see downriver now. The space between his troops and the river was even wider there, another large flat plain, completely open. This cannot be, he thought. No, this must be a feint, a ruse. They will start moving, downstream, a few miles, maybe Skinker's Neck, possibly down to Port Royal. But that would be the last chance. Below Port Royal the river widened to over a half mile, and was deep enough for larger boats. And, as the river snaked far down below the plains of Fredericksburg, there were thick woods lining both sides and any crossing would be difficult, easily defended with smaller numbers of troops. He stopped the horse, looked back across to the heights. And so there they sit, he thought. And it will be . . . *here.*

Above Stafford Heights he saw something, the sun reflecting off an object high in the air. He had heard of the balloons, the new observation platforms held aloft by the big bags of hydrogen. And now he saw more of them, downriver, and he knew they were watching him, knew by now he was digging in. He shook his head. They were waiting for . . . what? Does Burnside think I will attack *him?* he wondered. No, he is coming. And we will be patient.

Behind his hill more men were moving up, wagons were unloaded, more guns were pulling in. He saw horses climbing up toward him, saw Taylor, and another man, a red hat: artillery. It was Colonel Porter Alexander. They reached him, saluted, and Alexander said, "General Lee, a fine day, sir."

"Appears so, Colonel. What do you think of this position?"

Alexander smiled, and Lee saw the youth, a man not much older than Taylor, saw a bright and efficient student of war. Alexander said, "General, we have batteries all along the hill, we have a solid anchor on the north, covering the river, and by tomorrow the batteries will be positioned in those trees down to the south. We will be able to cover the entire open ground, all of it." He paused, looked down toward the town, then closer, the bottom of the steep hill, the stone wall.

"General Lee, do you think they will come at us here?"

Lee looked again to the river, said, "Colonel, the Federal Army is massed together across that river watching us prepare for them. If I were General Burnside . . . no, I would not attack here, I would move back upstream, come across above us. But General Burnside is not a man with the luxury of flexibility. He is being pushed from behind, by loud voices in Washington, by newspapers who demand quick action. We are here, and so he will attack us here."

"General, we have positioned guns to cover every inch of the open ground. If they try to cross that canal, it will slow them down, and we will hit them from every angle. Sir, a chicken could not live on that field."

Lee looked at the young man, saw the intensity, the enthusiasm for the deadly job. He suddenly felt excited, a quick rush, looked back down toward the town, thought, Yes, let them come.

To the south, along the ridge, a lone horseman worked his way along, through the lines of laboring soldiers. Taylor motioned, and Lee turned his horse, watched the man move closer, then saw Captain James Power Smith of Jackson's staff.

Smith saluted, knocking a thin crust of mud off his hat, said, "General Lee, sir. General Jackson sends his respects, and advises that his corps will begin deploying to the south of this position by tomorrow, per your instructions, sir."

Lee nodded, looked back across the river, raised his eyes and looked into the dull gray sky. He gave a prayer then: *Thank You for this place, for this ground.* He lowered his gaze, stared at the blue mass across the river, covering the distant hillside, the patchwork of white tents and black guns, thought, You had your chance, General. Now we are ready.

28. JACKSON

DECEMBER 1862

I T HAD BEEN A GOOD DAY, THE MEN HAD KEPT THE COLUMNS TIGHT, moving with good speed. There was no dust, the roads crusted each morning with a thin frost, a light cover of snow. He had sat on his horse, watching them pass, had seen the bare feet, the bloody impressions, and he felt a deep pain, a sadness. He did not talk about it, did not show what he was thinking, and his staff had learned to keep their distance; that when he moved away from the column, sat alone like this, watching the men, there would be no orders, no messages; that he would stay in one spot for a long while, just watching. The troops would often cheer him, recognized him now, knew the worn and ragged coat he wore, the same major's jacket he had worn at VMI, the small crumpled cadet hat he pulled tightly down on his head, shading his eyes.

Today he sat off to the side of the road in the shadows of a tall pine tree, and they did not know he had cried, talking quietly to God. He sat upright in the saddle, stiff, feeling the sharp burning in his side, knowing it was sent there by God, a lesson in the pain of his men. He had pleaded, *Please, make it stop, yes I understand, I see them. They are all good men, and I have so little to give them.* But the pain had not stopped, had been with him all day, and now, after the march, the cold night covered them all. Finally, as he sat alone in his tent, the pain had gone away.

As they rested in the comfort of the Shenandoah, his army had grown. If there was one success from the Maryland invasion, it had been to rid northern Virginia of Federal troops, and the farms had prospered, the harvest had been a good one, and so the army had been fed, had grown much healthier, and new recruits and veterans with healing wounds had added to the numbers.

He did not want to go to Fredericksburg. From his position in the valley he was still a threat to Washington, and he had tried to convince Lee that this was the greater value. But Lee had finally been firm, had ordered him to march, and so he moved his men with the same energy they had come to expect. He did not understand the importance of Fredericksburg. There was no way to pursue a beaten enemy back across the Rappahannock. He had favored a line farther south, along the South Anna River, and Lee had agreed, but now Burnside had taken that option away. The fight was to be at Fredericksburg, and so he did not question, began to see it now in his mind, his guns and his troops flowing forward to strike the enemy again with all the fire and deadly energy God would provide.

Outside the tent, his staff gathered around a sack of mail, dropped by a weary courier. There was a light snowfall, and the air was quiet and cold. They would not disturb him when he was in his tent, had learned that he would often pray for long periods, but now there were nods, and it was his chief of staff, Sandie Pendleton, who moved toward the tent.

He stopped, stood at attention by the canvas wall, said, "Sir? Forgive me, General. . . ."

Jackson sat inside on a small wooden stool, had been staring at the back of the tent, staring at the glow from a small oil lamp. He turned toward the voice from outside, did not speak, and Pendleton waited. After a moment Jackson focused and his mind returned to the tent, absorbed the young man's words. He said, "You may enter, Captain."

Pendleton lifted the flaps, leaned into the warmth of the dull light, said, "There is a letter for you, General. It's a bit late, but the courier was slow today. I thought you would want to see it, sir."

Jackson reached out, took the letter from Pendleton's outstretched hand and glanced at the envelope. It was a woman's writing, but not Anna's.

Pendleton said, "Good night, sir," and was gone, the flaps dropping back down to seal out the cold.

He stared now at the letter, felt a cold lump in his stomach. Anna had been pregnant again, and he had not seen her since he heard the news. They had been together briefly the previous spring, in Winchester, prior to the great battles, his great triumphs over the Federal armies in the valley. He had not mentioned the pregnancy to anyone, not even his staff, had feared if word got out, God would not be pleased, would punish him somehow. His fear for Anna was so great that he would not think of her at all, would coach himself to think instead of God. If he revealed too much, if God knew that he was afraid for her, if he did not trust completely in God's care, He would take her from him, as He had taken Ellie, as He had taken his daughter.

Jackson did not recognize the writing on the envelope, saw that it was from North Carolina, where Anna had gone to spend the long months with her family. He took a deep breath, tore open the envelope. His hand shook slightly as he held the paper out, catching the lamplight.

> My Own Dear Father,
>   As my mother's letter has been cut short by my arrival, I think it but justice that I should continue it. I know that you are rejoiced to hear of my coming, and I hope that God has sent me to radiate your pathway through life. I am a very tiny little thing. I weigh only eight and a half pounds, and Aunt Harriet says I am the express image of my darling papa . . .

Tears filled his eyes, and he wiped with his sleeve, then began to search down the page, came to the line he had sought:

> My mother is very comfortable this morning . . .

He put the letter down, smiled, wiped more tears away, then looked up, through the walls of his tent, said in a low voice, *"You did not take her from me. Thank You, thank You."*

He sat staring for a minute, then read the letter again, saw the final words, signed: "Your dear little wee Daughter." He smiled again, stared into the walls of the tent, closed his eyes, staring far away into the dark, and saw the face of his mother, her face with a smile like he had not seen before, a glow from her that filled him with a sudden energy, a bright light deep inside him. He knew it was a gift, that his new and precious daughter would fill that place, the lonely dark hole that his mother had left, and he thought, Yes, she will be named for you, she will be called Julia. Then the image began to fade, but deep inside he felt her smiling still.

HIS MOOD WAS DIFFERENT. HE DID NOT RIDE OUT TO WATCH the troops. He rode at the head of the long column, stared out to the front. The staff noticed, but no one asked about the letter. They had learned early what he expected of you and what you did not do. His division commanders had served with him long enough to witness his irritability and intolerance for inefficiency. Now, he too was involved in a conflict with A. P. Hill; the fiery temper and fragile ego that had plagued Longstreet were now tormenting him as well.

Hill had shown a tendency to march his division with too much haste, stringing out his men into a sloppy line, leaving behind many stragglers. On the march into Maryland, Jackson had ordered one of Hill's brigadiers to halt, to allow the unit to close up and regroup. Hill had furiously protested, and Jackson responded by having him arrested, had ordered him to march at the rear of his division. In the weeks that followed, Hill had been granted a brief reprieve, the opportunity to lead his division at Antietam, but even his timely heroics there had not changed Jackson's mind about his need for discipline, and a long series of letters and accusations from both men had poured across Lee's desk.

Lee tried to soothe feelings on both sides, with little success. Jackson was unbending, and Hill demanded a full court of inquiry, a disruption even in the best of circumstances, and Lee knew the army could not afford to be tied up with such administrative energy. And, despite Jackson's anger, and Hill's talent for annoying his superiors, Lee knew that Hill was an essential division commander. Faced with the inevitable assault by Burnside's superior numbers, Lee needed all the capable commanders he had at hand. Thus, the conflict had to simmer until Lee chose to pursue it further. He had no plans to do so.

A month earlier Lee made the corps system in his army official. With the approval of President Davis, Longstreet and Jackson were promoted to the rank of Lieutenant General. Longstreet was still the senior, which Davis had heartily approved, since he had never been comfortable with Jackson's independent spirit. Lee understood that Davis had to be convinced that Jackson was not a threat to Davis's sensitive illusion that he held tight control over the army. Lee had insisted that Jackson was as important to the army as Longstreet, and he had finally defused Davis's uneasiness.

Jackson received the news of the promotion without comment, saw no reason to change his routine. His staff had wanted to offer some celebration, but he would not have it.

He still carried the letter in his pocket, had ridden all day without telling anyone, did not want the congratulations, did not want God to see too much happiness. Now, as this day ended, they were approaching the hills of Fredericksburg. He ordered them into camp, resting the army within a short day's march from Longstreet's defensive lines.

After the evening supper, he returned to his tent, read the letter again, had waited all day for the quiet moment. He thought, I must answer, there will be time tonight. Tomorrow they would begin the deployment of the troops, spreading the divisions to the south of Longstreet's strong solid line.

He rose from his small hard seat, stepped out into the camp, saw the campfire, and his staff noticed him, began to gather. He walked stiffly to the fire, raised his hand high over his head, stretching his back, feeling for the pain in his side. He looked at the faces, saw Pendleton, tilted his head, asking a silent question, and Pendleton nodded, bowed slightly, was quickly gone. The others watched, did not understand. Jackson held his hands up to the fire, absorbing the heat.

Captain Smith moved closer, said, "General, I have seen the deployment of General Longstreet's troops. We are in a very strong position, sir."

Jackson looked at him, said nothing, then looked past, saw Pendleton hurrying back toward the fire, carrying a small wooden box. Jackson waited, and Pendleton lifted the lid, revealing small yellow balls nesting in a soft bed of straw: lemons. Jackson reached for one, held it up in the firelight, pulled out his pocketknife and sliced it in half. Smith glanced at Pendleton, who replaced the lid on the box, slid away toward Jackson's tent, placed the box inside the flaps, then returned to the fire. Smith watched Jackson stuff the half lemon into his mouth, looked again at Pendleton.

Pendleton said under his breath, "A gift . . . from Florida. They come all the time . . . from the same place. . . ."

Smith whispered, "Who . . . ?"

"Don't know. I don't ask."

Jackson paid no attention, stared deep into the fire, bathing his throat with the tart juice.

Pendleton turned toward a noise, and now there were voices, and they saw the rider, the huge German, Von Borcke, from Stuart's camp. He rode clumsily, his wide girth spilling over both sides of his straining horse, seemed ready to tumble to the ground with every step of his much pitied animal.

"Greetings, vat ho!"

Hands were extended, and Von Borcke looked past the men toward Jackson, who still stared into the fire.

"General, goot evening. I come . . . bringing you a present!"

Jackson's head jerked up, suddenly aware, and he stared at the huge man with wonder. Heros Von Borcke was unlike any man in the army. He was still an officer in the Prussian Dragoons, had slipped through the Federal blockade at Charleston, had crossed the Atlantic with a strange obsession to fight with the rebel army, finally arriving in Richmond with much fanfare and a public plea to be allowed to fight.

It was Stuart who had caught Von Borcke's attention. He had read of colorful and daring and often exaggerated exploits in the Richmond papers, and Stuart recognized a fine opportunity, as well. Von Borcke's adventures would be fine entertainment for the European newspapers, and so, despite Von Borcke's limited use of English, Stuart insisted that the Prussian serve with him as a staff officer. Impeccably dressed, with all the trappings of military ceremony, he had become Stuart's favorite messenger, and his arrival always resulted in a gathering crowd. Stuart had been so impressed by his enthusiasm for service that he recommended Von Borcke receive an official commission in the army, and now it was Major Von Borcke.

Jackson began to smile, and his staff caught the mood. Von Borcke laughed along with the others, who were laughing at him, and he waved to the growing number of men who had moved closer to this odd spectacle.

"General Chackson ... I am *grreatly* pleased to bring you this present from General Shtuart. The general has gone to *grrreat* lengths to secure for you ... this!"

Von Borcke held out a package wrapped in brown paper, and Jackson stared at it, did not move. Pendleton reached out, took the package, said, "Would you like me to open it, sir?"

Jackson looked up at Von Borcke, then at Pendleton, nodded silently, and Pendleton tore at the paper and held up the neatly folded gray of a new uniform.

"Wowee, General, this is some fine material. Look here, there's gold braid. ..."

Jackson stared at the gift, began to reach out a hand, to touch the new cloth, then stopped, withdrew. "Major, you may tell General Stuart that I deeply appreciate his present. Please assure him that I will regard it with the greatest of care, and will see that no harm comes to it. Captain Pendleton, will you kindly place the uniform in my tent, and keep it neatly folded."

Von Borcke's expression changed, the smile faded. "No, General, no, you do not understand. General Shtuart vas most insistent that you try it on. He will certainly ask how vas the fit. Please, General. Try it on."

Jackson looked at Pendleton, who smiled broadly, holding the uniform out to him. Jackson reached out slowly, felt the material, then took it, cradling it with both hands, and without speaking turned and walked to his tent.

In the dark, men began to move closer, and Pendleton turned, motioned for quiet. Officers began to appear and there were questions. They saw Von Borcke, and so the men were kept at a distance, but were allowed to stay.

A few minutes passed, and the impatient Von Borcke walked thunderously over to Jackson's tent, did not have the staff's wariness of Jackson's moods, called out loudly, "General, can I be of assistance?"

There was no sound from the tent. Then the flaps were pushed back and Jackson stepped out into the firelight, stood up straight, placed a large black hat on his head.

"*Mein Gott,* you are a splendid sight!" Von Borcke made a deep bow, and around the fire his staff began to applaud, weakly at first, uncertain. Then, as Jackson noticed the gathered troops, he raised the hat, held it high above his head, and the men exploded into cheers. He stood still for a long moment, could not hide a smile, then placed the hat back on his head.

He said to Von Borcke, "You may tell General Stuart that I thank him deeply for this gift. The hat . . . my wife sent it to me, and I never thought . . . it was quite right. . . ."

"General, it is perfect . . . perfect! Please, General, allow me to leave. I will report to General Shtuart that his gift is a success."

"Yes, certainly, you are dismissed, Major."

Von Borcke hurried heavily to his horse, climbed up with a great grunt, began to move away through the crowd of men. Some of the troops followed after him, calling out, and he waved wildly, nearly falling from the horse.

"*Vat ho!*" And the men yelled it back to him, none having any idea what he meant.

Pendleton moved closer to Jackson, admired the gold buttons, the gold stars on the collar, the elaborate braiding on the sleeves.

"General Stuart must have gone to a great deal of trouble, sir. This is fine work, probably came from Richmond."

Jackson had stopped smiling, stared at the young man, said, "We will move at dawn, Captain. General Lee will be expecting us."

Pendleton knew the festivities were over. He took a step back, raised a salute, said, "Yes, sir. Good night, sir."

Jackson removed the hat, leaned over into the tent, and the flaps closed behind him. He tossed the hat down on his blanket, thought of Anna, the silly gift that he thought he would never wear. I am a lieutenant general, he thought. She is proud. I must tell her, No, do not be proud of me—thank God for what He has given us. He ran his hands down the smooth material of the uniform, so different from the old ragged jacket that lay now on the ground by his feet. He began to undo the buttons, thought of sleep, the day ahead, then he saw the laughing face of Stuart, thought, I suppose I cannot insult the kindness of General Stuart. But it is clear he has too much time on his hands. We will have to see what we can do about that.

He sat on his blanket, leaned over to the small lamp, snuffed out the light. He lay down, pulled the blanket over the fine gray cloth, and now it was dark and quiet and the cold began to seep into the tent. He stared up, began to think of Fredericksburg and the wide river, of bayonets and flashing cannons and driving the enemy back, over the edge, into the icy water.

29. HANCOCK

DECEMBER 1862

THE PONTOONS HAD FINALLY COME INTO FALMOUTH THE LAST few days of November, came piecemeal, a convoy that had stretched itself thin on the softening mush of the roads. Now they lay in long rows on the bank of the river, patrolled by nervous engineers, the men who would push them out into the icy water and lash them together side by side, until they reached the far shore. Once in place, planks would be laid on top, and the huge army would begin to cross on a narrow strip of bouncing wood. Hancock had walked among them, had heard the comments. They had waited for nearly two weeks for the pontoons to arrive, and now that they were there, the order had not come. There was only silence from Burnside's headquarters.

Hancock had stayed away from headquarters, from the frequent meetings, meetings that Burnside also avoided, choosing instead to hear a summary of the comments from his staff, feeling out the mood of his commanders. When Burnside did attend, it was to persuade his subordinates that loyalty was their primary concern, not the soundness of his plan. Now, there had been another meeting, and Hancock had been summoned specifically, had gone with no expectations, and the crowded room had been loud and hostile, the commanders speaking their minds more openly now, criticizing their commander's strategy. The meeting was chaired by Sumner, and the old man had finally given up, had dismissed them with a weary wave of his hand. As the men flowed out of the grand old house, no one spoke, the mood of the generals reflecting the mood of the army. Hancock had paused, waiting for Couch, but Couch passed by him with red-faced anger, did not want to talk, and the others had gone quickly as well.

Now Hancock stood alone in the winter ruins of the wide garden, stared far across the river toward the heavy lines of Bobby Lee, admired the scene again, the snow on the wide-open fields, the pleasant waterfront town, and felt like this was all unreal somehow, that there was no war, that nothing would happen to disturb this peaceful countryside.

He put one foot up on a low brick wall, thought, No, this is very real, and we do not have a leader. Behind him he heard a voice, turned, saw Sumner coming toward him. The old man was pulling on a heavy coat, his breath in short bursts of white, and he walked closer to Hancock, who pulled his foot from the wall, turned, stood at attention.

"Easy, General. Saw you out here, wondered what you were doing. You didn't say much this morning, but there's a lot in your face. A lot of them . . . they're getting pretty casual with what they're saying about General Burnside. Not good . . . not good for an army to let down like that. The disrespect . . . He is *still* the commander."

Sumner stared out across the river, and Hancock looked at the old face, the heavy eyes.

"General, we can go inside if you like. No need to stand out here in the cold . . ."

Sumner looked at him, shook his head. "Makes no difference, General. Sometimes, I feel the cold worse inside than I do out here. Old bones . . . this old coat . . ." He raised an arm, and Hancock saw the dull brass buttons on the sleeve, an old army design he had not seen before. "Had this old coat since . . . hell, I don't know, since the beginning. No West Point back then, no place for a soldier to get any training except out here, the field. It was better . . . smaller . . . simpler. A general gave commands and the army carried them out, and the job was done. You in Mexico, General?"

Hancock nodded. "Sixth Infantry."

"Oh, so you were with Scott. Winfield Scott . . . now, there was a commander." Sumner paused, looked again at Hancock. "Your name . . . you were named after him."

Hancock smiled. "Yes, sir. My father had a great admiration for him. I even met him once. He came to West Point. He asked for me, for *me* in particular, saw my name on the list of cadets. He told me we had a responsibility to each other . . . said he'd promise not to disgrace my name if I didn't disgrace his. He scared me to death."

Sumner laughed, a rough cough, and Hancock realized he'd never seen him smile before. But the smile did not last, and Sumner shook his head, said, "It is a different army. General Scott didn't have to hold meetings to find out what he should do, to tell him what people thought . . . he didn't give a *damn* what people thought. He was the *commander*, and everyone understood that, even the President. Hell . . . several Presidents. But he made a great mistake—he got too old, and now they replace him with this damned Halleck, a politician. Runs the army like a puppetmaster, pulling strings. If he thinks you're in his corner, he supports you. If he doesn't, you don't get your damned pontoons when you're supposed to. Scott would never have done that . . . that foolishness." He turned sharply to Hancock, leaned closer. "This bother you, General? You think maybe I'm talking out of turn?"

Hancock shook his head. "You're saying what a lot of the men have been saying, General. Even the foot soldiers seem to feel the same way, seem to understand what a mess we're in."

"You think we're in a mess . . . here?"

Hancock paused, told himself to be careful. He knew he had better choose his words. "We might have a difficult time taking those hills, General."

"General Hancock, last week I showed General Burnside a map, given to me by one of the engineers. It showed a deep canal, cutting across that open field behind the town, the field we will have to cross. I pointed out the location of the canal, that it will present a difficult obstacle in the face of artillery fire. General Burnside looked at the map, then looked at me, and said there is no canal in that location, that the map was wrong. I thought, well, he could be right, I suppose he has access to better information than I do. So I came out here, stood on this spot with field glasses, and looked across the tops of those church steeples, and pretty plain I could see it, right where the engineer said it was. Now, General, what am I supposed to do? I have spent over forty years in this army accepting the word of my commander as gospel, carrying out my duty." He paused, wiped at his nose with a handkerchief. "The commanding general says we are to cross this river and take those heights. So, that is what we will do."

Hancock nodded, said, "It's possible. Down to the left, we could push through, maybe turn Jackson's lines, push him back, trap Longstreet on top of the hill, surround him. It's possible."

Sumner cocked an eyebrow, chuckled again, said, "You trying to be a politician too? Turn Jackson's lines? No, General, we will meet him head-on and it will be a bloody mess. And we will march up to that hill over there, and we will eat their artillery fire all the way across that field. But the important thing is, regardless of the outcome, we will be able to look at ourselves in the mirror and say we are good soldiers, we did what we were told. And if we are not successful, we can say, well, it was a good plan, but there were . . . circumstances, and Mr. Lincoln and General Halleck and Secretary Stanton will pace in their offices and fret over what we should do next. And *you*, General, can one day go back to your hometown and tell the families of your men that they died doing their duty. And they might even believe you."

Hancock felt the cold numbing his hands and feet, began to move slightly, nervously. "Is there no way to change his mind? We should have crossed upriver, at the shallow fords."

"Oh, certainly that has been suggested, General. Try to imagine President Lincoln's response if General Burnside said to him, 'Sir, if you don't mind, we're turning the army around, going back up where we just came from and starting over.' " He chuckled, rubbed his chin with the handkerchief. "I'd like to be there for that . . . ought to be a good one."

Hancock nodded, tried to smile. Sumner turned, began to move back toward the wide doors of the house. He paused, kicked softly at the snow, turned up something with his foot, and Hancock saw color, bright yellow, red, a child's toy. Sumner bent over, picked it up, shook off the snow and held it for a long moment. He said nothing, and Hancock waited, then moved closer to the old man, saw his face, saw red anger, hard red eyes, and Sumner tossed the toy out of the garden, over the low brick wall.

"General, we will be moving across the river very soon. There has been too much talk . . . too much loose talk. I want it shut off, stopped. Any further criticism of General Burnside's plan of attack will be considered insubordination and will be dealt with severely. Am I clear?"

Hancock stiffened, felt the old man's anger, said crisply, "Yes, sir. Very clear, sir."

"Good. Now, return to your division, General. The engineers will be receiving their orders very soon. Be ready." He climbed up the short steps, reached for the door, did not look back, and Hancock watched him disappear inside. He stood still for a minute, absorbing what Sumner had said, thought, Of course, he has no choice, it is all he has ever been. The rest of us . . . we have the luxury of youth, of better education, of better choices after all this is over. He's just an old soldier, and his time is up. And he will go out doing his duty.

He turned toward the river again, to the far hills, felt a shiver flow across his body, pulled his coat tighter. He walked over to the low wall again, looked down the hill, saw the deep scars in the snow where the toy had rolled, saw broken pieces, the remnants, and he thought of Pennsylvania, and going home to the families of his men.

30. BARKSDALE

DECEMBER 11, 1862

I T HAD BEEN A STEADY STREAM, A SOLID SAD LINE MOVING SLOWLY, by foot, by cart, out and away from the town. They were old and young, women and children and their grandparents, the sick and infirm. Some were veterans of earlier fights, men who carried their wounds. Some were fit to be soldiers but had escaped, by politics or by money, but now they were all part of the same tragedy, moving together, and they all understood, they were giving up their homes, leaving behind them all that they could not carry, because the great destruction of the great war had finally come to crush their town, and the two armies, who squatted on the hills around them, could not offer them safety, but only ensure them that if they stayed, they would suffer the most.

He had kept his men by the side of the road, allowing the long line to pass, making room for squeaking carts and richly upholstered carriages, and the people looked at him as they went by, some saluting the uniform, but few said anything, there was no cheering, no mindless patriotism.

The civilians had grown used to seeing the war through the newspapers, sipping tea on sunlit porches, boasting of the great Lee and the mighty Jackson, cursing the demon Lincoln. They had read of the horrors of other cities, Charleston, Norfolk, pitied the people in the smaller towns, Sharpsburg, Manassas, Harper's Ferry. Some of them worked on the river, loaded goods from boats and barges to trains and wagons, watched the food and supplies move away, sustaining their soldiers off in some far distant field, some other valley. Some had expected this, were prepared, neatly packed boxes, wagons piled high, and others did not believe it still, wanted to stay, fight the Yankees just by being there, showing their spirit. But the order had come from the hills beyond, from Lee himself, and so they would not disobey. Across the river they could see the big guns and the mass of blue, and they understood at last that all they could do was leave, get out of the way.

He moved his men into Fredericksburg before dark, quietly, with no fanfare, and they did not have to work, no trenches or earthworks, but had filled the basements and the lower levels of the houses and stores perched along the riverbank. Every window, every small gap in old brickwork, any place a man could fire a rifle, was filled with the men of his brigade. Sixteen hundred rifles pointed at the river, and during the long dark night, they made coffee and played cards, and talked of the Yankees across the way.

Barksdale stood at the edge of the water, at a small boat launch, the hard street flowing right down into the water. It was still early, there was no light, and he could feel the thick, cold air, the heavy fog that filled the valley. He strained his eyes, stared across the quiet water, listened hard for any sound. There were small voices, conversation, then the sound of tin, coffee cups and plates, and soon the voices became louder, more intense. The conversation had become official, commands and replies, and now there were new sounds, tools and heavy wood, and still he could see nothing.

The fog began to glow, a light gray, the dim light of dawn finding its way down to the streets and the water, and now he watched his boots, had perched his toes right on the edge of the smooth glaze of ice, gauging the motion of the slowly moving river. He looked out again, and still there was only the fog, and after a minute he looked down again, and saw: his boots were wet—the water had come out from under the ice, a small disturbance on the still water, pushed toward him by something . . . something wide and heavy moving into the river from the other side.

He turned quickly, ran up the short hill to the quiet streets, and now he saw his staff, the men waiting for the order, and he sent them fanning out through the houses and stores, passing the word to the men: the Yankees were coming across.

He walked back to the edge of the river, stared hard into the fog, heard now the splashing of oars, heavy boots on hard wood, the orders of the engineers. He tried to measure the distance, had memorized the far bank, the positions of the idle pontoons, now began to draw a bead. There was no breeze, and so he knew the sounds were true and straight. He raised his pistol, pointed blindly at the sound of a man's voice, held the pistol steady for a long second and fired a single shot.

On both sides of him, his men responded to his signal, and a volley of rifles opened with bright flashes, sending a shower of lead toward the unseen voices.

There were splashes, the sound of cracking ice. Men screamed and orders were yelled, and suddenly the voices moved away, back in the distance: they had gone back to the far shore. He waited, listened; there was no sound from the river, no movement on the water. He took off his hat, waved it high above his head and gave out a whoop, a single piece of rebel yell, and from the basements and windows came the muffled reply, the cheering of his men.

Barksdale's brigade of Mississippians had been ordered into the town as the first line of defense, and the division commander, Lafayette McLaws, had told him there would be no support. Barksdale's orders had been simple and brief: delay the building of the pontoon bridges, then retire back to the safety of the high hill, the hill above the stone wall known as Marye's Heights.

William Barksdale had come to the Confederacy with the background as a newspaperman and a hard-line secessionist. He was gray-haired and clean-shaven, a neat and educated man, and had shown an unusual ability to lead troops, unusual because Lee had learned through bitter experience that the more political a commander, the less likely he was to be a good soldier.

The fog showed no signs of lifting, and now he heard the noises again, more heavy boots on hard wood, sharp voices and cracking ice, and he waited, let them begin work again. He tried to picture the scene in his mind, the engineers scrambling over the fat pontoon boats, pulling them together into a line, hauling the long planks, laying them across. He knew they would be looking his way, wondering where the shots had come from and when the next volley would come. He smiled, raised the pistol again, and fired into the fog. And from all along the riverfront his men responded with their rifles, and the cries were louder this time, more men fell into the ice, collapsed into the boats. He did not yell, heard his men take up the refrain on their own, and he knew this would work for a while, but he was only one brigade, and surely someone over there would do something to push him out of the town and away from the river.

Barksdale stared hard at the fog, could see out into the river now, maybe forty or fifty yards. It was fully daylight, and the fog was beginning to lift. Now the noises returned, and he could hear men farther down the river, another bridge, knew he had men stretching far enough to cover the entire waterfront, that any landing along the town would be a hot one. He raised the pistol again, picked out a single sound and took aim, and suddenly there was a loud rush of sound, a low scream, and behind him a shell exploded, digging a hole into the hard street. Then another one fell into the building on his left, splinters and bricks scattered across the street, and he heard voices, his staff behind him, and he turned and ran up the short street. Men were waving at him, and he went that way, and another shell hit the street, then another went through the porch where his men had stood, and he was hit with a spray of broken glass and shattered timbers. He saw more men and moved that way, ran with his head down and reached a stairway, dropping down below the level of the street. He jumped toward the bottom, fell hard and then felt himself pulled by the arms into the dark coolness of a basement.

The shelling kept up for several minutes, and when his eyes grew accustomed to the dark space, he counted seven men, all huddled against the heavy walls. Above them the terrible screams of the shells were muted, the sharp explosions dulled by the thick mud of the walls.

He could see faces now, smiles, nods, the heavy sounds from above blotting out their voices. He ran his hands over his legs and arms, no wounds, felt a painful ankle from the long jump down. He thought, It is just like this, all along the river, men in small groups, sitting in low crouches, waiting. But the cannon will have to stop, or soon they will hit their own men, the men on the lengthening bridges, and so we will just sit and wait.

The shelling began to slow, then abruptly stopped. He stood up, reached for the low ceiling with his hand, could not quite stand upright. He went to the small window, looked to the river, and saw the first glimpse of the men on the water, one ghostly figure standing in a shallow boat. Suddenly, there were shots, a scattered volley from his men, who did not wait for the signal. They could begin to see on their own now, and he saw the man fall, a splash of water and thin ice. Now he could see more, straight out in front of him, could see the buttons of their coats, officers yelling and pointing and their men moving in quick, short motions, scampering over the boats like big blue mice, trying to find cover in the wide-open middle of the river. His men kept firing, and now the figures disappeared back into the thinning fog, pulling away again, and his men stopped firing and he waited, knew what was coming, listened for the first high sounds. Then they came, shrieking overhead, shattering the walls of a house on the street behind them. He sat back down on the cold floor, saw the faces watching him in the small dark space, and he nodded, smiled, and they waited again.

31. HANCOCK

DECEMBER 11, 1862

THEY WERE TIGHT TOGETHER, A SEA OF MEN STANDING TOgether by regiment, muskets pointing high, and they could not move.

They had begun to form along the edge of the river at midmorning, moving through the thinning fog. The engineers had started earlier, and the bridges now reached well out into the river. All morning the musket fire from the far side had whistled past them, blindly piercing the clustered masses of men who waited on the bank. The officers kept them together, and they all knew there was nowhere to hide, no cover, that if the small lead ball was meant for you it would find you, and they flinched and ducked and held their position.

Hancock had watched it all, had been out early with the engineers. The order to begin laying the pontoons came the night before, passed through his hands, and it seemed something positive was happening at last, and he saw they would finally have their chance, and thought it might work. Then, as he stared into the fog, watching the workmen falling into the ice, the angry shelling of the town that drove no one from their holes, his excitement faded and he began to feel angry, a boiling fire of fury.

He looked back, over the heads of his own men, up the hill to the mansion, said aloud, "You won't move them out with guns!" and his men heard and cheered him, an outburst that betrayed their mood.

He saw Sumner now, riding down the hill, below the firing of the guns, thought, Fine, come see for yourself. The general's staff followed close behind, made an elegant procession. Hancock pulled his horse through the crowd of men, slowly, carefully, moved to meet him. Couch came down the hill as well, from another direction, and now Hancock saw Oliver Howard, another of Couch's division commanders, making his way to the spot where they would meet.

Now there was a pause in the shelling, and behind him the engineers tried again, more visible now to the riflemen on the other side. Hancock did not watch, stared ahead to the gathering commanders.

Sumner was in a new uniform, sat tall in his saddle, his back straight, the thin face set square and firm, and Hancock suddenly knew that this would be all for him, the last fight. He knows that this will not work, Hancock thought, but he has no choice. He suddenly felt pity, watched the old man's face with a great sadness.

Sumner looked at him, showed nothing, no emotion, said, "General, are your men ready to move across?"

"Quite ready, General."

Sumner turned to Howard, who was trying to steady his horse, said, "And you, General? I want you to be the first. Move your division through the town, spread them out on the streets, protected from those far heights. Keep them inside the line of buildings."

Howard said, "Yes, sir, we await the order to move, sir."

Hancock looked at Couch, who was staring down toward the river. "They're coming back again."

They all turned, and Hancock saw the men running along the wobbling pontoons, toward the safety of the near shore. Now, from above, the shelling began again. The ground rumbled, and across the river they could see the flashes of light, black smoke rising through thinning fog.

Hancock looked at Sumner, wanted to say . . . something, thought again of suggesting the crossing upriver, coming into the town from above, clearing out the sharpshooters from behind. Sumner stared at the river, and Hancock said nothing, let it go.

A rider yelled out, the man pushing his horse through the crowded troops. There were shouts, indignation, and the man kept moving, forced his way closer.

"General Sumner, Colonel Coppersmith of General Franklin's staff. General Franklin has asked me to report, sir, that we have completed the laying of the pontoon bridges downriver. If you are ready to cross, sir, we will move on your signal."

Sumner looked at the man, did not change his expression. "We are not ready to cross, Colonel. Tell General Franklin that he can begin his own crossing at his convenience. We will move across when we can. We have a bit of a problem up here."

"Well, sir, General Franklin has not been successful in convincing

General Burnside that he should not wait. General Burnside has expressed to General Franklin that the army move together. I was there, sir, when General Burnside said that we should . . . 'sweep across as one mighty wave' . . . sir."

A smile escaped from the man's face, and Sumner said nothing.

The man cleared his throat, said, "General, if I may return to General Franklin, I will advise him of your situation."

Sumner nodded, and the man saluted, turned his horse and began to push again through the lines of men.

Hancock looked at Couch, questioning, and Couch shook his head, looked at Sumner. Sumner turned again toward the river, to the clearing scene on the far side. The houses could be seen now, and the impact of the shelling.

Sumner said, "They are still there." He turned to Couch, said, "Pick some men who know how to row a boat. Send them across directly, with good speed. It might help to clear out those damned riflemen."

Couch said, "Immediately, sir," and Hancock saw his expression, a sudden flood of energy. Hancock turned his horse, his men clearing a path, and Couch moved quickly down toward the river.

The regimental commanders were assembled, and Hancock gave the instructions. Within minutes men were filling the pontoons and the wide boats were moving out into the river. Hancock watched them from the bank, saw the small flashes coming from the far side, from small holes under piles of debris, the sharpshooters still in place. More boats moved out from the shore, farther up, the oars breaking through the thin ice, and the rifle fire came across the river again, aimed this time at the boats. But the pontoons were heavy and the men kept low, and soon boats had reached the other side, men pouring up the banks into the town. Now the firing did not come across the river. Rebel soldiers began to appear, emerging out of their holes, moving back through the streets. There were more orders, loud voices beside him, and the engineers started forward again, the workers moving with new courage, without their officers prodding them.

Hancock rode back up the hill, glassed farther down the river, could see Franklin's bridges stretching across the still water, saw no troops, no lines of blue. There was no crossing. He thought, Another day, we have lost another day.

It was after dark before Sumner's men could begin moving into town. Howard's division crossed as ordered, and set up camps in the streets. But the army had run out of time, and Hancock's men would have to wait until the next morning, and so he lay on his blanket, staring past the walls of his tent, thinking about the sharpshooters across the river, the small brigade that had kept eighty thousand men from moving all day. Outside, the fog began to fill the valley again, and across the way more gray troops arrived to fill the high ground.

32. JACKSON

HE DID NOT LIKE DIGGING TRENCHES, BUT PUT HIS MEN TO work all down the line. They did not have Longstreet's great advantage of the steep hill, the stone wall. They were in the trees, mostly thick woods, and so they cut and dug and piled tree limbs and dirt, and soon they would be ready. The flat plain in front of him was nearly two miles across, and there was no cover, and so when Sumner's engineers were being killed by Barksdale, Jackson could only watch as Franklin's engineers did their work, laying their pontoons across the icy water. He had wanted to advance, place a line of rifles along the bank, but the Federal guns on Stafford Heights made that impossible. He watched through his field glasses as the long bridges gradually found their way to his side of the river.

They had not known what Burnside was going to do here, below the town. Lee thought he might cross lower, downstream, at Skinker's Neck, and so he sent General Early there, commanding the division of the wounded Dick Ewell. Daniel Hill had been sent farther down, protecting the crossing at Port Royal, and Jackson's own division, commanded now by William Taliaferro, set up close by at Guiney's Station. Only A. P. Hill's division was below Longstreet's lines, around the place where Jackson sat, across from the new bridges.

As the fog lifted and the bridges grew, Burnside finally showed his hand. Now the instructions came from Lee: Jackson would bring the corps together. He had sent his staff out quickly, the call for his units to come together here, below Longstreet, forming a heavy line down through the trees. Below Fredericksburg the river curved away slightly, and the plain between the woods and the river was wider than in front of Longstreet. But it was open and flat and there would be nowhere to hide.

On his left, toward the base of Marye's Heights, he linked up with Longstreet's right, the division of John Bell Hood. It was slow going in the thick trees, but if the Federal crossing was not rapid, if they did not mass an attack today, there would be time.

The new uniform stayed behind, in his tent. Jackson had thought about it, felt the fine material again, rubbed his fingers gently over the new gold braid, but it was not time. He did not want to appear too . . . taken with it, with the grand appearance. He would wear it for the men, had seen how it inspired them, but not today; today they were working, their duty was clear, and so there was no need.

He sat stiffly on the small horse, stared through the glasses, focused past overhanging branches, bare and brittle, but behind him the trees were thick enough to hide his men. The ground rose up toward him, and he was high enough to see the white of the water and the thin lines of pontoons, the new bridges. He focused closer, scanned across the wide, flat ground, and it made him ache. It would have been so simple, such a good place to form strong lines, cover the river with thousands of muskets and cut them to pieces as they came across. But then he raised the glasses, looked to the far heights above the river, saw the vast cluster of black, more than a hundred long-range cannon, better guns, more accurate than the Confederate batteries, and he knew they would have to wait, sit back in the trees while the Federal Army crossed at will, unmolested.

It was getting late now, the light fading fast. He scanned the horizon far down to the right, downstream, saw balloons, wondered how much Burnside knew, how much he could see. The trees were thick along the river there, and any troop movement might be exaggerated, the numbers inflated by nervous observers. Small units had been left to guard the crossings downstream. They were ordered to keep moving, marching back and forth, showing themselves in the small openings in the trees. It had always worked with the Federal lookouts, who seemed anxious to embellish their reports of vast gray armies prowling the ground in front of them.

Jackson knew that today he had been vulnerable, too spread out, but it had to be—at worst, the divisions had been within a day's march of each other, could delay the crossing at any point long enough for support to arrive. But then, gratefully, Burnside did not cross at all, sat still while Lee played the chess game, watched Burnside's plan unfold, and now Jackson was moving everyone into place, and through the trees down to his right more men were filling the lines.

He saw movement, glassed toward the river, saw troops, blue dots appearing suddenly on his side of the river, climbing up, reaching the top of the steep embankment that lined the river there. He looked beyond, to the bridges, expected to see great masses of troops, but there was only a thin line now, men moving across in single file. So few, he thought, why are they not coming? It's nearly dark, but . . . there is no opposition, they have a free passage.

He put the glasses down, rested his eyes, thought, Are they waiting for dark? But he knew the Yankees did not like to march in the dark. He shook his head, it made no sense. Upriver, to his left, the heavy shelling in the town had long stopped, and now the street fighting slowed. There was no mass crossing there either, he thought. Barksdale's muskets held them up. So, it would be tomorrow.

He looked to the right, down his own lines, saw movement on the long narrow road through the darkening trees, wagons and guns and new flags. It was Early's men, and they were spreading out, deploying into the woods. Jackson smiled, nodded silently, thought, We are stronger still.

Behind him Sandie Pendleton was directing the couriers, the men returning from the distant units, placing them at a discreet distance from Jackson, telling them to wait for further orders. There was a commotion in the trees, riders moving through the troops, and Pendleton saw the flag of D. H. Hill's division, and Hill himself, leading a small staff.

Pendleton called out, "General Jackson, sir, General Hill . . . *Daniel* Hill . . . is approaching."

Jackson turned, smiled, saw the small frame of his brother-in-law moving up the rise toward him. Hill threw up a formal salute, which Jackson acknowledged.

"General Hill, it is a pleasure to see you. Ride with me, if you please."

The two men moved away from the staffs, rode forward, out of the woods, down into patches of snow and tall brown grass and a fading glimpse of sunshine in the cold blue sky.

Jackson turned to look at Hill, saw the hair more gray, the forehead taller, the bright professor's eyes a bit more weary, and he said, "How are you, Daniel? How is Isabella?"

Hill was surprised at Jackson's personal question, concern for his wife, nodded. "Very well, thank you. Allow me to congratulate you on the birth of your daughter."

Jackson turned abruptly, glanced over his shoulder, still had told no one. He wondered how Hill knew, and Hill saw his surprise.

"Isabella wrote me, the letter came this morning." He was puzzled by Jackson's glare, and then Jackson returned to the smile, nodded. "Of course. Anna's sister . . . Isabella. Women must reveal all, I suppose."

"Is it a secret, General? Be assured, I will tell no one." Hill turned away, hiding a smile, looked across the clean white of the field, knew Jackson well enough to understand that there need be no explanation for Jackson's secrecy.

"Daniel, it is best if we keep good news . . . happy news . . . to ourselves. If we spend our energy spreading these . . . things . . . God is liable to take them away. I would rather use my good feelings thanking Him for the gift." He turned toward the river, spoke, thinking out loud. "I must tell Anna. Do not put our precious daughter at risk. We must not be too happy. Thank God, thank Him."

Hill lifted his field glasses, was watching the river. "They're on this side," he said. "They're coming across."

"No, not yet. Too few of them, maybe a skirmish line. They will cross tomorrow."

Hill put down the glasses, looked at Jackson, said, "Do you think it's a feint? Maybe they're still going to move downriver. We have pulled out of Port Royal. I could turn the men around. . . ."

"No. Once they began building the bridges it was settled. How could they go anywhere else? It is too easy here, they control the open ground with their guns. We cannot even slow them down from back here. How soon will your men be up, be ready to deploy?"

"By morning, first light."

"Good. It will happen tomorrow. They will do nothing more tonight."

Jackson pulled at his horse, and Hill followed. They rode back up toward the trees, quietly, and Jackson thought of Lexington, of Hill the professor, and he turned, smiled at Hill. Hill did not understand, and did not ask, and saw Jackson pull something yellow from his pocket.

33. LEE

DECEMBER 13, 1862. DAWN.

I T DID NOT HAPPEN AS JACKSON HAD HOPED. A FULL DAY PASSED, and the attack did not come. The Federal troops had finally crossed the bridges, slow, thick lines marching on fragile ribbons of wood, finally gathering on Lee's side of the river, but they did not advance, stayed close to the water, spreading out on the plain in a huge sea of blue. The fog had shielded them at first, then lifted late in the morning, and by then the spectacle of it was immense, and Lee had sat on the top of his hill and watched with barely concealed excitement. It was a grand show, and Burnside was doing exactly what Lee wanted him to do. The chess game was over, now it was straightforward and honest and brutal, and Lee would do no more now than watch and wait.

In Fredericksburg the streets had filled with Federal troops, and Lee could see them crowding between the buildings and the houses, setting up their camps in the shattered ruins. He did not give the order to the artillery, would not do as Sumner had done—would not shell the town.

The day had passed, and the armies watched each other, one growing, feeling its strength, while the other sat back firmly against its hills. Lee made no attempt to move forward, knew the guns on Stafford Heights were still there, would still control the open fields, and so he spent the day moving men about, small adjustments in a line that needed very little adjusting. When the darkness came, there had been nothing, only slight noises from the town, no campfires, Burnside making sure his men were not seen from Lee's hills. Lee had thought, How foolish, depriving your men of the warmth of their fires, while bitter winds hurled down the valley. It was an order straight from some textbook, and Lee knew that in the morning, the Federal troops would be weary and stiff and grumbling.

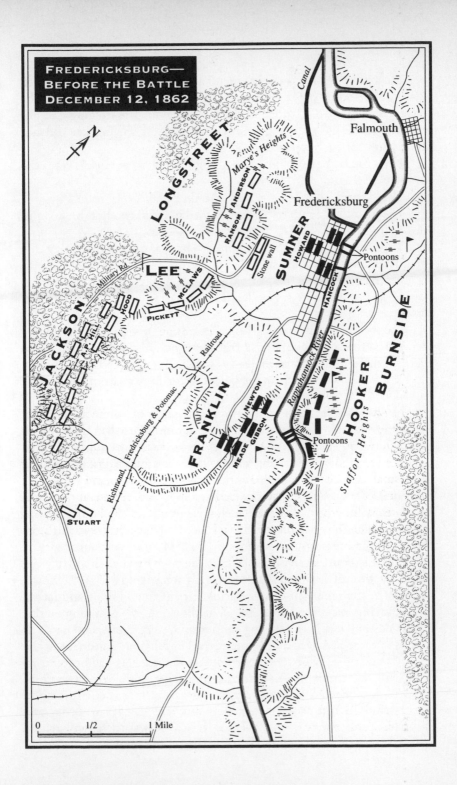

FREDERICKSBURG—
BEFORE THE BATTLE
DECEMBER 12, 1862

N

Canal

Falmouth

LONGSTREET

Marye's Heights

ANDERSON

RANSOM

Fredericksburg

Stone wall

SUMNER

HOWARD

Pontoons

LEE

MCLAWS

PICKETT

HANCOCK

Military Rd

HOOD

JACKSON

A.P. HILL

Railroad

BURNSIDE

HOOKER

Rappahannock River

Fredricksburg & Potomac

FRANKLIN

NEWTON

Pontoons

MEADE GIBBON

Stafford Heights

Richmond,

STUART

0   1/2   1 Mile

He awoke before the light, met Taylor beside the small fire, tried to see stars, and of course there would be none. The wide valley, the entire scene, was again bathed in thick fog. Taylor was holding a cup of something hot and steaming, offered it to Lee, knowing Lee did not often drink coffee, but it was very cold.

Lee said, "Yes, thank you, Major. Have you sent for the commanders?"

Taylor nodded. "Yes, sir, they should be here very soon."

Lee held the cup up to his lips, pulled it away, too hot, blew on it, tried again.

Taylor said, "General, I do hope we have some activity today. It's a mighty cold place to just sit."

Lee nodded, turned away from the fire, walked over to the horses. A groom was brushing Traveller. Lee raised a hand, and the groom backed away silently.

Lee reached out to the horse, stroking his neck, still feeling the sore stiffness in his hands, and thought, Taylor was right, this cold . . . these old hands need to be warm. But it will happen today, and by tonight we will again sit before great fires and not care about the cold.

He had not felt this way before, this sense of comfort, of confidence. He had eighty thousand men around him, more than the Confederate Army had ever put on one field. He had the ground, he had the commanders, and he was facing a man who was unsure and cautious. He said a small prayer, *By Your mercy, we will not lose many, our friends . . . Please deliver us . . .* and the prayer faded from his mind, he could not ask for more, realized he had already been given much.

Traveller lowered his head, waiting, and Lee scratched him between the ears, was lost for a moment, saw Mary, the younger girl he had married, courted right over there, across the river in that great house, the beautiful gardens. It was so very long ago. . . .

There were more noises, the army stirring, men joking and laughing in the cold mist. They understand, he thought, God is smiling on this army, and they feel it. All during the autumn, since the second battle at Manassas, there had been a growing revival of religious sentiment in the army. Tents had gone up at every camp, more preachers had begun traveling with the army, and Lee had felt the spirit, the growing sense of Providence filling the men, watching over them. It was comforting to him, because he still ordered them forward, still sent them to die, and this made it easier somehow, a balance—that God was there, understood their cause, would watch them, keeping them a little more safe.

There were few trees on his hill, and the light began to find the ground. He could see movement, men walking about in the dull gray of the morning. He turned, looked for Taylor, saw the fire and walked over. Taylor was quickly there, chewing on something. He tried to swallow too quickly, and Lee raised his hand as if to say no, it's all right, please continue eating. But he knew Taylor, was thankful for his pure devotion, and Taylor cleared his throat, was red-faced, embarrassed, caught his breath.

"Sorry, General . . . I was just—"

"Major, please, go and finish your breakfast. We have little to attend to until the others arrive."

Taylor saluted, still rubbed his throat, moved away to the wagon where the other staff had gathered. Lee thought, A biscuit would be good, maybe one more for his pocket, and he followed behind Taylor. Down the hill, from the south, came a horse, the first loud sound of the morning, the true beginning of the day. Lee watched, saw the figure approach in the fog, the wide black-plumed hat, the grand entrance of Stuart.

Lee raised a hand, a quiet acknowledgment, moved quickly to the breakfast wagon and grabbed a pair of biscuits. Stuart waited close to the fire, warming gloved hands. Lee climbed back up the rise, said, "General Stuart, are you well this morning?"

"Quite well, General, quite." The voice was high, excited. "Sir, we are extending the far right flank of General Jackson's line. I have scouted forward, determined that the Federal position rests along the river, then out toward General Jackson to a point near the Richmond Road. The way is open for the enemy to attempt to flank—"

Lee held up his hand, said, "Wait for your report, please, General. I would like the others to be here, to hear what you have learned. It will be just a few minutes, I am certain."

Stuart stopped, began to look past Lee toward the food, the smell of coffee. "General, if you will permit? It was a rather chilly ride up this way."

"General, help yourself to some breakfast."

Stuart moved quickly toward the table, passed Taylor, who came up beside Lee, to the fire.

"General Stuart is full of energy this morning. His cavalry will serve us well today."

Taylor tried to speak, his mouth distressingly full again, and he made a small grunt. Lee hid his smile as behind them another horse approached, at a slow deliberate trot, from the opposite direction. Lee knew without turning it was Longstreet.

Longstreet dismounted, moved to the warmth, and now Lee could see the face clearly, the fog had a bright glow, and Longstreet saluted, removed the floppy-brimmed hat, was smoking a short cigar.

"Any movement to your front, General?" Lee asked.

"Nothing. Can't see anything . . . just like up here . . . but there's some sounds. The picket line sends back regular reports . . . they're eating breakfast, most likely. Won't do much until the fog clears. Nothing to shoot at yet."

Lee stared down at the fire, said, "They are all so . . . cautious. I often wonder if God has done that . . . made them slow. It evens up the fight a bit. They have the numbers . . . the guns."

Longstreet stared at Lee, put the hat back on, moved the cigar in his mouth. "Could be," he said. "Could be they just don't have the heart for this fight. The generals, I mean. The troops . . . they're the same boys we served with before. I've talked to some of the prisoners. Not much different from these boys up here. They go where they're told, shoot when they're told to shoot. But they don't have much respect for the officers. And the officers don't have much respect for the generals. It's not very . . . healthy."

Lee watched the fire, thought of the troops, said, "No, General, they are not the same. These men . . . our men are fighting for something that means more to them than obeying their orders. I feel sometimes like God is with us . . . God is protecting these men. He knows they are looking to Him."

Longstreet chewed on the cigar, said, "Maybe. I'm not sure if God is in all the places we want Him to be."

It was an odd statement, and Lee still looked down, thought, No, He is with you too, General. He thought of Longstreet's children, how Longstreet could not even plan the funeral. It was George Pickett, his old friend, who had made the arrangements, and Longstreet had not even attended, could not watch his children laid in the ground, and so did not hear the words of the minister, the comforting blessings, the lesson of God's will. Lee thought, It was a mistake, he should have been there, God would have given him peace.

Lee also thought that Longstreet had come back too soon, returned to duty too quickly. But Longstreet would not speak of it, would not talk of his wife, of the experience. Instead he pulled himself into a quiet darkness. Lee felt pain for him, wanted to give him something . . . some comfort from God, show him that God would help him, but there was no opening, and so Lee knew there would always be that difference between them, a different way of seeing . . . everything, the enemy, the war.

Jackson appeared now, at a quick gallop from the same direction as Stuart. Lee thought, No, it can't be. Then he saw the face, the sharp nose and glaring blue eyes from under a wide black hat, and yes, it was him, but . . . he was dressed in a new uniform, gold buttons shining down the front of his coat, crisp gold braiding on his sleeves, a gold braid around the wide black hat. Lee did not know what to say, thought, This is very strange.

Stuart was back, held a heaping plate of food, said loudly, "Well, General Jackson, you are a beautiful and most gallant sight this morning. Von Borcke told me it was a fine fit, but I had no idea . . . the uniform suits you most elegantly."

Jackson did not speak, seemed embarrassed, moved toward the fire and removed his hat, saluted Lee. "Thank you, General Stuart. Your gift was appreciated. Very kind."

Longstreet had said nothing, began to laugh, said, "General Jackson, this was a gift? Well now, was there some special occasion? I apologize for not being better informed."

Stuart began to move about, excitedly, spilling food from the plate. "No, General, it was just . . . something I felt this army could use. We have a quite famous man in our midst. It seemed appropriate for him to dress the part."

Jackson frowned, and Longstreet said, "Well, yes, I understand that. The papers up North are giving our good Stonewall here credit for bad weather in New England and a poor harvest in Illinois. Certainly, he should dress the part."

Jackson put the hat back on, stared down, hiding his face, which was bright red. Lee was still speechless, had never known Jackson to look like anything other than a rugged mess.

"I must say, General," Lee began, "the change is . . . a positive one. Yes, General Stuart, you are to be commended for your good taste. It puts the rest of us . . ." He looked down to his own simple gray coat. "Well, let us say that we had best be careful walking among the troops . . . there will be confusion as to who is in command." It was a rare joke from Lee.

Jackson looked up, concerned, said, "Oh, certainly not, sir. Forgive me, General Stuart, but perhaps this was a mistake. I did not mean to suggest anything of my own . . . I did not wish to appear grandiose. . . ."

Longstreet was still laughing, said, "Nonsense, General. I feel to-day that you are the new symbol of this army—gold braid and all. You have truly inspired us. Perhaps I will go and polish my boots."

This was very good, Lee thought, they are all in good spirits. But he knew this would go on until he stopped it, and he said, "Gentlemen, we must address the matter at hand. Please join me." He motioned, and they moved toward a small table.

Taylor jumped ahead of them, unrolled a map, and Lee said, "General Longstreet, please show us where your troops are positioned."

Taylor held a small piece of pencil, laid it on the map. Longstreet tossed the cigar aside and began to make short straight lines with the pencil.

"We are anchored on the north by Anderson's division, up on the bend in the river, then General Ransom's division is in several lines along and below the ridge of Marye's Heights, with Cobb's brigade dug in down on the road, behind that stone wall. To their right is General McLaws, and farther down, in the woods to the right, are Pickett and Hood. General Hood is my right flank, and is connected in those heavy trees with General Jackson's left. Up here, on the heights, are the Washington Artillery, with Colonel Alexander's batteries in support. It is a very strong line, General."

"Very well, General. General Jackson, would you please extend the line for us?"

Jackson took off the hat again, leaned forward slightly, said, "General Hill . . . A. P. Hill is on the left, adjoining General Hood. His position is supported . . . here . . . by General Taliaferro and General Early. To the right flank and behind is Daniel Hill. General Lee . . ." He paused, ran his finger along the map. "We have completed construction of a road, running behind the lines for our entire length. We can move troops as is necessary. If the enemy penetrates our line at any point, the reserves—Taliaferro and Early—can change their position rapidly. If the enemy makes an attempt to cut our center, or if General Pickett is pressed, we can move to his aid. Our right flank is anchored here." He pointed to a straight line, a road that led away from the river, out to the west. "General Stuart has advised that the enemy has placed his flank on this road, and does not threaten farther southward. Daniel Hill is positioned to move farther down if the enemy changes his direction."

Lee stared at Jackson, and there was a brief silence. Jackson had not built his reputation by defensive tactics, and even Longstreet nodded, impressed, said quietly, "Good, very good."

Stuart was moving impatiently, and Lee said, "General Stuart, are you protecting General Jackson's flank?"

"Yes, sir. We are covering the enemy's position from the river, as far out as General Daniel Hill's position. If the enemy begins to threaten downriver, to turn General Jackson's line, we can block his advance until the line is moved."

"Very well." Lee leaned over the map, studied the positions, the ground. "General Jackson, there is a large area of trees extending out toward the enemy from the center of your line. That area could be vulnerable. There could be good cover there for the enemy's advance."

Jackson leaned forward, squinted, said, "A. P. Hill is dug in along that position, sir. I will confirm that he is aware of that possibility."

Lee nodded. "Very well. I have confidence in General Hill. He will not leave himself at a disadvantage."

Behind the men, out toward the open field that stretched toward the town, the batteries of the Washington Artillery were set into shallow pits. The men were manning the guns, watching the fog slowly drifting in the growing breeze, a fine, cold mist. The sun was higher now, and across the river the far heights could be seen, the flags of the Federal headquarters, the closely spaced guns of the enemy. Now, the fog had settled downward, into the town, and rising above the dense gray were church spires, the only sign that there was a town there at all. The meeting was concluded and the four men walked out toward the guns, walked behind the crews, who stood stiffly, quietly, reverent respect for the four generals.

Lee moved closer to one of the guns, placed his sore hand on a spoked wheel, said aloud, "How odd. The fog is lower. . . ."

Now other pieces of the town began to appear, the rooftops of the taller buildings, and he began to see some of the destruction, the black skeletons of burnt-out houses. A breeze blew sharply up the hill, and below, the fog was moving, breaking into smaller layers. Thick puffs of white began to move past the town, clearing the plain, and suddenly they could see far below, down the river.

Stuart said, "My God. They're coming."

On the wide plain in front of Jackson's woods, a vast checkerboard was taking shape. Neat formations were moving out slowly on the clean snow-covered field, the sharp squares of blue spreading out on the stark white, and Lee stared, amazed, had never seen anything like this. The troops had nothing to protect them, nothing to hide them except the fog, and now it was clearing rapidly.

Longstreet moved up next to Lee. "Beautiful."

Lee said nothing, stared down from the hill, resting on the wheel of the big gun. The soldiers around them were still quiet, absorbed by the stunning sight, and he began to count, the regiments, the strength. From the river's edge out into the plain he tried to estimate, could see . . . fifty . . . sixty thousand troops. They were not advancing yet, were not spread into battle line, and so it was like a grand review, some great blue parade.

There were always trees, hills, obstructing the view. You saw them coming in pieces, sometimes wide lines, maybe a whole brigade. But the smoke would come, the battle would be on before the rest came forward, and so you knew the strength, knew the numbers in your head, would make a good guess where they would hit the hardest, where the farthest units would be thrown in at your own lines, but you would never see all of them, the whole army. Not like this. He even saw the reserves, more blue masses across the river, crowding the bank. And he thought, Longstreet is right, God help us, but it is a beautiful sight.

Guns began to fire now, far down the line, Jackson's guns, but not many. Lee knew it was reckless, would be stopped quickly, and from the far heights the Federal guns answered, and he could see it all, the bright specks of light streaking across the river, landing in the woods. The great blue masses began to move forward, thinning out, shaping into long lines, and the Federal guns opened again, more of them, a massed artillery barrage on the woods where Jackson's men crouched. Lee turned, saw Jackson looking through field glasses, said, "General, it seems that your men will open the day."

Jackson turned, put down the glasses, and Lee saw the look, the blue fire, the raw, silent screaming in the eyes. Jackson did not speak, gave a short salute, and Taylor was there, had his horse. Jackson climbed up and pulled his hat down low on his head, hiding his face.

Longstreet said, smiling, "General, there's an awful lot of them out there. Don't they scare you just a bit?"

Jackson tilted back his head, glared at him, said, "We will see if now I will scare *them*." He turned the horse, and with a quick flash from his eyes, a last glance at Lee, he was gone down the hill, toward the growing thunder filling the trees.

Lee turned back to the blue troops, to the steady sound of the Federal cannon. Far out, beyond the lines, down where Stuart's troops were holding the flank, he saw something, movement, a small team of horses, then another, wheeling two guns out into the open field. He put his glasses up to his eyes, heard Stuart say, "My God, those are *our* guns . . . it's Pelham. Those are Pelham's guns."

Lee strained to see. The guns were firing now, small dots of men scrambling around them, then firing again. The first wave of blue was advancing toward Jackson's woods, moving out through the open fields, and now puffs of smoke came from their lines, the impact of Pelham's shelling, the firing right into their flanks, right down the long blue lines.

Stuart began to cheer. "Hoooeeeee, that's Pelham all right. Hoooeeeeee!"

Lee focused on the two small guns, saw a great ball of smoke and fire near them, a Federal gun directing its fire in their direction. Quickly, the horses were hitched and the guns moved a short distance. Then their crews were back on them and both guns began to fire again. Lee looked closer, toward the Federal lines, saw gaps opening, the line wavering, and still Pelham's guns kept firing. Now more Federal guns were pointing that way, trying to find the range. Once again the horses were hitched and the guns shifted. Lee saw one explosion, a bright flash of light, and one of the guns was in pieces, and he thought, Well, it's over, but it was a good effort. Now the smoke cleared and he was amazed. He saw the other gun, still moving, and now firing again, and the Federal line was breaking up, pulling back. Lee focused on the blue mass, saw the lines behind through the smoke, trying to advance, bogging down, stopped by the shattering of the line in front.

Stuart was still yelling, and the men around them, the gun crews, began to cheer as well. The Federal lines were still well away from Jackson's position, but were being delayed and disrupted by the one man, John Pelham, one gunner from Stuart's command. Now Stuart grew quieter, said, "All right, pull out . . . that's enough . . . save the gun. You've done enough."

Lee could still see the lone gun firing, shells impacting around it, close, and Pelham moving again, still firing. He turned to Stuart, said, "General, you had best return to your troops. I don't want that gallant young man to fight this battle by himself."

Stuart was smiling, saluted. "At your service, *mon Général*." Then he reached for his horse, climbed up, and with a wave of his tall hat rode away toward the battle.

Longstreet was glassing down toward the town, saw little movement, said, "It's all down that way . . . nothing is happening in front of us. It's Antietam again. One piece at a time."

Lee looked toward the town, glassed the buildings, saw masses of blue in the streets, knew Longstreet was right. The fight was not here, but down there, on the right, and Burnside would wait and see what happened there first. Lee shook his head, turned toward the sounds, searched again through his glasses for the lone cannon, the heroic gunner. "It is well this is so terrible," he said. "We should grow too fond of it."

34. JACKSON

H E SAW THE RED SHIRT FROM A DISTANCE, RODE THAT WAY. Shells were still falling in the woods to his left, out toward the front of the line and the edge of the wide plain. Military Road, which the soldiers had built through the thick trees, was clear, open; the shells had not reached that far back. He rode quickly, kept looking toward the sounds of the explosions, felt the earth bouncing under the horse, the horse not flinching at all.

Jackson reached the group of men, the man in the red shirt, A. P. Hill, directing the rest, and he pulled the horse up. He tried to hear what was being said, and they turned to him, Hill saluting. But the sound of the artillery barrage drowned out the voices. Hill was pointing toward the front, said something to Jackson he could not hear, and Jackson motioned to him: move back, behind the road, away from the shelling.

Hill mounted his horse and followed Jackson back into the trees. They passed over lines of crouching men, Taliaferro's lines, and the men saw him, began to cheer, waving hats. Jackson tried not to notice them, and Hill looked self-conscious, usually heard the same thing from his own men, but not from the rest, and it was clear they were cheering Jackson, not him.

When they reached a small clearing, two of Jackson's staff, Pendleton and Smith, rode up quickly from behind. Both men were sweating in the cold air, and Jackson reined his horse and waited.

Pendleton said, "General, we were told you had returned. Sir, we have a gap in the line, you need to see this. . . ."

Jackson looked at Hill, who said, "Yes, yes, it's that swamp, the thick trees. Do not worry, General, no sizable force can move through that ground. It's a wide creek bed, the ground is a muddy swamp. I spoke with a local farmer. He told me he never uses that land. With respect to your staff, General, my lines are sound."

Jackson said nothing, reached for the piece of paper offered by Pendleton, a small, crude map showing the units, the woods. He studied it, and there was a long, quiet moment, a lull in the shelling. "I must ride out," Jackson said. "I must see what is happening. Mr. Pendleton, you will stay with General Hill. You may find me on this road, or forward, at the edge of the trees. Captain Smith, please accompany me."

Jackson spurred his horse and Smith followed. They were quickly beyond the clearing, moving toward the front. Hill still offered a salute, which Jackson did not see, then dropped his hand with a sarcastic flourish.

Now, the shelling began again, still in the trees in front of them. They reached the road and Jackson pulled the horse, moved farther down to the right. He turned again, eased the horse to the left, up off the road, forward through the brush, and came to a shallow trench filled with Hill's men. Carefully, he jumped the trench, and the men cheered him again. Smith waved at them furiously, quieting them, because now they could be heard by the enemy.

As they reached the edge of the trees, the shelling came in to their right, down the line. Jackson raised his glasses, tried to find the blue line, the advance of the Federal troops.

"I can't see. Too low. Let's move forward." And he spurred the horse out into the clearing, into the tall grass. Smith rode out beside him, then to the front, and Jackson did not notice that Smith was placing himself between him and the enemy lines.

They reached a small rise. Jackson stopped, brought up the glasses again, said aloud, "Over there, they're coming toward the point of trees."

The blue lines were barely visible, stretched out for several hundred yards, but they were moving forward again, still a long way off. Behind him there was no sound. The shelling from the Federal guns had stopped and Hill's guns were not firing, not yet. He turned, looked back to the line of trees, could see nothing, no sign of his men, and he turned toward the advancing enemy, said, "They don't know where we are. Let them come . . . much closer. We must get back to General Hill, tell him to hold his fire, keep the guns quiet until they are much closer."

He pulled on his horse, and Smith said, "Look!"

Out to the front, two hundred yards away, a single soldier, a blue

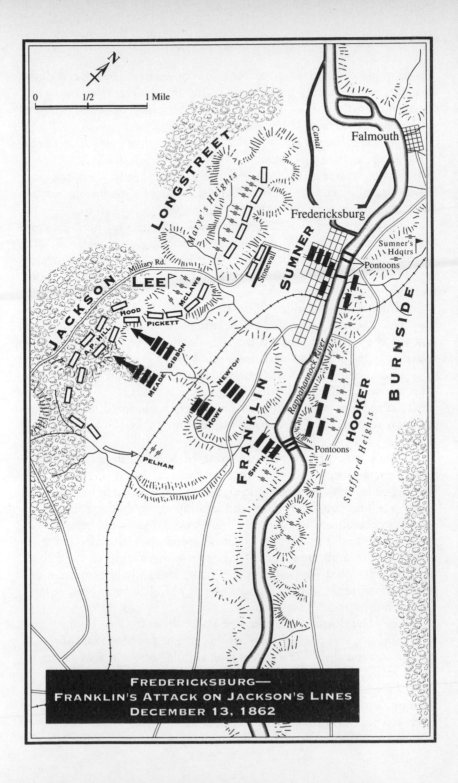

FREDERICKSBURG—
FRANKLIN'S ATTACK ON JACKSON'S LINES
DECEMBER 13, 1862

uniform, stood in the tall grass. He raised his musket, and they did not hear the shot, but only the whistle of the lead ball. It hissed between them, missed them both by a couple of feet, and the man dropped down again, hidden by the grass.

Jackson calmly said, "Why, Mr. Smith, you had best return to the trees. They're shooting at you!"

Smith did not smile, looked for the soldier again, knew the man was reloading. Jackson abruptly laughed, pulled on his horse, and the two men rode back into the trees.

They found Hill in the road, more staff around him. Jackson pulled up, said, "General, the enemy is advancing on those trees, that swamp. Order your artillery to hold their fire, allow the enemy to move close. We cannot be seen, and I am certain they do not know our strength, or our position."

Hill nodded, motioned to the staff officers, and they rode out into the trees, toward the lines and the positions of the guns. Jackson turned quickly away, moved forward again, rode through the woods until he found an open space, a small rise behind Hill's lines. The enemy was visible now, blue coats moving toward them through the snow and the grass. He watched them through his glasses, sat straight and high on the horse, raised one arm high in the air, the palm upturned, held it there for a few seconds, then reached down, into his pocket, and pulled out a lemon.

The advancing troops were those of Meade's division, of Reynolds's First Corps. Jackson watched them close on the trees, saw the flags through his glasses, and then from behind him and from down the lines on both sides the cannon opened, the thunderous sounds of dozens of big guns. The blue lines became obscured, bathed in the thick deadly smoke, and Jackson stood up in the stirrups, tried to see, caught a glimpse of the lines reforming, trying to hold their position. He could see behind them now, a gap in the smoke, more lines moving up in support, and knew it was a full division, several thousand men.

They had slowed under the first volley from the cannon, but now they came on, still pressed forward. He scanned to the front of them, in the direction they were moving, and could see the mass of trees to Hill's front, the swamp Hill had so confidently dismissed. Jackson knew Hill had been wrong, they were going into the woods at that position, it offered the best cover, was the first safe place they could reach after surviving the murderous fire in the open fields. And it was *winter*. The swamp, the soft muddy ground, would be frozen hard. He snatched his hat off his head and yelled out a furious sound. Behind him Pendleton moved forward, looked at him, waiting for instructions, but Jackson continued to stare ahead at the long point of trees that split Hill's lines.

From each side Hill's muskets began to fire, squeezing the blue lines together, pressing them with the deadly fire, and so they would reach the trees even more compactly, moving where the fire was the least, where Hill had no muskets. Jackson saw it happening, saw the gap in Hill's lines suddenly filling with a strong flow of blue. They began to move into the swamp, pushing forward, driving a wedge between Hill's brigades.

Jackson pulled on the horse, began to move back toward the road. Smoke was drifting across now, and he could see very little. The sounds of muskets filled the woods, and he did not see Hill. He moved down the road, toward the point where the blue advance would come, saw General Maxcy Gregg and the troops that lay behind the swamp, that would next feel the thrust of Meade's advance.

"General, prepare for the assault. The enemy is cutting our lines . . . they are pushing through the swamp, between the brigades of Archer and Lane."

Gregg nodded. "Yes, General, we have seen them coming. Can we expect some support?"

Jackson turned, saw his two aides following up close behind him. "Captain Pendleton," he said, "go to General Early. Tell him to advance his men here, toward these woods. He may direct himself by the sounds of the battle. Captain Smith . . . go to General Taliaferro, tell him to advance his men here as well." He turned back to Gregg, who saluted and was quickly gone.

The battle was closer now, the minié balls clipping leaves and small branches around him, high shots from lines of men who knew they were breaking through the enemy, men who would not stop unless you *made* them stop. He looked down the road in both directions, still did not see Hill, and now in the road in front of him, not a hundred yards away, smoke boiled out of the trees, a fresh volley from moving troops. He saw a cluster of blue, the men pouring out into the road like the flow from a great blue wound, lining up against Gregg's troops, who were moving up from the woods in the rear.

Suddenly, he was blinded by a swirling cloud of smoke, the hot sulfur smell. Jackson turned the horse, rode back into the woods, tried to find a clear spot, someplace he could see. In front of him and to the side new smoke poured from the lines of muskets, and he could hear nothing but the steady crack of the rifles, the enemy yells, and the screams of his shattered troops.

He rode farther back, tried to escape the smoke, to find someone, Early. We have the reserves, he thought, we are strong. They never should have pushed this far, cut through our lines. He thought of Hill, felt a violent twinge, saw the man's small figure, the ragged beard, the red shirt that he now saw as obnoxious, foolish bravado, and he wanted to kill him, grab him with his fists and squeeze the life from him.

He jerked the horse through the trees, ducked under low branches. He rode up onto a small ridge, could see out through the woods, thinner trees, the dense clouds of smoke hanging in the branches. The sounds kept moving, a steady flow, pushing his men back, and he knew this was bad. If they send in more strength at the gap, he thought, they can turn our lines completely, cutting behind the bigger hills, surrounding Longstreet's position. He faced the sounds, tried to determine the direction, glanced up at the sun, now high in the sky, and gauged the direction. No, they had not turned yet, were still coming straight through, straight across the road.

The firing began to slow now, the men deep into dense woods, seeking out a target. For a short few minutes the Federal troops had no organized lines in front of them, no enemy they could see. Jackson heard the shouting, officers calling to their men, trying to bring them back together, forming the companies into some organized shape. From his right he heard a new sound, a piercing shrillness, a long, high wail that he had not heard since Manassas. He moved the horse, prodded it along the ridge, toward the sound. Taking off his hat, holding it high, he stared at the sound with the blue fire in his eyes. . . . It was the rebel yell.

From back behind the heavy trees a new force was advancing into the confused positions of Meade's men. It was Early's division, and they flowed into the woods, strong, heavy lines of fresh troops. Now the muskets began again, and Jackson felt it, felt the surge. *Yes, push them back.* Close in front of him he heard new sounds, of the wounded and dying, and of blind panic, and the sounds began to shift back toward the road. Meade's men were falling back.

EARLY'S DIVISION PUSHED THE FEDERAL ADVANCE COMPLETELY back out of the trees, and then the Confederate position was strengthened, units moved out into the frozen swamp. The gap was sealed, the reserves brought forward, and the Federal forces wilted under the steady barrage of cannon and muskets. Alongside Meade, Gibbon's division, which had pushed up against the brunt of Jackson's defense, could only hold its ground in front of the line of trees, and now was pulling back as well. It had not been pressed as hard, but Gibbon had expected help, support from the vast number of troops behind him.

For most of the morning the rest of Franklin's Grand Division, the rest of the sixty thousand men who had crossed the river, stood in formation, ready to follow Meade across the plain, into the woods. The plan had been for Meade to push through and break the lines, but when he tumbled back out of the woods, flowing back out into the plain with broken lines and panicked troops, Franklin watched without responding, and did not order a new advance. The call went instead across the river, to Burnside, a request for new instructions, and from high up on Stafford Heights, from the man who still believed in his own plan, no orders came. If Franklin's troops could not carry the day, could not push through Jackson's woods, then it would be Sumner and the troops in the town.

Outside Burnside's headquarters, while Franklin's courier waited for instructions, the commander stared through his glasses toward the hills beyond the town, where Sumner's troops would make the final push, a glorious assault that Burnside knew would sweep Lee's army from the hills in one broad stroke.

35. HANCOCK

DECEMBER 13, 1862. MIDDAY.

THEY MOVED THROUGH THE STREETS, BEGAN TO FORM ON THE edge of town, out past the last of the houses. They could still hear the guns down to the left, the destruction of Meade's division, but their attention was focused on the hill a half-mile across the open ground in front of them.

Hancock rode through the forming lines, stared out at the field, could see fences, rows of posts and rails that would slow and therefore devastate his lines when crossed. Farther, he could now clearly make out the canal, crossing the field at a slight angle, the canal that Burnside said did not exist.

Out beyond his lines the division of William French was already in battle formation, would be the first across the field. Behind him, still strung out down the streets of the town, Oliver Howard's division would follow Hancock. This was Couch's Second Corps, and on them would fall the responsibility for salvaging Burnside's great plan.

Hancock rode back into the town, saw the last units of his men gathering, easing slowly through the last rows of buildings. Officers were prodding the slow movers, and when they saw him, their pace quickened. He rode toward the river, glanced up at the heights beyond, to the Federal headquarters, to the silent guns. He lowered his head, thought of the irony. The great force of artillery that had blasted so much of the town to ruins was now totally useless. The range of the guns commanded the flat ground they would cross, but could not reach the hills, and so, since Lee had not moved forward, had not made any attempt to cross that ground, the big guns had nothing to shoot at, could only point silently above the backs of his men as they marched toward the high ground.

He saw a flag, quick riders: Couch. Hancock moved that way, and Couch saw him, halted the group, motioned for him to ride forward, leaving the staff behind.

"General," Couch said. "Your division about set?"

"They are. French is ready as well. Howard should be able to move out once we start forward."

"Good."

Hancock saw the face, tight and grim, said, "Any further word . . . from over there?" He motioned back across the river.

"Sumner has been ordered to remain in his headquarters. He will not accompany his Grand Division in the fight."

Hancock stared up at the far mansion, thought of the old man, said, "Burnside ordered him to stay back?"

"I think General Burnside feels that General Sumner is at risk today, might do something . . . dangerous. General Sumner is not pleased with the order."

"No, I would imagine he is not pleased at all." Hancock waited, expected something further from Couch, but Couch said nothing, looked downriver toward the sounds of the fading battle. Hancock followed the look, said, "It did not go well, I expect. Jackson held his lines."

Couch took off his hat, held it up, blocking out the sun. "They did not expect General Jackson to put up much of a fight. They tried to drive him back, break his defense with two divisions, two of Reynolds's divisions. They left the bulk of Franklin's forces idle. General Smith's corps was ordered to guard the bridgeheads . . . his *entire* corps. Guarding them . . . from what?" Couch lowered the hat, slapped it against his leg, said, "Burnside's order said to keep the lines of retreat open. Have you ever received an order like that? Your commander emphasizing your need for retreat?"

Hancock stared away, thought of Reynolds, a good man, a general who knew how to command a field, all his fight taken away by a weak commander. How could they not expect Jackson to put up a fight? He shook his head, said, "Was it bad?"

"Don't know. Heard Meade made a good advance, but Franklin didn't support him. Had Hooker sitting across the river with thirty thousand reserves and didn't use them. Now, they're *our* reserves. Likely, by tonight, they'll still be over there."

Hancock looked toward the hill and Lee's army, said, "We'll try, though. It's all we can do."

Couch looked at him, turned to his staff and waved them

forward. "General Hancock," he said, "return to your division. I will give General French the order to advance, and you will allow him to move out approximately two hundred yards, then you will move your men in line behind him. The orders you received this morning still apply. You will advance in brigade front, spacing your brigades that same distance. Your objective will be the stone wall at the base of the hill. You will drive the enemy from his position and move up the hill." He stopped, stared away, back across the river. "Do you understand, General?"

Hancock nodded. "Yes, sir, I understand."

Couch turned toward him and his expression changed. Hancock saw something, concern, a soft look in the eyes, and Couch suddenly put out a hand, said, "Take care, Win."

He took the hand, embarrassed; the staff was watching, lines of marching troops were passing by. He released the hand, snapped a salute, said, "General . . . we will see you this evening . . . up on that hill."

Couch nodded, said nothing, and Hancock turned and rode through the streets toward his men.

He moved the horse carefully, and the men in the street gave way, moved respectfully to the side. There was some yelling, a few catcalls, nervous comments from the men who would do the bloody work. He did not look at them, did not know them—they were Howard's men. He could see his own lines now, the formation nearly complete, and he rode out among them, into the open field. Beyond the end of his lines he saw Couch, riding quickly through the last row of houses, moving forward, toward French's lines.

Suddenly, the hills in front of them began to speak, small flashes and puffs of white. There was a silent pause, a frozen moment, the men turning, waiting, and now came the sounds, the high screams, the whistles and shrieks. The shells began to fall, shaking the ground, blowing quick holes in the neat blue lines. French's men moved forward, wavering slightly from the impact of the explosions. Gaps had already opened in the line, men dying before they could even begin the attack. Hancock saw Couch riding back toward the town, the order given, the assault under way.

Hancock moved the horse up through his own lines. Sam Zook, one of his brigade commanders, another Pennsylvanian, was waving at French's men, leading a cheer, watching them move away. Then he saw Hancock. "You're the first line, Sam. Clear the way."

Zook was smiling broadly, ready for the fight, and he yelled out,

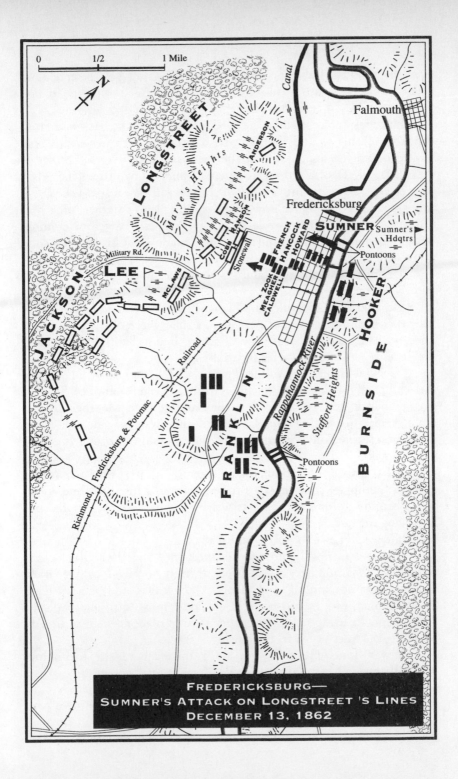

FREDERICKSBURG—
SUMNER'S ATTACK ON LONGSTREET'S LINES
DECEMBER 13, 1862

over the sounds of the incoming shells, "General, you best tell old French to hurry it up, or move out of the way! We're headin' for the top of the hill!"

Hancock forced a smile, nodded, pulled his horse back and faced the front of his second line, the Irish Brigade—Meagher's men. He looked down the line, saw that the men had put green . . . *things* in their hats, pieces of anything they could find. Above them the green flags of the regiments moved slowly. They will be easy to follow, he thought. He saw Meagher now, standing, fragile, his staff helping him up onto a horse, and he rode that way. Meagher saw him coming, straightened himself up on the horse, glanced down at his leg. Hancock saw a wide cloth, a thick bandage.

Meagher was holding a salute as Hancock pulled up, and Hancock said, "General, are you fit?"

Meagher tried to smile, and Hancock saw he was pale, weary. He had taken a minor wound at Antietam, a small piece of shrapnel in his knee. It had been no cause for concern, but it hadn't healed, and the knee was bad now, the leg in trouble.

"General Hancock, I will lead me brigade. We are a-headin' up that there hill, and I will personally spit in the eye of old Bobby Lee. Sir."

Hancock nodded, looked at the bandage, and Meagher saluted again, said, "General, I *will* be leadin' this here brigade. Have no doubt about that, sir. We will do the old Emerald Isle proud this day, that we will."

"I have no doubt about that, General." He returned the salute, spurred the horse, rode through the men toward his third line, Caldwell's brigade. John Caldwell was waiting for him, impatient, did not like being the last in line.

"General Hancock, sir, we are ready."

"General Caldwell, do not advance until the Irish Brigade has moved out two hundred steps. Count them if you have to, General." Caldwell was not smiling, and Hancock knew he could be a bit reckless, too much in a hurry, but still, he could move his men, could be counted on to bring up a strong line. Caldwell nodded, was already watching the lines to his front, waiting.

It was done. He rode out along the edge of the formation, watched through his glasses as French's men reached the first of the fences, the lines slowing, men pulling down the wooden rails. The shelling was following them out, like a violent storm that moves with you, the gunners adjusting the range, hurling their solid shot through French's lines with vicious effect. Hancock saw a great black mass hit the ground, splattering dirt and men, and the black ball still coming, rolling and bouncing across the patches of snow and grass, then burrowing into the lines of his own men. He moved his horse forward, looked down the rows of his lead brigade and saw Zook riding out in front, waving his sword. Now the whole thick line, the First Brigade, began to move, and Hancock moved forward with them.

Up ahead French's men were still holding their formation, but the fences were slowing them down. Zook's brigade began to close the gap between them, the artillery taking a heavier toll, the blasts and rolling shot cutting through the bunched-up lines. The smoke began to hide the hill, and Hancock could see French himself, riding down through his men, waving and yelling, and now he understood. They had reached the canal.

Men began to drop down, out of sight, then Hancock saw them coming back up, climbing a short embankment. There were small bridges, thin rails, and the rebels had removed the planking, so the men could only cross single file. The gunners on the hill had been prepared for that, had the range and were close enough for the smaller shot, the grape and canister. Men began to fall into the canal, blown apart by the unseen swarms of hot metal.

The smoke was thicker still as Hancock reached the canal. He could not see French's lines at all, wondered if there were any lines left. His men began to jump down into the freezing water, nearly waist deep, splashing through the thin ice. Down the line he saw Zook, raising his sword at a small group of men who were moving back, pulling away from the canal, and Zook turned them around and over they went, pushed along now by the second line, closing the gap again. He thought, No, this is not good, wait, and he saw the green flags, saw men moving toward him with the green in their hats. He looked for Meagher, other officers, saw one man leading a company, rode to him through the clouds of smoke.

"Wait . . . hold them up, slow the line!" Hancock shouted. "You're moving up too fast!"

The man looked at him, stunned, did not understand, and Hancock saw: a lieutenant with the face of a scared child. He looked up, tried to see farther down the line, saw Meagher now, riding toward him, and Meagher was yelling, telling his men to wait, let the front clear out. Hancock watched him, admired him until a shell hit the ground between them, a blinding flash. A mound of dirt blew straight up in the air, and he could not see. He thought, Keep moving, General.

Some of his men had found makeshift planking for the bridges, had laid it across the rails, and now the men were quicker. Many of them did not have to jump down into the frozen icy stream. Hancock dismounted, moved with the men over the bridge, holding his horse. Once across he could see through the smoke, a ragged line out in front. French was still advancing, was moving past a small farmhouse, and Hancock rode quickly to the front of Zook's men, saw the lines straightening, the last of the barriers cleared. It will be faster now, he thought. We are getting close. He turned toward the hill, looked up the long slope, saw the mouths of the big guns pointing down at his men, the gaps still blowing through the lines, and felt a new rush of blind fury. He yelled out . . . something . . . not words, turned and saw Zook leading them on, laughing madly, wild eyes, and now they moved past him, toward the face of the hill.

Behind him, he watched for Meagher, saw the specks of green coming on, saw horsemen, the officers, bright flags in the wall of smoke, and then he saw Meagher, rode quickly toward him.

Meagher waved, had his sword high, yelled above the steady roar, "There she be, General. We're a-gettin' close. It's a hot one, that's for sure!"

Hancock did not speak, looked toward the hill, at another small farmhouse, the last of the structures. Then he could see the base of the hill and French's men out in the open, moving faster now. Some men began to run toward the hill. He saw a short stone wall, a long line running along the base of the hill. There was movement from the wall, and suddenly the entire front of the hill was a sheet of flame, a single crushing blast of massed musket fire. French's lines simply collapsed, melted away in the shower of lead. Smoke flowed across the open ground from the face of the hill. Hancock could not see, but he heard the sound again, another volley, and the balls were reaching his men now. Men were going down, small cries and grunts, the horrible slap and crack of the balls against flesh and bone, and he could begin to hear the wounded, sharp screams, and there was another volley, and around him his men were dropping down, some firing blindly toward the hill, some beginning to run away from the terrible flashes.

From the smoke in front of him, men were moving back toward him, the survivors of French's lines, lines that were completely gone. Across the field, through small clearings in the smoke, Hancock could see bodies everywhere. He looked behind him, saw his own lines still holding together, still advancing, and he yelled out, waved them on. The men saw him, still cheered him, raised their hats and held their muskets high. They moved steadily toward the great mass of guns that waited behind the stone wall. They began to pass French's men, the men who had survived by lying flat on the ground, trying to hide from the rifles. They had found a slight depression in the ground—the last hundred yards to the stone wall was up and over a small rise, and the men had found blessed cover.

Hancock saw that this was a good place to reform the lines, bring them together for the last push. He rode forward, could see over the rise to the wall, thought, Not too close, remembering Meagher's words: "A general's not much good to anyone if he gets himself killed." Zook's men were gathering below the rise now, and some of French's men were regrouping, standing with them. He saw Zook calling to them, and they began to move again, up the hill. They reached the crest and now stood within fifty yards of the wall.

Many of the men were stopping to fire, their first chance to see the clear face of the enemy, and then they were wiped away, whole groups falling at once. Hancock watched from below the rise, yelled, "No, do not stop!" but there was no one to hear him.

Behind him, dropping now into the depression, came the Irish Brigade, and he saw Meagher waving the men on, and then Meagher was falling, awkwardly, from the horse, and Hancock rushed that way and dismounted.

Meagher was surrounded by his men, the men in the green hats, and he waved them away. "No, go on, I'm all right!" He saw Hancock, pointed at the knee, the dirty bandage, and Hancock saw a neat black hole. Meagher said, "I'll be a-takin' this leg off, that's for sure. Damned thing keeps drawin' fire."

Hancock leaned over him, and Meagher looked around, began waving at his men. "Go on, move! You're almost up the hill! Go!"

He's all right, Hancock thought, and joined the line of Irishmen moving forward on foot.

They went to the crest, saw the wall, and the men kept going, broke into a run, did not stop to shoot. He watched them close in, saw the faces of the men behind the wall, many, many faces, and there was another volley, and then another, and again he could not see, and now behind him it was Caldwell's brigade. He did not see Caldwell, but still screamed at the men, and they obeyed, climbed up, moved forward with the rest. Now he had no one else to send, tried to see through the smoke, through eyes watering from the thick smell of burning powder.

He expected to see the blue coats, his men, climbing the stone wall, moving over the top, pushing the rebels out. But the smoke was too thick and the muskets were still firing. He dropped down to his knees, moved up, out into the open, crawled over a body, then another. There was a lull, and the smoke was drifting back, over his head, and now he could see, and the faces were still behind the wall, looking out over the field with the black and hungry stare of men who have not had enough, the ground in front of him spread with a vast carpet of blue.

36. CHAMBERLAIN

DECEMBER 13, 1862. LATE AFTERNOON.

HOOKER'S RESERVES DID FINALLY CROSS THE RIVER, MARCHING shakily across the bouncing pontoons and through the burning and shattered town, forming their lines at the edge of the open field. It was late afternoon, and Sumner's attack had run its course. Steady streams of bloodied and hobbled men now crossed the field toward them, many passing right through the lines without speaking, others cursing their own luck, or warning the fresh troops what awaited them out there, beyond the low rise. Chamberlain did not watch them, kept his eyes to the front, stared out across the smoky plain toward the half-hidden hills, the steady roar of the muskets, the constant pounding of the big guns.

There had been no official word. No report had come down this far, but they knew the day was not a good one. Before, from across the river, they could not see what was happening in front of the stone wall, but now, as the broken units out in front of them hugged the ground and broken men flowed from the field, Chamberlain understood. His men were the reserves, and they were being sent in.

The Twentieth Maine was part of the Third Brigade of Griffin's division, Fifth Corps. Griffin's other brigades were already moving out, and Chamberlain watched them go, growing smaller and fading into the drifting smoke. Now he heard new bugles, and Ames, down the line, the familiar voice, "Advance . . . the Twentieth!" and the line began to move slowly forward.

They marched in lines three deep. Chamberlain looked to the side, down the short rows, thought, We are not very many, and this is a big damned field. To his left he saw the other regiments, men from New York, Pennsylvania, Michigan. Men like these, he thought, just farmers and shopkeepers, and now we are soldiers, and now we are about to die. The thought struck him as a certainty, and it shocked him. He did not feel afraid, felt no emotion at all, only the slow rhythm of his steps kicking through the thick grass, small, hard lumps of snow.

He had been hearing the constant sounds all day, and nothing had changed, and so it did not affect him. The sounds were closer, maybe louder, but they were the same sounds. He became curious, thought, We will see, now, won't we? We will learn something, what this is like, what it has been like for the men in front of us, the men who were in front of us at Antietam, who have done this before.

From the brigade in front of him he saw a man break, turn and run back toward him, closer, and he saw the face, the animal eyes, the pure terror. Down the line his men began to yell, taunting, and he suddenly knew that it was his job to do . . . something.

He felt at his belt, grabbed his pistol, pulled it from the holster and pointed it at the man's head. The man looked at him, the eyes clearing for a few seconds, and he stopped running, stood a few yards in front of him. Chamberlain was still moving forward, his feet in a rhythm by themselves, and the man stared at the pistol, abruptly turned and began to walk forward again, by himself, out in front of the regiment.

Chamberlain lowered the pistol, amazed, heard cheering from his men, and he stared ahead at the back of the lone soldier, thought, All right, it's all right. The instinct is in all of us, to save ourselves. But what happened to that man, what was it that made him suddenly turn?

He began to feel afraid now, a sudden wave of sickness filling him. What if I run? No, do not do that. You think too much. This is not about thinking, it is about . . . instinct, a different instinct than survival. He tried to think of the *cause*, yes, focus on that . . . the reason for . . . all of this. He tried to picture it, slavery, the rights of all men. . . . But the men . . . why are they doing this? No, this wasn't working. His mind was numb, he felt no great fire, no passion for any cause. Where had it gone, the excitement and enthusiasm for doing something that was so . . . necessary, his trip to the capital, to the governor? It was all vague, faint memory . . . and out in front of him the puffs of smoke and the small flashes were all that was real.

The shells began to reach them now, and the rhythm of his steps was jarred, the ground rolling and bouncing him up, and dirt spraying him, pushing him aside with a breath of hot wind. But he did not fall, looked back toward the explosion, saw . . . nothing, a gap in the line. He turned to the front, the rhythm returning, thought, There had been a man there . . . several. But his mind would not let him focus on that, and he stared ahead, saw the backs of the men out in front of him, saw the lone soldier still marching by himself. The noises were growing now, loud hisses, high screams. The ground began to bounce again, and now he could hear something else, the sounds of men, and he still focused ahead, saw the lines in front bunching up, the men gathering together, crossing a canal, and for the first time he said something, made a sound, called out to his men.

"Hold up the line, halt!" They were looking at him, would do what he told them to do, and he thought of that, of being in command, felt a strength, a new rush of energy.

He held them back, moved out by himself, closer to the canal, looked at the small fragile planks, the last of the Second Brigade crossing, forming again on the far side. He turned back, raised his sword, looked along the line, then saw, off to his left, toward the right flank of the regiment, beyond, saw . . . *nothing*. There had been other units on the right flank, two more regiments, and they were not there. He suddenly felt a cold panic, moved over that way, looking back, then saw the lines, lagging a hundred yards behind, and he saw Ames with them, in front of them, yelling angrily, bringing them on, and he felt a sudden rage, impatience. This is no time for mistakes, for stupidity.

He yelled aloud, over the heads of his men, "Get up here, on the right flank! Step it up!" and his men were turning, looking back with him, and now he saw: Ames was moving them up. Other officers, their own officers, were yelling and moving quickly along the lines, closing up the brigade.

He turned back toward the canal, felt his hands shaking, the rhythm broken now. He walked forward, stepped onto the small bridge. He waved the sword forward, and they began to form a line, began to move across on the planks. To the other side, the left flank, he saw the other regiments, saw there were no bridges, and the men began to move along the canal toward him, to the one dry crossing. No, he thought, it won't work, and he saw other officers waving swords, and now the men began to jump into the water, moving across where there was no bridge. He looked down into the canal, thick masses of blue, like piles of rock, but the men were walking around them, careful, and he saw the rocks had arms, the bottom of the canal was deep in the bodies of blue-coated men. Suddenly his stomach turned, and he shook, held it in, looked up, away, fought for control.

There was a loud rush of sound, a sudden splash, and he was sprayed with cold water. He looked down again, and there were more bodies, fresh bodies. At the far end of the canal he saw a bright flash, a rebel battery firing straight down the canal. Another great splash of water blew over the small bridge and men below him were suddenly swept away. His men began to cross with more speed, and the men now down in the canal pushed across, climbing out quickly, knowing this was not a place to wait, this was not cover. Now he was caught up in the heavy flow of men, pushed through, moved out in front waving his sword. They began to spread out again, forming the lines, and again they marched forward.

There was no rhythm now, each step was deliberate. He tried to see, to find the men in front, and there was nothing, a field of thick gray smoke. Then a hand was on his arm. It was Ames.

"You have command of the regiment! I must take charge of the right side of the line. The commanders are down. . . . God help us!" and he was gone.

Chamberlain suddenly felt awake. He climbed out of his thoughts, saw the faces looking at him, waiting for him to lead them. He pointed the sword toward the thick unknown, yelled, "Men! Forward! Keep it up!"

The sounds came by him one at a time now, the single terrible whiz of the musket ball, the hot whoosh of streaking shrapnel, the air hitting him in short, hot bursts. He still could not see, moved forward through the thick smoke, did not look at the bodies as he passed, the red and blue poured out into great heaps over the white snow. He looked back to his men again. They were still with him, and he gripped the sword hard, dug his fingers into the steel of the scabbard, but it was not enough. He reached for the pistol, held it tightly in his other hand, still moving forward.

There was a break, a small gap in the flowing smoke, and he could see a wide depression in the ground and a shallow rise, men in blue crouching down, some with muskets, firing, reloading, vast numbers that were just . . . bodies. Beyond, he saw a stone wall, and he raised the pistol, his hand shaking with a boiling rage. He was not thinking, his mind did not tell him what to do. He began to yell, screaming now at the muskets pointing at him from behind the wall, the face of the enemy, and his voice blended with the great roar around him. There was a burst of flame from the wall, and around him men fell, and he aimed the pistol, fired, and fired again.

THERE WERE MEN ALL AROUND HIM, VOICES AND CRIES, AND HE lay without moving, staring up at the darkness, the night sky. What was left of the regiment, and of the brigade, was lying flat around him in the depression, out in front of the stone wall, and for today it was over.

He could feel the cold of the ground under his back, felt it creeping up, into his hands and arms and feet, and he thought, This is not good . . . we will freeze to death. They had heavier coats, of course, had left them in the town, had left everything in the town except what they would need to fight. But they were still out here, still facing the enemy, and would have to wait through a freezing night before anything else would happen, before there could be any relief.

He began to shiver, flexed his fingers, wrapped himself with his arms, and now shivered more. He raised his head just slightly and looked around him, saw a great field of black shapes. He began to move, slid along the hard ground, moved up alongside one of the shapes, said in a low, hoarse voice, "You, there. Are you wounded?" He waited, then reached out a hand, touched the blue cloth, prodded harder, poked the man's stiff body, and he understood.

"Truly sorry, old fellow. But . . . I need to . . . " He slid closer, pressed his body up against the mass, grabbed the man's loose coat, unwrapped the body slightly, pulled a flap out over him and lay still again, but it was not enough. He rose up, saw another mass a few feet up the rise, pulled himself along, prodded again, and again, there was no reply. As he slid back down, he grabbed the man's foot, pulled him down the hill, put the man on the other side of him, pulled another flap of coat out over him. Now he lay between them, thought, All right, so now you will be warm. He pushed up hard against one man, pulled the other closer still, then lay his head down, his hat for a pillow.

It had been dark for about an hour, and he began to hear new sounds, the numbness of the shock, the natural anesthetic of the wounded giving way to the raw pain. The sounds began to grow, spreading out over the entire field, soft cries broken by short screams, words and meaningless noises, curses and prayers. The sounds filled his mind, there was no shutting them out, and he stared up at the stars, tried to see beyond the sounds, but they pulled him back. There were other voices now as well, the men who were not wounded, who were scattered through the others, through the lifeless forms, as he was, and they began to shout, some of them yelling at the wounded to stop, to be quiet. Some were angry, loud hostile screams, others begged, pleaded. He kept staring up, distracting himself, trying not to hear, but the sounds were now filling every space, and his head began to throb . . . *the sounds were coming from inside, louder now, no voices, no words, but a steady, high scream, and he felt his head would burst, his mind shattering, blowing into a thousand pieces, the pieces of the men around him. . . .*

And then he was suddenly awake. The sound was gone, and he felt the cold again, felt the hard masses pressing on him from either side. Above him there was a face, a man crouching low over him, and the man pulled the flaps back, looked at him, and Chamberlain said, "Excuse me, but I was sleeping. . . ."

The man jumped, lurched back, said in a burst, "For the love of God!" and crawled away, sat for a moment in the dark, said in a whisper, "Sorry. I thought you was with the Beyond."

Chamberlain raised himself up, could see across the field now. The moon had come up, and men were moving around, crawling among the dead, pulling off coats and shirts and boots. There were men with stretchers, lifting some of the wounded, carrying them back toward the wagons waiting far behind the lines. The sounds of the wounded were still there, but not as many, softer sounds, and he thought, Many have died, maybe the lucky ones.

He propped himself up on his elbows, told himself, You are in command, maybe you should . . . This had never been discussed; Ames had not told him what to do in this situation. Ames . . . he wondered if he was alive. He crawled out from the shelter of the bodies, slid along painfully, then saw more of the stretcher bearers, standing, and he rose to his knees, tried to look around. He wanted to say something, to call out, how many were still alive . . . Tom. *Tom!* He felt a burst of cold in his gut.

"Tom!" The noise exploded through the cold night, and he listened, waited, and then he heard other voices, other yells.

"Tom!" and laughing, and he looked that way, over the hill, toward the stone wall, and now there were more voices.

"Tom! You home, Tom?" and along the hill, across the field, his own men began to take up the call.

"No Tom here!"

"Hey, Tom! You got a message!"

He felt a rush of anger, wanted to yell again, and now he heard another voice, one single sound from below him, down in the bottom of the wide depression:

"Lawrence!"

He started to rise, to stand up, thought, I can see, the moon is bright, maybe I can see where he is . . . and suddenly there was a flash, several more, and he dropped down, lay flat, and around him other men began to yell, "Keep it down, stay down. You'll draw fire!"

He lay still for a minute, raised himself up slowly, thought, He is alive, thank God. He turned, crawled back up to his bed, slid in tight between the bodies, pulled again at the flaps of cloth.

There were clouds now, moving across the face of the bright moon, and he could see fewer stars. There was a new sound, the wind, a steady growing breeze, and he thought, No, please, no storm, no snow, not tonight. But the clouds were thin, and the moon was still there, shining through. The breeze flowed across the field, and he rose one more time, felt the sharp chill, lay back down, said in a low whisper to the bodies, to his shelter, "God forgive me."

He lay still for a long time, watched the clouds slide past the moon, and the wind began to change, to shift direction, and suddenly there was a noise, a rustle, a knocking. He sat up, looked to the side, up over the rise, saw a dark shape in the distance, a battered house. The noise came from there, but he could see nothing. He lay back down, and the noise kept coming, and he tried to imagine what it was, pictured a house in his mind, the wind, thought, A *window*. And he knew it was a curtain, a blind, slapping against an open window frame. He felt relief, let out a long breath. He lay still again, and the noise still came, the sound growing, pushing everything else away, and his mind was filled again, and the noise became words, a hard, cold whisper.

"Never, forever . . . never, forever . . ."

H E WOKE TO THE DIM LIGHT OF A FOGGY DAWN AND THE sound of muskets. There were scattered shots, small protests from the stone wall, and his men learned quickly that they had no choice but to stay low, keeping their heads barely above the surface of the ground. The depression gave them cover, broke the clean line of fire from the wall, but higher up, on the face of the hill, the big guns still watched over them, and so Chamberlain stayed put.

The word had been passed, the Ninth Corps would advance, come up behind them, renew the attack, a strong force moving up to replace them. It had the logic of something official, and so he believed it, did not distrust that it was only the wishful thinking, the careless fantasies of pinned-down officers. By mid-morning there was no attack, only the scattered firing, and he could see up the rise, across the shallow hill, could easily pick out the men who were still alive, the ones who held a musket as they took their careful shots, reloaded while lying down, then took aim again. There was little action anywhere else, no distant sounds, no long-range guns. He began to think about the army on the hill in front of them, wondered if they were coming, to sweep away this small line of troops who lay flat in the thin snow.

He tried to reach a better vantage point, make some reconnaissance, slid on his stomach, and a rifle ball plowed into the snow beside him. He backed down the hill, said to himself, All right, so much for *that*. He passed beside more bodies, pulled one down with him, lay it on the uphill side, above his head, toward the enemy, thought, He would understand, I would want them to do this with me. Then he pushed that from his mind, was not at all sure if it was the truth.

There was no reaching Tom, and he had not seen Ames. He heard some talk that orders were being issued, and it sounded like Ames was moving about, farther back, on safer ground. He realized that Ames might think he was dead. I need to get word to him somehow, he thought, find out what I should be doing. Suddenly, there was a flurry of musket fire, and he turned, looked out over one of the bodies and saw a line of gray soldiers moving beyond the crest of the hill, coming out, forward, firing into the open flank of the men in the depression. He yelled out, a warning, and others were yelling as well, and now the shots were being answered, his men firing at the new line of skirmishers. He pulled the pistol out, laid it across his chest and raised his head slightly, just to see past the body beside him. He saw a man raise a musket, spotting him, and he dropped his head down, heard the crack and the dull slap of lead against his protector. Now there were other shots, balls whizzing inches above him, and more lead hit the man beside him, thuds and thumps. He could feel the impact, the shock passing through the man's body, and he wanted to sit up, fire the pistol, felt a new anger, wanted to yell out, "For the love of God, let him lie in peace." There was more firing now, from below him, and he heard yelling and new sounds, and a line of his own men began to push by him, toward the rebel line. Now the volleys were slow and scattered, and he could hear his men, talking, yelling, they had pushed the rebels back.

He sat up, saw the blessed blue coats moving slowly back down the hill, spreading out just above him, and he said, "Hey! Good work ... good work, thank you!"

A man moved down toward him, slid heavily along the ground, and he saw the round face of the Irishman, Kilrain.

"Well, Colonel, me laddie, we was a-wond'rin' if you was still among the living." He looked at the bodies on either side. "Got to hand it to you, Colonel, you have a talent for pickin' your friends. This one's . . . done his bit. . . ." He reached across, rolled the other man toward him, and Chamberlain saw the expression change, the bright smile vanish, replaced by a look of recognition and horror.

Kilrain said, "Oh, Mother of God." He let the man go, turned away, stared down at the ground.

Chamberlain wanted to ask who it was, felt the bulk of the man still pressing against his side, thought, No, don't, let it go.

Kilrain shook his head, looked at Chamberlain, said, "We lost many a fine man . . . a few fine *boys* too. Don't seem like we can do much of anything today. Nobody coming up to help us, it appears. We're scattered out all over this field, the whole division, more. The rebs . . . they seem pretty happy to sit tight. We run off that one bunch. A few of them didn't make it back. . . . Don't expect they'll try *that* again."

"Sergeant . . . I need to get back . . . to find Colonel Ames. Can you . . . is it all right to move back down the hill? You seem to have been able. . . ."

"Come on, Colonel, just keep your head down. The rest of ya too. Stay low."

Chamberlain slid out from his human shelter, fought the urge to look at the face of the man Kilrain knew, and they began to move down the hill. Others were moving up now, strengthening the skirmish line, and across the wide hill he saw the men in a solid snaking line, lying just below the crest, just out of the line of fire from the wall, and most were waiting, ready. He wondered, Will the order come, the new attack? He was beginning to feel the excitement of a new day, thought, Yes, we can do it again . . . we're already here. There just aren't very many of us. He could see back across the field, all the way to the town. There were still vast numbers of men, some in formation, strong lines of blue, and the sight thrilled him. Yes, come on!

They reached the bottom of the depression, and Kilrain led him along, over the mass of bodies, and now Chamberlain could see horses, officers, flags, some organization, back out of range of the muskets. He began to walk upright, heard a musket ball whiz overhead, and he ducked.

Kilrain watched him, said, "Colonel, me darlin', if that one was meant for you . . . there'd be no need to be duckin'."

He stood upright again, looked at the officers, finally saw Ames. He felt another thrill, wanted to run up to him, show him he had survived after all, and Ames looked at him, nodded, a quick, short smile. Chamberlain understood, saw now General Griffin, and Colonel Strong Vincent, of the Eighty-third Pennsylvania. Griffin was speaking.

". . . while Stockton is unable. Colonel Vincent, you are now in command of the Third Brigade. Keep the men in position here until dark. You will be relieved as soon as possible."

Vincent saluted, said, "Yes, sir," then noticed Chamberlain, stared for a second, said, "Colonel . . . are you all right?"

Chamberlain nodded, said, "Yes, sir. I was pinned down . . . up on the rise . . . the wall." He felt suddenly very tired, looked at Ames, who smiled again.

Ames said, "General Griffin, Colonel Vincent, this is Lieutenant Colonel Chamberlain. I spoke of him earlier."

Griffin held out his hand, caught Chamberlain by surprise, and he stared numbly. Griffin waited, kept the hand out, and Chamberlain reached for it weakly.

Griffin said, "Fine work, Colonel, keeping your men up close like that. Not many men made it that far . . . fine work."

Chamberlain felt the hand release, and he nodded, felt himself smiling, a big stupid grin, tried to control it, saw the faces of the others watching him, said, "Thank you, General. Are we going to attack?"

There was a silent moment, and the others looked at Griffin, who stared down at the ground, then looked hard at Chamberlain. "Colonel," he said, "there are no new orders. The commanding general has not given instructions to General Hooker, and General Hooker has not given instructions to me. You have done your job, Colonel. All of these men on this field have done their job. Unless something changes, that job is complete."

Chamberlain stared at Griffin's face, saw deep lines and tired eyes, and he looked at Ames, and Ames raised his hand, cocked a finger, a small quick signal to move away, *follow me.*

Ames moved slowly, stepped over bodies. Chamberlain struggled to keep up. His legs were not working well. "Colonel," he said, "what happened? How can we be through?"

Ames stopped, said, "Because we are. It's over. We sent forty thousand men across this field, Colonel, and it was not enough. They are still up there." He pointed to the hill, and Chamberlain could see it clearly now, the entire hill in front of him, the guns perched high on top, small flags waving. "They're waiting for us to try again. It was suicide, Colonel. It would be still."

Chamberlain stared at the hill, then looked down, across the wide field, the crouching lines and small groups, the living and the dead, and he felt something swelling inside him, something painful and sickening, and he wanted to be angry, to say something important, some loud pronouncement against the raw stupidity, the tragedy of the waste, sorrow for the dead. But he had nothing left, he had given all he had the day before, and Ames turned away, moving toward the long rise. Chamberlain began to understand, to accept the truth, that there was nothing left to do but wait for the sun to drop and the field to grow dark. Then they would lead the men back across the field and pull away from the guns of the enemy.

37. LEE

A S THE SUN WENT DOWN, IT BEGAN TO RAIN, COLD, HARD DROPS, and he found shelter, stayed near his tent. He had been at the top of his hill all day, waiting, watching. His eyes were worn, tired from the long hours of looking through the field glasses, and he felt a great need for sleep. Taylor had brought him a plate of food, and he sat now just inside the flaps of his tent, gave a silent blessing, *Thank You*, ate gratefully, and thought again of the great open field below him: *Thy will be done.*

He had expected a new attack, all of them had, and the sunken road behind that wonderful stone wall was lined with fresh troops, anxious men who could see the field in front of them, the horrible piles of blue bodies, and they were ready for more, ready to resume the slaughter.

He thought of Thomas Cobb, the fiery clean-cut Georgian whose brigade had first filled that road, and Maxcy Gregg, the charming, educated man from South Carolina—both were dead. There had been many . . . good soldiers, good leaders. Where would they come from now?

He cleaned the plate, wiped at thick gravy with a hard biscuit. It was still raining, and he pushed back the flap of the tent, looked out, saw men around a sputtering fire, thick smoke.

Taylor saw him, came over quickly, splashing through mud. "General, can I get you anything?" he asked. "Was the supper acceptable?"

Lee nodded, handed him the plate, said, "Thank you, Major, it was fine, quite good. I would like to speak with General Longstreet. Please send someone to his camp. Be sure to express my apologies for bringing the general out in this weather."

"Sir!" Taylor stood upright, saluted, and moved toward the fire. Lee watched, saw one of the staff move quickly away. He let the flap drop again, moved over to his cot, lay down and closed his eyes for a moment, just a quick rest, his mind drifting out ... *over a wide flat ocean, thick waves of blue, rolling against a rocky shore, the sweet soft rumble of the surf, and the voice of* ... Longstreet.

"General, forgive me for waking you."

He blinked, tried to see, sat up and shook his head. "No, please, General," he said. "I will join you." He stood, pushed aside the flaps, stepped out into the chill. The rain had stopped, giving way to a light breeze. Longstreet stood towering before him in a heavy overcoat, his face hidden by the wide floppy hat. Lee moved to the fire, held out his hands, felt a thick cloud of smoke engulf him. He backed away, said, "Too wet. Winter ... we should not be out here."

"We won't be, much longer."

Lee looked toward the voice. "General, do you have some information?"

Longstreet removed the hat, pulled out a short cigar, lit it behind his dirty white gloves, said, "They spent all afternoon digging trenches, by the town. Those men out there, in the field: they will be gone by morning. The skirmishers down below have been talking to them, taunting them a bit ... you know how it goes, sir. 'Come and get some more,' all of that. The Yanks are talking pretty freely about ... about all of it, I suppose. Mainly, they're pretty sure they've been left out there alone. Not many kind words for Burnside. General McLaws brought me a prisoner, an officer, Pennsylvania man, says he's not going back, thinks he's been led by fools, a lost cause. Says there's no attack coming, the generals have no stomach for another day like yesterday."

Lee stared at the struggling fire, said, "Dangerous talk from an officer. You believe him?"

"He says they're expecting us to advance, drive them back. That's the reason for the trenches. They think we'll try to push them across the river."

Lee shook his head, rubbed his fingers through his beard. "No, there will be no advance. We have no cause to move off the good ground. We have beaten them from this ground ... we will do it again."

"I don't believe they will give us the chance."

"I hope you are wrong, General. This has been a war of missed opportunities. We have let them get away before. I do not wish to make that mistake again. We cannot continue to lose men . . . good officers. . . . We cannot trade casualties with an enemy that has much greater numbers and much greater resources. If we are to win this war, we must strike a decisive blow . . . force him to admit defeat." He turned away from the fire, walked slowly toward the crest of the tall hill, toward the wide, dark field. "He will try again . . . maybe to the south, below General Jackson. It should have been his plan from the start . . . not here, not against these hills. We must tell General Stuart to observe him closely, watch for movement by Franklin's forces. General Reynolds is down there. He is a good commander, knows how to position his troops."

Longstreet stayed close behind him, and Lee still moved forward, reached the crest and began to walk down, between the batteries. The clouds were thinning now, the moon reflecting on the flat plain. There were scattered shots from below, from the base of the long hill to the left, the men in the sunken road firing at motion in the moonlight.

Longstreet chewed on the cigar, put the hat back on his head, said, "Sir, John Reynolds will not move anywhere Burnside does not tell him to move. It is still Burnside's army. We have beaten him. There will be another day, but it will not be here."

Lee said nothing, watched the shadows of the small clouds move across the field, and suddenly there was a bright flash, a searing band of color jumped out of the sky, and he flinched, raised his hand up to his face. But there was no sound, it was completely silent, and now he saw a wide sheet of green, and the light spread out over him, rippled, then was gone. To the north there was another, turning slightly red, and around them the men began cheering, yelling.

Longstreet said, "The aurora . . . the northern lights."

Lee kept staring up, the lights dancing and flickering, then spreading out wide, then moving away. "My God . . . I've never seen anything like this before. Are you . . . certain, General?"

"Oh, yes, sir. Used to see them once in a while in Pennsylvania, when I was at Carlisle. Quite a show sometimes." Longstreet began to chuckle, was enjoying the spectacle.

Lee said, "No . . . it is more than that, General. It is a sign. We have pleased God. He is honoring the dead. A sight like this cannot be . . . just an accident. This is Sunday . . . the Sabbath. No, it is no accident."

Longstreet said nothing, stared upward, and the calls were echoing now, across the field, soldiers on both sides absorbing the wondrous sight. Longstreet looked down at the flat ground, saw the colors reflecting off what was left of the snow, thought, We are all sharing this . . . both sides. If God has smiled on us, then He will also smile on them.

DECEMBER 15, 1862

THE FOG RETURNED, AND HE WOKE TO MORE WET COLD, AND AN army still shivering. Lee pushed out of the tent, could see up toward the top of his hill, rolling mist and dark shapes. He looked for Taylor, for the others, saw no one, thought, They cannot be sleeping, must be . . . breakfast. He thought of going toward the food, tried to pick up the smells, but the heavy mist was in the way, and he walked the other way, back up over the crest. He saw small groups of men gathering around the guns. Someone saw him and hats were raised quietly. They knew by now not to shout, not to alert the enemy. Down the hill he could see nothing, just a sea of thick gray, and he listened hard, heard voices, movement, the sound of tin coffee cups, nothing else.

He turned, climbed back up to the crest, toward his tent, saw a man kneeling, working on the fire, wet wood and quiet curses. The smells began to reach him, coffee, fresh bread. He shivered, felt a growl in his stomach, saw men moving toward him, carrying plates, and Taylor quickly hurried up to him.

"Sir, I have been looking for you. A courier is here, from General Jackson." He turned, looked for the man, and Lee spotted him, the young Pendleton, carrying a plate piled high.

Pendleton saluted with his free hand, cleared away a mouthful of food, said, "Good morning, General. Sorry . . . we have not yet had breakfast in General Jackson's camp. Sir, General Jackson offers his respects and reports that the enemy is no longer in front of our position, sir. The general made a reconnaissance in force early this morning, hoping to catch the enemy in the fog . . . and they were no longer there, sir."

Lee looked for a stool, moved over, sat, said, "Are you referring to the forces under General Franklin? Captain, you're talking about sixty thousand troops. They did not just vanish. Has the general spoken with General Stuart . . . have they scouted downriver?" His voice began to rise and he felt a tightening in his chest.

"General, the enemy has withdrawn back across the river. When our troops found no resistance, they kept going. They reached the edge of the river and they could hear the enemy, on the other side. The sound carries very well in the fog, sir. The pontoon bridges are gone, sir, cut loose from the bank."

Lee stared up at the young face, thought, It cannot be . . . Longstreet was right. He straightened his back, said to Taylor, "Major, summon General Longstreet. I want to know what is down below us here. I do not wish to wait for the fog to lift to find out. Captain Pendleton, you may return to General Jackson. Please express my appreciation for his diligence. And please remind General Jackson that we do not wish to give the enemy an opportunity by exposing our troops to those guns on the heights. When the fog lifts, your advance will surely receive a concentration of artillery fire."

Pendleton saluted, nodded. "Yes, sir. General Jackson has already ordered the men back. There is only a line of pickets at the river, sir."

Lee thought, He has done all this . . . so early? He remembered the joke, passed along by his staff: to Jackson, dawn is one minute after midnight.

"Very well, Captain. You are dismissed."

Pendleton slid the contents of the plate into his pockets, moved quickly to his horse and disappeared in a flurry of muddy hoofprints. Lee leaned forward, rested his arms on the tops of his thighs, felt another shiver. Longstreet will be here soon, he thought, and I must know. He stood, flexed the stiff, sore hands, moved toward the warmth of the growing fire.

THE MEN AT THE BASE OF THE HILL ALREADY KNEW. MANY HAD ventured out, another night of scavenging, taking from the dead what they no longer needed. But this time they found that most were buried, shallow and crude graves, dug with bayonets and shell fragments. It was one thing to strip a dead man, but once he was in the ground, in the earth, it was a line they would not cross, and so they had come back to the safety of the wall with few new prizes.

McLaws had ordered more of them out now, a more organized line, probing, easing slowly along, down the slope of the incline, into the depression. Like Jackson's men, when they did not find the enemy, when there was no rifle fire, no obstacle, they pressed on, gradually picking up speed, stalking less quietly and with more courage. They had gone all the way to the edge of the town, crossed over the trenches dug the day before, and once they knew there was no one there, they began a party, a feast on the spoils left behind, knapsacks and blankets.

Word had gone back to McLaws, then to Longstreet, and Longstreet had come to Lee.

The fog was nearly gone now, and the sky began to clear, cold and blue. Lee and Longstreet reached the edge of the town together. Lee moved Traveller carefully down, across the fresh trench, and Longstreet followed, and in front of them nervous skirmishers began to move out through the streets of Fredericksburg, probing through the remains of the houses, making sure there was no one waiting.

Longstreet pointed, said, "Over the river . . . they're back on the heights. They may begin to shell us . . . the town."

Lee stopped the horse, stared over to the far hill, said nothing. From the right, toward the far edge of the town, they heard horses, and the foot soldiers dropped down and raised their muskets. Lee saw a flag and a man in a tall, plumed hat. In the street an officer yelled out to hold fire. It was Stuart.

"Good morning, General! General Longstreet. I heard you were riding into town. I hope you don't mind if I join you."

Lee nodded, said, "Of course, General, you are always welcome." He saw a broad smile, a man full of victory. "General Stuart, it was risky for you to ride across that plain with your flag. The enemy could certainly see you clearly."

Stuart bowed. "Thank you for your concern, General. We did not unfurl the flag until we reached the safety of the buildings. Besides, General, my staff and I have a way of escaping the guns of the enemy. Their marksmen are no match for a good horseman."

Longstreet made a sound, and Lee did not look at him, said, "All the same, General . . . there are too few of us to present the enemy with careless opportunity."

The smile faded and Stuart nodded solemnly, a scolded child.

Lee moved the horse forward, saw an officer running through the streets toward them, waving, yelling. "General . . . it's barbarism! The devil himself! You have to see . . . !" The man turned, waved them on, ran back down the street.

They rode ahead, followed the man's path, rounded a corner and reached the first row of houses, many still partially intact. Lee stared, looked down the street to heaping piles of debris, saw many more piles beyond, shattered furniture. He dismounted and the others followed. He walked toward the homes, felt the cracking of glass under his feet. The street was covered with the contents of the houses. There were mirrors, smashed from their frames, paintings ripped and torn, clothing—dresses, men's suits, a bridal gown—soaking up muddy water. He turned, walked down a side street, saw more of the same, began to move quicker, to the next main street, saw a huge pile of broken furniture, pieces of porcelain, grand vases and small pitchers, dishes, cups, all shattered into pieces. In front of one house a pile of books lay in the mud of the yard, covers ripped off, bindings split, and finally he stopped, felt the hot anger tighten his chest. He clenched his fists through the soreness, lowered his head.

"God . . . " He fought the anger, felt the sharp edge of the curse rising inside him, held it hard, pushed it back, away. "God, *forgive* them for what they have done."

Longstreet moved up beside him, and Lee still stared down, his eyes closed now, and Longstreet tried to think of something, said, "It's a real war. This is what war can do."

Lee did not look up, said, "No, General. This is not the work of soldiers. That man was right . . . it is the devil himself. It is the rape of the innocent." He raised his head, looked around again, and Longstreet saw tears, red swollen eyes. Lee turned then, walked back through the great piles of destruction. Longstreet heard a voice, Stuart, raw indignation, angry sounds, and he came up beside Longstreet, wanted to say something to Lee. Longstreet held up an arm, held him back.

Stuart said, "The whole town . . . barbarism . . . everything is destroyed! He has to do something about this!"

Longstreet watched Lee mount the horse, said, "He will, General, he will."

38. HANCOCK

December 15, 1862

THE SNOW WAS NEARLY GONE ON THE HEIGHTS, THE WARMER
rain washing much of it away into the river, and the hillside
was slick and muddy. All day the troops had moved up the hill,
forming camps behind the long rise, spreading out behind the guns.
What was left of his division was now far back in the trees, behind the
old mansion.

He had spent most of the morning with the paperwork, his great
talent, and this time it was not supplies he counted, but men, the casualties. Word came up, passed from the squadrons, to the companies and
regiments, and then to the brigades, and while other commanders were
still tending to their own staffs, or the replacement of horses, Hancock
was working with the papers. He had to know.

He had taken over five thousand men to the stone wall, taken
them to within twenty-five yards, the closest anyone had gotten, and
all three of his brigades, Zook and Meagher and Caldwell, had been
decimated. They had lost nearly forty percent of their strength, over
two thousand casualties. Once he saw the figure, he handed the report
to his staff, could not complete it, not yet, and left the men behind. He
walked back to the river, passed through the undamaged batteries that
still watched the town, the guns that could not help them.

Hancock moved with careful steps, his boots sliding in the soft
mud and small patches of ice. He walked upriver, away from the army,
walked to the place in the river he had seen before, where the cattle had
come across, where his men could have crossed days earlier. A decision,
he thought. A command decision.

He understood command, understood the value of discipline, it
was the most basic lesson a soldier could learn. If you were asked, you

offered your input, your suggestions, and in the end you did what the commander told you to do. It was simple and straightforward, and it was the only way to run an army. And this time it had been a horrible disaster.

He found a rock, climbed up, found a dry spot and sat down. Across the river he could see the burnt and crushed buildings in Fredericksburg, the debris piled along the streets, the scattered ruins of people's lives, lives that were changed forever. His men had done that. Not all of it, of course. The whole corps had seemed to go insane, had turned the town into some kind of violent party, a furious storm that blew out of control, and he could not stop it. The commanders had ordered the provost guards at the bridges to let no goods leave the town, nothing could be carried across the bridges, and so what the men could not keep, what they could not steal, they had just destroyed. And now, he thought, the people will return, trying to rescue some fragile piece of home, and they will find this . . . and they will learn something *new* about war, more than the quiet nightmare of leaving your home behind. They will learn that something happens to men, men who have felt no satisfaction, who have absorbed and digested defeat after bloody stupid defeat, men who up to now have done mostly what they were told to do. And when those men begin to understand that it is not anything in *them*, no great weakness or inferiority, but that it is the leaders, the generals and politicians who tell them what to do, that the fault is *there*, after a while they will stop listening. Then the beast, the collective anger, battered and bloodied, will strike out, will respond to the unending sights of horror, the deaths of friends and brothers, and it will not be fair or reasonable or just, since there is no intelligence in the beast. They will strike out at whatever presents itself, and here it was the harmless and innocent lives of the people of Fredericksburg.

He stared at the town for a long moment, the church steeples that still rose high and had somehow survived. At least you will have that, he thought. He wondered how strong their faith could be, after . . . He glanced up, looked toward God, something he rarely did, said to himself, *All right, help them. Give them some strength to start over, rebuild what they have lost. If this is Your will, then explain that to them. I surely cannot.*

He could see rebel soldiers in the town, men on horses, flags, but they were not in force, were not there to set up a line of defense. The big guns were still up here, after all, and by now Lee would know there was no need for a defense. It was over.

In the river below him the pontoon bridges were still fastened to the near shore, but had drifted down with the current, lay flat against the bank, and he could see men moving beside them, starting their work, untying them, salvaging what was worth keeping. He laughed, a humorless chuckle. It will be a long time before this army crosses a river on those things again, he thought. Maybe we should just cut them loose, let them drift in long strings down the widening river. They might make it all the way to the ocean, or hang up, clogging the river, preventing supplies from moving up this way. Might be a better weapon than these damned guns.

He rubbed his face, told himself to keep it under control. He knew he was angry, and an officer cannot be angry, does not have the luxury of the good old-fashioned cleansing temper, of walking up to headquarters with a pint of whiskey and two hard fists, kicking down the door and launching a bolt of lightning through the face of the man who did this. He felt himself shake. Yes, that would be very damned nice. The whiskey would be easy, there was always some around. He could even picture the scene, the whole thing, the staff officers moving to stop him, and he would brush them aside, the pale and weak men who did not dirty themselves with soldiers' work, and there would be Burnside, the fat round face staring up at him with raw terror, and he would pull him up by the collar . . . no, he would grab the sides of his face by those ridiculous whiskers, and Burnside would scream out, "Have pity, mercy!" And he would say, "They are all gone. You sent them across that river and watched them die . . . *you fat, bloody idiot.*"

He lay his face down in his hands, felt it pour up out of him, tried to cry, felt his eyes fill, and then it cut off, would not come. He could still see the looks on the faces, the pieces of broken and blasted men, *his* men, still running at the wall, right into the face of the muskets; and after the blinding flash, if they were still standing, they still ran forward. How can we expect them to keep doing that? It is not just training, you do not train a man to face death, he either will or he won't. And so many of them *will*.

He thought of Burnside again, thought, At least he knows what he did. Hancock still loved McClellan, would always consider him a friend, but McClellan did not understand, did not seem to grasp why a battle was lost, that he might have done something differently, better, faster. He would never blame the men, of course, but always looked behind him, to Washington, always found a conspiracy, some way to blame . . . *them.* But Burnside had accepted his failure, had even tried to lead another assault, ride out in front of his old Ninth Corps by himself, lead them up to that damned stone wall, die as the others had died.

It was a foolish gesture, and no one ever considered letting him go, and even he had understood that the absurd plan would kill a great many more good soldiers in yet another suicidal assault.

Lincoln will certainly replace him, Hancock thought. He went through the names: Franklin, Sumner, Hooker. None of them seemed to inspire much of anything. There was Reynolds, Baldy Smith, even Couch: a better group than the first, probably. But there was always the issue of rank, of seniority. And this was still the army.

He saw clouds forming now, a long low bank far to the west, back behind Lee's hills, more dark winter. We will do nothing for a while, he thought. Good, let them rest. Christmas . . . He thought of his son. My God, he is nearly ten years old. And he wants to be a soldier. He remembered Mira's last letter, the toy gun, fighting imaginary rebs in the backyard. No, he will not get the chance. The war may last . . . but he will not go, not *ever*.

He stood up, stretched, felt a stinging pain, his stomach, a wound he had not even noticed until it was over. Something . . . a ball, shrapnel, had torn his shirt, grazed a raw red line on his skin. Lucky man, he thought. If it had been an inch closer . . .

He stepped down from the rock, slid in the mud, steadied himself. Best get back, he thought. They're probably looking for me. Ought to find Couch, talk to him. And Meagher, his leg. He started back along the hill, was surprised to see a man higher up the hill, sitting against a tree, a civilian. The man was writing, had a pad of paper perched on his knee, and Hancock turned, climbed up closer, and the man looked up, surprised.

"Hello . . . you're . . . a general. One of the *leaders* of our fine young men." There was heavy sarcasm in his voice, and Hancock let it pass, nodded.

"Hancock. Winfield Hancock."

The man looked up again, wide eyes, said, "Oh, General Hancock. It is a pleasure to meet you. Not too many generals on this field to whom I could say that. You are very highly regarded, General . . . which is also a rare comment."

Hancock watched the man, who kept writing; a small man, older, thin gray hair, wire-rimmed glasses.

"I don't know you, sir. Are you an artist?"

The man laughed, put down the pen, said, "Well, yes, certainly I am. In the same way as you, I suppose. Anyone who rises to the top of his profession must have some artistry. In fact, I am a reporter. Have you heard of the *Cincinnati Commercial*?"

"No, sorry, I'm from Pennsylvania."

"No matter. There's a good many in Cincinnati who haven't heard of her either."

"You're writing about what happened here?"

"What happened here has already been dispatched. By this morning my paper, and most others, have already given the people the news. Another chapter of disaster in the ever lengthening tragedy. No, General, I am writing a column, a commentary. From time to time there are people in Cincinnati who actually seem to care about what I think."

"So, may I ask?"

"What I think? What does it matter, General? You have only one duty, only one opinion to guide you, that of your commander. We civilians have little influence over either your actions or your thoughts. My audience is interested in hearing the point of view that does not flow through a headquarters, is not censored by the official rationale that, alas, war is a necessary evil, and thus any tragedy or idiocy is just a small part of the greater curse, which of course you all deplore. The people have heard all that, General. What they do not often hear is some honesty, the uncensored view of someone outside of your bloody little fraternity."

"I assure you, Mister . . ."

"Bolander, Cyrus Bolander."

"I assure you, Mr. Bolander, we do not all share the same official view of events. The commanding general has a responsibility to speak for his army, but he does not tell us what to think."

The man looked at his pad, then back at Hancock, said, "Hmmm, well that may be, General. All right, fine. Here." He handed the pad up to Hancock. "That's my column. Forgive me if you find my words a bit harsh."

Hancock turned the pad around, saw the writing of a skilled hand, neat straight lines, and he began to read. "It has never been possible for men to show more valor, or generals to manifest less judgment . . ."

He stopped, looked at Bolander, said, "No, sir. I do not find your words too harsh. Perhaps they are not harsh enough."

PART
FOUR

39. CHAMBERLAIN

JANUARY 1863

CHRISTMAS HAD BEEN WHITE AND COLD, AND THEY DID NOT talk about the men who were no longer there. Griffin's division moved out away from the river, spread out into winter quarters around an obscure place known as Stoneman's Switch.

They had dug shallow pits in the hard ground, piled logs around for short walls, then capped the huts with what had been their tents. It was cramped and dark, but it kept them warm. But the warmth also softened the ground beneath them, and so the huts became soggy dens of mud and sickness.

They did not celebrate the New Year. Burnside would not allow the army to sit quietly while his great failure haunted him, and so he sent troops out, up the river, small reconnaissance patrols and larger probes, as though by the effort he could somehow discover some soft vulnerability in Lee's lines, some undiscovered part of the countryside where the army could redeem itself, and thus redeem him. Chamberlain led the regiment on such a probe, had done nothing to create any miracle, only the men having passed the time over the New Year without having to huddle together in the crude huts.

His feet were cold. They were always cold. He walked among the huts, could hear the squishing sound of his boots now, the ground softening, the weather warming slightly. He looked up to the sun, thought, So, what now? An early spring? The weather over Christmas had been brutal, a heavy, wet cold that even the men from Maine found miserable. Now he felt a slight warmth, looked into the bright glare above him. Damned strange. He thought of Maine, the dependability of the winter. By November it was there, without doubt, and the snow would come, and it was consistent and definite, and you worked around it, understood it was simply part of life. It would stay there often until April, and then you began to think once more of spring. He thought of the simplicity, the four seasons. It was a good system. But in Virginia there was no system. The cold gave way, a day or two of warm air, and the snow would melt, turning the ground to soft glue, and then without warning it would snow again, sometimes a foot or more, or a hard freeze would catch them by surprise, torturing the men, who had begun to lighten their load, letting down their guard. And so they would prepare for the worst again, scramble into the huts, and then it would warm up again. Chamberlain thought, I will not miss this.

They were nearly three weeks into the new year, and did not believe anything serious would happen until an honest spring came upon them, but now there were orders, and most of the huge army was stirring around them, new activity. Ames had come around early, told Chamberlain to bring the men together. They were to begin a new march.

There were no announcements, no send-off, and even the bands were quiet. All they knew was that Burnside had a new plan, and they were to move back up the river, to cross the Rappahannock where many had insisted they cross two months before, the shallow fords above Fredericksburg.

Again Burnside assumed he would outsmart Lee, would make a bold and quick assault from the north, catch Lee by surprise, coming at him from behind. Burnside waited until the roads were firm, the weather fair, and now he would lead his men to the victory they had no chance of finding in December.

Chamberlain did not ride, led his men on foot, and they filed into place on the wide road that would lead them along the river. He heard little talking; there was no sense of adventure now, the energy drained away. He saw Ames, on his horse, sitting beside the road ahead. Ames was talking to another officer, a man missing an arm. Chamberlain walked toward them, stepped down off the surface of the road, and his feet slid suddenly away, slipped sideways into the depression that ran beside the road. He caught himself, one hand landing hard in the wetness, and Ames saw him. The other man said something, laughing, then rode away.

"Are you all right, Colonel?"

Chamberlain straightened, shook his hand, looked for something to wipe the mud away, and behind him, a voice: Tom.

"Lawrence, you hurt? Here . . ." Tom had a handkerchief, held it out, and Chamberlain took it, grateful, and wiped his hand.

Chamberlain looked at Ames, said, "Just a clumsy fall, Colonel. These roads are a bit of a mess."

"No, they are not, Colonel. I have just been told—that officer was Colonel Markey, of General Griffin's staff—these roads are now ideal for a new and glorious advance of this army. That is, in so many words, part of General Burnside's orders. So, Colonel, you see, you did not slip in the mud. There is no mud."

Chamberlain stared at Ames, heard the bitterness, something new, looked at his hand again, the handkerchief. "No, sir. No mud here."

Ames abruptly turned his horse, rode away along the edge of the wet road.

Tom said, "He's in a fine spirit today, eh, Lawrence?"

Chamberlain handed the cloth back to his brother, realized Tom was wearing a new uniform. "So . . . it's official."

"Ain't it grand, Lawrence? Got it this morning. Look . . ." He pointed to the shoulder, the gold bar of the lieutenant. "Lawrence, I tell you . . . it's real different. They *salute*. Even those boys from Bangor—the Capper brothers? I was always afraid they was gonna whip me for no good reason. Now, they call me *sir*!"

It had been Ames, and Captain Spear, who had recommended Tom for promotion. Chamberlain had stayed out of it, knew better, but it was clear that Tom had done his job well enough to attract the praise of the others. And now there were many vacant positions for officers.

Chamberlain smiled, said, "A uniform does strange things to people. Good things, I suppose. It has meaning . . . we're trained to accept that. We see that bar on your shoulder . . . the eagle on Ames's. We don't even have to see the face, the *man*. I guess that means we're soldiers."

"Lawrence, I was gonna write to Papa today, tell him about the promotion . . . the new uniform. Anything you want me to say?"

Chamberlain watched the line of troops moving past, momentum pushing them into the rhythm of the march. "I suppose . . . tell him we did good. You and me both. We did as good a job as soldiers are supposed to do. He'll appreciate that. Probably mean as much to him as anything else we could say."

"All right, I will. They're proud of both of us, Lawrence, you know that."

Chamberlain watched the last of the regiment move past, saw new officers, the next unit in line, knew they had better move along, catch up. "Yep, I know that. But please, stop calling me Lawrence."

Tom smiled, saluted, then turned and ran, falling into line at the rear of his company. Chamberlain climbed carefully up to the road bed, walked with a quick step alongside the lines of troops, thought, We follow symbols, we follow the commands of men who have stars on their uniforms. The man doesn't matter, the face or the name. Unless . . . he makes some bloody awful mistake, then the stars are given to someone else. He looked at the ground, felt his boots sink slightly into softening dirt, thought of Ames's words. Of course, Ames understood, it is happening again.

He passed Tom, kept moving forward, moved by the other familiar faces, made his way toward the front of the line. He glanced over to one man, saw Kilrain, who was looking up, and Chamberlain followed the look, a brief glimpse toward a thick gray sky, and then he felt it, hitting his cheek, one cold drop of rain, and he looked back toward Kilrain. The heavy round face was looking at him, the hard look of a man who also understood, who had seen all the stupidity, who knew, after all, that the gold stars were often mindless decoration, that the army was led not by symbols, but by the fallible egos and blind fantasies of men.

I T RAINED ALL NIGHT AND ALL THE NEXT DAY, AND STILL DID NOT stop. On the far side of the river Stuart's men watched from under the dripping rims of wide hats as Burnside's new plan, the quick and daring assault, was swallowed by the deep ooze of the Virginia mud. The great lines of wagons pulling the salvaged pontoons, the small field guns and heavier cannon, the tons of food and supplies, sank deeper and deeper, until Burnside had no choice but to halt the march and give the order to return the army back to Falmouth and the winter camps across the river from Fredericksburg.

By the end of January the army had settled into a new sense of gloom, defeated not only by Lee and Jackson, Stuart and Longstreet, or by the forces beyond the control of man, the rain and the cold. They had been defeated by the mind of one man, a kind and affable man who had a disastrous lack of talent for command. And thus Lincoln again made a change. Burnside was removed, as was Franklin, and Sumner was forced to retire. Fighting Joe Hooker was given command of the army. Lincoln's appointment to the new commander concluded, "Go forward and give us victories."

40. LEE

February 1863

HE WAR WAS SPREAD NOW OVER MOST OF THE SOUTH, AND there were new threats to the Atlantic coast. Burnside had been given his Ninth Corps again, and had been sent by boat to the southern coast of Virginia, below the James River. This effort could open a new front which would threaten the valuable supply routes that came from farther south, the fragile system of railroads through the Carolinas and Georgia. There was still the fear that by occupying southern Virginia, the Federal troops might again push inland, south of the James River, and once again threaten Richmond, this time from below.

The Federal threats to the Southern coast had never been serious enough to warrant Lee splitting up his army. He had found this part of the Confederacy a convenient place to send those commanders who had proven they were not fit to lead large armies in times of major crisis. Gustavus Smith, Chase Whiting, and even Beauregard, whose ego did not mix well with Lee's style, were in command in various regions along the coast. But with the new threat, Lee knew he had to send someone who could hold the line against a serious advance, and at the same time hold the various Confederate commands together into some sort of cohesive unit, not governed by each general's temperament.

He had first responded to the Federal move by sending Daniel Hill to North Carolina, to organize new volunteers into some sort of effective defense. Additional troops had been sent down under General Robert Ransom, and while Lee knew that neither man had proven himself in independent command, both were diligent and trustworthy soldiers. The detachments from Lee's already outnumbered army, which still looked across the Rappahannock at the massive Federal force, did not satisfy the agitation that the new threat had given Jefferson Davis. Davis believed the threat to Richmond called for a more drastic response, and so, despite Lee's small numbers, Davis insisted the army be divided further, and that a much larger force be sent to southern Virginia.

THERE HAD BEEN SNOW AGAIN, A FEW INCHES, AND THE HILLS and fields were again a solid white, a clean blanket for the fresh graves and torn earth of the great battle. Lee walked along his hill, Taylor behind, and the gun crews came alive, stood suddenly, shaking off the cold, a show for the commander which he did not need. He raised his hand, nodded to the men, and hats were raised, cheers went down the line. The sounds carried below, to the troops in their cold-weather camps, and the men crawled out from snow-covered hideaways, knew what the sound meant. No matter how often they saw him, they would give up the small warm place in the ground to see him again.

He moved back over the hill, dropped down behind the lines, saw a huge fire. There were few big fires now, there was no wood left, the trees and fences long gone. The men had formed details, hauling firewood over the rough country roads from farther and farther away. As the army sat in one place, it pulled at the country like some great dirty sponge, soaking up a widening circle of food and fuel.

The big fire was slowing, and the men saw him coming now, more cheers, and now he saw it had been a wagon; one spoke wheel leaned crookedly from the edge of the black ash. There was one officer, a captain Lee did not know, and the man was hesitant, saluted with a glance toward the fire, and Lee nodded, did not speak, did not ask if the wagon was usable or not.

He stood close to the shrinking heat, looked at the men who spread along the far side of the fire, away from him. They would not get too close, though more than once, when he would ride through the camps, someone would approach, carefully, a dirty hand extended, just to touch him, to touch the horse. He did not understand that, it always embarrassed him, but he rarely stopped them, left that to the officers or his staff, who might keep the men away with a shout, or the empty threat of a raised sword. He stared beyond the fire now and saw the faces of the men, the faces of his grand and wonderful army. Now there were more faces, to the side, behind him, men gathering from all directions, all along the hill, and he looked out, to all the dark eyes that watched him quietly, and he felt his throat tighten, could not swallow, fought it, said a silent prayer, *Thank You, for the love of these men.* Yes, he thought, I love them as well.

He tried not to look at the faces, saw the army instead, saw the filthy rags most were using for clothes, the small pieces of cloth many had wrapped around their feet, but not all—there were many bare feet, red and hard on the snow. He saw now the thin frames of men who did not eat because there was little to go around. The soft sadness gave way now, replaced by anger, toward the Federals, toward this war. And toward Davis, who would not come out here, who did not see these men in their rough and cold camps, and so did not take seriously his urgent requests, and those of others, to provide better for these men, soldiers who spent their time now in basic survival, a glorious fighting force that was slowly starving to death.

H E WAS IN HIS TENT, HOLDING A GIFT FROM A LOCAL MERCHANT in the town, an old man, a candlemaker, who had brought his family back to their home and found their whole lives reduced to the litter of war, scattered into the streets of Fredericksburg. The man had crossed the canal, climbed the hill, looking for Lee, asking, following the sad directions of weak soldiers, and finally had found him. He had come only to give him the one piece of his family's history that he had found intact, their Bible. The old man looked at Lee with eyes that unsettled him, eyes that dug deep inside, a man whose faith was now firmly with this army, and so he accepted the gift without protest. Now, he sat alone and read the inside cover, crude handwriting, the old man's simple message: "To General Robert E. Lee, May God bless you, and the good work you do."

Work. He did not think of what he did as work, not as a job. When he had been back in Richmond, in the drab office with the piles of paper, that had been work. Leading these men . . . he shook his head, thought, Maybe that is what we need now: work. These men do not need generals now, they need someone who can supply them, feed them, the work of the people who stare at piles of paper. And those people have not done a very good job.

He rose, put the Bible down on his cot, pushed out through the flaps of the tent and looked for Taylor, who was standing over two men, trying to keep a small fire lit.

"Major, if you please." Taylor turned toward him, began

to move, and Lee said, "Major, please send my respects to General Longstreet, and request that he meet with me as soon as he is able."

Taylor nodded, began to move again, and Lee said, "And ... please request that the general bring along two of his best ... no ... that is vague. Request that the general be accompanied by General Pickett and General Hood."

Taylor absorbed the message, nodded again, and Lee went back to the warmth of the tent, began again to read the old man's Bible.

I T WAS LATE IN THE AFTERNOON, AND MORE CLOUDS WERE MOVING in, more thick gray, and Lee knew there would be snow yet again. He heard them first, a dull rumble, then saw the horses coming up the rise from the direction of the larger hill, Marye's Heights. Longstreet wore the wide floppy hat, held the reins with a new pair of white leather gloves, and Lee smiled, thought, It has to be a gift, he would not wash the old ones.

Behind Longstreet the other men were a marked contrast. Lee knew the bulky form of Hood, a bigger man than even Longstreet, and beside him Pickett, the small, thin frame topped by rolls of curling hair bouncing below his small cap. They reined up, dismounted heavily, and Lee stood, hands on his hips, stretched his back, then felt a tightness in his chest.

He pushed his arms out wide, said, "Gentlemen, it is a pleasure. Please, let us go inside, it's a bit warmer."

Lee backed into the tent, and Taylor held open the large flaps for the others. Longstreet bent, moved inside, and Lee pointed to a small stool. Longstreet did not speak, sat down with a small groan. Hood moved inside, quickly found a place on the ground, and now Pickett, and suddenly the tent was filled with a smell, and Lee felt his face contract, bombarded by the peculiar odor.

"My goodness ... what is that ... ?"

Longstreet laughed, pointed a gloved hand at Pickett, who said, "General Lee, with all respect, I come today wearing the latest gift from my dear Sallie, a sample of the finest and most recent import from Paris. It is called 'Fleur de ... Fromage,' or something. ..."

Lee thought, Flower of cheese? and Longstreet said, "General, please forgive General Pickett, he does not have a gift for French. And as for his taste ..."

"My taste is quite the envy of Richmond, sir. I assure you, if the other gentlemen in this army would allow themselves to partake of the good life that still abounds, it would make for a much more pleasant if not high-class atmosphere."

Hood moved slightly, increased the distance between him and Pickett, said, "General, it is not often my good fortune to share such close quarters with you . . . for which I am now grateful . . . but I respectfully point out that there are a great many fine officers in this army who are *not* gentlemen, and who would not be caught dead smelling like that."

Pickett looked at Hood with surprise, then frowned. "Pity . . ."

"Gentlemen," Lee said, interrupting. "We must address matters at hand. I, for one, will accept General Pickett's . . . adornment. However, it compels me to make this meeting a brief one."

Hood nodded, said, "Bless you, sir."

Lee looked at Longstreet, who waited, was not smiling now, had removed the gloves and pulled a short cigar from his coat. "General Longstreet, we are faced with a problem . . . two problems, actually. The first, and most immediate, is the supplying of this army. This is my priority. The second problem concerns the Federal advance along the Virginia coast, below the James River. That is President Davis's priority. I believe we have a means to deal with both situations. We must begin by dividing this army. . . ."

A S THE FIRST TRUE SIGNS OF SPRING BEGAN TO SPREAD OVER the hills and farms of Virginia, the march began. The two divisions under Hood and Pickett would move to the trains, travel south, establish a defensive front below the James River, and unite the efforts of the other commanders there to prevent any further Federal advance. Longstreet was placed in a position of independent command, with two important conditions. One was that he begin immediately to secure supplies for the army from an agricultural area that was still relatively abundant, and send a steady flow of these supplies to northern Virginia. The second condition was that Longstreet be prepared, at quick notice, to make use of the railroads, and return his troops to Lee's command if Lee required it. Lee was now left with a force of only fifty-five thousand, less than half the size of the Federal Army that sat in winter quarters above the Rappahannock, a Federal Army with a new commander, who had a sharp eye toward the end of the miserable winter.

H E HAD RIDDEN INTO THE TOWN, AN INVITATION FROM A GROUP of women. It was a brave show of normalcy, a formal and social gathering by citizens crushed by the weight of destruction and rebuilding, and Lee could not refuse them.

The snow was gone now, the wide field beginning to fill with large patches of deep green. There were still signs of the battle, many signs, and he rode past them now without looking down. He looked up to his hill, to the long row of hills, thought, Will they do it again? It was hopeful, but he knew it would not be. The new Federal commander would not follow the same disastrous path of his predecessor.

He began to climb, and the gun crews waved to him, welcoming him back. He stopped the horse, climbed down, had a sudden need to walk, to kick through the new growth. Behind him, his staff was surprised, began to climb down as well, and he turned, waved them on, said, "No, go ahead. I just want to walk."

Taylor stayed behind, sat on his horse, holding Traveller's reins, and the others rode on up the hill, between the big guns.

He began to climb, quick short steps, a fresh energy, his boots digging into the soft dirt, and he looked down, saw bees dancing among the first of the new flowers, small yellow circles climbing out of the layer of thick brown. He was breathing hard now, paused, reached down, thought of Mary, flowers in her hair, and there was a sudden pain in his throat. He tried to straighten up, felt the pain moving into his left arm, a sharp burn, and looked at the arm, the hand, expected to see blood, a wound, but the gray coat was unchanged. He sank to one knee, held the arm, massaging, feeling, but the pain did not go away. He looked up the hill, to the guns, saw the troops watching him, coming toward him, and from deep inside he felt something swell up, long icy fingers wrapping around, gripping his heart, and he looked down, saw the flowers, saw them fading behind a cold black curtain.

H E WAS ON HIS COT, STARING INTO A GLOW OF LIGHT, THE RE-flection of the sun on the canvas. He saw Taylor, and Walker, and now he saw more, realized the tent was full of people, and there was a doctor . . . the man who had set his injured hands. He tried to turn his head, felt the pain in his throat, froze into stillness.

The doctor said, "Hello, General. Welcome back. We were a bit concerned, I must say."

He said nothing, looked at Taylor, saw teary-eyed relief, then tried to turn, and again the pain stopped him cold.

"Easy, now, General. No need to move about."

"What . . . ?"

Taylor bent over him, said in a hushed tone, "We thought you had left us, General. You collapsed . . . we brought you to your tent. The doctor says you'll be all right. Just rest. If you need anything . . ."

There was a sound outside the tent, a voice, yelling. "He's awake. He's all right!" and now there was more noise, the sounds of cheering, and Lee listened, did not move, looked at the doctor, a question.

The doctor said, "General, if I may have a private word?"

Lee looked at Taylor, who turned, spoke to the others. "Out! Leave the general alone now. We must leave him."

The men began to file out, and the tent seemed suddenly cavernous, hollow. The doctor sat down on the stool, said, "General, I believe you have a problem with your heart. You seem better now . . . actually, you seem in perfect health. But sometimes it can sneak up on you. The best advice I can give you is take it a bit easier."

Lee spoke quietly, testing his voice. "Doctor, there is an army out there. They are not likely to allow me much of a rest."

"General Lee, I can only offer that you will not serve our cause well if you are flat on your back. The best way for you to get back on your feet, or onto your horse, is to rest now. Your young Mr. Taylor seems to be quite capable of managing this headquarters."

Lee stared at the canvas, nodded slightly. "Doctor, can we do anything to keep this matter somewhat . . . private?"

The doctor laughed, said, "Actually, no."

Lee smiled. "No, I suppose not."

The news that he was not seriously ill spread through the army with the same speed and energy that propels word of a great victory. The troops began to find ways to pass by his headquarters more often now, and gifts began to flow into the camp, from the town and from the countryside. He did not stay on his cot long, and within a few days even Taylor could see no difference, none of the tormenting signs of age. Lee began to ride again, to move among the troops, to ride down the broad hill, through the guns and the fields of flowers, staring hard at the hills across the river.

41. JACKSON

APRIL 1863

HE STARED DOWN AT THE PAPER, HELD THE PENCIL TIGHTLY, frowned. There were no words. Abruptly, he stood up and walked around the small table, a quick search for inspiration, then sat back down, stared again at the blank page. He tried to recall the battle, could see it all, the smoke and the men, could hear the violent sounds. But . . . he could not write it down, the simple explanation of what happened.

He had gone too long without tackling this job, the painful and annoying paperwork of command. Lee had insisted. There was a lull in the fighting, the army was still in winter quarters, and there would be no better time. But Jackson was not a writer.

He stood again, thought, Pendleton will help, of course. He wondered why he had not thought of that before—his staff. They had been on all the fields, they saw most of what he saw. They would know whose regiment and whose brigade led which advance. To Jackson, once the sounds of the battles had rolled across the field, it was all automatic. The troop movements and the positioning of the lines were instinctive. He did not ever recall thinking that he would have to write it all down afterward.

Yes, he thought, I will tell them: Pendleton . . . Smith. They can do this. I will read what they recall, and if it seems accurate, I will sign it. He nodded, pleased with himself, his aggravation resolved. He thought of lemonade then, realized he had a great thirst, knew the women in the house would always accommodate him. He looked around the tent, spotted the wide black felt hat that Anna had sent him, reached for it, and heard a small sound outside. He stopped, silent, peered toward the flaps, saw a small movement along the bottom and smiled, then moved quietly closer to the sound with slow, light steps. He could hear the sound again, the small giggle, and through the flaps came a small pink hand, then more, the tiny face, a beaming smile. Jackson knelt down, surprised the little girl with a quick grab, pulled her up and into the tent, and she burst into loud and happy laughter. He held the child up above him, toward the top of the tent, and the surprise passed. She was smiling now, reached for the hat on his head, and he set her down.

"No, child, you cannot have my hat. It might be a bit large. . . ." He removed it, saw the strip of gold braid that wound around the hat, pulled, and it came loose in his hand. He tossed the hat aside, wrapped the gold braid around the girl's head and tied it up around the fine golden hair.

"Well, now," he said, "I believe that suits a young girl better than an old soldier."

She laughed again, touching the braid.

"Now, I was just about to go for some lemonade. I would very much like the company of one beautiful five-year-old girl."

She nodded, smiling brightly, and he led her out of the tent. He picked her up and set her gently down on his shoulders, her oversized dress bunching up, covering his face, and he stumbled about. "Oh no, I cannot see," he said. "How shall we find the house?" She began the high sweet giggles again, and he staggered unevenly across the yard, went up to the porch and into the house.

In the yard, near the other tents, Jackson's aides had watched the scene, and Pendleton said, "No soldier, on either side, who has ever shared the field with Stonewall would ever believe what we have just seen."

The others laughed, heads were shaking, and the group began to disperse, attending to their own duties. Pendleton went toward Jackson's tent, held a handful of new reports, ducked inside, looked for a place to set them down and then saw the blank paper on the table. He understood Jackson's difficulty with battle reports. There were small dots—a dozen pencil marks where Jackson had tried to begin writing. Pendleton sat down in Jackson's chair, thought of what he'd just seen out in the yard. Around the fires, at dinner, Jackson would sit quietly while the staff joked and kidded, and when he would laugh, it was sudden and awkward, and Pendleton thought, He laughs like a man who doesn't know how. Yet, out there, with the little girl, he had been as open and free as a child himself, nothing reserved, no shy withdrawal. Pendleton picked up the pencil, began to write:

The Official Report from the Second Corps, Lieutenant General Thomas J. Jackson Commanding: The Battle of Fredericksburg . . .

THEY WERE CAMPED ON THE VAST GROUNDS OF MOSS NECK, A plantation spread out a few miles below the plains of Fredericksburg. It was the home of Richard Corbin, his wife and child, and his larger family, some of them refugees from other places, places now consumed by the war. Corbin himself was away, assigned to duty with the army, and so the women commanded the household, and the little girl, five-year-old Jane, commanded General Jackson.

Jackson had been invited to stay in the house itself and declined. He'd had the staff tents pitched across the wide yard. On occasion, however, he would allow himself and the staff to enjoy the luxury of a supper on the white linen of the Corbin dining room. Mrs. Corbin was a most courteous hostess, but it was her daughter who brightened the long days of winter quarters.

They stood in the hallway, at the kitchen door, waiting. The request had been made, and Jackson stood at attention, the little girl reaching her hand high to hold his, and together they filled the doorway. The girl's aunt, Kate Corbin, was busy stirring a pitcher.

"My, General, we do appreciate the gift. Where do you get all these lemons?"

Jackson stared ahead, said, "It is a kind Providence that provides kindness. . . ." He paused, tried to rephrase that.

"Why, General, you are quite the poet!"

He was suddenly embarrassed, said, "No, it is God who provides. . . ."

"Yes, General, I know what you meant. Here, for goodness sakes, enjoy your lemonade."

She handed a tall glass to him, and a small cup to the little girl, and he stepped away from the door and bent over, a formal bow to bright blue eyes. Jane bowed toward him, then they both drank from their glasses. Afterward, wiping at wet chins, they repeated what had become their ritual, closed their eyes and together said, "Mmmmmmmmmmmm!"

Kate wiped her hands with a small towel, said, "I swear, General, if you spoil your own child like that . . . you will have your hands full."

He looked at her, and Jane suddenly leapt forward, grabbed his leg and wrapped one arm tight around his knee. "Miss Corbin," he said, "it will give me great pleasure to spoil my daughter. I intend to give her many opportunities to spoil me as well." He looked at the small bundle now clinging to his leg, and he drank from the glass again. "How easy it is to forget . . . all that we must do . . . all the horrors that we have seen . . . simply by staring into the face of a small child. There is Providence here . . . in that. The children are blessed."

He reached down, pulled the little girl up, lifted her onto his shoulder. She still held the small cup, splashed lemonade on his uniform.

Kate said, "Oh goodness, here, General, let me put a damp cloth on that."

Jackson glanced at her, a gleam of blue mischief in his eyes, said, "Oh, that won't be necessary, Miss Corbin, because Jane and I . . ." He paused, grinned devilishly at the little girl, and giggles rolled over him. Suddenly, he was running down the hall, out the front of the house, carrying her at all angles. He gently set her down in the green grass and rolled on the ground beside her, and there were gales of laughter from both of them.

A few feet away, Captain Smith was staring in utter amazement, then turned toward the sound of an approaching rider.

THE FEDERAL ARMY HAD BEGUN TO STIR. WHILE THERE WAS NO clear evidence of a plan, Lee knew that the new commander, Hooker, under the stern eye of Washington, could produce a quick threat, and so he ordered Jackson to move his camp up from Moss Neck, to be closer to the hills behind Fredericksburg. Stuart's vigilance along the river above the town had given Lee some hint that the Federal Army would again plan a move in that direction, and he took a chance, pulling Jackson's corps away from Port Royal. He anticipated that Hooker would do what Burnside should have done from the start, cross the river to the northwest, behind the hills, using the convenience of several shallow fords. Below the crossings, the roads ran together, intersecting with the main roads leading westward out of Fredericksburg. The intersection was named for the family that lived there, was called Chancellorsville.

The tents had been struck, the troops moved well up the road, and Jackson rode his horse back along the line of moving men, went toward the house for the last time. Kate Corbin was on the porch, had watched the troops leave. The last of the staff was cleaning up the yard when she saw Jackson and waved sadly. He rode up close to the porch, dismounted and said, "Miss Corbin, if you please, I would like to say good-bye to your niece. I shall miss her."

"Certainly, General. She is not feeling well today. There seems to be some illness in this house. All the children have come down with a fever. Please, come in."

He followed her into the house, he felt the heavy layer of quiet, and lightened his steps, self-conscious of his boots on the hard floor. She led him into a small parlor, and he saw Mrs. Corbin, Jane's mother, bending over a small blanket. She turned, looked at him, smiled weakly, and he went to the little girl, saw the blond hair spread over a small white pillow.

"Well, now, what is this? How can I play with my friend if she insists on staying in bed?"

He waited for the laugh, the small giggle, but she only smiled up at him, held up a hand and tried to reach his short beard. He saw the look in her eyes, suddenly straightened, said to Mrs. Corbin, "I will have my doctor, Dr. McGuire, attend to her. I will send him immediately." She nodded, grateful, and he backed away, saying, "I must return to my men. I will send Dr. McGuire."

Then he turned and marched from the house.

T HEY WERE CAMPED NOW IN A LARGE FIELD, IN SIGHT OF THE broad plain where Jackson had held his lines against Meade. The staff filed from the small mess tent, had enjoyed the unusual and rare gift of a smoked ham sent to the headquarters from a local farmer, who clearly had a talent for hiding his bounty. Jackson was last out of the tent. He rubbed his stomach, listened to the casual talk from the others, how long they would be in this spot, the warmth of the spring weather. He thought of writing a letter, had received a new note from Anna detailing the joys of his tiny daughter, and he began to form his words, maybe a prayer, but heard the sound of horses. There were two riders out on the road. It was Pendleton . . . and Hunter McGuire.

McGuire was not much older than the young staff officer, had come to Jackson's staff from Winchester, a choice made mainly because he was well known among the others. He was a well-educated man, even by medical standards, had received formal training at the University of Pennsylvania. By now he had built a solid reputation for medicine, advised many of the older surgeons, and no one doubted he was the best man Jackson could have chosen for the job. Jackson had an instinctive respect for the neat and efficient young man, and as Pendleton and McGuire walked toward him, there was something in the doctor's face that turned Jackson cold. He did not move, waited. Pendleton saluted, and Jackson did not look at him, kept his eyes on McGuire.

The doctor glanced down at the ground, said in a low voice, "It was scarlet fever. The children are all right. I gave them some . . . they will be fine. Except . . . I am terribly sorry, General. The little girl . . . Jane . . . did not survive. She has died, sir."

Jackson stared at him, did not speak, fixed his eyes on McGuire's face, and McGuire turned away, could not look back at the sharp glare of Jackson's eyes. Abruptly, Jackson stepped away, marched out between the tents, out into the field. Pendleton began to follow him, the others as well, but they slowed, stayed back, watched as he moved away through the thick green grass. Then suddenly he sat, on a short stump, put his head in his hands and began to sob.

Pendleton stayed a short distance away, felt McGuire's hand on his arm. "What is it?" Pendleton said. "He's never cried before . . . not for all the blood and all the death. There was something about that little girl. . . ."

McGuire nodded quietly, said, "A general cannot cry for his men. They cannot even cry for each other now. This army has cried all its tears."

"But he has not."

They stood, and around them troops gathered, curious. They saw Jackson now, and no one spoke. They watched in silence as Jackson poured out his grief, and they did not move, stayed quietly around him as the dark night filled the field.

42. CHAMBERLAIN

APRIL 1863

THERE WAS NO OTHER EXPLANATION: THE SERUM WAS SIMPLY bad. He did not understand medicine, knew that his unit had done well compared to others, that they made it through the winter without losing many. Now, Hooker had made it a priority: the army would improve its health. Hygiene would be practiced, the camps would be cleaner. And . . . there would be vaccinations, protection against the always present danger of smallpox. Except . . . the serum had been bad.

Around the camp, officers were working quickly, men in white masks directing the troops, digging the small signposts into the soft ground. Chamberlain moved closer, saw the troops back away, keeping their distance, and he walked around, saw the sign: DO NOT ENTER—QUARANTINE AREA.

He waved at the men. "Hello, how are you today?" and smiled, thought of the absurd bad luck. The serum could possibly have infected the entire regiment with the disease, and so, of course, they would have to stay put, together, no contact with the rest of the army until the danger was past. He stared at one man, a doctor who was waving the troops away, their work done.

Chamberlain walked over to another signpost, where a man was nailing up fence wire. "Enjoy your work, do you?" he asked.

The man looked at him, covered his mouth, said, "For the love of God, man, stay away! I got a family!"

Chamberlain turned, walked toward the tents, shook his head. If the enemy cannot kill us, he thought, the army can.

The rest of the army had begun to move, along the same roads that had swallowed them up in January. Hooker had done much for morale, for the sense that maybe—this time—it would be different. Chamberlain did not know the mission, knew the army was moving away to the northwest and that the Twentieth Maine was not going anywhere.

He had not seen Ames, who was not in camp, and he wondered if quarantines applied to the commanders. It brightened him for a moment. Maybe he could somehow just order the disease away, the privilege of rank.

He saw men on horseback approaching the edge of the camp, then dismounting, and he moved toward them. They were officers, among them a major, who stepped back. It was a reflex Chamberlain was beginning to find extremely annoying.

"Sir . . . you are Colonel Chamberlain?"

"Certainly am, Major."

"Sir, I have a message for you . . . from Colonel Ames. Under the circumstances, Colonel . . . would you mind if I read it? I am not to cross the quarantine line, sir."

Chamberlain nodded. "Fine, Major, read the message."

"Thank you, sir."

> To Lieutenant Colonel J. L. Chamberlain . . . I am pleased to inform you that I have received appointment to General Meade's command, as a staff officer. I deeply appreciate your fine work as second in command and wish to advise you unless I return, you are in command of the Twentieth Maine Regiment of Volunteers. I regret that the regiment, which has performed with consistent valor, should have been victimized by such an unfortunate turn of events. However, I have been assured that in a few short weeks the quarantine will be lifted and the regiment may return to active duty. Please assure the men that they are in my thoughts. Signed, Colonel Adelbert Ames.

"That is all, sir."

Chamberlain nodded. "Thank you, Major. You may return to the land of the unafflicted."

He walked toward his tent, thought, So Ames *did* escape. And he made certain I did not. Men were watching him, some had heard the order, and they began to gather. He stopped, stood with his hands on his hips.

One man said, "Colonel, sir, how long are we to be kept here? They're treatin' us like prisoners."

Others began to speak, angry questions, and he held up his hands, said, "Please, quiet." More men moved up, they were in a circle around him, and he saw Tom and the other officers. "The army is on the march, and we cannot go with them, not for a while. It's as simple as that. You already know the danger, why we are behind a fence. There is simply nothing we can do about it."

"Colonel . . . " Ellis Spear moved forward, through the men. "I've been talking to . . . well, sir, the Eighty-third Pennsylvania is under the impression that they are moving up to meet the rebs pretty quick, they're expecting a good fight. My men . . . they feel like we're gonna miss out on something big. Surely the army can find something for us to do."

The men responded, the voices rising, and Chamberlain held up his hands again, said, "If we're going to have a fight soon, then we are going to miss it. I have no say in this. General Hooker himself knows of our predicament. I did volunteer us . . . that we be allowed to lead the attack. If we were to infect the enemy, it might be an effective way to end the war." There was laughing and men nodded.

"But the high command did not think it a practical and humane strategy. Wars should be fought by noise and violence, not by subtle diseases. So . . . we will stay behind."

He began to move through them, and their protests faded, the officers breaking them up, moving away. He reached his tent, heard a sound, music, listened. It was a band, far out on the road, leading another column of men away. The sounds faded, and he thought, So, we will miss this one, and maybe . . . there will not be any more, maybe it will end here, one more great fight. And we can go back home and say . . . nothing. We weren't there. He leaned into the tent, realizing what a terrible thing it was to hope for . . . that the war go on just so they could be a part of it. But he could not help it, sat on his cot now, stared at the side of the tent, remembered the stone wall, the smoke, the screams. His heart began to pound, and he thought, Please, someday, let us have one more chance. . . .

43. HANCOCK

Thursday, April 30, 1863

H E HAD BEEN WRONG ABOUT THE PONTOONS. THEY WOULD BE
used again, were already in place when he led his division
to the site, the wide clearing along the river. There had
once been a bridge here too, at this place called, strangely, United
States Ford. As at every good crossing, the bridges were long gone,
small burnt memories lingering in crooked shapes. But here there
was no opposition, no hidden muskets on the far bank, and the men
crossed quickly and easily, and Hancock knew they were ready for a
fight.

Hooker had done for the army what Burnside could not. He had
put them into position, quickly, with efficient use of engineers and
time; put them into position to crush Lee's army from the rear. The
plan was basic military logic: keep Lee occupied by a large force, Sedgwick's corps crossing the Rappahannock again below Fredericksburg,
threatening to move across the same fields where Jackson had defended
against Meade, while Hooker moved the larger bulk of the army upriver, to the shallow fords. By occupying all three of the main crossings, the army would move with more speed, down separate roads,
converging due west of Lee's position, to his rear. With pressure then
from Sedgwick, Lee would be caught along his row of hills in a vise
grip of nearly 140,000 Federal troops.

By now Sedgwick was in place, a formidable blue mass that was
already on Lee's side of the river, and their complete parade-ground
visibility would clearly demonstrate that it was a large enough force to
hold Lee in place, a threat he could not ignore.

Hooker had given the army something else besides another good
plan. In the months of waiting, while the ground hardened and the

warm air of spring filled the valley, the army had been trained constantly, their diet improved. He did away with Burnside's system of Grand Divisions, bringing back the more efficient corps system. And, knowing the sad state of troop morale, Hooker devised a symbolic, though effective means of instilling pride. Each corps was given their own identifying insignia, with the color of that insignia reflecting the specific divisions. The new insignias were sewn on the soldiers' hats, and the response was immediate and positive. The men eagerly accepted this small bit of identity, and the officers knew that in the heat of battle, it would be much simpler for the men to stay with their own units, or locate them after the fight.

The new commander also dealt with poor morale by pardoning deserters and stragglers, and guaranteeing the men that they would have a predetermined opportunity for leave, so that desertion would no longer be necessary. For all of Hooker's shortcomings, he had done a great deal to bring the army back up to fighting form. Now, with the new spring and the new march, Hancock understood that something good had happened to the army, to his division. Now they would learn if Hooker could satisfy Lincoln's request to "go forward and give us victories."

The army was spreading below the river quickly, moving down the roads toward the hub of the wheel, the intersection of Chancellorsville. Hancock's division was now the First, still a part of Couch's Second Corps, and in the new organization of the army, Couch was an informal second in command to Hooker. Hancock felt some comfort in that, some sense that at least Couch would be there, would hear it all and have his say, and surely, *surely*, they would not stumble into another bloody disaster.

They marched south, left the river, and the road led them through a thick and dense woods. Couch rode beside him, and they led the column, trailed by the staffs and Sam Zook's brigade.

"This is rather like Florida."

Couch looked toward Hancock's gesture, said, "Really? I would imagine Florida to be more . . . green."

"Green, yes. And thick, impossible to see. Down there, it was palmettos, and some kind of damned thick sticker bush, something called catclaw. This looks about as bad—you can't see anything."

Couch looked toward the other side of the road, saw more of the same, said, "It's called the Wilderness. I heard it wasn't always like this, but the big trees were all cut—there's some ironworks around here, use a lot of wood fuel, and after the trees were cut, the woods just grew up

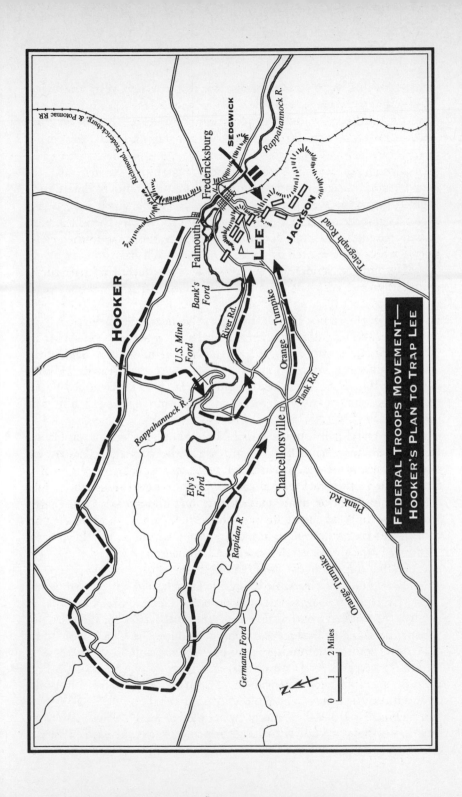

Richmond Fredericksburg, & Potomac RR

SEDGWICK

Fredericksburg

Rappahannock R.

JACKSON

LEE

Telegraph Road

Falmouth

Bank's Ford

HOOKER

River Rd.

Orange Turnpike

U.S. Mine Ford

Rappahannock R.

Plank Rd.

Chancellorsville

Ely's Ford

Plank Rd.

Rapidan R.

Germania Ford

Orange Turnpike

FEDERAL TROOPS MOVEMENT—
HOOKER'S PLAN TO TRAP LEE

2 Miles

0   1

N

thick like this, bushes, scrub trees. Maybe in a few years the bigger trees will come back."

"A few years . . . don't expect we'll see much of this country in a few years. Hope not. I'd rather be back in Pennsylvania, looking at green grass."

Couch smiled, nodded. Hancock was still staring into the brush, said, "We going to move out of this stuff soon? No place for a fight."

"Our orders are to advance to Chancellorsville, then turn east, toward Fredericksburg. The ground clears away once we move east a bit. If we've done as well as the reports say, we'll have an easy march well beyond the Wilderness before we run into Lee. Last I heard, he still hadn't moved away from the hills." He paused. "This may actually work."

Hancock did not answer, thought, I've heard that before.

There were shouts to the front, calls from the pickets, and from around a curve a rider appeared, a courier. The man sat straight in the saddle, pulled his horse up and turned with expert precision, a good show for the generals. He was smiling through a short clipped beard, waited for some acknowledgment, and both men looked at him, said nothing.

The man finally spoke. "General Couch, sir! It is a pleasure to see you this fine day. Your corps is moving with great speed, I must say! And General Hancock, you are looking fit and well."

Couch looked at Hancock, said, "Do you know this man?"

Hancock shook his head, suddenly had no patience for the over-done show of good cheer.

The man said, as though of course they would recall, "Lieutenant Colonel Earle, sir, General Slocum's adjutant."

"What can we do for you, Colonel?"

Earle pulled his horse up alongside Couch, said with the smugness of a man close to it all, who knows much, "General Slocum sends his regards, and wishes you to know that his Twelfth Corps, and the Fifth Corps of General Meade, are encamped around the Chancellor house and await your arrival, so they may begin the assault."

"Await our arrival? Why?"

"General Hooker's orders, sir. The army is to assemble into one grand force, to strike the fatal blow into the rebels!"

Hancock felt his stomach twist. Couch said, "Why have they not moved forward . . . is there any opposition to the east? Where is Hooker?"

The colonel's expression began to change. Couch's response to his good news was not what he had expected. "Uh . . . I am not sure, sir. General Hooker has not yet arrived on the field. Perhaps the general would care to accompany me back to General Slocum? It is a short ride now, sir."

Couch glanced at Hancock, said, "Keep your column moving, General," and spurred his horse, moving quickly away, leaving the colonel behind. Earle jerked his horse forward, and then both men were gone in a spray of dust.

Hancock turned, saw the puzzled faces of Couch's staff, said, "Don't worry, he'll be back. It seems the plan has changed."

"GENTLEMEN, THIS IS A GLORIOUS DAY INDEED!" There were nods, some low sounds, and Hooker held his glass high, waited, and gradually the arms went up, the others joining in the toast.

Hancock and Couch stood under a great chandelier, and the large room was filled with the elegance of the great plantations and thick with the smell of cigars. Hooker had arrived after dark, a grand show, taking personal command of the attack, which now would begin the next morning.

Hancock held his glass high, had said nothing, glanced at Couch, who was not smiling, and he felt the shared anger, the sense that yet again they were led by a man who did not inspire respect. There was something else about Hooker that made Hancock uneasy. Unlike the personable and mildly buffoonish Burnside, Hooker was a man clearly focused on his own goals, behaving more like a politician than a soldier. Hancock heard it in the idle talk, the conversation of the others: Hooker was generally disliked by everyone who served close to him. They had respected his treatment of the army, but the rise in morale had not spread through the headquarters of the commanders. They would wait, instead, for the results of this new plan. Their gloom was lifted by the quick march, the efficient crossing of the river, but now, despite Hooker's attempt to create a party, a celebration of some unnamed success, Hancock felt it clearly, through the toasts and the bouyant salutes. There was nothing yet to celebrate.

The troops were camped close to the small town, spread out in tiny clearings that dotted the thick Wilderness. Hancock understood, they all understood, that had they pushed on, turned to the east, they would be out in the open ground, closer to Lee's position, where they could see what lay in front of them. There had been no official explanation from Hooker why he had slowed them down, just some vague talk of uniting the army. And so the afternoon had passed without contact with any major force from Lee, nothing to slow down the assault except the sudden caution of Joe Hooker.

The toast was concluded, and suddenly there was a wooden box, a case of whiskey, a common commodity around Hooker's headquarters. There were more toasts, and Hancock knew this would go on for a while yet. Other corps commanders had arrived, his friend Oliver Howard, who now commanded the Eleventh, and Dan Sickles of the Third. The great room was filling quickly, and Hancock felt a stifling heat, a need for air. He left Couch's side, began to move toward the wide front door of the grand house. There was a sudden shout, a man calling for quiet, and slowly the talk hushed. Hancock waited, turned to see Hooker's aide standing on a chair, holding a paper.

"Gentlemen, you have all received the commander's General Order Forty-seven, but ... on this occasion, I feel it should be read aloud."

There were nods, mostly from the junior commanders, who had not yet seen the order.

" 'It is with heartfelt satisfaction the commanding general announces to the army that the operations of the last three days have determined that our enemy must either ingloriously fly or come out from behind his entrenchments and give us battle on our own ground, where certain destruction awaits him—' " He was interrupted by cheers, a show of enthusiasm that Hancock tried to share.

Now Hooker spoke up, raising a glass, and shouted above the voices, "God Almighty will not be able to prevent the destruction of the rebel army!" There were more cheers, but they faded quickly, and Hancock saw stunned and uncomfortable expressions, the men who held dearly to their faith, who were absorbing what their commander had just said.

He had heard enough, quickly opened the door, passed by eavesdropping guards, stepped down away from the light. He climbed up onto the horse, moved the big mare along the road, thought of the ridiculous boasting, daring God to stop them, felt suddenly very sad. He tried to convince himself it did not have to depend on those men

. . . the real success could still come from the good work of these good soldiers. We do have the numbers, he thought, and we may have indeed surprised Bobby Lee. He rode on toward the camps of his men, thought of Hooker's words, wondered if Lee would ever be pursuaded to "ingloriously fly."

44. LEE

April 30, 1863

H E WAS STILL ON THE HILL, LOOKED DOWN TOWARD THE RIVER, to the spreading mass of blue, a force too strong to be a simple diversion. But they were not coming, not advancing toward the woods where Jackson's men waited, again.

Jackson was watching him, sat on a log, then stood, felt the itch of the new fight, paced for a moment, then sat again. Lee walked alone, still stared at Sedgwick's troops, then turned and moved back up to the crest of the hill, toward Jackson's impatience.

"That is not the main attack," Lee said. "They are waiting for something."

"We should punish them, now. Hit them before they can get set."

He turned to Jackson, saw the fire, the violence in the sharp face. "No, General, the guns, remember the guns. They are still on Stafford Heights, it would be a costly advance if we showed ourselves across that plain. It is no different now than it was in December. We must wait for *them*."

Jackson looked toward the far hills, across the river, knew of course that Lee was right. He put his hands behind him and his shoulders sagged slightly.

Lee said, "General, I must know where the rest of them have gone. We must wait for General Stuart. Sedgwick has come across with only one or two corps. Hooker would not repeat Burnside's plan. Do not focus your energies on those troops."

It was not a command, but the softer advice, a father to an overeager son. Lee understood the impatience: the target was in plain sight, open and vulnerable. That was exactly why he did not believe it, did not believe Hooker would attack with just those troops.

Stuart had observed heavy columns moving above the river, out to the northwest, and Lee knew they would cross somewhere upstream, as they should have done in December. To the north and slightly west of Lee's left flank lay Bank's Ford, where the river made a sharp U downward, and he understood that there must be no crossing there, it was dangerously close to his rear, and so he had strengthened that position, sent Anderson's division back, off the hills.

Richard Anderson commanded one of the two divisions of Longstreet's corps that had stayed with Lee, and Lee knew that though Anderson was not one for ingenuity, he could be counted on to stand his ground. Lee had instructed him to push out farther west, as far as the next major crossing, United States Ford. It was there that Anderson met the first of Hooker's strong columns, advancing southward. As instructed, he pulled back, and now was spreading his division in a north-south line, protecting both Bank's Ford and the two main roads that led from Chancellorsville straight into Lee's position. But Lee still did not know how many troops Hooker was pushing across the river there, or just where they might be heading.

Jackson was still frustrated, paced again. The meeting seemed to be over, and he looked for his horse, was ready to return to his troops, and Lee held up his hand, said, "General, please, sit down. We can do little else until we hear—"

There was a shout, the voice of Taylor, running along the hill. "General . . . it's Von Borcke, Major Von Borcke!"

Lee saw him now, the huge form riding with some difficulty up the side of the hill. He was on a large black mule, and the mule seemed intent on moving in other directions than where the Prussian intended.

"Vat ho! General Lee . . ." Suddenly the mule turned, began to go back down the hill, and Von Borcke jerked the head around, gave a heavy kick to the mule's side, and it began to climb slowly again.

Jackson moved up close to Lee, and Taylor stepped forward and grabbed the reins of the mule. Abruptly, Von Borcke swung a huge leg over and leapt from the mule in a great awkward flight, landing thunderously on both feet.

"Only vay I can get off the damned thing. He shtill vants to run off to play." He looked now at Lee, saw no smile, saw the deep glare from Jackson, straightened himself, said, "Forgive me, Herr General, I am not used to riding such animals as you have here. I beg to report on behalf of General Shtuart, that a column of the enemy has crossed the river at Germanna Ford, and is moving south, toward Chancellorsville.

General Shtuart has determined it is the Twelfth Corps. He has also observed units of the Eleventh."

Lee said nothing, looked at Jackson, and Jackson said, "They would not move two corps that far behind us for a feint."

"No, they would not." Lee nodded toward the big German, said, "Major, you may return to General Stuart, and request in the strongest terms that General Stuart join me here. Please go now, Major. I regret your difficulty with your mule. We do not have the luxury of thoroughbreds." It was not a criticism, but Von Borcke suddenly felt foolish, complaining to a man who clearly knew of all the army did not have. He backed away, saluted, and Taylor held the reins tight as Von Borcke struggled up to the mule. Then he moved quickly away.

Lee did not watch him leave, turned again toward the south and the blue stain that spread along the edge of the river.

"General Hooker expects us to stay here, watching *them*. And that is the trap."

Jackson nodded, said nothing, understood now that Lee had been right.

Lee motioned to Taylor, said, "Major, my horse please," and then turned to Jackson. "General, we do not yet know where General Hooker is intending to lead his army. He is either intent on holding us here, assaulting us from behind, or he may move farther south, toward Gordonsville. He could easily cut the Orange and Alexandria Railroad, and cut us off from the Shenandoah. If he drives in that direction, we will have to withdraw from here, move down to the South Anna River and make our defense there."

He felt an anger rising up from deep inside, thought, How much more must we do? All the grand successes, the great bloody efforts to push them out of Virginia, and now they were coming again, unstoppable, into the heart of his home. He suddenly kicked at the ground, sent a spray of dirt flying, was breathing heavily, closed his eyes. No, keep control.

Jackson stared at him, and Lee turned toward him, looked hard into the sharp blue eyes. Jackson did not look away, and Lee said, "General, once again God is challenging us, offering us another opportunity. We must strike the enemy before he can go any farther." He looked away now, across the open fields, the town, the river. "I had thought . . . we had done enough . . . that He would be pleased. . . ."

Jackson stared at him, at the soft white beard, the face of a man growing old, then he looked up, beyond, said, "General Lee, if it will please God, we will kill them *all*."

I T WAS DARK WHEN STUART REACHED LEE'S CAMP. HE LED HIS
troops through lines of marching infantry, Lee's men withdrawing from the great safety of the long row of hills, moving out now
toward the west. Stuart's route had taken him along the roads that
ran below Chancellorsville. He understood the necessity of staying
clear of the Federal positions, but had still met a regiment of Federal
cavalry, a short and confused fight on a dark road, and so it was
becoming clear that Hooker was not passing them by, was not
moving away toward Gordonsville, but was spread out around
Chancellorsville, had stopped in the vast, thick Wilderness. Lee had
not heard the shooting, but Anderson had, knew it was more than
nervous skirmishers. He had sent word to Lee, and so when Stuart
finally reached Lee's camp, Lee had not been sleeping, but anxious
and alert.

The infantry was still moving down off the hill, would move all
through the night, and Lee heard the shouts, tried to see in faint firelight, to see the man on the horse, the hat held high in the air, absorbing the cheers of the troops.

Stuart finally saw Lee, dismounted, made a deep bow. "General
Lee, I am at your service."

"I am pleased to see you, General. I understand you had some
difficulty tonight."

Stuart was grinning. "That we did, sir. The Virginians did themselves proud, both regiments, the Third and the Fifth. We sent a
good-sized flock of Yanks scurrying back home!"

"That is good news, General, but I do not need you engaged with
the enemy just now. You must be of greater service to this army."

Stuart bowed again, serious, said, "Yes, sir, I understand. Fact is,
General, we did not look for the fight. We just ran into them. There's
not many places to hide on these roads, sir. The Wilderness is not a
place for horses."

"Very well, General. Do you mean to say that the Federal cavalry
is advancing below the main body of infantry?"

Stuart seemed surprised, said, "Oh, no sir. They're *gone*. We ran
into a regiment . . . just one regiment . . . some boys from New York.
The main body, most of Stoneman's entire strength, is moving away,
down south. I sent your son . . . that is, I sent General Rooney Lee to
keep after them, stay close, and keep me—the army—informed." He
stopped, Lee waited for more, saw the smile again. "General Lee, I

believe that General Stoneman is trying to ride clear around this army, sir." He waited for Lee to absorb that.

Lee said, "General, are you suggesting that General Stoneman is attempting to duplicate your . . . accomplishments?"

"All I can tell, sir, is he's taken several thousand men, is moving down along the Orange and Alexandria Railroad, trying to tear up whatever he can, and he has already sent some units toward the east, well below us, sir. By now he is completely cut off from General Hooker's command. They may even be heading toward Richmond, sir! Maybe General Stoneman . . . well, maybe he wants to see his name in the Richmond papers."

Stuart was glowing now, and Lee could not believe it. If Stuart was right, Hooker's cavalry, the critical eyes of the Federal Army, was on their own, possibly to make a sweep through central Virginia that would be an annoyance, but little else. Stuart had made the same type of ride, twice before, had severely embarrassed the Federal command by riding completely around their army without any serious obstacles, and without any substantial gain. It was not something of which Lee approved, but the grand show, the sheer audacity of it, had been of great benefit to morale and was trumpeted loudly by the newspapers, both North and South. Surely, Lee thought, there is more than that . . . this cannot be just a glorified parade.

"General, please keep me informed what the young Mr. Lee reports. I do not want ten thousand Federal cavalry suddenly appearing on our flank."

"There will be no surprises, General."

Lee turned, walked over to a small fire, and Stuart followed. It was very late, and Lee suddenly felt a great need for sleep, a thickening fog in the brain. Taylor was poking the fire, trying to stifle a yawn. Lee said, "Major, you may retire. We will have a long day tomorrow."

Taylor stood, felt another yawn coming, clamped it down, saluted, and quickly moved away. Lee felt his own yawn building, and he stretched his back, twisting slightly.

"General Stuart, in the morning, General Hooker will find that we have moved out to meet him. We are constructing a line of defense from the river to the north, down across the main roads. I do not believe the force that is below Fredericksburg is a threat at this time. I have ordered General Jackson to move his corps away from these hills, to support General Anderson and General McLaws. General Jackson will be in command of the field."

Stuart looked out along the top of the hill, started to say something, and Lee said, "We are not abandoning these hills, General. I have placed General Early's division up here, spread out in a thin line. He will do what he can to convince General Sedgwick that we are still up here in force." The fog in his brain had cleared. He felt a rush of energy, and the words came quickly. "I do not believe General Hooker wants the fight to be below Fredericksburg, and so I do not believe General Sedgwick will advance against us. But I do not want General Hooker to move the rest of his army any farther south. General Stuart, you will do what you can to impede his movement that way, toward Gordonsville. If there is to be a fight, we must make it quickly, before General Sedgwick learns we have pulled away from him. If he sees there is only weak opposition, he will certainly move up and occupy these hills. We cannot fight a battle in two directions. . . ."

Stuart listened hard, stared at Lee. It was plain and clear, and Stuart suddenly felt overwhelmed, felt something rising in him, loud and excited. He smiled again, wanted to put his hands on Lee's shoulders, show him the affection, but it would not happen, and he tried to hold it in, abruptly made another deep bow, swept the ground with his hat.

"Yes, sir. I will keep you informed, sir."

Lee nodded, was finished. The words had drained him, and he felt the fog returning in a heavy wave. He turned away from the small fire, moved wearily toward his tent and with a soft voice said, "You are the eyes of this army, General."

45. HANCOCK

Friday, May 1, 1863

THE FOG HAD BEEN THICK, WAS NOW BURNING AWAY. THE MEN had been up since first light, had formed early and waited in the roads, but there were no orders. Now, finally, the word came from the old mansion and they began to move.

They were to advance eastward on three roads, the two direct routes toward Fredericksburg, the Orange Turnpike and Plank Road, and by a third route, River Road, which left the Wilderness above and moved in a direct northeast line toward Bank's Ford. Two divisions of Meade's Fifth Corps had this assignment, with the intended goal of opening up that crossing for Federal troops and creating a more direct line of communication and supply between Hooker's main force and Sedgwick's corps below Fredericksburg. Slocum's Twelfth Corps would advance on Plank Road, to the south, supported by Howard's Eleventh, and between these two routes, George Sykes's division of Meade's corps would lead the way, followed by Couch's Second Corps, with Hancock in front, close behind Sykes. The Third Corps, led by Dan Sickles, would remain north of Chancellorsville, acting as a general reserve. This advance involved a force of nearly seventy thousand troops.

Hancock rode behind the last of Sykes's column, watched thin clouds of steam rise out of the thick brush on both sides of the road. The fog had given way to a light rain, but it had been brief, thankfully, had not mired the roads, and now it was clear and warm, and nearly noon.

They would not have far to march before the Wilderness would break, give way to the open fields, precious room to maneuver, to

place the cannon where they could actually see their targets . . . if there
were any targets.

Couch had been with him earlier, before the march, expecting the
quick order to move out, and when the orders did not come, Couch
had gone back to see Hooker. Hancock did not know if the orders had
finally come because of anything Couch had done, but he knew—all
the commanders knew—something was wrong at headquarters. The
soldiers still had the high spirit of the day before, knew they had done
something important, a quick and successful march by this huge army,
and the campsites had been lively places. This morning they had not
delayed falling into line, were moving now with the quick step of men
who have the sense that this time they had the upper hand, that the
fight would be theirs.

The line in front of Hancock began to make a long slow climb
toward a slight rise that lifted the ground far out on both sides. He
could see the advance now, up in front, small flags, and suddenly there
was a long thin line of smoke, but not heavy. It was the skirmish line,
the first opposition to their grand sweep toward Lee. Sykes's column

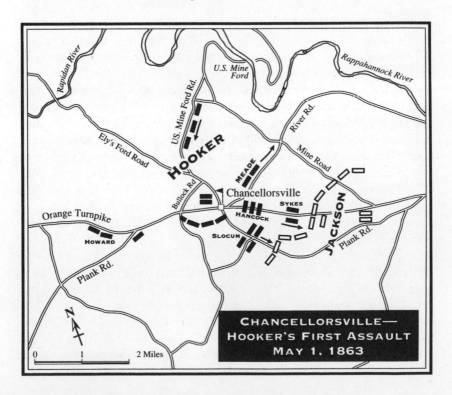

CHANCELLORSVILLE—
HOOKER'S FIRST ASSAULT
MAY 1, 1863

began to disperse, moving with difficulty off the road and into the wiry brush. Hancock rode forward, past shouting officers, intent on finding General Sykes, to see if he knew yet what was in front of him.

There had been no word from either of the other advance columns. The terrain made it impossible for communication, but there were no sounds, not yet, no deep thunder of the battle, and so they would press on.

Sykes's lines did not slow, pushed the rebel skirmishers back up the long hill, and Hancock still rode forward, past more troops. He saw Sykes now, a cluster of blue uniforms, and Sykes was directing his officers, spreading the companies out across the road.

Sykes saw Hancock, raised a hand, said, "Ah, good morning . . . good day, General. All is well so far. We seem to have awakened a few rebels. No matter, they've scattered away."

"A skirmish line, General?"

"Barely. They didn't really try to slow us down, just took a shot and moved out. Probably a scouting party. Any word from the rear?"

"Not yet. I expect General Couch to return soon. Have you heard anything—"

"From Meade? No, and nothing down below us either. Looks like easy going, General."

Hancock focused on the far woods, tried to hear . . . something. Sykes's men began to file back into the road, reforming the column, and now they were moving again, up the long hill.

Sykes was waving to more officers, directing them forward, and he said to Hancock, "If you can, General, ride with me. Your men are close behind, stay in front for a bit. We should break out of this infernal thicket just beyond that hill, give us a little room to move. Should be able to see Slocum's lines, down to the right. How does it feel?"

"Feel?" Hancock shook his head, didn't understand.

"Knowing you're running right up the back of Robert E. Lee? We may have him this time . . . finally have him. I always thought it would have been McClellan, we would have done this, ended this with Mac. Never figured Joe Hooker to be the one."

Hancock nodded, said nothing. Maybe it was true. If Lee felt the threat from in front, from Sedgwick, and then felt the greater force coming in behind him . . . he might simply be gone, pulled out. With his smaller numbers, he thought, it might be the smart move to withdraw south of Fredericksburg, dig in closer to Richmond, make Hooker bring the Federal Army *to* him. And we will have gained . . . what? he wondered. Ground? But maybe more important, Hooker will have driven Lee back, and once that begins, we may be able to keep driving him back. He is outmanned, outgunned, outsupplied. And maybe today he was outmaneuvered.

Hancock began to feel some excitement, thought, Yes, it is working, the quick march, dividing the army. He looked at Sykes, who was focused to the front, to the moving line of troops.

"Yes, General, press on! My men are anxious to see the backs of Lee's army!" He felt foolish saying it, the kind of mindless boasting heard so often around the camps, around the headquarters of bad commanders.

Sykes looked at him, smiled. "Yes, and don't forget that Stonewall. Let's see how fast he can run!"

There was more firing now, a rolling wave of muskets, and toward the front of the line the men were spreading out again. Sykes began to ride, moving forward, and Hancock followed, sped the horse closer. Now they could see the crest of the hill. Spread on both sides of the road, out through a narrow clearing in the deep brush, was a solid gray line, and the muskets began again, fresh and regular volleys, and Sykes was yelling, directing the men. Hancock saw that this was not a skirmish line, Lee had come out to meet them, was waiting for them. He stared ahead for a moment, then turned the horse, rode back down the hill toward the front of his division. His staff was there, waiting, expectant faces, and he thought of the ridiculous conversation with Sykes, the arrogant notion that Stonewall Jackson would ever run.

T HEY HAD MET THE LINES OF ANDERSON AND McLAWS. JACKson did not want to wait, knew that once the Federal columns came out of the Wilderness, they would have the advantage of mobility. While Jackson's own divisions were quickly moving toward the field, preparing to link up with Anderson, Jackson was already there, had reached the strong defensive lines Anderson had prepared during the night, the trenches and felled trees. It was a strong line, but Jackson would not wait for the slow advance of the Federals, had ordered Anderson and McLaws forward, out of the trenches, toward the edge of the Wilderness.

Hancock pointed from the center of the road, spreading his regiments out into the woods. He could still see Sykes's lines moving forward, still climbing the hill, and now his own men were ready, began to advance up, close behind Sykes. The sounds were steady now, a dull echo in the dense mass of brush. Down to the south he could hear more sounds: Slocum was engaged as well; Jackson's lines were spread down across both roads.

Hancock stood in the stirrups, tried to see beyond the brush, but it was hopeless. How can they put up that much of a front? he wondered. His mind began to turn quickly. If Lee is here, he thought, if he has come out to meet us, then who is on the hills in front of Sedgwick? So, if Lee has turned this way, then it is up to Sedgwick to come up over and around the hills, and we can still squeeze Lee between us.

His men were pushing slowly through the thickets, still moving up the hill, and now he saw a flag, riders. It was Couch.

Couch pulled the horse up, stared forward toward the crest of the hill. "General Hancock, are your men engaged?"

"No, sir. But Sykes is pushing them back. He appears to have control of the high point of the hill. The clear open ground is not far beyond. If we can advance out of this mess, we will have an open field of fire."

Couch turned to the south, listening. Hancock said, "Slocum is engaged as well. If the rebels are giving way, it must be a thin line in front of us. We have the momentum, and it seems we have the strength."

Couch nodded, looked back to the north. "Meade is still advancing on the River Road. I left headquarters when we heard the first sounds from out here. But so far Meade is unopposed. Lee will surely have some force guarding Bank's Ford, but with two divisions, Meade should be able to clear them out." Couch was staring hard, intense, bright flashing eyes, and Hancock did not recall seeing the small man with such energy, such animated movement.

"Sir, what of Sedgwick? Is he advancing?"

Couch did not answer, still stared ahead to the fight.

"Sir, is General Sedgwick advancing on Lee's position? If Lee has moved a strong force this way, the hills above Fredericksburg could be taken without—"

"General Hooker has ordered Sedgwick not to attack, to just make a demonstration. General Hooker has ordered Sedgwick to dig in, to prepare to *receive* an attack."

Hancock leaned forward, stared at Couch, was not sure he understood. "An attack? From where?"

"From Jackson . . . from Lee's forces on the hill."

Hancock was confused, said, "Then who is that in front of *us*?"

Couch waited, looked again to the north, heard nothing, said, "If we had some cavalry, we might have the answer to that."

Ahead of them the fighting began to slow, and they could see blue troops on the crest of the hill. Couch began to ride forward, and Hancock rode with him, leading their staffs. The crest of the hill was covered with bodies, and the dead were being pulled aside, off the road. All around them wounded were being attended, men from both sides. From the top of the hill they could see to the east, out past the edge of the Wilderness. Well below, the gray lines were reforming, had been pushed back, but now the Federal forces had the high ground, and far in the distance they could see the dark shapes of the hills between them and Fredericksburg.

The ridge ran north and south for miles, and down to the right they could begin to see Slocum's lines, also in numbers too great for the thin line of Jackson's defense.

Couch was looking through field glasses, watching the emerging lines of blue. Hancock saw Sykes riding up toward the crest, back from the advance lines of his troops.

Sykes saluted, said, "General Couch, welcome to the field, sir. We have won the day . . . we have prevailed! The rebels have been pushed back to the edge of the open ground, and I am ordering my guns up to this hill. Have you heard from General Meade, sir? I must report to him."

Couch shook his head, pointed toward the north. "He's still up there, as far as I know. If he's had as good a day as you have, he may be sitting at Bank's Ford."

Sykes looked toward the rear of his lines, saw horses bringing up the first of his field guns. There was an officer leading, and Sykes yelled, "Here, over here, there's a small clearing. . . ." The horses moved that way, a clatter of wheels, and Sykes said, "General Couch, do you have any orders, sir? Should we press the attack?"

Couch turned, looked back at Hancock's troops, who had filled the road behind them, down along the hill. Hancock looked with him, thought, Yes, we cannot be stopped. We are too many.

In the distance there was a man on a horse, moving awkwardly along the side of the road, pressing hard up the hill toward them. Couch said, "That's Loveless . . . from Hooker." They waited, and the man made his way up the hill, waving a piece of paper.

"Sir . . . your orders, sir!"

The man had called out with unusual energy, was looking now to the front, cautiously, where a few bursts of musket fire still echoed through the woods.

Couch took the paper, read quietly, and Hancock watched his face, tried to see. Couch's expression did not change. Suddenly, he gripped the paper hard, crushing it, stared ahead at nothing. "We have been ordered to withdraw."

Hancock waited for more, said, "You mean, my division?"

Couch looked at him, grim and hard, said, "No, General. Both divisions. The *army*. General Hooker is recalling all units back to Chancellorsville. We are to form a defensive line, back where we began this morning."

Sykes stared at Couch, his mouth open slightly, and he turned to the east, pointed. "Sir, we have pushed the enemy back! The field is ours, we must advance . . . General Meade . . . I must find out if General Meade knows—"

"No, General. The order clearly names your division as well. There is no mention of General Meade. I would assume he has received an order just like this one."

Hancock looked to the south, toward the far clearing where Slocum's troops could be seen. "They're leaving. Slocum is withdrawing already."

Couch followed Hancock's gaze, said, "Of course, he follows orders. We all follow orders."

Sykes was shaking his head, waved an arm wildly, said, "No! If Slocum pulls back we are exposed! Our flank is open!"

Hancock was still looking toward the south and the small sounds of distant muskets. He looked to the clearing beside the road, to Sykes's cannon, the men unhooking and turning the guns, pointing toward the east. He looked back at Couch, who was listening to Sykes still protesting, his voice getting louder.

Men were beginning to gather, men who knew their commander to be a solid leader, a soldier who led a tough division, mostly regulars, veterans of many bad and costly fights. Now the men were beginning to understand, heard Sykes say, "We cannot withdraw! General, we simply cannot!"

The soldiers began to close in around the men on the horses, and Hooker's courier was glancing sharply around, nervous. A man yelled out, "We ain't turnin' back! We got the rebs on the run!"

There were more calls now, and men began to shout at Couch, at Hancock, knew their own commander would not back away, not from a fight they were winning.

Couch looked out at the faces, said nothing, then looked at Hancock, and Hancock now understood. The order was clear and direct, and they would obey. Couch turned to Sykes, who was silent now, in wide-eyed disbelief.

Couch said, "General Sykes, you will form your division and march in column toward Chancellorsville. General Hancock's division will protect your flanks and rear and then will follow your column."

Sykes looked at Hancock, then back to Couch, and around them men were yelling, angry and defiant. Sykes started to say something, waved his arm again, and Couch raised his voice, said with a dark anger, "There will be no further discussion! You will carry out your orders, General!"

Sykes nodded, looked at Hancock, and Hancock could not stay still, pulled his horse away and moved back down the hill, toward his own troops. Behind him officers were giving the commands to Sykes's men, and suddenly there were horses moving quickly by him—Couch and his staff riding hard, back to the west, toward the headquarters of their commanding general.

H E MOVED BY REFLEX, HIS MIND IN A FOG AS HE DIRECTED HIS men through the small clearings east of the Chancellor mansion. They still faced toward the enemy, had now joined alongside Sykes. He gave the new orders, and the company commanders supervised the labor—trenches and earthworks were dug, trees cut.

His division was now fully deployed, and Hancock rode back along the road, toward the Chancellor mansion. He still did not believe it had happened; there had to be something else, some major piece of the puzzle missing, some great disaster. Of course, it could have been Sedgwick. Perhaps Sedgwick had been beaten back across the river. Longstreet could have returned; his divisions could have surprised Sedgwick from the south. And there was Meade, up along the river. There could have been a major obstacle there, something unexpected. But—and there were many buts—there had been no sounds of battle, no distant rumble of guns from Fredericksburg. Meade had not been engaged, the sounds would have been clearer still. He caught himself, realized this had happened before. McClellan had often done it, magnified Lee's strength into huge numbers, great numbers of the enemy everywhere at once, had talked himself into seeing the ghosts of an army that wasn't there. But today they *were* there, Hancock thought. We were right in front of them, and there weren't that many . . . it was our field. And we gave it back to them. Now Lee will move his guns up to that high ridge, will look down on us while we sit tight in our trenches, wondering what to do next.

Hancock reached the grand house, saw officers standing in small groups, men leaving on horses, others arriving. He climbed down, moved slowly, heavily, up to the porch. A guard opened the door, and Hancock saw blank and pale faces, then heard voices, loud and angry. His mind cleared and he moved in noisy steps on the hard floor, went into the large living room, the room with the chandelier. Couch was waving his arms in the air, red-faced; and sitting behind a large table, Joe Hooker.

Hancock did not hear what Couch had said. He stared at Hooker, surprised, did not see anger. The clean-shaven face was staring up at Couch with a small, weak smile. Suddenly Hooker stood up, looked around the room, looked at Hancock without seeing him, looked past several other men, said, "It is all right, General Couch. Gentlemen, it is all right. I have got old Bobby Lee right where I want him. Now he will have to come to us, on our own ground!"

Couch stood still for a moment, then abruptly turned and moved quickly toward the door. He passed Hancock, saw him, a quick glance of recognition, and Hancock followed him outside.

Couch went to his horse, and his aides began to gather. He looked at Hancock, said, "He ran out of nerve. When he learned that we had run into opposition, he stopped believing in his own plan. He just ran out of nerve. Meade . . . Meade had nearly reached Bank's Ford . . . *unopposed*, when he was called back. Howard's corps never even had time to leave their camp. Sedgwick still doesn't know what happened. Now we're digging in . . . as though Almighty God Himself is leading an army against us!"

Hancock wanted to say something, knew Couch was as angry as he had ever seen him, and Couch put a hand up on his horse, grabbed at the leather straps, turned again to Hancock, calmer now. With a long, slow breath, he said, "He is a whipped man."

Couch climbed up on his horse, and his staff moved in behind. Without speaking, he turned and rode away.

It was nearly dark, and Hancock climbed on his own horse, moved slowly across the yard, nodded at familiar faces. He moved out onto the road, felt completely drained now, like waking up from a long and deep sleep, rising slowly out of a horrible nightmare, but now there was no relief, no feeling that it was over, only the same heavy dread that they had done this before, the utterly foolish mistakes, and if the leaders had not learned, certainly the soldiers had—that these mistakes would always turn into bloody disasters.

46. JACKSON

FRIDAY, MAY 1, 1863

H E REACHED THE INTERSECTION, LOOKED DOWN BOTH ROADS. Troops were everywhere, small fires and stacks of arms. He did not yet see Lee. He pushed the horse along, and the men saw him now, hats went up, and the subdued cheers. They were, after all, a tired army, a stiff march and a good sharp fight, and Jackson tried to see the faces, the men who had done their duty. He glanced upward, raised a hand, said a silent prayer, *We do all we can to please You,* and he felt a calm satisfaction, knew God would be pleased by such a day as this.

He had thought it too easy, the heavy columns of Federal troops pulling away, giving him the field, abandoning the fine, long ridge from where the guns could find the long range. Now his own three divisions were in place, alongside Anderson and McLaws, and he knew that with this army, no one could stand in their way, that Hooker must know that as well and would pull away, completely, back across the river. He nodded silently, pulled a lemon from his pocket. *Yes,* you had best be gone tomorrow or we will give you the bayonet.

He stopped the horse, looked around through a small grove of pines, saw more troops, watching him, and now he saw Lee, riding slowly through the grove, heard the new cheers from his men. Lee dismounted, raised a hand, a warm greeting, and Jackson pulled the horse off the road, into the grove.

Lee's staff was arranging something to sit on, old wooden boxes marked U.S. ARMY, and three boxes were placed together, two chairs and a table. They were near a fire, and a dim glow spread over the flat wood. Lee moved toward one of the boxes and sat down.

Behind him, Jackson's aides had moved up, closer, and someone took the reins from his hand. He walked on soft ground toward the fire, tossed the flattened lemon aside, sat down on the other "chair," watched Lee from under the short bill of the old cadet cap.

Lee removed his hat, ran a stiff hand through gray hair, glanced toward the fire, and Jackson saw the old face in the firelight, heavy, tired eyes. Lee said, "Fine work, today, General. We were in a difficult situation. It could have been very different."

Jackson did not respond, absorbed the words, was not sure what Lee meant. He leaned forward, put his hands out on the box between them, as though holding it down in place, said, "We pushed them hard, and they ran away. There was nothing difficult about it."

Lee looked at him, hid a smile. "General, from what we have observed . . . there are nearly seventy thousand Federal troops beyond those trees, digging in around Chancellorsville. Sedgwick has nearly forty thousand spread out along this side of the river in front of General Early. There are possibly thirty thousand more back along the river, north of here, that we have not yet located. I give you credit for a fine day's work, General. But we are not in a position of strength here. We owe a great deal to the unexplainable, to the mystery of General Hooker. He has allowed us to maneuver freely between two parts of an army that is more than twice our strength. I am concerned, General, that we do not yet understand his plan."

Jackson leaned back, looked at Lee again from under the cap. "He has no plan. He is waiting for us to take the fight to him. He is, right now, digging trenches, building a defensive line. He is already beaten."

Lee nodded. "Perhaps. He may yet be planning a move toward Gordonsville, move around below us, cut us off from Richmond. We must not forget about General Sedgwick, on the river. He shows no signs of moving, but that could change."

Lee turned, motioned to Taylor, who stood beside the fire, and the young man came close, handed Lee a rolled-up paper, which Lee spread on the box. It was a map, faint pencil lines on wrinkled paper, and Jackson leaned closer, tried to focus in the dim light.

Lee pointed to the Rappahannock, to a point above them, said, "They are anchored against the river, up here. Their line is continuous, down below Chancellorsville, then curves along . . . here."

Jackson nodded. "Yes, we observed that . . . their lines curve around these open clearings . . . then toward the west."

"Then what, General? Do you know where their right flank is, where they are anchored to the west?"

Jackson stared at the map, said quietly, a small defeat, "No. Not yet."

"We must know that, General. If he begins to march in that direction, he could threaten our flank, or be gone toward Gordonsville before we can react."

Jackson shook his head. "If he moves, it will be north, across the river. . . ."

Horses came at a fast gallop on the road, and both men turned, saw a small squad of cavalry and the tall dark plume on Stuart's hat.

Stuart jumped from his horse, moved quickly toward where the men sat, removed the hat with the usual flair, said, "General, may I be allowed to join your meeting?"

Lee smiled slightly, nodded, and Stuart looked around for his own box to sit on, saw nothing, then moved around, away from the fire, so as not to block the light, and leaned over the map.

"General, I have some interesting news."

Jackson leaned his head back, tried to see Stuart from under the cap, said, "They are digging in."

Stuart looked at him, nodded, "Oh, yes, sir, they are digging in. But that's not the interesting part." He looked at Lee, put his finger on the map. "Out here, to the west . . . along the turnpike here . . . their right flank is completely exposed. It's the one place where they are *not* digging in. Clearly, they do not expect any pressure there. Their flank is completely in the air."

Lee glanced at Jackson, leaned closer to the map, said, "Who is on their flank?"

"The Eleventh Corps, Oliver Howard."

Lee continued to look at the map, reached a hand out. "Are there any roads, down this way, below the turnpike?"

Stuart began to move now, shifting from one foot to the other. "Yes, sir, indeed there are. Good roads." He pointed. "That's Catherine's Furnace, and there's a road . . . wait . . ." He pulled a stub of a pencil from his pocket, drew a ragged line. "Here, there's a road, over this way."

Jackson said, "Then we will hit them *there*. We can move around their flank." He looked up at Lee. "And they will have nowhere to go but back across the river . . . or we will destroy them."

Lee nodded, said, "Those roads . . . they are too close to their lines, they will observe any movement. We must find another road, farther down. Do we have someone here, someone we can trust, who knows the area?"

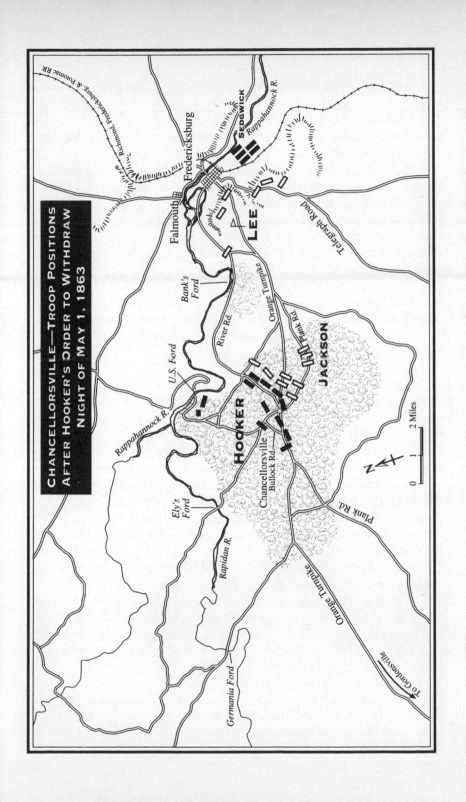

CHANCELLORSVILLE—TROOP POSITIONS
AFTER HOOKER'S ORDER TO WITHDRAW
NIGHT OF MAY 1, 1863

Richmond Fredericksburg & Potomac RR

SEDGWICK

Rappahannock R.

Fredericksburg

LEE

Telegraph Road

Falmouth

Bank's Ford

River Rd.

Orange Turnpike

Plank Rd.

JACKSON

U.S. Ford

Rappahannock R.

HOOKER

Chancellorsville
Bullock Rd.

Plank Rd.

Ely's Ford

Rapidan R.

2 Miles

0   1

N

Germania Ford

Orange Turnpike

To Gordonsville

Jackson abruptly stood, stepped toward the fire, to a small group of men who straightened as he approached. "Mr. Pendleton, find Chaplain Lacy."

There was a voice, a small sound, and a man moved closer to the fire, said, "Begging your pardon, General, but I am here, sir."

Jackson turned, moved back toward the map and Lacy followed, shyly. Jackson said, "General, this is my chaplain, the Reverend Tucker Lacy. He has family in this area, sir."

Lee stood, offered a hand, and Lacy hesitated, then reached out, took it with a gentle grasp. Lee sat down again, looked at the map, said, "Reverend, it would be very helpful if you could find us a safe route around the enemy."

Lacy leaned over slightly, said, "Well, sir, I'm sorry . . . I'm not that familiar with the back roads . . . but . . . there." He pointed to the spot marked Catherine's Furnace. "I know a family, the Wellfords. I would suggest a visit there. We may find ourselves a guide."

Jackson said, "Please go there at once, Mr. Lacy. Find us someone who can tell me how I might proceed."

Lee smiled, said, "Then we have decided, General, that this mission will be *yours*." He nodded, smiled to himself. "I would not have it any other way."

I T WAS SURPRISINGLY COOL—A DAMP MIST BLEW THROUGH THE trees. The meeting was over, the men who had a job to do were out on the road. Pendleton was adding wood to the fire, stirring it with a small stick, and Jackson was searching the ground, began to kick at some pine straw, pushing it together, forming a bed. He coughed, a loud, raspy sound.

Pendleton turned, said, "General, you sound like you might have an affliction. Are you feeling all right?"

Jackson nodded, cleared his throat, realized he felt very weak, tired, and it was very late. "We will rise early, Major. The men must be up and moving quickly. General Lee will be expecting to see me well before dawn." He coughed again, rubbed his chest, took a deep breath, felt a slight pain, and sat down on the pine straw.

Pendleton was watching him. "General, please . . . take this . . . here," he said, and he removed the black rubber overcoat, moved over toward Jackson, held the coat out.

Jackson looked up, shook his head. "No, Major. Do not discomfort yourself on my account. This night will pass quickly."

Pendleton began to pull at the coat, separating the long lower flap from the topcoat, a series of small metal snaps.

"At least, sir, take the bottom part. I will not need more than this."

Jackson saw the young face, genuine concern, and he nodded. "All right. Thank you . . . bless you, Major. Now, let us get some sleep."

He lay flat on the straw, felt something hard, realized he had not removed his sword. He sat up, unbuckled it, then turned and reached out toward a tall pine, leaned the sword upright against the trunk of the tree. He saw Pendleton, lying still now near the fire, and he said a prayer, a quick thought for the boy. Above, the wind blew the thick mist down through the trees, a sharp, cold breeze. Jackson fought against a cough, stood, walked quietly to where Pendleton lay, heard the faint, steady breathing of the tired young man. He draped Pendleton's coat over the young man's legs and moved back toward his own bed. Jackson stretched out on the damp straw, another small cough, and he rolled over, lay on his side, the side that did not hurt. Now a new breeze came through the tops of the pines, a hard whisper, swirling toward the sleeping soldiers. The sword, held by the glow of the faint firelight, was lifted by the voice of the wind, suddenly slid away, dropped down hard on the straw-covered ground.

Saturday, May 2, 1863

HE WAS A BOY, BUT HE HAD SPENT HIS YOUNG LIFE IN THESE woods, had seen the brush thicken into a vast tangle, covering the old trails, and so he had made new ones, had explored the creeks and climbed the hills. Now he would guide the army, the army he was too young to join. He would lead them away from the eyes of the Yankees.

Jackson had been up for a while, had barely slept at all, and now he was on his horse, moving slowly among his troops, the troops that would soon be on the march.

Lee was still asleep as Jackson eased toward the pine grove and dismounted. In the faint light he could see one of the staff, working on the fire. He walked through the grove, and the young man watched him, nodded, said nothing. Jackson eased closer to the dark form on the ground, paused, watched the slow breathing, then said, "General Lee?"

There was motion, and Lee's bare head peeked from under a blanket.

"What? Time? Oh . . . thank you, General. Be right with you."

Jackson backed away, moved toward the boxes. The map was there now, spread out by the young aide, and the man went quietly back to the fire.

Lee, in the firelight now, putting on his coat, looked up at thick darkness, said, "General, your Mr. Lacy came to me . . . late . . . earlier this morning. He told me there is another road, a road that will take you well below the Federal lines."

Jackson sat, leaned over to the map, said, "Yes. The boy—the Wellford boy—has explained it to me. He knows the route. He will ride with me."

Lee sat back, glanced toward the warmth coming now from the growing fire.

Jackson was still staring at the map, said, "There. We will march to that point, where this road rejoins the turnpike. Then we will turn east and attack the flank."

"Very well, General. And what do you propose to make this movement with?"

Jackson looked up, seemed surprised at the question. "Well, General, with my whole corps."

Lee was not surprised at the answer, flexed his stiff hands in the cool air.

"And what will you leave me?"

Jackson looked at the old face, thought he saw a smile, said, "Why, the divisions of Anderson and McLaws."

Lee stood, walked to the fire, began to understand. Of course, it was the only way. The risk was extraordinary. He would be left with barely twelve thousand men, spread in a thin line facing Hooker's mass of seventy thousand. But if the plan were to work at all, Jackson would need the strength, a sharp hammer blow to the Federal flank, enough force to do more than surprise. If Hooker had already shown a reluctance to charge into a hot fight, Jackson's assault could unnerve him enough to fulfill Jackson's prediction and withdraw back above the river.

It was Jackson's job to lead thirty thousand troops quietly and discreetly through the countryside, and it was his to keep Hooker from realizing how weak the forces were that he was defending against. If Hooker pushed out of his trenches, even a short and brief advance toward Lee, or if he made an aggressive move toward Jackson's marching column, he could destroy not only the plan, but possibly the army.

Lee held up his hands, warmed them toward the fire, shook his head. And of course, there was still Sedgwick along the river. . . . How long would he sit and stare at a near-empty hill? This is not an accident, he thought. We are led by Divine hands. He turned, saw Jackson standing now, saw the familiar look, knew Jackson was anxious, ready to leave, and Lee nodded, said, "Well, go on!"

I T WAS AFTER DAYLIGHT, DANGEROUSLY LATE. THE MARCH WOULD cover twelve miles, an easy distance for Jackson's foot cavalry if there was no obstruction and no opposition.

They filled the road quickly and quietly—instructions had gone down, all the way to the lowest levels—this was a quiet affair. There would be no cheering, no shouts, and no stragglers.

The three divisions would march in a column of fours, led by Daniel Hill's men, commanded now by Robert Rodes. Behind Rodes were Jackson's own division, led now by Raleigh Colston, and in the rear, the division of A. P. Hill.

Lee sat on Traveller at the edge of the trees, watched them forming column lines, and now he saw Jackson, riding with a hard, fixed

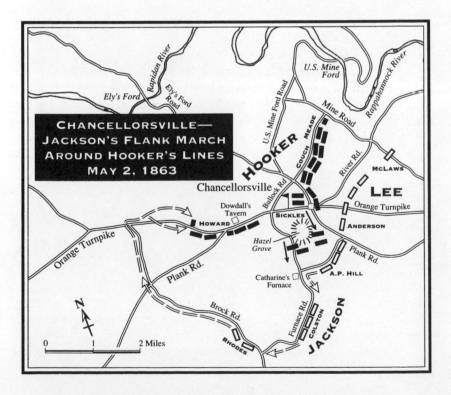

CHANCELLORSVILLE—
JACKSON'S FLANK MARCH
AROUND HOOKER'S LINES
MAY 2, 1863

stare, moving alongside the troops. The men did not respond. The mood was clear, something was going on, the march would not end with tents and rations, but a hot and bloody fight. If they did not hear it in the orders, they saw it in Jackson's face.

He rode up to Lee, tilted back his head, was still wearing the old cap, and Lee saw the eyes, nodded sharply, did not smile.

There were few words, small nods, and suddenly Jackson reached out an arm, pointed down across the intersection, to the route they would take. Then he spurred the small horse, Little Sorrell, moved out across the road. Lee watched him move away, lowered his head, a small prayer, *God be with you, General,* and in front of him the great column began to move.

47. HOWARD

MAY 2, 1863. MIDDAY.

H
E LET THE EMPTY SLEEVE HANG LOOSELY, DID NOT ROLL IT UP
and pin it as most of the others did. The arm was lost at Fair
Oaks, on the peninsula, and the loose sleeve reminded him
constantly. He did not want to forget. And it made a good show. The
Eleventh Corps did not accept his appointment with enthusiasm, and
with this bit of dramatics, the loud message that he was a veteran, had
made the sacrifice, he thought they might respect him a bit more.

The Eleventh had been identified as Sigel's corps, had consisted
mainly of German immigrants, farmers and factory workers, mostly
from New York and Pennsylvania. The men of the Eleventh were an
untamed and rugged bunch and had pride in their heritage. When Sigel
was relieved, the corps was given to Howard, a disciplinarian and a devout Christian. Neither trait opened any doors.

Oliver Howard had earned the promotion, served well under Mc-
Clellan and since. He was the first division commander, under Couch,
to enter Fredericksburg the winter before. He was a man with no outstanding talents, but he understood command, and it was a natural pro-
gression for him to eventually lead a corps. But even he understood
that command of the Eleventh was a questionable reward. The Ger-
mans were not highly regarded as fighters, and were rarely put into the
thick of the action. Now they were the far right flank of Hooker's
army, well out of harm's way, the last line of defense, facing an empty
section of the Wilderness.

They had finished breakfast, and the men were not looking for
a fight. There were small groups, circles of blue, card-playing mostly,
some stretched along the side of the turnpike, the opportunity for
extra sleep. The trenches they had dug faced south, alongside the

turnpike, and they were not deep. The fight was well to the east, far off to their left.

To the north, above the turnpike, the river was three miles away. There were no troops positioned above them. It was the far rear of the Federal position, the safest place on the field.

Howard rode slowly down the line of trenches, was met by small nods, the trained show of respect. It had only been a month, and he still did not know many of them, the regimental commanders, long and unpronounceable names. He had been patient with the accents, but often they would speak German around him, and he would say nothing, stare them down, and they would return to English, or say nothing at all.

He rode on the turnpike itself, toward the west, came to the end of the line, saw two brass guns pointing straight down the road, out toward nothing. It was the only place guns could be positioned; the road was the only clear line of sight. He turned toward the right, moved the horse off the road, saw the flags of two regiments, not quite a thousand men who lined up at a right angle from the road, refusing the line to the north. Here, they had not dug trenches at all. He rode alongside the distinct edge of the thickets, tried to see out through the dense tangle, and he saw a man, emerging with curses, carrying an armload of wood. The man tried to free himself from a thorny vine, dropped the wood, said, "Dammit, tore my sleeve."

He saw Howard, did not salute, bent over to retrieve his firewood, said, "No fit place for a man, General. Damned near got lost."

Howard nodded, did not smile, pushed the horse along.

There was a flurry of noise back on the turnpike, and he turned in the saddle, saw riders, flags. He spurred the horse, moved closer, saw now it was Hooker, his staff stretching out behind him like a small parade. Hooker raised his hand, stopping them. Howard rode up onto the road, saluted with his left hand.

Hooker said, "Good morning, General Howard."

Hooker was smiling broadly, in high spirits, and Howard forced a smile, said, "General Hooker. I am honored by your presence."

Hooker accepted the flattery, sat straight up in the saddle, looked out to the trenches, the official eye of the inspection. Men were standing now, lining the edge of the road, and Hooker said, "Yes, good. Good, indeed. Very strong, very strong."

Abruptly, he turned the horse around, moved through his staff, followed closely by his color bearers, and shouted back, "Keep it up, Howard!" and the parade moved quickly away.

The men began to spread out again, the show was over, and Howard stayed up on the road, pushed the horse slowly, followed the direction of Hooker's ride, moved back toward his own headquarters.

Howard did not move with any haste, expected few official tasks to fill the day. He let the horse walk slowly, gradually approached the building, the old tavern known as Dowdall's. In front there were horses, those of his staff, and another, which he did not recognize. He was still up on his horse, and an officer emerged from the tavern.

"General Howard, I am Major Montcrief of General Hooker's staff. The general has sent me to alert you, sir. There is a movement of rebel infantry and wagons on the roads south of this position."

Howard stared at the man, an unfamiliar face. "General Hooker . . . was just here, not an hour ago. He said nothing—"

"No, sir. The news just came from General Sickles. There is a heavy line of rebel activity moving south and west of General Sickles's position. General Hooker is most pleased to advise you, sir, to be alert for this activity."

"Pleased?"

"Why, yes sir. The general has expressed his congratulations to his men for prompting the retreat of the rebel army."

He thought, Of course, it has to be. They are moving away, probably toward Gordonsville. Stoneman's cavalry raid likely did serious damage to their supply and communications lines.

"Thank you, Major. You may return to General Hooker and convey to him that we are prepared to pursue the enemy on his command."

The man jumped down the steps, climbed his horse, and with a quick salute was gone.

Howard sat back in his saddle, thought, Yes, this army is finally moving in the right direction. He thought of going inside, maybe some coffee, but suddenly he felt stronger, awake, and he pulled the horse around, moved back down the turnpike, to once again ride along the strong lines of his men.

H E JOINED THE MEN AROUND THE SMALL FIRE, ASKED SLOWLY, "Might I enjoy a cup of your coffee?"

They had stood quietly, watching him approach, dismounting from the horse. There were nods, looks between them, and a cup was offered.

"Thank you, it has been a while since I had a cup of *real* coffee."

He put the cup to his mouth, felt the rush of steam. "Ah, yes. Thank you."

He looked to the faces that were looking at him, uncertain, curious, and now more men were moving closer, word was spreading, the aloof and hard commander was down with the men.

"Gentlemen, you may not know this yet, but this is a day to remember." He paused, heard voices, men saying "Sir," and he looked around, saw General Devens, the commander of the division, moving through the men.

"Ah, Devens, hope you don't mind my taking the liberty . . . I smelled the coffee, had to stop."

Devens saluted, glanced at the men, said, "No, General Howard, certainly not."

"General Devens, do any of your men climb trees?"

There was a pause, and one man said, "I been a good climber since I was a boy. Never seen a tree I couldn't top."

There were laughs, small jibes, and Howard said, "Well, that's mighty fine. I tell you what, soldier. You go over there, across the road, and pick out one of those tall ones, and when you get to the top, you tell me what you see."

The men were talking and moving now, accepting the challenge, and Devens moved closer to Howard, more curious, but Howard would say nothing, was enjoying the moment. Yes, this was a fine day indeed.

The soldier pulled off his coat, wrapped hard hands around the trunk of a tall, thin tree, began to shin his way up the limbless trunk. Men circled around the tree, cheering him on, and the man reached the first of the small limbs, pulled himself up quicker now, and Howard stood in the middle of the road, looked up through the branches, said, "All right, soldier. Anything to report?"

The man looked around, parted the leaves with his free hand, and then looked down at Howard, shook his head, and Howard raised his hand, pointed to the south, said, "How about that way?"

The man slid around the trunk of the tree, parted more leaves, and suddenly he stood up higher, leaned out away from the tree, said, "Hoooeeee. It's rebs! A whole army!"

Faces turned to Howard, and now other men began to move up the tree, and other trees, some without success.

Howard rocked on his heels, listened to the sounds of the men, and the excitement spread all along the lines.

Devens stood beside him, said, "May I assume, sir, that the rebel army is in retreat?"

Howard smiled at him, said, "Yes, you may, General." He looked around, saw one of Devens's staff, said, "Captain, please take a message to General Hooker."

The man moved up, pulled a pad of paper from his pocket, and Howard said, "Tell the General . . . from General Devens's headquarters, we can observe a column of infantry moving westward. . . ."

THE SOUNDS CAME RUMBLING UP THROUGH THE BRUSH, FROM down to the southeast. Howard was back at his headquarters, at Dowdall's, had returned from the woods to the south, from the direction of the fight. Sickles had been watching the enemy movement all morning, could stand still no longer, and so had sent a division down, toward Catherine's Furnace, to drive hard into the moving column. Howard had received a request from Hooker to lend a hand, to move one of his units down in that direction, protecting Sickles's right flank. The orders were carried out, and now Howard was back at his headquarters, stood outside the tavern, listened to the sounds of the fight, smiled. Yes, Bobby Lee, we will chase you after all.

He had wondered why Hooker did not begin to form the army, move out in pursuit, but Hooker had seemed content to stay put, let Lee move away. The victory, the great success of his plan, was to be savored.

Sickles had pressed down, into a portion of A. P. Hill's division, and Hill had brought his long line together, pinching at Sickles from both sides. Within a short time the battle had faded, and Sickles had the token reward of a regiment full of prisoners and the satisfaction of a man who has pressed the action, who, unlike his commander, was not content to watch the enemy flee. Since the bulk of the rebel column had already passed on the Furnace road, Sickles was content to settle his forces down in their new position, well below the rest of the Federal defenses. The brigade that Howard had sent for support had left a wide gap on the east side of his lines, but with Sickles down below, there would be no need for strength at that point. His men in the treetops could still see the rebel column moving far away to the west.

He thought again of coffee, maybe something stronger. It was mid-afternoon now, and he was not a drinker, but . . . it was such a glorious day, for an army that did not have many glorious days. He climbed up the steps, and now there was a rider coming from the west, and the man seemed anxious, was yelling.

"General . . . General . . . Please!"

Howard watched the man dismount in a tumble from his horse, and the man came forward in a rush, saluted wildly, said, "General, Major Rice reports that the rebel column has turned and is now to our west, sir. The major requests instructions, sir!"

Howard held up his hand, said, "Easy, young man. I am aware of the rebel movements. Tell your major to keep his eye on them. There is no cause for alarm. Have you reported this to General Devens?"

The soldier stared at him, said, "No, sir. The major thought this was . . . a high priority, sir."

"You tell Major Rice that in the future he will report his observations to his division commander. I do not have the time to entertain every courier from every outpost."

The man nodded, said, "Yes, sir. Sorry, sir. I will tell him."

He backed away, climbed up on the horse, and Howard raised the hand again, trying to ease the man's agitation. The man saluted, calmer now, and Howard returned it, nodded, and the man rode back to the west.

DEVENS WAS WATCHING THE MAN IN THE TREETOP, BALANCED precariously, and the man was struggling, trying to stay upright. Below him others were shouting, *"Hang on!"* and suddenly the man fell, down through the branches, dragging the thin limbs with him, and another man, below him, tried to slow the man's fall, and he began to fall as well, and there was laughing, and in a slow jerky motion, limbs cracking one by one, they slid downward, the two men grasping each other, then dropped into the clear, fell the final few feet to the ground. The crowd of men cheered now, and the men were helped to their feet, limping and scraped. Devens smiled, saw no major damage, except of course to their pride. He looked through the crowd of men and the men beyond, thought, This is very good, this has been very good for morale. Now . . . we may finally see some change, some real success.

He walked back up to the turnpike, looked at the pair of brass guns, pointing away down the far road, and he heard the voice of his aide. "General Devens, sir, a messenger."

He looked for the voice, saw his young lieutenant, and another man in a heavy sweat. The man saluted him, said, "General Devens, sir,

Major Rice reports that a large body of the enemy is to his front. He suggests . . . he respectfully advises . . ." The man paused. "General, he ordered me to say . . . 'for God's sake make some disposition to receive them.' "

Devens stopped smiling, said, "Sergeant, have you seen this large body of Major Rice's enemy?"

"Well, no sir. I'm the courier, sir. The major commands the lookout, sir. Don't care much for heights myself."

"Well, then, Sergeant, you go back and tell Major Rice that there is no need in trying to panic either you or this division. I will forward this report to General Howard. But I would suggest you return to Major Rice and tell him to calm down. If he cannot perform his duties with appropriate decorum, we may have to find someone else for the job. Is that clear?"

The man snapped to attention, said, "Perfectly clear, sir. Please allow me to return to the outpost, sir."

Devens returned the man's salute, said, "Dismissed, Sergeant." He stared wearily at the lieutenant, rested his hands on his hips. "I suppose you should ride to General Howard's headquarters. Tell him of the report. Tell him I have seen no evidence that the enemy is doing anything more than leaving."

The man hurried away, mounted his horse, and galloped down the road, then slowed, rode the horse at a trot, knew that when he reached Howard's headquarters he would hear the same reproach, would receive the wrath of the annoyed commander: that these observers, the men who watch the enemy, are always jumpy, always exaggerate, and that the commander certainly understood the situation—it was his *job* to know what was going on.

48. JACKSON

H E STEPPED QUIETLY THROUGH A CLUSTER OF SMALL BUSHES, thick and green, and the ground suddenly dropped away, down a long flat hill, and there, along a wide road, was the Federal line.

He had never been this close, felt like giggling, a wild adventure. His guide, the man who had brought him to this spot, was beside him: Lee's nephew, Stuart's brigade commander, Fitz Lee.

"There they be, General. The whole lot of 'em."

They were sitting around small fires. Some were reading, playing cards, and back, behind them, a small herd of cattle was being lined up, the preparation for tonight's dinner. Jackson rubbed his hands together, wiped them on his pants leg. This was an incredible sight.

Lee backed away, through the bushes. Jackson didn't want to leave, but knew he had to get back, to move the column farther to the west. This was the point where they had thought the flank could be assaulted, but there were too many blue troops, and the line ran farther west, along the road. So the march would continue, until his men were far around the last of the Federal lines.

He followed the young Lee back to the horses, said nothing. Lee climbed up, smiling, waited for the compliment, the acknowledgment of a fine piece of scouting. He was well taught in the Stuart school of soldiering, appreciated the glamour of the cavalry; they all basked in the bright light of Stuart's reputation. But Jackson had climbed up on the horse, was already far away, and Lee frowned, would have to find the pat on the back elsewhere.

They moved quickly back to the road. A squad of cavalry was waiting, and Jackson looked past them, pulled the horse around, began to move alongside the marching column of troops, toward the front of the line.

He reached an intersection, the last leg that would take the men up to the turnpike, and saw Robert Rodes and the young boy who had guided them. Rodes's division was now crossing the intersection, and Jackson rode close beside the men, said, "Keep it up, move up."

They looked up at him. Most were smiling, and he did not notice the hollow eyes, a toll from the warm day and the lack of food. There had been few rations for the march, and those men who had not eaten early that morning had likely not eaten since the morning before. Despite Jackson's enthusiasm, and the constant pressure from the officers, the march was taking far longer than he had expected.

He pushed through the line of troops and moved up beside Rodes. Raleigh Colston came quickly along the road, followed by a small staff, and Jackson waited. When Colston reined up, Jackson said, "Very soon now. General Rodes, you will begin to deploy your men on either side of the turnpike, brigade front. General Colston, how soon will your men be up?"

"We're right behind, General."

Jackson nodded, was now seeing beyond the men, out past the thick tangle of woods, already watching what was yet to come.

Colston and Rodes had both been instructors at VMI, and both were well acquainted with Jackson's manner and his moods. Neither man spoke, and they glanced at each other as Jackson stared quietly beyond the road. Suddenly, he reached into his pocket, pulled out a small pencil, a rough piece of crumpled paper, held the paper flat against his saddle and wrote a brief message.

". . . I hope as soon as practicable to attack. I trust that an ever kind Providence will bless us with great success . . ." He concluded the note, stared at it, and behind him Pendleton moved closer, anticipated the order. Jackson started writing again, a small postscript. Pendleton had motioned for a courier, and the man was up quickly, held out his hand when Jackson turned with the note. Jackson stared at him, thought he should know the man's name. He had forgotten it, stared for a long minute, tried to recall. The man glanced at Pendleton, uncomfortable, and Jackson abruptly handed him the paper, said, "Take this to General Lee."

Pendleton said something to the man, precautionary instructions that Jackson did not hear, and then the courier was quickly moving, leading the horse back along the edge of the road.

There were more horses now, Fitz Lee's squadron of cavalry

moving past, alongside the road, and Jackson turned and watched them. Lee slowed, waved the men on, and Jackson looked at him from under the cap, said, "Take your men up past the turnpike. You must observe the roads that go to the river, protect our flank."

Lee saluted, smiled. "Already on our way, General."

Jackson watched the cavalry move away, sat back in his saddle and smiled. He looked at the two men, said, "The Virginia Military Institute will be heard from today!"

Rodes smiled, glanced at Colston. Both men had wondered often if Jackson even recalled their former relationship.

The column reached the turnpike, and Rodes quickly led a line of skirmishers out, down the turnpike to the east, toward the farthest point of the Federal position. The men filed out into the brush, began to feel their way through. Jackson sat high in the middle of the road and watched. Now he could hear the guns, from far out in front of him, a roll of low thunder. He gauged the distance, knew it was Anderson, McLaws, and Lee on the far side of the Federal position, and he nodded, thought, Good, they are still engaged, still in place. He felt the thrill again, the excitement of knowing the entire Federal Army was right in front of him, between him and Lee, *right there*. Others were beside him now, his own staff, and now Rodes was back, and his division was filling the road, spreading out in thick battle lines into the woods.

Jackson began to rock in the saddle, a small rhythm, back and forth, pushing the men into position. With each forward movement he said to himself, Go, move forward. The men were having some difficulty, it was slow going, and he wanted to yell, tell them to hurry, but there could be no noise, and so he prodded them from inside his head, leaned out over the horse's head, then back in the saddle. It was getting late, but he would not look at the sun, far behind them now, dropping quickly toward the distant trees. He saw his own shadow on the road, long and dark, and closed his eyes, would not see it, kept pushing them, rocking.

It was Colston now, and the second division moved into lines behind Rodes, the men swarming past Jackson's horse. Most did not look up now, knew it was soon. Then Colston was beside him, wanted to say something. He was nervous, had not led a division into battle before, and still Jackson rocked, his eyes closed. Colston watched him, let it go, turned to his troops again.

Jackson suddenly stopped moving, looked sharply behind him, saw Pendleton and said, "Where is Hill?"

Pendleton was startled, moved closer. "General Hill will be up with his lead brigade very soon," he said. "He is not more than a mile behind. His last two brigades are well back, sir. They have not been able to make up for the lost time, for the fight with the Yankees."

Jackson turned, closed his eyes again, was suddenly furious, felt a stab of pain in his side. His chest tightened and he tried to breathe, opened his mouth, and the tightness gave way. *Hill again.* It was good Hill was last in line. They could move without him if they had to.

Rodes was still close by, heard the brief conversation, felt defensive about Hill, said, "Sir, General Hill was pressed by a large force of Federals. I am certain he is bringing his men up as quickly as he can."

Jackson stared at him, a withering glare, and Rodes looked away, had crossed a dangerous line with his commander. Jackson closed his eyes and slowly began to rock again. Colston's lines were almost in place now, and Jackson spurred his horse, moving down the road toward the back of Rodes's troops, with Rodes moving quickly to catch up with him. Jackson reached the line of men, leaned over and tried to see out into the thick brush. The line disappeared in both directions, the men slowly moving forward with small noises, the officers keeping them in line. Jackson heard curses and nervous laughter, could hear the sounds of the brush, the men stepping through the tangle. He looked down the road, lifted his field glasses, stared ahead and saw two small black eyes, the silent stare of Howard's cannon. Lowering the glasses, he reached into his pocket and pulled out a small gold watch: five-fifteen. They would have two hours of daylight.

Rodes said nothing, waited, and Jackson now looked at him, hard, tried to see into the man's soul, measure the strength of his heart. Rodes still waited, felt the power of Jackson's cold blue stare.

Jackson said, "Are you ready, General Rodes?"

"Yes, sir." Rodes did not pause.

"You can go forward, sir."

Rodes turned, and there was a quick shout and a bugle sounded, and out in front the first line began to crush through the tangle of briars and thickets. From far out in both directions came the sound, the high, screaming wail, of ten thousand men; a solid line a mile wide pushing and clawing through the brush in one great mass of motion. The terrible sound echoed far in front of them, carried forward by the wind, and before them, beyond the brush, in the wide clearings along the road, heads began to turn, and plates of hot food were spilled, and the men in blue coats stood, staring at the impossible, the impenetrable thicket, stared as the deer and the rabbits and the birds ran and darted and flushed out before the great wave. Before the first man was seen, or the first musket aimed, the men in blue were swallowed by the sound, by the raw terror, and they began to run.

H E RODE CLOSE BEHIND THE FIRST HEAVY LINE, PUSHED OUT into the first clearing. His men stopped, raised their rifles in one sweeping motion, and there was a long blast, the echo filling the space. In front of them the flight of many soldiers was cut down. They ran on again, passed untouched stands of muskets, campfires and tents and wagons. They could see the enemy in a desperate scramble to get away, and, like the hound who finally sees the prey, they quickened their pursuit.

Devens's division was in total chaos, stampeded past the trenches of Schurz's division, the next in line. Schurz's men turned, formed a line of fire, and a volley came at the front of the gray wave, but it was the poor aim of panic, and the tide quickly rolled over them, driving those who could run into the escaping mob.

There were more trenches now, earthworks dug by men who had expected a fight, and they were quickly covered by the swarm. Jackson rode up, pushed the horse onto a long mound of dirt, could see his troops far in front, continuing to press on. Men were coming up behind him, Colston's first line.

Jackson turned, yelled, "Press on! Forward!"

They looked at him, and he saw the fire in their faces, *his* fire, and they went over the embankment, fighting their way through felled trees. Shots whistled past him now, return fire from small pockets of men in blue, the few who stood to fight. But even the most determined, those who would never run, soon realized that the line washing over them was too wide and too many, and if they did not finally move out, join the great wave, they would be quickly captured.

He pushed on, rode through the earthworks, saw beyond to the next obstructions, and there was more solid fire now, coming through the thick brush, splintering branches and limbs. His men slowed, the lines ragged now, and there were new shouts from officers. Jackson yelled to them all, "Form the lines! Keep it up!"

Now there were more volleys, from both sides, and he saw men falling, right in front of him, Rodes's men—*his* men. He rode past them, toward a building, glanced at the sign, DOWDALL'S, and reined the horse. Across the road he caught a glimpse of blue, hidden by the brush, and a roar of muskets blew into the line behind him. He turned back, saw a dozen men, a neat straight line, still pointing their muskets forward, and the men were all down, had fallen together. Now there was another sharp blast, farther behind him, toward the brush, screams, and men stumbled out toward the road, blue coats and new stains of red, and his line moved on by, kept going. He looked at the fallen men, men from both sides, a few feet apart, and raised his hand, held it high, the palm up, a silent prayer. Colston's second line was passing by him now, watching him, and suddenly there was a cheer, echoing down through the roar of the guns and the rising smoke. It spread, grew into a high scream, rolled into a new chorus of the rebel yell, and he watched them now, shouted out again, "Keep it up! Move forward! Stay together!"

The smoke was heavier now, shells ripping the air, bursting in the road, tearing through the brush. Federal batteries were turning, meeting the wave, and his lines began to shatter. He turned to the side, rode along a thick patch of the dense woods, saw a small group of men standing, unsure, and an officer. He yelled to the man, "Get them together, press them on!"

The man looked at him, appeared stunned, and Jackson yelled again, "Get them into line!"

There was a hot rush of air, and the brush in front of him was suddenly swept away; then a bright flash, a deafening, horrible sound, and the officer and men were gone. He had started to yell again, his mouth open, the words forming, and he stopped, turned, would not see, would still push them on.

Jackson jerked at the horse, moved back into the clearing, to the road, began to follow the line again. Now the firing was more to the front. They were still pushing the Federal troops back. He looked behind him, to the tavern, saw a farmhouse and knew they had come two, maybe three miles. He spurred the horse, moved up quickly, did not look at what lay around him, the vast spread of debris, shattered guns and wagons, and the broken bodies of men. He moved out toward a grove of trees, saw there were blue soldiers, crouching, aiming, and a volley ripped by him, struck men moving up behind. He saw a line, Colston's men, moving into the grove, and there was another volley, in both directions, a thick mass of smoke spreading out right in front of him. He strained to see, raised his pistol, ready, then saw the blue bodies, swept from their cover. Colston's men moved forward, and now Jackson saw one man, with the face of a boy, still standing, facing the oncoming line. He was trying to reload, and now Colston's men were on him, and the boy was trying to raise the rifle, and there was a flash of steel, the quick rip of the bayonet, and the boy was down. Jackson turned away, the image hard in his mind, thought, We must kill the brave ones, we must kill them *all*.

Far in front of him, beyond the heavy lines of smoke, one man sat high on his horse, held a billowing flag, the Stars and Stripes, taken in a rush from his headquarters. He clamped it tight against his body with the stump of his arm, the empty sleeve waving wildly, held his pistol high with the other hand, yelled, screamed, pleaded with the men who ran by him, "Stop, for God's sake . . . turn and fight!"

They did not stop, would not look into the face of their commander, knew only that behind them was the certain terror of hell on earth, and somewhere, if they kept going, they would find the river, would get back across, to where it was safe; that maybe they would fight again, become an army again, but not today.

49. HANCOCK

MAY 2, 1863. LATE AFTERNOON.

"COLONEL MILES, THEY'RE COMING AGAIN!"
The young man followed the extended arm, saw movement deep in the brush, the wave of brown and gray, and
raised his pistol. All along the skirmish line the other officers yelled
out the order, and now the line exploded into a single blast, a careful
volley that stopped the advance cold, and the gray lines melted back
into the dense brush.

They were beside a long, narrow creek bed, had spent the night
digging shallow trench lines, clearing the woods to their front for a
clean line of fire. Behind them, back up the rise, the main body of Hancock's division was dug in as well, waiting for the grand assault by
Lee's army.

Hooker had ridden by earlier in the day, full of pomp and compliments. Hancock had been polite and formal, endured the inspection
as a soldier had to endure inspection, but Hooker's predictions had not
come true, there was not yet a heavy attack, just this constant skir-
mishing, wave after small wave, against the strong lines that had so
pleased Hooker, the lines that would butcher Lee's army.

Hancock heard the new assault, the brief volleys, saw the thin
line of smoke rising, again, from the trees below. He saw an officer
moving in a run up the rise, and the man stopped, the young face
smeared with mud and the gray stain of battle. He spoke through
heavy breaths, saying, "General, it's nothing but . . . more of the same.
They've been beating us up all day with a single line of skirmishers. It
doesn't make sense, sir."

Hancock stared across the wide depression, past the trees that
covered the creek bed, toward the position of Lee's unseen troops, and

now, to the south, in front of the Twelfth Corps, a new burst of artillery, shells bursting in the air, shattering trees, and far down in the woods there was a rebel yell and a clash of muskets, and both men watched, waited, and then it stopped.

Hancock looked down at the dirty face, found the clear eyes. "Colonel Miles, I will send you a bit more strength, beef up the line again. But I don't believe you will be pushed very hard. Not now . . . it's too late in the day."

Miles looked back down the hill, said, "Doesn't make sense. You can't get anything done with a skirmish line."

Hancock looked across the crest of the ridge, the trenches and heavy lines of troops, his division, still waiting, rifles still pointing toward the trees below, rifles that had been quiet most of the day. They had not moved, had kept the sharp eye to the east, where Lee's army had moved in close the night before. All day, Lee had just . . . played with them.

He waved an arm, and an aide moved closer. Hancock said, "Go tell General Meagher to pick out another squad, have their commander report to Colonel Miles, down below."

The man saluted, began to move along the crest of the ridge.

"Go on back to your line, Colonel," Hancock said. "I'm sending you some Irishmen this time."

Miles raised a dirty hand, saluted, and Hancock turned his horse and rode to the south, toward the sounds of the last assault. He could see the turnpike now, saw a long, deep line of blue, the trenches of the Twelfth Corps, and riding up the ridge toward him, a flag, a small parade. It was Slocum.

"General Hancock, greetings. How are things up this way?"

It was a rhetorical question. Hancock had not known Slocum long, had never received a good impression, but Slocum had impressed someone in Washington enough to secure command of a corps, and seemed to enjoy the show of it, the long trail of staff under the flutter of flags. He was a small, wiry man, with a short clump of beard perched below a long, thin face, and he smiled pleasantly, waiting for Hancock's rhetorical answer.

"We're looking at the same thing you are, General. They're just bumping into us every so often."

Slocum still smiled, waved an arm slowly, toward the east. "Ah, but it would have been glorious. It could have happened right here, right on this spot. We could have ended it all."

Hancock watched him, sat quietly. Did Slocum really believe Lee would throw himself against this position? he wondered.

"So now, tomorrow, we have to start chasing them . . . all the way to Richmond, I imagine."

Hancock said, "What? What do you mean?"

Slocum looked at him, smiled again, said, "Why, they're gone, in full retreat. Have you not heard?"

"No, I haven't. I've been attending to this fight in front of me."

"General, I'm surprised. I received word from General Hooker's headquarters hours ago. The Confederate Army is in full retreat, toward Gordonsville. They've been marching west all day. I thought you knew."

"No, I have not heard that. Is this . . . certain?"

"Definitely, General, I heard from my own lookouts early this morning, and Sickles moved some units down to harass their supply trains, and ended up capturing an entire regiment of Georgians. He was too late to disrupt the retreat further, they were already by him. My latest orders are to prepare to pursue in the morning. As I said, General, it's a shame we couldn't fight them right here, from this wonderful position."

Hancock looked to the east, down toward the woods where Miles was strengthening his lines.

"General, if Lee is in retreat, who is it that keeps charging my lines?"

Slocum rubbed his chin, said, "Well, to tell you the truth, that question had occurred to me. Not like Lee to leave anybody behind."

Hancock thought, Lee has never *had* to leave anybody behind. "Excuse me, General, I must return to my division. And it seems clear that I must find General Couch."

Slocum watched him go, still smiled, and down below, in the trees, there was another high yell, and the trees came alive again with the rattle of the muskets and the sounds of a new charge.

COUCH HAD RIDDEN ALONG THE LINES EARLIER, SHORTLY AFTER the tour by Hooker. Hancock thought, It's not like him to keep me in the dark. Why had he not sent word?

Hancock rode toward the orange glow of the sun, lowered the brim of his hat, let the horse keep herself in the road. Behind him there were more shells bursting, a new artillery barrage, and he thought, If Lee is gone . . . would he leave his guns behind? He began to feel a small rumble in his gut, a small clench, thought of Slocum's words, then suddenly reined up the horse, stopping in the middle of the road.

He looked down, toward the south, recalled the map, the roads that led away, then ran parallel, far out to the west. There were more shells falling now, all along the ridge where his troops waited, a steady roar from a heavier assault, heavier than he had heard all day, and he thought, This could be it, I should go back. He rode hard back to the crest of the hill, pulled up, listened, and the shells slowed, stopped, and now the sounds of the skirmish came again, exactly as before, all along Miles's line. He waited, expected to hear much more, but in a few minutes it was over again.

He stared down the hill, watched the white smoke gradually clearing, and the rumble in his gut began again, and a familiar word suddenly flowed into his brain, a word from the textbooks, from old lessons. Suddenly, he felt utterly stupid, knew they had all listened to Hooker, had accepted instinctively, blindly, what the commander told them, and even if they did not truly believe it would happen, that Lee would hurl his army against a solid wall, they still waited, firmly in their trenches, inflexible and mindless. The word came into his brain again: *demonstration.* Now he understood why the attacks were regular and brief, with just enough muscle to hold his division in their trenches. Now he understood what Lee had done.

He spurred the horse hard, jerked the reins, and began to gallop into the deep glow of the sun, toward the Chancellor mansion where the generals waited. It was a short ride, and he pulled into the yard, jumped down hard, stumbled, and men were watching him, some were laughing. He stood, felt a sharp pain in his knee, looked up toward the porch, saw, sitting at a small table, holding a teacup, Joe Hooker.

"General, try to maintain a bit of dignity. There are enlisted men present."

There was laughter, and Hancock saw the faces of the others. Officers and their aides spilled out onto the porch, drawn by the commotion, and he saw Couch now, coming out of the house. Couch saw the look on his face and did not laugh. On the road behind him there was a sound, the clatter of wheels, and he turned, followed the gaze of the others, saw a horse, a fast gallop, pulling an empty wagon, and there was no driver. He watched the wagon move past, heard more laughter, looked back to Couch, would talk to him, find out what was happening, the truth. On the porch, one man looked past Hancock, looked toward the last of the sunlight, through the trail of dust from the single wagon, said, "Good God . . . here they come!"

Hancock turned, saw on the road, across the clearing on both sides, a ragged mass of troops, no coats, no hats, without guns. There was the rattle of another wagon, then many more, still without drivers, terrified horses, pulled along by a growing tide of running men.

On the porch Hooker yelled out, and men began to move. Above the house, in a wide clearing, there was a line of resting troops, a reserve division of Sickles's corps, and now orders were flying, the men scrambling into formation. Hooker shouted from the porch, "Move into line, move around, move into line! Give them the bayonet!"

Hancock grabbed his horse, jumped up and spurred the big animal out into the road, saw now that this was not the enemy, these were men in blue. *Our* men, he thought, and felt the great weight of the wave. If they keep going, they will run right over the backs of my men.

He could hear guns now, well to the west, scattered cannon, but mostly muskets, the vast flow of sound finally reaching the clearing. There were more wagons, men on horses, and the mad stampede was moving past the mansion. Hancock looked for officers, someone in control, saw the line of Sickles's fresh troops swinging around, moving toward the road, trying to stop the panicked mob. From the thicket below the road more men appeared, torn uniforms, still running, and he raised his sword, swung it down hard, hit a man flat across the shoulder, knocking him down. The man looked at him with raw terror.

Hancock shouted, "Get up! Stop running!" and the man was back on his feet, seemed to understand. But then another rush, and the man was caught up and gone again. Hancock turned the horse, rode quickly down the road, fought his way with the tide, moved past, tried to get out in front, to reach his trenches before the tide swept over.

He crested the hill, turned back, saw fewer men running now. Many had simply collapsed with exhaustion. But others came on, and now they reached his own troops. His men were turning, standing, surprised, and muskets were raised, but they saw it was blue troops, not the enemy, and did not shoot. The first of the wave poured away, down the hill, into the woods, across the stream where Miles's men waited, and many still ran, farther, plunging through the vines and the brush and into the arms of Lee's astonished troops.

50. JACKSON

MAY 2, 1863. EVENING.

THE VOLLEYS WERE SLOWING NOW. THE BIG GUNS STILL THREW shell and canister toward him, but the dark was spilling heavily over the ground, had filled the thick woods, and even the open clearings were growing dim. He saw Colston, and rode that way. Colston was yelling at an officer, directing the man to form his company, saw Jackson and stared with wild eyes.

"We have stopped, sir! Can't see! The lines are tangled . . . we're mixed in with Rodes's men. It's confusion, sir! We need Hill to come up . . . Hill's men can move on by us!"

Jackson turned, looked to the rear, tried to see past the dark thickets. He heard the sound of troops, fresh troops, said, "Yes, General. Try to form your men. I will tell General Hill to push on! We must not stop! They are running. They will keep running if we press them!"

He turned the horse, rode back toward the oncoming lines, now saw A. P. Hill leading his staff. Hill saluted, unsmiling, and Jackson stared hard into the thin face. "Keep them moving, General," he said. "Keep the pressure up. We have broken their flank. We can crush them now, cut them off. We must not give them time to organize. Take your division forward, then press on to the north, toward the river. Move toward United States Ford . . . they must not escape!"

Hill stared at him, said, "General . . . it is dark. I don't know the ground."

Jackson turned around, looked, saw his own staff beginning to come together, saw Captain Boswell, the engineer, and yelled out, "Boswell, report to General Hill. Find a way through the woods . . . to the northeast. Find the rear of the enemy's position. We will cut them off!"

Boswell moved up, saluted Jackson, and Hill looked at him, knew there would be no argument.

Jackson turned away now, his orders clear, and he rode forward down the dark road. In front of him a sudden burst of shelling was answered from both sides, the woods cut down by aimless blasts of metal. He rode farther, listening, looked up into the black, wanted to ask God to please let them keep on . . . but he did not, thought, *You have given us much today.* To the south, away from the turnpike, he could see a red glow, and then another. Now, the staff eased up closer behind him.

A voice said, "Fire . . . the woods are burning," and they waited, watched.

Another man said, "Oh my God . . . the wounded . . ." Jackson held up his hand, waved them back, pushed the horse forward, listened. The shelling had stopped now. Scattered musket fire echoed through the trees, and he watched the fire, could hear it, fueled by the dry and dense brush.

He wanted to ride forward, to the confused tangle of Rodes's and Colston's lines, to tell them not to stop, to keep going, move forward . . . but he felt the sudden deadweight of hopelessness, could not see anything at all in front of him, knew they could not as well, that a night attack rarely made sense, not in a place like this. He looked up, said another prayer, *Thank You for our success,* and through the tops of far trees, saw a white light, the great brightness of the rising full moon. Around him the light was cutting through the shadows, and now he could see the shapes, the wide path of the road. Yes, he thought, God is still showing us the way!

He turned, and the staff came up again. He saw the boy, the young man who knew these woods so well, and Jackson said, "Is there a road . . . that way, toward the United States Ford?"

"No, sir, not here. There's some old trails, but farther up, there's the Bullock Road. Some trails off that . . ."

Jackson nodded impatiently. "Show me! Now . . . we must not waste time!"

The boy moved forward, Jackson followed, and the staff trailed behind.

They turned down a small road, moving slowly in the growing moonlight, and Jackson strained to hear, stopped the horse, heard troops out in front of him, digging in. There was the clear sound of axes, the chopping of trees, and so they would be Federal troops. Still, he thought, sound carries far at night, they might not be as close as the sounds, there must still be a way. The boy was watching him. He motioned, and they began to move along the trail again.

Behind them there was the deafening blast of a big gun, one of Hill's, a pointless blind shot toward the Federal lines. Then came the answer, several bright flashes, and around them limbs shattered, dirt flew up, and both sides turned quiet, nervous fingers wrapped on tight triggers, waiting for some movement, some telltale sound.

Jackson felt the chill of the night, the damp sweat in his uniform, reached behind the saddle for the black rubber overcoat, pulled it quietly over his shoulders, and they kept moving, into solid dark broken by small pieces of moonlight. Behind him the staff drew up, closer. A burst of fire came from the Federal troops, a short volley from a line of muskets exploded in the woods from the right, then he heard a low voice behind him, and a hand touched his shoulder.

It was Lieutenant Morrison, Anna's younger brother. Morrison said, in an anxious whisper, "Sir . . . we are beyond our lines. This is no place for you, sir."

Jackson stopped the horse, raised his hand, halting the group. He understood now, it could not go the way he had hoped. It would have to be in the morning.

"You are correct. We will return to the road."

He turned the horse, began to move quickly now, and the others followed. Now, below them, close in the thick brush, a man's voice. "Halt! Who is that?" and another voice, a sharp command, "It's cavalry! Fire!"

There was a quick sheet of flame, and behind him, Jackson heard the cry of horses and men falling.

One of the aides rode toward the troops, shouted, "No, stop firing . . . you're firing on your own men!"

Then came a strong hard voice, the voice of a veteran who has seen cunning and deceit, and who understands that his men are the front of the line, and that before them is only the enemy. "It is a lie! Pour it to them!"

The second volley was better aimed, the moonlight silhouetting the men on horseback. Jackson spun around, tried to reach the shelter of trees beyond the trail, and he felt a hard tug at his hand, a hard, hot punch in his shoulder. The horse lunged, terrified, began to run away from the noise, jumped and jerked, and now it was Morrison, beside him, grabbing the reins that Jackson had dropped. He felt himself sliding, tried to reach for the saddle, could not grab with his hand, slid down the side of the horse and fell hard to the cold ground.

There was more yelling now. Horsemen were coming toward them on the trail. It was Hill and his staff, and Hill yelled toward his lines, said, "Hold your fire. These are your men here!"

His staff rode quickly toward the line of rifles. Hill came forward, saw the bodies scattered beside dying horses, and he dropped down from the horse, moved through the dark, said, "Oh God . . . what have they done?"

He saw one more man on the ground, and another man kneeling and Hill said, "Who is this?" He saw the face of young Morrison then, and Morrison was crying.

Hill moved around. A small piece of moonlight crossed Jackson's face. "Oh . . . God . . . General . . . are you hurt?"

"I am afraid so, I am hit in the shoulder . . . and . . . here." He raised his right hand, turned it in the faint light, tried to see it, to see where the pain began.

Now there were more shots, from above the trail. The Federal lines were moving forward, and Hill turned to one of the aides, said, "Get an ambulance . . . a litter! We need a litter!"

The aide hesitated, stared at the blood flowing from Jackson's shoulder, soaking into his uniform, said, "Oh my God . . ."

"*Move!*"

The aide looked at Hill, then turned and was gone.

"We must leave here, General. Can you walk?"

Others had gathered, and a tourniquet was wrapped high around his left arm. He bent his knees, tried to stand, and there were hands around him, pulling him up.

They began to move quickly down the trail. He tried to run, felt the hands holding him up, saw others coming up the trail toward them, carrying a litter.

He stared at the soft, dirty cloth, thought, No, I will walk, heard a familiar voice, Captain Smith, and tried to see the young man's face. But the hands pulled him down, laid him down, and now he was on his back.

Smith leaned close to his face, said, "General, are you in pain? Can I give you something? Here . . . take this, it will help."

He put a small bottle to Jackson's mouth, and Jackson thought, No, I don't need anything. The liquid wet his tongue, burned his throat, and he wanted to say no, but the liquid burned down deep, the warmth spreading through him. Then Smith took the bottle away, and Jackson smiled at him.

"Mr. Smith, I should have a word with you about this. . . ." He felt himself rising, lifted up, could not see Smith's face now, only the tops of the trees, the moonlight, small specks of light, the stars. He tried to feel the pain, could not, knew it was not just the whiskey, thought, Thank You. He tried to lift his head, but the litter was bouncing, and he remembered . . . Hill . . . fresh troops. We should not have stopped.

There was a sudden roar of fire, a new burst of light. Federal cannons were firing blindly into the rebel positions, and now the men dropped down, lay flat. Overhead, limbs and small branches flew into pieces, wood and dirt rained over them. A body was suddenly across his, and now he saw Smith's face, close, shielding him from the debris. He wanted to speak, to say something to the young man, tell him thank you, but there was no voice, and he knew he was now very very weak. I will die here, tonight, he thought. He tried to see God, to ask why . . . this place? But his mind was foggy, swimming, he could no longer see the trees.

The shelling stopped, and they rose in unison, picked up the litter, and four men held the corners as they again moved toward the road. Now, musket fire, more Federal troops, and there was a small, sharp crack, lead against bone, and one of the men suddenly grunted and crumpled, dropping the litter. Jackson rolled off to the side, landed hard, felt a sharp pain in his side, slicing through him. He was suddenly alert again, tried to twist, to roll off the pain, his mind screaming inside, Make it stop, and the hands were on him again, and he was mercifully on his back and they were moving again.

They reached the road, and now more soldiers were around them, the lines of his men. Hill was suddenly moving quickly, saw an officer, a captain, the man questioning, and Hill said, "Tell your men nothing. It is a wounded Confederate officer." The man looked past him, tried to see, and Hill heard horses, the ambulance, and he pushed the man aside.

The man went over to the litter, looked down into the face of Jackson, suddenly dropped to his knees, said, "No, oh dear God, no . . ."

Jackson heard the man, but his mind was now moving far away, and he turned his head, could see beyond the trees, the rising red glow of the fast-moving fires. He looked to the man again, tried to see, but the face was framed by the wall of red, and Jackson stared hard, eyes wide, saw the flames now moving toward him, laughing and dancing, and he looked back to the face, wanted to say . . . to ask . . . would talk . . . must talk to God, but now the face went away, and there was

only the fire, the pain burning him from inside, and he was too weak
to stop it, to fight it, and his mind finally gave in, and he drifted further
away now, beyond the fire, felt the strong hands lifting him again,
and he slept, believing that it was God's hands, and He was lifting him
toward Heaven.

T HE LITTER WAS UP AND IN THE AMBULANCE, AND HILL LOOKED
at Smith, said, "Where will you—"
"Dr. McGuire is at Dowdall's. We have sent word. I will keep
you informed, General."

Hill nodded, turned, saw his aides and moved toward his horse.
He knew it was his responsibility now, that this army was in confusion, that daylight would bring a dangerous fight from a huge number
of Federal troops, troops that were digging in hard in front of them.
He sat in the saddle, looked past the trees in front of him, then pulled
the horse, moved down across the turnpike. Beyond, there was more
scattered shooting, and he dismounted again, waved a courier forward,
thought, I must find Colston and Rodes, get word to Stuart . . . and
Lee. He began to put words together, forming the messages, and the
courier followed. Hill looked up to the trees, the moon, tried to pin-
point the sounds of the guns, to get some bearing.

Now the heavy roar of the cannon filled the woods around him.
Suddenly, there was a ripping pain in his legs. His knees gave way and
he rolled forward, made a sharp cry. His men were quickly down,
holding him, and he tried to feel the wound, touched the backs of his
legs, felt the blood, nothing deep. He looked up at the faces, said, "No,
it's all right . . . just my legs, it's all right." They tried to lift him up,
and his legs would not hold him, he could not stand, and he fell back
down, fell forward onto his hands, stared into the dark, thought, I am
in command . . . I must . . . I am in command. . . .

He tried to stand again, and there was no feeling in his legs. He
rolled to the side, sat, thought, So, God is with Stonewall after all. If *he*
cannot command, then it is not to be me. He looked at the faces
around him, said, "The command of the Second Corps should pass
now to General Rodes. But General Lee would not place him in that
position, he does not have the experience. Captain Adams . . ."

The man bent over, said, "Yes, sir, what can I do, sir?"

"Take a message to General Stuart, he is up at Ely's Ford, I believe. Tell him of our situation, and request that he ride here as quickly
as possible. He must take command of the corps. And send a message

to General Lee, for his approval. I do not see what other choice we have, but General Lee might disagree."

"Sir . . . right away!"

There was a flurry of motion, and horses began to move away.

He put his hands around the wounds on his legs, tried to feel. . . . He reached into his pocket, held up a gold watch, tried to catch the moonlight, saw . . . nearly three A.M.

"Well, we will soon learn if Joe Hooker is still running."

D R. McGUIRE WAS TALKING TO HIM. "WE'LL GET THIS TIGHT-ened up first." And he felt a tugging in his shoulder. McGuire looked at him, saw the sharp blue eyes. "Well, General, welcome back. Can you hear me? How are you feeling?"

Jackson tried to see the shoulder, and a sharp pain stopped him. He opened his mouth, made a sound, "Ummghh." His tongue felt like cotton.

McGuire reached out, brought a cup up to his mouth. "Here, this may help. . . ."

It was cool and wonderful, and he tried to swallow, felt his throat harden into a knot, and the water spilled down the sides of his face. McGuire lifted the cup, and Jackson shook his head, tried to lift up.

McGuire said, "All right, here, try again."

This time he swallowed, just a bit, then more, and now he laid his head back, moved his tongue, said, "I . . . am I not dead?"

McGuire laughed. "Certainly not! I may take offense at that, General. You are in my hands now."

Jackson tried to smile, then saw other faces, more men, and the faces were dark and serious. He suddenly realized he was on a bed. "Where am I, Doctor?"

"Field hospital. For tonight, anyway. Tomorrow, we'll move you away from the . . . fighting."

McGuire was not smiling now, knew the word would have an effect. Jackson suddenly tried to sit, to pull himself up. He reached for the edge of the bed, saw his right hand was bandaged.

"What . . . I'm shot. . . ."

"General, the hand is minor. The ball lodged under the skin. It is the other wounds. . . ." He paused, looked up at the other men, and Jackson heard the sound of a table being moved, saw the faces closer now. "General, you were wounded twice in your left arm. The artery in your upper arm has been severed, the bone is broken. You were very fortunate you did not bleed to death. In cases such as this, the removal of the arm is . . . required." McGuire paused, waited for a reaction. The other men were around the top of the bed now.

Jackson said, "Doctor, I have absolute faith in your abilities. You must do what is necessary."

McGuire nodded slowly, said, "We have chloroform . . . it will make this much easier for you." Jackson shook his head, and McGuire said, "No argument this time, General. You will not please God if you endure pain needlessly. This is not a test of courage."

Jackson smiled, knew that McGuire understood him well. He closed his eyes, a brief prayer, *Forgive me . . . but I must follow orders.* He looked again at McGuire, and now the smiles were gone. McGuire said something to one of the other men, and there was a hand above him, and a white cloth, and Jackson closed his eyes, felt the soft cotton against his face, took a long, deep breath.

His mind began to spin, a swirl of light, and above him, far away, he heard music, faint, soft. Then it grew, swelled into a loud and glorious march, deep and rhythmic, the smooth and regular cadence of soldiers on the move, men who could do anything. . . .

51. STUART

SUNDAY, MAY 3, 1863

H E SAW RODES FIRST, RODE UP QUICKLY TOWARD THE LARGER
tent. Then the others came, Colston, Harry Heth, and more,
men he did not know.

He had ridden alone, left his men up at Ely's Ford, a crossing
that was now dangerous because it offered the Federal Army a clear
route behind their new position, the ground they had won by the collapse of the Federal flank. Late in the day, Jackson had sent him up to
prevent anyone from coming that way, if there was a Federal commander who recognized the opportunity. They were surprised to find
the ford already occupied by a large force of Federal cavalry, Averill's
brigade, and Stuart knew he did not have the manpower to drive them
away. But this night, there was much edginess, and it would only take
a good, solid surprise to hold them back, keep them nervously dug
into one spot.

But the attack had begun without him. A. P. Hill's courier had
reached him with the message, and he did not wait, gave Von Borcke
the job: strike fast, retreat, then strike once more.

He had pushed the horse hard, reached the turnpike at a fast gallop, pulled up now at the new headquarters, near Dowdall's, close to
the former center of Howard's position, but now well behind their
own lines.

He did not bow, did not sweep the ground with the ridiculous
hat, looked hard at the men waiting for him, saw the eyes of confident
soldiers who know they need direction.

There were salutes, and they let him pass by, followed
him into the tent. It was warm, from the dull heat of an oil lamp. He
saw a small table, a wood chair, sat and motioned to small seats

446

spread around the tent. They followed, quiet now, looking at him, waiting.

"Do we know if General Jackson is alive?"

Rodes looked at the others, spoke up. "He is seriously wounded, his arm . . . not sure where he is now, but we have not heard more since he was taken from the field."

"General Hill was with him." Heth stood now, tall, nervous. "General Hill was wounded shortly after . . . not seriously, but he cannot walk. He has appointed me. . . . As senior brigade commander, I have assumed command of his division. If you do not object, sir."

Stuart motioned. "Please, General Heth, please sit. This is a difficult time for us all. We must pause, say a prayer for General Jackson, and keep our heads cool. Yes, I quite agree with General Hill. Unless General Lee requests otherwise, you are now in command of Hill's division."

Heth sat down again, all knees and elbows, stared at the ground, said, "General, have you been informed who it was . . . how General Jackson was wounded?"

"Is it important? Our concern is with his recovery and his return to the field. Revenge cannot be—"

"Sir, it was our own troops. General Lane . . . it was the Eighteenth North Carolina."

Stuart stared at him, absorbed, said, "My God . . . are you certain?"

Heth nodded, still looked down. After a long moment Heth said, "They are aware . . . it was dark and they were close to the enemy. It was a dangerous place for the general to be."

"The Eighteenth North Carolina . . ." Stuart felt sick, took a long, deep breath. "They will carry this with them for the rest of their lives."

Heth looked up with sad, tired eyes. "We all will, sir."

Colston cleared his throat, said, "General, we have all been praying for General Jackson. The whole army . . . word has spread, it could not be helped. I suppose that even the Yankees know by now. We may be in serious trouble."

Stuart did not know Colston well, knew only that he was new to command and had risen through the ranks of Jackson's own men, the division that Jackson himself organized two years earlier: the heartbeat of the entire corps, the Stonewall Brigade.

"General Colston, the sun will rise very soon on a field where the enemy has been beaten badly and is of a mind to withdraw. The advantages are all ours."

Colston seemed unsure, looked at Rodes, and Rodes said,

"General Stuart, we welcome your authority to command this corps. We will do what you order us to do, sir. But these men . . . my division is scattered all over these woods, sir. I don't even know how many men I can put into line. General Colston has the same situation. The only fresh troops we have, men who have even had something to eat . . . are Hill's . . . General Heth's division. The Federals are digging in, building heavy defensive lines. They are expecting us to advance against them at daylight. I'm not sure we have much to send against them."

Stuart looked at Heth, said, "General, is your division in place? Can you press forward an organized attack?"

"Yes, sir. The men were not heavily engaged yesterday. They will be strong."

"Good. Then they will lead the attack. Gentlemen, I do not believe General Jackson would have had us sitting here moaning about our problems. He would have one word, for all of us: *attack.* That is what we must do. Once we can see . . . once we can determine what the enemy has done to prepare for us . . . then we will find his weaknesses, and move against him."

There were nods, and he stood, led them back out of the tent. Riders were coming into the camp. He looked at faces, and saw his own men, reports of the success at Ely's, and then he saw Sandie Pendleton, Jackson's chief of staff. Pendleton climbed from the horse slowly, and Stuart watched him, was suddenly very afraid, waited.

Pendleton said, "General Stuart, I come from General Jackson's bedside. I reached the general just after he awoke from surgery. Dr. McGuire has amputated his left arm. . . ." He paused, choked on the words.

Behind Stuart, Colston said in a soft whisper, "Good God."

Stuart stepped forward, raised a hand, some comfort, and Pendleton straightened, felt the hand on his shoulder, continued.

"Sir, General Jackson has been informed of General Hill's wounds, and of your taking command, sir. The general has every confidence in your abilities."

"Can you tell me, Major . . . does the general have any orders?"

"He said only for you to do what you think is best, General. It is your command."

Stuart turned to the others, and they waited. He thought, No, Stonewall is still in command, they will do it for him, they will do what he would want. I must remember that.

"Gentlemen, this has been a difficult . . . a long day. I suggest we tend to our troops, try to get them fed, and find some breakfast for ourselves."

They looked past him now, to another rider. He turned and saw Jed Hotchkiss, Jackson's mapmaker. Hotchkiss limped from the horse, moved tenderly, held out a paper, said, "General Stuart, I have a message for you, sir, from General Lee. Please forgive me. . . ." He slumped, fell to one knee, and Pendleton was down beside him.

"All right, Hotchkiss, all right. Does Lee know . . . ?"

"Yes, yes, he had been informed by Wilbourn when I got there. I had to ride down a long way." He stood, steadied himself on Pendleton's arm, and Stuart unfolded the paper, read quietly, then turned to the others, read aloud.

" 'It is necessary that the glorious victory thus far achieved be prosecuted with the utmost vigor, and the enemy given no time to rally. As soon as it is possible, they must be pressed, so that we may unite the two wings of the army. Endeavor, therefore, to dispossess them of Chancellorsville.' "

He stopped, there was a silent moment, and he said, "The plan is clear, gentlemen. We will form in lines to press hard to the east, toward Chancellorsville, and by doing so, we can move our right flank around to the southeast and link up with General Lee's lines. The enemy has already demonstrated a great willingness to leave this field. We will do what we can to speed them along."

The meeting was over, and men and horses began to move away. Hotchkiss sat down beside a small fire. Pendleton watched him, lowered his voice, said to Stuart, "It has been difficult for us all. Captain Smith is with the general now . . . I had best get back as well. I will keep you informed."

Stuart nodded, patted the young man's shoulder again, said, "Tell General Jackson that we will finish the work. This day too will be ours."

Pendleton tried to smile, nodded, moved slowly toward the horse. Now both men turned, saw it together, the first white glow of the dawn.

HE HAD RIDDEN OUT FIRST TO THE SOUTH, TO THE RIGHT FLANK of their lines, followed the advance as it pushed forward, smashing with full fury into the first of the Federal positions. The right flank was little more than a mile from Lee's left, but in between, Sickles's corps had dug in, well below the turnpike, and so

Stuart could not reach Lee without first confronting the deep lines of the Third Corps.

Heth's lines were nearly two miles wide, and they swept forward in a continuation of the assault the day before, straight down the turnpike, toward Chancellorsville. Colston's lines were moving up behind, and in the rear, Rodes was organizing what was left of his division. Stuart knew that he could count on barely twenty-five thousand exhausted and underfed troops, and in front of him was an army of nearly ninety thousand men, many of whom—the men under Reynolds and Meade—had yet to see any action at all.

To the north, Reynolds's First Corps and Meade's Fifth had worked all night, dug a long solid line, blocking any advance toward the river, the advance that Jackson would have pressed the day before had he not run out of daylight. Around Chancellorsville, Couch and Slocum were entrenched in a near circle, Slocum facing south and west, and Couch facing east. Between his headquarters and the Confederate lines, Hooker had dug four solid lines of entrenchments.

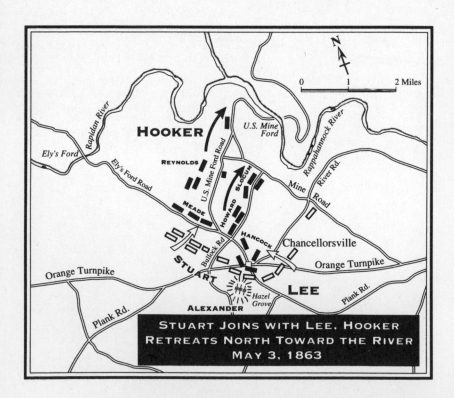

Stuart rode close behind the first line, as Jackson had the day before. He waved his sword, yelled, "Remember Jackson," and they watched him, shouted back. They all knew it was not yet a victory, that the long day ahead of them would prove whether the great, bold plan, the sheer audacity of Lee and Jackson, would be enough after all.

They could see the abatis now, the great piles of thick brush, cut trees, spread high in front of the first entrenchments. The lines kept moving, pushed ahead through smaller thickets, short clearings. He pulled the horse along, stepping over the unburied dead, tried to pick his way through the roar of musket fire. Behind him, he could not see the next line, hidden in the thick brush, and he turned the horse, called out and waited. Then came the great rumble, from the batteries far in front, and low screams, the high whistling shrieks, and the brush began to fly apart around him. Great blasts of splinters blew by him, and he turned again, ducked low on the horse, saw the backs of his men pushing forward, yelled, "Keep moving, forward!"

He rode back to the south, toward the right flank, looked for officers, horses. The orders were plain, Lee had sent another message: link their two armies together, move around below the Federal lines. He pushed the horse into a thick mass of vines. The horse stopped, and he yelled, "*Move!*"

A shell tore through the brush behind them, a sharp spray of dirt hitting him in the back, and suddenly the horse lurched, tore through the last of the thicket, and he was in the open. I know, he thought, this is not what cavalry horses do. He laughed now, patted the horse's neck, moved farther. Smoke was filling the clearings. He saw a man on a horse and rode that way. The man was directing his men through the thickets, and now the troops in front of him were gone, out of sight in the dense brush.

Stuart reached him, saw he was a major, said, "You'll have to dismount! Move with them . . . stay with them!"

The man looked at him without recognition, and Stuart was quickly past. The man stayed on the horse, and Stuart was looking in all directions, could see no other horses, just lines of moving men. He saw the major again, thought, He might know . . . where his commander is.

The man was watching him now, yelled, "This is no place for a fight . . . we can't stay together!"

"Dismount! Move into the brush with your men, Major. The fight is in front of you!"

The man stared at him, still not moving, and now another man rode up, through the thickening smoke, said, "General Stuart! Please ride down this way . . . General Archer is pushing the flank, sir!"

Stuart jerked the horse, moved with the man, and the major stared, wide-eyed, was quickly down from the horse, began to plunge into the brush after his men.

Stuart followed Archer's aide closely, their horses still stepping over scattered bodies. Then he saw Jim Archer, a vague, ghostly form in the smoke. The heavy shells were whistling higher overhead now, finding the lines behind them, and now in front of them a steady rattle of muskets began, from places they could not see.

Archer saluted Stuart, yelled hoarsely through the sounds, "Good morning, sir! It is an honor to be under your command, sir! We have a strong position in front of us, it appears. The Yankees are still in these woods! We did not expect to find them this far below the roads!"

Stuart tried to see to the front. The musket fire was growing still, and now the men behind them were moving up, the second line, and hats went up, cheers. Stuart waved, but did not yell, knew these men did not need anything else to inspire them.

There was another officer beside them now, a captain, and he was pointing up to the left, from where Stuart had just come. "General, we have lost contact with McGowan's flank! We are in the open, sir! It's too thick to see!"

Archer spurred his horse, said, "Excuse me, General, I must see to my flank," and he rode forward, moved quickly through a grove of short trees.

Stuart watched him. It could be like this all along the line, he thought, hard for them to stay together, to see each other. He dug hard at the horse's side, rode farther down to the right, toward the end of the line. He could see a long clearing now, then up a large hill, in front of them, and on top the steady flashes of the Federal guns, a high and clear position, a perfect place to throw fire into the oncoming lines of his troops. Stuart heard more guns now, down in front, farther east, and he thought, *Lee's* guns. Lee was pressing the attack as well.

He turned the horse and rode back toward the turnpike, passing between lines of gray troops, all moving east. He came to a small road, was amazed to see a long line of guns, *his* guns, strung out far down the road, men on wagons and horses, just sitting, waiting. He thought, No, something is wrong. Why are they not in line, firing? He saw an officer, a red cap, and the man rode toward him, saluted, said, "General Stuart, we are ready, sir. We need that ground!"

Stuart stared at the man, then recognized him, it was Porter Alexander.

"Colonel, why are these guns not in position? They should be answering those batteries up on that hill!"

"General, that is exactly where we're going . . . that hill. All I'm waiting for is your troops to clear those batteries away. We will advance as soon as we can."

Stuart looked toward the hill, could see only smoke, and the musket fire below was a strong and steady roar.

"Colonel Alexander . . . you are assuming—"

"Yes, General, I am. We will push them back, and clear that hill. That is the objective, isn't it, sir?"

Stuart nodded, yes, of course. The infantry must move against the hill, push on up. He thought of the cavalry, the plan . . . go around, ride in quick and surprise them from the rear, but this was not cavalry, and he had no one to send except the foot soldiers. He was beginning to appreciate the infantry commanders. There was nowhere else to go but right *there*, straight ahead.

"Colonel, prepare your men to move! I will give you that hill!"

Stuart turned the horse, rode along the small road, followed the sounds of the muskets. Now there was a new sound, high and loud, and he saw men all around him, yelling, some beginning to run. He stopped, saw a long bare pile of dirt, and men flowing across, down into the trenches beyond. They had reached the first entrenchments, had pushed the Federal soldiers out and away, and many of his men were still going, pushing forward, disappearing into the smoke.

He rode behind them, felt the ground rising, knew they were on the big hill, and he stopped, tried to hear. There were more muskets farther to the left, some back behind, and he had a sudden burst of cold in his gut, thought, We are not together, there are no lines. The fight is . . . *everywhere*. He turned now, rode along the base of the hill, suddenly saw a clearing and a line of blue troops, firing into the brush beyond. He jerked the horse, rode farther to the rear. He saw lines of his own men now, moving toward the Federal troops, and they were not watching him now, did not focus on the men on horses, were driving forward, staring in one direction. Men were stopping, firing, and others falling, dropping down in solid heaps or flying back, arms wild, heads back. He pulled the horse again, fought more vines, more brush, and now he was in the clear and back on the turnpike.

The shelling was coming from the north now, and from the east, from Chancellorsville. The trenches dug by the Federal troops the night before were behind them, and he could see ahead, to the next line of trenches. His men were moving that way, shrouded by the smoke.

Colston's lines were advancing past the first entrenchments now, and they moved by him. Many hats went up and they began to yell. Stuart sat still, beside the road, suddenly stood in the stirrups and waved his hat in a wide circle, began to yell himself. They felt it, began to run, pushed through the woods in a new wave. Now, in front of them, where the muskets met across small spaces, and men stared into the faces of their enemy, the gray wall pressed and pressed. The men in blue pulled out, left the second entrenchments, swallowed by the screaming wave of gray.

It was no longer the stampede of raw panic, and the gray wave began to slow. There were more muskets in front of them now, heavier, solid blue lines. He rode into a small clearing, saw his men moving out beyond the second trenches, and now straight in front the trees exploded with one mighty flame, and canister tore through the brush and through the lines of his men. He stared, could see nothing through the new wall of white smoke, turned, and the horse would not run, was suddenly limping. He looked down, saw a flow of red, thought, No, not here, I must get to the road. The horse began to move, stepping awkwardly. He guided the animal past mangled bodies, heaps of men, reached the road and dismounted. It was a bright gash, a deep and deadly wound. The horse dropped its head, one knee buckled, and he patted the soft neck, stepped back, took off his hat, pulled out his pistol and ended it.

Men were running back along the road now, the wave had turned, and the shells began to fly past, heavy shot and the hot whistle of canister. He ran down into the trees, began to yell, "Stop . . . turn and fight!" He could not see, did not know what was happening, but could not move on the road. It was the one clear line of sight for the Federal gunners, and they were sweeping the road with steady firing.

He moved back, reached the first line of trenches, saw they were filled now with his men, most with heads down, shielded from the vicious firing.

"Up, you men. Up! You must keep moving forward! On your feet!" Men were looking at him. Some began to rise, officers appearing, and he watched one man, grabbing at the men around him, pulling them up, and he yelled, "Yes! Stonewall would be proud! Do it for Jackson!"

Now more were moving, forming a solid line, and they began to move out of the trench. In the trees a blast of muskets rolled over them, an advancing line of blue troops, and the men melted back, down into the trench. The firing went both ways now, blue soldiers behind trees, moving forward in small groups, and the men in the trenches, and Stuart knew this was not where he should be. . . .

He reached the edge of the road again, past the bodies of many men, had stepped across solid layers of men. Bodies were scattered in a thin layer all across the road. He saw a group of officers and ran toward them. They watched him come, stared at him, and there were loud shouts, commands, and suddenly he was handed the reins to a horse.

"Do you have orders, sir?" It was Rodes.

He steadied himself on the horse, sat straight in the saddle, said, "General Rodes, we must advance with all our strength. We are being driven back. We do not have the numbers, the defenses are too strong. Are your men ready?"

Rodes looked behind him, saw officers riding along the edge of the woods, pointing, shouting orders, and he said, "We are ready on your command, sir."

"Then, advance your men. Fast. Press them hard. If we do not push them back they may counterattack."

"Sir, for General Jackson." He saluted, turned to the officers behind him.

Stuart spurred the new horse, pulled him back toward the roar of the muskets, said under his breath, "Yes, for General Jackson."

ARCHER'S BRIGADE CONTINUED TO PRESS UP THE LONG RISE, toward the top of the wide hill known as Hazel Grove. Beside him McGowan's brigade did the same, but it was two separate attacks, a fight by two units who could not stay connected to each other. Gradually, the lines of Federal soldiers withdrew all along the hill. Sickles had asked for help, to strengthen that part of the defense, but his lines were well below the main strength of Hooker's trenches, and Hooker was more inclined to pull Sickles back, tightening the circle around Chancellorsville. As Archer's men reached the top of Hazel Grove, they saw Sickles leaving, the heavy guns pulling away, the shallow gun pits empty and waiting for Porter Alexander to climb the hill.

"HERE! SIR!"
Stuart heard the voice, saw the wave, rode toward the man in the red cap. Around him the guns were unlimbering, men scrambling down from caissons and wagons, and Stuart saw Alexander pointing, holding his arm out straight. Now Stuart saw, pulled up the horse, stared across the green thickets below them, toward the northeast: a short mile away, toward the next rise, another hill, open, a wide clearing, and one large and imposing mansion: Chancellorsville.

"My God . . ."

"Yes, sir. As I said, sir. We will begin firing very soon now. This should take the pressure off the infantry, quite a bit, I'd say, sir."

Below them, down in the trees, the musket fire was steady and spread all around them. Stuart rode forward, did not feel like a commander. There was no control to this battle . . . it was being fought by small groups of men, regiments, led by low-level officers. He had tried to find many of the commanders himself, found small units that did not know who was leading them. So many of the officers were down, so many of the names he knew were either separated from their units, lost themselves, or dead. Companies were being led by sergeants, regiments by captains. Frank Paxton, the only general that Colston had under him, the man picked by Jackson to lead the Stonewall Brigade, was dead. Stuart stared out across the sounds, to the grand old house, thought, This must end soon. We are running out of men.

The order was yelled, there was a shot from a pistol, and the batteries began to fire, thundering across the wide hill. Stuart moved back, stood beside Alexander, raised his field glasses and saw the first puffs, the small flashes of light. He nodded. Yes, Joe Hooker, he thought, we have found your headquarters. Quickly, the house was covered with smoke, and he could see small fires, knew the house would not last long. It was, of course, the first target for men who had been waiting for a target.

Now all the batteries were firing, and the ground was shaking under him. He steadied the horse, tried to see. The wide fields around the house were alive with the impact of the shells, and smoke covered most of the hill. Federal batteries began to answer, from new positions beyond the house, and around them a few shells were beginning to land. He turned to Alexander, said, "Colonel, this is your hill. You know what to do."

Alexander was smiling, said, "If you happen to see General Hooker, please thank him for this wonderful gift."

Stuart nodded, smiled, began to move the horse, would move back up to the north, toward the turnpike. He thought, I must try to form them . . . some kind of line, press them forward. Then he saw riders coming from the east, moving out of the woods, into the clearing. They were officers, men in gray. He stopped, waited, then spurred the horse, rode hard toward them, waved the hat high.

"General Lee!"

He pulled up, jumped from the horse, made the low bow, and Lee said, "Well, I did not expect to find you up here. Very well, General. It seems we have joined the two corps. Anderson's division is below us now, and I believe they have located General Heth's flank. How is the fight here, General?"

Lee was not smiling, and Stuart stood at attention, said, "Sir, we have pressed the enemy hard. We have beaten him back from his defenses, but . . . we are outmanned, sir. They have pushed us back."

"We are always outmanned, General. We need to press on." He stopped, saw now the focus of the guns, saw Alexander riding up. "This is a fine position, Colonel. Your guns will do good work from here."

Alexander saluted, was still smiling. "We will do our best, General."

Lee looked down at Stuart, who reached for the horse, pulled himself up, said, "General, perhaps I should return to my . . . to General Jackson's troops."

Lee nodded. "That would be a wise decision, General. Press them. Press them *hard*."

Stuart saluted and moved the horse away, back down the wide hill, where the guns continued to fire in a steady rhythm.

Lee watched him, thought of Jackson now. The mention of his name sent a hard, dull pain through his chest. We have lost many . . . so many, he thought, and God does not judge one man better than the next. But I cannot help it. *Dear God, You must save General Jackson. This army has no better man.*

Lee put it from his mind, would not see the face, the sharp blue eyes, stared out in the direction of the cannon fire. He raised his field glasses, saw the house, burning now, tall flames and black smoke, and he thought, General Hooker has lost his headquarters, and so he must move, and when he moves, he will take the army with him.

52. HANCOCK

THEY HAD BEEN PRESSED SINCE FIRST LIGHT, HEAVIER WAVES coming out of the woods to the east, and it was clear that no one had retreated from in front of his division.

The fight was coming now all along their lines, down, across the front of Slocum's position, then in a wide arc to the right, in a wide U-shaped front, and from the crest of the ridge he commanded he could hear the worst of it back behind him, toward the west.

He had put the young Colonel Miles in command of the first lines, had given him enough troops to spread out in a heavy skirmish line all along his front, dug into their muddy trenches. Lee's troops had pushed and charged and sent volley after volley against them, and Miles did not break. This part of the line will hold, Hancock thought.

He rode along the crest, down toward his flank and the junction with Slocum, heard more steady musket fire and a few big guns. He saw Slocum, who moved toward him, waving, his staff riding at full speed to keep up. Slocum slowed the horse, yelled, "General, we are running out of ammunition! Have you any reserves?"

Hancock looked at him, saw no smile now, only the dirty sweat of the battle. "We are holding our lines . . . but . . . no, I have received no supplies. The wagons are up above the mansion. Have you sent back to headquarters?"

Slocum waved his arms, seemed frantic. "Of course I've sent to headquarters! There is no support there! Hooker will not send any aid . . . says we are fighting for our lives!"

Hancock saw the look, a man who believed they were done, a commander who would infect his men.

"General Slocum, we are not giving way! There are not enough rebel soldiers to drive us from this ground! Can you hold your position?"

Slocum stared now down toward his lines, then turned to Hancock with a new look, a dull sadness. "We will hold out as long as we can. If Sedgwick does not come to our aid . . . it cannot last."

Hancock thought, Sedgwick? Why do we need Sedgwick? Is he still on the river, below Fredericksburg? He was feeling the old anger again, the heat rising in his chest.

"General Slocum, I must tend to my division. I am sorry that headquarters is not cooperating with you. I will try to find General Couch. He may have some help to give."

He pulled the horse away, left Slocum sitting, rode back toward the turnpike, toward headquarters, the Chancellor house.

There were guns now, long lines, wagons and caissons, moving up into the wide clearing, coming from the south and the west. They moved up past the house, to the north, began to unlimber, officers screaming orders, gunners pulling their cannon into position. He reined the horse, thought, Why are they back here . . . and suddenly, in front of him, a bright flash, a hard slap of wind, and the air came alive, bright red streaks, blinding explosions. Now he understood: We have pulled back, the lines are closing in.

He pushed the horse, could see the house, saw a shell hit directly into the walls, shattered brick blown high in the air, a stone chimney collapsing. Men were running, scattering, riderless horses were galloping toward him. He tried to keep going, the house now hidden by smoke, and he heard men yelling, approaching, saw flags now, officers. He waited, thought, Keep moving, but no, there will be no one there now, and that whole damned clearing is a target. He heard his name then, a hoarse voice. He turned toward the sound, saw men on horses, Couch. Other officers were trailing behind him, and they were moving fast, away from the house, toward the east, moving closer now, toward the turnpike. He pulled the horse around, met them on the road.

Couch said, "Are your lines holding, General?"

"Yes, we have not withdrawn from our original positions. Where are the rebel guns firing—"

"From Hazel Grove. We have pulled back. Our commander has decided we are too weak, and so we are concentrating the lines. We are too goddamned weak!"

He saw Couch's face, red rage, knew that it was all falling apart, and Couch said aloud, as more men gathered around them, "General Hooker has been injured. It is not serious . . . he seems to be stunned.

He was at the house when the shelling began and was struck . . . quite possibly by the hand of God." There were nods, small laughs from the men, and Hancock saw that Couch was not smiling.

"The general has transferred command of the field to me. His last orders were . . . that the army be withdrawn . . . that we seek the safety of the river. It is the commanding general's feeling that this army has been beaten on this ground. I do not agree with that assessment . . . but the order has been given. I have sent word to Sickles and to Slocum to begin pulling back from contact with the enemy."

Hancock stared down to the south, toward Slocum's lines. He could see wagons moving, men filling the road. Behind them, around the burning house, shells continued to fall, and the Federal guns there were now answering. From the far side of the clearing, from where the stampede of the Eleventh Corps had come the day before, columns of troops were marching toward them, Sickles's men. Couch watched silently, and the men around him did not move, waited. Hancock looked at Couch, thought, He wants to turn them around, to fight . . . he cannot just *leave*.

Couch turned, said, "Gentlemen, let us move to a safer place. We will soon be the front lines."

He spurred the horse, and Hancock looked east, toward his troops, could hear nothing, sounds drowned out by the fierce chorus of blasts from the clearing.

He yelled toward Couch, rode quickly to catch up, and Couch slowed, looked at him. Hancock saw the face of a man who had had enough, the anger now fading, replaced by deep sadness. Couch said, "You will protect our flanks. . . . We will pull back to the north, toward the river. Reynolds will cover the west flank, you will cover the south and east."

Reynolds? he thought. "Sir, did the First Corps give way? I did not know they had engaged—"

"The First Corps did not have the chance to give way. They have not yet seen action. General Reynolds is dug in above the turnpike, and will withdraw toward the fords above him."

Hancock stared blankly at Couch. Reynolds . . . the First Corps, maybe the best they had . . . *was not even engaged*.

Up the road leading toward the river, riders appeared, came through the smoke, turned, moved toward them. Hancock saw the flag of the Fifth Corps, the Maltese cross. It was Meade, and with him, John Reynolds.

The aides stayed back, and Couch moved forward. The three men began to speak, and Hancock waited, could hear nothing. Then Couch turned, motioned to him, and he pushed the horse closer. Meade was staring away, toward the sound of the guns, and Reynolds was looking at him, hard, cold.

Couch said, "General Hancock, do you understand your orders?"

"Yes, sir. I am to protect the withdrawal of the army."

Reynolds was still staring at him, said quietly, "The withdrawal of the army . . . gentlemen, this is pure madness. General Hooker is not in control. Couch, you can override him, you are in command of the field. I can advance my men in line to the south, flank the enemy to the west. It is not too late to save this!"

Meade was still looking away, watching the lines of troops moving up the road, away from the sound of the guns. "We did not even have a fight." He turned, stared at Couch. "We did not even have a fight! Most of them . . . my men never even *saw* the enemy!"

Couch nodded, spoke with slow, careful words. "Gentlemen, General Hooker's last order was clear. The general made his decision because . . . General Sedgwick did not pursue the enemy with vigor. General Hooker feels that had Sedgwick come in behind Lee's lines, we would not be forced to withdraw. But we have already begun the withdrawal. It is now . . . the only course left to us."

Reynolds leaned forward, glared at Couch. "Sedgwick? So . . . that's to be it, eh? Sedgwick is the cause? We will blame one corps?"

"Gentlemen . . ." Couch raised his hand. "You may all prepare your own reports of this battle. But we have our orders. They will be carried out. General Hancock . . ." He turned, and Hancock looked again into the sad eyes. "You may return to your division."

THEY HELD THE LINE UNTIL THE TROOPS BEHIND THEM HAD passed, moving quickly now, the retreat pushed hard by the panic of defeat, the spreading disease of fear—that the enemy was coming, right behind them, that if they did not move quickly, the massive army would be crushed. On the roads the columns had little order, and the guns, from Hazel Grove, from the main roads in both directions, poured a steady stream of solid shot and exploding shells into the ranks. Many of the units lost all order. Men began running into the thick brush, away from the deadly open roads, knew that if they just kept moving north, they would find the river.

Those who did not share the panic, the corps and division commanders, were now coming to understand that this tragic and expensive defeat had not come from the weakness of the troops, but from the collapse of one man.

Hancock stayed on the turnpike, watched the stream of blue move over the wide fields, past their own guns, still firing, punching holes in the advancing lines of Lee's army, slowing the pursuit. To the south one division was holding a solid line, a rear guard, withdrawing more slowly than the others. It was Geary, of Slocum's corps, and now he was being flanked. The lines had broken, and they came out of the brush in a run, guided by the high column of smoke from the big house. Hancock knew it was time to pull his own people in, back along the ridge, wrap their lines across the wide field, hold the advancing rebels away until the army could reform itself behind him, protect the crossings at the river.

Below him, along the creek, Miles was still holding out. There had been no breakthrough there, but he had sent the word down: withdraw, move up to the trenches on the ridge.

He waited, watched the trees below, and they were not coming. He looked for a courier, the staff following him closely now, yelled out, "Go down there, repeat my order to withdraw! No delays . . . they could be cut off!"

The man saluted, a young lieutenant, began to gallop down the rise. Then Hancock saw horses, and a blue line emerging from the trees, and behind the horses, men were carrying a litter. The lieutenant reached them, turned, waved back at Hancock, and he spurred the horse and moved down. Shells began to fall around him, up behind, along the trenches, and he knew Lee's guns were closing in.

Hancock reached the horses, did not think, just followed the man's wave, pointing, and he saw officers, a captain, and the man saluted him, ran up to the horse.

"General, Colonel Miles is wounded, sir. . . ."

He jumped from the horse, moved to the litter. Miles was black with mud, his face barely recognizable, and he saw Hancock now.

"General . . . why are we pulling out, sir? The line is strong. . . ." He turned his head away, and Hancock saw the blood, the front of his uniform, a dark stain flowing down onto the litter. Hancock looked to the captain, saw no answers. They were waiting for him to say something, and he looked below, into the trees, saw Miles's men coming, moving slowly up the hill.

He said to his lieutenant, still on the horse, "Find the surgeon! Now! Tend to the colonel!" The man pulled the horse away, galloped up toward the crest of the hill. Now Hancock looked at the others, saw another officer, a familiar face, and men were stopping around him. They had heard that Miles was down, most had not seen him until now.

"Gentlemen, we must not delay. Keep the units in line, rejoin the division. We are the rear guard. We are covering the retreat." He paused, saw muddy faces and no expressions, and he could not let it go, had to tell them.

"You men performed as well as any army ever has. Officers . . . tell your men, make sure they all know this. You did not lose this fight! The soldiers . . . in this division, in other divisions . . . you did not lose this fight! I am honored to command you." Miles raised an arm, and Hancock stared down, surprised, did not know he was still conscious. And Miles put a dirty hand to his forehead, made a weak salute. Hancock turned, suddenly could not look at him. There was nothing he could say. He climbed onto the horse, spurred it hard, moved quickly up the hill.

B LUE TROOPS WERE STILL COMING UP FROM THE SOUTH, AND there was little order, men running alone and in small groups. Now the musket fire was growing, and men were falling. Hancock could not yet see, but knew from the sounds that Lee's advance was closing in, a tightening circle in the thick brush. He stayed on his horse, moved behind the new lines, could see the last of the flames from the mansion below him, now out in front of the lines. The guns were pulling away behind him, could no longer support his troops, the fight was coming in too close. He watched the muskets, bayonets pointing out, all down the line. They were not firing, no targets yet, and then he saw horses, officers, a fast gallop toward his lines, more men in blue. There was shouting, and his men were standing, gathering. He rode in that direction, heard the frantic, screaming voice.

"Charge, you cowards! Charge! They're right behind us!"

It was John Geary. Hancock moved closer, and Geary kept yelling, was turning back, looking toward the thickets and the last of his own retreating men. They moved by, passed through Hancock's line, many with wounds, moving slowly, and Geary yelled again, at Hancock's troops.

"Charge them, you cowards!"

Soldiers were closing around the horse, and Hancock saw a musket raised, pointed at Geary. A soldier said, "There are no cowards in this line!" and others began to yell at Geary as well, angry taunts. Geary was staring at the musket, the point of a bayonet.

Hancock moved up, said, "General Geary, I am in command here. You will not give orders to my men. These men have had their fill of watching this army retreat. I would suggest you retire to the rear with your troops."

Geary stared at Hancock, mouth open, and Hancock turned the horse away, had nothing else to say, knew he could not pour out his anger on this one man, a man who after all was doing what he was told.

He heard hoots, yelling behind him, knew it was directed at Geary, the men calling after him as he rode back, away from the fight. Now there were new voices, men calling out, and he felt a sudden rush of hot wind, a high zip of a musket ball, then more, rushing past him on all sides and below, down past the last dying flames of the mansion, they came from out of the brush, a row of muskets, bayonets, and the ragged lines of the enemy.

The long lines on either side of him erupted instantly, a quick and heavy volley, and a thick blast of smoke rolled across the wide field. Now the answer came back, and he began to move, looking for the commanders. He had not seen Meagher for a while, and Caldwell was up ahead somewhere. He rode quickly, and the smoke stayed out in front of them, like fog rolling down a hill, so the firing from below was blind, balls whizzing over him, high and wild. He saw Caldwell on his horse, moving down the line, and Hancock motioned, back, away from the lines, and Caldwell turned and moved with him toward a small grove of trees. Hancock turned the horse, tried to see, and felt a quick shiver from the horse. The horse was searching the ground, plucking slowly at the green grass. Hancock jumped down, saw a steady trickle of blood, a clean shot through the head. He stood back, watched the animal, grazing, thought of the talk of the wounded, men who are dying, who fade slowly away, drifting back to some other place, some peaceful memory, and he thought, You too, old girl, and the front legs quivered, then buckled, and the horse fell over on its side and did not move.

Behind him, Caldwell's aide had grabbed another horse, led it to him. Hancock stared at the animal, much smaller than his, and climbed up, his boots nearly brushing the ground.

Caldwell was staring back at his own lines, the smoke drifting toward them, and he said, "General, we cannot hold out against a strong assault. Where are the reserves?"

Hancock pulled the horse around, said, "You will hold your lines until I tell you to withdraw. There are no reserves, the rest of the army is withdrawing to the river."

Caldwell stared, wanted to ask, saw the hot glare in Hancock's eyes and nodded. "I understand, sir."

Hancock spurred the horse, and it moved toward the smoke. He was suddenly engulfed in a thick cloud of sulfur and ash. He tried to turn, to move off to the left, but was swallowed now, felt himself choking. He moved farther, kicked the horse hard, and saw a clearing and his other lines, facing east, and below, a new volley, a fresh wave of the enemy coming from the woods where Miles had held them away. Then it was Meagher's lines, and he rode forward, saw the green flag and Meagher pointing, shouting. There was a long, single explosion of muskets, and quickly, another. He moved up behind the line, could see down, a thick mass of men pouring out of the heavy trees, coming toward them. They were stopping to shoot, then running again, and he heard it now, the high, terrible scream of the rebel yell.

He rode back toward the black skeleton of the mansion, could see the gray troops moving in one long mass up that side of the rise, and now he knew it was done, his men could not stay here, were being pressed from both sides. He moved quickly, waved to the couriers trailing behind and yelled, "Go to the commanders! Pull back, to the north. Retreat in line, keep firing!"

The men were away, and he rode up the road toward the north, where the rest of the army was crowding the banks of the river, digging in, a quick defensive line protecting the withdrawal from the rushing tide of Lee's tightening ring.

He turned, saw his men falling back on both sides of him, the lines backing toward each other, the distance between them closing rapidly, the deadly fire from the rebel muskets now striking his men from behind, some shots flying farther, reaching out and dropping men far across the field, in the lines of their own advancing troops.

The smoke came toward him again, and he pulled the horse away, slowly, stayed on the road. His men were still moving back, a good solid line, no break, no panicking flood. He halted the horse, sat still now, and suddenly the light wind shifted again, cleared the smoke away, and now he could see it all, his men moving backward. He felt himself shake, an icy stab in his chest, that this was some kind of absurd, horrible joke. He kept staring at them, watched them come closer, backing toward him, and now he felt a sudden release, the small hard place inside him that he could not open, could not touch months before, on the muddy banks of the Rappahannock. But now it came, an unstoppable flow of grief, the weight inside him pouring out, and it was not for the dead, for the men who would hurt no more, but for these, the living, the men in front of him now, men no different from him; soldiers who would carry this with them for the rest of their lives, who would always know that they ran in the face of the enemy they should have beaten, not because they were cowards, or because there was weakness in their hearts. They ran because they were told to.

53. LEE

MAY 3, 1863. MIDDAY.

H E HELD THE HORSE BESIDE THE ROAD, ALLOWED THE GUNS TO pass, the sweating mules and creaking wagons. He saw the clearing now, rode farther, his staff behind, climbed the short rise and could see across the wide-open ground. The remains of the grand house were a smoldering mass of twisted black. He moved that way.

His army was already ahead of him, had pushed beyond the clearings, concentrating on the withdrawal of the Federal troops. Now, guns from Hazel Grove, from the batteries to the west, were moving up, repositioning. It was barely past noon, and he watched them, thought, We can still do it today, there is plenty of time.

He dismounted, walked by himself toward the ruins of the house, stopped close to the edge of the smoldering ash. He tried to feel some joy, the familiar thrill, the wild pursuit of a routed enemy, the glory of victory. It would not come. Men were passing around him, keeping a respectful distance. He heard the shouts.

"We whipped 'em good!"

"The bluebellies are still runnin', General. . . ."

He looked toward the voices, men waving at him, hats and muskets high, and he waved back, weakly, stared down again into the ashes.

Taylor kept the rest of the staff back, on their horses, and moved forward slowly, walked the horse up behind Lee and stopped. Lee did not look up. Taylor said, "Doesn't seem right that General Jackson isn't here to see this."

Lee shook his head, said, "No, Major. It doesn't seem right at all. But it is the will of God."

Lee tried to pull himself away, thought about the army, Jackson's troops coming together, reorganizing, the regiments and companies reuniting now after the massive confusion, the headlong rush through the thick woods. He had seen the face often, peering out from under the old cap, and Lee had to keep telling himself, He is all right, he just lost an arm. Lee had even sent a message, tried to be lighthearted: "Rejoin us on the field, won't you, General?" But it was not sincere, there could be no joy, and then he had said, "You have lost your left arm, I have lost my right. . . ." And he knew somewhere deep inside, that was the truth, that no matter what happened now, Jackson would not return, would not be here to carry the fight.

And there was still a fight. Sedgwick had finally pushed hard into Early's forces, moving up into Fredericksburg and then out, across the same ground where Burnside's army had marched into a massacre. But this time Early was too few, and Sedgwick understood that if the men kept running, did not stop in front of the stone wall, did not try to shoot their way across, the wall could be reached and overrun. So now Early was pushed back, withdrawn safely down to the southwest, below the hills, and Sedgwick controlled the heights and was moving out this way.

Lee had turned McLaws around, marched him out the turnpike to meet Sedgwick's advance head-on. They still held Bank's Ford, on the river just northwest of the town held by Cadmus Wilcox's brigade. McLaws would now spread south, in a heavy line, a long, high ridge that ran beside a small brick building, Salem Church. Sedgwick would find that he was not advancing against the vulnerable and unsuspecting rear of Lee's position, but was moving instead into the teeth of a division full of the good fight, men who had learned that no matter what the enemy sent them, they would turn him around.

Wilcox had used his men to delay Sedgwick as long as he could, withdrawing slowly back toward the church, and Sedgwick found himself strung out in long lines of march, could not organize in the face of Wilcox's tormenting skirmishers. When McLaws showed himself and the volleys began, Sedgwick's lead units were run piecemeal into the fight.

Lee could hear the sounds of battle now, from the east. He turned and stared out. Taylor said, "McLaws . . ."

Lee was moving, went quickly toward his horse, climbed up, said, "Major, send a courier to find General Anderson. I do not want General McLaws overrun."

Taylor moved toward the waiting staff, and a man was quickly out, moving back down the rise. There were more riders now, from the south, a small flag, and they rode toward Taylor and stopped. There were salutes and low voices. Taylor turned, moved toward Lee.

"General, it is Captain Hodges, sir, a message from General Early. He has reformed his division, sir, behind the Fredericksburg hills, and he requests—"

Lee raised his hand, stopped him. "Captain Hodges, you may come closer. Please tell me what you have observed, what General Early has on his front."

Hodges removed his hat, seemed hesitant, said, "General Lee, sir, the Yankees . . . the enemy has pulled most of its force to the northwest of the heights . . . up near the river. General Early believes, sir, that they are moving now toward . . . here." He looked around, saw no entrenchments, no defensive lines.

"Captain, you may return to General Early and tell him this: McLaws's division is in contact with the enemy, between here and the heights, at Salem Church. I am sending reinforcements to assist his efforts. Please request that General Early move northward with all speed. I believe, Captain, that General Early will discover that he has a great advantage in front of him. He may find he can close on the enemy from their flank and rear."

Hodges looked toward the new sounds of battle, nodded, said, "Thank you, General, it will be done, sir." He threw up a salute, made a short bow, and led the group of riders away in a gallop.

Taylor was laughing, said, "Pardon me, sir. He rode up here and started whispering, said he didn't want to disturb you, sir."

Lee watched the small flag disappear on the road, said nothing. He looked toward the low thunder in the east, growing, spreading, and now he saw Anderson, more riders, and Anderson was moving slowly, a calm procession moving up the turnpike. Lee stared, thought, Was I not clear? There is a fight growing behind you. . . .

He heard a loud whoop from the other direction, turned and saw Stuart, another staff and more flags. Stuart reached him first, stayed on the horse.

"Greetings, *mon Général*! It is a fine day, sir! We have done Old Stonewall proud!"

Lee felt a rush of anger, his hands clenched on the reins of the horse, and Anderson was close now, lifting his hat to the men around them, basking in his own glow. Lee felt his jaw tighten, said, "Gentlemen, if you please. This day is not over. We have a fight on our right flank. Sedgwick's corps is on the move, has pushed General Early from the hills and is moving to join forces with General Hooker. And, gentlemen, before we engage in celebration, let us be reminded that just north of our position here, we are attempting to contain an army that outnumbers us by three to one."

Stuart lowered his head, again the scolded child, said, "General Lee, the Second Corps is reforming in a tight arc, sir, and will move against Hooker's forces at your command, sir!"

"No, General, rest them for now. They cannot continue to press the attack without some replenishment. This is not the cavalry, General, we must make time. Get the smaller units together, determine who is in command. We have lost a great many fine officers." He paused, took a deep breath.

"It is our objective to drive General Hooker against the river. If we bring a strong line against his forces, we may cause them considerable discomfort. They can no longer withdraw in a slow methodical retreat. They will be very limited in how quickly they can cross the river, and then we will have them. We have an opportunity to destroy them, gentlemen, with their backs to the river. General Anderson, you must take your division back to the east, toward Salem Church, and strengthen General McLaws's lines. Early's division will be advancing from the south. If we can tie up Sedgwick until General Early arrives, we may be able to press him hard against the river as well." He was suddenly very excited, putting it into words. He realized now the magnitude of the opportunity in front of them. Anderson saluted, backed the horse away, and Lee stared out to the north, where the Federal Army was digging in to their last line of defense.

He heard Stuart move up closer, beside him, and Lee said, "God has given us an opportunity. It is very clear now. There is a much greater prize, we can do so much more than merely claim this field. If we can crush the enemy right here, against the river . . . we may force him to surrender. We have paid the price . . . what God has taken . . . is General Jackson. It is a message. He is saying, 'Here is your opportunity, and here . . . is the cost.' " He looked at Stuart, and Stuart was watching him with wide, round eyes, the eyes of a small boy absorbing the words of his father.

"Remember that, General, there is always a price."

EARLY DID NOT REACH SEDGWICK'S POSITION UNTIL VERY LATE IN the day, and Anderson's lines were slow in spreading, and so by dark Sedgwick had concentrated his forces, made a strong defensive line backed up against Bank's Ford. In front of Stuart, Hooker's army was tightly in place, a sharp U, with its back toward the United States Ford.

All the next day, McLaws, Anderson, and Early pounded hard against Sedgwick's position, but it was difficult ground, and the numbers were nearly even. Sedgwick was pushed harder into his defensive line, but could not be moved. Around Hooker, the divisions of Jackson's corps harassed and threw light punches all day. Hooker could have pushed out of his own defenses at any time, but Lee had guessed correctly that Hooker would not attack, that still he was waiting for Sedgwick, had pinned all hopes of any Federal victory on one small separate piece of his army.

The next day, Tuesday, May 5, it began to rain, a hard, soaking storm, and so both armies lay down hard in their muddy positions, waiting. Lee could feel his greatest opportunity to end the war flowing away, like the fresh streams of mud that poured away into the river. That night, with Hooker himself already across, the Federal Army made its way over the rocking pontoons. Lee had his men fed and their guns ready, and in the first light of the new day he sent out the fresh and rested troops, the final crushing blow, and they would push out hard and fast and find only empty trenches.

54. JACKSON

D AYS BEFORE ... HE HAD LAIN AWAKE, LISTENING TO THE steady roar, the thunder of the big guns in the woods beyond the field hospital, and then muskets, waves of shooting, and sometimes, he thought, It had been very close. McGuire gave him something ... he had wanted to ask, but his mind would cloud, thick fog, and the pain would be stopped. He could see McGuire's face, calm, confident, and so he would not object, would accept the medication, the prick of the needle. It had been Sunday ... the Sabbath. We should not have to do that ... to fight on His day, he thought, but now he lay quietly, did not know what day it was ... how long it had been.

The fog had cleared, gradually. He could see the room, saw something new, a white ceiling, remembered, We are no longer in the field. ... His eyes followed a small crack in the plaster, a long curving line, and he stared at it for a long time. The voices and the men were around him, and then it was quiet. He did not know if he was awake or asleep, but then the thin line would grow, move closer, heavier ... *and he saw now it was a snake, blue and fat, and he watched it move and twist, injured, wounded, rolling madly, convulsing, and he saw men, soldiers, bayonets, and the snake would not die, kept twisting* ... and then he knew he was awake, because now the snake was gone, was just a long, thin crack in the plaster.

The hospital had been a dangerous place. The shifting flow of the battle had put it close to the shelling, and McGuire and Smith had made arrangements for him to be moved. Jed Hotchkiss and the engineers had led the way, cleared the small road of the refuse of the fighting, shattered trees and sharp holes, and the steady flow of men and wagons had stood to the side, men with hats in their hands, sad salutes and soft crying as the ambulance had passed.

McGuire had received permission directly from Lee to accompany Jackson away from the field. He had hesitated to ask, knew of the common practice of men of high rank, who often treated their army's doctors as their personal physicians, the foolish exercise of privilege that left wounded soldiers unattended. But Lee had no hesitation, had ordered the move, knew that if Jackson was to recover, there was no one better than McGuire to guide him through it.

The Chandler house lay along the railroad line, below Fredericksburg, at Guiney's Station. The war had made Guiney's a busy place, and the Chandler plantation had suffered, as did all the rich farmlands of central Virginia. But for now it was safe and comfortable, and Jackson had agreed, remembered many kind invitations to make their home his headquarters. Now it would be his hospital.

They had brought him to a small building below the main house, a simple, square two-story structure, two rooms down and two up, and in one of the lower rooms, a bed had been placed, with fresh linens. He was carried there, could see out a tall, narrow window to the trees beyond and the bright warmth of the sun.

He was beginning to feel stronger, was awake more, less drugged sleep. McGuire set up the other downstairs room for his medical office, bandages and dressings, and he was completing his examination of Jackson's wound, the surgery.

"Hmm . . . yes, General, very good. It is healing nicely. Is there any pain . . . here?"

Jackson felt the probe, the pressure in the shoulder. "No. No pain."

McGuire stood, nodded. "All right, then, we'll dress that again, and I'll check it in the morning. How's the hand?"

Jackson raised the clump of bandages, turned it, moved the fingers. "It seems fine, Doctor."

"It was not bad, should heal completely . . . sore for a while, but you'll have full movement in a week or two."

Outside, there were horses, voices, and the outer door opened, boots on the wood floor, and Jackson heard a quiet voice.

"Is it all right, Doctor?"

McGuire moved away from the bed, said, "Certainly, Captain Smith, please come in. The general is doing quite well today."

Smith moved toward the bed, bent down to one knee, said, "General? You feeling better?"

Jackson looked at the young face, the sad eyes, said, "Don't concern yourself about me, Mr. Smith. I am in God's care now. But . . . tell me . . . how are we faring . . . ?"

"The fight? Oh, General, the enemy is gone, across the river. We've secured the high ground around Chancellorsville . . . and along the river. General Stuart did well by you, sir. And the Stonewall Brigade . . . right in the middle of it, sir. They were fighting for Stonewall, I heard that all day."

Jackson nodded, smiled, thought, Why must they do that? "Captain, I would appreciate it if you would not refer to me that way. There is too much of the self-seeking . . . the name Stonewall belongs to the men who earned it, the men who fought at Manassas. God would not be pleased if I carried a label I do not deserve."

Smith looked down, stared at the floor, smiled to himself. This man would never be known as anything but Stonewall.

"Sir, the men . . . they honored you . . . a good fight. They all think of you, sir."

"The men . . . Captain, many years from now those men will be able to recall this war with the unique pride of the soldier, something no one will ever take away. They will be proud to say they served in the Stonewall Brigade. But they did not serve me . . . they served God."

Smith nodded. "Yes, sir." There was a silent pause, and Smith stood up, said, "General, I have the ball. Dr. McGuire allowed me to keep the musket ball he took from your hand, sir. It is a round smoothbore, sir. It has to be one of ours."

Jackson nodded. "Yes. I heard . . . they thought I was asleep. Pendleton . . . I heard them talking. It could not be helped. There is no blame in war. God understands, we must all forgive."

"Yes, sir . . . it was the Eighteenth North Carolina—"

Jackson lifted the bandaged hand. "No . . . it was the war. We will not place blame. Tell them . . . do not be sad . . . they were doing their duty."

He began to feel weak, the alertness fading, and he turned, stared at the blank wall. Smith watched him, said, "Sir . . . ? Are you all right?" He stepped back, went to the door, called across to the other room, "Doctor? The general—"

McGuire moved past him, went to the bed, said, "General? Are you getting tired? We can leave you now. You should be resting . . . let the strength return."

Jackson looked at him, saw the dark heavy eyes, said, "I'm fine,

Doctor. Tired. I should rest now. Tell me, Doctor, when was the last time *you* slept?"

McGuire smiled. "I'm not certain. We should all be concerned with . . . less duty and more care for ourselves. Captain, would you mind leaving us for a while?"

"Not at all, sir." Smith bent down again, one knee on the floor. "I'm right outside, General."

Jackson looked at him, tried to focus, but the fog was flowing through his brain again, and now the strength was gone, and he felt himself rising, drifting out . . .

. . . he heard the shots, the fresh volley, heard the hard slap of lead, splitting the skull of the man beside him, and the man crumpled, dropped in a solid mass, and the litter turned, spilling him, and he hit the ground hard, on his side, and the pain tore through him, burning, the hot hard stab of the bayonet, and now he was staring up into the dark, could not see the tree-tops . . . and now saw the shadows, the window, thought, I'm still in the bed, the clean white room. But the searing blast of pain did not fade, was still there. He reached over, tried to feel it with his left arm, the hand not bandaged, felt the hand move across his body. He tried to touch the hurt and could not, tried to probe with the fingers, could feel them moving, and he held the hand up to his face, but there was nothing there, no dark shape. Now he was awake, his mind clearing, and he knew there was no hand . . . no arm. But . . . he had felt it . . . the fingers . . . and he tried to feel it again, but . . . the pain would not stop. Now he moved the other hand, the heavy bandages, touched the side, pressing, but the pain was deep inside, a burning hole in his lung. He lay still, tried to breathe, deeply, a slow rhythm, calm, heard now other breathing, tried to see, the foot of the bed . . . McGuire was there . . . sleeping on a small, hard couch. He relaxed again, thought, No, do not wake him. It will pass. He stared up at the dark, prayed, *God, please give comfort to them all. They care for me . . . the men are concerned . . . too much. It must not turn them away from their duty.*

The pain began to ease, and he kept his thoughts focused away, the men . . . General Lee. There is more for me to do. God does not want me yet. The enemy is still there . . . waiting. . . .

. . . the field . . . the thick brush, the dense tangles. His heart was racing, and he thought . . . the high ground, we must place the guns. He saw the lines now, his men, rolling forward, the enemy falling back, the edge of the river, falling, jumping in, panic, and his men were there, at the edge of the water . . . the river churning hot and red, and he could hear the yells, the screams of the enemy, and now they began to move across, his troops,

marching across the river, above the bodies of the enemy, pressing on, into the tall trees on the other side. . . .

THURSDAY, MAY 7, 1863

S HE HELD THE BABY, STEPPED DOWN FROM THE TRAIN, HELPED now by men in dirty uniforms. They stood aside, made a clear path for her. There was a carriage, and a man held the door. She nodded, tried to smile.

Her brother was behind her, held a large cloth bag, motioned up to the top of the carriage, and other bags were lifted, tossed up. He climbed in, sat beside her. They did not talk, and the carriage began to move.

He knew it was his responsibility to bring the news, to bring her here. They both knew that Jackson had allowed him to serve on his staff because of her. She did not want him near the fight. This way he could still be a soldier, and, even if Jackson took his own fight close to the front of the lines, something she tried not to think about, his staff, and her brother, would be safe.

It had taken him two days to reach her, the delay caused by Stoneman's cavalry raid. The train that brought them was heavily armed, would fight their way through if necessary, but finally the tracks from Richmond had been cleared, and now they had reached Guiney's Station.

There were troops in the yard, small groups, dirty, ragged, and officers, some familiar. She saw women now, coming out on the porch of the big house, waiting for her. She was led, a gentle arm, soft words and sad faces. She watched her brother moving away toward the small cottage, and men saluted, and she thought, I should see him now, but they were pulling her away. She looked into the faces now, saw the concern, the deep sadness, and knew something was happening, something her brother had not told her, and she tried to turn, said, "I must see my husband. . . ."

Mrs. Chandler nodded, said, "Yes, my dear, yes. You should talk to Dr. McGuire first."

She stopped, turned, knew they were not going to tell her anything, and she said, "Please, take me to him." The baby began to cry now, and she looked at the small face, thought, It has been a difficult trip. She looked at Mrs. Chandler.

Now, a girl moved closer, said, "Please, Mrs. Jackson, allow me to put the baby in bed. We have a place made up special, for both of you."

Anna saw the eagerness, soft kindness. "I suppose . . . all right," she said. "I will rest a bit."

They led her into the house, up to her room, and she lay the baby down in a small bed. Her bags were there now, and she looked at the faces of the women again, and began to feel overwhelmed, the anticipation, the stress of the trip passing.

She sat wearily on the edge of the bed. "I must have a moment . . . please. Thank you for all your kindness."

The girl was leaning over close to the baby, and Mrs. Chandler said, "Lucy, let us allow Mrs. Jackson to rest. Please, excuse us, Mrs. Jackson. . . ."

The woman nodded, a faint smile, and Anna looked to her bags, and the door closed softly behind her. She stood, felt a deep yawn rising in her, moved to the baby, sleeping again, and she smiled and said in a whisper, "Soon . . . we will be a family again . . . this will be over. . . ."

She moved toward the sunlight, a tall window, looked out over the thick green grass of the wide yard, saw troops, men with shovels, and they were digging hard, throwing dirt into a wide pile, and she felt a sudden cold shock. *They are digging a grave.* She tried to see, could not, her eyes thick with tears. She stayed at the window, thought, Why have they not told me? Behind her there was a soft knock at the door. She turned, angry now.

"Yes?"

The door opened, and she saw the face of the young doctor. He bowed slightly, said, "Hello, Mrs. Jackson, may I be allowed to come in? I would like to speak to you before you visit your husband."

"Visit him?" Her voice was rising, tears running down her cheeks. She pointed toward the window. "So, am I allowed to visit my husband before he is buried?"

McGuire was puzzled, looked toward the window, said, "Buried? He . . . is not . . ." Now he saw the men, the shovels. "Oh my . . . no, no, Mrs. Jackson. That is not a grave. Well, it is . . . but, not, oh no . . ."

She wiped her eyes, looked out, watched them working again. Now men jumped down into the hole, began to lift something, and she felt her stomach turn slowly, thought, What is happening? A long box appeared, was slowly lifted, and several other men moved closer, lifted it farther, away from the hole.

"Ma'am, that's the body of General Paxton, Frank Paxton. He was killed during the fighting. His body is being moved, taken back to his home in Lexington."

She stared down at the box, said, "Yes, I know Mr. Paxton . . . General Paxton. He is our neighbor. His wife . . . she cried when he left. I suppose she knew something like this would happen." She was calm now, looked at McGuire, waited.

"Lieutenant Morrison . . . your brother has told you about your husband's wounds. We removed his left arm, patched his right hand . . . it is healing well, I am very pleased. But . . . there is a new problem. I believe he now has pneumonia."

She stared, felt the words, said slowly, "May I see him, Doctor?"

"Certainly. He is weak, I have given him medication, to help him sleep. He is in some pain. The medication makes him . . . drift away . . . in and out. He may not recognize you, but I am certain your presence would be most welcome."

McGuire stood aside, and they moved downstairs together. Anna suddenly stopped, a familiar smell, saw the young girl and said, "Oh, Miss Chandler . . . Lucy . . . do I smell lemons . . . lemonade?"

The girl smiled, said, "Yes, ma'am. We received a box of lemons yesterday . . . a gift . . . someone from Florida. Mother is making lemonade for the soldiers. Would you like some?"

Anna smiled, said to McGuire, "Please, go on ahead, Doctor. I wish to prepare a surprise for my husband."

SHE SAW HER BROTHER, AND CAPTAIN SMITH, AND SHE WALKED toward them, carried the tray carefully, and now her brother moved to her quickly, said, "Anna . . . here, let me. Very kind—"

"No, Joseph, it is not for you, it is for Thomas. Before I see him . . . would you please see if he is awake, and offer him this glass? I would like it to be a surprise."

He smiled, said, "Of course. Captain Smith, may I take this inside . . . for the general?"

Smith bowed, nodded to Anna, tried to smile, said, "Please do, Lieutenant. I heard the general talking just a few minutes ago. He is awake."

McGuire was beside the bed, saw the lieutenant come in, and the young man nodded, motioned to the glass. McGuire understood, said, "General, we have a treat for you, something you may have been missing."

Jackson lifted his head, saw the glass, said, "Another of your medications? Very well, Doctor."

"No . . . well, not mine, actually. But should do you some good." He held the glass, lowered it to Jackson's mouth.

Jackson took a short drink, then turned his head, said, "Ahhhgggg, it is so *sweet*. Too much sugar. Always the problem with my *esposita's—*" He stopped, and McGuire was smiling, and Jackson saw Morrison now, and he said, "She is here."

"Yes, General. Lieutenant, would you please escort Mrs. Jackson in?"

Morrison went out, and now McGuire backed away, waited, and the young lieutenant had his sister's arm, led her into the room.

She stared down at the clear blue eyes, saw the weakness, something she had never seen, and suddenly she could not look at him, at the wounds. She dropped down, laid her head on his chest, held his right arm, careful not to touch the bandages. Behind her McGuire made a small noise, motioned, and the two men left the room.

He felt her, soft sobs, and he wanted to wrap his arms around her, pull her into him the way he always had, and he tried to feel the left arm, pull it over her. It would not move, and he began to cry now, softly, small tears falling onto the pillow, and he closed his eyes, said softly, *"Esposita . . . esposita . . ."*

SUNDAY, MAY 10, 1863

He was staring out at the river, and across, the enemy was lining the banks, preparing, long battle lines, and he felt the horse rear back, and he waved the sword, and now the guns began, a solid line of fire poured across the river, and his men moved forward, over and across the water, and the sounds rushed around him, the rebel yell, the steady roar of muskets, and the enemy faded back, away, the lines utterly destroyed. Now his men pushed on, into the far woods, and the yells continued, echoing, softer now, drifting back toward him. Around him, more lines, his men still coming up beside him, and he yelled out. . . .

"Order A. P. Hill . . . prepare for action! Pass the infantry to the front!"

McGuire heard the words, moved closer, listened. Jackson had not slept well, had burst into long streams of speech, nonsensical, gasping, and McGuire understood, the medications, the morphia, were no longer effective. He listened to the breathing, the short quick rhythm, worse now, worse each day.

He moved out, through the doorway, into the other room, where his equipment, the towels and bandages, lay in organized rows. He stopped, stared at the instruments, a black leather pouch laid open on the table, shining steel blades, tongs, small, pointed scissors. He folded the pouch, rolled it up, carefully tied it closed with the small attached ribbon.

He went to the window, looked out toward the big house, saw more troops, a whole company of men. There was no fight now, and the army was regrouping. Many of the men had come here without permission, and the officers did not question them. There were no bands playing now, no typical sounds of the camps, and each morning the men had been given a prayer service, led by Chaplain Lacy. But now Lacy was gone, had returned to the corps to lead services for the army, observing Jackson's emphatic belief in the importance of the Sabbath.

He saw Anna now, coming down from the porch of the house. She carried a bundle, and he shook his head. No, he thought, this is not a good idea. She had insisted, said it could only help, and McGuire understood that he had no place to deny this, that it was for them, both of them, that even if Jackson was far away, did not know them, the mother would always be able to tell the child—he saw you before the end.

He moved to the door, and it was opened. He saw Smith and Anna's cousin, Dr. Stephen Morrison, who had been Jackson's personal physician before the war, and now Sandie Pendleton was there, from the corps headquarters. They all came in, quiet, and McGuire looked at the child, the small soft face, and the child smiled at him, waved its arms in a quick flurry of motion. He felt something deep, pulling at him, and they passed by him and continued into the room where Jackson lay.

The only sounds came from Jackson, high and quick and rasping, and no one spoke. The men stood close behind Anna, glanced at McGuire. They did not know what to expect, waited, would be there, unless . . . she asked them to leave.

Anna bent over, held the baby out, set her down on the bed. The baby made a small noise, and Jackson's eyes opened and he stared up, far away. McGuire moved closer, thought, He could make a sudden move, but then he saw something in Jackson's face, and Jackson's eyes turned to the side, and now they were clear and sharp, and he looked at Anna, then turned, saw the small blanket and the moving hands, and closed his eyes, smiled, said, "My sweet daughter . . . my little Julia . . ."

Anna reached out, sat the baby up, and the small hands began to wave, the high sounds came again. McGuire moved closer, stood at the foot of the bed, felt something now, in the room, looked around, the plain simple walls, and the room was suddenly alive, the dreary darkness fading, the sun suddenly flowing in, clearing out the dark spaces. McGuire looked back to the bed, watched them both, heard the sounds, Jackson's hard, short breaths, and the sweet small sounds from the smiling child.

Jackson began to drift away again, his eyes turning dimly toward the ceiling, and Anna picked up the little girl, glanced at McGuire and nodded, a quiet thank-you. He looked at the child, thought, She was right, it can only do some good ... a small piece of life to break through the darkness of this terrible place.

The group filed back outside, and soldiers began to move toward them, expectantly, waiting for some word. Smith waved them back, silently, and Anna carried the child back to the big house.

McGuire did not go with them. He moved to the small, hard couch, sat in the growing shadows, watched Jackson breathing. Minutes passed, and he heard the door again, did not stand, saw Anna alone. She looked at him, said, "Dr. Morrison tells me that it will be over soon, that it is certain. Is that so?"

He nodded, resigned.

"Does he know?"

McGuire shook his head, said, "I have not told him."

"Then I will. He must know. He must be prepared. He must know it is the Sabbath, it will comfort him."

He looked toward the bed, said nothing, understood now, for the first time, that his job was truly done, that he was no different now from the rest of them, the soldiers outside, the chaplains, praying for miracles, and the newspapermen, gathering slowly in the distance. There was nothing to do now but wait.

• • • He could still smell the baby, the scent was still beside him, and he tried to see her again, tried to focus, but there was nothing, only a soft white, the glow of sunshine through the thick woods. The sounds began to come back, the fight now distant, but the low thunder still reached him, and he thought, No, I am too far away, they have gone ahead ... too fast. He stared now at the river, his army was far across, and around him there was no one, a quiet calm, and he caught the baby's scent again, and he saw something, out in the river, a figure, a woman, and he wanted to say ... no, it's dangerous, the fighting ... but now the sounds had gone, the army was far away, and *he watched the woman, drifting across the surface of the water, moving slowly toward him. He stood motionless, waited, and now he knew her. It was his mother, young, the face as it had been, before, without the pain, the illness, the woman who laughed and played with him. He stared, tried to speak, but there was no sound, and she smiled, moved closer still, and now he reached out, and she shook her head, no, not yet. Suddenly he was very small, and they were at the swing, and he was pushing his baby sister, and his mother was laughing, a sweet sound like soft music, and he turned to her, and she said something, playful scolding, that's enough, it's time to go. He turned now, and the swing and his sister were gone, and he was not a child, saw now, the uniform, his hand, the bandage, the empty sleeve, and she was leading him out of the woods, out to the water. He saw the trees beyond, filled now with a soft light, large wide oaks, a carpet of soft leaves, and she held her arms up to him, spoke to him, faint, soft words, It is time, He is waiting. In the trees, the light began to glow brighter, and he could feel her now, all around him, her warmth, her happiness, and there was no pain, no sickness, and he put his hand on his chest, no bandage now, suddenly felt the last hard breath, the last hard stab of pain, and the light from the trees began to wash over them and she spoke to him again, and he could hear her now, from deep inside, her voice filling him.*

"Let us cross over the river, and rest under the shade of the trees."

T HEY ALL STARED, HEARD THE WORDS, AND NOW THERE WAS SIlence in the room. On a small mantel a clock was ticking, and McGuire looked at it, had not heard the sound before, saw: threefifteen. Anna was sitting beside the bed, reached out, touched the bandaged hand, then leaned both arms onto the bed, put her head down. Pendleton stood behind her, looked at McGuire. The doctor nodded, and Pendleton eased away with quiet steps, left the room and went outside.

In the yard, men had gathered, most stood, with hats off, waiting, and now Pendleton stopped, looked at the faces of the men, and no one spoke. He said, "The general has died."

The sounds began to flow across the open spaces, low and heavy, and men began to cry. Some collapsed to their knees. Now, Smith came out, said to Pendleton, "We must wire General Lee."

Pendleton nodded, said nothing, and Smith waited, said, "I can take care of it . . . I'll go to the station."

Pendleton looked at him, put a hand on his shoulder, nodded, still did not speak, and Smith moved away, slowly, past the soft sounds of the men.

Anna sat up now, stood, and around her the others still said nothing, would wait for her. She looked around the small room, said, "Thank you . . . for all you did."

Dr. Morrison moved closer, said, "May I escort you back to the house, to your room?"

"Thank you, Stephen." She looked at her brother, standing at the foot of the bed, and the young lieutenant moved around, took her other arm, and she turned, a last look at her husband before they led her slowly from the room. McGuire waited, heard the outer door close, then moved closer to the bed and pulled the blanket up, over Jackson's face.

Outside, Anna saw Tucker Lacy, climbing down from a carriage, and Lacy moved quickly, alongside them, said to Dr. Morrison, "I just heard . . . men, out on the road." He looked at Anna, moved in front of her, said, "Take comfort, he is with God now."

She looked at him, deep black eyes. "There is no comfort in this, Reverend. My husband is dead . . . my child has no father."

Lacy held up his hand. "Seek comfort in God . . . He is there for you."

"Is He, Reverend? All I have ever asked is that He give me back my husband . . . allow him to survive this war and come home to his family. There is nothing else I have ever wanted."

Lacy lowered his head, said, "Please . . . rely on your faith, do not turn away. He will comfort you."

"Will He? Would it not be of greater comfort if He did not allow this war to happen at all? How much comfort must He give . . . how many wives and children need His comfort now?"

Lacy lowered his head, and Dr. Morrison said, "Please, Anna, let us get some rest. This has been hard for all of us."

She felt a sudden wave of weakness, slumped against him, and now both men held her and they moved past Lacy, who wanted to say more, raised the hand again, but she was gone now, up the steps, into the house.

McGuire was alone in the dreary room, sat down on the hard couch, stared at the bed, at the lifeless form. He heard the outer door open, and now Pendleton was there, stood in the doorway, looked at the bed, then moved to a corner of the room, sat on the floor and stared down between his knees.

"What will become of us now?"

McGuire looked at the young officer, said nothing, did not know what soldiers were supposed to do, it was not a question he could answer. He listened to the ticking of the clock, began to think about the arrangements, the casket, the memorials, the funeral, imagined a long procession through weeping crowds. . . .

Suddenly there was a new sound, from outside. He looked toward the window, and Pendleton raised his head, and the sound began to fill the room, loud and piercing. Outside, the soldiers had gathered close to the cottage, and through the tears their voices rose together in one high chorus—the rebel yell.

55. LEE

SUNDAY, MAY 10, 1863

H E HAD SENT THEM AWAY, TAYLOR, THE OTHERS, REPORTERS and well-wishers, was alone now in the tent. The desk was covered with paper, a hundred requests, promotions, supply, and he could not look at any of it, sat in the small, stiff chair and stared at the blank walls of the tent.

On the table was also a wire, from Jefferson Davis, requesting he come to Richmond, discuss the new strategy. He would go, of course, do it all again, knowing that soon Hooker would be gone and someone else would fall into the role, and the war would start up, all over again, as though none of it had happened before.

He had tried not to think of Jackson, of the death, had kept his mind on the papers, but there had to be the moment, this moment, when the distractions would fade, when he must talk to God, to ask, *Why?* There would be no reply, of course. The answers were all in his faith, that it was all God's will, and that there was nothing else he could do but go on believing, and accepting that in the end there was a Plan. But he had never thought . . . there were already so many challenges, they had overcome so much, fought the good fight when anything less would have cost them the war, when it all would have been lost. He could not help but wonder . . . have we done something wrong? Has the cause become something else, some misguided effort? And he could think of nothing that had changed, why he was fighting, why the war must go on.

Now, the face came to him, the clear image, and he let it come, could not block it out, saw the lightning in the ice-blue eyes, the old cap, and he felt something inside him give way, and he leaned forward, put his face in his hands, and began to cry.

MAY 20, 1863

TAYLOR WAS STANDING BESIDE HIM, AND TOGETHER THEY WERE reading the lists for promotion. They heard the horses, and Lee stood up, moved outside the tent, the sun high and hot, and he saw the big man dismounting, the short cigar.

Longstreet had returned to the bloody ground around Chancellorsville several days after the fighting had ended, and the ultimate result of the excursion south had not been so positive. He had succeeded in sending sorely needed supplies north, but his own goal of pushing the Federal presence out of southern Virginia was not realized, and he had reluctantly pulled his troops away from the outskirts of Suffolk, which the Federal Army still occupied. It had taken a firm order from Lee to bring him back, but now Pickett and Hood had added to the strength of Lee's recuperating forces.

Lee had spent several days in Richmond, had found Davis to be more fragile than ever, infected with a growing paranoia about the defense of the capital, and so Lee now knew there would be no further support, no reinforcements. Davis would not interfere in Lee's strategies, but any plan Lee had would have to be accomplished with the troops he had on hand. After the difficult fight in the Wilderness, many in the army had gone home, many were no longer fit to serve, and so even with Longstreet's return, he had little more than forty thousand effective troops. In the North a paralyzed Hooker was still in command. The wheels of change were slow, and so Lee knew the next move would be his.

"General Longstreet, welcome."

"General." He touched the hat, and Lee suddenly held out a hand, something he rarely did, and Longstreet took it, and there was a short, quiet moment. Longstreet said, "I am deeply sorry for the loss of General Jackson."

Lee nodded, motioned toward the tent, and the two men went inside.

They sat, Lee behind his small desk, and he stared at the piles of papers, said, "We should not regret the loss of General Jackson. He is sitting with God. There is no unhappiness in that." Longstreet looked down, said nothing, and Lee watched him, said, "Still . . . we may grieve. God does not deny us that."

Longstreet nodded, looked at Lee, felt a sudden wave of affection, said, "How are *you*, sir?"

Lee saw the soft look, the concern, tried not to look away, felt suddenly emotional, weak, thought, No, there has been too much emotion. He stared hard at the papers, said, "The army is well, General. With the return of your divisions, and the confidence of these troops now, we have an opportunity."

Longstreet let it go, knew that Lee would not reveal much, said, "We have had many opportunities."

Lee nodded. "Perhaps. Each one is different. And there will not be many more. We cannot continue to win these fights and allow the enemy to escape. We do not have the reserves, the wealth of supply. We cannot continue to fight this war on our own ground, destroying our own land. We have bloodied him and swept him from the field, but there is no victory to be gained by simply pushing him away time and again. He will return, he will always return, with more men and more equipment, and eventually . . . they will find someone, a commander who understands . . . who is capable. They do have many good men. I have been grateful. God has blessed us with their choice of commanders. I have never understood any of the choices . . . not since George McClellan."

Longstreet said nothing, thought, We have been very very lucky. If it had been Couch . . . or Reynolds . . . or the reckless Sickles . . . He thought of McClellan finding Lee's orders, the one time Lee's luck was bad, said, "We tried moving north. . . ."

"It was not the right time. God showed us that. But now . . . if we are to end this war, we must *win* this war, and I believe it is the only way."

He stood, straightened stiff legs, stepped around the small desk. Longstreet watched him, and Lee said, "President Davis has agreed . . . we must not only take the fight out of Virginia, but we must take it out of Tennessee and Carolina and Louisiana as well. In Virginia we are winning the battles. Elsewhere, it has not gone as well. The more time that passes, the more we are simply used up, and so, General, we are losing the war, and that will not change unless we take the war . . . unless we strike them right in their heart. We must point our guns straight into Lincoln's door, and then it will end."

"Attack Washington? Directly? Sir . . . the fortifications—"

"No, General. We do not have to attack the city. We just have to convince them that we *can*, that if they do not end this war, we *will!* Lincoln is already under pressure . . . great pressure. Their own generals hang their heads in public and ask forgiveness as the dead fill their cemeteries. The *people* have had enough of this. We have paid a terrible price, and so God has opened the door. We must march through it."

Longstreet stared at him, was surprised at the show of anger, sat quietly for a moment, said, "We can move up, as we did before, Maryland, then Pennsylvania. They will not know where we intend to strike."

Lee looked at him, waited, had hoped he would finally agree to the plan.

Longstreet thought again, said, "All we need is some luck . . . didn't have it last time, McClellan learning about the plan . . . but we can push the army fast, good roads, good time of year, move around to the northeast, cut off Washington from Philadelphia . . . New York. Even if they react, move to meet us quickly, we will be on *their* ground."

"Yes, General. And the civilians in the North will not stand for that, nor will the politicians."

Longstreet nodded, and now he glanced toward the opening in the tent, said, "General . . . forgive me, sir, but have you chosen a new commander for the Second Corps?"

Lee moved around the desk, sat again, pushed through the papers, held up one, studied it, said, "It is a difficult situation, General. We have lost so many. I do not believe we have one man who can assume that level of command. This is what I have proposed to President Davis, and it will become official very soon."

He handed the paper to Longstreet, and Longstreet studied it. His eyes widened. "Two corps? Dividing it into two corps? A. P. Hill . . . Dick Ewell. Ewell has returned?"

"Yes. He is healthy again, has a wooden leg now. General Jackson placed great confidence in General Ewell. And General Hill . . . there is no denying that he is a fine commander . . . in the field."

Longstreet nodded, a small laugh. "Now the only superior officer he can aggravate is you."

Lee had no humor, was weary of the conflicts with Hill. "That is the new system, General. There will now be three corps. General Stuart will resume command of the cavalry."

"Have you told him that? He might not be too happy—"

"General Stuart understands that he is better suited for that command. He acquitted himself adequately in General Jackson's absence, but he is eager to return to the cavalry. And if we are to succeed, we will require General Stuart's talents."

Lee stood, the signal that it was over, and Longstreet was up, ducked out through the tent. Taylor moved up, saluted, said, "Sir, the newspaper reporters are waiting . . . they keep asking about the rumors, sir. I don't know what to tell them."

"Rumors?" Longstreet looked at Taylor, and Taylor said, "Yes, sir. There's talk in the North . . . the papers, that General Lee is going to invade Washington, that the capital will be under siege." He looked at Lee. "Please, sir, will you speak to them? Or . . . please tell me what to say to them. They are mighty persistent, sir."

Lee looked at Longstreet, smiled slightly, said, "Major, tell them I am too busy at present to speak with them, and that it is . . . imprudent of us to discuss our plans."

"But, sir, what about the rumors? Do I tell them not to print—"

Lee raised his hand. "Major, I would never tell these men what they should not print. There will always be rumors. Sometimes, that is not all bad."

JUNE 1863

THEY DID NOT SPEND TIME IN MARYLAND. THERE WERE NO longer hopes that the neutral state would provide help to their army. So he rode the tall horse, and they moved quickly and with purpose. The papers in the North began to tell of the new invasion, and the Federal Army drew in closer to Washington, but Lee did not move that way, drove north, crossed the border into Pennsylvania. He led a great column of men who understood it would end soon, they were moving up to strike the deciding blow, and there were none among them who doubted they would do it. This was an army that had never been beaten, and that knowledge made them all stronger still.

It was hot now, and even the green hills did not give them relief, but they carried the memory of Jackson, and they knew how he would have pushed them, and so stragglers were few, and the strength of their morale gave them a shield against the hot march.

It was late in the day, long shadows crossed the road, and in front of them was the town of Chambersburg. He had ridden with Longstreet, had sent Ewell and Hill on a parallel route, farther east, and though they had met no opposition, he was beginning to feel concern, to wonder about the movements of the Federal Army.

Longstreet had ridden back, had sent word down the line, Keep a sharp eye, had sent his own scouts away, into the countryside. Now Lee heard him coming, pushing the horse quickly along the edge of the road. Then Longstreet slowed, moved beside him.

"Still nothing from Stuart. Not a sign, not a word!"

Lee heard the anger in his voice, said, "We will hear from him soon. I am certain of that. He understands the importance."

"He is not where we need him to be."

Lee stared ahead, did not answer, thought, General Stuart understands his orders. . . .

Far to the east, Stuart's cavalry raced northward, separated from Lee's army by the advancing column of Federal troops. He was trying, again, to make the glorious ride, encircle the blue army, reclaim the reputation, now that he was again with his own beloved horse soldiers. But Lincoln had moved again, and the Federal Army now had a new commander, George Gordon Meade, a man who did not suffer from the heavy burden of defeat, whose troops withdrew at Fredericksburg because they had not been supported, who had withdrawn at Chancellorsville because Hooker had collapsed. But now the army was his, and they were on the move, above the capital, moving with a new energy to confront the invasion. And this time Stuart could not ride fast enough. It was no longer a weak, lethargic army around which he was playing.

Lee rode out, toward the edge of the camps, looked across the church steeples and small buildings of the quiet town. He stared out to the east, to the deep and quiet darkness, thought, Any time now, there will be horses, the high yell, and he will ride in, jump down in front of me like a small excited boy, bend over and sweep the ground with that hat. But there was still the quiet, the dark, and somewhere, deep inside, he felt a dark hole, small but growing, the enthusiasm for this army's great mission, the final crushing blow now slowly slipping away. He reached down, patted Traveller on the neck, then pulled on the reins, turned the horse back toward the camp. It will be tomorrow, he thought. He will certainly be here tomorrow, and then . . . we will know: where the enemy is, what is in front of us.

Miles beyond the trees, past low hills and thick green woods, another army was in its camp, and their cavalry was already out in front, feeling out, seeking, and tomorrow they would ride forward again, probing the roads in front of them. They would crest a long rise and pause at a small cemetery, high above the peaceful farms and quiet streets of a town called Gettysburg.

AFTERWORD

"... And Thou knowest O Lord, that when Thou didst decide that the Confederacy should not succeed, Thou hadst first to remove Thy servant, Stonewall Jackson."
— BENEDICTION GIVEN BY FATHER HUBERT, OF HAYS'S
LOUISIANA BRIGADE, AT THE UNVEILING OF THE JACKSON
MONUMENT IN NEW ORLEANS, 1881

MARY ANNA MORRISON JACKSON

She is the widow now of the South's most beloved hero, and readily accepts the responsibility of that role. From the first memorial services in 1863, throughout the rest of her life, she represents her husband's memory at ceremonies, presentations, statues, and monuments for Jackson and for the Confederacy. Her daughter Julia survives only to age twenty-six, dies of typhoid fever, leaving a husband and two children. Anna retires finally to North Carolina, and never considers remarrying. While covering her invited visit to President Taft in Washington, D.C., in 1910, a Washington newspaper reported:

> Those who had the great honor of meeting Mrs. Jackson found her a fragile little woman with keen bright eyes, and the alert air which characterizes those whose interest in life and its best endeavors is undimmed by sorrow or the passing years. Time seems to have passed over her lightly. Having known her worst grief when life was young, she had been enabled to take up the thread again and to weave some brightness into what was left. She delights in recalling old

days and she speaks now with calmness which comes only from Christian resignation.

She dies in March 1915 of heart disease and is buried beside her husband and her two children beneath the Jackson Memorial in Lexington, Virginia. (Jackson's first wife, Ellie, and her stillborn infant are buried nearby.) One of Anna's funeral party is the Reverend James Power Smith, the final surviving member of Jackson's staff.

MARY RANDOLPH CUSTIS LEE

She outlives her husband, maintains a home in Lexington, Virginia. The great mass of the memorabilia of George Washington had been confiscated by the Union occupiers of Arlington, is stored after the war in Washington. She petitions the government for the return of her family's cherished heirlooms, but Congress still regards Lee as the enemy, and refuses. Widowed by her husband's death in 1870, she yearns for one last visit to the old homestead of Arlington, and even as an invalid, makes the difficult journey with her youngest son, Robert, Jr. In 1872, returning to Lexington, she is with her daughter Agnes when Agnes is stricken ill and dies. Mary Lee thus outlives not only her husband, but two of her daughters (Annie had died in 1862). Her grief at this irony is overwhelming, and Mary dies soon after, in November 1873.

ALMIRA RUSSELL HANCOCK

Left nearly penniless after Hancock's death in 1886, she receives an outpouring of generosity from his many friends of influence, and is provided several homes, finally settles in New York City, where she writes her own memoirs of her remembrances of Hancock's life and career.

Hamilton Fish, an old friend, and the Secretary of State to President Ulysses Grant, wrote of her that "she was always so bright, so gay, so full of sunshine." Known always as a woman who stood close beside her husband throughout his extraordinary career, she is considered the shining ideal of the Soldier's Wife. Thus, when she dies in 1893, it is a strange and unexplained contradiction that she is buried not beside her husband, but in the Russell family plot in St. Louis.

FRANCES "FANNIE" ADAMS CHAMBERLAIN

Her marriage is never without great stress. At the conclusion of the war, she receives her husband's return from the army with much graciousness, but his subsequent political career, and thus frequent absences from their home, take a serious toll. Withdrawing often into long depressions, she even confides to her closest friends of the unthinkable possibility of divorce. She is eventually stricken with blindness and failing health, but their marriage endures until her death in 1905.

THOSE WHO WORE GRAY

MAJOR GENERAL DANIEL HARVEY HILL

Jackson's brother-in-law serves in the defense of Richmond while the battle rages in Gettysburg. Promoted to Lieutenant General of North Carolina after the battle, he is sent to Tennessee to assist Braxton Bragg in the defense of Chickamauga, and is embroiled in a controversy by claiming Bragg is incompetent. But President Davis supports Bragg, and so relieves Hill and refuses to recommend Hill's promotion to the Confederate Congress. He serves the remainder of the war in command of volunteers in North Carolina. Returns then to academics, and in 1877 becomes president of the University of Arkansas. Later, he heads the Georgia Military Academy, until his death in 1889.

MAJOR ALEXANDER SWIFT "SANDIE" PENDLETON

After Jackson's death, is appointed by Lee to General Ewell's staff, in the newly organized Second Corps, and Ewell promotes him to Lieutenant Colonel. However, the cordial relationship between Ewell and Jackson's former staff quickly dissolves, as the men who were accustomed to Jackson's aggressiveness observe Ewell's sluggishness at Gettysburg and his monumental failure to capture the high ground of Cemetery Hill. Pendleton writes, "Oh for the presence and inspiration of Old Jack for just one hour!"

When Ewell's health begins to fail, Jubal Early is given command of the Second Corps, and Pendleton is one of the very few who gains the respect of the disagreeable Early, serving with him through the campaigns of the following year in the Shenandoah Valley. In late 1863 he receives a brief leave, and marries Kate Corbin, the young aunt of the tragic five-year-old girl who had so captured Jackson. In September 1864, during a battle for the town of Winchester, he is mortally wounded, and dies the next day. He does not ever see the son that Kate bears him the following November. The infant is named Sandie, but does not survive his first year.

Of Pendleton, his friend James Power Smith writes: "His intellectual powers were of the highest order . . . the readiness with which he approached his duty . . . was equaled by the celerity and skill with which he performed it. As a staff officer he had no equal."

DR. HUNTER H. McGUIRE

From his early association with Jackson's first command of the First Virginia Brigade (the Stonewall Brigade), his reputation exceeds that of any other medical officer in the Confederate Army. After Jackson's death, he serves in Ewell's corps, and thus will return to his beloved Shenandoah, where he is eventually named Medical Director for the Army of the Valley. After the war, his career continues to earn him great honor and respect. He establishes the College of Medicine at the University of Virginia, serves there as Professor of Surgery until 1878, and later is named President of the American Surgical Association, and then of the American Medical Association. He survives until 1900.

MAJOR GENERAL JOSEPH E. JOHNSTON

Recovers from his wounds at Fair Oaks, returns to command the Department of the West. His feud with Davis, and his lack of cooperation and communication, continues, and he is thus blamed for the defeats at Vicksburg, Chickamauga, and Chattanooga. He cannot bring enough forces to the field to impede Sherman's assault on Atlanta, and so is relieved in July 1864 by John Bell Hood.

After the war, he goes into private business, serves briefly as a congressman, and eventually settles in Washington, D.C., as a railroad commissioner. He dies of pneumonia in 1891. It is observed that he is in many ways the complete opposite of George McClellan: great skill in the field, with a total lack of administrative abilities.

BRIGADIER GENERAL WILLIAM BARKSDALE

At Chancellorsville his brigade fights alongside Early's division on Marye's Heights, which eventually gives way to the vastly superior numbers of Sedgwick's corps. He leads his decimated forces into battle on the right flank during the second day at Gettysburg, engages Sickles's corps at the Peach Orchard, where he is mortally wounded. He dies the following day.

BRIGADIER GENERAL ROBERT RODES

After Chancellorsville, Jackson's former colleague is promoted to Major General, leads his division with distinction at Gettysburg and afterward. Assigned to the Shenandoah Valley with Early's corps, he is killed at Winchester the same day as Sandie Pendleton.

PRESIDENT JEFFERSON DAVIS

Continues to deteriorate mentally as the war goes on, pulls all available troops close around Richmond, and so, around himself. When Richmond falls, he moves the Confederate government to Charlotte, North Carolina, and finally is captured in May 1865 at Irwinsville, Georgia. He is imprisoned for two years, but never stands trial, is released by a government anxious to move beyond the lingering taste of the war. P.G.T. Beauregard later writes that the Confederacy "needed for President either a military man of high order, or a politician of the first-class without military pretensions." Regrettably for the Great Cause, Davis proved to be neither. He survives until 1889.

THOSE WHO WORE BLUE
GENERAL IN CHIEF WINFIELD SCOTT

He is given no significant role in the war after the first appointment of McClellan in 1861, and thus the grand old man of the army spends much of the war years writing his memoirs. He dies in 1866, at the age of eighty, and is buried at West Point. For his extraordinary abilities as both a strategist and a leader of men, he is still regarded as one of the greatest soldiers this nation has ever produced.

COMMANDING GENERAL GEORGE B. McCLELLAN

Runs unsuccessfully for President against Lincoln in 1864, later becomes Governor of New Jersey. He writes an autobiography, defending his military decision-making and emphasizing his success in organizing the army. But even his staunchest supporters concede that his genius as an administrator was never carried forward to the battlefield. He survives until 1885.

Major General Ambrose E. Burnside

Reassigned to the Army of the Ohio, he performs adequately through several engagements, though at Petersburg is again blamed for poor command decisions. After the war, he becomes a successful railroad administrator. In 1866 he is elected Governor of Rhode Island, and after two terms is elected United States Senator, serving until his death in 1881.

Ulysses Grant describes him as "an officer who was generally liked and respected, he was not, however, fitted to command an army. No one knew this better than himself."

Major General Darius N. Couch

On May 22, 1863, he requests a leave of absence, tells the War Department he can no longer "lead his men to senseless slaughter" under Joe Hooker. When he is turned down, he tenders his resignation. His service to the army is considered too valuable to allow him to retire into civilian life, and so in June 1863 he is appointed commander of the new Department of the Susquehanna, and given the duty of organizing local militia to defend Pennsylvania against the threatened Confederate invasion. After Gettysburg he goes west, commands a division in Tennessee. Following the war, he resigns from the army, runs unsuccessfully for governor in Massachusetts, and later enters private business, though he still serves in the volunteer army until his death in 1897. After Chancellorsville, Couch is replaced as commander of the Second Corps by Winfield Scott Hancock.

Colonel Nelson A. Miles

Surviving his wounds at Chancellorsville, he is eventually promoted to brigade and then division command under Hancock. He receives the Congressional Medal of Honor for his brilliant stand against Lee's continuous attacks at Chancellorsville. He is promoted to Brigadier General in the spring of 1864, then after the war, to Major General. He is appointed custodian of the prisoner Jefferson Davis, and afterward moves to the West to continue building his solid reputation as a fighter in the Indian wars. Named General in

Chief of the Army in 1895, he commands the victorious U.S. forces during the Spanish-American War. He retires from the army in 1903, one of this country's most decorated soldiers, lives the peaceful life of the dignified hero until 1925. He is one of four pallbearers at the funeral of General Hancock.

Major General Joseph Hooker

Relieved of command in June 1863, he is reassigned to command under the forces of Ulysses S. Grant in Tennessee, where, surprisingly, he distinguishes himself at Lookout Mountain and Missionary Ridge, receives a commendation for gallant and meritorious service at the Battle of Chattanooga. Grant, however, writes of him: "I regarded him as a dangerous man . . . he was ambitious to the extent of caring nothing for the rights of others." Paralyzed by a stroke in 1868, he survives until 1879. Of the disastrous failure at Chancellorsville, Hooker later confides to a friend that he had simply lost confidence in Joe Hooker.

Major General Edwin V. "Bull" Sumner

The old loyal soldier, who shares none of the political egotism of his colleagues, is not named in Burnside's sweeping indictment of his commanders after the debacle at Fredericksburg. By staying back across the Rappahannock River, he is therefore spared much of the stigma the other commanders will carry. However, his personal failures weigh heavily, and in the spring of 1863, less than two months after his forced retirement, he dies.

Colonel Adelbert A. Ames

On May 20, 1863, he is promoted to Brigadier General after a vigorous campaign on his own behalf, and receives command of a brigade in the Eleventh Corps, under Oliver Howard. He is later awarded a Congressional Medal of Honor for his gallantry at First Manassas (Bull Run). After the war, General Grant assigns him to Mississippi as the military provisional governor. In 1876 he is forced to resign by an uprising in reaction to his unpopularly liberal views. Returning to the army, he commands a brigade in the Spanish-American War. He dies in 1933, at age ninety-seven, and is thus the oldest surviving general officer of the Civil War.

BRIGADIER GENERAL THOMAS F. MEAGHER

His Irish Brigade is so decimated after Chancellorsville, he resigns from command, believing his usefulness to the army has passed. By December 1863 he is given command of forces under William T. Sherman. After the war, he receives a gold medal from the state of New York for his brilliant leadership of the Irish Brigade. But he leaves the postwar turmoil of the East, goes to Montana, becomes Territorial Governor. He dies by drowning in the Missouri River in 1867.

AND FROM THESE PAGES

ROBERT E. LEE, JAMES LONGSTREET, LEWIS ARMISTEAD, A. P. HILL, JOHN BELL HOOD, GEORGE PICKETT, J.E.B. STUART, PORTER ALEXANDER, HARRY HETH,

AND

WINFIELD SCOTT HANCOCK, JOSHUA LAWRENCE CHAMBERLAIN, JOHN REYNOLDS, GEORGE GORDON MEADE, JOHN BUFORD, OLIVER HOWARD, DAN SICKLES

In July 1863 they will share the field again, the low hills and open farmlands around Gettysburg, for the three bloodiest days in American history. But that is another story. . . .

ABOUT THE AUTHOR

JEFF SHAARA was born in 1952 in New Brunswick, New Jersey. He grew up in Tallahassee, Florida, and graduated from Florida State University in 1974. For many years he was a dealer in rare coins, but sold his Tampa, Florida business in 1988 upon the death of his father, Michael Shaara.

As manager of his father's estate, Jeff developed a friendship with film director Ron Maxwell, whose film *Gettysburg* was based on *The Killer Angels*. It was Maxwell who suggested that Jeff continue the story Michael Shaara had begun.

Gods and Generals is Jeff's first novel. He and his wife, Lynne, live in Missoula, Montana.